The MARQUIS, the ESCAPE & the FOX

WHAT READERS ARE SAYING

ADULTS

Jenny L. Cote is, without a doubt, a truly gifted storyteller. God has blessed Jenny with the ability to create characters and storylines that come to life and make the reader feel as if they are traveling back through time on these incredible historical adventures. I believe Jenny is more than just a storyteller, though. Jenny has proven herself to be an incredible historian who painstakingly strives for accuracy and truth in her journeys through time. This book is not only entertaining but an important history lesson as well.

—**Mark Schneider,** Historian and Colonial Williamsburg's
Marquis de Lafayette, Williamsburg, VA

C'est magnifique! In this witty and engaging yarn, you'll get to know "America's Favorite Fighting Frenchman" like never before. Ms. Cote's high-spirited writing style and endearing animal characters will entertain you from the first page. Meanwhile, she re-creates revolutionary events so vividly that you feel like you are strolling arm-in-arm with General Washington and young Lafayette across the pond. *Ooh la la,* this EPIC tale unfolds as smoothly as melted brie. *Bon voyage!*

—**Libby McNamee,** Richmond, VA
Author of *Susanna's Midnight Ride* and *Dolley Madison and the War of 1812*

Jenny leaves no historical stone unturned in her zeal to tell America's founding story. She has once again interweaved her exhaustive research into a fun gem of a read to inspire the next generation of Patriots.

—**Richard Schumann,** Colonial Williamsburg's Patrick Henry,
Williamsburg, VA

With her latest book—*The Marquis, the Escape & the Fox*—Jenny L. Cote has done it again! Her command of the historical record, her buoyant imagination, and her ability to write fluent but easily understood prose make this book a worthy addition to any preteen's or teenager's library. Bravo!

—**Alan R. Hoffman,** President, The American Friends of Lafayette

Jenny L. Cote's newest historical novel could be her best one yet! *The Marquis, the Escape & the Fox* is everything a young reader could want. Ms. Cote provides non-stop action and perfect historical references—all the while sprinkling in important life lessons. This book should be on every teenager's bookshelf.

—**Chuck Schwam,** Chief Operating Officer,
The American Friends of Lafayette

Mrs. Cote takes us on a thrilling ride from start to finish. The dashing young Marquis de Lafayette is an inspiration. Elsa is one of my favorite characters yet. I enjoyed all the history I learned. Mostly, I marveled, once again, at the audacity of the Americans who took on the most powerful kingdom in the world in service to their dream of freedom from tyranny. Time and again they endured dire conditions and experienced miraculous escapes that they might live to fight another day.

—**Claire Foltz,** AP Social Studies Teacher, Milton, GA

Jenny L. Cote is a master storyteller, weaving the events of history with intricate detail that showcases the beautiful tapestry that is America's story. I found myself embarking on an adventure of epic proportions, marveling at the way our Maker clearly had His hand on America's journey to Independence. What a beautiful story, masterfully presented by Jenny's anointed pen. 'Can't wait for the next adventure! HUZZAH!

—**Christl Watt,** Teacher and current Homeschooler,
Canberra ACT Australia

With the cast of both sides of this Revolutionary conflict growing, Jenny weaves a masterful tale best summed up as EPIC. Battles are fought in the field of war; the shadows of espionage begin to emerge, and the hearts of people grow resilient as the infant nation of America stubbornly cries 'No!' to the British crown. The stakes are higher than ever, as the Order adds mortal allies to their team to battle the Evil One's minions right under human noses. Numerous twists and turns had me on the edge of my seat breathlessly wondering what would happen one moment and cheering in victory the next. Huzzah and bravo for another Epic tale! Keep writing Ms. Cote, and we shall all keep reading!

— **Emma Raczek,** 20, The Author Conservatory, Mosinee WI

Jenny L. Cote has done it again! This is a wonderful, engaging story that is a rare blend of learning and enjoyment, all about our nation's founding. Well worth reading!

—**John Maass,** Alexandria, VA
Author of *The Road to Yorktown* and *George Washington's Virginia,*

Anyone can be an American, but it takes knowing who you are to be a Patriot. You must have an identity to succeed in life, both as an individual and a country. Jenny isn't just telling us America's history; she's telling us who we are.

—**Dr. Paul Mims,** Chaplain, Palmetto, GA

KIDS & TEENS

I was six, sitting on my bed, holding in my hands the first book of what I would soon realize was my all-time favorite book series. Eight years later, I hold in my hands the ninth book in a truly epic series. The cover is gorgeous, but it's nothing to what's inside. History and faith, bravery and treachery, life and death. All beautifully told from the perspectives of animals. I've always loved reading, but this book, and its whole series, has captured a place in my heart that no other can take. I cannot recommend these books enough with the words I know, but I can only say that this book will bring a new meaning to American history.

—**Tatiana Brubach,** 14, Homeschooled, Deland, FL

As a freshman, I know highschoolers don't enjoy history and are tired with facts or dates and tend to forget what they learned after the test has passed. Yet growing up reading Jenny L. Cote as a child honestly allowed me to love history for what happened, not for the dates and locations. And *The Marquis, the Escape & the Fox* really takes that to a level any teenager can enjoy. Just because there's a dog and cat on the cover doesn't mean it's a picture book. Reading about the battles that took place in New York and George Washington's struggles has allowed me to learn more than I've learned from any history book or movie.

—**Chad Velez,** 15, Homeschooled, Houston, TX

This book is incredible! Jenny has always been my favorite author, but *The Marquis, the Escape & the Fox* is next level! The storyline is very complex and weaves together the characters' stories in a fascinating way that demonstrates God's miraculous hand at work at this pivotal time in history. Each of the Order of the Seven plays a significant part to help secure America's freedom, yet the way in which Jenny wrote the book does not change the overall historical accuracy. I also loved how Lafayette is so passionate about the American cause and gives his all to get to America to fight for *'liberté.'* I can't wait to see what happens next! Keep writing, Jenny!

—**Danalyn Lamos,** 12, The Kings House School Windsor, Windsor Berkshire, United Kingdom

It is incredible to me how Ms. Cote's books continue to engage and entertain me from ages 6 to 16. *The Marquis, the Escape & the Fox* is no exception. I learned more about history from this book than I ever did in a history class, and I was completely immersed while doing so. Ms. Cote describes history in a way that makes it happen only yesterday and brings historical people to life as if they were old friends. I sat in breathtaking suspense, hanging on to each word, even though I already know the way the story ends. With plot twists, heart-wrenching moments, espionage, intrigue, and a call for *"liberté!"* this book is an absolute must read!

—**Savannah Jones,** 16, Homeschooled, Dadeville, AL

Jenny L. Cote brings history, animals, and God all into a single book! My family loves her writing! Her descriptive words place me right with Max and Jock running across battlefields or with Nigel and Liz as they edit the Declaration, as well as with Veritas soaring through the skies and with Kate as she runs around invisible and unseen! My favorite character in the book is Jock. He is always willing to learn and progress. I also love Lafayette, always seeking *liberté!* Altogether, Jenny is doing one of the most important things anyone can do! She is keeping HIS-Story alive!

—**Liam Cole,** 14, Homeschooled, Carlisle, PA

As an Australian, I never thought I'd find American history quite so fascinating and engaging, but Jenny has done it again. I couldn't wait to get my hands on this next part of the saga, and it didn't disappoint. Jenny's masterful writing and unexpected plot twists had me on the edge of my seat, and I couldn't put the book down. It made me feel like I was actually there, experiencing history with the animals, and I loved it! Now to read it again whilst I wait for the next one!

—**Jayden Stubberfield,** 14, Homeschooled, Central Coast NSW, Australia

Reading through this latest installment, I was able to understand to a greater extent how much the Patriots sacrificed for liberty. The plot was entangled with many spies and traitors. There is a great cast of characters, both new and familiar, who helped goodness to prevail in the end. Throughout the pages you will see Scripture and God incorporated in the story of our country's struggle for freedom. This is a must read for history fans!

—**Nathaniel Gade,** 11, Homeschooled, Cary, NC

Piles of rich detail, witty characters, action, adventure, and most importantly a God-honoring account of American history, *The Marquis, the Escape & the Fox* is a must-read for all ages! Jenny's writing makes the divine hand of the Creator clearly evident in every single event of the American Revolution, no matter how minuscule, and makes me proud to call America the country of my birth.

—**Pristine Tam,** 15, Wilson Hill Academy, Oakville, ON, Canada

This is Ms. Cote's best book yet! I felt like I was with George Washington fighting the Redcoats! I highly recommend this book if you are a fan of the Revolutionary War! If you aren't yet, you soon will be!

—**Kyle Klubnik,** 10, Logos Preparatory Academy, Needville, TX

It is mesmerizing to watch Ms. Cote weave her plot lines together into an EPIC story! I adored Elsa and the brilliant fox hunting theme. The way the Continental Army never gave up was so inspiring! You can feel the suspense and revel in the victories along with the Epic Order of the Seven. As always, I learned so much. I love the story of the Marquis de Lafayette and am looking forward to learning more. So well done, Jenny! *Vive la liberté!*

—**Eva Bellig,** 16, Homeschooled, New Ulm, MN

This is by far the best book Jenny L. Cote has written! I felt like I was right there alongside Max and Jock on the battlefields . . . right beside Liz and Nigel at Congress, and alongside Kate, "Our Dog in Paris." I can't wait until the next book comes out!

—**Judah White,** 11, Homeschooled, Woodbury, MN

The Marquis, the Escape & the Fox is [sure to be] another bestseller by Jenny L. Cote! The best one yet in her Epic Order of the Seven Revolutionary saga! I loved every single page. Each page is overflowing with information, adventure, and excitement! I felt like I was a part of the story taking place—from the pivotal signing of the Declaration of Independence to the danger of the Revolutionary War battles. Ms. Cote has brought history back to life in a way suitable for all ages. With adventure, history, spies, and incredible insight on the secrets of the American Revolution, I simply couldn't recommend it more. HUZZAH!

—**Christopher Watt,** 14, Homeschooled, Canberra ACT Australia

The Marquis, the Escape & the Fox is a MUST READ for any history buff, young or old. Jenny L. Cote, in her 9th book, has managed to make this her most EPIC one yet! It starts with a heart-pounding prologue, then it jumps into pages filled with drama, heroes, villains, betrayal, and conspiracies. I absolutely loved this book, and I know you will too.

—**Edan M.,** 18, High School Student, San Jose, CA

I absolutely loved this book! Jenny truly brings history to life, and I so enjoyed watching the Revolution unfold while getting to know Lafayette and so many other historical figures as real people, not just names on a page. I was reminded of how God is truly in control of everything and uses even trials and difficult circumstances for His purposes and ultimately our good.

—**Addie Harris,** 14, Homeschooled, Liberal, KS

Wow! I have been a fan of Jenny L. Cote since I was six years old, and I am still enthralled by each and every one of her books. This book was the cream on top! I simply could not put this book down once I received it and cannot wait for the next in the series. My only regret is that Max, Liz, Al, Nigel, Kate, Clarie, and Gillamon do not exist in real life and that I cannot meet them!

— **Ethan Ballough,** 16, Homeschooled, Vero Beach, FL

She's done it again! Another masterpiece! Just like with all her other books, she has masterfully intertwined history with the Epic Order of the Seven. This book is definitely my favorite. It is a thrilling and awesome read!

—**Emily Sylvan,** 15, Homeschooled, Dallas, GA

I love Jenny L. Cote's work! It's so inspiring! It has taught me tons of HIStory and biblical knowledge. I love how each book is even better than the last! *The Marquis, the Escape & the Fox* is so interesting that I could barely put it down! I love the way that Jenny shows how difficult it was for America to declare independence from Great Britain. My favorite character is Jock. It's fun to see how he is directed by Gillamon and his grandsire, Max. If you wish that you knew what animals were thinking or that they could talk, you'll love these books! This series is a true masterpiece. I can't wait for the next book!

—**Eli Harris,** 12, Homeschooled, Liberal, KS

Jenny has done it again! *The Marquis, the Escape & the Fox* had me sitting on the edge of my seat the entire time. My favorite character is Jock. I love his ability to control the weather and the way it is tied into Revolutionary battles. I also enjoyed the newest character, Elsa, and her sassy, easygoing personality. Once again, Jenny's newest Epic Order of the Seven book made me laugh, cry, and smile! This book is my favorite one so far (but of course, every single book of hers is really good, so how could I possibly choose just one?!).

—**Mikayla Badenhorst,** 12, Liberty Baptist Academy, Sarasota, FL

C'est magnifique! Madame Cote has crafted yet another EPIC piece of literature! *The Marquis, the Escape & the Fox* relays the intrigue surrounding the Marquis de Lafayette's escape from France to join the fight for *liberté* in America. Utilizing her sophisticated French, British, Dutch, German, and Colonial American vocabulary, Ms. Cote transports readers to the 18th century, immersing them in the suspense of narrow escapes, constant espionage, and false façades. Ms. Cote has researched the American Revolution for over a decade—and it shows! Fascinating facts not found in your history textbook flow from every page. Lightening the mood with her lovable cast of characters, Ms. Cote once again proves her skill as a storyteller is unparalleled. Bravo!

—**Ethan Both,** 14, Veritas Classical Schools, Roswell, GA

I have read hundreds of books in my life—everything from Shakespeare to Oscar Wilde. None have had such an impact on my life as Ms. Cote's books. I've grown up with the Epic Order of the Seven. I'm in a college AP US History class, and the credit should go to Ms. Cote for that. She made me realize how important our history is and that if we don't know it, we're doomed to repeat it. *The Marquis* is just another example of her brilliant writing and incredible storytelling, and I truly believe that it has been written for such a time in our country as this. I may be Canadian, but Ms. Cote's books have made me fall in love with America. Now I live here, in the land of the free and the home of the brave. I can't thank you enough, Ms. Cote, for making me fall in love with your country, years before I even considered the thought of living here. *Vive La Liberté Américaine!*

—**Mackenzie Alspach,** 16, Calvary Christian School, Independence, KY

I grew up reading the Epic Order of the Seven, and I'm super excited that it's going through my favorite time in history. I'm always blown away at how much research goes into these books. I love how Ms. Cote weaves fantasy in with history and then tops it off with all the classic characters, plus a Scottish terrier puppy and a German fox. After all, CUR NON??!!

—**Megan Canfield,** 17, Homeschooled, Carrollton, TX

This is my favorite book yet! I was always excited to read the next chapter. I've learned more from this book about the start of America, the Revolutionary War, and France than from any other book I've read. Jenny has such an amazing writing style. She makes her characters come alive so vibrantly. All the animals are active and engaging. And she always points everything back to God. I love seeing Lafayette's quest for both his and America's freedom. I love Jenny's books, and I can't wait for the next one!

—**Nathan Wilson,** 15, Homeschooled, Spokane, WA

EPIC ORDER OF THE SEVEN

The
MARQUIS,
the ESCAPE &
the FOX

JENNY L. COTE

LIVING INK BOOKS
Writing Worth Reading

Epic Order of the Seven®

The Marquis, the Escape, and the Fox

Copyright © 2023 by Jenny L. Cote

Published by Living Ink Books, an imprint of AMG Publishers, Chattanooga, Tennessee (www.amgpublishers.com).

Print Edition ISBN: 978-161715-605-2
ePUB Edition ISBN: 978-1-61715-602-1
Mobi Edition ISBN: 978-1-61715-603-8
ePDF Edition ISBN: 978-1-61715-604-5

First AMG Printing-July 2023

EPIC ORDER OF THE SEVEN is a trademark of Jenny L. Cote.

Cover and internal illustrations by Rob Moffitt, Chicago, Illinois. Interior design and typeset by Katherine Lloyd, theDESKonline.com. Editing by Richard Cairnes, Walworth, Wisconsin.

Proofreading by Rick Steele, Ringgold, Georgia (steeleeditorialservices.myportfolio.com). Historic Maps from the Library of Congress Maps Division.

Internal images by shutterstock.com. Back cover author photo by Mary Denman Photography, Greenville, South Carolina.

Printed in Canada.
24 25 26 27 -M- 6 5 4 3

To Mark Schneider

With that first enthusiastic stomp of your boot,
hands held high in the air, and your exuberant French greeting,
I knew I wanted to write about the Marquis de Lafayette.
Thank you for making history live for me and countless others
as you don uniforms, ride horses, and make magnificent speeches.
You've kept my quill sharp with your vast knowledge
of French and military history,
and you've kept me from writing like a girl.

Merci beaucoup, mon cher ami.
VIVE LAFAYETTE!

This book contains fact, fiction,
and fantasy—in that order.

For the purely factual accounts of the remarkable history
contained herein, please see the sources
listed in the bibliography.

. . . He marked out their appointed times in history . . .
Acts 17:26

CONTENTS

PART FIVE: THE GREAT ESCAPE
(FRANCE, DECEMBER 1776 – APRIL 1777)

Acknowledgments

When in the course of writing events, it becomes necessary for an author to research the history to get it right, to write so a manuscript is produced, to publish so a book is printed, and to publicize so the world will know about it, a decent respect to the proper credit due requires that the author should declare the people who impel her to succeed. I therefore make this DECLARATION OF DEPENDENCE, *because I clearly did not write this book alone. I had help—a noble train of it.*

God You knew when I happily ran around the battlefields of Yorktown as a toddler and skipped down Duke of Gloucester Street in Williamsburg that I would someday write the story of the American Revolution. Thank you for allowing me to grow up immersed in the place where America herself was a toddler and grew to Independence. Thank you for ensuring that I would be raised as a proud Virginian by my godly history-loving parents. I will ever be Your most humble and obedient servant to command.

Richard Schumann Thank you for making Patrick Henry come alive for me, and for patiently helping me to do the same for others in these books. I'm happy that you were not only my Revolutionary muse, but also became my dear friend. I'll always be your devoted scribe. And you'll always be "my Henry."

Mark Schneider You first introduced me to Lafayette and Banastre Tarleton, and made me want to write their stories. Thank you for your military, historical, and French eagle eye to get their stories right, your tireless assistance, your treasured friendship, and keeping me from writing like a girl in battle scenes. You're my favorite fighting Frenchman, my favorite antagonist, but above all, my dear friend.

Epic Historians and Historical Sites Whenever kids ask me what the best part is about being an author, I always answer with an enthusiastic, one-word answer: "RESEARCH!" I've amassed over three hundred books to write this Revolutionary saga, but books alone are insufficient to drill down to the nitty-gritty details of history. You must go see where history happened, so I have. I've been to nearly every major locale of the American Revolution, attended as many re-enactments as I can, and travelled to France multiple times to research Lafayette (it's for the *children*). You also need to pick the brains of historians who know the subject inside and out. I'm grateful to an endless list of epic historians (and historical sites) who have endured my questions, my repeated visits, and even my "slipping behind the curtain" moments when I should have remained seated in the audience.

Family, Friends, Critique Team Thank you for your love, encouragement, prayers, feedback, and inspiration while I researched, traveled, spoke, and wrote: My husband Casey and son Alex, my parents Dr. Paul and Janice Mims, my EPIC muse Claire Roberts Foltz, and my EPIC "spoon sister" and fellow author Libby McNamee.

Publishing Team An EPIC thank you to the people who take what comes out of my pen and turn it into something beautiful to hold, read, and share! Illustrator Rob Moffitt, Editor Richard Cairnes, Proofreader Rick Steele, Interior Designer Katherine Lloyd, Literary Agent Paul Shepherd, and the AMG Publishers Team: Steve Turner, Amanda Jenkins, Ebony Sims, Donna Coker, and the support staff.

Readers It is my joy and honor to write for you. My passion is to inspire the next generation to know and love America, and I pray I have done so with this book. Thank you for your prayers, encouraging notes, letters, pictures, cards, e-mails, Tweets, and Instagram and Facebook posts. They make me smile, and you encourage this author's heart more than you could ever know. I would love to hear how this book inspired you or about something you learned at jenny@epicorderoftheseven.com. I'll keep writing as long as you keep reading!

    With Epic Love,

Main Character Profiles

Max: a Scottish Terrier from (where else?) Scotland. Full name is Maximillian Braveheart the Bruce. Short, black, with a large head, always ready to take on the bad guys. Faithful leader of the team who started with their first mission on Noah's Ark in *The Ark, the Reed, and the Fire Cloud*. Loves to mess with Al, "encouraging" him to work on his bravery. Can't swim. Immortal.

Liz: a petite, French, black cat from Normandy. Full name is Lizette Brilliante Aloysius. Brilliant, refined, and strategic leader of the team, beginning with Noah's Ark. Loves the study of history, science, the written word, culture, and languages. Prides herself on knowing the meanings of names, and simply adores gardens. Immortal.

Al: a well-fed, Irish, orange cat. Full name is Albert Aloysius, also called "Big Al" by his close friends. Hopelessly in love with his mate, Liz, since Noah's Ark. Simple-minded, but often holds the key to gaining access to impossible places, and figuring out things everyone else misses, including deep spiritual truths. Lives to eat and sleep. Afraid of everything. Immortal.

Kate: a West Highland White Terrier, also from Scotland. The love of Max's life ever since they 'wed' on the way to the Ark. Has a sweetness that disarms everyone she meets. Is also a fiery lass, unafraid to speak her mind. Always sees the good in others and sticks up for the underdog. Immortal.

Nigel P. Monaco: a jolly, British mouse. Possesses impeccable manners and speech. Wears spectacles and is on the same intellectual level as Liz. An expert Egyptologist who joined the team in *The Dreamer, the Schemer, and the Robe.* Taught Liz all about Egypt, giving her the endearing title "my pet." Travels quickly via carrier pigeon and has an affinity for music. Immortal.

Gillamon: a wise, kind mountain goat from Switzerland. Moved to Scotland, where he raised Max (an orphan) and served as his mentor. Died before the Flood but serves as a spiritual being who delivers mission assignments from the Maker to the team. Can take any shape or form and shows up when least expected.

Clarie: a sweet little lamb from Judea. Shepherds gave her to Mary and Joseph as a gift for Baby Jesus in *The Prophet, the Shepherd, and the Star.* Died enabling the family to escape to Egypt without harm and joined Gillamon as a spiritual being member of the team. Serves as all-knowing guide in the IAMISPHERE when the team goes back in time to observe historical events. Can take any shape or form.

Open your ears to what I am saying,
for I will speak to you in a parable.
I will teach you hidden lessons from our past—
stories we have heard and know,
stories our ancestors handed down to us.
We will not hide these truths from our children
but will tell the next generation about the
glorious deeds of the Lord. We will tell of his power
and the mighty miracles he did.

—PSALM 78:1–4

PROLOGUE

ESCAPING THE KING

BAYONNE, FRANCE, APRIL 17, 1777

Pink ribbons streaked across the lightening purple sky, causing the half-moon to slowly fade from view. A single beam of sunlight amplified by a swirl of dust crept into the hundred-year-old barn as a rooster strutted back and forth across the entrance. His head jutted forward with each step, and he emitted a quiet 'bawk, bawk, bawk,' to warm up his vocal cords.

Liz stifled a giggle at the iconic French rooster. The sleek black cat lifted her dainty paw and smiled. "Whenever you are ready, *monsieur.*"

"Bon, madame," the rooster answered, stopping in place, and blowing her a kiss with the tip of his wing. He threw back his head, took in a deep breath, and closed his eyes. "COCK-A-DOODLE-DOOOOOOOO!"

Lafayette moaned, hearing the rooster greet the day. But he didn't budge.

"Do it again, if ye don't mind," Kate whispered to the rooster. The little white dog smiled. "I know how ye like ta own the morn."

"Avec plaisir, madame," the colorful rooster proudly answered with a gravelly French accent and a wink to the white Westie. "It is what I do best, no?" He cleared his throat, lifted his red beak high in the air, and stretched out his blue-green metallic wings for the wind-up to really belt it out. His red throat feathers flared and violently shook as he let it all go, screaming, "COCK-A-DOODLE-DOOOOOOOO! COCK-A-DOODLE-DOOOOOOOOOOOOOOOOOOO!"

"Oui, I heard you the first time," an irritated Lafayette muttered, rolling over on the straw. "And the second, and the third . . ." His sleepy mumble trailed off. In a moment he let go a snore.

Kate frowned, shaking her head at the exhausted young Frenchman who refused to wake up. She looked from Liz to the rooster and shrugged her shoulders.

"Humph! I know when I have been insulted!" the rooster huffed, embarrassed by the teenager who ignored some of his best work. *"Adolescent typique, pfft!"* he blustered as he lifted his chin and strutted out of the barn toward the farmhouse. He would press on, crowing to rouse the rest of the local inhabitants in this ancient town perched on the southwest coastal border of France and Spain.

"*Le coq français typique, no?*" Liz said, sharing a giggle with Kate.

"Aye, jest like Jacques," Kate answered. "Yer typical French rooster."

"*Oui,* and a typical teenager as our rooster friend said of our marquis," Liz agreed, gazing at Lafayette's black shirt and burgundy breeches as he nestled comfortably in the hay. Her tail curled up and down, and she looked around the old barn, thinking.

"He needs ta get up," Kate muttered with a frown. "We don't want ta get caught here after how far we've come. We're almost there!"

"Do you know what the local Bayonne peasants did in the mid-seventeenth century when conflicts arose with the Spanish, and they ran low on gunpowder and projectiles?" Liz asked, walking over to a bench with tools.

Kate cocked her head. "Nooooo, Liz. Ye know I enjoy yer history lectures, but I don't think this be the time . . ."

"They simply attached long hunting knives to the barrels of their muskets, and *voila* they had makeshift spears," Liz continued, ignoring Kate's comment. She picked up a small, iron spike and turned, wearing a big grin. "And do you know what the peasants of Bayonne called them?"

Kate sighed, "Um, *no,* lass."

"Come, *mon amie,* think!" Liz encouraged her excitedly. "*C'est simple!*" She walked over to Lafayette and held the spike close to his back side.

Kate's eyes widened as she saw Liz lift the spike in the air. "Bayonets!"

"*Oui,* which is the *point* of this lecture!" Liz answered gleefully, poking the spike into Lafayette's behind, causing him to bolt upright and shout as she darted behind a barrel.

Lafayette frowned and rubbed his backside, looking around him. He saw no one, only the sun now pouring into the barn and the hay scattered about. All he heard was the rooster crowing in the distance and his brown horse in the far stall, seemingly snickering at him. The young man shook his head, his red hair mussed and dangling around his shoulders. He felt around the hay and his hand landed on an iron spike. "Ah, I must have rolled over on this." He chuckled, tossed it back into the hay, and stretched out his arms and back, trying to come to life.

Kate stepped outside the barn because she heard something that Lafayette didn't yet hear—the sound of a swift pair of horses galloping up the road. Alarmed, she ran to the hedge and spotted what she had hoped she would not see. It was Fumel's men!

"It's them!" she barked, alerting Liz. "They've followed us here!"

Lafayette heard a dog barking and hurriedly slipped on his boots. He walked over to peek out of the barn and spotted the two horsemen as they passed by. He withdrew into the barn, his heart racing as he leaned his back against the old wooden door. *They've followed us here!*

The nineteen-year-old quickly put on his long, charcoal coat and three-cornered hat and ran to the stall to grab the horse by the reins. "Shhhh, we must be quiet, *cheval.*" He gently rubbed the horse's neck and led him to the entrance of the barn. He mounted the horse and looked both ways. No sign of the horsemen. He exhaled and directed the horse onward. Once he got to the road, he frowned. "We cannot meet Mauroy and the coach back at the inn as planned. Fumel's men will surely be there," he muttered to his horse. "He will have to figure it out and meet me at San Sebastian." He patted the horse on the neck. "I know you are tired from our long journey yester-day, *cheval,* but I need for you to run a bit longer, as fast as you can." The horse whinnied, as if protesting the coming ride. Lafayette clicked his tongue, squeezed his legs tight, and hoarsely whispered, *"Allons-y!"*

Liz ran out to meet Kate, and they watched the Marquis de Lafayette gallop away from Bayonne. "We must get to Clarie and the coach to let her know he has gone on ahead!" Together the two friends ran down the dirt path to the town center to find their friend.

The sun was high overhead now, and Lafayette kept looking behind him as he rode his horse hard and fast toward San Sebastian. It was twenty-eight miles from Bayonne to reach the port city where his ship awaited him. It had been three weeks since he left *La Victoire* in the care of General de Kalb and the shipload of officers waiting for him to sail to America. After all he had overcome to reach this point, he could not afford to be apprehended by those police officers. They were only following orders, but the orders they followed were to arrest the outlaw, and they were issued by none other than King Louis XVI of France.

The gravity of his escape weighed heavily on his mind, spurring him on to escape arrest, to escape the king, to escape his father-in-law, and to escape a meaningless existence at the Court of Versailles. If he could finally make this one great escape, he would not only win liberty for the Americans, but also for himself. The Marquis de Lafayette would attain glory on the battlefield fighting for a righteous, glorious cause.

Lafayette slowly felt his horse begin to struggle with the pace he had held now for twelve miles. The horse's breathing grew labored, his pace slowed, and he began jerking his head against the reins. *"Je sais, je sais, mon cheval,* you have run so far, and so well," Lafayette consoled him, slowing to a walk.

Lafayette frowned and patted the horse's neck, feeling how drenched it was with sweat. The horse's heavy breathing was mixed with an occasional wheeze. He needed watering, and now.

Suddenly Lafayette heard behind him what he most dreaded, especially at this moment. A pair of horses were galloping toward him, kicking up the dust a mile distant. "No, no, no, no!" Terror filled his eyes and he looked down at the struggling horse. He quickly looked around to get his bearings when he saw a welcome sight. There in the distance was a small crescent-shaped harbor and the little town of St. Jean-de-Luz. He leaned over into the horse's ear. "One mile more, *mon cheval!* Then you can rest. But for now, I need you to run!"

The young Frenchman snapped the reins, pressed his knees into the horse's sides and once more took off at a fast gallop. Lafayette leaned over the horse as low as he could, his coat flying behind him. His heart pounded as hard as his horse's hooves against the road. He looked behind him, and it appeared that the men were gaining on him. "Almost there, *cheval!*" he shouted.

Within a few moments, he galloped into town and hurried to the familiar barn behind the inn. He quickly dismounted and brought the horse inside to a watering trough. The young man's chest heaved, and he put his hands on his knees, trying to catch his breath. His legs felt weak from fear as much as the rigorous ride. He stood up and wiped his face with his upper arm. He then leaned over and stroked the horse's neck, burying his head gratefully into its black mane. *"C'est bon, c'est bon. Merci, mon cheval. Merci."*

"Monsieur?" came the soft voice of a lady at the entrance to the barn. She had a basket of fresh eggs draped over her arm.

Lafayette snapped his head up quickly, and his face flooded with relief. It was Madeleine. Her eyes suddenly widened with recognition, but then frowned as she saw that he was now dressed like a common courier, not a gentleman. She tilted her head in question, but before she could say anything more, the two police officers came clip-clopping up the street in front of the barn. Lafayette quickly put a finger to his mouth and then raised a fist in the air, mouthing the word, *"LIBERTÉ!"*

"Mademoiselle! Have you seen the rider that came this way?" one of the officers asked.

"He rode a brown horse," the other officer added.

Madeleine didn't bat an eye but walked over to join the men in the street, diverting their attention away from the barn. *"Oui,* I've just seen him. He wore a long, dark coat and burgundy breeches, no?"

The officers looked at each other and nodded. *"Oui,* that's him!"

The young French girl smiled and pointed in the opposite direction. "That way."

"*Merci, mademoiselle,*" the men answered in unison, tapping a finger to their hats. In seconds they galloped off in pursuit of the elusive outlaw.

Lafayette heard the horses ride off and closed his eyes in relief. He slumped down to the cool stone floor, drawing his knees up and resting his head on his arms.

Madeleine reappeared in the door. "I did not expect to see you again . . . especially dressed like that, and not in your carriage . . . and being chased by riders." She wore a look of suspicion. "Who were those men, *monsieur?*"

Lafayette looked up and smiled, a sweaty mess with his damp red hair sticking out from his hat. "I cannot begin to thank you enough, *mademoiselle.* You are an angel sent from God!" He looked up and gave another exhale of relief and then got to his feet. He took her hand in his and kissed it. "*Merci, merci, merci!*" He smiled and clasped his hands together as if praying. "*S'il vous plaît,* believe me, I am not a criminal. There has been a terrible misunderstanding, and those men have not yet received word to explain things. I cannot go into the details, but I am in pursuit of doing something noble."

Madeleine tilted her head and smiled. "Noble like Vercingetorix? *Liberté?*"

"*Exactement!*" Lafayette exclaimed with a hand up. His eyes widened. "Vercingetorix!" He ran to the stall belonging to the wild white stallion. "He is still here!"

"*Oui,* he is still here," Madeleine answered.

"You have already done more for me than I could ever ask, but I must ask you for one more favor," Lafayette implored. "Please, allow me to exchange my brown horse for Vercingetorix. I must continue on my way, especially if those men come back looking for me here. I cannot allow you to experience trouble on my behalf."

"But *monsieur*, we are yet to ride him! You remember that he has bucked off every man who has tried," Madeleine answered.

"Did they use whips?" Lafayette asked, now staring at the horse, who walked right up to him.

"*Oui,* I believe so," she answered. "How else could they control him?"

Lafayette looked the beautiful white horse in the eye and stroked his nose. "Do you also want *liberté,* Vercingetorix? Let me take you away from here, *cheval.*" The horse didn't flinch but kept his gaze on the young Frenchman, who slowly opened the gate of the stall, stepping inside. Lafayette came over and gently rubbed the horse's side, allowing the horse to smell him and get reacquainted with him.

Madeleine looked on and marveled at how the young man and the horse interacted. "Are you certain you wish to take him?"

Lafayette slipped his arm under the horse's head, standing close while the horse nuzzled him. *"Oui,* I can ride this horse. Plus, I do not have a choice. I must escape from here." He whispered in the horse's ear, "Show me that you are the fastest *cheval* in France."

Madeleine lifted a hand and shrugged her shoulders with a grin. *"Très bien. Mon père* will be relieved to have you take him off his hands."

"Merci beaucoup, mademoiselle!" Lafayette exclaimed, patting Vercingetorix. *"Bon!* Let me transfer the saddle and harness, and we will be on our way." While he took care of the horses, he told her, "You were quick on your feet to tell those men I rode in the opposite direction."

"I did not exactly do that, *monsieur,"* she answered with a sly grin. "I told them I had just seen you—which I had, in the barn—and then I simply pointed and said, 'That way.' I didn't say you had *gone* that way."

Lafayette threw back his head and laughed. "You are an angel indeed!"

Soon he was ready to mount up and handed her several gold coins. *"Pour vous, merci."*

"Merci beaucoup, monsieur!" she exclaimed, wide-eyed at the money he had given her. "You honor Vercingetorix—both of them!"

Lafayette bowed with a hand over his heart. *"Merci. Au revoir."*

Madeleine curtsied and grinned. *"Au revoir, et bonne chance, monsieur."*

With that, Lafayette guided the white horse out of the stall. He calmly put a foot into the stirrups and climbed up into the saddle. The horse whinnied and moved his head side to side, a bit anxious. Lafayette calmly patted his neck and spoke to him. "Shhh, *bon cheval, bon cheval."* He gently applied pressure with his knees and Vercingetorix started walking forward. Lafayette and Madeleine exchanged glances of delight. Once he was at the door, he tipped his hat to the young lady and stepped outside.

Within moments Lafayette and Vercingetorix raced down the street toward San Sebastian. "But first, *mon cheval,* I will take you to *la mer."*

The white horse gave a neigh of exhilaration as they took off toward the sea, his mane flying behind him. He snorted with anticipation, smelling the salt air he longed for. Lafayette had never ridden a faster horse! He guided him down the coast and to a remote beach below the craggy shoreline where the cliffs towered above the azure sea. When they got to the beach, Vercingetorix ran right into the water, galloping happily along. Lafayette threw his head back, laughing with joy. He already was madly in love with this horse who shared his craving for freedom.

Lafayette allowed the horse to go where he wished, back and forth and up and down the beach, frolicking. After a while, Vercingetorix slowed and simply stood in the water, gazing out to sea, panting. He snorted and bobbed his head up and down.

Lafayette leaned over and rubbed the horse's shoulder. *"Mon cheval de mer."* He sat back up. *"Bon,* now we must get to *La Victoire."*

It was now nearing dusk, and the pink ribbons in the sky that began the day started to appear, this time bringing the half-moon back into view as the light started to fade.

Once Fumel's men had ridden a few miles, they decided to backtrack, having seen no sign of Lafayette anywhere on the main road. They decided that if the outlaw were going anywhere other than Marseilles, it would be to San Sebastian to catch his ship. Off they went, now in the direction of the port. If they didn't find the ship, they would head back to Bordeaux. Once they crossed over into Spain, they would be out of their jurisdiction to arrest Lafayette. At least they could report what they learned, but their aim was to catch the outlaw before he reached the border.

As Lafayette neared San Sebastian, he suddenly heard the two riders in the distance. He turned to see them a mile behind him. Had they spotted him? He quickly pulled on the reins and directed Vercingetorix off the road and into a cluster of trees in a thicket near the cliff. He prayed a quick prayer for an answer about what to do next.

If they caught him here, his dreams of sailing to America would be over.

PART ONE

THE BRITISH ARE HERE

April 1776 – June 1776

GEORGES ON HORSES

MANHATTAN, NEW YORK, APRIL 13, 1776

"New York! I'm happy to be back in my home colony, but I've never been to the big city before," Jock exclaimed. "Some of these buildings are *four* stories high!"

The little Scottie's eyes widened as he gazed up at the buildings overlooking the water at the southern tip of York Island. Dutch-styled houses of wood and red or yellow brick were perched along the wide, tree-lined avenue called Broadway. Known as Manhattan, or 'Mannahatta', as the Native Americans called it, this normally bustling city housed twenty-five thousand people in less than a square mile, but a third of them had already fled with war knocking on their door.

A few small sailing vessels clipped along with a stiff breeze through the blue waters of the Upper Bay, which bounded the south of York Island. The Hudson River lapped against its western shore and the East River against its eastern shore. This small, hilly island was eleven miles long and roughly two miles wide at its widest point. The Harlem River bounded York Island on the north at King's Bridge, which connected the island to the mainland. From King's Bridge for ten miles down to the city limits, the land was lush with green wooded forests and marshy wetlands abounding with wildlife, flowing streams, and rocky outcroppings carved long ago by moving glaciers. Several grand country estates and farms were scattered throughout the countryside.

The Upper Bay of New York Harbor was dotted with several tiny islands and flowed down through a small channel between Staten Island and Long Island called The Narrows. From there, it emptied into the Lower Bay, which opened out to the Atlantic Ocean. Inbound ships trying to reach Manhattan first had to navigate the waters by a spit of land with a lighthouse called Sandy Hook, then cross the shoals through the Lower Bay rimming the New Jersey shoreline and sail through The Narrows to the Upper Bay. In such a busy seagoing city of merchants, traders, and shipbuilders, sailing vessels of all kinds kept New York harbor full of white sails. But several British warships floated beyond The Narrows to remind the city's inhabitants of just who owned and controlled these waters.

Seagulls cried out overhead, and the warm sunshine lit up the bay so brightly that Jock had to squint against the glare. He ran along the water's edge at the Battery next to Fort George and gazed around the harbor and back over to the hilly, green stretch of land rising on the other side of the East River. "Me mum always told me about how grand the city were, but we lived way out in the country in Setauket over there on Long Island." Tears quickened in his eyes, and a lump grew in his throat. "She said we'd come here someday, but then . . . I lost her, along with the rest of my family . . . to that beast."

Jock felt a burly paw on his shoulder and turned to lock eyes with a pair of big brown eyes under scruffy black eyebrows. "Not yer *whole* family. Ye've got *me* now, gr-r-randlad," Max said with a resolute yet compassionate voice. The older Scottish Terrier nuzzled the little dog with his square head. "I lost me mum young, too, so I know how ye feel. But I'm yer gr-r-randsire, an' I'll never leave ye."

Jock closed his eyes, leaned gratefully into Max, and smiled in relief. "Aye, Grandsire. I'm so happy Gillamon found me and brought me to you! We've only been together a couple of months, but it's already been a grand adventure."

"Aye! Life's always a gr-r-rand adventure when ye're with Maximillian Br-r-raveheart the Br-r-ruce!" Max heartily agreed. "Ye'll get ta meet yer grandmum Kate when we're together again. For now, she's on mission for the Maker in France ta help Lafayette, an' we Br-r-ruce men be on mission here in New York. We've got ta watch our humans as they get r-r-ready ta face the British here in this big city." Max nodded in the direction of a team of horses in the distance that slowly clip-clopped down Broadway. "Me human, General George Washington, has the fate of a new nation ridin' on his shoulders."

The Continental Army first descended on the city when the Commander-in-Chief George Washington sent his best General Charles Lee here in early February to begin building fortifications to secure the city before the British forces arrived. New York was the strategic epicenter for all the colonies, linking New England and the south with transportation, communication, and commerce. Because ships could enter the deep waters of New York Harbor and sail up the Hudson River with troops to access Canada via land up through the Lake George/Lake Champlain corridor (or from Canada down to New York City), this city became the next strategic target for the British to bring the rebelling colonies under control. Their strategy was simple: capture New York, cut off New England from the south, and the rebellion would be crushed. Or so they surmised.

Washington thought that British General William Howe would come to New York after the Patriots had driven his besieged army out of Boston a month ago. Humiliated and needing to regroup, resupply, and wait for reinforcements from England, Howe sailed not to New York but to Halifax, Nova Scotia. But Washington and the inhabitants of this city knew the British would eventually come here to New York to establish their military base. They could come any day—the question was, when? And how many ships and men would they have when they arrived? For Washington, the most important question was, would his small army be ready to defend New York and take on one of the most powerful armies and formidable navies in the world?

The young Scottie nodded and stood erect, stiffening his spine to the tip of his upraised tail. "Aye, and *my* human, Colonel Henry Knox is one of Washington's most loyal officers. I'm glad he let me come on ahead with you while he gets all the guns and stuff moved here. But he petted my wee head and told me he'd join us in New York soon. Anyway, I'm happy I got to help him with his first mission to get the guns from Fort Ticonderoga."

Max grinned proudly. "Those guns dr-r-rove General Howe an' those R-r-redcoats out of Boston!" He patted his grandlad and winked. "Of course, Knox didn't know it were his little Jock Frost Knox that whipped up the kind of weather he needed ta haul those guns in the snow an' sneak them up on Dorchester Heights in a single foggy night."

"I like making weather!" Jock agreed, wagging his tail, and lifting one of his frosty paws streaked with silvery fur.

"I'm glad to hear it, as you'll have plenty of opportunities to make more weather as the war unfolds," came the voice of Gillamon as he walked up to them in the form of an old soldier. He was the leader of the Order of the Seven team and could take any shape or form. Today he was dressed in a hunting frock and brown breeches and was known by the humans as Mr. Atticus. He puffed on his intricately carved pipe, and the sweet smell of cherry tobacco filled the air as smoke curled around his three-cornered hat. Gillamon's smiling blue eyes twinkled as he reached down to pet the pair of Scotties. "Well done on the long march from Boston."

"Gillamon! I wondered when we'd see ye again," Max exclaimed happily. "Aye, two hundred-twenty miles were a long way through Massachusetts, Rhode Island, Connecticut, an' down through Westchester County, but most of the humans made it in two weeks. Some rode in carriages, some on horses, an' a few traveled a wee bit by water, but most of the eight thousand lads had ta march on foot. Some still be on their way, includin' Jock's human, Colonel Knox."

"Aye! We walked about twelve hours a day, going five or six miles before we even ate breakfast!" Jock added. "The poor humans had to carry their heavy packs through the rain and mud, dragging wagons, but they kept up the fast pace that Washington set."

"Aye, the warm welcome an' cheers lifted the army's spirits as we went from town ta town," Max added. "The humans lined the streets, an' gave all sorts of dinners an' toasts ta honor General Washington an' the army as we marched through."

"Yeah, all of America must be happy about the Continental Army fighting the British!" Jock enthused, wagging his tail.

"Not all, lad," Gillamon corrected him. "Especially not here in New York."

"What do you mean, Gillamon?" Jock asked, wide-eyed. "Doesn't every American want independence?"

Gillamon puffed on his pipe and shook his head. "No, young one. Only a third of the people in these colonies want independence." He turned his gaze and spotted an unusual statue behind them. "Follow me."

"Those wantin' independence be called Patriots," Max affirmed as he and Jock followed along behind Gillamon.

Gillamon led them away from the waterside over to Bowling Green—a small, oval park of green grass enclosed by a black, wrought-iron fence with golden crowns atop each fence post. In the center was a large equestrian statue raised on a white marble pedestal fifteen feet high. An oversized man wearing a laurel crown and flowing robes sat atop a normal-sized horse, sculpted out of lead and gilded in brilliant gold.

"Who's that?" Jock wanted to know while walking around the base of the statue that towered above them.

"*That* is King George III," Gillamon answered, pointing his pipe at the golden statue that glimmered in the sunshine.

Jock cocked his head. "He looks like an ancient Roman emperor."

Max frowned. "Aye, an' he *acts* like one, too, lad. All tyrants think they be bigger than they are."

"This statue was erected in *gratitude* to the king after he repealed the 1765 Stamp Act," Gillamon explained.

"Thanks ta the Voice of the R-R-Revolution, Patrick Henry! His bold speech against the hated Stamp Act started the ball of the R-r-revolution r-r-rollin'!" Max interjected. "Henry's fiery words inspired Patriots ta form the Sons of Liberty all over the colonies. He called *this* George on a horse a *tyrant!*"

Gillamon nodded. "But in the years that followed, King George and Parliament kept imposing taxes and stripping away the liberties of the people. The Sons of Liberty and other dedicated Patriots began the movement to break away from Great Britain toward independence. But not every American wants to separate from the Crown. One third of them want to remain loyal to King George III and are called Loyalists, or Tories."

"Aye, an' the rest of them be undecided aboot wha' side ta take, but that choice will get harder an' harder as the war heats up," Max added.

"Both Patriots and Loyalists are putting pressure on the undecided ones to join their cause and seek to punish those who don't support them," Gillamon explained. "It's not just a revolution, but a civil war that is happening in America. It's sadly tearing families apart as the humans choose which side to take. Merchants are losing their businesses, and many have boarded up their shops and fled from New York just as they did in Boston."

"Tarrin' an' featherin' be popular with the Sons of Liberty who be tryin' ta *convince* every non-Patriot ta join their side," Max explained. "They get a bit r-r-ruff, but they be passionate aboot the cause of liberty."

"So, Americans aren't just fighting the *British*. They're fighting each other," Jock realized, frowning at the state of things in America.

Gillamon chuckled. "Remember that every citizen in these colonies *is* British. At least up until now."

Jock laughed at himself. "Aye. So why did you say that the humans would especially not be happy here in New York?"

"Because unlike Boston, New York is full of Loyalists who own two-thirds of the property here. This city is full of wealthy, prominent families who have strong, royal ties with King George," Gillamon explained. "Merchants have become rich by trading with England and are therefore extremely loyal to their business partners over three thousand miles away. You'll see many churches here in New York, but it is the Church of England that dominates the people, who see King George as the head of their church as well as their homeland. They will not betray their faith, which would be the same as betraying the mother country."

Max frowned. "But the Church of England—bein' Trinity Church here in New York—also owns a big tr-r-ract of land north of here called 'The Holy Gr-r-round' where anythin' but holy things happen. Lots of bad people gather there, an' Washington's already worried aboot his men bein' tempted by strong drink an' lewd lasses. It's a wicked, filthy slum district full of bad places! I jest dunnot understand why the church allows that land ta be used in such a way. The army's enemy won't jest be the Br-r-ritish army but *badness*. Young, naive lads away from home for the first time will be hard ta keep in line."

Gillamon nodded. "Indeed, Max. Washington took command of this hodge-podge of soldiers from different colonies, backgrounds, and beliefs and seeks to inspire them to be disciplined men of honor, good character, and virtue. The army's routine includes daily prayer and Sunday worship, which the General models himself, never missing services. But a soldier's behavior always comes down to his individual, personal choices. Washington knows he cannot impose his beliefs on his men, but he hopes to inspire them by setting an example with his own conduct. He strives to bring order from chaos, and cleanliness from filth. Washington first seeks to inspire his men to choose to behave in a worthy, dutiful manner. But if that fails, he won't hesitate to punish poor behavior and bad choices. His task is a difficult one also because the men fight among themselves, disliking those not from their own colonies. These thirteen colonies are not one united nation yet. Washington is doing all he can to unite them, especially before they come face to face with a powerful enemy army on the battlefield."

"Ye see, Jock, r-r-right now these men jest be fightin' *against* things, like taxes, tyranny, an' injustice," Max further explained. "Until the Continental Congress also stops fightin' between themselves as separate colonies an' becomes unified with some sort of declaration of independence, they won't have anything ta fight *for.*"

"So that's what Liz and Nigel are doing for their part of the mission in Virginia and Philadelphia?" Jock queried, referring to two other members of the Order of the Seven team. Brilliant French cat Liz and British mouse Nigel were skilled at history, politics, and the written word, so were assigned to help with that side of the quest for independence. "While we're here on the battlefield, they're working on giving the colonies something to bring them together for the same purpose—independence as one nation?"

"Perfectly stated, young one," Gillamon answered with a smile. "One nation under God."

Suddenly they heard horse hooves echoing off the cobblestones and looked over to see General George Washington riding toward them sitting atop a beautiful white horse named 'Blueskin.' The magnificent horse was a blue roan breed with a dark coat beneath its white hair. In the summer months, his shorter hair gave him a blueish appearance. In winter, Blueskin's coat would thicken and appear pure white. Washington loved Blueskin for his speed and performance, and Blueskin was proud to be one of Washington's favorite horses.

At six feet, two inches, Washington was taller than most men, and had a muscular build with broad shoulders, a strong face, prominent nose, and grey-blue eyes. Always impeccably dressed in a resplendent blue and buff uniform trimmed in gold buttons and epaulettes, sky-blue sash and black polished boots, and black three-cornered hat, forty-four-year-old Washington exuded confidence and ease in the saddle. He was considered the best horse-man in Virginia, riding with grace, power, and skill whether it be on the chase in a fox hunt at his home of Mount Vernon or leading his men into battle as he did in the French and Indian War.

"*Two* Georges on horses," Jock noted. He looked from George Washington back to the statue of King George III. "I'm proud to be a Patriot pup and fol-low George *Washington!*"

Max beamed. "Aye! That's me lad! The Maker has gr-r-rand things planned for America, an' he's chosen *this* George ta be the one ta lead the way. I'm honored ta be the one charged ta pr-r-rotect him. I'm glad that the march from Boston went as smooth as silk."

"Speaking of silk and protection," Gillamon said, pointing to the painted white silk flag waving in the breeze that was carried by a handsome soldier with dark hair, a dark complexion, and a muscular build. He and a half-dozen soldiers mounted on horseback escorted Washington. "Washington was wise to create the Life Guard before leaving Cambridge."

Max nodded, looking to see who was carrying the flag. "Looks like the general gave Thomas Hickey the honor ta carry the flag inta New York today. He's one of Washington's favorites."

The flag was painted with a guardsman holding the reins of a horse while receiving a flag from the 'Genius of Liberty,' a woman leaning on the red, white, and blue shield of stars and stripes. Standing next to her was a bald eagle, and above them a banner with the motto, 'CONQUER OR DIE.'

Jock cocked his head. "Why does Washington need Life Guards?"

"Important leaders throughout history have always needed protection," Gillamon explained. "Enemies think that attacking or eliminating the head of an army, a government, or a cause will allow them to triumph. Of course, this isn't always the case. Sometimes such enemy attacks have the *opposite* effect."

"I'll never forget how them Philistines came after young David after he were anointed king of Israel," Max growled. "Ye can be sure that the minute the Maker gives ye anythin' worth fightin' for, the Enemy will come an' try ta destr-r-roy it or take it away. But when ye've got the Maker on yer side, ye'll be more powerful than those fightin' against ye. An' the only way ta get str-r-rong comes from the fight."

"Well said, Max," Gillamon agreed. "And as David was divinely anointed, so, too has this infant nation been anointed and destined for greatness. America will be a beacon of light in a dark world, and the Enemy wants to destroy it before it can even be born. So, because the Continental Army is so young and fragile, the Enemy knows that if Washington is eliminated, the army will fall."

"And if the *army* falls, the fight for independence will also fall," Jock realized, frowning.

"That's right, little one," Gillamon affirmed him. "It doesn't matter if the colonies declare independence if they don't have an army to fight and defend their bold words. Humans have long debated which is mightier—the pen or the sword. But I hope you're starting to understand that for America to be a free and independent nation, *both* must be mighty."

"Aye, words an' actions must both be str-r-rong an' back each other up!" Max agreed. "So now that Washington's on the move, security be a top pr-r-riority ta keep him safe from surprise attacks. Fifty Life Guards have been assigned ta pr-r-rotect Washington. They'll also pr-r-rotect the general's baggage an' the official papers of the Continental Army, which are kept in a big r-r-red trunk."

Washington dismounted Blueskin to enter what would become his military headquarters at No. 1 Broadway. The stately, yellow-brick townhouse known as the Kennedy Mansion faced Bowling Green in front and overlooked the Hudson River in back.

"So, the cause of independence depends on the army, and the army depends on George Washington. Everything is riding on *that George* on his horse!" Jock realized. "Being a Life Guard is a more important job than I thought! How did those soldiers get picked?"

"Well, bein' the orderly leader he is, Washington gave str-r-rict instructions for who could be a Life Guard," Max answered, keeping an eye on Washington as he walked up the steps into the townhouse. "Besides the officers an' the r-r-rank an' file soldiers, there be six drummers, six fifers, an' a dr-r-rum major."

"Washington asked each regiment to provide four men, so the entire army was represented by each colony," Gillamon added. "He required them to be five feet, eight inches to five feet, ten inches tall, well built, clean, sober, intelligent, of good character, and reliable men."

"I like their motto, 'Conquer or die.' It doesn't leave r-r-room for anything else in between," Max stated with a furrowed brow. "I'm glad ta have those lads helpin' me ta pr-r-rotect Washington. He'll have lots of enemies here in New York, comin' at him fr-r-rom all sides."

"Including from the *inside* as we experienced in Boston with that traitor Dr. Church," Gillamon warned them. "We must be vigilant at all times and watch out for other Loyalist traitors in our midst. While the Loyalists dominate New York, many of them have fled, including the royal Governor of New York, William Tryon. But he didn't flee very far."

"Where is he, Gillamon?" Jock asked.

"He fled to a ship called the *Duchess of Gordon* and is out there floating in New York Harbor below The Narrows, protected by the British warship *Asia*. He no doubt has a network of spies throughout the city. I'll need you two to be the eyes and ears around Washington and his military staff to keep on the alert for any Loyalist plots."

"Ye can count on us, Gillamon!" Max exclaimed, chest puffed out and head erect, pointy ears up. "Conquer or die."

"Aye!" Jock agreed, assuming the same stance as his grandsire. "Conquer or die!"

Gillamon nodded and reached down to give Max and Jock another pet. "Good lads. While you look after things here, I have to make a short trip to Philadelphia. I won't be gone long and will check back in with you when I return."

"Are ye goin' ta help them paper pushers in Congress?" Max asked.

"Not right now," Gillamon answered. "I rather need to go *prevent* some paper pushing."

2

A Treacherous Pattern

MORTIER MANSION, MANHATTAN,
NEW YORK, APRIL 17, 1776

"Now, please take this large blue trunk to the upstairs bedroom, and that box of dishes to the dining room," Martha Washington instructed workers with a full, clear voice as she walked around the chaotic foyer of this elegant manor house, inspecting the numerous crates, trunks, and boxes brought in from the carriage and wagons. She had finally arrived to join her husband here in New York as she had in Cambridge, bringing with her clothes, fine china, silverware, stemware, crates of food, and other supplies. The attractive forty-five-year-old, five-foot tall Martha was a petite powerhouse of organization, but she delivered instructions with such warmth that everyone gladly did her bidding, with a smile.

The Mortier Mansion was located roughly two miles north of Washington's military headquarters at No. 1 Broadway and stood on twenty-six beautiful acres with a commanding view of the Hudson River and the distant New Jersey shore. Previously occupied by wealthy British deputy paymaster general, Major General Abraham Mortier, who fled the coming conflict, the beautiful white house was five bays wide and three bays deep. Its double-decker columned porches offered ample outdoor seating to enjoy the beauty of the tall oaks, fragrant gardens, and serenading songbirds. Former Commander-in-Chief of the British army in North America, Sir Jeffrey Amherst, had used the Mortier house as his headquarters at the close of the French and Indian War. Now it would be used by the Commander-in-Chief of the Continental Army, who would soon face the powerful British army. Not only was the estate a beautiful retreat for George and Martha, but it was also seen as an ideal place for Washington's Life Guards to provide optimum security.

"Steady as a clock, busy as a bee, cheerful as a cricket," Martha exclaimed with a singular clap of her hands as the two men lugged the heavy blue trunk upstairs to the Washingtons' bedroom. She stood with one hand on her hip, and another touching the white lacey mobcap under her stylish bonnet to make sure it was securely in place.

Suddenly Max and Jock came bounding up the steps and inside the house. They ran over to Martha, who smiled and squatted to happily pet the two Scotties. "Why, Max and Jock! How are my two favorite Scots? Did you two protect the General on the trip from Boston?"

Aye, that's exactly wha' we did, lass! Max whimpered, licking Martha's hand, and wagging his tail.

Jock nudged in his nose for some affection, furiously wagging his tail. *And we'll keep you safe here, too!*

A man walked into the foyer with Martha's beloved basket of quilting materials. "I'll take that, there's a good lad." She picked up her current quilting project and lovingly draped it over her arm with a gentle pat. "We'll bring order out of this chaos soon enough."

"Mrs. Washington, may I say how fortunate General Washington is to have such an efficient yet genteel *commander* to manage his domestic affairs?" Captain Caleb Gibbs of the Life Guard offered, carrying a large bearskin rug into the house. Two Life Guards brought in a large red trunk and set it down next to him, catching their breath and respectfully standing at attention.

Martha's hazel eyes twinkled, and she emitted her infectious giggle. "I thank you kindly, Captain! Becoming a widow with small children at twenty-six, I was baptized by the fire of running a large estate overnight. I had to learn how to do everything from pay bills, plant crops, fix buildings, feed and clothe people, care for animals, and even order *fish* nets. When one must learn to do so many important things *quickly,* one tends to figure out how to do them *efficiently.* " She tapped the bearskin that was used to drape the important red trunk holding Washington's military papers. "But you shall have the greater task of managing the operations for this household to oversee the General's safety with these fine men and the house staff." She swept her hand before the three men standing there. "I take great comfort in knowing that *you* are in charge, sir."

Captain Gibbs put a finger to his hat. "I humbly thank you, ma'am. We'll have two armed sentries at the front entrance of the house and two positioned at the back. The men will take shifts, with guards posted around the clock. As the General moves during the day or night, so will his appointed Life Guards. And one guard will be assigned to always watch over the General's trunk. Since these are all new operating procedures, we will be conducting drills to make sure the men are well prepared for any sudden emergencies."

"So, you *too* must learn to do many important things quickly, and efficiently," Martha quipped with a smile.

"I like it. Sounds like the lad has a solid plan," Max whispered to Jock. "Security must be a top pr-r-riority. All it would take is one shot of a musket or one swipe of a blade ta kill Washington."

Martha pointed to the big red trunk. "Very good, Captain. Now this needs to go to General Washington's study, just down the hall."

"Proceed, men. I'll be right with you," Captain Gibbs told the Life Guards who took the trunk as directed. A middle-aged woman walked into the foyer and curtsied. "Mrs. Washington, allow me to introduce Mrs. Mary Smith. She will be the head housekeeper to supervise the house staff, run the kitchen, and oversee the General's day-to-day expenses. She comes highly recommended from several prominent families in the area."

"Splendid!" Martha answered, extending a hand of greeting to the lady. "I'm delighted to meet you, Mrs. Smith. Thank you in advance for the important service you will render to General Washington and his staff here."

"Thank you, Mrs. Washington. It will be my honor," Mrs. Smith replied with a soft voice. She pointed to the quilt topper. "Is this your work? It's lovely."

Martha lifted the quilt topper in process. So far it was a simple hodge-podge of patchwork stars. She pulled from the basket some cloth swatches in various colors. "Yes, thank you. I'm always sewing something. I am working on a special quilt to reflect the General's new command."

"How grand!" Mrs. Smith exclaimed. "It is always wonderful to watch disorganized pieces of cloth come together to make such beautiful quilts."

Martha held up a finger. "The end result must always be thoroughly envisioned before one begins a quilt. It takes careful planning and precise measuring, cutting, and placement of fabrics. One must work from the center out until reaching the desired size. But if done right and well, the pattern always emerges."

"It takes skillful talent to bring order from chaos," Captain Gibbs complimented her with a smile and a finger to his hat. "Excuse me, ladies."

Mrs. Smith watched the captain walk away. "Is there anything in particular that our kitchen could prepare for your first dinner this evening?"

"I'm quite fond of fish, and the General loves peas," Martha replied, leaning in with a wink. "If it's quite convenient."

Mrs. Smith smiled and nodded. "Certainly, ma'am. I'll make sure those dishes are included on the menu."

"I wanna be *her* best friend to help out in the kitchen!" Jock whispered to Max.

"Very well, thank you," Martha replied. "Now, shall we get back to work?"

"Ma'am," Mrs. Smith replied with a nod, curtsying, and turning to go to the kitchen.

Suddenly they heard the heavy footsteps of General Washington coming up the stairs and entering the foyer. "Welcome, Mrs. Washington," he said with a subdued smile, coming over to take her hand in his and kiss her on the cheek. "I trust you had an uneventful journey?"

Martha gazed happily up into her husband's eyes. "I did, Mr. Washington, thank you. I'm so happy to be here with you now."

Washington towered over his wife and forced a smile. "I'm happy as well. I've missed having you by my side."

Martha wrinkled her brow. "Something troubles you."

Washington looked around to ensure they were alone. He never openly showed emotion, or discussed sensitive matters in public. He lowered his voice to a whisper. "Many things. Uppermost of course are unfinished fortifications to defend New York before British forces arrive. The task is formidable. But we've had word of Loyalist plots everywhere in the city. While he was here, General Lee learned that Governor Tryon was running all sorts of underhanded operations from his ship. Somehow, *from his ship,* Tryon arranged for his former servant James Brattle to spy on the Continental Congress by becoming a personal valet to New York delegate James Duane. He copied Duane's congressional session meeting notes at night in Philadelphia and sent them to Tryon here in New York. When he was discovered, he quickly fled." Washington clenched his jaw. "Tryon's influence and reach are extensive."

Martha's eyes widened in alarm, and she hoarsely whispered, "Why he's like a scheming spider spinning a web out there on that ship!"

Washington nodded. "It gets worse, I'm afraid. When General Stirling took over things here after Lee departed for South Carolina, he uncovered another wicked scheme. Tryon is actually bankrolling an effort to bribe Patriot soldiers to switch sides and fight for the British forces."

"Oh! How dare he think of luring our boys!" Martha protested. "You already struggle with having enough men to fight."

Washington closed his eyes and put a finger to his mouth so Martha wouldn't speak so loudly. "Tryon must be cut off from the city, so I will draft a letter to address the issue with the local authorities."

She gave him a determined nod, cupped her small hand in the crook of his arm and gave him a confident squeeze. "Then I shall pray for the wisdom you need, General Washington. And we shall discuss things in detail later this evening. Off you go then. Get to it."

The Commander-in-Chief gratefully bowed, the corner of his mouth slightly upturned. "Yes, Mrs. Washington."

As Washington's footsteps sounded on the hardwood floors heading to his study, Max and Jock looked at one another, frowning.

Max growled. "Why that floatin', schemin' governor!"

"How do we find out how Tryon's doing all this stuff?" Jock wondered with worried eyes.

"Like Lady Washington said aboot her quiltin', a pattern always emerges," Max told him. "We jest need ta find the exact pattern of Tr-r-ryon's web an' how he's plottin' ta catch our soldiers."

"A pattern?" Jock asked.

"Aye," Max said, heading to Washington's study. "A tr-r-reacherous pattern."

MORTIER MANSION, MANHATTAN, NEW YORK, APRIL 18, 1776

"So, this is the letter Washington wrote last night to the New York Committee of Safety?" Jock asked, cocking his head as he and Max read over the letter that Martha was in the process of copying for her husband, as she frequently did to assist him. "Even *he* calls it evil! But what does it mean?"

It is therefore Gentlemen that I have taken the Liberty to address you on this important Subject, relying upon your Zeal and attachment to the Cause of American Liberty for your assistance in putting a Stop to this Evil, and that you will cooperate with me in such measures as shall be effectual, either to prevent any future Correspondence with the Enemy, or in bringing to Condign punishment such Persons as may be hardy and wicked enough to carry it on, otherwise than by a prescribed mode, if any Case can possibly arise to require it.

"Well, he's sayin' that visitors be comin' an' goin' ta Governor Tryon's ship as they please, bringin' supplies an' all sorts of communication," Max explained. "Washington's gettin' tough, orderin' that from now on, anyone who communicates with Tryon won't jest be br-r-reakin' r-r-rules, but committin' tr-r-reason. If we're fightin' a war, an' Tr-r-ryon's the enemy, then no one best be helpin' him!"

Jock's eyes widened. "Ohhh, I see. That means that no little boat in the harbor will be allowed to row out to any British ships, especially the *Duchess,* anymore. But there are lots and lots of boats out there! How are the Patriots going to stop them all?"

Max frowned. "That's the problem, lad. Between the br-r-ribin' an' the dark of night, that schemin' governor can ferry supplies an' spies back an' forth, an' keep controllin' the city even while sittin' on his ship down in the Narrows."

"So, it's going to be a fight between Washington and Tryon on who really runs this city," Jock realized. "What can we do to help the humans?"

"Gillamon said for us ta be eyes an' ears, so that's wha' we'll be," Max replied. "We're goin' ta patr-r-rol up an' down the streets of Manhattan ta see wha' we can find out from the humans. Let's go."

"Aye, this is war!" Jock agreed, following Max out the door.

DUCHESS OF GORDON, THE NARROWS, NEW YORK, APRIL 19, 1776

Waves lapped against the hull of the ship that gently rocked with the swells of tidal currents in New York Harbor. The *Duchess of Gordon*, along with the British ships *Asia, Phoenix, Mercury, Lively,* and a handful of transports had been driven here outside the Narrows, out of reach of rebel cannons and gunmen. Forty-seven-year-old British-born Governor William Tryon had shivered through the bitter cold winter aboard the *Duchess* as he spun his web of espionage and clandestine activity to undermine the rebels at every turn. It was now spring, but the bitter cold had intensified his bitterness at being confined to a rocking ship instead of a palatial mansion on dry ground to run the affairs of this colony for the Crown.

New York City Mayor David Matthews, newly appointed by Governor Tryon, watched the wine sway back and forth in the goblets as the ship moved. He dabbed at the corners of his mouth with a linen napkin. "I must say, Governor, that you serve a bountiful table despite being confined to the *Duchess*. Those oysters were outstanding, as was the mutton." He took a sip of madeira and set his goblet on the table. "But I'm afraid this will be the last time I can safely come to you with this newly announced resolution by the New York Committee of Safety. The Continental Army has already begun enforcing these measures."

Tryon held the freshly inked resolution brought by Matthews up to his face in the dim candlelight with one hand while gripping a dinner fork with the other. He had a nasally, high-pitched British accent coupled with a mocking tone of disdain as he read aloud what Washington had asked the Committee to relay to the inhabitants of New York:

"*Resolved and ordered, that no inhabitants of this colony, upon any pretense, or for any purpose whatsoever, either in person or in writing, directly or indirectly, do presume to have or maintain any intercourse whatsoever with any ship or vessel belonging to or in the service of the King of Great Britain,*" Tryon spat, angrily crinkling the paper. "*. . . or with any person or persons on board of the same, upon being dealt with in the severest manner, as enemies to the rights and liberties of the United North American Colonies.*" He suddenly balled up the resolution and threw it across the cabin. "Curse them!"

Matthews shrugged his shoulders and cleared his throat. "I'm afraid that means the delivery of goods including the sale of food will be prohibited, and while you have your sources to get whatever you wish, this will certainly drive fear into the people you deal with in the city. Your bribes will no doubt need to increase to offset their risk. It also will make it difficult for me to communicate here with you in person. I'll have to have documented, approved visitation from Washington's officers, stating my official business and reason for seeing you."

"The utter absurdity of it all! I am Royal GOVERNOR of New York! And yet I am a prisoner on my own ship in MY city, bah!" Tryon shouted. He leaned forward with squinty eyes, pointing with his fork. *"He did this, you know! Washington!* George Washington has been a thorn in my side long enough. He's taken *my* city from me! He has made my loyal citizens flee New York for sanctuary and turned the city into a cesspool of rebels!" Tryon spat, waving his hand in the air. "And he humiliated His Majesty's forces in Boston, causing them to flee *that* city! He's a thorn in the side of *every* Briton. I dare say that if it weren't for him as the Commander-in-Chief of their pathetic little army, there would *be* no army." He got up from the table and paced back and forth for a moment. He then stopped at the window to gaze out at the lights dotting the darkened harbor, letting go a heavy sigh following his rant.

"Before your appointment here in New York, you were known as the 'Butcher of North Carolina' when you were governor," Matthews noted. "You were able to subdue the so-called Regulators when they rebelled against what they considered to be oppressive taxes in 1770—one tax was to build your personal mansion, I believe, 'Tryon's Palace.' How did you successfully crush *that* rebellion?"

"Those were dirty, poor farmers," Tryon answered, waving them off with a hand in the air. "My militia rounded up their leaders and quickly tried and sentenced them on the spot. Hanging the rebel leaders made the protesting peasants fall into line. It was easy to snuff out that rebellion." He paused and clucked his tongue. "But it would not do to treat the New Yorkers as I did the Regulators; they are a very different kind of men. Parliament would never allow me to hire my own militia and send them running through the streets to kill rebels at will. No, I must do things differently here."

"Well, Governor Tryon, you have done an admirable job of turning ordinary citizens into willing soldiers ready to take up arms in pockets all over New York," Matthews noted. "You've already bribed most of the New York gunsmiths to supply arms when needed. And your efforts to bribe rebel soldiers from local militias and the Continental Army to switch sides is showing great promise."

"Yes, yes, yes, but we need to do *more* than that, something grander," Tryon interjected, clasping his hands behind his back. He paused a moment and then slowly turned to grin at Matthews. "We don't need just *any* soldiers to switch sides. Not just local militia, or even enlisted Continental soldiers." He came over and rested his knuckles on the table in front of Matthews, impishly twirling his tongue in his cheek. "We need to get to rebel soldiers on the *inside*—in Washington's inner circle."

Matthews leaned forward. "I'm listening."

Tryon's mind was racing with a plot so sinister that not even he could formulate words fast enough, such was the dark pleasure of his intent. "When the Howe brothers and our British forces arrive in New York City . . . we're going to kill him. We're going to assassinate George Washington."

3

A Goot Man

PHILADELPHIA, PENNSYLVANIA, APRIL 25, 1776

"*Counterfeiting is easy. The hard part is getting the right paper.*"
Isaac Ketcham frowned as those words echoed over and over in his mind. They were uttered not by himself but by a criminal named Henry Dawkins. Ketcham could see the smile of this shady character leaning over the table as light illuminated his grimy face. Dawkins licked his fingers to pinch out the candle's flame, his words mingling in the air with the curl of smoke in the darkened room. Ketcham got up from the table and slipped quietly out the door of the house where Dawkins was hiding. But despite the late hour, the dark night, and their careful secrecy, watchful eyes saw Ketcham leave the house belonging to his friends, the Young brothers.

Dawkins had been released from prison in January, but instead of learning from his mistakes and starting with a clean slate, he ran straight back into darkness. A silversmith and an engraver by trade, he was an honest, prosperous artisan before he turned to a life of crime. Coming from London to Philadelphia in 1754, he embarked on an exciting new life in America. He enjoyed a profitable, rewarding career for two decades. But as tensions rose between Great Britain and her colonies, demand dwindled for things like book plates, maps, coats of arms, seals, and rings for wealthy Philadelphians. So, the starving artist went to New York to see if he could make a living there. But Dawkins made bad choices, and fell into bad company with bad actions, and bad consequences.

While in prison he was visited by a man named Israel Young who was looking for someone with Dawkins's skills. Young had just bought a printing press and needed an engraver. Together they hatched a plan to set up a counterfeiting operation in Young's house in Cold Spring Harbor, Long Island, with Israel's little brother, Isaac. The three men would make easy money forging counterfeit bills. Counterfeiting was a thriving business in the colonies, as it was difficult for the authorities to effectively monitor and control the practice. Real money looked so shoddy that it was easy to make fake currency. One only needed to make sure there were enough imperfections in the bills so it wouldn't stand out as being *too* perfect. Authorities now had their hands full with preparing to fight a war. Small scammers like the trio of counterfeiters could easily hide away printing money in their attic and avoid detection while making a small fortune. They had the printing press, the engraver, and the ink. All they needed was paper. And there was only one place where that paper was made for such exclusive use—Philadelphia.

Ketcham thought about what he was getting ready to do. He wasn't a criminal; He was a *good* man, an honest family man. But he was out of work. And he had six children at home with no mother to care for them. How was he supposed to put food on the table and care for his children? *Oh, my love, how will we ever make it without you?!* Ketcham's grief was fresh, as he had only recently lost his wife. *I'm glad you're not here to see what I'm doing.* He shook his head at himself and his situation. *I don't want to be part of this scheme, but I feel like I have no choice. If only I had a way out.*

As his horse clip-clopped down the streets of Philadelphia, Ketcham pulled from his pocket a tiny piece of paper and stared at it with a frown. It was a sample of the exact paper that Dawkins and the Young brothers needed to print their counterfeit currency. The Young brothers had approached him with an idea to make some easy money. All he had to do was travel to Philadelphia, find the right papermaker, make the purchase, travel back to Long Island, and deliver the paper to them. That was it. The young widower would have no further part to play in the secret operation taking place in the hidden attic in Cold Spring Harbor. He would be paid for his part once the press started rolling. Ketcham was already coming to Philadelphia to sell two horses, so he hadn't made this trip *just* for the counterfeiters. Getting the paper was merely a side errand. He would buy and deliver the paper, return to his six children in Huntington, Long Island, and be done with it. *Then* he'd find a way to make an honest living.

The Youngs had instructed Ketcham to stop in Brunswick Landing, New Jersey, on the way, and talk to a man named Levi Lott. This man had knowledge of paper mills and could provide him with information on where exactly to find the right paper in Philadelphia. But Lott only gave Ketcham a sample of the paper that he cut away from a full page of real Continental currency. Ketcham would have to show the paper sample around to merchants in the city and find the right papermaker on his own. *Counterfeiting is easy. The hard part is getting the right paper.* Ketcham rolled his eyes. *No kidding,* he thought to himself.

Ketcham had already sold the two horses as he planned, so his original purpose for coming to Philadelphia was accomplished. *Maybe I should leave now and wash my hands of this other shady business.* But he was already here.

Why not just complete the task, get the money I so desperately need, and then start doing the right thing to earn money? No real harm done, other than to my conscience.

The struggling man dismounted his horse and tied it to a post in front of a row of merchants. He pulled out the sample paper, clenched his jaw, and started walking in and out of shops, making inquiries about the paper mill he needed to find. As he left the third shop, a tall, blonde-headed Dutchman followed him out into the street.

"Hallo. I couldn't help oferhearing yer question about de paper," the Dutchman said, pointing to Ketcham's hand with his ornately carved pipe. His exaggerated, bushy blonde eyebrows humorously extended out over his striking blue eyes. "Dis merchant is a frient of me."

Ketcham wanted to chuckle at the funny looking and sounding man, but simply grinned before looking both ways to see who was near them in the street. He opened his hand to reveal the sample paper. "Good day, sir. Uh, yes, yes. The paper. I've come to Philadelphia to find the paper mill that makes this particular stock." He leaned in to show the sample to the Dutchman. "Are you familiar with such paper?"

The Dutchman took the paper in hand and studied it, puffing on his pipe while his bushy eyebrows wiggled up and down, causing Ketcham to smile. Ketcham hadn't smiled in a week from the heavy burden he carried. He was glad for the comic relief. The Dutchman nodded and handed the paper back to Ketcham. "Ja, I know dis paper." He leaned in to stare Ketcham right in the eye. "Dey won't sell it ta ye."

Ketcham frowned and leaned back, surprised. "Excuse me, sir, but why do you say that?"

The Dutchman tapped the paper with his pipe. "Dis is *official* paper. Dey are sworn."

"Sworn?" Ketcham asked.

"Ja, sworn. De paper mill has sworn dat dey will only make dis paper for official use," the Dutchman explained. "Anyway, if ye carry dis paper, what will ye tell men if dey stop ye?"

Ketcham didn't answer. He couldn't answer. The Dutchman was right. If he were stopped by the authorities and found with stacks of official *blank* Continental currency paper, they would know exactly what he was doing. He would be locked away in prison for counterfeiting. *Then* what would his children do? He looked at the paper sample and closed his fist over it. His stomach grumbled, and he quickly put his balled fist over his belly.

"*Van de hand in de tand leven?*" the Dutchman asked with a firm gaze that seemed to pierce Ketcham's soul. It was as if this man knew how dire

Ketcham's financial situation was. The Dutchman put a hand to his mouth. "Ye are lifing hant ta mous?"

Ketcham looked down to the ground and nodded. "Yes, I am living hand to mouth. Plus, I have six children to support," he blurted out, suddenly feeling the need and the freedom to unburden himself to this stranger. He threw his hand up and let it fall to his side, his voice trembling. "I . . . have no work."

The Dutchman clasped his hands in front of him and leaned forward. "Go home, ja? Go home ta dose children. Forget dis paper business. I am sure ye can fint some work, ja? *Beter ten halve gekeerd dan ten hele gedwaald.*"

Ketcham wrinkled his brow, obviously convicted that the Dutchman was right, and relieved to have someone affirm the right thing he needed to do. But he again didn't understand the Dutchman's words. "Pardon, sir?"

"It's better ta change direction halfway dan ta be wrong all de way," the Dutchman replied, twirling his finger in the air.

"Indeed, you are right, sir," Ketcham answered, looking at the ground.

"If some *gladjakker* sent ye here ta get dis paper, I would forget it! *Al is de leugen nog zo snel, de waarheid achterhaalt haar wel.*"

Ketcham looked blankly at the Dutchman.

"A *gladjakker* is a smoos talker who tells ye what ye want ta hear," the Dutchman explained. "Howefer quick a lie may be, the truse will ofertake it."

"However quick a lie may be, the truth will overtake it?" Ketcham repeated, to make sure he heard the Dutch-accented English correctly. He nodded, chagrined that the Dutchman suspected he was up to no good.

"Ja. Lies won't last. Da truse will always come out," the Dutchman reiterated. He reached into his pocket and handed Ketcham a handful of coins. "Get a goot meal. Go home. Da Lort will profide when we ask for help, ja? He's no *gladjakker*—He does what He says, for yer highest goot!"

"Thank you, sir. I don't know how to thank you," Ketcham said, humbled by the gesture of this kind stranger. He gave a single chuckle, gratefully took the coins in hand, and bowed his head in respect. "Sometimes I feel like God is the opposite of a *gladjakker*—telling me what I *don't* want to hear. I've never been much of a praying man."

"Well, now is a goot time ta start, ja?" The Dutchman winked at Ketcham under his bushy blonde eyebrows. "No matter how hart things are now, remember what we Dutch say, 'Eferything has an ent except Got.'"

"Everything has an end except God," Ketcham clarified. "I'll have to remember that."

The Dutchman gave a singular nod and gripped Ketcham by the upper arm. "Goot man. I will be on my way now. All will be well, ja? Haf a safe journey back to New York." With that he abruptly turned and walked away, leaving Ketcham in the street.

Ketcham watched the Dutchman turn the corner, and suddenly felt a burden lifted from his shoulders. His decision was made. He would not look any further for the paper the counterfeiters wanted *him* to take the risk of buying. He wanted no more part of this underhanded business. He smiled and lifted his chin as he walked to his horse. He couldn't wait to get home to his children. *Wait a minute. How did he know I was from New York? Maybe it was my accent. After all, it was the Dutch who first settled New York.* He looked up to the sky and whispered a soft prayer. "Well, 'Got,' you'll have to show me what to do next to be a 'goot' man. If you're there, please . . . help me."

The Dutchman leaned against a brick wall and watched Ketcham ride out of town. Gillamon grinned to himself. "Oh, He will, dear boy. His help won't be what you expect but trust Him anyway. You have no idea where this counterfeit business will lead, and the important role you will play to change history. 'Got' will show you what to do. As will I . . . back in New York."

SLURPING OYSTERS AND THREATENING CHOCOLATE

"He was a bold man that first ate an oyster," Major General Henry Clinton repeated with a laugh, quoting Jonathan Swift, as a servant placed a platter of freshly shucked oysters in front of him as he sat alone in his cabin. His large blue eyes squinted at the ocean through his open window while squeezing a lemon over the raw oysters on the half-shell. "As was the first man who dared to sail over that horizon." He mindlessly picked up an oyster and slurped down the raw delicacy. The bright noonday sun brought warmth to this spring day, but the monotonous, mastless ocean view irked the pudgy, second-ranked of Great Britain's commanding trio of generals who last year had come to America to squash the rebellion.

In January, Clinton had sailed south from Boston on orders from General Sir William Howe to execute a new southern strategy ordered by the Crown. But a month ago, the *northern* strategy suffered a setback. The besieged British were humiliatingly driven from Boston after the American rebels placed cannons atop Dorchester Heights, exactly as Clinton had warned Howe and Burgoyne they would. "But did they listen to me?" Clinton sarcastically grumbled to himself. He picked up another oyster and slurped it down. "Of course not."

Clinton sat aboard the sixth-rate man-o'-war *Mercury,* which had sailed south with the sloop *Falcon* and two transports carrying a pair of light infantry companies. Together they had spent seven gale-battered weeks to reach the treacherous Frying Pan Shoals before dropping anchor here at the mouth of the Cape Fear River. Upon their arrival on March 12th, they had expected to find a promised British fleet from Ireland and an army of North Carolinian Loyalist Highlanders ready to fall under Clinton's command. But no one was here.

The four southern royal governors of Virginia, North Carolina, South Carolina, and Georgia had all been chased from their provincial palaces by the American rebels and were themselves living aboard various ships. They had assured the Crown that it would not require an excessive amount of force to set things right in the south, as an abundance of loyal colonials would rally around the king's army. King George III enthusiastically agreed with the new southern strategy of sending an armada to assist the so-called 'good American' Loyalists to bring an end to the conflict with Great Britain, at least in the southern colonies.

"Every means of distressing America must meet with my concurrence," the king wrote within two hours of reading British Prime Minister Lord North's plan, quickly identifying British regiments in Ireland and two artillery companies to send to Cape Fear. Commodore Sir Peter Parker commanded the royal fleet sailing from Cork, Ireland, which would meet up with General Clinton and his fifteen hundred regulars sailing down to North Carolina from besieged Boston. Together they would gather the supposed throngs of North Carolina Loyalists and overwhelm the rebellious southern colonies to regain British control.

But in February, the impatient Loyalist Highlanders decided not to wait for Clinton to arrive. They led a failed skirmish at Moore's Creek Bridge with a thousand swords against a thousand muskets and rifles fired by Patriot militia and Continentals—and were defeated in three minutes. Tartan kilts floated around the fallen Scottish warriors drifting along in the creek's current, creating a colorful tapestry of Loyalist defeat. The civil war that had exploded in the colonial south now found the victorious Patriots with the upper hand, even more emboldened for the cause of liberty.

"Their courage was not war-proof," Clinton scoffed, reading the reports of Loyalist desertions leading up to the failed battle and after their stunning defeat. Now he would see what the British fleet could do for the other half of this southern strategy. It would be up to the British Navy to bring reinforcements and to turn the tide of this rebellion. But where were they? They were to have set sail in January. He had been sitting here slurping oysters for five weeks, waiting for the promised fleet of ships sailing from Ireland, but the horizon remained vacant of British canvas.

Clinton frowned, pushed back the empty oyster platter, belched, and wiped his hands with a linen napkin. He stood and picked up his violin, holding it under his cleft chin to play as he walked slowly back and forth in his cabin, thinking. He closed his eyes and his dark bushy eyebrows moved with the rise and fall of the notes of Haydn's melody.

The only child of a British admiral, forty-five-year-old Clinton was born in Newfoundland and spent his early years in New York, where his father served as the royal governor from 1743 to 1754. Socially awkward and shy, Clinton had poor interpersonal skills and was politically weak. Like Howe, he hadn't volunteered for this mission, but had reluctantly come on orders to serve here in America. But he was the most strategic thinker of the three generals, having learned military tactics while serving as an aide-de-camp to Prussia's brilliant Field Marshal Ferdinand on the battlefields of Europe. He spoke too freely, giving bold advice to his superior General Howe, who was more inclined to ignore it. As friction between them developed, Howe was more than happy to send Clinton south.

Clinton's suspicious nature kept him guarded, which kept even his colleagues guessing. But he was always thinking about the next move, many times while playing his violin. While studying Caesar's *Commentaries,* Clinton was more interested in what the Barbarians did to avoid battle than what strategy the Romans executed against them. The Barbarians refused to be pulled into an uneven fight. *The American rebels have done the unthinkable in the north and now appear to be doing so in the south,* he thought, pulling his bow across the violin strings. *These American 'Barbarians' know the fight is uneven. So, when we engage them in battle, we must crush them then and there—and not allow them to escape as Howe did in Boston after Bunker Hill.* Clinton frowned and shook his head. *We could have ended this rebellion then, but Howe would not listen to me when I wanted to chase the retreating rebels. He let them escape.*

The frustrated British general turned his attention back to the task now at hand. *How do we subdue not just another army but a* population *in rebellion? How do we gain the hearts and subdue the minds of America? This southern strategy is already not working, with Dunmore's defeat in Virginia and now the Loyalists' defeat in North Carolina. For South Carolina, attacking Charleston will be very difficult and will do little to win back the South. We should instead make a show of force in the Chesapeake and then rejoin Howe in New York for a concentrated campaign.* He stopped playing and held his violin as he gazed out to sea from his cabin window.

There in the distance, he saw a single ship appear on the horizon, the first of the Cork fleet to arrive. But he suddenly grew sullen about what they would accomplish in the Carolinas. *Any further maneuvers here in the South will only serve to inflame minds and sacrifice friends of the Crown to the rage and fury of the multitude of rebels.*

⚜

HMS *BRISTOL*, OFF THE NORTH CAROLINA COAST, MAY 3, 1776

Major General Lord Earl Charles Cornwallis sat reading on his bunk in this newly launched fifty-gun flagship of the caravan from Cork, the *Bristol.* He felt the furry cat at his feet roll over and drape a chubby leg across his boot. Cornwallis peered from around his book at the orange-striped feline. He smiled, shaking his head at the humorous stowaway that had been his cabin-mate for three long months at sea. "Perhaps you shall prefer American oysters to Irish whitefish, tabby cat." Little did he know that the cat he addressed was not only Irish, but a true connoisseur of fish. The cat's pickiness was due to seasickness.

After weeks of supplying and boarding troops in Cork, Ireland, the con-voy of forty-four ships including five men-o'-war and twenty-seven transports set sail on February 12th. But on the first day out of port, a fierce Atlantic storm tossed nine ships back to England, and after three weeks at sea, only fourteen vessels remained in the convoy. Violent gales, contrary winds, and storm-tossed seas left the convoy's troops seasick and battered. Commodore Sir Peter Parker and Cornwallis were unsure of just how many vessels would actually make it to Cape Fear, North Carolina, but they projected that the *Bristol* herself wouldn't arrive until the first of May.

Thirty-eight-year-old Cornwallis had charge of seven infantry regiments and two artillery units for this expedition. The mild-looking man had been promoted to major general in 1775, but had long served the king, beginning at age 17 when he acquired his first commission as an ensign. A year later he purchased a captaincy in the 85th Foot Regiment. He saw action as an aide-de-camp at the Battle of Minden, where the Marquis de Lafayette's father was killed in 1759. He was promoted to lieutenant colonel in the 12th Foot in 1761 and in 1766 became Colonel of the 33rd Foot. He was not the type to push and claw, nor scheme and manipulate his way to the top, but enjoyed rapid advancement due to who he was rather than what he had achieved.

Cornwallis was born into a distinguished English family, the eldest son of the first Earl Cornwallis, succeeding his father as the second Earl in 1762. Schooled at Eton and Cambridge, he was struck in the face while playing field hockey and suffered a permanent disfigurement, leaving him with a fixed, odd expression. He married happily, however, in 1768, and he and Jemima had two children. He was respected for his strong character and resolute principles. He wasn't particularly social and didn't gamble, drink heavily, or womanize as did many of his boisterous comrades. Although he had been sympathetic to the Americans in matters such as the 1765 Stamp Act, voting against the mea-sure, he felt they had crossed the line in Lexington and Concord. Cornwallis was fiercely loyal to the Crown and felt it was his duty to volunteer to fight against the rebellion and restore order to His Majesty's colonies.

King George III knew Cornwallis well, having given him several royal appointments over the years. The king was delighted to quickly accept Cornwallis's offer and gave him his own 33rd Regiment to take to America as part of his invasion force. Cornwallis's wife, however, was aghast and did everything she could to keep him from going. But nothing Jemima said mattered. Cornwallis was heading to America, and along with him, a young "blood" upstart named Banastre Tarleton.

Tarleton was among Cornwallis's troops currently plying the massive ocean swells across the Atlantic, but he was aboard a smaller vessel. Al was assigned to both Cornwallis and Tarleton. The comfort-loving cat knew the accommodations and food would be better with the senior officers, so decided to take up lodging with Cornwallis in his handsomely appointed officer quarters. But the queasy kitty surprisingly found himself turning his nose up at scraps of fish that Cornwallis offered him, which was completely out of character for the ever-hungry cat.

Al's whiskers twitched, and his eyes moved rapidly underneath his closed eyelids. He licked his chops as the aroma of hot chocolate in his dream brought back the vivid moments with Nigel at the Cocoa Tree Club in London back in December. Gillamon wanted them to witness an important scene with Al's human assignment, the roguish Banastre Tarleton.

The rich, spoiled son of a slave trader from Liverpool, Tarleton had squandered his inheritance within two years with wining, dining, and gambling while neglecting his law studies at Middle Temple. Joining the military was his only option after failing out of law school and running out of money.

In his dream, Al turned to see the twenty-one-year-old soldier flirting with a young lady before his friends called him over to their table in this famed chocolate house.

Tarleton was below middle height but obviously fit; his tailored scarlet coat accentuated his toned arms and broad chest. He was polished from head to toe, with a white ruffled shirt, buff waistcoat, buff breeches buttoned at the knee, and tall, polished black boots. One silver epaulet on his left shoulder signified his rank of cornet, and the dark blue facings of his scarlet coat indicated he served with the King's Dragoons. A long saber in a leather scabbard was strapped to his side.

Tarleton picked up his cup, closing his eyes as he smelled the chocolate aroma. "Ah, chocolate—the *eighth* deadly sin." He looked around at the men at his table and gave a wicked grin. "Brought to us courtesy of the Mayans, who would add sacrificial blood to their chocolate." Tarleton lifted his steaming cup of chocolate. "To the Mayans and to Medici!" He took a sip and closed his eyes with delight, licking his lips with satisfaction. "My favorite concoction."

"What exactly is in this 'Medici's Elixir?'" wondered Francis.

Tarleton swirled the chocolate and leaned forward with the cup for the men to get a whiff of the aromas. "Jasmine, cinnamon, vanilla beans, musk, ambergris, and citrus peel. This recipe was developed by Florence's chocolate-loving Grand Duke of Tuscany, Cosimo III de' Medici."

"When Medici visited London he frequented the other chocolate houses at St. James's, but someone stole his secret concoction to serve here at the Cocoa Tree," James added. "Some suspected that Medici sometimes would lace his special concoction with poison to murder his enemies."

"Death by chocolate. What a *delicious* way to slay your enemies," Tarleton jested, taking another sip. "The right people can do the wrong things, as long as they do them with good taste."

"Ah, so I assume you would adhere to Machiavelli's advice to Cosimo's Medici predecessor," Francis posed. "The ends justify the means?"

Tarleton set down his cup and casually draped his hands over his crossed legs. "But of course. Machiavelli plainly wrote of how the world *is*, rather than how it *should* be. So, the pursuit of the public good necessitates that those in power sometimes take action that private ethics or religious values would condemn as immoral or unjust."

"I like macaroni," Al said dully.

Nigel facepalmed and shook his head. "Mach-i-a-velli, a fifteenth-century Italian philosopher, diplomat, and writer during the Renaissance. His writings are so scandalous that they've been banned by the Pope and denounced here in London as pure evil! He boldly asserted that princes like the Medici should treat deception, murder, and other violence as *normal* and *necessary* to protect the republic and to remain in power. Machiavelli had quite the poison quill, I assure you!"

Al wrinkled his forehead. "Well, I'd stay away from his inkwell, then."

"Machiavelli dedicated *The Prince* to Lorenzo di Piero de' Medici, but I am of the school of thought that it was a satire," Richard said. "His subsequent *Discourses on Livy* perfectly lay out how a republic should be established and structured, based on Ancient Rome. How can you encourage a tyrant to ruthlessly hold on to power and yet serve as an architect for a healthy republic for the people at the same time? Surely he was jesting in *The Prince!*"

"Machiavelli forgives Romulus for murdering his co-heir and brother Remus to attain absolute power in order to establish a civil way of life for the masses in founding Rome, the greatest empire the world has ever known," Tarleton noted. "Again, the end always justifies the means."

"But I doubt Romulus used poisoned chocolate to kill his brother," James jested. His face then grew serious. "But using such philosophy, the sugar needed to sweeten this chocolate comes from the slave trade. Your father's sea merchant business included trading sugar and slaves while lining his pockets, which in turn helped build Liverpool into the important city that it is. So, the wickedness of slavery justifies our pleasure and the establishment of a city?"

"Absolutely," Tarleton unhesitatingly retorted, not batting an eye.

"He is *insufferable!*" Nigel fumed, pulling on his whiskers.

"Steady, Mousie," Al uttered calmingly.

James sat back and crossed his arms over his chest, clearly at odds with Tarleton on the issue of slavery. "And like Machiavelli, you don't care what people think about getting one's hands dirty. One should embody spirited, immodest ambition and pursue glory at whatever cost, is that it?"

Tarleton grinned and slowly nodded his head. "Machiavelli could not abide public indecision or leaders agonizing over hard decisions that must be made. I agree and likewise favor those who make swift, bold decisions. There is no glory without risk." Tarleton raised his chin. "Fortune favors the bold."

"But fortune does not favor the *reckless,* as I'm sure Tarleton's purse can attest," Nigel spat. "This cheeky fellow will be dangerous on the battlefield. He appears willing and eager to gamble with lives as much as with money."

"Machiavelli wasn't the first one in history to observe and write of that which results from ambition and spiritedness," Richard interjected. "War is inevitable as part of that streak of human nature. Look at your very attire, Sir. You are heading off to fight because the rebels have exhibited such bold spiritedness. Would you applaud them?"

"I would *slay* them for defying His Majesty!" Tarleton countered. "And no doubt I *shall* slay them to restore the balance of power for the Crown."

"Are you off then to America?" James asked. "You've been training and serving with the King's Dragoons."

"Indeed I am. Although I purchased my cornetcy in the King's Dragoons, when I heard that the 16th Regiment of Light Dragoons was being called up to quash the unrest of the hated rebels in America, I requested the King's leave and immediately volunteered to join Major General Lord Cornwallis," Tarleton reported.

"*He* didn't buy that cornetcy," Al told Nigel. "His *mum* Lady Jane did, for eight hundred pounds."

Nigel's eyes widened. "After wasting his entire inheritance, this spoiled, pompous soldier had the nerve to ask his *mother* to purchase a commission for him?"

"Ah, Burgoyne's Light Horse," spoke Francis with an approving nod. "Gentleman Johnny Burgoyne's elite light cavalry regiment, formed back in the Seven Years' War. Good show. I hope you get to serve under General Burgoyne himself while in America."

Richard held up the latest *Norwich Mercury.* "Now that Howe has replaced Gage, I'm sure that Burgoyne and Clinton will command part of the regiments arriving with Lord Cornwallis."

"Bow, wow, wow!" Al exclaimed, never forgetting how the three generals who sailed away aboard the *Cerberus* last spring were reported in the headlines. "Gillamon said Burgoyne's on his way back here to England, bein' too bored in Boston. He's comin' home to ask for somethin' big to do back in America. Of course, these here gents don't have that kind of intelligence yet . . ." he paused and coolly swiped back his whiskers, ". . . as does this kitty."

"Burgoyne's Light Horse," Nigel repeated to himself. Suddenly it dawned on the little mouse what Al had told him earlier at Gage's house. He began to chuckle. "My dear boy, when Gillamon told you about this human assignment, he spoke about Tarleton of Liverpool as a *dragoon,* not a dragon."

Al shrugged. "Same difference to me."

"A dragoon is an infantryman who rides a horse," Nigel explained. "Dragoons took their name from the *gun* that French dragoons used called a *dragon.*"

"Like I said," Al replied, lifting his nose to smell the intoxicating aroma of a fresh pot of hot chocolate being poured next to them. His mouth watered. "Seems like everything here tonight starts with the French—dragoons, dragons, and chocolate."

"Well, with our three best generals now in command, those rebel Americans will indeed find their spirited revolt crushed to a pulp," Tarleton confidently predicted.

"But that traitorous General Charles Lee is a disgrace to the British Army!" Francis exclaimed with a frown. "Can you imagine? He fought valiantly with Burgoyne in the Braddock campaign back in the Seven Years' War."

"Yet he readily resigned his commission in the British Army and renounced his half-pay," Richard added. "And for what? To fight with the rebels against King George?!"

James threw a hand in the air. "Absurd treachery! Lee deserves a traitor's death!"

Banastre Tarleton tightened his jaw as he listened to the news of General Lee's deplorable actions. For a British general to turn sides and fight for rebellious citizen-soldiers was a major affront to the British. General Lee possessed what Tarleton longed to achieve, yet he threw it away with both hands, and right back into the face of the British Army.

"If General Lee prefers the company of rebel dogs to His Majesty's finest soldiers . . ." Tarleton's hand slowly drifted to his saber, and he grabbed the handle. Suddenly he scraped back his chair, rose to his feet, drew his saber, and thrust it into the air, narrowly missing a low-hanging chandelier. Through clenched teeth he boldly and loudly declared, "With this sword, I'll cut off General Lee's head!"

Everyone stopped and turned to gaze upon the daring officer waving his sword. After a moment, some gambling men huddled together and started to place wagers on whether Banastre Tarleton would indeed cut off the head of the turncoat general.

"I believe you would," James responded, smiling as Tarleton replaced his saber and took his seat.

"Machiavelli would approve of your bold declaration," Francis added.

Richard lifted his cup. "And something tells me you'll be willing to die trying."

"Death or glory," Tarleton coolly replied with a confident grin, gulping back his last swig of chocolate, and slamming his empty cup on the table.

Al and Nigel looked at one another in shock. Al wrapped a paw around his throat, swallowing hard. "Remind me to never get on that dragon's bad side. I'm a wee bit fond o' me head." The fat cat's ears flattened. "Why do I always get stuck with the bad lads?"

"Perhaps you were right about Banastre Tarleton being a fiery dragon after all," Nigel worried with a frown.

Al smiled weakly. "I tried to tell ye, but I wish I were wrong."

Nigel straightened his spectacles with a determined look. "And I see now why Gillamon wanted us to witness Banastre Tarleton in action here tonight. We now know of a specific, direct threat to Washington's best general. We'll have to inform the others in the War Room. You and Max shall need to be on high alert once you reach America."

"LAND HO!" came the shout of the seamen above decks.

Al's eyes fluttered open with a start, and he rolled off the side of the bunk, landing on the floor with a thud. He shook his head, coming to after his deep sleep and dreams of being with Nigel and Banastre Tarleton in London. *Land! That sounds even sweeter than chocolate to me right now!*

Cornwallis sat up on his bunk, laying aside his book as a knock sounded on his door. "Come."

"Cape Fear dead ahead, Sir," came the ship's steward, poking his head inside the general's cabin.

"Splendid," Cornwallis answered, getting to his feet, and putting on his scarlet coat. "At long last!"

As Cornwallis exited the cabin to get topside, Al sat on the floor with wide eyes. "Cape Fear, *dead ahead?*" He gulped. "Get it together, kitty. Time to face the Cape o' Fear. At least it means gettin' off this ship!" The chubby cat scurried after Cornwallis to see just what was so scary about this ill-named part of North Carolina.

5

To Appear So, It Must Be So

CHÂTEAU DE VERSAILLES, FRANCE, MAY 2, 1776

King Louis XVI of France closed one eye and squinted into the brass key lock that was affixed to the ornate, gilded jewelry box belonging to his young queen, Marie Antoinette. She had misplaced the key and could not open the multi-drawered box containing her most coveted—and, probably not by coincidence, costly—jewels. As a boy, Louis was fascinated by locking mechanisms and studied how to open them as one of his hobbies. The twenty-one-year-old monarch welcomed the opportunity to tinker with the jewelry box for his beautiful queen. He enjoyed figuring out how things worked despite having countless servants who could do everything for him.

France's Minister of Foreign Affairs, Comte de Vergennes, stood in front of the king's table as he worked, hands held behind his back, waiting in silence. King Louis unrolled a felt cloth containing several metal instruments and spotted the specific tool he needed. "Ah, *voilà.*" He held up the tool and smiled at Vergennes before inserting it into the lock and jiggling the mechanism. Concentrating with a furrowed brow, the king looked up at the ceiling as he felt for just the right movement of gears, listening carefully. They soon both heard a 'click.' "*C'est ça.*" The king smiled broadly and opened the chest door to reveal the sparkling treasure inside.

"Bravo, Sire," Vergennes complimented the king. "I did not know you were so skilled at working with locks."

King Louis lifted a diamond sapphire necklace and held it in the air. Sunlight streamed in from the window and caught the priceless jewels, reflecting a bright prism of light on the far wall. "I've enjoyed tinkering with locks since I was a boy. It simply requires the right tool to serve as a key, no?" He replaced the necklace and shut the door. "If only I had the power to *lock* the queen's spending habits."

Indeed, Vergennes mentally agreed. *But today you shall match her in your spending.*

Marie Antoinette refused to listen to anyone about curbing her expenses. She was determined to progressively outdo herself in the grandeur of her parties, balls, fireworks, and food, sparing no expense. The twenty-year-old set the pace and stage for what was fashionable at Versailles, whether it be wigs, dresses, politics, or entertainment. The lively queen's new favorite card game was called 'Le Boston.' French sentiment about the goings-on in America had shifted ever since the first shots were fired at Lexington and Concord. The French cheered the underdog Americans who boldly trounced France's hated enemy at Bunker Hill, laying siege to the British in Boston before driving them victoriously from the city.

While the Queen of France found the American revolt to be "fashionable" in her salons, the King of France was more reticent. King Louis XVI did not want to be pulled into a war. The gentle king only wanted to be loved and popular, and to spend his days on the hunt galloping through the vast forests of Versailles. But international events of the past year were closing in on the young monarch, and Vergennes was delicately leading him toward a course that would change history. Rather than convince the king that assisting the Americans would be an act of revenge against France's oldest enemy after the humiliating defeat in the Seven Years' War, Vergennes sought to help him understand that it was the king's *duty* to defend the honor of France and protect her from future danger with a potential new enemy—an independent America. The best way to do so was to secretly assist the Americans in their revolt against King George III. Vergennes used intelligence from spies in America and London to convince King Louis to help the rebels.

Last December, Vergennes sent French spy Achard de Bonvouloir to secretly meet with Benjamin Franklin and John Jay in Philadelphia. Thanks to Franklin's embellished picture of America's unity and readiness, Bonvouloir sent Vergennes an overly glowing report of how eager and how well-positioned the Americans were to take on the British lion and set things in motion for France and America to secretly begin working toward an alliance. The Americans now knew that France supported them and had decided to send Connecticut Congressman Silas Deane to Paris with letters of introduction. But to make sure that Bonvouloir's claims of friendship with France were true, they also sent instructions to their agent in London, Arthur Lee, to feel out the sentiments in Europe. But Lee had done more than simply feel things out—he had pursued the playwright-turned-spy Pierre-Augustin Caron de Beaumarchais to act as a potential French agent to secure arms from France. The enterprising Lee convinced the dramatic Beaumarchais of America's eventual victory, and Beaumarchais in turn convinced the strategic Vergennes. Both agents were telling their respective countries what they wanted to hear, but it was based on impressions that far surpassed the reality of the situation.

At one of Marie Antoinette's masquerade balls last year, Beaumarchais whispered in Vergennes's ear about the American agent who had replaced Benjamin Franklin in London: Arthur Lee. The playwright had come to the masquerade ball dressed in a harlequin costume as his *Le Barbier de Séville* character 'Figaro.' In between frivolous, playful conversations with the queen, Beaumarchais told Vergennes about a dinner he had recently attended at the home of London's Mayor Wilkes. Beaumarchais struck up an immediate friendship with Lee, who enlightened him about everything that was happening in the American colonies. For the past year, the spy had turned from writing plays to writing Vergennes letter after letter about why France should help the Americans.

Beaumarchais's most insistent letter was a dramatic paper that he had entitled *La Paix ou la Guerre—Au Roi seul:* Peace or War—To the King alone. Beaumarchais repeatedly requested to have just fifteen minutes in front of the king to make his case about a plan to secretly help the Americans. Vergennes held back for months, but the time had finally come to approach the king, given what Beaumarchais had penned:

> *The famous quarrel between America and England will soon divide the world and change the system of Europe . . . While a violent crisis is approaching with great rapidity, I am obliged to warn your Majesty that the preservation of our possessions in America, and the peace which your Majesty appears to desire so much, depend solely upon this one proposition: the Americans must be assisted . . .*

It was an operation that would allow the French to secretly arm the Americans without leaving any fingerprints belonging to King Louis XVI or his ministers. And it would eventually provide trade that might help to 'enrich France,' or at least help pay for Marie Antoinette's parties and fireworks.

"*Bon,* now let us discuss another treasure box before I unlock it," King Louis said, getting up from the table to walk over to his royal desk. Vergennes followed the king and took a seat in front of the monarch, who lifted a paper in the air. "*Monsieur* Beaumarchais and this scheme of his. Are you certain that he can and *will* do as he writes in this plan?"

"*Oui,* Sire," Vergennes replied. "As we have discussed, Beaumarchais will set up a fictitious trading company to purchase our outdated and surplus guns and equipment, arrange for shipments to America through the West Indies, and loan the Americans funds to purchase the supplies from him. The

Americans will repay the loan by refilling the ships with tobacco, rice, indigo, etc. Beaumarchais will sell those items for a profit and recoup the money he loaned the Americans. Essentially, your million-*livre* investment will find its way right back into your pocket after two shipments."

A grin spread across the king's face. "And who will know about this scheme?"

"Only you, Sire, as well as Beaumarchais, and I," Vergennes replied with a coy grin. "Once the arms reach America, no one there or in France will truly know how they got there. The English will of course discover the origin of the arms as having come from France and British Ambassador Lord Stormont will no doubt come and complain to me. But I will tell him that since France is a *neutral* nation, we have no control over merchants who buy and sell our discarded arms to buyers anywhere in the world."

"Meanwhile, we shall build up our French armaments with new guns and supplies and be ready to take on the English after the Americans have worn them down with a war," King Louis added.

The two men stared at each other for a moment, then burst out laughing.

"Although I do not like his play, I do love how *Monsieur* Beaumarchais is playing the part of Figaro to secretly help America break away from the arrogant English," King Louis observed with a chuckle, referring to Figaro's scheming character in *The Barber of Seville.* He opened a silver box on his desk and lifted out a bank note embossed with the official seal of the French Treasury. He dipped his quill in an ornate silver ink well. *"Très bien."* He signed his name to a check for one million *livres* and handed it to Vergennes. "I have unlocked the treasure chest of France for America. Make sure *Figaro* plays his part flawlessly."

Vergennes stood, bowed, and took the check in hand. *"Merci,* Sire. I shall see to it."

Kate, a white Westie on mission for the Order of the Seven, peeked from around the curtain as the two men stood and left the room to go for a stroll in the vast, lush gardens of the palace to further discuss the particulars. "It's done! Now Washington an' his brave lads will soon get the guns an' powder they need! They'll be ready for Lafayette when he comes ta help them fight." She waited until the coast was clear and then scurried down the hall and outside to follow behind King Louis and Vergennes.

The eighteen-year-old, wealthy Marquis de Lafayette was Kate's human assignment for this mission. He was baptized as Marie-Joseph-Paul-Yves-Roch-Gilbert du Motier, le Marquis de Lafayette. The Westie had kept watch over him since he was a toddler in his childhood home of Chavaniac in the south of France, protecting him from wolves and anyone who sought to harm him. When he was two years old, his father was killed by the British at the Battle of Minden, and his mother died when he was only thirteen, making him the richest orphan in France. After Lafayette came to Paris for school and married the beautiful Adrienne de Noailles, Kate re-entered his life as a new little white dog that he affectionately called 'Bibi,' after his childhood dog by the same name. Little did the Marquis know that Kate was the same *chienne* that had been with him since before he learned to talk.

Lafayette was descended from a long line of warriors who achieved glory on the battlefield. Despite his wealth and position as an aristocrat, Lafayette wanted nothing to do with the shallow lifestyle as a courtier at Versailles. He wanted to also fight for glory on the battlefield. He was a Black Musketeer for the King of France, but that involved merely pomp with no action. As a wedding gift, his father-in-law the Duc d'Ayen purchased a commission for him as a lieutenant in the cavalry regiment of Noailles Dragoons. He was promoted to captain, and along with his brother-in-law Louis Vicomte de Noailles, attended summer training in the French city of Metz. But with France not at war (at that moment), summer training was the extent of his soldiering.

As newly appointed *Marèchal de France,* Lafayette's father-in-law had other ideas about what would be best for his son-in-law. He had arranged for Lafayette to become the personal guard of King Louis's dull brother, the Comte de Provence. When Lafayette learned of this pending appointment, he was mortified! He had to escape that looming, dreadful existence at court and do as he had written as a boy. He wrote in an essay that at the sight of a whip the perfect horse would throw off its rider and gallop away to freedom.

Throughout his young life, others had made decisions for the young Marquis, but now he needed to chart his *own* life course. So, he did the unthinkable. At the same masquerade ball where Beaumarchais whispered in Vergennes's ear about assisting the Americans, Lafayette purposely insulted the Comte de Provence. The next morning as Lafayette and his embarrassed father-in-law stood before the king's brother and endured his angry rant, the Marquis's heart soared with the exhilaration of freedom when the Comte relieved Lafayette of his pending post. While the Duc d'Ayen frowned, the Marquis smiled, for his next destination was the only place suited for him: military training in Metz.

It was there in August 1775 that Lafayette attended a fateful dinner with none other than the King of England's rogue prince brother, the Duke of Gloucester. Lafayette's ears perked up at hearing about the Americans' growing rebellion and quest to be free and independent. The Marquis knew in an instant that he wanted to give his heart and his sword to their cause. He rose from the table, pulled his sword from its sheath, and held it proudly in the air with his valiant declaration. But his commander, the Comte de Broglie told him to sit down and put his sword away.

Lafayette's idealist enthusiasm and zeal for liberty was quashed as soon as it was expressed, but that night his life's course became clear. Kate and Liz were there to observe what the Order of the Seven team leader Gillamon had told them would be the first of three dinners to mark Lafayette's life purpose: 'a princely dinner of light.' Since childhood Lafayette had dreamed about one day becoming like Sir Lancelot, the gallant French member of King Arthur's Knights of the Round Table. Liz and Kate wondered if the second significant dinner, 'a knightly dinner of swords,' could possibly mean a dinner with Lafayette and George Washington. The third coming significant dinner for Lafayette's purpose, 'a legacy dinner of liberty,' was unclear.

For now, budgetary cuts made necessary by France's wartime debt and Marie Antoinette's spending habits would soon place the Marquis and other officers on reserve status. This left Lafayette with nothing to do other than to attend Marie Antoinette's endless balls and parties at Versailles. But Lafayette's fire for *liberté* and his dream of fighting for America still burned inside his chest. He only needed to wait until the right time came. Once America declared her independence, France would no doubt join in the fight against her hated enemy, the British. And then Lafayette would officially offer his sword and fight for the cause of freedom.

While she didn't understand everything about this mission, Kate knew that the Marquis de Lafayette would be crucial to the success of the fledgling colonies in achieving their independence. And she knew therefore that the evil forces set against freedom and the new nation of the United States of America would do anything to stop that from happening. Kate and Max had protected young Lafayette from a massive wolf known as the Beast of the *Gévaudan*, but their evil serpent adversary Charlatan had enlisted the defeated wolf into his services with a second chance to kill the Marquis among other assignments. Named *Espion*, the now invisible wolf would not be allowed access to Lafayette until he first proved his worth in the cause of evil against the Americans.

Kate refused to lower her guard, and never liked being far from Lafayette while she stayed informed of developments in France for the mission at hand. After following King Louis and Vergennes around the manicured pathways wending through the gardens and lovely fountains of Versailles, she ran happily back to *Hôtel de Noailles,* current home of the Marquis de Lafayette here at Versailles.

When King Louis and Vergennes walked by a fountain on their way back to the palace, the water in the fountain began to boil. Frogs leapt from the lily pads to escape the hot water, jumping away to the nearby stretch of green grass. Suddenly a massive black snake rose from the water and hissed as the men discussed Beaumarchais's plan to assist the Americans, along with acquiring additional funds from Spain.

"You foolish, inexperienced, pathetic little king! That one million livres *for the Americans will be on* your *head!"* Charlatan hissed. The snake then stopped as a thought occurred to him. He shuddered with wicked delight, sliding onto the side of the fountain. *"Sssssince you are sssso eager to ssssssupport the American Revolution, I'll make sssssure you have one of your own here in Francccccce."* He noticed the statue holding a basket and slithered up to peek inside. *"And when the people of Francccccce hold out a basssssket for repayment, you will pay with your head!"*

CHÂTEAU DE VERSAILLES, FRANCE, JUNE 5, 1776

The flamboyant Beaumarchais took his seat across from Vergennes's desk, flipping back his royal blue silk coat tails and planting his gold satin and buckled shoes firmly in place as he sat on the edge of his seat. His deep brown eyes danced with excited anticipation, and his heart raced as he waited on the ever-calm Minister of Foreign Affairs to begin.

"To *appear* so, it must *be* so. We are secretly giving you a million *livres*. We shall get Spain to contribute an equal sum; with these two millions and the cooperation of other parties who may invest in your enterprise, you will establish a large commercial house and, at your own risk, supply America with arms, munitions, equipment, and all other necessary matériel for carrying on a war. Our arsenals will give you arms and ammunition, which you can replace or pay for. You will not demand money of the Americans because they have none; but you will demand payment from the produce of their soil, and we will help you distribute it in this kingdom."

Beaumarchais nodded and giddily gushed, *"Oui, oui,* of course, just as you say, *Monsieur le Comte!"*

Vergennes gave a singular nod and continued. *"Bon.* After our initial support, the operation must afterward feed and support itself; but because we reserve the right to favor its continuance or put an end to its operation, you shall render us a regular accounting of your profits and your losses, and we will determine whether to grant you fresh assistance or discharge you of liability for previous grants."

"Oui, je comprends!" Beaumarchais agreed eagerly. His palms grew sweaty with anticipation as Vergennes held the king's check in the air.

"In order to add a layer of security, I had the king make the check out to my fifteen-year-old son *Monsieur* Duvergier," Vergennes explained, lifting a quill, and dipping it into his red crystal inkwell. "I now shall endorse it over to you for deposit. Do you have a name for your fictitious trading company?"

"*Oui,*" Beaumarchais answered with an impish grin. "Roderigue Hortalez and Company."

Vergennes grinned back. "Very well, *Monsieur.*" Vergennes proceeded to endorse the check to *Rodrigue Hortalez et Cie* and blew on the ink before handing it to Beaumarchais.

Beaumarchais carefully took the check with both hands and stared at it in sheer disbelief. He had worked and persevered to get the attention and the approval of Vergennes and the King of France. He knew it was the most important check ever written in world history, for it would change the balance of power in Europe and the world by helping to launch a new nation, the United States of America. He looked up at Vergennes and smiled broadly. "*Merci, Monsieur.*"

The minister rose from his chair. "From this point on, know that the king of France shall have no further hand in the affair because it would compromise the government in the eyes of the English. You are now on your own. *Bonne chance.*"

Beaumarchais rose from his chair, dramatically draped one hand over his heart, bowed low, and flung his other hand high into the air. "*Merci, Monsieur le Comte.* And Senior Hortalez thanks you and the king as well."

With that, the playwright-turned-spy-turned-businessman rose, tucked the million-*livre* check into his coat pocket and walked out the door, humming a Spanish tune in anticipation of his next show-stopping performance.

6

THE VOICE OF THE REVOLUTION

SCOTCHTOWN PLANTATION, VIRGINIA, MAY 2, 1776

Ages yet unborn, and millions existing at present, must rue or bless that Assembly, on which their happiness or misery will so eminently depend. Virginia has hitherto taken the lead in great affairs, and many now look to her with anxious expectation . . .

Patrick Henry paused as he reread the words penned by his longtime friend and fellow Virginian, Richard Henry Lee. He furrowed his brow, stopping a moment to think about the gravity of what he was getting ready to do. Lee was a delegate to the Continental Congress and had hurriedly sent this letter to him from Philadelphia, along with a pamphlet on framing a new government, written by John Adams. Lee knew that Patrick Henry was heading to Williamsburg for the Fifth Virginia Convention, and he was urging him to once more be the bold Voice of the Revolution and lead the charge toward independence. On the question of independence, the nation looked to the states, the states to their people, and the people of Virginia to Patrick Henry.

"Happiness or misery," Patrick repeated aloud, sitting on the bench he had placed in this garden for Sallie. The early morning sunshine felt warm on his face. He spotted a daisy that had bloomed overnight and smiled to see new life coming from the dead stems of the previous winter. He leaned over to graze the soft, delicate petals with his finger. "Liberty or death. And this time, my words will most certainly lead to death if liberty is not achieved." He heard his children laughing as they played hide-and-seek in the boxwoods. "What I do next will determine the happiness or misery of my children, their children, and 'ages yet unborn.'" He looked at the daisy and nodded resolutely to himself. "So be it."

As Patrick shot up from the bench with Richard Henry Lee's letter in hand, Liz followed him into the large house and to his office. He needed to finish penning the resolution he would present on the floor of the Convention. Liz smiled to see the fiery orator dip the bald eagle Cato's feather into the inkwell. She knew that his words would provide the foundation stone on which a new, figurative statue of Libertas would be sculpted, this time for America.

After Patrick completed his work, he put his papers into the leather satchel on the floor and got up to finish packing for the trip to Williamsburg.

When he wasn't looking, Liz smiled and slipped Cato's feather into the satchel. *Do not forget your chisel,* mon *Henry.*

Within the hour, Patrick was galloping away from Scotchtown on MizP. And Liz and Nigel were shadowing him from above, on the wings of Veritas, son of Cato the bald eagle.

PALACE GREEN, WILLIAMSBURG, VIRGINIA, MAY 6, 1776

Liz and Nigel sat next to a tree and watched a small flock of sheep slowly nibble their way down the green pasture stretching from the Governor's Palace to Duke of Gloucester Street.

"Ah, there is nothing like the pastoral scene of sheep peacefully grazing whilst their shepherd stands watch. Such tranquil imagery no doubt inspired David's beloved Psalms," Nigel presumed, closing his eyes, breathing in the fresh air, and basking in the warm sunshine. "Since Lord Dunmore no longer resides in the palace, there seems to be a greater atmosphere of peace in Williamsburg, don't you agree, my dear?"

Liz opened her mouth to reply, when suddenly the sheep bolted and started running in every direction, screaming, "BAAAAAAAAAAA! BAAAAAAAAAAA! BAAAAAAAAAAA!"

"Good heavens, has the British lion returned to attack the flock?" Nigel cried in alarm.

Liz then spotted a high-stepping, long-legged, slender black and tan dog with one ear up and one ear down, nipping at the heels of the sheep. She giggled. "It is not a lion, Nigel, only a special 'monshter.'"

"What on *Earth* do you mean?" Nigel wanted to know, watching the panicked sheep.

Liz pointed. "Archer is chasing the sheep—remember General Charles Lee's funny dog we met back in Cambridge? And there is Spado the black Pomeranian in the distance by the palace entrance. General Lee always has his dogs with him."

Nigel placed a paw over his heart and chuckled. "What a relief! I did not realize that General Lee had stationed his men here in Williamsburg. After he assessed things in New York, Congress sent him southward to oversee the new Southern Department, but I thought he might head to the Carolinas."

"It appears he has taken over the palace as his headquarters," Liz noted, watching soldiers entering and exiting the building.

"I'm shpechial!" Archer greeted them, running up happily with his tongue hanging out.

"Yes, we *know,*" Nigel answered the goofy dog. "We've met before, in Cambridge."

Archer's eyes widened, and he grew a broad smile. "Heyyyyyyyyyyyy, I remember YOU!" He nudged Nigel with his nose.

Liz giggled. *"Bonjour,* Archer. We are Liz and Nigel if you do not recall our names. How long have you been here in Williamsburg with General Lee?"

"Since Marchish," Archer replied, sitting down next to them. "I'm living in the PALACE, so that proves I'm shpechial! Only I keep getting lost in the maze out back."

"Now *that* is hard to believe." Nigel rolled his eyes and stifled a snicker. "I say, how long do you think you will be in Williamsburg?"

Archer shrugged his shoulders. "I dunno. I guessh 'til we leave."

Just then they heard General Lee shouting, "ARCHER! COME!"

"My mashter's calling! Bye!" Archer exclaimed before trotting off down the green back to the palace.

Nigel shook his head good-humoredly. "How the simple mind must enjoy life."

Just then Patrick Henry came striding down the path heading toward Duke of Gloucester Street when General Lee intercepted him.

"We must hear what they are saying," Liz urged, running in their direction. She and Nigel hid under a bush while the two men spoke about the break with Great Britain and what was transpiring with the Congress in Philadelphia.

The tall, thin Lee looked unkempt as usual, dressed in a well-worn drab shirt and green sherryvallies—overbreeches with leather stripes that buttoned from the knee to the hip. His large nose cast a shadow over his face with its high forehead and small, deep-set eyes. He intermittently shouted at the dogs that kept chasing the sheep around Palace Green.

"I see you still have your dog companions in tow, General," Patrick observed, watching the yapping dogs.

Lee answered with a nod. "The strongest proof of a good heart is to love dogs and dislike mankind. Although I feel like one of them myself at the moment."

"Sir?" Patrick asked.

"I feel like a dog in a dancing school," Lee admitted. "I don't know where the British might strike next. Dunmore's small fleet is marauding along the coast in the Chesapeake, but a larger British fleet under Clinton could easily pounce on the Carolinas and then turn quickly to come here."

"I understand your dilemma, Sir," Patrick replied. "Yet I know you have the keenest military mind in the Continental Army despite your uncertainties, and feel Virginia shall be well protected under your military direction."

"As Virginia will be protected *politically* under yours," Lee answered, leaning over into Patrick's face. "I urge you to push for independency, Sir. The spirit of the people, except a very few in these lower parts of Virginia whose little blood has been sucked out by mosquitoes, cry out for this declaration, the military in particular."

Patrick furrowed his brow and nodded. "Aye. The mood of the people is ripe for independence, and I agree with them. My only concern is when to act upon it. In my correspondence with John Adams and Richard Henry Lee, I know they seek to move Congress toward a formal declaration of independence. They also seek the establishment of a formal confederation of the colonies and an alliance with France. I am in agreement with them that we need all three, but I have strongly urged that the Congress not declare independence until we have laid the groundwork for a French alliance, which to me is everything. But Mr. Adams believes that all of these things will happen quickly, so it will not matter in what order they occurred."

Lee frowned, the corners of his mouth turned downward in exaggerated creases. He clenched his jaw, as if he wanted to speak, but hesitated. "I admire your liberal way of thinking, Colonel Henry. I know you will lead this Virginia Convention to the right course. Independency is the only one left to us."

Patrick bowed slightly in respect. "I thank you, General. I shall do my best. Now, if you will excuse me, I must get to the Capitol."

As the men parted ways, Liz's tail slapped up and down on the ground as she studied General Lee, who stepped forward as if to follow Henry. He gripped his hand in the air as if to say one more thing, then allowed it to fall by his side. "General Lee is not telling Patrick something he knows."

"What do you suppose it is?" Nigel asked.

"I do not know, but if it will help *mon* Henry to make up his mind about when to present his resolution, he must act quickly," Liz answered.

As Liz and Nigel shadowed Patrick Henry down the Duke of Gloucester, they observed him meeting one of the newest delegates of the Virginia Assembly as they walked inside the Capitol.

"He's rather a diminutive young fellow, that James Madison of Orange County," Nigel observed.

"Well, big things can come from diminutive young fellows," Liz teased, nudging the tiny mouse with her paw.

"Quite right!" Nigel agreed wholeheartedly with a chuckle.

Once inside, the convention of one hundred thirty-one delegates began with many of the tried-and-true leaders back in their seats. But as they were joined by a large number of new delegates, including James Madison and Edmund Randolph, it quickly became clear that things would be slow going at first to get the novice burgesses up to speed on how things worked. Edmund Pendleton was once more elected President of the Convention, and John Tazewell appointed Clerk to keep the minutes.

Nigel yawned after a few hours of routine business and going over old minutes from the previous convention. "I daresay we shan't be getting to the exciting new business of independence anytime soon. This convention must first tend to the needs of the colony and the military demands of the moment."

"But I am glad they have at least called for a day of Fasting and Prayer soon to seek the Maker's help as they proceed ahead," Liz offered. "This is of course the wisest thing they could do, no? And it appears Patrick is letting bygones be bygones with his former treatment at the hand of Edmund Pendleton and the Committee of Safety. He raised no objections to Pendleton's election as president."

"Indeed, it is a great person who can put aside personal slights for the highest good of all," Nigel agreed.

"From listening to the delegates murmuring among themselves, it sounds as if the people of Virginia have overwhelmingly instructed them to push for independence."

"And 'bid His Britannic Majesty a good night forever,'" Nigel added, quoting Cumberland County's instructions. "The question remains, 'When?'"

CAPITOL BUILDING, WILLIAMSBURG, VIRGINIA, MAY 14, 1776

After a week, things were finally ready to progress, including Patrick Henry himself. General Lee had written to him the day after they chatted, confiding in him that he had received intelligence that things were already underway with France. Liz was thrilled to see Patrick's face light up as he read that Silas Deane had been sent to Paris in March to begin secret negotiations with the French. He would need to keep this information quiet, of course. But now that Patrick Henry knew his primary concern was addressed, he was ready to make his move for independence.

Liz had watched him last night as he spread his resolution out on the desk to make minor revisions here and there. He wrinkled his brow when he found Cato's feather in the satchel, scratching his head, as he did not remember packing it. Liz smiled as she watched Patrick's funny habit of twirling his wig atop his head as he read and reread his resolution, making small changes until it was just as he wanted it.

"Finally, we can get on with this declaration business," Nigel cheered as the motion was made for the convention to move into a Committee of the Whole. He and Liz were in their hiding spots under Secretary Tazewell's table.

"*Oui,* and *Monsieur* Nelson is ready to present *mon* Henry's resolutions!" Liz echoed. "It was of course brilliant of Patrick to have Thomas Nelson, Jr., read them on his behalf."

"Then our fiery orator can take the floor and set the hearts and minds of everyone here afloat toward the wistful shores of independency," Nigel agreed, frowning as he spotted Robert Carter Nicholas. "Well, almost everyone."

Edmund Pendleton stepped down from the Speaker's Chair and was replaced by Archibald Cary, who would preside over this meeting of the entire assembly as one big committee. The subject was independence, and Thomas Nelson, Jr., held up his hand.

"The Committee recognizes Mr. Thomas Nelson, Jr., of York County," Archibald Cary announced as John Tazewell penned the minutes of each action into the convention's journal.

Thomas Nelson, Jr., rose from his seat and locked eyes with Patrick Henry, who gave him a firm nod of approval and encouragement. He cleared his throat and looked around the room at the delegates, who sat up at attention, anticipating what was to come.

"Gentlemen, we have reached the subject that we have anticipated since our convention opened—that of independency. We have heard from the people who elected us to represent them here today, and they have instructed us toward this juncture," Nelson began. "We are all fully aware of the import of what declaring independence means—the difficulties we face in arming and equipping our inexperienced military forces, and the very real dangers ahead. But everything we have done to avoid this measure has failed, leaving us with only one course. Permit me to read the following resolution." He held up Patrick Henry's resolution and adjusted his spectacles, clearing his throat again.

"It is time, my pet!" Nigel hoarsely whispered to Liz. "How thrilling to hear the first words uttered before an elected body of people, calling for a Declaration of Independence!"

Liz's eyes brimmed with joy. "*Oui, mon* Henry's words."

"As the humble petitions of the Continental Congress have been rejected and treated with contempt; as the parliament of Great Britain so far from showing any disposition to redress our grievances, have lately passed an act approving of the ravages that have been committed upon our coasts, and obliging the unhappy men who shall be made captives to bear arms against their families, kindred, friends and country; and after being plundered themselves, to become accomplices in plundering their brethren, a compulsion not practiced on prisoners of war except among pirates, the outlaws and enemies of human society. As they are not only making every preparation to crush us, which the internal strength of the nation and its alliances with foreign powers afford them but are using every art to draw the savage Indians upon our frontiers, and are even encouraging insurrections among our slaves, many of whom are now actually in arms against us. And as the King of Great Britain by a long series of oppressive acts has proved himself the tyrant instead of the protector of his people . . ."

"Here it comes!" Nigel exulted, clinging to Liz in anticipation.

"We, the representatives of the colony of Virginia do declare, that we hold ourselves absolved of our allegiance to the crown of Great Britain and obliged by the eternal laws of self-preservation to pursue such measures as may conduce to the good and happiness of the united colonies; and as a full declaration of independency appears to us to be the only honorable means under Heaven of obtaining that happiness, and of restoring us again to a tranquil and prosperous situation;

"Resolved, that our delegates in Congress be enjoined in the strongest and most positive manner to exert their ability in procuring an immediate, clear, and full Declaration of Independency."

Thomas Nelson, Jr., held up the paper. "Gentlemen, I urge you to pass this resolution. Americans cannot return from war with the cordiality of subjects to a king which seeks their destruction." He bowed slightly, and walked over to the secretary's table, handing the resolution to Tazewell.

"Is there a second?" Archibald Cary asked, looking around the room.

"SECOND!" Patrick Henry quickly replied, rising to his feet from the long, green cushion topping the narrow wooden bench.

"The gentleman from Hanover, Mr. Patrick Henry," Cary announced with a nod.

"This is your moment, cher Patrick," Liz whispered softly. "This is why you were needed in this room, and not in the field. You are the Voice of the Revolution."

Patrick Henry stood and nodded respectfully to Cary, who sat in the Speaker's Chair. "Sir." He bowed his head respectfully to Thomas Nelson, Jr. "Thank you, Mr. Nelson." He then looked around the room and softly tapped the dark wood railing in front of him. He wrinkled his brow as if in profound consideration of what he was about to say.

"Indeed, we are at a critical moment, and have anticipated its arrival. But I submit we have done so not just since the 6th of May," Patrick Henry began. "In truth, we have anticipated it since we gathered in this very room some eleven years ago." He looked up to the ceiling and all around, holding out his hands. "After Virginia raised her voice of opposition against the hated Stamp Act, our resolutions spread throughout the colonies like wildfire, leading the way for the voices of our sister colonies to unite with ours. In short order, the Act was repealed. *Eleven years ago,* gentlemen. Although the thought may have only brushed the deep recesses of our minds, none of us wanted independence then. But ponder for a moment all that has happened since." He paused and allowed the memories of the past eleven years to sink in as he moved from behind the bench to the center of the room.

"He is starting off slowly, as he always does," Nigel noted with a grin, crossing his arms over his chest. "It is classic Patrick Henry."

"I think we all here would agree that independence is not something *any* of us *wanted,* and still many of us walk to the threshold of decision with reluctance, dragging our feet with understandable dread," Patrick continued, taking slow, deliberate steps, and glancing at Robert Carter Nicholas as he passed the elder statesman who sat erect on the straight-backed, green-cushioned bench.

"Least of all, *Monsieur* Nicholas," Liz whispered, looking around the room. "I believe he is the only one who opposes independence."

Patrick turned at the end of the room and stood with lifted hands to the portraits of the King and Queen. "There is good reason to dread such a decision. The very fact that we have been fighting for a year yet have not taken the step to declare independence shows what a fearsome, and a sorrowful step it will be. We shall not just be resisting the king; we shall be utterly *rejecting* him. As Englishmen we have long revered our sovereigns. The thought of severing ties with all we have ever known is a difficult one, a painful one. But it is also a *deadly* one, as we shall all be branded as traitors to the crown." He took a step forward. "Declaring independence is a formidable step. In order for a child to grow, he must cut the knot with all he has ever known and stand on his own two feet." He paused and looked around the room. "But this is more than one child stepping out into the world to naturally launch his independence. This cause is larger than one individual. It is larger than any of us and should supersede any self-centered ambitions we may have."

Nigel cupped his ear. "Are you listening, Mr. *Pendleton?*"

"This is a cause in which we *all* must join in order to stand firm as we step into the unknown darkness of independence." He proceeded to walk around the assembly room, making eye contact with the delegates. "Such a cause will put at stake our very lives and fortunes. Yet while it is a cause greater than any of us, a decision for or against independence must be made by every individual, but only after counting the cost. And it must be made without intimidation or force, but of free will." He paused at the secretary's table and lifted the resolution. "Because once the decision is made, it will require more than a piece of paper to bring the words which declare it to reality. It will require our sacrifices, our hard work, our money, our commitment, our perseverance. It will require our compromises." He gave a knowing look to Edmund Pendleton. "It will require our blood, for nothing great is ever achieved without the shedding of blood. So, consider first what you must do and what it will cost you. For once the exuberance of making a decision to declare independence is celebrated and our course is set, a time will come when weariness will weigh heavily on our shoulders from the difficulty of the journey through the wilderness, just as it did with the children of Israel. The weariness of the journey was great enough to cause them to look back over their shoulders and believe that their former captivity was not so very horrible. In their exhaustion they even longed to return to Egypt! But as with the children of Israel, a return to captivity will not be possible for us. There will be no retreat until one of two things is realized: liberty or death. And I assure you, it will be one or the other."

"Brilliant strategy to revisit his former clarion call while alluding to the journey to the Promised Land!" Nigel cheered.

"But how curious that he seems noncommittal to the cause himself," Liz posited, furrowing her brow.

"Eleven years ago, gentlemen," Patrick restated, setting the resolution back down on the table. "Virginia led the way and the tide turned in the favor of the colonies. Today all eyes of the nation are once more trained upon us. What shall we do? In these dark days shall we once more be the beacon of light for our sister colonies? There is a promised land which the people of this nation long to possess. *America* is that Promised Land! America—thirteen disparate colonies now coming together like the twelve tribes of Israel to reach a land flowing with milk and honey. And just as the nation of Israel followed a pillar of fire to reach the Promised Land, the spirit of the people of Virginia shall be the pillar of fire to light the way for our brethren!"

"Hear, hear!" cheered some of the men of the assembly.

Robert Carter Nicholas sat there with arms folded across his chest, shaking his head.

Patrick held up his hand as if he held a torch. "Virginia must boldly step into the darkness and declare our independence for the sake of this nation, lighting the way to liberty! The other twelve colonies will follow our light, and together we shall march to the Promised Land, united as *states.*"

Liz put a paw to her heart. "He is sculpting an image of Libertas in their minds!"

"As I told you last year, we shall not fight our battles alone," Patrick continued. "There is a just God who presides over the destinies of nations and will raise up friends to fight our battles for us."

"*Oui,* the French are coming, *mon* Henry!" Liz exulted in a whisper. "You were right, and we have seen to it."

"Patrick knows he cannot yet reveal what he knows about the steps we have taken with the French," Nigel whispered back.

"I must admit that my greatest concern has not been *if* we should declare independence, but *when* we should declare it," Patrick confessed, placing his hands over his chest. "But I have come to the realization that unless we first declare our independence, our friends will be *unable* to come to our aid. I submit that we all needed that dose of *Common Sense* to prod us forward. And to remind us of why we are fighting. So let our steps be ordered rightly and well," he continued, placing one foot in front of the other as he walked back to his seat. "Let us cut the knot, declare independence, forge alliances, and then with the help of Heaven, attain our long-awaited liberty."

Robert Carter Nicholas raised his hand to be recognized as Patrick Henry took his seat.

"Now comes the laborious opposition," Nigel lamented. "We shall hear every argument against independence that has been brought forth over the past eleven years! Our army is *inexperienced.* It is too *difficult* to obtain crucial supplies to execute a war. There is no *guarantee* that foreign aid will come despite our declarations . . ."

"And how this country will tear itself apart," Liz added. "*Monsieur* Nicholas is right in that this shall be a civil war, no? And he speaks truth of our desperate situation, but this is where faith must come in. I was once the same. Logically, it is doubtful that with only one third of Americans wanting independence, it can be achieved, no? America is truly David against Goliath."

"Ah, yes, the earlier 'you' whose intellect so blinded your mind that a leap of faith was much too fearsome to consider," Nigel reminded her, twirling a whisker. "But David was an army of one who only needed one, smooth stone."

"*Oui,* and he *did* defeat that horrible giant with the Maker's strength and aim," Liz recounted. "That was a miraculous day."

Nigel nodded as they listened to Nicholas drone on about everything Nigel had said he would. "Well, at least this chap's heart is sincere, and he is indeed speaking his true mind."

"Now if he will only keep his voice silent when it comes to a vote," Liz suggested. "Then *mon* Henry's resolution will pass."

WILLIAMSBURG, VIRGINIA, MAY 15, 1776, 7:00 A.M.

MizP leaned her muzzle on the fence rail where Liz and Nigel sat. They were getting her caught up on everything that had happened so far.

"Essentially, Patrick's resolution calls for Virginia to declare her independence and for Virginia's delegates in Congress to propose that all of the colonies declare independence as one voice in Philadelphia," Nigel explained. "Meriwether Smith and Edmund Pendleton also proposed resolutions, but theirs were rather brief, and did not go as far as Patrick's."

"So, what did 'Old Fiddlehead' propose?" MizP asked.

Liz giggled at Patrick Henry's wry horse. *"Monsieur* 'Fiddlehead' Smith called for Virginia to establish her own government with a Bill of Rights but does not mention a separation from Great Britain."

"Right. And Pendleton's resolution states that due to the barbarous nature of King George and Parliament, all union betwixt the colonies and Great Britain should be dissolved, but it stops short of anything further," Nigel added. "Neither of the other two resolutions is as comprehensive or drastic as Patrick Henry's."

"Of course they aren't! No one is as bold and radical as our Pahtrick," MizP snorted proudly. "He's not called the Voice of the Revolution fuh nothing."

Liz smiled. "I agree, *mon amie*. So, *Monsieur* Pendleton is preparing one resolution that combines all three of them. It will hopefully be adopted today."

"Well, the humans are gathering around the Capitol like flies on my back side in July," MizP noticed. "I know they're just as anxious outside those walls as the men are inside that brick building. They best leave those windows open so the people can hear what happens when they vote."

Liz looked up at the British Union Jack flapping in the breeze above the cupola. "And if Virginia declares her independence from Great Britain, the first thing the humans must do is to raise a new flag."

CAPITOL BUILDING, WILLIAMSBURG, VIRGINIA, MAY 15, 1776, 10:00 A.M.

"The Assembly is *packed,"* Nigel whispered, looking around as the delegates found their seats. "MizP was right, the humans are eager for what this day shall bring."

"I am happy that the windows are open," Liz agreed.

Edmund Pendleton rose from his seat and cleared his throat. "Gentlemen, I have taken the liberty of preparing a composite of the three resolutions proposed by my esteemed colleagues Mr. Smith and Mr. Henry, and by myself." He glanced over at Patrick Henry. "A *compromise,* if you will." Patrick nodded respectfully in response.

"Please Maker, let it be perfect!" Nigel whispered, his paws clasped together in anticipation.

As Pendleton began reading a summary of the grievances as put forth by Patrick Henry, Liz watched Patrick squirm and purse his lips. "I believe *mon* Henry does not like the toned-down nature of the beginning, but it does present the case that despite repeated attempts, reconciliation has not been possible. This compromise will get the job done, no?"

"He's made the case," Nigel said eagerly. "Now for the punch line of the resolution!"

"Wherefore appealing to the Searcher of Hearts for the sincerity of former declarations, expressing our desire to preserve the connection with that nation and that we are driven from that inclination by their wicked councils and the eternal laws of self-preservation.

"Resolved unanimously that the delegates appointed to represent this colony in General Congress be instructed to propose to that respectable body to declare the United Colonies free and independent states absolved from all allegiance to or dependence upon the crown or parliament of Great Britain and that they give the assent of this Colony to such declaration and to whatever measures may be thought proper and necessary by the Congress for forming foreign alliances and a confederation of the Colonies at such time and in the manner as to them shall seem best: Provided that the power of forming government for and the regulations of the internal concerns of each colony be left to the respective colonial legislatures.

"Resolved unanimously that a Committee ought to prepare a DECLARATION OF RIGHTS and such a plan of government as will be most likely to maintain peace and order in this colony and secure substantial and equal liberty to the people."

As Pendleton lowered his paper and looked around the Assembly, a sense of awe filled the room. The very air was heavy with what they were about to do. History was being made, and they knew it.

"Now to see how they will vote," Liz whispered as the formal vote was taken with the one hundred twelve members. "And what Robert Carter Nicholas will do."

As votes were taken, the people outside leaned in to hear the roster of votes recorded, delegate by delegate. When they got to Robert Carter Nicholas, he abstained, neither voting for nor against the resolution. When they reached the final delegate, the answer was, 'Aye,' making it a unanimous vote for independence.

"The vote is unanimous. The resolutions pass," Tazewell announced.

"*C'est magnifique! Mon* Henry did it! The Voice of the Revolution has once more led the charge!" Liz exulted, hugging Nigel.

Nigel's whiskers quivered with excitement as he squeezed Liz with joy.

Immediately the chamber erupted in celebration as the delegates streamed out of the building to the loud, exuberant cheers of the people. A young man ran up the steps to the cupola and immediately lowered the British Union Jack before raising the new Continental Grand Union flag high above the Capitol. Liz and Nigel scurried outside under the legs of the humans, who didn't notice them, but who wouldn't have cared if they had. Fifes and drums started playing, and preparations immediately got underway to celebrate with a public reading of the resolutions, a parade, a party for the soldiers, toasts accompanied by the shooting of muskets and artillery, and illuminations to light up the city of Williamsburg.

Virginia had declared her independence, and they celebrated accordingly. But before they took another step, they needed to ask for God's direction and blessing.

WILLIAMSBURG, VIRGINIA, MAY 17, 1776

"I didn't think Pahtrick would evuh stop playing that fiddle last night," MizP told Liz and Nigel. "I was glad tuh see him so happy again. I don't believe I'd seen him play since he lost Sallie."

"*Oui,* it was a wonderful day of celebration, and Patrick led the charge even in that," Liz replied, wiping a happy tear from her eyes. "I have not seen him smile and laugh like that in so very long."

Nigel played an imaginary fiddle in the air. "I daresay that Patrick Henry even had Edmund Pendleton and Old Fiddlehead tapping their toes at the Raleigh."

Veritas stretched out his wings as he perched on the fence. "You should have seen it from the air. Williamsburg was a beautiful sight to behold."

Liz beamed. "But today was an even more beautiful time at Bruton Parish Church, MizP. The sermon was preached from the most perfect verse for this day of fasting and prayer."

Nigel cleared his throat and lifted a paw in the air to recite 2 Chronicles 20:15: *"Thus saith the Lord unto you: Be not afraid, nor dismayed, by reason of this great multitude; for the battle is not yours, but God's.* The humans filed out of the church feeling encouraged and ready for the challenges that lie ahead."

"Amen!" MizP exclaimed. "I couldn't have picked one better myself. The greatest friend tuh fight our battles for us is the *Maker."*

"Exactement!" Liz answered with a wink. "But He will allow the French to help."

"Now what?" Veritas asked.

"The convention shall get busy in drafting a Virginia Declaration of Rights and a Constitution for her new state government," Nigel answered. "Patrick Henry has already been added to the committee to draft them, so he shall be quite busy in the days and weeks ahead."

Liz nodded. "Meanwhile, Thomas Nelson, Jr., will hand deliver the resolutions and instructions to the Virginia delegates in Philadelphia to make a formal declaration of independence at the Congress."

"Gillamon instructed us to go there next, so we shall ask you to bear us upon your sturdy wings to Philadelphia soon, my good fellow," Nigel told the young bald eagle, petting him on the shoulder.

"My pleasure," Veritas told them.

"This is the start of a new and glorious era for Virginia!" Liz declared happily. "Not only has she declared her own independence, but she is leading the way for all the colonies to declare independence for the nation as a whole."

Nigel now pretended to chisel an imaginary statue. "Right you are, my pet. The foundation for liberty has been struck, and with each blow of the chisel, America's 'Libertas' will take shape."

"So, it is only fitting that Virginia has provided America with two of the three instruments needed to sculpt Liberty and the Revolution," Liz added. "Patrick Henry is the Voice, and George Washington is the Sword."

"And what is the third?" MizP asked.

"The Pen!" Nigel answered, pretending to write in the air. "To write the Declaration of Independence for America."

"I just realized that *mon* Henry might be saddened if he finds Cato's feather missing were I to borrow it to take to Philadelphia," Liz frowned, staring at Veritas. "But whoever the Pen of the Revolution will be must also use a special quill to write the Declaration of Independence for America."

The bald eagle smiled and reached back to pull one of the feathers from his shoulder. He handed it to Liz. "It would be my honor if he used mine."

Liz's eyes filled with tears, and she kissed Veritas on the cheek. "Oh, *cher* Veritas!"

Nigel also wiped away a tear from underneath his spectacles. "How utterly fitting for the next generation to participate in the next step of independence."

"Well then, I suggest you get tuh Philadelphia and arrange for a young Virginian tuh do the honors," MizP urged them with a droll smile. "Virginians must be at the head of this business, after all."

A PATTERN EMERGES

"He sure does write a lot of letters for a General," Jock noted as he and Max looked over Washington's desk, sitting close to each other on Washington's leather chair.

> To Major General Charles Lee
> New York May 9, 1776
> My dear Lee,
> Your favour of the 5th Ulto from Williamsburg (the first I have received from you since you left this City) came to my hands by the last Post. I thank you for your kind congratulations on our Possession of Boston—I thank you also for your good wishes in our future oper-ation's—and hope that every diabolical attempt to deprive Mankind of their Inherent Rights and Privileges, whether made in the East—West—North—or South, will be attended with disappointment and disgrace; and that the Authors—in the end—will be brought to such punishment as an injured People have a right to Inflict.

"Aye, that's wha' Commanders-in-Chief have ta do," Max agreed. "Washington has ta give lots of orders ta his commanders not jest here in New York, but up north in Canada, an' down south for General Lee facin' the Br-r-ritish in the Carolinas. Plus, he has ta talk a lot ta Congress aboot wha' he needs ta fight the war with soldiers an' supplies, an' how best ta fight the British. He may be the Sword of the R-R-Revolution, but Washington still has ta wield a pen then."

Jock nodded. "He sure gets *mad* when humans ignore what he writes! That was fun when we overheard all those sneaky humans bribing the local sentries on the docks to let their boats pass at night and then barked the alarm so other soldiers saw what was happening. But when Washington found out that supply boats were still delivering stuff to Tryon out on the *Duchess* after his orders forbidding it, he wrote to the New York papers so *nobody* would miss his orders!"

"Includin' Tr-r-ryon himself! Aye, don't mess with the General's orders!

He means wha' he says," Max grinned. "He made sure every human in New York knows that if they be caught helpin' the governor, they'll be guilty of treason an' punished by the army. Them be fightin' words! Washington knows that it's still goin' ta be impossible ta stop them all, but he sent a clear message ta that schemin' spider floatin' on his boat."

"The humans will think twice about helping Tryon now," Jock asserted.

Max frowned. "Aye, but the thing aboot schemers be that they always find a way ta work ar-r-round things. Let's go back downtown an' sniff out more tr-r-rouble, lad. I've never known a schemer workin' for the enemy that didn't smell funny."

BROADWAY, MANHATTAN, NEW YORK, MAY 10, 1776

Max and Jock darted in and around the legs of humans as they walked up and down the streets of Manhattan. They ran down to the docks and listened to the dock masters for any word of illegal boats rowing out to Tryon's ship but came up empty. They decided to walk along Broadway to see what they could see. It was such a beautiful spring day that shops and taverns kept their doors open to allow the fresh air inside. The humans paid the two Scotties no mind except for an occasional pet or chuckle. Soon the dogs came to an alehouse named Hull's Tavern and sat outside watching and listening.

"Do you smell anything yet, Grandsire?" Jock asked. "How do you smell out bad guys anyway?"

"Not yet. Jest normal smelly humans who haven't had a bath in weeks." Max sniffed the air. "It's hard ta explain, but I have the ability ta smell when somethin's jest not r-r-right in the air. The Maker made me smeller extra sensitive. I've been this way ever since me first mission with Noah. When ye done faced an' smelled pure evil in the flesh, ye don't forget it. For me, it's as easy as smellin' bacon fryin' for br-r-reakfast." He looked around at the people coming and going. It was a mix of soldiers, citizens, merchants, and shady characters.

Just then a gust of wind lifted their fur. Max caught a whiff of something and raised his nose in the air. Then he put his nose to the ground and began to follow a scent. "Got somethin', lad. It's faint, but let's see where it leads."

"Oh, boy!" Jock exclaimed, following Max, and trying to smell what the older dog smelled. They crossed the street, and Jock looked up to see a sign swinging in the spring breeze above them. "Gunsmith. I've never been in a gunsmith shop."

"No? Well, let's pop inside then," Max offered, looking up at the sign. "There may be somethin' here."

As they quietly slipped in the door, they saw sample muskets and rifles mounted on the wall, wood scraps and shavings all over the floor, bars of iron, brass plates, and wooden blocks holding numerous iron tools for filing and shaping. A thickset, short man wearing a white coat stoked a hot fire with a piece of iron before pulling it out and taking it to an anvil where he proceeded to hammer it. Sparks went flying everywhere with the clank of iron hitting iron. Sweat poured from the man's brow and ran down to the tip of his nose before falling to the anvil with a sizzle.

"Is that the gunsmith?" Jock whispered to Max.

"Aye. The jack of all trades himself. A gunsmith has ta know how ta be a blacksmith, a machinist, a woodworker, an' an engraver ta make all these guns," Max explained. "He makes every part of the gun—lock, stock, an' barrel."

"No wonder he's so sweaty. That's a lot of work," Jock noticed. "Even *I* can smell him."

The gunsmith didn't notice when a man stepped inside the shop. "Good-day, Forbes!" the man shouted to be heard above the clank-clank-clank of the gunsmith.

Max's head shot up as he got a whiff of the man. A low grumble vibrated in his throat.

The gunsmith turned and gave a singular nod before plunging the iron rod into a barrel of water that hissed with rising steam. "Webb." The gun-smith wiped his hands on the apron tied around his waist and went over to the counter where the man rested his elbow. He looked around the shop to make sure no other customers were present.

"I've got good news. Your twenty guns were delivered safely to the *Duchess* last night," Webb reported in a whisper with a satisfied grin. "Nine rifles and eleven muskets. I delivered them myself, just as I promised."

Forbes tightened his lips and nodded. "And my payment? Did Governor Tryon send it back with you?"

Webb held up his hands. "Don't worry, Forbes. Tryon is good for the three guineas apiece that he owes you. He didn't give me the money but has someone else bringing it to you. Someone *important.*"

"Who?" Forbes asked with a perturbed expression, resting his knuckles on the dusty counter.

"Mayor David Matthews," Webb answered with a wink.

Forbes's eyes widened. "The Mayor? But why send him to *me?*"

Webb shrugged his shoulders. "For the Governor to send him, I imagine it involves more than just paying off a gunsmith for smuggled guns to give to willing Loyalists." He handed the gunsmith a piece of paper. "He said for you to meet him tomorrow night."

Forbes took the paper in hand and nodded. "Very well. I'll go meet him. Now let me get back to work."

Webb tapped the counter and sent a small cloud of dust into the air. "I must do the same. Millstones don't make themselves. Until next time, Forbes—which I imagine will be sooner rather than later."

When Webb left the shop, Forbes tapped the paper in his hand and smiled before tucking it in his pocket and returning to his iron.

Max nodded to Jock, and together the two slipped out of the store to the street. "I knew it the minute that Webb came inta the store! I smelled somethin' r-r-rotten! So this Gilbert Forbes the gunsmith be sellin' guns illegally ta the Governor."

"And now the Mayor himself wants to see him," Jock added.

"Aye, must be somethin' bigger than guns," Max surmised. "All I know for sure is that we'll be at that meetin', too. Time ta find out jest wha' this scheme's all aboot."

BROADWAY, MANHATTAN, NEW YORK,
MAY 11, 1776

A lamplighter busily refilled the oil and trimmed the wicks of the lamps mounted at every seventh house along the streets of Manhattan. There was just enough light to see where you were headed, and where you'd been, but darkness ruled the streets of New York. Max and Jock stealthily followed Gilbert Forbes to the designated meeting place with Mayor Matthews, a popular Loyalist tavern called Houlding's.

They slipped inside the boisterous room filled with mug-ringed tables carved by a thousand rowdy customers. The walls were yellowed from pipe smoke, and the floors were sticky from spilled ale. A handful of customers were tucked away in black painted booths in the corners. A single lantern illuminated the face of Mayor Matthews as Forbes came to sit across from him. Max and Jock slipped under an adjacent table, unseen in the darkened room.

"Mr. Forbes, thank you for coming," Matthews greeted him with a smile. "Can I buy you an ale?" He motioned for the bar maid to bring over two mugs.

"Sir, thank you sir," Forbes said, clearly uncertain about where this was heading.

"The Governor sends his compliments on your excellent craftmanship of the guns you sent with Mr. Webb," Matthews began. "I will be visiting the *Duchess of Gordon* myself soon and will be getting the £65 pounds owed to you."

"Thank you, Mr. Matthews," Forbes replied with a puzzled expression. "But why have me meet you to tell me this?"

Matthews smiled. "I thought we might discuss . . . other things as well. Perhaps even *add* to the amount I'll bring to you." He leaned forward. "Surely you realize that after showing such allegiance to the Crown with the gun sale, you are part of the Governor's network of brave, dependable individuals here in New York. Among a long list of other loyal individuals, we have a shoemaker who ferries passengers to the *Duchess*, a millstone maker that acts as a go-between communicator, and now a gunsmith to provide arms. But what the Governor and I are curious to know is, would your long list of talents include the ability to recruit soldiers?"

Forbes raised his eyebrows in surprise. "I wasn't expecting this. Go on."

Matthews pointed a hand to the gunsmith. "You have a shop in the heart of Manhattan, just blocks away from General Washington's headquarters. Continental soldiers surround you in nearby barracks, and no doubt stop in your store should they need something for their guns. *They* frequent taverns, and *you* frequent taverns. You are an expert at the one thing a soldier depends upon to preserve his life—his gun. The Governor is recruiting citizens to take up arms when the time comes, but he wants to recruit rebel *soldiers* to fight for our side as well and will pay them in coin and land. Specifically, he wants soldiers who will be ready to act when British forces arrive, which will be very, very soon." He leaned in. "What if I brought you not just £65 pounds, but £115 pounds to serve as our primary recruiter here in Manhattan?"

"I like the sound of that," Forbes answered. "But what if I want some of what the Governor is offering the new recruits? Land."

"Well, if you raise enough men for the Crown, you could have your own company and receive an officer's commission to lead them when the British forces arrive," Matthews offered. He leaned in. "Officers will receive even larger parcels of land. What say you now?"

Forbes leaned in. "I'd say it sounds like you found yourself a new recruiter."

The two men lifted their mugs and clinked them, exclaiming, "God save the King!"

Max turned to Jock. "This smells r-r-rotten alr-r-right. Now we can see the pattern startin' ta form. Tryon pays Matthews who pays Forbes who will pay the soldiers he recruits."

"But who will Forbes recruit?" Jock wondered in a whisper.

"Once we know that, we'll be able to figure out the rest of the pattern," Max answered. "But one thing's for certain. That tr-r-rail will lead str-r-raight ta Washington's men."

CITY JAIL, MANHATTAN, NEW YORK, MAY 13, 1776

"Get inside, all of you!" a guard shouted, shoving the prisoners down the hall and into four separate cells.

Henry Dawkins, Isaac and Israel Young, and Isaac Ketcham had all just been arrested for attempted counterfeiting. Suspicious neighbors alerted the New York Provincial Congress, reporting unusual activity at the Youngs' house in Cold Spring Harbor, Long Island; therefore, the New York Congress sent a militia captain to recruit men for a raid on the house. Finding a hidden door, they found a passage to the attic. After scouring the hidden upstairs room, they found the printing press, engraving tools, counterfeit plates, and an imperfect copy of a forty-shilling Connecticut bill. Because someone had seen Ketcham interacting with the trio of counterfeiters, he also was rounded up and hauled to New York to await trial before the Provincial Congress. To prevent the four men from collaborating on a story to excuse the evidence and accusations, they were separated from each other.

Ketcham sat on the dirty floor and buried his face in his arms, his knees tucked up under him, weeping. "My poor children," he softly sobbed. "They have no one to care for them."

During the night, a new guard came on duty and slowly walked the halls of the dingy jail in the basement of City Hall. Upstairs from the jail was the chamber where the New York Provincial Congress sat. Up there was law and order, truth, and justice. Down here were disorderly lawbreakers, deception, and wickedness. The jail crawled with vermin and was filled with Loyalists who had been caught for a myriad of plots to upend the Patriot cause. The worst offenders were shackled to the wall. The guard stopped at Ketcham's cell and looked upon the sobbing man.

"What are you crying about?" the guard asked.

"I weep not for myself, but for my six children," Ketcham explained, lifting his head, and wiping his eyes. "I didn't do anything wrong, but they will suffer."

"If you didn't do anything wrong, I doubt you'd be sitting where you are," the guard replied.

Ketcham looked up at the guard. "I started to . . .," he began, and then threw up his hand at the futile attempt to defend himself. He shook his head. "Even doing the right thing landed me in prison."

"Hmmm, sounds like Joseph," the guard retorted.

Ketcham wrinkled his forehead. "Who?"

"Joseph, from the Old Testament. Don't you read the Holy Writ?" the guard answered. "He did the right thing and still landed in prison. Stayed there a long time, too."

"If he was in the Bible, that just goes to show how God treats people," Ketcham scoffed. "You can't win with him, eh?"

"You must not know the rest of the story," the guard offered with a grin. "After Pharaoh called for him, Joseph was released from prison and made the second highest ruler in Egypt. So, in the course of an hour, he went from being in a place like this," he said, banging the prison bars, "to living in a palace."

"That sounds like a fairy tale," Ketcham answered, but curious.

"Doesn't it, though?" the guard asked. "God's Word has lots of incredible but true accounts of people who faced impossible injustice before God turned the tables on their enemies. Take Mordecai and Haman for example."

"Who?" Ketcham asked.

The guard looked up at the ceiling and shook his head. "You clearly need to read the Bible, lad. At the very least, those six children of yours deserve to be told these stories." He came closer and leaned on the bars. "An evil man named Haman served as the king's chief advisor. He hated the Jews and convinced the king to kill all of them by a wicked decree. Haman especially hated a Jew named Mordecai who refused to bow to him, so unbeknownst to the king he had gallows built to hang Mordecai. What the king also didn't realize was that his beautiful young queen named Esther was a Jew, and Mordecai was her cousin. One day long before any of this happened, Mordecai was sitting by the gates and overheard two of the king's guards discussing a plot to assassinate the king. He reported the plot, and the guards were arrested and executed. It took a while for anything good to come from the right thing that Mordecai had done. But just as Haman finished building the gallows to hang Mordecai, the king couldn't sleep and ordered that he be read the journals of his kingdom. He heard how Mordecai had foiled the assassination attempt, and the next day ordered Haman to parade Mordecai through the streets with honor to thank him for saving his life. The best part of the story? After Queen Esther informed the king of Haman's wickedness, justice was served when Haman himself was hanged on those gallows, not Mordecai. And then Mordecai took Haman's job. You see, injustice might appear to win at first, but God always has the final say, because the truth always comes out. Everything has an end except God."

Ketcham shot a quick glance at the guard who turned and walked away, leaving him alone with his thoughts. *That's what the Dutchman said,* he remembered.

MANHATTAN, NEW YORK, MAY 14, 1776

"I'm tellin' ye, Gillamon, that gunsmith be the key ta figurin' out Tr-r-ryon's pattern for turnin' Washington's soldiers against him," Max reported.

He and Jock filled Gillamon in on everything they had uncovered so far. "Excellent work, Max," Gillamon answered. "You and Jock have done well to start connecting things with Tryon, Matthews, and now Forbes. Keep following your nose to see where it leads."

Gillamon then filled them in on the counterfeiters and Ketcham now in prison.

"What about Ketcham's poor kids?" Jock wanted to know. "Who's going to care for them?"

"Don't worry, young one," Gillamon assured him. "I'm seeing to their care and will make sure they have food and whatever else they need."

"But wha' do Ketcham an' these counterfeiters have ta do with anythin'?" Max asked. "They be small time cr-r-rooks, not big players like the Governor and Mayor."

"Time will tell. It always does," Gillamon answered with a knowing grin. "Meanwhile, I've got 'Mordecai' positioned in jail. Now I just need for you to locate the 'king's two guards' to put in jail with him to talk about their plot."

8

THE PEN OF THE REVOLUTION

PHILADELPHIA, PENNSYLVANIA, JUNE 3, 1776

John Adams leaned back his head and blinked a few times, allowing the salve to cover his eyes. It was bittersweet to use this medicine, for while it was a tremendous help for his eyestrain, it had been given to him by the first spy and traitor to America. But Dr. Benjamin Church's betrayal had also opened the mental eyes of John Adams and George Washington among others, teaching them to be wary of anyone who could compromise their cause. So much had happened in the past year, but these leading men of the Revolution had grown in knowledge and wisdom. The lessons learned best are often the hardest ones of them all.

Patrick Henry and John Adams shared the same bold yet wary vision and had become fast friends when Henry attended the First and Second Continental Congress sessions in Philadelphia. After Patrick left the Congress to serve as Colonel of Virginia's forces, John Adams and Richard Henry Lee continued the conversation in Philadelphia as to what form a new American government should take. Encouraging one another to put pen to paper, Adams produced a pamphlet called *Thoughts on Government* and Lee a broadside called *Proposals for a Form of Government* that was reprinted in Williamsburg. Patrick Henry read both papers and wrote his friends accordingly. On May 20th, Patrick Henry wrote to John Adams:

> *The sentiments are precisely the same I have long since taken up, and they come recommended by you. Go on my dear friend to assail the strongholds of tyranny. And in whatever form oppression may be found, may those talents and that firmness which have achieved so much for America, be pointed against it.*

Patrick Henry also updated Adams on the developments in Virginia:

> *Before this reaches you the Resolution for finally separating from Britain will be handed to Congress by Col. Nelson. I put up with it in*

the present form, for the sake of unanimity. 'Tis not quite so pointed as
I could wish . . . Would to God you and your Sam Adams were here. It
shall be my incessant study to so form our portrait of Government that
a kindred with New England may be discern'd in it.

On May 27th, Thomas Nelson, Jr., arrived from Williamsburg and presented to Congress Virginia's declaration and instructions for the Virginia
delegates to propose independence. Liz and Nigel wished they could be in two
places at once—Williamsburg and Philadelphia—to see to the rapid developments happening toward independence in Virginia and in the Continental
Congress. But for now, they knew they needed to secure the perfect human
to write America's Declaration of Independence, and that that person needed
to be a Virginian. A year ago, John Adams had been the one to propose the
Sword of the Revolution—George Washington—as Commander-in-Chief.
Since they felt Adams would be the best one to also propose the Pen of the
Revolution, they set out to learn all they could by watching Adams and the
Virginians here in Philadelphia.

Nigel looked on from the shadows while the dim candlelight illuminated
John Adams's writing desk. He had been reading Adams's daily journal, which
noted details on the members and events of Congress, but tonight the little
mouse was eager to read Adams's reply to Patrick Henry. He waited until the
weary Massachusetts man finally rose from his chair to retire for the night and
then scurried over to scan the words of one Revolutionary giant to another:

I know of none so competent, to the task as the Author of the
first Virginia Resolutions against the Stamp Act, who will have
the glory with posterity, of beginning and concluding this great
Revolution. Happy Virginia, whose Constitution is to be framed
by so masterly a builder . . .

Your intimation that the session of your representative body
would be long gave me great pleasure, because we all look up to
Virginia for examples and in the present perplexities, dangers,
and distresses of our country it is necessary that the supreme
councils of the colonies should be almost constantly sitting . . .

The Decree is gone forth, and it cannot be recalled, that a
more equal Liberty, than has prevail'd in other parts of the
Earth, must be established in America.

"And indeed, it shall, Mr. Adams," Nigel whispered with great satisfaction. He then scurried out the door to go find Liz, who had followed Thomas
Jefferson to his lodgings here in Philadelphia. There they would compare notes.

JACOB GRAFF HOUSE, PHILADELPHIA, PENNSYLVANIA, JUNE 4, 1776

"Is he gone?" Nigel asked Liz, peering into the second-floor parlor where light streamed in from the tall windows.

Liz turned from where she sat on the table and smiled at the little mouse. *"Oui,* he left a while ago. The coast is clear, *mon ami."*

Nigel walked into the room, admiring the hunter green molding, marble fireplace, and simple yet handsome furnishings. Rather than be in the city center, Thomas Jefferson had opted to reside in this newly built three-story brick house located at the corner of Market and 7th Streets. It sat on the outskirts of town where the air was a bit fresher and the hustle and bustle a bit slower. For the tall Virginian who thrived in the tranquil countryside of Monticello, the Graff House was the perfect place where he could gaze out at the horse stable and surrounding fields. He rented the entire second floor consisting of a furnished parlor and bedchamber. Jefferson's fourteen-year-old slave Bob Hemmings tended to his personal and domestic needs and ran errands all over the city while Jefferson attended the daily sessions of Congress.

Liz was engrossed with her reading while Nigel made his way over to the table on which were spread an assortment of letters and documents. He stopped when he noticed the underside of a Windsor chair. "I say, what is this contraption?" He stood on his back legs to inspect the unusual chair. "This chair has two seats that appear to rotate on a central iron spindle," Nigel noted as he studied the mechanics. "There are rollers set in a groove between the two seats. By Jove, this is a revolving chair!"

"Oui, the rollers were made from the window sash pulleys," Liz told him, pointing up to the windows.

Nigel used his paw to move the seat. "Alas, if only I were not so very small; I should like to take this chair for a spin. This is truly a *revolutionary* chair."

"Monsieur Jefferson is quite the intelligent inventor. Come up here and I will show you my personal favorite," Liz told him.

Nigel made his way to the table where sat a small, handsome mahogany writing desk. A hinged writing board was attached to a rectangular box that had a drawer with compartments to hold paper, ink, and pens.

"Jefferson designed this lap desk, which was made by a Philadelphia cabinetmaker named Benjamin Randolph," Liz explained. "Jefferson lodged with *Monsieur* Randolph last year and also when he first arrived to Philadelphia in May before moving to this house."

The little mouse walked around the writing desk. "How exquisite! I should think Mr. Jefferson could write anywhere with this desk setting atop his lap."

"*Oui,* it is quite unusual," Liz agreed, running her paw along the edge. "I would love to have a . . . *laptop* such as this, no?"

Nigel walked around the table, scanning the papers lying there. "It appears our Mr. Jefferson is also quite the prolific writer. I am surprised to see such a profundity of thought, seeing how he hardly speaks at the Congress. He is clearly no Patrick Henry in that regard!" The mouse gave a jolly chuckle and adjusted his spectacles. "I say, what is this? A draft for a Virginia Constitution?"

Liz nodded. "By the time Jefferson arrived in Philadelphia on May 14th, Congress had already passed John Adams's resolution that each of the colonies adopt their own form of government. Of course, he did not know this, but Virginia was already in the process of doing so. *Monsieur* Jefferson immediately wrote to Thomas Nelson, Jr., proposing that Virginia wait and hold a special election for an assembly to draft Virginia's government. Of course, this is not possible or necessary. So, when Mr. Nelson arrived with Virginia's declaration news of May 15th, Jefferson began working on his own version of a constitution for his home colony. I believe he will send it soon, especially now that he has heard that Virginia is proceeding without him. The last place he wishes to be is Philadelphia."

"So, Mr. Jefferson would prefer to be in Williamsburg 'inventing' a new government there." Nigel twirled a whisker as he read. "Well, from what I see here, his preamble of charges against King George III of establishing 'a detestable and insupportable Tyranny' could be used in a Declaration of Independence." He looked at Liz. "By Jove, do you suppose Mr. Jefferson is meant to be the Pen of the Revolution?"

"I believe so, *mon ami.* Among the Virginia delegates in Philadelphia who could pen a Declaration of Independence, we have Richard Henry Lee, George Wythe, Benjamin Harrison, Francis Lightfoot Lee, Carter Braxton, and Thomas Jefferson," Liz recounted, picking up one of the small, white quills from a pewter cup on the table. "As MizP suggested, we should select a talented *young* Virginian, like Veritas, representing the next generation."

"Right. Richard Henry Lee is to present the resolution, as the best orator here in Philadelphia. He, his brother Francis, and George Wythe are of the older guard, Harrison is not liked *at all* by John Adams, and Patrick Henry believes that Braxton's ideas on government are 'silly,'" Nigel relayed.

"And Thomas Jefferson is the *youngest* of them all at thirty-three years of age. He and Patrick are friends, so I think *mon* Henry would approve," Liz surmised. "How well I remember that Christmas party when Patrick first met young seventeen-year-old Jefferson heading to Williamsburg to attend the College of William and Mary. So much has happened since then!" Liz looked around at the table and back at Nigel. "Given what we see here, *oui,* I believe that Jefferson is the right human for the job."

Nigel clasped his paws together. "Splendid! And from what I've read in John Adams's daily journal, he has already taken note of Jefferson's 'reputation of a masterly pen' after reading Jefferson's tome, *Summary View of the Rights of British America.* So now we can be on the alert for how to best assist the freckle-faced young Virginian with his assignment."

"But Congress must first propose independence, and Richard Henry Lee is the right human for *that* job," Liz offered with a smile, replacing the small white quill. "When the time is right, we shall give the right quill to the Pen of the Revolution."

⚜

SECOND CONTINENTAL CONGRESS, PENNSYLVANIA STATE HOUSE, PHILADELPHIA, JUNE 7, 1776

"So far, a handful of other colonies have given their delegates the authority to vote for independence *if the issue is brought up,*" Nigel reported. "But no colony besides Virginia has instructed their delegates to make a motion to *declare* independence. As usual, it is up to the Virginians to get the ball rolling. The Adamses and the Lees are leading the charge here in the Congress toward independency, but there remain those hesitant to proceed, being primarily the delegates from New York, Pennsylvania, and South Carolina."

"*Oui,* but as goes Virginia, so goes America," Liz reminded him, gazing over at the table of Virginia delegates. Thomas Jefferson leaned against the windowsill next to their table, his arms folded tightly over his chest. The light coming in from the window spilled over the lanky Virginian's coppery hair. As usual he was finely dressed but remained silent and guarded, showing no emotion, no reaction to anything said.

"I see why Mr. Adams says everyone looks up to Virginia as they shall do today, but the stocky Mr. Adams and the short Mr. Hancock must literally do so!" Nigel whispered to Liz from their hiding spot in the assembly room. "Jefferson and Richard Henry Lee are over six feet tall. General Washington is as well, of course, but he is not present. It was splendid to see him here after his departure from Boston and settling the Continental Army in New York."

Liz nodded. "I was also happy to see Max and Jock if only for two days.

But it was timely for the members of Congress to hear directly from General Washington about the situation they face in New York. I believe it put a healthy fear in these humans to hear that King George has hired 17,000 German Hessians to fight alongside British forces here in America against General Washington's seven thousand Continental soldiers."

"Well, let us hope that the David and Goliath scenario rallies these delegates rather than makes them cower in fear," Nigel worried, glancing around the room.

John Hancock slammed the gavel. "The chair recognizes the delegate from Virginia, Mr. Richard Henry Lee."

"This is it!" Liz whispered expectantly.

The polished Virginian bowed and held up his right hand, holding a piece of paper summarizing the instructions from Patrick Henry and the Virginia Convention. His left hand remained at his side and was wrapped in a black silk handkerchief to hide the loss of two fingers from a swan hunting accident years ago. "Gentlemen, I have received from the Virginia Assembly the following resolutions that I move for consideration:

"That these United Colonies are, and of right, ought to be, free and independent States, that they are absolved from all allegiance to the British crown, and that all political connection between them and the State of Great Britain is, and ought to be, totally dissolved;

"That it is expedient forthwith to take the most effectual measures for forming Alliances;

"That a plan of confederation be prepared and transmitted to the respective colonies for their consideration."

"SECOND!" John Adams quickly added, followed by the cheers of some and the jeers of others.

"Since we are obliged to attend to other business, we shall put off debate on Mr. Lee's resolutions until tomorrow," Hancock announced. "At that time, we shall move into a Committee of the Whole for discussion."

"To hear *mon* Henry's call for independence in those resolutions fills me with such happiness!" Liz exclaimed, enveloping Nigel in a hug. "We have just witnessed history!"

"Indeed, we have, my pet," Nigel answered happily. He then frowned as he watched Pennsylvania's John Dickinson and James Wilson huddled in talks with South Carolina's Edward Rutledge and New York's Robert Livingston. "But I'm afraid the opposition to independence is formidable. Until those other colonies get on board, Mr. Jefferson will not have to lift a quill."

SECOND CONTINENTAL CONGRESS,
PENNSYLVANIA STATE HOUSE, PHILADELPHIA, JUNE 8, 1776

Candlelight flickered off the windowpanes, and streams of smoke rose to the ceiling from brass wall sconces and candles placed at every green table around the room. The delegates fanned themselves with folded papers and dabbed the sweat from their brows. Some removed their scratchy wigs to wipe the perspiration from their bald heads. Others slouched in their chairs or leaned against the tables only to suddenly jump and slap their stockinged legs when bitten by one of the flies that had invaded the room. The men looked weary and unkempt, their wigs disheveled and five o'clock shadows peppering their upper lips and chins. Sweat rings penetrated their silken waistcoats and jackets from the stuffy room. Hot air rose from the candles as well as from the unending bickering on this sweltering June night.

"It is not that we are not *friends* of the measure for independence, but the timing of it that concerns us," twenty-six-year-old Edward Rutledge of South Carolina exclaimed. He was the youngest delegate and the grandest peacock of the entire congress in his mauve silk coat and breeches, ruffled shirt, and powdered wig of layered curls.

"We must wait for the voice of the people to guide us," John Dickinson of Pennsylvania echoed. He led the charge for trying to restore harmony with the crown. He beseeched the Congress to send the futile Olive Branch Petition he had penned, but it went unread by the king.

"We *are* the voice of the people, Sir!" John Adams spat back. "They elected us to represent them here, and they now wait for *us* to lead the way."

Robert Livingston shot to his feet. "Until we hear the clear mandate of the people, we will *not* vote for independence!" He was on edge, knowing full well that the British armada would soon arrive at his home colony of New York.

"The time for independence is *now!*" Richard Henry Lee shouted, pacing about, and swatting at a fly that buzzed around his head. "The largest colony of Virginia has boldly declared her independence and is proceeding to form a new government. We must do the same for this union of colonies."

Liz watched Thomas Jefferson squirm at Lee's words.

"We would sooner secede from the union of this assembly than to rush ahead of the people," Dickinson threatened.

"Or make an alliance with France!" added Livingston. "Would you trade our British king for a French one who could just as easily impose his will on America in the guise of helping us to win our independence?"

"We cannot conduct trade nor make alliances with any European powers until we declare ourselves a sovereign nation," John Adams insisted. "General Washington has told us very plainly that the current military campaign may be unsuccessful, gentlemen! We *must* have foreign assistance for guns, ammunition, and supplies. There is simply no time to lose!"

Liz looked at Benjamin Franklin, who sat quietly at the Pennsylvania table, gripping the top of his cane with both hands, and wearing a frown as the debate raged around him. *"Monsieur* Franklin remains silent like *Monsieur* Jefferson, even though he knows far more about the French alliance than anyone here. If only he knew that his meeting with Bonvouloir convinced Vergennes and the French to send aid!"

"Yes, but unfortunately the lingering suspicion of the French from the bloody French and Indian War remains with some in this assembly," Nigel pointed out. "And nerves are wearing quite thin from this long day of debate. The humans simply need more time. South Carolina is hesitant, and Maryland, Pennsylvania, Delaware, New Jersey, and New York have not yet been empowered by their colonial legislatures to vote for independence. If John Hancock moves for a vote before the colonies are unanimous in their decision, it could spell disaster."

"Oui, it must be a unanimous vote," Liz agreed, looking at the little mouse. "Or perhaps a unani*mouse* one. I have an idea!" She held up Veritas's feather. "But I shall need some ink and paper."

SECOND CONTINENTAL CONGRESS, PENNSYLVANIA STATE HOUSE, PHILADELPHIA, JUNE 10, 1776

"I am grateful the Congress does not meet on Sundays," Nigel whispered as he and Liz watched the delegates file back into the room after a day of rest. "The delegates had some much-needed time to cool off, physically as well as emotionally."

"I agree, *mon ami.* Now to see if the humans will agree to our suggestion to delay the vote," Liz replied. She watched Rutledge pick up the note that Nigel had left on his table and then huddle with his fellow delegates. She then looked to see Adams pick up the other note she had penned for him to find. "And to form a committee to prepare a Declaration in the meantime."

John Hancock sounded the gavel and called the session to order, resuming the assembly in the Committee of the Whole.

Rutledge stood to his feet. "The delegates of South Carolina would like to propose a delay for the vote on independence in order to receive further instructions from our colony. We believe the middle colonies also seek such instructions from their constituents. Twenty days should be sufficient."

"Second!" Adams answered, holding the note that Nigel had left on his table.

"Very well, we shall delay the vote on Mr. Lee's resolutions until July 1ˢᵗ," Hancock declared.

"Might I suggest that we form a committee to prepare an official Declaration in anticipation of the vote lest any time be lost?" Adams suggested. John Hancock looked around the room. "Any objections? Mr. Dickinson? Mr. Livingston?"

"No objection, Sir," Livingston replied, looking over at Dickinson, who nodded in agreement.

"Mr. Adams, please form your committee," John Hancock instructed.

"Brilliant! We have assisted them with time," Nigel exulted.

Liz watched as Adams gazed over at Thomas Jefferson. *"Oui,* now to assist them with words."

CITY TAVERN, PHILADELPHIA, PENNSYLVANIA, JUNE 11, 1776

The epicenter of politics in Philadelphia was not the Pennsylvania State House, but the lively City Tavern located down the street. Considered to be the finest dining establishment in America, the five-level building housed kitchens, a bar room, two coffee rooms, three dining rooms, a large upstairs ballroom, five lodging rooms, servants' quarters, and stables out back for travelers' animals. Many delegates of the Continental Congress had stayed here, including Patrick Henry, and it was here George Washington and John Adams first met.

But it was also here the delegates came to discuss privately what had been debated and discussed publicly in the Congress. These fashionable rooms were not just for enjoying the freshest, most deliciously prepared food in Philadelphia, they were for politicking, planning, negotiating, and deal-making. Delegates came here not just as individuals, but often as informal committees. Given the dozens of committees appointed by Congress and the overwhelming time required for members to meet, committees sometimes worked through dinner.

Although Thomas Jefferson's lodgings were located on the opposite side of town, he kept an open tab here at City Tavern to pay for meals and refreshments throughout the long days and nights of the Congress. After John Adams had received permission to form a committee to draft a Declaration of Independence, he quickly secured the Committee of Five for the task: Thomas

Jefferson of Virginia, Roger Sherman of Connecticut, Benjamin Franklin of Pennsylvania, Robert R. Livingston of New York, and himself, John Adams of Massachusetts. While it was a prudent mix of delegates representing the broad spectrum of opinion on independence, Adams knew that only one person could draft the document. And he knew that the right person was Thomas Jefferson. Given the tense debate on the floor, Adams arranged for the committee to first meet here at City Tavern to start off on a positive, genteel note. "A word, Mr. Jefferson, before the others arrive," Adams requested, taking Jefferson by the elbow, and guiding him to a corner table in the front room.

They deposited their three-cornered hats on a peg rack and took their seats. "I am pleased to serve with you on this committee, Mr. Adams," Jefferson told him. "I am sure you will draft a fine declaration."

John Adams leaned forward with a furrowed brow. "Not I, Mr. Jefferson, but YOU."

"Why?" Jefferson asked, folding his arms over his chest, and leaning back in his seat.

"Reasons enough," Adams replied, looking around the room and spotting Rutledge and Dickinson making their way to a table.

Jefferson maintained a deadpan expression. "What can be your reasons, Sir?"

"Reason first: You are a Virginian, and a Virginian ought to appear at the head of this business," Adams replied, glancing around at the room, and feeling as if all eyes were trained on him. Reason second: I am obnoxious, suspected, and unpopular—I'm as obnoxious as a honking goose." He turned back to Jefferson and lifted a hand to the elegant young Virginian sitting in his blue silk clothes and polished shoe buckles, legs crossed and comfortable in his own skin. "You are very much otherwise. In Virginia, all geese are *swans*. Reason third: You can write ten times better than I can."

Jefferson pursed his lips and raised his eyebrows as he glanced down at the table before raising his gaze. "I am currently working on a draft for Virginia's new constitution and am anxious to send it with Mr. Wythe when he and Mr. Lee return to Virginia in two days' time. With the Virginia delegation spread thin, I will have to daily be in attendance and serve as well on the other committees . . ."

Adams held up his hand to interrupt him, shaking his head. "Mr. Jefferson, we *all* face pressing demands. I serve on twenty-three committees and expect to be placed on three more this week, including the Board of War. I simply do *not* have time to draft the Declaration. As you've expressed to me in previous conversations, you do not possess a gift for oratory, and as you have surmised by now, oratory is one gift I seem to never tire of dispensing on the floor of the Congress. I must use it to continue to pull sway on every impulse toward independency and assist with supplying General Washington and the Continental Army. Neither I nor this committee have time to waste. We must hurriedly produce this draft and have an edited, fair copy ready to present on the floor of Congress in three weeks."

"Three weeks for a written masterpiece that will change the world," Nigel whispered aloud to himself as he listened in. "Just like Handel had three weeks to compose *Messiah,* another masterpiece to change the world."

Jefferson furrowed his brow. "It appears you have made up your mind, Mr. Adams."

"I have, Mr. Jefferson." Adams slapped the table decidedly. "I will announce to the committee that you should make the draft, and I shall then expect you to accept and proceed with your draft immediately."

Jefferson took in a deep breath through his nostrils and exhaled. "Well, if you are decided, I will do as well as I can."

"And you shall have some assistance," Nigel added with a grin before noticing the headlines from a newspaper lying on a nearby table. His eyes widened behind his spectacles. "Huzzah! Virginia has done it! I must make haste and get this to Liz!"

JACOB GRAFF HOUSE, PHILADELPHIA, PENNSYLVANIA, JUNE 11, 1776

Liz watched from behind the fireplace screen as Bob Hemmings lit the candles around the room and neatly arranged Thomas Jefferson's mail just as he liked it when returning home from Congress. The slave tidied up the parlor and proceeded to lay out Thomas Jefferson's night clothes in the bedroom. Liz frowned, considering the fourteen-year-old boy's situation. He had a kind, pleasant master, of course, but he was not free. The French cat continually struggled with the horrible reality of slavery that existed in the colonies, but she held on to the words Gillamon had shared with her. Freedom for all would come step by step, but it would take time. After Bob left the room, Liz jumped up onto the table to continue reading Jefferson's draft for the Virginia Constitution.

Nigel startled her when he arrived with his exuberant greeting. "The Pen of the Revolution has been aptly selected and given his charge!"

Liz looked up with a broad grin. *"Monsieur* Jefferson, no?"

"Right you are, my pet! I heard John Adams sternly inform Thomas Jefferson that he simply had no choice in the matter but to draft the

Declaration," Nigel recounted. "The Committee of Five had their first gathering and laid out the basic elements for Jefferson to include."

"I assume they wish to pattern it after the declarations their ancestors have written in England time and again before them, starting with charges against the King," Liz supposed.

"Yes, and Adams informed Jefferson that the Declaration must be drafted, edited, and ready to present to the Congress in three weeks," Nigel went on. "It occurred to me that three weeks also was the amount of time Handel took to compose *Messiah.*"

"Only three short weeks to produce such a masterpiece," Liz marveled.

"Precisely my thoughts before I stumbled onto this in the City Tavern!" Nigel answered happily, laying a copy of the June 6th *Pennsylvania Evening Post* on the table. "This is the first draft of Virginia's Declaration of Rights! Mr. George Mason has been the primary architect, and with his committee has crafted eighteen specific rights for the people of Virginia."

"*Magnifique!* Oh, let me see!" Liz exclaimed. She and Nigel began poring over the document.

A DECLARATION OF RIGHTS

Is made by the representatives of the good people of Virginia, assembled in full and free convention which rights do pertain to them and their posterity, as the basis and foundation of government.

SECTION 1. That all men are by nature equally free and independent and have certain inherent rights, of which, when they enter into a state of society, they cannot, by any compact, deprive or divest their posterity; namely, the enjoyment of life and liberty, with the means of acquiring and possessing property, and pursuing and obtaining happiness and safety.

"Perhaps Mason and the committee wish to share their draft to inspire the other colonies," Nigel supposed. "But they must be close to completion if this was printed on June 6th here in Pennsylvania."

Liz nodded and wrinkled her brow. "I do not know why, but for some reason June 6th has a feeling of destiny about it."

"How so, my pet?" Nigel wondered, adjusting his spectacles as he traced his paw down the page.

"I cannot explain it. My heart just feels heavy about this date, no?" She shook her head to wave off the feeling. "But this is *happy* news from Virginia. I am so very proud of the work *Monsieur* Mason has done."

"Indeed, George Mason has been the primary author of this exquisite document," Nigel agreed. I am also certain Patrick Henry and the committee have been astute contributing editors," he added.

"I hear the voice of Dr. Mazzei in these words as well," Liz recalled. "Remember that he is friends with Mason and Patrick, and of course is Jefferson's neighbor. I believe this Virginia Declaration of Rights will be an important resource for *Monsieur* Jefferson as he pens the Declaration of Independence."

"Quite so. Jefferson also has his own work on a proposed Virginia Constitution that entails a splendid list of grievances against King George III." Nigel put his paws on his hips, looking at the documents on the table. He placed the Virginia Declaration of Rights on top of the stack of incoming correspondence. "Our young Virginian will assume this *Pennsylvania Post* was delivered with his mail."

Liz nodded. "Perfect! He has what he needs to inspire his thinking. I have no doubt he shall also pull from his understanding of the 1689 English Declaration of Rights as *Monsieur* Mason has done, no?"

"Undoubtedly so. From what I've seen, Mr. Jefferson's mind is a walking library of texts from which to pull, including even the poetry of Defoe," Nigel posited, clearing his throat and lowering an imaginary sword:

"When kings the sword of justice first lay down,
They are no longer kings, though they possess the crown.
Titles are shadows, crowns are empty things,
The good of subjects is the end of kings."

"Bravo, *mon ami!*" Liz exclaimed, clapping her paws together as Nigel took a bow. She took out a blank piece of paper and dipped Veritas's feather in the inkwell. "Now, I shall leave *Monsieur* Jefferson this special quill, along with a note. Given his affinity for nature and Indian culture, I am sure having a revered bald eagle feather for drafting the Declaration will inspire him. I shall leave it next to his stack of correspondence."

Just then they heard Jefferson coming up the stairs. Liz folded the note and placed Veritas's feather inside. She and Nigel jumped to the floor and darted behind the ornately carved brass fireplace screen. Here they could easily watch Jefferson at work while remaining in the darkened shadows of the unused fireplace during this sultry Philadelphia evening. Jefferson went over and raised a window to allow fresh air to circulate, then removed his coat and draped it neatly over a side chair. He leaned over to inspect the mail before taking his seat in the revolving chair.

Jefferson tilted his head as he lifted Liz's note and saw Veritas's feather fall to the table. His eyes widened and he picked up the beautiful eagle feather, pulling it through his fingers and admiring its deep grey-brown hues with the tuft of white at the base. "What a fine specimen, but where did it come from?" He then opened Liz's note. "From a true friend of liberty. May this quill inspire every word you write.—VERITAS."

"Veritas—*truth*. Who could that be?" Jefferson muttered, gripping the feather now as a quill. He eagerly leaned forward and dipped it in the ink to test it, writing his signature on the bottom of Liz's note.

Th Jefferson

He smiled, pleased with the smoothness of the quill and the weight of it in his hand. He rested it in the inkwell and reached for the *Pennsylvania Evening Post*. Immediately his eyes fell to news of the Virginia Declaration of Rights, and he devoured every word, his lips moving as he read silently.

"I believe the Pen of the Revolution is quite pleased with his new instrument," Nigel whispered to Liz.

Liz smiled. "And he is equally pleased with Virginia's Declaration."

After a few moments, Jefferson nodded and laid Virginia's Declaration in front of him, along with his draft of the Virginia Constitution. He reached over to a stack of blank paper and lifted a sheet, setting it on his writing desk. As he pulled the desk onto his lap, a fly darted in from the open window and proceeded to buzz around his head. He lifted a hand to swat it away and then dipped Veritas's feather in the inkwell. He paused a moment and took in a deep breath before quickly exhaling. He leaned over and wrote the header that mirrored the opening of Virginia's Declaration:

A Declaration by the Representatives of the UNITED STATES OF AMERICA, in General Congress assembled.

He leaned back in his revolving chair and slowly turned back and forth as he thought about his next words. "Whereas . . ."

The fly came buzzing by again and bit him on the leg. "Blast these flies!" he scoffed, slapping his leg, and angrily setting the writing desk on the table. He got up and forcefully shut the window, mumbling under his breath as he gazed out at the horse stable. He swatted at the fly before it rested out of his reach on the wall above him.

He folded his arms over his chest and began to pace in front of the window, yawning. "Whereas . . . whereas . . . whereas . . . no, that's not how to begin."

The fly came back again and harassed the tall Virginian. Jefferson stomped his foot in exasperation. "I am too tired to fight flies or write another word tonight." He yawned again. "I will rise early and start fresh in the morning."

"It appears he is stopping for the night," Liz whispered to Nigel as Jefferson left the parlor and retired to the bedroom.

"Indeed, my dear, but I believe that Mr. Jefferson has all he needs for now to assist him with the Declaration of Independence," Nigel replied. "Whilst he labors on the draft, I feel we must return to Williamsburg to assess the finalization of this Virginia Declaration of Rights and to see the progress on the new Virginia Constitution. Then we can return here once the committee begins editing the document."

"*Oui,* I agree. We can go there tonight," Liz agreed. "But first I believe *Monsieur* Jefferson needs some assistance to get started with the Declaration. I think he wishes to set this document apart from previous declarations, for it will be an unusual audience who will read it."

"It shall be a grandiose 'break-up letter,' if you will, with Great Britain, so he intends for the king to feel the sting of his pen," Nigel offered with a chuckle, twirling a whisker. "And the audience will include the people of America, whom he hopes to rally to the cause, including soldiers to win the war."

Liz nodded. "This is true, *mon ami,* but I believe this Declaration is meant not just for King George or the people of America, but primarily for my country! *Oui,* while it is a 'break-up letter' with England, it is also an invitation for France to have the next dance with America."

"By Jove, you're right!" Nigel realized, wide-eyed. "Vergennes has made it clear that before France can fully assist the Americans, a Declaration of Independence must be issued. And this Declaration shall declare to France that America is not simply a downtrodden group of colonies in a rebellion against a monarch, but is its own sovereign nation, ready to take its place in the world."

"*Oui,* but it needs to be written for the ear as well as the eye," Liz shared, pointing to Jefferson's beginning page. "This Declaration of Independence will be read aloud as well as printed, so it must romance the French ear as well as the American ear."

"I read in Mr. Adams's diary that Jefferson is fluent in French," Nigel told her excitedly.

Liz's eyes sparkled in the candlelight. "*Bon!* That means that as *Monsieur* Jefferson writes, he will be able to think of how the French will receive *La déclaration d'indépendence.*"

"Very true. But you are right, my pet. He does appear to be stuck in how to begin the preamble," Nigel observed, folding his arms over his chest. "It must have a musical cadence to it if it is to be read aloud."

"And it needs to capture its audience immediately with some powerful opening words." Liz then spotted Jefferson's violin kit sitting on the table next to where Nigel stood. "Well, just as you played your tiny violin in Handel's ear as he slept to inspire the music for *Messiah*, perhaps I can whisper a few words in Jefferson's ear as he sleeps in order to inspire his words."

"Brilliant, my dear!" Nigel exclaimed. "How do you think you shall begin?"

They suddenly heard Jefferson snoring in the other room. He had collapsed from exhaustion into bed and promptly fell asleep. Liz grinned. *"Mon Henry needed just seven little words to rally a nation to independence, so I shall give Monsieur Jefferson seven little words to begin its déclaration."*

Nigel wiggled his whiskers excitedly as he followed Liz from the parlor to the bedroom. "I simply cannot wait to see what you whisper to the Pen of the Revolution!"

Liz softly jumped onto the bed and made her way over to Jefferson's pillow. She then leaned over to whisper, *"Lorsque, dans le cours des événements humains . . .*

9

OUR DOG IN PARIS

THE WAR ROOM, JUNE 6, 1776

Kate blinked her soft brown eyes a few times to clear away the dissolving white mist that had enveloped her while transporting to this secret War Room. Gillamon arranged for the Order of the Seven to have this dedicated place to meet, share information, and receive vital instructions for their missions. To get here, the animals simply had to dip a quill or paw into milk, stand on the text of Genesis 3 and write the letter "W." Instantly they would be transported to the War Room.

The white Westie shook from head to tail, once more awed by the magnificence of the circular room with no door. She stood on the mahogany table laden with books, maps, and implements of espionage. Her mouth watered when she noticed a plate of French madeleine cakes and a dish of water sitting there on the table. She licked her chops and lifted her gaze to the red, massive, Order of the Seven seal sculpted on the ceiling. Glowing candlesticks and wall sconces illuminated the large room. Between two large bookcases hung Benjamin Franklin's picture of the dismembered snake labeled with the initials of the colonies. Spread across the curved walls were detailed maps of the colonies, of England, of France, and a huge map of the world and its oceans. Also hanging on the wall was a single panel of time used to view moments from the past as well as the present. Next to the table stood a colorful globe cradled in an ornate golden pedestal. A one-hundred-eighty-degree curved bar hovered over the surface of the globe with markings to indicate distance. A metal Order of the Seven seal rested on the bar and could be used to slide across the bar to mark a location. When leaving the War Room, one would place the marker on a desired location and press the seal to transport there. A wide horizontal platform encircled the globe, large enough for the animals to walk around. Intricate relief images of mountain ranges and oceans filled the globe with depth, but something spectacular was happening. The globe was moving ever so slowly. Sunlight shimmered on the globe's surface across daylight time zones while shadows spread across nighttime zones now covered in darkness. Kate cocked her head as she saw a tiny ship bobbing across the surface of the ocean off the coast of France.

"Hello, little one," came Gillamon's familiar, warm voice as he walked over to her, now in the form of an older human man wearing spectacles and a three-cornered hat, and puffing on an intricately carved pipe. The aroma of sweet cherry-tinged tobacco drifted into the air. He pointed to the ship with his pipe. "That would be your next human assignment soon to make port in Bordeaux, Mr. Silas Deane."

Kate wagged her tail happily. "Hello, Gillamon! I were wonderin' aboot that." She looked around the room. "Where be the rest of the team? I got yer message in the garden ta meet here, an' sneaked away from Lafayette's house in Versailles the first chance I got."

Gillamon softly chuckled and scratched Kate behind the ears. "Today's meeting is just for you and me, sweet Kate." He set his pipe on a round ceramic dish with the word *HUZZAH!* etched in blue and took a seat in one of the red leather high-back chairs with scrolled mahogany arms embellished with the Order of the Seven seal. He glanced at the plate of French madeleine cakes and smiled. "I have some important things to share with you."

"With *me?*" Kate asked, wide-eyed, sitting down in front of the team leader. "That makes me feel special, Gillamon! Ye usually tell the important things ta Max, Liz, or Nigel."

"Indeed, Max, Liz, and Nigel do tend to have the most *visible* roles in our team," Gillamon agreed with a nod. "Clarie of course is continually taking different forms and works closely with me on secret missions. And Al can't help but be visible regardless of what he does." He shared a chuckle with the little dog. "But you, little Kate, have always been content to serve in a less visible role behind the scenes to help the humans and special creatures. By no means is your work of love, protection, and compassion any less important than what the others do. Remember, the Maker sees not only everything that is visible, but also everything that is *invisible*, including what is in the heart. He cares about our *motives* as much as He cares about our actions. He loves a selfless, humble servant heart such as yours, little one."

Kate lowered her gaze and smiled shyly. "Thank ye kindly. I don't mind bein' in the shadows, Gillamon. I love ta make humans and other creatures happy. I don't need ta be in the spotlight."

"Which is why I've decided that it is time for you to take a more prominent role for this next phase of our mission to help birth a new nation," Gillamon added, leaning forward to look the Westie in the eye. "You are our dog in Paris and will be the eyes, ears, and paws to oversee one of the most important elements needed to secure independence for the Americans—the French Alliance. And you'll do so *invisibly.*"

Kate wrinkled her brow. "Do ye mean I have ta sneak around like I did for a while until I were reunited with Lafayette? I've learned how ta hide in the shadows while keepin' watch on things, but it's not easy ta do. I can't always get ta places I want ta reach."

Gillamon smiled and shook his head "no" while sliding the tray of French madeleine cakes in front of the little dog. "Please, take one."

Kate's mouth watered. "I love biscuits! Especially these French ones! Lafayette's wife Adrienne serves them all the time." She happily picked up the buttery, cake-like cookie shaped like a beautiful shell with scalloped edges. "Hmmmm. Delicious!" she muttered.

Gillamon sat there with his chin propped up by the tips of his fingers, elbows resting on the arms of his chair, grinning as the little dog enjoyed the madeleine.

"Thank ye, Gillamon, for the treat," Kate said. "So wha' did ye mean by me bein' invisible?"

Gillamon's twinkling eyes met hers with a knowing look, and he lifted a mirror to set on the table. "What do you see?"

There was a moment of silence before Kate exclaimed, "Gillamon! Where am I?"

"Don't be alarmed, Kate. You're right there on the table as before," Gillamon assured her. "You are simply invisible from eating the madeleine. This will be a new special power you possess whenever it becomes necessary for you to move about without being seen."

Kate giggled. "I can't believe it, Gillamon! Ye mean I can jest eat a biscuit an' become invisible?"

"Indeed, little one. It need not be a madeleine," Gillamon explained. "Any cookie or 'biscuit' will do. Not only shall you be invisible, but anything you carry in your mouth will be as well." He placed a small white pouch on the table. "If you ever need to carry anything, this pouch will also conceal its contents while you carry it in your mouth."

"How grand! It reminds me of the seed sack that Al carried for Liz ta the Ark! But how long does this invisibility last?" Kate wanted to know.

Gillamon pointed to the dish of water. "Take a sip and see."

Kate lapped up the water and slowly her white fur reappeared from head to tail. She looked down and saw her fluffy paws once more. "So I'll be invisible until I take a sip of water? That'll be easy! I think this be the most fun ability of any of the Order of the Seven team members! It certainly be the most *delicious.*"

Gillamon chuckled and leaned in to look at Kate from above his spectacles. "I'm afraid Al will want to exchange his iron claw ability for your eating power, so let's keep your new ability secret for the time being, shall we?"

"Aye, whatever ye say, Gillamon!" Kate agreed with a giggle. Her face then turned serious. "That evil beastie Espion that's out ta kill me human Lafayette walks around invisible, too. I'll be able ta use the same ability but for doin' *good.*"

"Indeed, Kate, the Beast of the *Gévaudan* that you and Max defeated behind Lafayette's childhood home of *Chavaniac* in the south of France now serves the evil team leader Charlatan," Gillamon agreed. "While you work to assist Deane, Lafayette, and the other humans in Paris, your invisible power will serve you as you search for their headquarters, starting beneath the streets of Paris."

"There be two hundred miles of tunnels below Paris, so it will take time, but I'll find out where those evil beasties meet," Kate predicted confidently.

"Liz will assist you in that quest when she arrives to help you with Lafayette's valiant escape from France," Gillamon noted. "Clarie will lend her aid as well."

"Lassie power!" Kate cheered. "So wha' do ye need me ta do first?"

Gillamon softly tapped the desk with an approving nod. "Very good. As you know, Silas Deane has been sent to France by the Secret Committee of Congress to secure artillery, arms, uniforms, and equipment to equip an army of twenty-five thousand men. In addition, the Secret Committee of Correspondence has tasked Deane with becoming America's first ever diplomatic envoy to seek out help from a foreign nation, namely France. He'll be their man in Paris, joined later by Arthur Lee and Benjamin Franklin. And although Deane has not been given the express orders to do so, he will be the one to arrange for French officers including Lafayette to receive a commission to serve in the Continental Army."

Kate wagged her tail and smiled happily. "How grand! He will be an important human then. I'll especially want ta help make sure Lafayette meets him."

"Indeed. And as you can imagine, there will be spies abounding in this mission who will try to interfere with Deane and all he seeks to accomplish," Gillamon told her. "Thankfully, the work that Liz and Nigel did with the French spy Bonvouloir, who met with Benjamin Franklin in Philadelphia last December, convinced the French foreign minister, Comte de Vergennes and in turn, France's King Louis XVI to begin secret aid. Vergennes combined Bonvouloir's report with the secret French agent Beaumarchais's proposal to make the case for supplying the Americans with French arms, gunpowder, and supplies."

"Aye, King Louis gave Beaumarchais one million *livres* ta set up a fake tradin' company," Kate reported with a nod. "Beaumarchais will use half of the

money ta buy old French weapons, gunpowder, clothes, blankets, etcetera, an'
he'll lend the other half of the money ta Congress. Some of the loaded ships
will sail right ta America, an' others will sail ta the West Indies, where smaller
American ships can smuggle the supplies in from there. After the stuff is
unloaded in America, they'll ask the Americans ta load the ships back up with
tobacco, rice, indigo, cotton an' lumber ta send back ta France. Beaumarchais
can then sell those goods ta buy more things the Americans need. He'll make
money ta cover his expenses an' keep the tradin' goin' for however long it
takes for the Americans ta win the war with England."

Gillamon petted the Westie on the back. "Well done, Kate! I'm so pleased
that you have a firm understanding of how this shall work."

"Ye should have seen when Vergennes met with the King aboot
Beaumarchais's plan," Kate recounted with a giggle. "After Vergennes
explained the details of how France could secretly help the Americans right
under the noses of the British, he an' the king stared at each other for a
moment, then burst out laughin'! The king don't really like Beaumarchais's
play *The Barber of Seville* like his Queen Marie Antoinette do, but he shook
his finger at Vergennes with a laugh, an' said that that unlikely playwright-
turned-spy Beaumarchais were actin' jest like his clever character Figaro with
his brilliant scheming."

"I would love to have been with you hiding behind the curtain to watch
that scene!" Gillamon slapped the table good naturedly and chuckled.

"The king liked Beaumarchais's plan so much that he not only agreed ta
the plan, but he gave Vergennes permission ta ask his Bourbon cousin the
Spanish King Charles III ta pitch in another million *livres*," Kate explained.
"Beaumarchais will need ta raise another million *livres* from private investors
ta make things look like he's runnin' a real company. But the key ta the whole
thing be that Beaumarchais has ta keep the French government out of this—I
guess ye'd say *they* need ta be *invisible* as well. The British mustn't find out that
they be behind this secret plan. Vergennes can't eat madeleines ta be invisible
while the British ambassador Lord Stormont storms around Versailles, sniffin'
out wha' the Frenchies be up ta."

"Right. This will be an elaborate game of cat and mouse that Vergennes
plays with the British ambassador. Lord Stormont keeps a close eye on the
French in Versailles and uses an extensive network of spies in every port and
seemingly in every café in Paris to report everything back to the King of
England and his ministers," Gillamon added. He stood and picked up a madeleine, took a bite then pointed at the map of Europe with the little cake.

"France and Great Britain are not at war—at this moment anyway—so
Vergennes must accomplish some tricky things in order to eventually reach

a formal French Alliance with America. First, he must convince the British that France and Spain want *peace* with them while secretly preparing for *war* by rebuilding the French navy and re-equipping the French army. But the very act of updating France's military arms will be the perfect excuse for why they must rid their armories of outdated weapons. Vergennes knows France will not have prepared soldiers, cannons, and modernized ships to fight the British until early 1778. Secondly, he must stealthily support the American cause with arms and supplies until a Declaration of Independence is made and the Americans can prove that they *can* and *will* fight to win the war. America's words of independence must be followed up by solid action."

Kate gave an affirmative nod. "I've always liked stickin' up for the under-dogs who are bullied. Why do ye think the French want ta help the underdog Americans? Wha's *their* invisible heart motive?"

"The French are eager to restore their honor in Europe and the world after the humiliating defeat by the British in the Seven Years' War. They no longer are *the* giant power in Europe when it comes to diplomacy and the actions of nations. France used to be the first country consulted," Gillamon explained, finishing his madeleine. "France possesses far more men, money, and materials than England. They have twenty-four million people with a standing army of one hundred forty thousand men as opposed to England's nine million people and only thirty-five thousand soldiers. France has far more material riches than England, and the best armament industry in the world, so to lose a war to the smaller, less fortified country was a bitter defeat indeed. England must hire Hessian mercenaries to fight its wars, and while it has a mighty naval force, it knows that a combined French and Spanish navy could readily outnumber and end Britannia's rule of the waves."

"Is that why the British aren't eager ta fight France again?" Kate asked.

"Correct, Kate. When they ended the Seven Years' War with the 1763 Treaty of Paris, England returned to France almost all of the land it had gained, except for Canada, and the Ohio Valley. The Spanish will take over the Louisiana territory and New Orleans," Gillamon explained. "They do not wish to have to repeatedly go to war with France and fight over the same territory against a mightier power. So, the British feel smug as victors in their generosity to the French, but they do not realize the resentment and shame festering in the hearts of Frenchmen who are eager for revenge."

Kate shook her head sadly. "Besides the heart motive of revenge, what else does France want?"

"France also wants to be first in line to trade with a new United States of America. France has watched Great Britain grow rich from commerce with the colonies, and they want in on that trade. Beaumarchais values and applauds the cause of American independence, for he sees in that struggle his own personal struggle against the French aristocracy in making something of himself. He admires America's quest for freedom, and will indeed be a friend to help her, but *his* heart motive as a clever opportunist and businessman is France's honor and glory above all."

Kate frowned. "Wha' aboot me human, the Marquis de Lafayette? Seems ta me his heart's different from the rest."

Gillamon smiled. *"Oui,* Kate. Lafayette alone truly embraces the American cause enough to fight and die alongside her for the Patriotic ideals of liberty and equality. Yes, he seeks the adventure and glory for France that his military ancestors achieved, but Lafayette will fight for underdog America because his primary motive is a just and noble cause for mankind. The rest of France will fight on behalf of *France's* interests and for their own personal gain and glory."

"And the Spanish? Wha' be their motive in helpin' or not helpin' America?" Kate wanted to know.

"The Bourbon cousin kings of France and Spain signed a Family Compact in 1761 to protect each other from the attack of a third party," Gillamon answered, tapping the map. "Neither King Louis XVI of France nor King Charles III of Spain seeks war, despite their mutual dislike of England. Louis dislikes the idea of interfering with the internal affairs of another country but has come around to Vergennes's way of thinking to support the Americans because it seems the moral thing to do, which could benefit France. Charles, however, is leery of the American cause and doesn't wish for their independent ideals to seep into Spain's New World colonies. Nor does he want the Americans to expand their territory into Florida or west beyond the Mississippi River. But Charles' longstanding grudges against England are greater than his concerns over helping America, so he will provide financial aid and open Spanish ports to American ships. When news of the Americans driving the British from Boston reached Spain last month, Charles agreed to match France's one million *livres* in aid, but he won't do much more than that to support the American quest for Independence. Spain will not fight alongside America."

Kate nodded with understanding. "So, America's only true *ally* in this war will be France. An' America's only true *heart friend* will be Lafayette. When ye understand *why* creatures do wha' they do, it helps ye know how an' *if* ye should help them . . . or stop them."

Gillamon nodded with a broad smile, setting a piece of paper in front of her. "Indeed, Kate. So, you already know more than our esteemed Mr. Silas Deane, who knows nothing of France's plans that are already in place to help the Americans. Here is some background on Deane."

Kate scanned Silas Deane's profile sitting on the table. "Let's see. He were a schoolteacher, businessman, an' lawyer from Connecticut who served in the First an' Second Continental Congresses. He'll pose as a merchant sent by Congress ta buy things ta trade with Native American Indians in America so as ta keep them friendly on the frontier."

"Very good. Of course, Deane has no money to purchase supplies so needs to buy things on credit," Gillamon added. He went over to the single panel of time, tapping it gently. The scene of waves lapping against the wharf at Bordeaux came into view. Seagulls cried out overhead and the harbor was filled with the sights and sounds of ships being unloaded, merchants arguing about broken crates, fishing vessels hauling their catch to the market, and sailors laughing and flirting with the young ladies purchasing fish. "I want you to meet this American as he steps onto the shore of France today." He suddenly got a faraway look in his eyes and softly whispered, "June 6th."

"Gillamon?" Kate asked, standing and walking across the table to reach him. "Wha's wrong?"

"Nothing, little one," Gillamon assured her with a thoughtful smile. "This is just the first of many layers of history connecting France and America. And it is the start of a beautiful friendship." He pointed to Deane's ship slipping into the harbor of Bordeaux. "Deane will soon make port. He has never travelled abroad. He doesn't know a single soul in France, nor does he speak a word of French. Thankfully, Benjamin Franklin and the Secret Committee sent instructions with Deane on trusted men to contact upon his arrival."

"I can imagine how anxious he must feel, not havin' a friend in the world, an' not knowin' the language," Kate posed.

"So, you will help to put him at ease with this, little Kate," Gillamon replied. He took from his pocket an English-French dictionary. "He need not know where this came from. Slip it into his valise as you see him to his lodgings. He'll rest there from his long voyage before he heads to Paris." He then pointed to the scene of the market at the bustling waterfront. "Now, do you see this fair maiden with her basket? She is an innkeeper's daughter from St. Jean-du-Luz, a southern French town on the border with Spain. She is in Bordeaux with her father today, but I want you to remember her face. She will play an important role for Lafayette when the time comes. You and she have a great deal in common, for you both have the gift of encouragement."

Kate wagged her tail as she gazed at the petite young woman with a tiny waist, beautiful brown locks tucked under her blue bonnet, striking facial features of a square-cut jaw, chiseled French nose, blue eyes, and a radiant smile. "She's a bonnie lass. I'm happy ta know she'll help me with the Marquis. Wha's her name then?"

Gillamon picked up a madeleine. "Guess."

"Madeleine!" Kate exclaimed. "Only she's not invisible."

Gillamon handed her the cake. "But *you* will be, little one. After you see Deane settled in Bordeaux, head to Paris to check on progress with Beaumarchais and his fake company. Wait for Deane there in Paris and help get him settled at the *Hôtel du Grand Villars* when he arrives. And remember, Kate, spies will be everywhere, so stay sharp as our dog in Paris—for our man in Paris."

"Aye, I'll try ta figure out the motives of all the humans as best I can, Gillamon," Kate assured him, eating the madeleine, and disappearing from view. She picked up the book, which also disappeared at her touch, went to the globe, and moved the marker to Bordeaux. She tucked the book into her pouch. "I'll be as invisible as the spies hidin' in plain sight."

BORDEAUX, FRANCE, JUNE 6, 1776

The thirty-eight-year-old American closed his eyes in relief as he set foot on the solid plank of the wharf. Having been at sea since March with setbacks in the West Indies necessitating the purchase of the sailing sloop *Betsy* in Bermuda, Silas Deane was grateful to stand on wood that wasn't moving. He wore a red coat with large satin-covered buttons, a white frilly shirt with white neck cravat, a grey waistcoat with silver buttons, red breeches, and a black three-cornered hat. Rather tall with a narrow face, straight nose, high cheekbones, and thick eyelashes framing his striking blue eyes, he looked around and took in the sights, sounds, and smells of this busy French port. The aromas of low-tide greyish muck and pilon-clinging barnacles mingled with newly applied black tar pitch on the underside of a nearby dry-docked ship, coupled with the salty smells from a large catch of fish, oysters, and eel that drew the locals to purchase tonight's supper. Deane heard two chefs arguing, but since he did not understand French, he didn't realize that it concerned a particularly large redfish for sale to serve at their respective cafés. He smiled when a lovely, petite young lady stepped between them and bought the fish while their argument turned from the snapper to which of them served the finest *Poisson à la Bordelaise*. She placed it in her basket and lifted her chin with a grin as she left the arguing chefs behind.

Kate grinned at Madeleine's "catch" and noticed Deane tip his hat at the young lady, who returned his smile and walked away toward the town. *If they only knew that they'll both soon help the Marquis de Lafayette. Humans seldom realize that they be more connected than they know.*

Captain Johnson of Deane's ship walked up to the American along with a young man who wheeled a handcart carrying two trunks and Deane's leather valise and loaded them into a waiting carriage.

"Mr. Deane, as requested I have instructed the driver to take you to a nearby inn of good reputation," the captain relayed, holding out his hand to the carriage. "I hope you have success in your business trip. *Bienvenue en France.*" Deane wore a confused look for a brief moment before the captain quickly followed, with a knowing smile. "Welcome to France. I recommend you learn the language as best you can."

Deane's cheeks flushed with embarrassment and the realization that he would now be on his own without a friendly English-speaking captain to assist him. He bowed, "Thank you, sir. Ah, but in French . . .".

"Merci," the captain offered as Deane fumbled for the right word.

"Merci, yes, that's it, *merci,"* Deane answered awkwardly, dabbing his brow with a kerchief as he stepped up into the carriage.

Kate shook her head and hopped invisibly onto the back of the carriage with the hidden pouch to follow Deane to the inn. *How in the world will the lad speak ta the French aboot anythin' if he can't even say 'thank ye?' I'll get this dictionary in his hands tonight, but our man in Paris better find a translator ta be by his side at all times or he'll be as lost as a redfish out of water.*

As the horse clip-clopped past them along the cobblestone street, two men put their heads together and watched as Silas Deane's carriage left the wharf.

Later that night Silas Deane lay snoring with his mouth open, utterly exhausted from his voyage coupled with the stress of obtaining a room and ordering a simple bowl of soup before turning in for the night. Kate had slipped the English-French dictionary into his valise and smiled when he furrowed his brow as he unpacked, wondering how it got there. His eyes widened with surprise as he thumbed through the bilingual dictionary that would aid him as he navigated through France. He turned the pages until he got to "S" and ran his finger down the words until he found "soup." *"Soupe/potage,"* he muttered. "The server called it *potage.* No wonder he understood me when I asked for 'soup.'" He then looked up 'bread.' *"Pain?"* He shook his head and chuckled at himself. "Man does not live by *pain* alone, but I may have to until I learn a few more menu items." He put the dictionary on the desk and yawned as he crawled into bed. "At least I won't go hungry with *potage* and *pain.*" He lay down and closed his eyes, quickly falling asleep.

Kate hopped onto his desk where sat the letter of instructions from Benjamin Franklin next to his dictionary. A list of names for Deane to contact included Arthur Lee, younger brother of Richard Henry Lee, who was the colonial agent in London that took Benjamin Franklin's place when he returned to America in 1775. Little did they know that Lee was also the one who first convinced Beaumarchais to help the American cause. But Lee had also diplomatically irritated Vergennes by prematurely and boldly writing to ask France to aid the American cause by sending two French engineers whom George Washington desperately needed. Other names included Franklin's old friends who were doctors and scientists in Holland, London, and Paris, with instructions for each:

> *With the assistance of Monsieur Dubourg, who understands English, you will be able to make immediate application to Monsieur Vergennes, Minister des Affairs Etrangeres, either personally or by letter ... acquainting him that you are in France upon business of the American Congress, in the character of a merchant, having something to communicate to him, that may be beneficial to France and the North American Colonies ...*

But the sixth name on the list caught Kate's eye: Edward Bancroft.

Mousie said Bancroft were the one friend who stood closest ta Benjamin Franklin in his velvet suit when he had ta stand in the Cockpit an' be humiliated by that awful Privy Council in London! He's an American an' a big supporter of the colonies, Kate realized happily. *He were also one of Deane's pupils whom he tutored in Connecticut, so they already know each other. Plus he's fluent in French!*

> *You will endeavor to procure a meeting with Mr. Bancroft by writing a letter to him, under cover to Mr. Griffiths at Turnham Green, near London, and desiring him to come over to you in France or in Holland, on the score of old acquaintance. From him you may obtain a good deal of information of what is now going forward with England, and settle a mode of continuing a correspondence.*

Kate let go a relieved sigh. *Oh, I'm so happy he will have at least one friend who can meet him in Paris! Next ta this invisible one, of course.*

10

THE SWORD OF THE REVOLUTION

MANHATTAN, NEW YORK, JUNE 6, 1776

We expect a very bloody summer at New York and Canada ... I am sorry to say that we are not, either in men or arms, prepared for it; however, it is to be hoped that if our cause is just, as I do most religiously believe it to be, the same Providence which has in many instances appeared for us, will still go on to afford its aid.

Washington rode along silently on Blueskin, recalling the words he had just penned in a letter to his brother while in Philadelphia. Over the course of the past two weeks, he and his entourage had traveled there and back for the purpose of conferring with the Continental Congress about military matters, primarily involving defending New York. Martha had traveled with him to Philadelphia, and they both decided that she should be inoculated against smallpox. While Washington was immune from having had a mild case when he was young, Martha faced great peril if exposed. If she insisted on being at the front lines with the Commander-in-Chief, then it was imperative that she be kept safe from the deadly disease as she interacted with the Continental Army. She stayed behind to recover in Philadelphia and would return to New York later in the month. Washington would miss her presence and counsel, but at least he now had with him his friend, confidant, and aide, Lieutenant Colonel Joseph Reed, whom he had convinced to rejoin his military family here in New York.

The discussions in Philadelphia resulted in two key decisions. First, Washington would expend the maximum effort of the Continental Army to defend New York. But he desperately needed more men. The Continental Army was spread thin between Canada, New York, and South Carolina.

Congress had attempted to convince Canada to join the thirteen colonies in their rebellion against Great Britain with the goal of depriving the British of a northern route to attack New York. But Canada rejected the idea, choosing to remain loyal to the Crown. So, an attempt was made to force Canada to become the fourteenth colony with an invasion by Washington's northern department. In April, Washington had sent Brigadier Generals William Thompson and John Sullivan sailing up the Hudson to Canada with ten regiments to reinforce Benedict Arnold's siege of Quebec. But before they could arrive, British General John Burgoyne arrived from England to rescue the besieged Sir Guy Carleton. The powerful British forces then sent the sickly, dwindling American forces fleeing south toward Montreal in a chaotic, disastrous retreat.

So, in answer to Washington's request, Congress drew up a plan to raise an additional 23,800 troops, who would be called up from militias in seven colonies, but it would only be for short-term service in the Continental Army. Ten thousand of them would be stationed at defenses in New Jersey to protect the capital city of Philadelphia, and the rest of the new recruits would be given to Washington to defend New York. Washington currently had roughly nine thousand troops, most of them with little military training or discipline. The Commander-in-Chief wondered if those "New Levies" (as they were called) would stand their ground under enemy fire. On top of the questionable military abilities of the Continental Army plus the new recruits to come, Washington's army waged war with another enemy—disease. Smallpox and dysentery ravaged his ranks from unsanitary water and living conditions in New York, giving him far fewer men in the field than what was shown on paper.

But even though they would be greatly outnumbered when it came time for battle, Washington expressed his confidence that they could gain a victory, or at least give the British another "Bunker Hill victory" with costly casualties. With the dismal news of the northern army's disastrous defeat in Canada, Congress knew that France would doubt America's resolve to fight for independence if Washington's army fled New York without a fight. They understood the reality of the situation—America's ability to fight and win this war ultimately depended on having financial, political, and military aid from France. And to obtain that aid, they had to declare the words of independence, backed up with solid action.

The second decision reached was the creation of a Board of War and Ordnance chaired by John Adams to coordinate matters between the Continental Army and Congress. This would streamline the process for Washington, allowing for swift, precise communication and decisions to execute the war. Washington and Adams were solid friends with tremendous mutual trust and respect, so this working relationship would give the Commander-in-Chief the ear and direction he needed.

As they entered the outskirts of Manhattan, Washington's brow was furrowed due to the burden of responsibility he carried. *Only a handful of men in Congress have military experience. While they debate the decision to declare independence, they all look to me to bring their ultimate decision to fruition. But little do they truly understand what it will take militarily to achieve that independence.*

Washington could now view New York Harbor as they traveled along Broadway. It wouldn't be long until that harbor was full of British warships. General Howe would soon arrive from Halifax, and his brother Admiral Lord Howe would also soon arrive from England with thousands of troops, including the fierce mercenary troops from Germany, the Hessians. The vast British armada carrying more than thirty thousand soldiers would attack swiftly and wherever they wished. *Our army is ill-prepared for the impossible task of defeating such a powerful foe. Yet all eyes look to me to ensure that victory is achieved. As I have accepted the charge to bear the responsibility, I must make it so. Dear God in heaven, show me how.* He thought back to his General Orders from two weeks ago:

> *General Orders, May 15, 1776*
> *The Continental Congress having ordered, Friday the 17th Instant to be observed as a day of "fasting, humiliation and prayer, humbly to supplicate the mercy of Almighty God, that it would please him to pardon all our manifold sins and transgressions, and to prosper the Arms of the United Colonies, and finally, establish the peace and freedom of America, upon a solid and lasting foundation"—The General commands all officers, and soldiers, to pay strict obedience to the Orders of the Continental Congress, and by their unfeigned, and pious observance of their religious duties, incline the Lord, and Giver of Victory, to prosper our arms.*

Lord, You are indeed the giver of victory, Washington thought. *It can come to us in no other way.*

"Sir, there are five regiments parading ahead to welcome your return to New York," Captain Gibbs gladly reported to Washington, riding up to him holding the Life Guard flag. "They are lined up near Bowling Green to escort you to Fraunces Queen's Head Tavern for dinner. I have already posted new Life Guard sentries there, and will relieve the men currently on post with you."

Washington gave a nod. "Very well, Captain Gibbs."

Life Guard drummer William Green struck up a rapid drum cadence accompanied by fifer James Johnson to announce the approach of Washington as they walked ahead of the Commander-in-Chief and his entourage. Washington sat straight and tall in the saddle as Blueskin carried him through the streets lined with cheering soldiers and citizens. He lifted his hand in greeting but showed little emotion other than humble gratitude for the warm reception.

"He looks like he's just returned from winning a battle or something, but I know he's under a lot of stress after this trip," Jock observed as he and Max trotted through the throngs of people. "Washington never wears his heart on his sleeve, does he?"

Max shook his head. "No, lad. I've known Washington since he were young. Not only does he always keep control of himself, but he always makes sure he appears confident in public. He's taught his generals ta do the same for the sake of the soldiers an' the people, always presentin' nothin' but str-r-rength. The commanders of the Continental Army must appear confident, disciplined, an' organized no matter wha's really goin' on behind the scenes."

"It must be hard to keep up such a brave face," Jock surmised. "It must be hard to be George Washington."

"Aye. No one knows how hard it truly be," Max agreed, watching the Life Guard flag flapping proudly in the breeze with the *Conquer or Die* motto. "He knows that if his army doesn't conquer, not only will his men die, but independence will die, too. An' then Washington *himself* will die. He'll be taken ta London ta stand tr-r-rial before King George an' Parliament, an' be executed as a tr-r-raitor."

Jock's jaw dropped in anger and alarm. He furrowed his brow. "We better make sure he conquers! Too much is at stake!"

Max nodded. "That it is, lad. That it is."

Together they watched the revelry and excitement of Washington's return as he dismounted from Blueskin and entered Fraunces Tavern. The Life Guard stood at attention until Captain Gibbs relieved them of duty and changed out the sentries. Green tucked his drumsticks into his knapsack and smiled at Johnson, who slipped his fife into his coat pocket. Together they walked off with other Life Guards Michael Lynch, John Barnes, and Thomas Hickey. The five of them were a close-knit group of friends, and usually spent their off-duty hours together.

"Welcome back to New York," came the voice of Gillamon. He was now in the form of Mr. Atticus and stood by a tree, arms folded across his chest.

"Gillamon! How gr-r-rand ta see ye!" Max exclaimed, wagging his tail.

"Hi, Gillamon!" Jock enthused. "We just came all the way from Philadelphia!"

Gillamon smiled and reached down to scratch Jock behind the ears with a chuckle. "And I just returned from seeing your Grandmum Kate off in France."

Jock's jaw fell open. "How'd you do that? Isn't France across the *ocean?*"

Gillamon winked. "Well, I have a special way of traveling quickly from place to place."

"I wish you'd share it with General Washington then," Jock retorted with a laugh.

"How's me bonnie Kate?" Max wanted to know.

"She's lovely as ever and on to her important new assignment of welcoming Silas Deane to France," Gillamon answered, giving Max a pat. "She sends her love to both of you. How are Liz and Nigel faring with things at the Continental Congress?"

"Well enough, I suppose," Max answered. "We only got ta see them a couple of times. But if any two beasties can get the humans ta pen a Declaration of Independence, it be Liz an' Nigel!"

"Aye, but General Washington has a lot on his shoulders. The humans want him to defend New York no matter what," Jock explained.

"Indeed, but it was for such a time as this that George Washington was precisely chosen to be the Sword of Revolution," Gillamon answered. "Everything that has been poured into his life up until now has prepared him for what he must do. And his continual dependence on the Maker will be the key to giving him the victory he needs."

"Amen," Max agreed. "I were glad ta get him away from this city for a couple of weeks. How be the Ketcham kids with their papa in jail?"

"Those little ones are managing as best they can," Gillamon reported. "I go see them each day and bring them food and tend to whatever needs they have. Meanwhile, I continue to act as Ketcham's main prison guard. Right now, I'm steering him in the direction of keeping his ears open for loyalist plots. There are many seedy characters in jail, and they like to talk when I'm not around."

"I never realized how a prisoner could be one of the best spies the Patriots could have," Jock offered.

Gillamon gave him a knowing look. "Precisely, small one. That is why he is sitting right where he is, although even he doesn't know it yet."

Max turned to Jock. "Gillamon always knows a wee bit more than he lets on then. He jest can't tell us everythin'. So, Gillamon, do ye have any new instructions for us? No tellin' wha' schemes have been cooked up while we've been gone with that smelly gunsmith workin' for the schemin' mayor an' governor."

Gillamon pointed at the group of Life Guards who were now off duty and headed north to a tavern. "Follow Washington's men tonight. See if you observe anything . . . interesting."

"They're his most loyal soldiers," Jock asserted. "I'm not worried about them."

Max's eyes narrowed as he observed the men. He sniffed the air. "We'll let ye know wha' we find out."

"I'm counting on it," Gillamon responded with a wink.

CORBIE'S TAVERN, MANHATTAN, NEW YORK, JUNE 6, 1776

Jock chased a butterfly as they walked along the road leading out of the city to follow the group of Life Guards, who were relieved to be off duty and back in New York. "Hey, we're almost back to the Mortier House."

"Aye," Max answered with a frown, wrinkling his nose. "These lads look like they're goin' ta Corbie's Tavern. It's jest down the road from Washington's nighttime headquarters."

As the men stepped inside the tavern, Max and Jock slipped in and darted under a nearby table. Over the course of the next two hours, the men drank and began to talk loudly.

"Did you see those regiments lined up to welcome Washington at Bowling Green?" Barnes asked, shaking his head. "Supreme commander, bah! The only thing he knows how to command is how many places to set at table with all the rich food that he and his busy-body wife eat with the officers every day."

"Cursh the Continental Army!" Hickey exclaimed, punctuating his chest with a finger. "I've served in a *real* army, and I know how they are *supposed* to operate. I sailed to thesh colonies as a soldier in the British army, and we had real dishcipline, fine uniforms, guns, and all the food we could eat."

"Yeah, because you took it from the colonists when you barged in and quartered in their houses!" snickered Barnes. "So why did you desert His Majesty's army if it was so great?"

"Hick's always looking for a better situation," teased Green. "Looking out for yourself, huh, Hick?"

"Thash beshides the point!" Hickey argued, slurring his words badly. "My point is that thish 'army' is the most pathetic army I've ever seen. We don't even have uniforms!"

"He does have a point," Lynch offered. "Our army lives in terrible conditions rampant with disease, we eat wretched food, and have constant shortages of supplies and guns. Washington has been our Commander-in-Chief for eleven months but hasn't even waged a proper battle to fight the enemy. The best officer we have isn't even here in New York but down fighting in South Carolina."

"Aye, General Lee was an officer in the British army, so he knows what he'sh doin'," Hickey agreed. He lifted his mug for a toast and belched loudly. "To General Lee!"

Barnes slapped the table in anger. "We work long, exhausting hours for bad pay that's hit or miss if we even get it. Plus, we're going to be picked off like helpless sheep when the sharpshooter British army arrives. All this for what?"

"Don't ye *know?*" Hickey offered sarcastically, now holding his hand up in the air. "It's all for the 'Glorioush Cause'! For the liberty that beats in our hearts." He blew a raspberry and slammed his fist on the table. *"I'm* me favorite cause!"

Max and Jock were about to break out from their hiding places to bark, snarl, and bite against the vitriol pouring out of these men who had taken the oath as Washington's finest soldiers to loyally uphold that Glorious Cause.

"I don't have your keen nose, Grandsire, but I don't need it to smell how foul these humans are," Jock huffed, disgusted by what he was hearing and seeing. "I'm so sad."

"I know, lad," Max answered with a paw on Jock's shoulder. "It's a hard thing when ye be disillusioned by those ye thought were good. It's one thing ta not like the conditions ye have ta live in, but quite another ta curse the cause ye serve."

"Come on Green, lesh crack on," Hickey slurred in an Irish accent with an arm hooked around Green's neck. "I'm knackered."

"He's more fluthered than knackered," Lynch joked, meaning Hickey was more drunk than exhausted.

Lynch, Barnes, and Johnson all stood to leave, putting on their hats and tossing a few coins on the table.

Green frowned and shoved Hickey away. "You crack on. I'm not ready to go home."

"Have it your way," Hickey retorted, mussing Green's hair. He scooped up his hat and put it askew on his head. He held a finger up to his lips and whispered. "Better not let Chief shee ush."

"Come on, mate," Barnes admonished the handsome Irishman, shoving Hickey along as the four Life Guards went out the door.

"Sleep it off, Hick, eh?" Green called after them with a wave of his hand.

Jock turned to Max with a frown. "If Washington saw his Life Guards acting like this, he'd be furious!"

"Aye, especially his favorite one of the bunch, Hickey," Max growled, shaking his head. "Ye jest never know aboot humans. They may polish up all nice an' clean, but behind the scenes they can be a r-r-real mess sometimes.

I've dealt with lots of messed up humans over time, an' it's never pr-r-retty. But all humans be fallen, lad."

"I guess that's the bad side of keeping up appearances," Jock answered. "Washington keeps up appearances to instill confidence in his men. But his men keep up appearances to fool Washington."

"That's wha' worries me," Max lamented. He wrinkled his forehead. "But the truth always comes out eventually."

Sitting in the corner was a man in a white coat who had listened in to the group of five Life Guards complaining about the conditions of the army. He went to the bar, got two mugs of ale, and brought them over to where William Green now sat alone.

"Sounds like you need another drink, soldier," the man offered, setting the mug down on the table. "Mind if I join you?"

Green looked up at the man with a quizzical expression. Then he smiled and held out his hand to the empty side of the darkened booth. He lifted the pewter mug in the air. "Thanks, friend."

"It's the gunsmith!" Jock hoarsely whispered to Max. "He's the one that Mayor Matthews gave all that money to!"

"Aye, an' I think he's aboot ta try an' use it," Max answered through clenched teeth.

Forbes took a seat and offered his hand out. "Name's Gilbert Forbes."

Green shook his hand. "The gunsmith? I've seen your shop downtown."

Forbes smiled and nodded. "I couldn't help but overhear you and your friends. So, you're just back from Philadelphia, I understand. Rumor had it that Washington went to Philadelphia to resign his commission."

"If only he *had*," Green replied with a smirk.

Max growled. "How dare Washington's *dr-r-rumer* say such a thing?!"

"You're right, Grandsire! I thought Green was a loyal Life Guard!" Jock scoffed, worried with a paw on Max's foot. "What should we do?"

"Let it play out," Max advised. "Let's jest see where this leads."

Forbes and Green started speaking in hushed tones. From where Max and Jock sat, they couldn't hear everything the men were saying. "Gr-r-r, stay here, lad," Max growled and darted over to get right under the table in their booth. He was careful not to let them feel his presence with their legs. It was all Max could do to not bite them.

"What if I told you I could get you out of your Continental Army post with guaranteed cash in hand *now*, steady pay from here on, and land?" Forbes asked. "Lots of land."

Green's eyes widened. "For doing *what* exactly?"

"For simply choosing the right side," Forbes answered plainly. "For choosing to fight on the side of the certain *victors*—the British. You already doubt that the rebels can win. Why not switch sides while you can, and even profit from it?"

Green took a sip of ale, wiped his mouth with the back of his hand, and narrowed his eyes. "I'm listening."

"For men ready to take up arms when the British forces arrive here to New York," Gilbert Forbes started, looking around and then leaning in to lock eyes with the drummer, "Governor Tryon will give five guineas bounty and *two hundred* acres of land for each man, *one hundred* for his wife, and *fifty* for each child, on the condition that they enlist in His Majesty's service."

William Green slowly nodded as a smile grew on his face.

The gunsmith smiled back. "Interested?"

"Absolutely," Green responded. "I think some of my friends will be interested, too. But how would you pay us?"

"Mayor Matthews himself gave me money from Governor Tryon," Forbes said with a smug expression, feeling important. "I find, swear in, and pay new recruits. Since you're the leader of your group of friends, I'll pass on my authority to you to do the same for any Life Guards you can recruit. Enlist them, swear them in with the oath of loyalty to the Crown, pay them, and wait for orders on what to do next."

Green leaned back in his seat with a laugh, clapped once, and pointed at Forbes with a dark expression. "*That,* I can do."

Forbes cocked his head to the side. "Even if those orders direct you to betray your Commander-in-Chief himself?"

Green stopped mid-sip, locked eyes with Forbes, and held his pewter mug in the air with a sinister smile. "Long live the King."

Forbes lifted his pewter mug. "Long live the King."

Green clanked his mug into Forbes's mug, sloshing ale all over the table. "And to new friends of the King!"

Max darted back over to Jock. "Forbes jest r-r-recruited Green ta switch sides. He's gonna betray Washington."

"Why that *traitor!*" Jock growled.

Max put a paw on Jock's shoulder. "Steady, lad. I want ta take that dr-r-rummer's sticks an' dr-r-rum his backside, too, but we have ta handle this quietly an' tell Gillamon. This actually be a good thing."

"A *good* thing?!" Jock protested. "How can it be a good thing, Grandsire?"

"We've finally figured out the pattern of Tr-r-ryon's spider web ta catch Washington's soldiers," Max explained. "We know exactly how that schemin' governor has r-r-recruited men all over New York ta br-r-ribe soldiers with money an' land. They listen out for possible men who might dr-r-rink too much an' then talk too loud aboot politics so they know wha' they think of Washington an' the army. These r-r-recruiters look for angry soldiers an' offer them not only a way out, but far more money an' land ta make them leap an' join the British."

"So, what do we do now?" Jock asked with a wrinkled brow.

"We wait a wee bit longer, an' watch which 'friends' Green pulls inta the plan," Max answered with a grin. "Then we tear the spider's web apart."

11

Spongy Trunks

FIVE FATHOM HOLE, SOUTH CAROLINA, JUNE 8, 1776

Swaths of red accentuated the blue horizon as twenty-five hundred British redcoats lined the rails of fifty ships flying the king's colors at the mouth of Charleston Harbor. Fierce grenadiers donned their tall bearskin caps, battalion companies their three-cornered black hats, and light infantrymen their leather caps as they gazed over at Sullivan's Island and the one obstacle keeping them from sailing six miles to reach the city of Charleston—Fort Sullivan.

A large brown pelican plunged sixty feet into the water with a terrific splash next to a transport ship, scooping up a fish and then sitting there bobbing along on the surface.

"It's a sorry little fort of palmetto logs and *dirt!*" Banastre Tarleton scoffed as he stood with his fellow soldiers aboard the transport *Jenny*. He looked through his spyglass at the pathetic structure of stacked palmetto trees to see a beehive of activity with sweaty shirtless rebels and slaves working together on the unfinished fortifications.

It was a square fort with a bastion at each angle, made with an inner and outer wall of stacked palmetto logs seven feet high and sixteen feet apart. Sand filled the space between the walls that had a parapet of oak planks for the men to stand on. The two sides facing the sea were complete, but the other two sides were not, making the fort vulnerable to an attack from the rear. On a solitary flagpole in the southeast corner flew a dark indigo blue flag with a white crescent and the word LIBERTY rippling defiantly in the stiff sea breeze.

A tall grenadier shook his head and gave a laugh. "If you can even call it a fort. These rebels are no match for His Majesty's forces. Our firepower alone will blow that fort to Hades itself, where all rebels belong."

Tarleton lowered his spyglass and grinned up at the tall, snarky grenadier. "Indeed, Sir. I've heard Commodore Parker shares your optimism. I like your draconian viewpoint, Mr. . . . ."

"Rafe. Call me Rafe," the grenadier replied, wearing a grin. "And you are Banastre Tarleton. I heard of your zeal against the traitor General Lee while

103

en route from Cork with friends of yours on another transport, the *Kitty*. You threatened to cut off Lee's head with your sword, I hear."

"Ban, didn't you see a girl named Kitty while we were in Cork? Come to think of it, you saw a girl named Jenny, too!" an infantryman named Smithy exclaimed. He elbowed Rafe with a snicker. "Ban always keeps a girl on each arm, eh? I bet every transport here bears the name of a girl he's wooed!"

"So, you're also a professional wooer of women, with a girl in every port?" Rafe jested.

Tarleton gave a laugh. "Yes, to *all* of the above." He spread his hand out to the vast flotilla of ships the masts of which filled the sky with canvas sails as numerous as the puffy clouds passing overhead. "And I look forward to seeing how many damsels I can woo in America once these vessels have done their hot work."

The soldiers laughed and gazed out at Commodore Peter Parker's armada with expectant pride. The fleet included ten warships, thirty transport ships, and other specialty vessels that carried twenty-five hundred British troops from the 15th, 28th, 33rd, 37th, 46th, 54th, and 57th Regiments of Foot, and two thousand seamen. The two largest ships were the flagship *Bristol,* and the *Experiment*, each with two decks bearing fifty guns. The frigates *Actaeon, Active, Solebay, Siren, Sphinx,* and *Friendship* were smaller three-masted ships rigged with square sails and built for speed and maneuverability, enabling them to patrol and provide escort. They were more lightly armed, with 28-, 22-, or 20-pound guns placed on a single, upper deck. The bomb vessel *Thunder* was designed to bombard enemy positions on land. It was fitted with six guns and two mortars that could fire high-trajectory shells over a long distance. The eight-gun sloop *Ranger* and six-gun schooner *St. Lawrence* rounded out the fleet carrying 300 cannons in all.

This Goliath fleet of the mightiest naval power in the world floated just offshore from the half-built David of a palmetto-and-sand fort with only 31 cannons to oppose the flotilla.

After their exhausting, treacherous sea crossing, the first of Sir Peter Parker's fleet arrived in Cape Fear on April 18th, followed by other ships that staggered into the North Carolina rendezvous point. Cornwallis's ship *Bristol* and Tarleton's transport ship *Jenny* arrived May 3rd, and the weary, sick soldiers and seamen spent the next few weeks recovering, regrouping, and reconnoitering the countryside and coastal areas.

Meanwhile, General Clinton, Commodore Parker, and Major General Cornwallis met to discuss next steps in the southern strategy. While Clinton favored an attack back up in Virginia on the Chesapeake Bay before joining General Howe's forces in New York, Parker sent two ships south to scout

out the waters around Charleston, the richest city and largest port in North America. They returned May 26th and reported that the only real deterrent to taking control of the port city by water was the small fort on Sullivan's Island that was still under construction and guarded the entrance to Charleston Harbor. It could be taken without much effort, so the commanders determined that they could take the fort, take the port, and establish an ideal base for British troops against the rebels in the southern colonies.

Meanwhile, after hearing nothing for four months from their supreme British commander, General Howe, Clinton finally received a dispatch from Halifax, informing him that Howe was sailing south to New York. He gave Clinton no specific timetable, nor sense of urgency for the southern forces to join him but did indicate that Charleston was "an object of importance to His Majesty's service." Clinton then received instructions from Lord Germain in London to avoid great loss in the southern expedition and proceed immediately to New York "if nothing could soon be effected to be of great and essential service."

Clinton was sold on the idea. After blockading the port, they would leave a small British force of infantry and artillery supported by one or two frigates to control Charleston harbor while the rest of the fleet sailed north to join Howe's forces in New York. Clinton had no intention of taking Charleston itself since they didn't have enough troops for a prolonged siege of the city. That would have to wait.

Their plan set, Clinton and Parker agreed to weigh anchor and head south to Charleston. Aboard the flagship *Bristol* were not only Lord Cornwallis and Sir Peter Parker, but the three deposed, floating governors Josiah Martin of North Carolina, William Campbell of South Carolina, and James Wright of Georgia. The fleet of fifty ships headed to Five Fathom Hole, where it took several days for their deep-drafted ships to cross the bar of shoals at high tide.

Charleston sat at the tip of a seven-mile-long peninsula that was hugged by the Ashley and Cooper Rivers, which emptied into a bay where they were joined by the Wando River. To cut off the city by land and sea required capturing the peninsula above the city, the harbor, and both banks of the rivers. In front of the city and up and down the South Carolina and Georgia coasts were sea islands separated from the mainland with salt marshes and mud-bottomed creeks that were full at high tide and empty at low tide. Either condition created a nearly impassible barrier for armies with horses pulling field guns. Two of these small islands provided a natural defense barrier for Charleston: Sullivan's Island on the northeast side and James Island on the southwest side. Both islands bore forts to protect the harbor—the fully built but lightly armed Fort Johnson, which sat far back on James Island, and the half-constructed Fort Sullivan, which sat on the water's edge of Sullivan's Island.

Sullivan's Island was a sandy, snake-like spit about three miles long and only a few hundred yards wide at its broadest point. Its fort held an especially strategic location to repel passing ships. A ship sailing to Charleston first had to cross several treacherous shoals and then pass by the southern end of Sullivan's Island. It first sailed with its bow straight ahead to Sullivan's Island, then turned with its broadsides exposed to the fort. It then had to turn again to sail up the U-shaped "Rebellion Road" channel, exposing its stern to the guns from the fort.

This is precisely why the Patriots decided to dig in and build a fort at the tip of the island with whatever material they could find. And what they found were thousands of spongy palmetto trees.

"So, what are we doing floating out here?" Smithy wanted to know. "When do we attack?"

"General Clinton and Commodore Parker have been assessing when and how we will land after we bombard the little rebel fort," Tarleton surmised.

"But word has it that they disagree on *where* to land," Rafe noted. "Parker wants to land our troops on Sullivan's Island, but Clinton insists that the surf is too rough. He's been sailing around to that other little undefended island down there next to it, called Long Island." The grenadier pointed to the northern end of Sullivan's Island and the small gap between it and Long Island.

"The surf looks calmer on Long Island," Tarleton observed through his spyglass. "Perhaps we could land there and somehow get across to Sullivan's Island through the marshes."

"I don't care where we land, just get me off of this boat, eh?" Smithy complained, leaning his forearms on the railing, and gazing down into the emerald water where a pelican sat on the water, eyeing him. Smithy wrinkled his brow. *I didn't know pelicans had blue eyes.*

Tarleton turned his attention back to the fort with his spyglass. He suddenly noticed a pack of yapping dogs following along behind a slim horseman dressed in an unusual uniform. "That rebel officer keeps like-minded company," he observed with a laugh.

Rafe smiled at the cornet. "Do you know who that is? He's famous for always keeping a pack of dogs with him. And he's the commander of the Southern Department of the Continental Army."

Tarleton quickly lowered the spyglass. "Who is he?"

"None other than the very man you threatened at the Cocoa Tree Club," Rafe answered with a sinister grin. "General Charles Lee."

The pelican lifted off and slowly flapped its wings as it flew just over the water's surface, heading to the fort.

FORT SULLIVAN, SOUTH CAROLINA, JUNE 8, 1776

Colonel William Moultrie lifted his hat in salute, revealing a receding hairline and high cheek bones as General Lee dismounted his horse and approached the fort. The thickset forty-five-year-old planter-politician was a former militia colonel who had been made commander of the 2nd South Carolina Regiment of the Continental Army. "Good-day, General. Welcome to Fort Sullivan."

General Lee wore a sour expression and lifted his riding crop to his hat as he approached, his dogs running about freely everywhere. He looked around the fort and shook his head. "Colonel Moultrie. Your men are busy, I see. I understand this fort when finished could hold one thousand men. How many do you have with you?"

"With the 2nd South Carolina Regiment and the 4th South Carolina Artillery, I have four hundred thirty-five men," Moultrie answered as the two men walked up to the parapet overlooking the sea. "We've been working on the fort since March, and as you can see, we have two walls complete."

Lee quickly pointed to the unfinished back walls. "And two walls *incomplete.*" He then pointed to the British fleet floating offshore. "With three hundred British guns aimed at you!" He shook his head and looked down his long, skinny nose at Moultrie. "This is a slaughter pen. I recommend you abandon it immediately."

Moultrie clenched his fists but lifted his chin with a confident smile. "It may be an act of faith to use such materials as we have, but I am confident this fort can defend Charleston, General. I've also positioned Colonel William Thomson at the north end of the island at Breach Inlet with three cannons and seven hundred eighty men made up of regimental, militia, and riflemen from South Carolina, North Carolina, and Virginia, plus Indian riflemen from four tribes."

"No doubt you've used palmetto logs there, too, to build a breastwork," Lee scoffed. "I'll be sure to ride down there to assess those fortifications. I have stationed fifteen hundred men at Haddrell's Point and am ordering a pontoon bridge built from the battery over here to Sullivan's Island since you must have an escape route. It'll be a makeshift bridge of hogshead barrels and boats with planks laid over them. Meanwhile, I'm reinforcing all other positions on the mainland. In all we've got sixty-five hundred men to defend a city that is in chaos with panicked civilians running about since those British ships arrived offshore."

"Understood, Sir," Moultrie answered. "I'm sure you will have Charleston in a ready state of defense."

"Humph, which is more than I can say for this fort," Lee grumbled as he walked along. "We'll see what President Rutledge says about this fort after I talk to him."

Charleston-born John Rutledge was President of South Carolina, and the elder brother of Edward Rutledge, who now sat in Philadelphia debating independence on behalf of South Carolina. Unlike Banastre Tarleton, who failed out of Middle Temple in London, John Rutledge received an excellent education there to launch his legal career. Moultrie didn't bat an eye at Lee's grumbling threat. He knew he had Rutledge's support, and they had no plans to abandon the fort.

General Lee stopped and held up a bony finger. "One thing I won't abide is *waste*. We have limited gunpowder, Colonel, so I give you an eternal rule that no cannon is to be fired at ranges greater than four hundred yards."

"Yes, Sir," Moultrie agreed. Just then they passed two of his junior officers who stopped to salute them. "General Lee, perhaps you have a word of encouragement for these men, Major Francis Marion and Lieutenant Colonel Thomas Sumter."

Lee stopped and eyed the officers. "I served with General Clinton in Europe, and I know him to be a *fool.*" He squinted at them with a mischievous grin. "Today he sent a rowboat under a white flag with a 'proclamation' advising 'the deluded people of the miseries ever attendant upon civil war.' He entreated them to return to 'their duty to our common sovereign.' I don't think that fool knows who he's dealing with, but we are anything but deluded, and our sovereign is liberty!" he declared with a clenched fist. "Always know your enemy and get as much intelligence on them as you can. Then dig in and be ready, men." He pointed out to the floating British fleet. "I'll challenge Clinton to a duel if the British don't attack soon."

"Yes, Sir!" Marion cheered.

"We'll be ready for them, Sir," Sumter agreed.

Lee gave them a definitive nod. As Lee and Moultrie walked off, Major Marion put his hands on his hips and grinned. "Those Indians from the last war didn't call General Lee 'Boiling Water' for nothing."

"He's been called a lot of things, including 'Liberty Boy.' It's said, 'He thunders, lightnings, opens graves, and roars,'" Sumter answered. He nudged Marion with a grin. "I wonder what your *nom de guerre* should be."

Francis Marion laughed. "It's always better if the *enemy* names you. That way it sticks." The men turned and went back to work.

Lee's high-stepping black and tan dog Archer was up on one of the walls, jumping along the palmetto logs like a spring. "Wheeeeeeee! Boing! Boing! Boing!"

A shadow passed overhead, and the pelican came in for a landing right where the silly dog bounced. It folded its six-foot wings into its side and shook its tail. "Hello, Archer."

"I'm shpechial!" Archer replied before abruptly stopping his bounce. His eyes widened. "Heyyyyyyy, how do you know my name?"

"I'm Clarie, part of the animal team that is working for the Maker, but I can take any shape or form," the pelican explained. "I see you are enjoying the palmetto logs." She cocked her head to the side, an idea coming to her. "Do you know how much you weigh?"

"Why would I know that?" Archer asked with a goofy grin, his tongue hanging out. He lifted a white-socked paw and nudged the pelican in the shoulder. "How much do *you* weigh?"

Clarie grinned at the scatterbrained dog with his wide-mouthed grin, one ear up and one ear down. "Nine pounds, but I can carry about twenty-four pounds of water in my throat pouch, which is about how much I think *you* weigh."

"Ooooooh, can you fly me around then?" Archer asked excitedly.

Clarie laughed. "I don't think you'd fit. But it looks like you're getting some good air with your bouncing. Go ahead, show me."

"Sure!" Archer exclaimed, taking off once more to bounce along the spongy trunks.

"ARCHER! COME!" General Lee called.

"Gotta go! My mashter's calling!" Archer reported before running back to Lee.

Clarie studied the funny dog as he returned to his master, and then looked out at the ships. She lifted into the air and calculated the perfect distance for a twenty-four-pound cannon ball to be hurled at the palmetto fort when the British moved the ships into position. She then flew over the shoals off the tip of Sullivan's Island to study them with her excellent pelican vision down into the shallow waters below. She laughed to herself. "Four hundred yards should do it—then I know exactly what those cannon balls will do when they hit those spongy trunks!"

DEATH OR GLORY

LONG ISLAND, SOUTH CAROLINA, JUNE 14, 1776

"Get . . . me . . . off . . . this BOAT!" Banastre Tarleton exclaimed. He felt the soft sand give way under his boots as he plunged into the salty water. He wasn't about to wait another moment as the flat-bottomed boat cramped with sea-weary soldiers scraped the sandbar just off the beach. It had already taken a week to unload two thousand men from Parker's fleet, with another thousand left to transport, along with supplies and ten guns to Long Island. The small vessel rocked in the foamy surf as the eager cornet went over the side. Tarleton didn't care about the trickle of water that oozed over the tops of his black boots. It felt good after the intense heat of this South Carolina summer. He sloshed his way through the shin-deep waves, crunching shells as he waded onto shore.

He stood in his soggy boots and surveyed the picturesque island with its greyish-white beach and tall dunes fortified by wheat-colored sea oats, green sea grass, yellow wildflowers, and strings of white morning glories crisscrossing the sand. He kicked over a dead horseshoe crab that lay upside down, and a flock of sanderlings hurriedly tiptoed ahead of him, picking morsels from the wet sand. Seagulls cried out overhead, and men were scattered up and down the beach, sitting, standing, and staring out to sea.

"Welcome to Long Island," a sweaty officer greeted him with a deadpan British voice, walking up to Tarleton and the others as they joined him on shore. He slapped the back of his neck and held out his hand to show the blood from a mosquito that bit him. "I am Surgeon Thomas Foster, and I need to make you aware of the hazards you shall encounter here."

"Lots of mosquitoes, eh, Sir?" Smithy asked him.

"A thick cloud of mosquitoes is present everywhere you go," Foster answered with a frown, swiping the air around his head. "And no place is entirely free from rattlesnakes. Spiders, too, their bodies are as large as my coat button. There are thick cobwebs to push through everywhere. When exploring the island, you'll be knee deep in rotten wood and dried leaves. Every hundred yards or so there's a swamp with putrid standing water in the middle, full of alligators. And the morning brings the most suffocating heat with not a breath of air stirring."

"Lovely," Tarleton muttered under his breath, exchanging perturbed glances with Rafe and Smithy. "What about food and shelter?"

"There is nothing to eat and drink but salt pork, bad rum, and brackish water," Foster answered drolly. "Nothing grows here. No other bed than the sand and no other covering than the sky. General Clinton and Lord Cornwallis have also arrived today and established their headquarters just over that ridge there." The British surgeon pointed down the beach, south toward Breach Inlet. "Manage as best you can." He slapped his face and walked away as another mosquito bit him on the cheek.

"Well, ain't *he* a real bundle of sunshine and joy?" Smithy chortled as he planted himself in the sand, tossing a seashell. "Sounds like we had it better back on the ship."

Tarleton clenched his jaw and tapped his hand on his thigh. "Infernal American soil." He took off walking down the beach toward Cornwallis's headquarters.

"Where are you going?" Rafe asked, following him.

"To volunteer to do something, anything!" Tarleton answered. "I'll not sit and wait for this hellish island to make me its victim."

Al ran and hid in a clump of sea oats on a tall sand dune after hearing the surgeon's dismal report about Long Island given to Lord Cornwallis upon landing. The picture of terror that Foster painted was more than Al could handle. He was afraid to move and covered his eyes with his paws, hoping nothing would bother him. *Sure, if I can't see them beasties, maybe they won't see me.* But hearing them was another matter.

Just as the scared Irish cat began to relax by listening to the gentle roll of the surf, he suddenly heard a rattling sound. Al quickly moved his paws to his ears, his eyes now wide open and his heart beating fast. *And if I can't hear them?* He gulped and slowly turned his head to see a five-foot Eastern diamondback rattlesnake coiled up behind him, its menacing, forked tongue sticking out while its tail rattled a warning. Terrified, Al felt the blood drain from his face.

"Uh, there, there, nice little snakey," Al stammered, his lip quivering in fear. He slowly tucked in his tail and turned his body to start backing away. "Yer only the largest rattlesnake in the world and the most venomous snake beastie in America," Al groveled with a gulp, "so bein' such an *important* snake, I'm sure ye have lots o' choices for dinner. I'd only make ye cough up one big, giant, orange furball, lad. Trust me, it wouldn't be a pretty sight for either o' us."

The snake drew back its head showing its fangs and rattled even louder. "That's me cue!" Al cried and took off running and tumbling down the sand dunes, screaming in a high pitch at the top of his lungs, "AHHHHHHHHHHHHHHHH!!!!" He ran as fast and as far as his chubby little legs would carry him before collapsing on the beach. He lay on his back, whimpering. "Why did it have to be a snake beastie?" A shadow passed overhead, and Al squinted up to see a pelican circling him. "Do pelicans eat kitties?!"

The pelican came in for a landing and Al got ready to run again before it spoke. "Steady, Al! It's only me, Clarie."

Al fell back onto the sand in a relieved lump, draping a sandy, striped arm dramatically over his eyes. "Thank the Maker!"

"I heard you screaming from way up there," Clarie told him, giggling. "You were screaming like a girl."

Al lifted his arm and frowned. "But it were a *snake!* A rattler!"

"There are all sorts of creatures on these rugged coastal islands," Clarie said matter-of-factly. "But pay attention. Now that you're on Long Island with Clinton, Cornwallis, and Tarleton, you need to know some things. I'm a pelican now, but I've assumed the position of a harbor pilot in dealing with the humans. I've already given Clinton some not-so-accurate information about Breach Inlet that was true, oh, about a hundred years ago. The redcoats will try to cross over to Sullivan's Island. I need for you to monitor their movements and inform me of their plans. I know you can be brave and do your part for the cause."

Al sat up and wore a look of importance. "Aye! I've got intelligence-gatherin' skills. But how will I tell ye stuff?"

"Use that pointer claw of yours to draw a big 7 in the sand, and I'll see it as a signal to come meet you here," Clarie explained.

"Okay, lass," Al replied, popping out his special iron claw. "I may have to use it if that Tarleton lad gets violent. He's runnin' with some bad company, methinks. Some big redcoat named Rafe."

"You should know that the grenadier known as 'Rafe' is not who he appears to be," Clarie told him with a serious look. "He's actually Kakia, the evil cat on Charlatan's team."

Al's eyes filled again with fear, and he put his paws up to his mouth. "She's the poison-lovin', Greek kitty that me Liz rescued from the Tower of London!

She tried to kill Washington and Patrick Henry and *did* kill Cato the bald eagle! And Rafe were the one who locked Mousie in the trunk on General Gage's ship, too!"

"Yes, and Rafe successfully took the life of Dr. Joseph Warren on Bunker Hill, among other Patriots in the struggle around Lexington and Concord," Clarie added sadly. "But remember, Al, greater is He who is in you than he that is in Kakia . . . or Rafe."

Al gulped. "That's what Paul always said then, aye. Do Rafe know I'm me?"

"I don't know, since you've been on assignment in London before now, so try to keep a low profile," Clarie cautioned him.

Al sucked in his belly. "That ain't happenin', lass."

Clarie chuckled. "Well, do your best and remember what Gillamon always tells us."

"Know that ye be loved, and ye be able," Al called with a paw cupped around his whiskers as Clarie took off.

"That's it!" Clarie called from the air.

Al smiled, feeling better. He looked around him on the beach, suddenly feeling self-conscious as an orange-striped kitty on the sand. He now had another beastie to watch out for, and this one was more deadly than all the rest.

BREACH INLET, SOUTH CAROLINA, JUNE 17, 1776

"This mile-long stretch is called Breach Inlet," General Clinton informed Tarleton, Smithy, Rafe, and a group of officers, engineers, and volunteers gathered in a circle around him. Cornwallis stood next to him. And Al hid in a bush. "A local harbor pilot has informed me that it's only eighteen inches deep at low tide, so we can wade across it to reach Sullivan's Island. The rebels have established fortifications on the other side, so you are to wade over and scout out the inlet, getting as close as you can to assess their strength. Proceed."

A swirling convergence of tides kicked up small whitecaps in the inlet as the afternoon winds increased. The soldiers entered the water while Clinton peered through his spyglass across the inlet. But instead of wading easily across, the soldiers quickly sank to their shoulders. The water soon proved to be seven feet deep. Smithy fell into a hole up to his nostrils and bobbed back up to regain his footing. Together the men withdrew back to the edge on Long Island, dripping wet and looking at their surprised commander for instructions.

"It appears you received faulty intelligence," Cornwallis stated quietly, airing the obvious.

Clinton grimaced, furious at what he saw, collapsing his spyglass in a huff. "Indeed. This inlet is too deep to ford, and too shallow for any of Commodore Parker's ships to provide adequate gunfire support. Dismissed!" He stormed off. "We will have to search for another way across to Sullivan's Island."

Tarleton took off his boots, draining the water as he glared out at the enemy-held island. He suddenly saw a dog running around and start jumping on the palmetto logs. Two other dogs appeared, including a small black Pomeranian. "LEE!" he shouted angrily, now hurriedly walking along the inlet beach to get directly across from the rebel fortifications. He could make out the general riding his horse.

General Lee was inspecting Colonel Thomson's defensive positions, having given him advice to move the gun placements back from the water's edge so that they were almost impossible to bombard from ships or from Long Island. Colonel "Old Danger" Thomson was considered the best shot in South Carolina, and he planned to make not only his rifle take deadly aim, but the cannons that Colonel Moultrie sent his way.

LONG ISLAND, SOUTH CAROLINA,
JUNE 18, 1776

Clinton ordered ten pieces of field artillery placed at the tip of Long Island in front of the British camp and at the adjacent Green Island and a tiny oyster bank that included four cannons, four mortars, and two howitzers. He had fifteen armed flat-bottomed boats that he considered using to ferry the troops across, but he knew the rebel forces would hit them with their deadly artillery. Frustrated that they couldn't wade across Breach Inlet as he had hoped, he spent three nights reconnoitering the bogs, looking for some other way for his troops to ford across to Sullivan's Island. And as before, Banastre Tarleton volunteered to help the General in an attempt to keep his name before the commanders. He had no more money to buy his way up the chain of command. His advancement would have to come from his blood, sweat, and tears alone, and he knew it would always be risky. *Death or glory* was his mantra at every turn of opportunity.

It was just before sunrise when Tarleton followed Clinton and a handful of other soldiers as they returned to the British camp. They were covered in wet mud and were coming back emptyhanded after an exhausting night of being eaten alive by mosquitoes and walking through sticky spider webs. Tarleton stopped to catch his breath while the others walked on ahead through the dense brush and trees. He lifted the canteen draped across his chest and shook it for a drink. Empty. He looked over at a still water bog and wrinkled his nose. It was indeed nasty, brackish water, but it was all they had.

Tarleton popped the cork from his canteen and squatted down by the water's edge. He dipped the canteen into the dark water, and bubbles gurgled as it filled. He closed his eyes and wiped his sweaty brow but didn't see the pair of yellow eyes gliding stealthily toward him. *Infernal American water,* he thought.

Suddenly, a nine-foot alligator lunged out of the water, its toothy jaws wide open! Tarleton screamed, slipping, and falling back onto the muddy bank with his hands sunk in the mud and his legs spread out before him. The gator lunged forward again and clamped down onto the canteen that was still strapped to Tarleton's chest, trying to pull the terrified soldier into the water. "HELP! HELP! A GATOR! HELP ME!" he screeched at the top of his lungs, digging his boots into the bank as best he could.

As the gator thrashed its head back and forth, the sound of a rifle exploded behind Tarleton with an ear-piercing shot, hitting the gator in the head. The cold-blooded beast immediately stopped thrashing, and blood oozed out of the wound.

Tarleton's ears were ringing, and his heart was racing so fast from terror that he thought he would pass out. He couldn't move; he was frozen with fear. Rafe leaned over and used a knife to cut the canteen strap from the paralyzed soldier's chest, tossing it back to the dead alligator that still had it clamped in its now-dead jaws. Together they watched the beast slowly sink into the bog as Rafe held his smoking "wolf gun" in the air in triumph. It was a .65 caliber rifled carbine made of dark walnut with a steel flintlock and trigger. Carved on the stock was a menacing wolf's head with an almond-shaped eye and razor-sharp teeth made from inlaid ivory. It was half the weight of the standard army Brown Bess musket and fitted with a socket bayonet, but it was clearly not a regulation army piece.

Smithy came running up to them, eyes wide at the scene. "Blimey, Ban! You were about to become a gatah-boy meal in the belly of that beast! You okay, mate?!"

"Thanks to Rafe here," he answered breathlessly, nodding. Rafe reached out his hand and helped Tarleton to his feet. He looked at the fierce grenadier. "I owe you one." He looked at the gun that had saved his life. "Nice gun."

"I'm sure you'll return the favor someday," Rafe replied with a grin. He held up his wolf gun. "It's brought me good fortune." It was the very gun that

Rafe had manipulated a gullible British soldier into firing at Lexington Green to ignite the war.

Tarleton shook his head and rested his hands on his knees, giving a nervous laugh. "Fortune favors the bold."

"Let's get back to camp," Smithy suggested, "before any of that gator's family shows up."

"Gladly," Tarleton agreed, patting Rafe on the back as he stumbled on shaky legs back to the marshy path.

As they walked away, Al emerged from the grass. "And Clarie thought *I* screamed like a girl! Tarleton had me beat by a mile."

The British and American soldiers were so restless that they took to lobbing shots at one another with their artillery guns across Breach Inlet. Random musket fire sounded in the night from trigger-happy soldiers anxious for a fight, but small arms were well out of reach to do any harm.

"To my unspeakable mortification and disappointment, the army will be unable to do little more than serve as a distraction while Parker's ships carry out the real attack on Sullivan's Island," Clinton grudgingly admitted to his generals Lord Cornwallis and Brigadier General John Vaughan. He sat at his field writing desk, tapping a pencil, dreading having to send the message to the *Bristol*. "All we'll be able to do is send a few hundred men in flatboats to Breach Inlet and hope we don't get blown to kingdom come. I believe that the rebels could have several thousand men in those fortifications."

Cornwallis sat with his legs crossed, nodding in agreement. "With impenetrable swamps, an inlet too deep to ford, and waters too shallow for any of Parker's frigates to provide covering fire on our position here at Long Island, I'm afraid that is the reality."

"We *could* attempt to attack Haddrell's Point and Mount Pleasant by rowing up Hamlin Creek on the west side of Sullivan's Island, but we would still need covering fire from Parker's frigates. Ships would need to sail over the shoals to reach the vulnerable back side of Fort Sullivan," Vaughan suggested.

"I shall suggest it to Parker," Clinton said. He rubbed his forehead and let go an exasperated breath through his nostrils. "Time is precious. I heartily wish our business was done and we were on our way to the north. So, I shall propose an attack on Sunday, June 23rd. General Vaughan, I'm sending you to the *Bristol* to explain our plan to Commodore Parker."

"Understood, Sir," Vaughan answered. "I know that communication has been poor between you and Sir Parker with the fleet anchored out at Five Fathom Hole."

"Indeed. Flag signals and intermittent messages have left both of us questioning what the other is doing," Clinton answered. He wrinkled his forehead and nodded. "Parker could use any able-bodied officer to instill confidence in his men. His seamen have lived on two-thirds rations for the past month and have not eaten fresh meat since we were in North Carolina. Some of those sailors are too weak to man their battle stations."

"Should we enlist volunteers for duty aboard the warships?" Cornwallis asked.

"Yes, we might as well send men to Parker," Clinton agreed. "Rather than have them sitting here, useless." He sighed. "Select fifty men to be sailed out to the fleet."

"Very good, Sir," Cornwallis answered with a nod. He turned and left Clinton's tent. "I'll see to it right away."

Al perked up. *I hereby volunteer to get off this island!* He followed Cornwallis back to his tent. The commander promptly sent his aide to deliver a message to the troops on Long Island, accepting volunteers for the impending sea battle. *I better see who's comin' along.*

"I can't wait to get off this island," Smithy complained, slapping another mosquito biting his neck.

"Did you hear? Once we attack Fort Sullivan, no quarter is to be given to any rebel," Rafe told them with an eager grin.

"No quarter? Brutally *perfect,*" Tarleton said gruffly, slapping his cheek. "Infernal American mosquitoes!"

"*And* they're offering £5,000 for General Lee's head," Smithy added. "Bring your sword, Ban!"

Tarleton's eyes widened. "Even better! I'll get *paid* handsomely for what I've already said I would do for free," Tarleton declared, walking off. "Mark my words. My sword will find General Lee!"

"Where are you going?" Smithy called after the ambitious cornet.

"To Cornwallis's headquarters. I must ensure that I'm one of the fifty volunteers to get in this fight, so I can get to Lee first," he shouted back. "Death or glory!"

"I'm coming too, eh?" Smithy declared, following Tarleton.

Rafe grinned at the eager British soldiers and murmured to himself. "And

I will also 'volunteer.' But I'll board the *Actaeon* and sail behind the fort to destroy the rebels."

Al swatted away a swarm of mosquitoes that buzzed around his ears as he hid in the middle of some sea oats. "I've got lots to tell Clarie now!" He looked around him on the blank canvas of sand and poked out his iron claw. "Time to draw her a big seven!"

CONQUER OR DIE

"If Mousie were here, I know *exactly* wha' he'd say," Max grumbled. "R-r-revoltin'! I've smelt more r-r-rats in these str-r-reets of New York than I've ever smelt in me whole life."

"Especially *those* two rats," Jock spat, frowning as they followed Washington's two Life Guards, Hickey and Lynch. "They fit right in here now after swearing an oath to fight for the British."

"Aye, so far Gr-r-reen has dr-r-rummed up half a dozen Life Guards ta betr-r-ray Washington," Max agreed with a growl. Ever since Max and Jock had witnessed drummer William Green's meeting with gunsmith Gilbert Forbes, they reported to Gillamon every soldier who had agreed to switch sides and betray the Commander-in-Chief for coin and land. Gillamon kept a running list of names as the Scotties quietly listened for any word of exactly how and when those men would act. "Gillamon will know the r-r-right time ta hand the list over ta the humans."

The off-duty soldiers walked through the dangerous slums of the 'Holy Ground,' where the worst kind of shady characters gathered for anything but what was holy. Debauchery, lewdness, drunkenness, and criminal acts of every sort filled this sector of Manhattan. Washington warned his soldiers to steer clear of it, but tonight two of his finest men had run straight to it.

Max frowned as he saw Hickey and Lynch dart down an alley behind a house of ill repute. He and Jock quietly followed them, keeping their distance, and hiding behind some wooden barrels in the darkened street. A woman with red hair and heavy make-up came out a back door with a lantern in her hand and greeted the men with a mischievous smile. "How are my brave boys this evening?" she asked, reaching up to cup Hickey under the chin.

"Jest grand," Hickey replied in his Irish accent, clasping her wrist with a smile. "We'll be even grander if ye brought what we asked, lass."

She laughed and pulled her wrist away from Hickey's grip. She reached into her cloth pocket to pull out a wad of bills. She waved it playfully in the air with two fingers. "Of course."

Lynch reached for the bills, and she quickly put her hand behind her back. "Ah-ah-ah, not so fast. Give me the *real* money first."

Hickey nodded. "Give her the money."

Lynch reached into his pocket and handed over a wad of Continental currency. "Here. But we'll examine the counterfeit bills before you go anywhere."

"Why, of course, soldier," the woman answered playfully, exchanging bills with Lynch, and holding up the lantern.

Hickey and Lynch put their heads together as Lynch held up a bill near the lantern to take a close look at the fake money. "Looks bad enough to be real money," Hickey joked. He took the woman's hand and kissed it. "A pleasure doin' business with ye, me lady."

The woman winked and headed back to the door. "Anytime. I know where to get more."

With that, the soldiers split the wad of bills, shoved them into their pockets and smiled. "Now *that's* how I prefer to double my money," Lynch stated with a chuckle.

"Aye! Now let's go use it to double our mugs," Hickey agreed, gripping Lynch's shoulder with a laugh as the two soldiers walked back down the alley.

"They just bought counterfeit money!" Jock exclaimed. "Ketcham's in jail because he was going to help counterfeiters make bills like that. These Life Guards are nothing more than common criminals!"

"Aye, now ta make sure they're found out," Max answered with a grin. "I think we've found the perfect way ta give Gillamon his 'two king's guards.'"

Together the two dogs followed the Life Guards out of the Holy Ground to the more respectable part of town. The soldiers popped into a tavern and sat down at a table, loudly ordering drinks from a young barmaid. After a few rounds it was time to pay their bill and return to the barracks.

"Please, allow *me* to pay," Hickey said with a snicker to Lynch. He leaned over and whispered, "Sure, and this lass wouldn't know a fake bill if it bit her hand."

"How *generous* of you, friend," Lynch replied, lifting his pewter mug with a wink.

Just as Hickey pulled out the counterfeit bills from his pocket, Max bolted over and grabbed the wad of money. He ran behind the bar and dropped it at the feet of the tavern owner before darting off under a table.

"Give that back, ye pesky mutt!" Hickey shouted, scooting back his chair, and chasing after Max.

The tavern owner picked up the counterfeit money and furrowed his brow, noticing immediately the imperfections on the unusually large amount of folded bills. He had seen a lot of this fake currency floating through his tavern lately, so he knew exactly what it was.

"That's me money!" Hickey declared. "That stupid dog grabbed it out of me hand."

"You *sure* this is *your* money?" the tavern owner asked, lifting a hand to a pair of local sentries eating shepherd's pie at a nearby table.

"Aye, that it is," Hickey boldly exclaimed, holding out his hand for the fake money.

The tavern owner grabbed Hickey's hand and twisted it behind his back. "Counterfeiter! Officers, arrest this man!"

The sentries quickly got to their feet pulling pistols just as Lynch made a move toward the door. One sentry intercepted Lynch before he could leave, and the other man grabbed Hickey by the collar. The tavern owner handed the counterfeit bills to the sentries. "Here, more of that same fake money from the Holy Ground!"

"Come on, let's go. Both of you!" the sentries exclaimed, roughly pushing the Life Guards out the door.

Max came out of hiding and winked at Jock. "I told ye, lad. The tr-r-ruth always comes out. Even if it needs a little help sometimes."

"You were brave to do that, Grandsire! What will happen to Hickey and Lynch now?" Jock wanted to know.

"They'll be thr-r-rown in the city jail," Max answered. "An' Gillamon will figure out wha' ta do with them next."

Jock smiled. "At least they won't be able to hurt Washington any time soon."

Max grinned broadly. "Aye, an' if I know Gillamon, he'll make sure those bad laddies end up *helpin'* Washington."

CITY JAIL, MANHATTAN, NEW YORK, JUNE 15, 1776

"Please, have you heard anything?" Ketcham begged the passing prison guard, holding up his shackled hand. "It's been a week since I sent my letter to the Congress. I'm desperate to help my children!"

Isaac Ketcham had written a letter to the New York Provincial Congress, throwing himself on the mercy of the court for the sake of his six children who were home alone with no one to care for them. He expressed his sincere regret and shame for the minor role he played in even considering purchasing the paper for the counterfeiters, even though he did not go through with the task. He pleaded with the court to allow him to at least go to his children for a few days to tend to their care.

Gillamon stopped. "Nothing yet. Perhaps they will read it when they reconvene on Monday. Don't give up hope. They are extremely busy with preparing the city for war with the arrival of British forces. The Provincial Congress needs a good reason to stop what they're doing to listen to your plea. But I'll keep my ears open." He paused and added, "You do the same."

Ketcham wrinkled his brow. *Keep my ears open?* He shook his head and buried his face in his hands, overwhelmed by crushing grief and regret. "My poor children. What have I done?"

Suddenly they heard shouting down the corridor as two new prisoners were brought into the jail. Gillamon turned and walked to meet them. *Right on schedule,* he thought. "Bring those men here. We'll put them in this cell."

As Hickey and Lynch were shoved into Ketcham's cell, Gillamon dropped a piece of paper near Ketcham, but none of the prisoners noticed it. Gillamon then walked out and turned the key in the lock behind him. Ketcham looked worriedly at the men and then at Gillamon, who gave him a knowing look of confidence before walking away.

Immediately, Lynch and Hickey began arguing.

"This is all your fault, Hick! *You* were the one with the brilliant idea to get those fake bills," Lynch accused him.

"That mangy dog grabbed them out of me hand! What was I supposed to do?" Hickey answered. "I wasn't about to lose all that money."

"All that *fake* money," Lynch corrected him. "When Washington finds out about this, we're done for."

Hickey sneered. "Yeah? Well, his high-and-mighty perfect commander-in-chief kin kiss me foot. I'm sick and tired of bein' stuck in his company all day anyway. It'll be a relief to get away from that assignment."

"Fake money?" Ketcham asked them. "I'm in for counterfeiting, too." He pointed out their plain clothes. "You're Continental soldiers?"

"Aye, Washington's Life Guards, at your service," Lynch scoffed, shaking his head.

Ketcham raised his eyebrows. "Sounds like you don't approve of Washington. I don't either. I'm a Loyalist, through and through."

"Well, God save the KING!" Hickey exclaimed, lifting an imaginary mug of ale in the air. "We're Loyalists now, eh, Lynch?"

"What do you mean?" Ketcham hoarsely whispered, looking around. "Have you switched sides?"

The urge to exact revenge on the Patriot authorities who locked them in this cell made both soldiers defiantly want to boast about what they had agreed to do against Washington and the Patriot cause. Ketcham sat there in his iron chains and just listened as the angry Life Guards cursed the colonies, cursed George Washington, and slowly revealed a plot so sinister that it was all Ketcham could do to not call the prison guard. These soldiers had landed in prison for passing counterfeit bills, but if the authorities really knew the crimes these men were about to commit, they'd keep them locked up and throw away the key. The Life Guards hadn't just *heard* about this plot. They were *in* on it themselves.

The Provincial Congress needs a good reason to stop what they're doing to listen to your plea, Ketcham thought, remembering the prison guard's words. Hope suddenly stirred in his heart. Perhaps they would listen to what he had just learned from these two soldiers. They weren't just any soldiers. They were Washington's very own Life Guards. He'd keep listening to them tonight and then request some paper and a pencil to write a short note to the Congress in the morning. *Two of Washington's guards! Just like Mordecai reporting the king's two guards.* He grinned to himself, leaned his head back on the prison wall. and breathed a silent prayer. *God, if I get out of here, that'll be the first story I read to my children from the Holy Writ.*

NEW YORK PROVINCIAL CONGRESS, NEW YORK, JUNE 17, 1776

President Nathaniel Woodhull slammed his gavel on the wooden desk to call the 9:00 a.m. Monday morning session of Congress to order. Twenty-six delegates from every county in New York got to work covering a myriad of problems facing the colony as British ships neared their shores. But even with the crisis of impending war at hand, the regular business of trying crimes and meting out punishment remained on their docket of responsibility. Around mid-morning, the secretary read a June 9th letter penned by one of the prisoners arrested as part of the Long Island counterfeit ring, appealing for leniency to care for his six poor children.

"The prisoner submitted this additional note yesterday," the secretary reported, holding up Ketcham's second note and shaking his head. "His spelling is atrocious." He cleared his throat and read aloud:

> *Sir I the subscriber hath something to obsearve to the honourable house if I cold be admitted Its nothing concearning my one affair But intirely on another subgyt. From yours to serve, Isaac Ketcham*

John Jay raised his eyebrows. "The prisoner's spelling may be atrocious, but I would like to hear what he has 'observed' in his cell below. It shan't take long to give him a personal audience."

Only three days before, the New York Provincial Congress had assigned John Jay to a secret committee that was formed at the request of George Washington. The Commander-in-Chief saw the pressing need for counterintelligence to uncover Loyalist plots running rampant throughout the city. Like the Board of War to assist Washington with swift military decisions, the secret Committee on Conspiracies was composed of a few select members to share intelligence, grant permissions for important actions, and to investigate plots. John Jay had already been involved in matters of secrecy back in Philadelphia. It was he who had joined Benjamin Franklin upstairs in Carpenters' Hall for three top secret meetings with the French spy Bonvouloir last December. John Jay not only was a brilliant statesman of high integrity, but he could be trusted for matters of extreme importance requiring the utmost secrecy.

"Very well, have the commanding guard bring Isaac Ketcham before this Congress immediately," President Woodhull ordered.

The secretary handed a written order to the attending guard to send for Ketcham. Within moments, the note was handed to Gillamon, who nodded and went to retrieve the prisoner. He stifled a smile as he walked down the corridor past the foul cells with dirty, grumbling prisoners and came to Ketcham's cell. He put his key in the lock and said, "Ketcham, your petition has finally been read by the Congress. You may present your case to plead for leniency."

"What about us?" Hickey shouted.

"Aye, when do *we* get to be heard?" Lynch followed.

"You'll get your hearing in due time," Gillamon brusquely told them as he unlocked the shackles on Ketcham's wrists. "You just got here. This man has been here a month. Ketcham, let's go."

Ketcham scrambled to his feet and rubbed his sore wrists. He quickly ran his fingers through his stringy hair, wiped his face with his sleeve, and gave a hopeful smile to Gillamon as he stepped out of the cell. Gillamon locked the door behind them and escorted Ketcham down the corridor.

"Maybe there's finally hope for my children," Ketcham muttered quietly with a lump in his throat.

"There's always hope. Just tell the Congress what they need to hear," Gillamon instructed him. "You will swear an oath to tell the truth. So, tell them the truth. *Every bit* of it." He paused and looked Ketcham right in the eye. "Do you know what God's Word says about truth?"

Ketcham quietly shook his head. "No, what?"

"The truth shall set you free," Gillamon answered with a grin, his blue eyes striking a chord of familiarity with the prisoner. This guard again reminded Ketcham of the Dutchman.

"Like Moredecai when he reported the king's two guards?" Ketcham asked with a smile.

"Something like that," Gillamon answered.

Ketcham patted his pocket where he had stashed the paper that he found on the prison cell floor. He assumed that Lynch or Hickey dropped it, as it listed the names of soldiers who had agreed to switch sides and fight for the British.

"Bring in the prisoner," ordered the guard from the committee room.

Ketcham and Gillamon shared a hopeful smile and the failed, counterfeiting, widowed father of six children walked into the courtroom, ready to tell the truth.

The New York Provincial Congress was in shock at what Ketcham had just told them.

"Please have the prisoner wait in the hall while we deliberate," President Woodhull ordered Gillamon, who promptly took Ketcham out of the room.

"Sirs, if I may. The seriousness of this report and the importance of complete secrecy demands that the Committee on Conspiracies handle this immediately," John Jay offered, nodding to Philip Livingston and Gouverneur Morris. "I recommend that we convene now to attend to this matter."

The twenty-six members of the New York Provincial Congress unanimously agreed. At this very moment, active conspirators endangered the life of General George Washington. Within moments, the committee sat at a table, discussing what to do and how to proceed.

"How can we be sure that Ketcham is telling the truth? What if he's making it up?" Morris asked, holding up the list of names that Ketcham had given them. "We obviously need to find other witness testimony to back up Ketcham's claim."

"Well, we do have several more cases to hear involving Loyalist plots. Perhaps their information will shed light on this plot against Washington. For now, though, the only ones who have knowledge of this specific plot are sitting in a cell twenty feet below us," Livingston added, pointing to the floor. "What do we do with Ketcham?"

"We offer Ketcham the opportunity to have the court look *favorably* on his unfortunate situation by doing exactly as we say," John Jay answered. He leaned in. "By learning all he can from those two Life Guards. I don't care if he must tell them he'll pull the trigger to kill Washington himself, in order to gain their trust. Allow him the time to get every bit of intelligence he can out of those traitorous soldiers."

"In other words, Ketcham is now a spy working for us," Morris stated with a grin.

"That's exactly what he is," Jay answered. "We need to get to the bottom of this sinister plot immediately, gentlemen, to prove if Ketcham's report is true. No one must speak or write another word about this matter outside of this chamber, aside for the one man I must tell." He rose from his seat. "I must go inform Washington of what we've heard this morning. There are other conspiring Life Guards still out there . . . and they could strike at any time."

MORTIER MANSION, MANHATTAN, NEW YORK, JUNE 17, 1776

"No one must know. *No one*," Washington emphasized to Jay as he closed the door behind the departing statesman.

Max lay quietly in the corner, scarcely able to believe what he had just heard over the hour that John Jay spent with Washington behind closed doors. Washington now sat alone, leaning over to rest his elbows on his knees with folded hands propped up by his thumbs under his chin. He had to gather his thoughts and regain his composure. When he walked out of this room, he had to exude confidence and show no fear despite the sickening wave of emotions washing over him. The Commander-in-Chief already had on his shoulders the weight of defending a new nation; now he had the added burden of knowing that an active plot to kill him and his top officers was afoot by men who had been chosen to *protect* him.

Washington pulled his hands slowly down his nose and mouth and sat back in the winged-back chair, gripping its upholstered arms, and letting go a deep breath. His mind raced with what Jay had revealed to him. It was unthinkable. Somehow, Governor Tryon had gotten to his Life Guards. At the first appearance of British ships in New York Harbor, they were to assassinate Washington and his top officers, disable the Patriot cannons by jamming spikes into the touchholes, blow up the powder magazine, and destroy King's Bridge, which connected Manhattan to the mainland. Even if none of this evil plot had yet been proven and was just the hearsay testimony of a failed counterfeiting prisoner, Washington had to act upon it as if every bit of it were true. He would make sure that none of the soldiers on the list was assigned to guard him until they were examined by Jay's secret committee. Meanwhile, Washington had to act as if nothing were amiss.

This wicked scheme violated every single point of honor and valor that Washington had tried to instill in his men to form an army worthy of the glorious cause of liberty. Not only was it a personal betrayal, but it was also a betrayal to the cause of independence. It was treason. If found guilty, every one of those traitorous soldiers would be deserving of Congress's newly penned resolution for how to prosecute enemies of the Colonies. When Dr. Benjamin Church was discovered and charged for his treasonous behavior in Boston, there was no penalty yet in place for crimes against America, only for England. While Church was confined in prison for his crime as the only appropriate punishment at the time, any soldiers found guilty of treason here in New York would now face the designated penalty matching the crime—death.

But Washington could tell no one for now—not even Martha upon her return to New York. Neither Washington nor the secret committee could tip their hand to the conspirators that they knew about the plot until they had gathered far more intelligence and identified the other players involved. John Jay and his committee needed time to work, and they would be working around the clock until they got to the bottom of things. Meanwhile, Washington would need to continue working around the clock to secure New York against the coming British forces and not let on that his life was on the line. Washington made it clear to Jay that no one must know about the specific threat to Washington's life as part of this larger plot that would be launched with the arrival of British ships. Any hint that the Commander-in-Chief's life could be in danger from would-be assassins, especially from within the Life Guard, would ignite panic in the hearts of his soldiers as well as the public. As always, Washington and his officers must project nothing but strength, confidence, and resilience.

Max quietly walked over to Washington and sat by his chair. *I pr-r-romised ta keep ye safe, but even I know I can't keep yer heart safe.* He softly lifted his paws up onto the general's knees, willing the burdened man to feel the support and comfort that the faithful dog longed to express. Washington gave a sad smile and scooped Max up into his lap, holding him tightly as if he were the only friend he had in the world.

Any one of yer men could tr-r-ry an' attack ye with a dagger in the back, Max thought, *but I know they've already plunged a dagger deep inta yer heart.*

PEAS, PLEASE

MORTIER MANSION, MANHATTAN, NEW YORK,
JUNE 23, 1776

"Good day, Mrs. Washington. I trust you had a pleasant journey," came the voice of Samuel Webb, Washington's aide-de-camp. "The General isn't here but is inspecting defenses at King's Bridge with his officers. I'm going there now and will give him word of your return."

"Thank you, Mr. Webb," Martha replied, a bit winded and exhausted from her journey.

"Welcome home, Mrs. Washington!" exclaimed the housekeeper, Mary Smith. "How are you feeling after your long ordeal and journey from Philadelphia?"

Martha Washington loosened the ribbon under her chin and removed her bonnet as she stepped into the cool tile foyer of the Mortier house. The windows were opened to allow a breeze to flow through the rooms on this blistering hot summer day. "Thank you kindly, Mrs. Smith. I've been riding in a bumpy carriage along hot, dusty roads for days in petticoats and stays," she answered, letting out a breath of relief. She leaned in with a wink. "Getting inoculated against the smallpox was far more delightful than *that,* I can assure you! I'd like nothing more than a cool bath to freshen up."

"Certainly. I'll draw you a nice bath with lavender water to help you relax after your long journey," Mrs. Smith answered with a warm smile.

"That sounds heavenly, thank you," Martha answered, closing her eyes at the thought, and dabbing her sweaty brow with a handkerchief.

"I've just purchased some fresh fish that I'll make for a celebratory dinner this evening, along with General Washington's favorite side dish," Mrs. Smith told her.

"Peas!" Martha exclaimed. She clasped her hands gratefully. "Splendid." Just then Max and Jock came bounding up to her to welcome her home. "Why hello, wee Scots! Isn't it wonderful to be greeted by our faithful dogs? They always seem genuinely happy to see us. I'm sure Colonel Knox was glad to be reunited with little Jock after he finally arrived here to New York."

Mrs. Smith chuckled. "That is true, ma'am. And with his hands full, he's

happy to have Jock stay here with us whenever he wishes. Jock tends to especially enjoy *helping me* clean up in the kitchen."

Aye! I pick up all the dropped food, Jock barked in joyous agreement.

"Come, Jock and Max, let Mrs. Washington get settled while we prepare
a celebration dinner," Mrs. Smith said, pushing the dogs toward the door
leading to the outdoor kitchen across the courtyard. The two rear door Life
Guards on duty nodded at the housekeeper as she walked past.

Max and Jock stopped in the courtyard to lap up some cool water where
the house animals drank. Chickens walked about freely in and out of the
henhouse, where they provided a daily supply of fresh eggs for the household.

"I'm glad Mrs. Washington's back safe," Jock pointed out happily. "Do
you think the General will tell her all that's happened?"

Max wrinkled his brow. "Not everything, lad. Not yet anyway. Washington
had ta tell Captain Gibbs, his new aide-de-camp Samuel Webb, an' several of
his top generals aboot the plot for their protection an' ta prepare the defenses
at King's Bridge. I'm sure he'll share with Martha how some things be unfol-
din' since he had ta send General Greene ta ar-r-rest Mayor Matthews over
on Long Island."

"Aye, he can't very well keep the arrest of the *mayor* a secret since everyone
knows about it," Jock agreed. "It only took five days from the time Lynch and
Hickey landed in jail to arresting one of the ringleaders for the whole plot!"

"Aye, not a bad few days of work, but the super secret committee has lots
more ta do ta make sure they've caught all the right humans involved," Max
answered. "Gillamon said that they've interviewed lots of witnesses an' discovered even more recruiters around New York that operated the same way the
gunsmith did ta turn soldiers. Mayor Matthews said it were all Forbes's idea,
an' that he be innocent. So, then they arrested Gilbert Forbes."

"That jail's getting awfully crowded!" Jock observed with a laugh. "Did
Forbes tell them it was Matthews who hired *him?*"

"Well, when they first arrested him, Forbes r-r-refused ta talk," Max
explained. "But this mornin' they sent a young minister ta visit him an' let
him know he only had thr-r-ree days ta live *unless* he offered ta tell them the
whole story aboot things."

Jock's eyes widened. "So did the gunsmith start talking?"

Max nodded. "Aye, nothin' like facin' eternity that makes a human speak
up! Now they know all aboot Matthews an' that this scheme goes str-r-raight
ta the top with Governor Tr-r-ryon."

Suddenly Jock smelled the aroma of hot apple pie coming from the
kitchen and licked his chops. His mouth watered. "Do you mind if I stay
with Mrs. Smith to help with supper?"

Max chuckled. "Ye do that, lad. I'm goin' ta do me r-r-rounds ta make sure all be well on the property with the Life Guards. Then I think I'll go meet Washington as he r-r-rides back from King's Br-r-ridge. I'll see ye later."

The two Scotties parted, and Max trotted off to walk the perimeter of the estate down by the Hudson while Jock headed to the kitchen. It was then that a shadow crept across the courtyard.

"There you are!" Martha exclaimed as Washington entered the foyer of the Mortier house.

"Martha," Washington answered with a tender voice, grateful to see his wife here safe and fully recovered. He took her hand in his and kissed it. "You have gladdened my heart with your return."

Martha smiled quizzically at her husband's rare public show of affection. "I share your joy, dear husband. I am happy to be back. How are you?" The tall general softly rubbed his wife's hand with his thumb and looked her in the eye but said nothing. She could see that the burden in his eyes had only increased since they had seen each other in Philadelphia. "Clearly we have much to discuss."

Washington gave a singular nod. "Indeed, but later."

The contagious, booming laughter of Colonel Henry Knox was heard behind them as the brawny twenty-six-year-old officer entered the door along with thirty-four-year-old General Nathanael Greene. The men were not only two of Washington's finest officers, but they shared a long-time friendship from back when Knox was a bookseller in Boston and Greene came to purchase military books on his trips from Rhode Island. They faithfully supported Washington at every turn and performed their duties with excellence. After Martha joined Washington in New York, these officers had their wives join them as well, along with their newborn children. Lucy Knox brought their little daughter Lucy, and Caty Greene brought their firstborn son, George Washington Greene. Martha was not only grateful for the friendship and loyalty that these officers gave her husband, but also for the friendship she enjoyed with their wives. Greene and Caty stayed where he was stationed over on Long Island, while Knox and Lucy resided downtown at No. 1 Broadway, upstairs from the military headquarters. But Washington insisted on having his 'military family' with him daily.

"Why if it isn't two of the brightest lights in the Continental Army," Martha exclaimed as the officers came and bowed politely in greeting. "How are your lovely ladies?"

"Good evening, Mrs. Washington. Welcome back. They are busy with *babies,"* Knox bellowed with a jolly chuckle. "I never knew such small creatures could require so much time, attention, and cloth diapers. My Lucy is a trooper."

"I heartily agree," Greene added with one hand in the air as he leaned on his cane with the other. He had a bad leg from an old knee injury. "I must admit that I find the preparations for war to be easier than taming the cries of a baby with indigestion. But Mrs. Washington, Caty sends her fondest regards and looks forward to welcoming the Washingtons and the Knoxes to our home soon for dinner."

"We shall look forward to that, thank you," Martha answered with her hands clasped in front of her. "For now, Mrs. Smith has prepared a special welcome home dinner. Come gentlemen, you must be famished after your long day."

While everyone gathered in the dining room, servants filled goblets and placed platters and bowls of food on the table. Max trotted in behind them and sat next to Washington's chair. Everyone lowered their heads for the blessing.

Washington stood at the head of the table and bowed his head. "Lord, we thank thee for this bountiful meal and for the hands that prepared it. We ask thee to bless this food to our bodies so that we may serve thee with strength. Amen."

"Amen. I see your Max, but where is my Jock?" Knox asked, looking around the table legs for the wee Scottish terrier.

"I suspect he is underfoot in the kitchen," Washington answered. His eyes lit up as he spotted his favorite dish next to General Greene. "Ah, pass the peas, please."

"Mrs. Smith told me that Jock is her *helper* in the kitchen," Martha reported with a chuckle. As a servant filled her goblet, she asked him, "Would you please ask Mrs. Smith to pop in to see us if it is quite convenient? I wish to thank her for preparing such a grand feast."

"Mrs. Smith hasn't been seen since this afternoon, ma'am," the servant answered. "She left to go buy some peas for dinner, but never returned."

Washington took the bowl of peas to spoon some on his plate. "Surely she returned, for here are the peas."

"Yes, Sir. A farmer delivered them," the servant explained. "He must have brought them right from the field if I might say so. He smelled something fierce."

Max sniffed the air and instantly knew that something wasn't right. His eyes widened as he saw Washington take the serving spoon to dish the peas onto his plate. A growl entered his throat and he jumped up to knock the bowl of peas from his hand, barking, *DR-R-R-OP THEM PEAS, GEORGE!*

Peas went flying everywhere, and Washington scooted back his chair with a huff, furious at the little dog. "MAX! Why in the name of heaven did you do that?" he scolded, brushing off his lap and chair where the peas had landed. He turned to the servant and pointed to Max. "Please take the dog outside, now." He clenched his jaw at the embarrassing scene and lack of decorum at table. "My sincere apologies for this unseemly behavior."

Max frowned and tucked his tail between his legs as the servant picked him up to carry him from the room. He growled but was glad to see another servant hurriedly rush in to sweep up the spilled peas. When the servant put Max outside, he immediately put his nose to the ground, picking up an evil scent. His heart was pounding as he grew worried for Jock. "I never shoulda let him out of me sight!" Max's legs took him lightning fast around the courtyard and then off down the path leading to the Hudson River.

Max ran for a half-mile until the evil scent began to dissipate. He stopped at the water's edge, his paws sinking in the muddy bank. "JOCK! JOCK LAD! WHERE ARE YE?"

All he heard at first was the sound of loons in the distance, and the gentle water lapping against the shore. Max squinted into the reeds, where he saw movement. A low growl rose from his throat, and he sprang into action, jumping into the reeds. "Who's there?"

Suddenly he saw Jock, curled up and whimpering, covered in mud. "Grandlad!" Max cried, rushing to the puppy's side. "Are ye alr-r-right? Wha' happened?"

Jock blinked his terrified eyes to shake off the shock. "G-g-grandsire? Is that you?"

"Aye, lad, it's me. I'm here now," Max assured him. "Are ye hurt?"

Jock looked at his swollen back paw. "It . . . it came out of nowhere . . . in the courtyard. I ran as fast as I could, but it lunged at me. Then it just vanished. I crawled into the reeds to hide."

Max furrowed his brow, examining Jock's paw. "Wha' were the beastie that chased ye?"

Jock locked eyes with Max, his lip trembling. "It was a snake."

Max's eyes grew large, and a wave of dread washed over him. He started vigorously licking Jock's paw. "Ye'll be okay, ye'll be okay, ye'll be okay!" he insisted. He looked at Jock's paw and saw two puncture wounds with swelling, but no apparent sign of venomous damage. "Maybe it struck ye but failed ta shoot its venom in ye. Let's get ye back ta the house so the humans can tend ye. Can ye climb on me back?"

Jock winced from the pain in his foot but managed to climb on top of Max's back.

"Okay, lad, hang on. I've got ye," Max told him, carefully balancing the little dog as he walked up from the muddy bank.

Jock's eyes welled up and he softly wept from the relief that he had been rescued. "Thank you, Grandsire, for saving me."

Max frowned. *I jest hope I didn't arrive too late.*

Once they were back at the house, Max took Jock to the water trough. "Here lad, drink some water while I get help."

Jock did as he was told and drank while Max barked to alert the humans. He then noticed that the chickens were lying on the ground. "Grandsire, what happened to the chickens?"

Max ran over to see that the peas were scattered all around the dead chickens. A growl rumbled in his throat. "I knew it. Them peas were poisoned! The humans done fed 'em ta these chickens."

"Poisoned?" Jock asked, lying down from the throbbing pain in his back paw. "Who poisoned the peas?"

Max thought a moment and growled. "Grrr, I think I know, lad. This has happened before. Back in 1774 for the first Continental Congress in Philadelphia, that wicked kitty Kakia took the form of a human an' tr-r-ried ta poison Washington an' Patrick Henry with dessert. I knocked the tr-r-ray out of her hand before she got inside the house, an' Gillamon sent her r-r-runnin' away."

Jock's mouth hung open. "But why are the peas out here?"

"Because I knocked the bowl out of Washington's hand," Max answered. "I smelled the poison, an' when I heard ye an' Mrs. Smith were missin', I knew something weren't r-r-right."

"So, was that Kakia that came after me before she poisoned the peas?" Jock wanted to know. "The snake didn't speak."

"Hmmm, I'm not sure, lad." Max furrowed his brow. "Maybe it were jest a regular snake beastie that bit ye an' had nothin' ta do with Kakia. I can't see why she'd bother bein' a snake."

"Grandsire, when I hid in the reeds after the snake vanished, the next thing I saw was a human walking back to the house with a basket," Jock offered. "He looked like a farmer."

Max's eyes widened. "Lad, did ye see wha' happened ta Mrs. Smith?"

Jock thought a moment. "Last I heard she was leaving to go buy some peas."

Max's mind raced with questions. "Did the snake smell?"

"Aye, something terrible!" Jock answered. "I've never smelled anything that bad."

Max gulped. "Maybe Charlatan himself were here. Maybe *he* were the snake that became the farmer who delivered them poisoned peas. If so, there's no tellin' wha' he did ta Mrs. Smith." He ran up to the Life Guards and barked, urging them to warn Washington in case the evil animal team leader was still around.

"What's wrong, boy?" one of the Life Guards asked.

The other Life Guard saw Jock lying in the shadows. Then he spotted the chickens. "We better inform the officers." He ran back inside and within minutes, Washington, Knox, Greene, and Capt. Gibbs of the Life Guards came outside to see for themselves.

"They're dead, General," Gibbs said. "Those peas were poisoned."

Washington clenched his jaw with the realization of what had happened in the dining room. "And Mrs. Smith is missing."

"Could *she* have been the one to do this?" Greene suggested, whispering out of earshot of the Life Guards. "Was she in on the plot?"

"Poison the general and his staff and then flee," Knox whispered. "It seems plausible, Sir."

"I perish the thought, but we shall have to wait to see if she returns," Washington told them. "Meanwhile, we need to treat this poisoning attempt as part of the overall plot. I will shift my headquarters to City Hall. Captain Gibbs, post extra guards."

"Understood, Sir," Captain Gibbs answered.

Washington saw Max sitting there, and it suddenly dawned on him what the little dog had done. "Max, you were trying to *protect* me," he exclaimed, squatting down to pet the dog. "You knew, didn't you?"

Aye, George. That I did, Max whimpered as he wagged his tail. *I know ye can't understand me, an' didn't know wha' I were tryin' ta say. I'm jest glad ye're alr-r-right.*

"Jock, there you are!" Knox exclaimed, coming over to scoop up the little dog in his arms. He heard the puppy yelp and immediately noticed his swollen back paw. "He's hurt. Looks like a snake bite. Let's get you cared for."

As Knox took Jock inside, Washington gently cupped Max by the ears and looked him in the eye. "Never will I doubt your warning again, boy. You can detect things we cannot. It is fortunate you were by my side, right where you belong."

Max grinned and closed his eyes with relief. *Aye, lad. That's why I'm here.*

"Come, let's be going," Washington announced, getting to his feet. "And don't worry about Jock. We'll take good care of him."

If that slitherin' snake himself were here, it must mean we stopped the humans' plans ta kill Washington. An' that means the Br-r-ritish must be gettin' close, Max thought, looking around the courtyard. He frowned. *But if it r-r-really were Charlatan, why didn't he kill Jock?*

A WARNING
TO EVERY SOLDIER

George Washington tugged on his buff waistcoat and straightened the sky-blue sash that crossed his chest, indicating his rank as Commander-in-Chief. He stared into the mirror with a frown as he positioned the black three-cornered hat on his head. He then clenched his jaw, nodded to himself, and lifted his chin with resolute confidence. *We are ultimately the product of our choices.*

The verdict from the June 26th court martial of Thomas Hickey was definitive: guilty. Yesterday, Washington met with his six senior officers to share the verdict he had received and to obtain their advice on appropriate action. They unanimously advised that Hickey receive the newly designated penalty by Congress for the crime of treason: death.

Washington and his officers next determined that the execution should be a swift, public statement not only to the army and the citizens, but to the enemy as well. The execution would be conducted in an open area so everyone could witness the consequences of treason. And this viewing would not be a suggestion, but an *order* by the Commander-in-Chief.

At 10:00 a.m. this morning, Generals Heath, Stirling, Spencer, and Scott would begin marching their respective brigades north through the streets of New York to an open field at the city limits where hastily constructed gallows awaited the accused. Ten thousand armed and uniformed soldiers would stand at attention and watch as the Provost Marshal slipped the single noose around the neck of Thomas Hickey, traitor and first soldier in the Continental Army to be executed for treason.

Washington knew what he had written for today's General Orders was appropriate. It was necessary. It was just. He turned and walked out of the room. *May God have mercy on his soul.*

THE COMMONS, MANHATTAN, NEW YORK,
JUNE 28, 1776, 11:00 A.M.

"There must be a few thousand humans out here," Jock guessed.

"Twenty thousand, to be exact," Gillamon corrected him. "Ten thousand soldiers, and the rest are citizens of New York and New Jersey."

"There's somethin' aboot humans that wants ta watch deadly justice in action," Max opined, shaking his head. "I've seen it ever since the Cr-r-ross an' the Colosseum."

"I just don't understand why Hickey is the only soldier being executed out of all the bad humans who committed the same crime," Jock lamented, confused.

"I know it's hard to understand, little one," Gillamon answered. "I'll try to summarize for you what happened with this entire plot against Washington and the Continental Army. When John Jay and the Committee on Conspiracies investigated all the witnesses involved, initially they confirmed five Life Guards as suspects but eventually learned there were eight men involved. Because they are soldiers, they were handed over to the military to be tried by a swift court-martial rather than by a civilian court."

"Hickey's character weren't good ta begin with," Max interjected. "He were born in Ireland an' served the British army, but he chose ta desert them after tr-r-rouble broke out here in the colonies. *Then* he joined the American army, but as soon as he saw opportunity ta benefit fr-r-rom it, he chose ta switch sides *again*. The lad showed that he don't care aboot law an' order since he chose ta br-r-reak it by passin' counterfeit bills. So, Hickey's choices show he has no loyalty ta anyone but himself, an' he has no r r-r-respect for authority."

Gillamon nodded. "Hickey was the only one who had two key witnesses from separate sources identify him by name to the Committee. Once they began the court-martial, four witnesses testified against him: Green, Forbes, Ketcham, and a man named Welch, who claimed Hickey tried to recruit him after telling him about the plot."

"But one of those witnesses was the drummer, William Green!" Jock argued. "He was the *ringleader* for the Life Guards. Why didn't they punish him, too?"

"They will, young one," Gillamon assured him. "There is still much work to be done to mete out justice to everyone involved in this plot. The other guilty soldiers and players may only be locked away in prison in Connecticut, but the authorities needed one of them to be the 'face of the conspiracy' *now*—someone to set the example of what happens to anyone who dares to commit treason against America. You must understand that the timing is *critical* with the approach of British forces. If Washington doesn't quickly put a stop to this plot by showing what will happen to anyone involved, it could unfold at any moment."

"Aye, so Hickey decided he were smart enough ta r-r-represent himself in court," Max scoffed. "He even *admitted* that he joined the scheme! But he said he only did it ta cheat the plotters by takin' their money."

"Hickey then arrogantly stated he thinks the British will be the victors in the coming battle," Gillamon added. "He admitted that he wanted to make sure he covered himself by having his name on the list of colonists who agreed to fight for the British and betray the Continental Army."

"So, it didn't take long for the court-martial ta decide the lad were guilty as dirt," Max declared. "Once they handed the verdict ta Washington an' his generals, they decided ta make Hickey's sad fate serve at least one good purpose—teachin' a hard lesson ta everyone. If ye *choose* ta betr-r-ray this country, ye best be r-r-ready ta pay the ultimate pr-r-rice for it."

Jock wrinkled his brow and shook his head. "I know he did the wrong thing, but I still feel sorry for him. I wish he had chosen to walk away from doing the wrong thing, like Ketcham did."

"Of course, no one wants to have to execute Hickey," Gillamon agreed. "Punishment is never easy, but it is always necessary and just. A crime must always be punished, as with any sin. It must be paid for, and someone must pay the price."

"That's wha's so amazin' aboot grace," Max stressed somberly. "Humans betrayed the Maker in the Garden, but the Maker loved them so much He decided ta give them a way out of payin' the price. They don't deserve it, but the Maker *Himself* paid the price an' freely *gives* grace ta them, jest for the askin'."

Jock nodded thoughtfully, thinking of the snake in the Garden. "Gillamon, Grandsire and I aren't sure about the snake that bit me. Why didn't it inject me with venom? Why didn't it keep chasing me?"

"Aye, if it were Charlatan, why wouldn't he kill Jock?" Max wanted to know. "I know that evil, slitherin' snake, an' nothin' would give him more pleasure than ta kill me own gr-r-randlad."

"Not every snake bite involves venom," Gillamon explained. "Many strikes are dry bites, which is what you experienced. There must be a reason. There always is, even when it isn't clear at the time." He reached down to put his hand on Jock's back. "Tell me, little one. Are you warm-blooded or cold-blooded?"

"I'm warm-blooded, I think," Jock answered.

"Yes, you are, but snakes are *cold-blooded,*" Gillamon replied. "That means that you can run and run and run for a long time, but a snake cannot. A snake can lunge but is limited in its ability to keep moving. That means that you can outlast it."

"Ye can outr-r-run them beasties every time!" Max affirmed.

"Ever since the Garden, snakes have symbolized evil, not because they are evil themselves . . ." Gillamon started to say.

"Except for Charlatan, that is!" Max interjected.

". . . but snakes represent how evil operates, by twisting," Gillamon explained. "Snakes move by twisting, as does evil. A lie happens when the truth is twisted. Evil happens when that which is good becomes twisted. So, just like snakes are cold-blooded, so is evil."

"So does that mean that I can outrun evil, too?" Jock asked.

"Precisely, small one," Gillamon answered with a smile. "Although evil can strike, it remains cold-blooded. That means it can have a quick, short victory, but it cannot sustain an attack. It cannot endure, no matter how strong or powerful it may appear at first."

"So, lies, hatred, an' betrayals all be cold-blooded, but the power of evil can only last a short time," Max relayed. "Evil always fails in the long r-r-run."

Jock raised his eyebrows. "So since good is *warm-blooded*, it will always outrun and outlast evil!"

Gillamon nodded and smiled. "That's why those who choose goodness must always keep running the race to persevere. Always press on with what is good, true, and right, and in the end, you will overcome and claim victory over evil."

"That makes me feel better about dealing with the enemy," Jock said, wrinkling his brow as he spotted Hickey walking toward them. "If only Hickey had run away from evil."

Suddenly twenty soldiers from each of the four brigades started walking toward the gallows, guarding Hickey as he walked defiantly between them. A chaplain accompanied Hickey to the scaffold, and they talked quietly for a few minutes. Hickey hunched his shoulders and wept as the chaplain turned to leave, but then quickly stood up straight and wiped the tears from his face, unwilling to show his weakness to the thousands of spectators gathered to witness his death.

As Hickey was escorted up the scaffold steps, he shouted, "Green! Unless he's very cautious, the design will as yet be executed against *him!*"

Hickey's heart pounded as the executioner tied a blindfold around his eyes. He took several quick breaths and then clenched his jaw, anticipating the end.

"Look away, little one," Gillamon told Jock, holding the puppy's face to his chest as the hangman released the trap door where Hickey stood.

After a few moments of struggle, Thomas Hickey was dead.

HUNTINGTON, LONG ISLAND, NEW YORK, JUNE 28, 1776, NOON

Isaac Ketcham crested the hill, and his heart caught in his chest to see his six children out playing under the tree behind his house. He was free, he was home, and his children were safe. *It may not be as grand a home where Joseph went right from prison, but this is the only palace I need.* Tears filled his eyes as he lifted a hand and began running to them, calling, "Children! I'm home!"

The youngest girl spotted their father and squealed with joy! "Papa's home!" Together with her five siblings she ran toward the man, who dropped to his knees with his arms opened wide to embrace his precious children. They fell all over him with hugs, kisses, laughter, and tears.

"Oh, let me look at you!" Ketcham exclaimed with a relieved lump of joy in his throat to see each child in turn. "I'm so sorry to have left you, children. I promise I will never leave you again. I'm delighted to find you looking so healthy and happy. How did you manage alone?"

"The nice man said you'd be home soon!" a boy reported. "He brought us food every day."

Ketcham wrinkled his brow, at a loss to understand. "How? Who was he?"

"We don't know who he was, but he made sure we had everything we needed," the oldest boy explained.

"And he left something for you, too!" the youngest boy said, pulling on his father's hand. "Come see, papa!"

Together the children brought their father to the tree where a blanket was spread with a basket of food. They plopped down on the blanket, and the youngest boy tried to lift a heavy book from the basket. "It's heavy!"

Ketcham reached over to retrieve the book. It was a leatherbound copy of the Bible. His eyes widened in disbelief as he opened the book to the inside cover and read the inscription.

Train up a child in the way he should go: and when he is old, he will not depart from it. -Proverbs 22:6

"But who was the man who gave you this Bible and took care of you?" Ketcham wanted to know.

"He never told us his name, but he had kind, blue eyes," a girl answered with a grin, pointing to her eyes.

"And he talked funny," the youngest boy added with a giggle.

The oldest boy tapped the Bible. "There sure is a lot of paper in that book."

Ketcham couldn't believe what his children were saying. *The Dutchman? No, it couldn't be.* His heart swelled with relief and gratitude to know that his children were okay, and that he had been given a second chance to be the kind of man his children needed him to be. A *goot* man. He smiled. "Well, whoever he was, *this* will be the kind of paper I will use to teach you in our home from now on." His children gathered around him as he turned the pages to find the book of Esther. "Starting with the story of a man named Mordecai."

HEADQUARTERS, MANHATTAN, NEW YORK, JUNE 28, 1776, 3:00 P.M.

After the heavy events of the morning, Washington returned to his military headquarters to continue the task before him—preparing for war. The general busied himself with correspondence, including a letter to John Hancock and writing the General Orders for the day. He reread what he had penned for distribution to every soldier in the Continental Army:

> *The unhappy Fate of Thomas Hickey, executed this day for Mutiny, Sedition and Treachery; the General hopes will be a warning to every Soldier, in the Army, to avoid those crimes, and all others, so disgraceful to the character of a Soldier, and pernicious to his country, whose pay he receives and Bread he eats—And in order to avoid those Crimes the most certain method is to keep out of the temptation of them, and particularly to avoid lewd Women, who, by the dying Confession of this poor Criminal, first led him into practices which ended in an untimely and ignominious Death.*

Washington tightened his mouth and exhaled through his nose. He regretted having had to execute Hickey, one of his favorite soldiers. The tragedy weighed heavily on his heart. Still, he knew they had chosen the right course of action. He prayed it would prevent any other young men from choosing the wrong path. He read over the rest of his General Orders and signed his name.

GWashington

Max and Jock sat in the corner. "The General must be sad," Jock whispered. "Aye, of course he is, lad," Max agreed. "Somethin' would be wrong if he weren't. Nothin' stings like bein' betr-r-rayed. Then he had ta give the ulti-mate punishment ta one of his own soldiers."

"The Continental Army isn't what he hoped it would be so far, is it?" Jock asked. "He's tried to make them good soldiers who will fight with bravery and honor. But so many have let him down."

Max nodded his head. "Aye, but it's all he's got ta face a powerful enemy comin' here ta New York. But Washington does have a small band of br-r-roth-ers with him, even though they still may be diamonds in the r-r-rough."

Suddenly an urgent knock sounded on the door, and Joseph Reed entered Washington's office. He served as adjutant general, or the army's administra-tive head.

"Yes, Colonel Reed. What is it?" Washington asked.

"Sir, a British ship has been spotted heading toward Sandy Hook below New York Harbor," Reed reported, swallowing hard. "It's the *Greyhound.*"

Max's eyes widened. "That's General Howe's ship!"

Washington slowly pressed his hands into the desk and rose to his feet, wearing a serious expression. He straightened his waistcoat. "Then, Colonel Reed, we must expect more ships to follow. Call in my senior officers for a Council of War."

"Right away, General Washington," Reed responded before quickly leav-ing the room.

"What's happening?" Jock asked in alarm.

"The Commander-in-Chief of Br-r-ritish Forces in North America has jest arrived ta New York, an' he'll have a whole fleet of ships r-r-right behind him," Max answered gravely.

"That means *today* would have been the exact day for Governor Tryon's plot to kill Washington to start," Jock realized, wide-eyed. "Now I see why executing Hickey had to happen so fast."

"Aye, that were close. The Br-r-ritish aren't jest comin' ta New York any-more, lad," Max answered, staring at Washington. "They be HERE!"

PART TWO

FIGHTING WORDS

June 1776 – July 1776

16

First in the History of the World

WILLIAMSBURG, VIRGINIA, JUNE 12, 1776

"It's already hotter than the outskirts of *Hades* this morning!" MizP carped with a snort and a stomp of her hoof. Her ears twitched at the sound of a mosquito buzzing around her head. "And these blood suck-uhs are nothing but trouble, especially for humans."

Nigel swatted at a mosquito that tried to land on his head. "Indeed, MizP, mosquitoes are such *dreadful* scoundrels! Liz, why did not Noah rid the earth of these vile creatures when he had the chance?"

"Ain't that the truth?!" MizP agreed.

"It was not for Noah to destroy but to save the Maker's creations," Liz answered with a frown, swishing her tail back and forth. "Even the pesky ones."

"Well, I'm glad you and Nigel have returned despite this Virginia heat and her pests, including the human ones in that Capitol building," MizP told them. "They've finally finished bickering over the Virginia Declaration of Rights enough tuh pass it today, but now they're bickering about the Virginia Constitution. Pahtrick has had tuh remain cool despite the heat."

"Do tell us the details, MizP. Who have been the pests?" Liz asked.

"The usual suspects, I presume?" Nigel asked. "Pendleton, Braxton, Nicholas?"

MizP nodded, her black mane flipping to the other side of her neck. "Archibald Cary was made head of a committee of thirty men tuh write those documents. Thirty men! How they evuh thought tuh get anything done with thirty men, I'll never know. There were too many ideas and not enough agreement on *anything*. Thank goodness George Mason rode intuh town with his pockets stuffed with ideas. He was late tuh the Convention but once he presented his plans for government, his swallowed up all the rest."

"*Oui*, we read *Monsieur* Mason's draft of the Declaration of Rights while in Philadelphia," Liz told MizP. "*Monsieur* Jefferson may even use that draft as he writes the Declaration of Independence!"

MizP whinnied happily. "Well, that makes this old mare happier than a lightning bug at dusk!"

"We could tell that Mason had pulled from the Magna Carta, the 1689 Bill of Rights, and philosophers like Voltaire and Rousseau, but do you know how George Mason came up with his list of rights?" Nigel wanted to know. "Did he have help?"

"Mason worked in a room at the Raleigh Tavern and wrote most all of it, but did have help from Thomas Ludwell Lee, that new young 'un-James Madison, and of course our Pahtrick Henry. The committee narrowed down the list of rights from eighteen tuh sixteen," MizP explained. "But that Carter Braxton thinks independence is nothing more than bait concealing the hook of a purely democratic government! He wants tuh keep the old type of British government, and Pendleton agrees with him, saying that a democracy that empowers the PEOPLE at large is the *worst* form of government possible! Pendleton actually said he prefers the English Constitution, since it combines the principles of honor, virtue, and *fear!*"

Liz's tail slapped the railing. "The thought of ruling people by fear angers me. Respect for authority, *oui*. Fear, *non!* This old system of keeping humans stuck in a certain level of society must end. Humans must be free to pursue whatever they wish to become with the skills and gifts the Maker has given them. Life, liberty, and the pursuit of . . . happiness."

"Well, I'm sure Patrick has continued to lead the charge to tear down that old Tidewater mentality of hereditary privilege and concentrated power in the hands of a few at the expense of hapless souls with no say," Nigel spoke out.

"Of course Pahtrick has! He believes in representative government *by* and *for* the people, and the rule of *law,* not privilege, tuh run society," stated MizP.

"Why, MizP, you sound as if you've been studying the law yourself," Nigel quipped, patting the horse on the neck.

"It's hard not tuh pick up Pahtrick's thinking after hearing him speak his mind," MizP pointed out. "But of course, he happens tuh be right, and the common people have always thought so. They'll follow him wherever he leads."

"*Oui,* so if Virginia needs to be at the head of this business of forming a new government, *mon* Henry needs to be at the head of *Virginia* as Governor," Liz declared. "I have thought about this ever since he had to step down as Colonel in February, and I now see how important Patrick has become to the future of not just Virginia but America as a whole!"

MizP's eyes widened. "You mean tuh tell me Pahtrick could be living in the Governor's Palace down the street?"

"Well, *oui,* but where he lives is not as important as what he does as

Governor," Liz answered with a coy smile. "But I must confess I like the idea of *mon* Henry moving in and taking over the house where that pesky Lord Dunmore declared him an outlaw."

"It does have a bit of poetic justice to it," Nigel offered, preening his whiskers. "The revolutionary outlaw moving in and taking over not only the Palace but the reins of power! But before we get to that step, which will no doubt come from the new Virginia Constitution, let us hear of Patrick Henry's involvement with the Declaration of Rights."

"Well, the two hot buttons with the Declaration of Rights have been slavery and religion, and Pahtrick sees freedom of religion as the key tuh both," MizP told them. "He *hates* slavery and thinks if this country offers complete freedom tuh worship, skilled workers will pour intuh America from the old world and eventually end dependence on slave labor. Pahtrick knows this will take time tuh change, and there are no easy answers, but he knows we have tuh start somewhere. When they started debating the draft, they argued a week over just the wording that first suggested freedom tuh slaves. That Edmund Pendleton finally came up with the idea tuh say that 'all men are by nature equally free and independent' but only enjoy certain rights 'when they enter intuh a state of society.'"

"And since slaves are not considered 'part of the society' to which the declaration applies, they are excluded," Nigel realized with a frown. He shook his head. "It is a poor excuse but sadly the only one they had in order to begin the process of independence. Regrettably, this issue of slavery will not be settled until America has first secured her independence."

"The humans have to hold their noses and muddle through terrible compromises," Liz lamented. "I do not like it, but this will simply have to do for now."

"You're both right. So, once they passed the slavery obstacle, they next had tuh deal with religion. And since Pahtrick has fought for religious freedom by defending the dissenters from the Church of England, everyone knows how passionate he is about that. The last two articles deal with virtue and religion. Mason wrote the fifteenth. Madison wrote the sixteenth, but Pahtrick introduced it and worked tuh make it *stronger*. Instead of just *tolerating* religious beliefs of others, Pahtrick pushed for the *right* of full religious liberty," MizP told them. "I suggest you two get tuh the Capitol for the vote. Pahtrick says this list of rights will be the foundation on which the new government will rest."

"Oh, I cannot wait to see the final document!" Liz cheered.

"Shall we away, my dear?" Nigel asked.

"*Oui,* and we shall see you later, MizP!" Liz answered, jumping off the fence with Nigel.

"Enjoy the rights and then work on getting Pahtrick intuh the Palace," MizP called after them. A horsefly bit her on the rump, causing her to kick up a hind leg. "If Noah had been wise, he woulda swatted both of those mosquitoes *and* two flies!"

FIFTH VIRGINIA CONVENTION, CAPITOL BUILDING, WILLIAMSBURG, VIRGINIA

"From what MizP said, it appears they have the most important rights addressed," Nigel whispered to Liz.

Liz looked out at Patrick Henry, who waited for the reading of the Virginia Declaration of Rights preceding the official vote. *"Oui,* but I am sure that *mon* Henry would prefer to have as many specific rights detailed with ink. He knows that unless things are explicitly written down and protected, then power-hungry humans will ever seek to trample those rights and have their way over others."

"Indeed. Let's see how well they have done to cover the fundamentals," Nigel suggested as the secretary began reading the list. "Article one guarantees the equal right of all men to freedom and independence."

"Once they have entered into *a state of society,* " Liz lamented. "Article two declares all power to be entrusted to and derived from the people."

"The third, that government should be for the common welfare and happiness of the people based on majority rule," Nigel summarized. "Splendid! The fourth replaces filling offices held by inheritance with *merit*—as it should be!"

Liz nodded. "Article five wisely separates the branches of government: legislative, executive, and judicial, and the sixth guarantees freedom of elections."

Nigel tapped his chin thoughtfully as he considered the next. "Article seven declares that the power of suspending laws should be exercised only by the body to which is entrusted the power of making laws. Good show, that one."

"The next few protect citizens from unjust treatment in criminal cases," Liz noted. "The eighth guarantees trial by jury in criminal cases, the ninth prohibits excessive bail and cruel punishments, the tenth prohibits general warrants, broad and lacking specifics, and the eleventh poses a jury trial as the best way to settle civil suits."

"Ah, and this one is especially dear to our hearts, my dear!" Nigel pointed out, squeezing Liz's arm. "Article twelve secures the freedom of the press!"

"Including *Anonymouse* articles, no?" Liz replied with a giggle. "Article thirteen declares a trained militia as the proper means for defending a free state, and that the military should report to the civil power. Although this was difficult for *mon* Henry as Colonel, it is an important safety measure to keep military commanders in check. I am glad the Congress agrees, and that General Washington must do the same, no?"

"Indeed, as long as that civil power is *balanced,*" Nigel agreed. At least Washington has John Adams as an ally on the Board of War going forward. Let's see now, Article fourteen logically prohibits the creation of a separate government within the bounds of Virginia."

"And now we get to the last two!" Liz cheered expectantly as the secretary read them aloud:

"Article Fifteen: That no free government, or the blessings of liberty, can be preserved to any people but by a firm adherence to justice, moderation, temperance, frugality, and virtue and by frequent recurrence to fundamental principles."

"*Magnifique! Mon* Henry always stresses that without virtue, government will not last," Liz reminded her mouse friend.

"He is quite right!" Nigel affirmed. "Here comes the final article with his signature affixed to its words."

"Article Sixteen: That religion, or the duty which we owe to our Creator and the manner of discharging it, can be directed by reason and conviction, not by force or violence; and therefore, all men are equally entitled to the free exercise of religion, according to the dictates of conscience; and that it is the mutual duty of all to practice Christian forbearance, love, and charity toward each other."

"This takes the biscuit!" Nigel cheered. "No longer shall humans have to get permission to worship as they choose. I am sure the Baptist ministers will especially rejoice at this one!"

"*Oui!* They will not have to be defended in court or go to prison for preaching their beliefs," Liz added. "I am sure that *mon* Henry will not be saddened to lose them as clients."

"Indeed not! I believe that Patrick Henry would be thrilled to work himself out of a job for each and every protected right granted to the people," Nigel agreed.

Liz and Nigel hugged as the delegates reached the unanimous vote to pass the Virginia Declaration of Rights and happily congratulated one another on the historic accomplishment.

"A firm foundation has been laid for a new government," Liz noted proudly.

"Now to erect the frame," Nigel added. "With a new Virginia Constitution."

WILLIAMSBURG, VIRGINIA, JUNE 29, 1776

"He did it!" Liz exulted, jumping up onto the fence railing and hugging MizP around the neck. "Patrick Henry is the first officially elected Governor of Virginia, 60 to 45!"

"I knew he'd beat that Thomas Nelson, Sr.!" MizP whinnied, stomping her foot happily. "I'm so excited and proud of him, I could run tuh Georgia and back!"

Liz giggled. "I am certain you could, MizP! This is a happy day!"

"I'm sorry Nigel had tuh leave, but I suppose with so much going on between Philadelphia and Williamsburg, it was best tuh divide and conquer," MizP told Liz. "That little mouse was itching tuh get back tuh Thomas Jefferson as he drafts the Declaration of Independence."

Liz nodded. "Besides, there was nothing left to do, as things finally came together here. George Mason drafted the Constitution using John Adams's plan that Patrick had published in the *Virginia Gazette.*"

"Did the Convention use any of Thomas Jefferson's ideas that he sent along?" MizP asked. "I know his draft arrived just as the delegates were ready tuh wrap up this business and get out of town."

"*Oui,* Mason's plan had already been printed and was ready for a vote when George Wythe arrived from Philadelphia with Jefferson's plan," Liz relayed. "No one wished to rehash every point that Jefferson posed, but they did use his detailed charges against King George III as the preamble to the Virginia Constitution, plus a few minor refinements and suggestions."

"So, what will Virginia's government look like?" MizP asked.

"Virginia's government will have three branches: legislative, executive, and judicial," Liz answered. "The legislative branch will be elected by the people and have a lower house of delegates and an upper house of senators. The legislative branch will elect the governor for no more than three consecutive one-year terms as well as elect his advisory council. Of course, *mon* Henry was not pleased that the governor will have limited power in some areas, especially with veto power. He fought quite hard against this, but the fear of tyranny from Lord Dunmore and King George was still too fresh for the delegates to change their minds."

"And I'm sure Edmund Pendleton and his friends are just as afraid of Pahtrick having power over them as Lord Dunmore," MizP scoffed.

"This is true, *oui,* so although they did not listen to Patrick's advice to give the governor more power, he agreed to serve," Liz replied. "I wish you could have heard him, *mon amie.* After the Convention voted on the Virginia Constitution, Patrick shot to his feet in triumph and exclaimed, 'Never before in the history of mankind have citizens been privileged to hear such a remarkable truth: 'No longer are you beholden to your government. Your government is now beholden to you.'"

"Virginia is starting out on the right foot with Pahtrick, who will be an *excellent* governor," MizP declared.

"Do you realize what *mon* Henry has accomplished, even before independence has been declared for the thirteen colonies?" Liz asked, suddenly overcome with a sense of awe. "Because Virginia has already declared her independence from Great Britain and written her own Declaration of Rights and Constitution, that makes Patrick Henry the *first* elected governor of a *free* republic under a *written* constitution in the history of the *world!*"

"Why am I not surprised?" MizP chuckled. "Pahtrick has always been first in *my* world."

"*Moi aussi,*" Liz agreed with a grin. "I suppose we shall have to share him with the rest of the world, no?"

"I shall agree tuh that only because we'll be moving intuh the Palace," MizP quipped, flicking her ears against a buzzing mosquito. "Maybe there won't be any mosquitoes at *those* fancy stables."

"Well, there is a pond behind the Palace, so I am certain the mosquitoes will be just as pesky there, MizP," Liz told her, giggling.

"Humph, as long as Pahtrick is happy, I'll be happy," MizP promised. "Do you think we'll move in soon?"

"No. Since General Lee and his men occupied the Palace after Lord Dunmore's hasty departure, I believe some work must be done to prepare for Governor Patrick Henry to reside there," Liz answered, smiling. "I assume you will briefly return to Scotchtown, and of course, he must be first sworn in as Governor a few days from now."

"Governor Pahtrick Henry. I do love the sound of that!" MizP exclaimed.

"Now that you have the good news, I must join Nigel in Philadelphia for the exciting events in Congress," Liz announced. "Hopefully we will be able to return for Patrick's official ceremony. I would not want to miss that, no? But first, it is time for America to follow Virginia and declare her independence!"

MizP shook her mane. "And that will be another first evuh in the history of the world."

17

Thirteen Clocks

JACOB GRAFF HOUSE, PHILADELPHIA, PENNSYLVANIA, JUNE 25, 1776

The tick-tock of the mantel clock grew louder with each passing moment as Thomas Jefferson waited for Benjamin Franklin or John Adams to speak. He walked over to open the window, letting in a warm breeze. He then strolled back to his chair and took a seat, crossing his legs and his arms.

"Tart words make no friends," Benjamin Franklin uttered as a fly flew in and buzzed around his head. He slowly twirled around in Jefferson's revolving chair and swatted at the fly with a page of the draft of the Declaration of Independence. "And a spoonful of honey will catch more flies than a gallon of vinegar." He stopped and looked at Thomas, who sat restlessly over in another chair, watching as he and John Adams reviewed his draft. "But Mr. Jefferson, your words for King George and the British people are anything but sweet. Why they have so attracted this fly, I do not know."

Nigel looked on from the molding high above them on the windowsill. He held a paw over his mouth to quiet a chuckle. Ben Franklin's wit never ceased to amuse him. The little mouse was happy to finally see his hero here, as a bad case of gout had kept Franklin home and missing many of the meetings not only of Congress but of the Committee of Five as they discussed Jefferson's work.

"There are indeed words and expressions in this document that I personally would not have inserted myself," John Adams piped up, then added, "but I shall defend every word you have written, Mr. Jefferson. Well done, Sir."

Jefferson shrugged his shoulders. "Some may think I overstepped my bounds with making the case for King George as a tyrant, but it is what I believe."

"I do agree that the King acted outside the bounds of law on the basis of bad advice from his advisors but was cruel only in an *official* capacity," Adams noted, "not in his *personal* character, which for me would make him a tyrant also by his *nature.*"

"Well, the Congress will decide what to make of King George III,"

Franklin interjected. "But I must prepare you, Mr. Jefferson. The southern states will not take kindly to your references to slavery."

"The institution of slavery is evil and must be abolished," Jefferson retorted with a frown.

Franklin held up his hand. "I *agree* with you entirely, as do many in Congress. But we must proceed step by step. We unfortunately cannot correct every fault in this land with a single stroke of the pen."

"If we lose the southern colonies at the outset, America cannot unite for independence and the war to win it," John Adams added. "Independence *must* come first in order to end slavery on these shores. I know that Patrick Henry and some of your other fellow Virginians wish for the institution of slavery to die on the vine, leading to full emancipation, but Virginia's sisters to the southward do not yet share such a vision. Just as it has taken time for the American people to come around to supporting independence, it will take time for them to come around to ending slavery."

Jefferson got up with a frown and pointed to the table. "Every word in this declaration was carefully chosen."

"And I *laud* you for it," Franklin offered, trying to assuage Jefferson's sensitive reaction. "We shall see what the Congress does with the major portions of this draft. For now, I propose that we and the Committee of Five focus on the preamble."

John Adams nodded. "I concur, Dr. Franklin." He held up page one, glancing over the second paragraph. "We hold these truths to be *sacred and undeniable.*"

Franklin swatted at the fly again. "But rather than 'sacred and undeniable . . .'" He contorted his mouth, searching for his words. "These truths are . . . self-evident, are they not?"

John Adams looked at Franklin and then at Jefferson. "Indeed, life, liberty, and the pursuit of happiness are naturally desired and recognized by every soul."

"Happiness inherently requires safety and security," Jefferson stated, sitting back down in his chair, and crossing his arms. "But they shall sit every man under his vine and under his fig tree; and none shall make them afraid . . ."

"Micah 4:4," Nigel mumbled, finishing the verse that Jefferson quoted. "For the mouth of the Lord of hosts hath spoken it."

"Self-evident," Benjamin Franklin repeated, reaching for Veritas's feather to dip in the ink. "We hold these truths to be *self-evident.* Shall I make that substitution?"

Jefferson shrugged his shoulders. "If you think it proper."

John Adams gave a resolute nod to Ben Franklin. "Self-evident."

Nigel watched Jefferson sigh as Franklin scratched through 'sacred and undeniable' and wrote 'self-evident' above. "No author enjoys being edited, Mr. Jefferson. It is painful at the time but ultimately produces a beautiful result," stated the little mouse.

After a couple of hours, it was time for Franklin and Adams to depart.

Everyone was exhausted, but no one more so than Jefferson.

"What do you gentlemen foresee with the vote for independence?" Jefferson asked as the men stood to leave.

"That is *not* self-evident," Benjamin Franklin quipped. He winced as he took a step to the door on his sore foot. "We still need to deliver Maryland, Delaware, New Jersey, New York, and my fellow Pennsylvanians. But I doubt John Dickinson will ever come over to our side to vote for independence."

"But the vote must be *unanimous* before we can even discuss this declaration," Jefferson said flatly. He lifted the now-marked-up draft from the table. "This paper might never see the light of day in the full Congress."

"Timing is everything, Mr. Jefferson, and I believe we can convince the other colonies to join us," Adams offered hopefully. "Some people must have time to look around them, before, behind, on the right hand, and on the left, and then to think, and after all this to resolve. Others see at one intuitive glance into the past and future, and judge with precision at once." The round-faced Patriot took his hat in hand and pointed to the mantel clock that continued its ceaseless tick-tocking. "But remember you can't make thirteen clocks strike precisely alike at the same second."

18

Busted Britches and Splintered Ships

BREACH INLET, SOUTH CAROLINA,
JUNE 28, 1776, 9:30 A.M.

Colonel Moultrie winced as he rode his horse to Breach Inlet to check on Colonel Thomson, his men, and their fortifications. His leg was stiff with gout that had been acting up. He tried to pay it no mind as he galloped through the live oaks covered in Spanish moss that hung over the sandy road.

The middle-aged colonel was dressed in his blue coat with scarlet facings, white breeches, and a black feather in his three-cornered hat. General Lee had continued to be critical of his fortifications and especially of his light-handed manner of disciplining his men, but President Rutledge had stuck to his guns about the guns stationed at Fort Sullivan. The "slaughter pen" would be fully operational during the coming attack, and they would not abandon it as Lee suggested. Still, Moultrie shared the critical general's concerns about their low supply of ammunition. He calculated that they only had two tons of gunpowder in their magazine, which would allow only about twenty-six rounds fired from each of his thirty-one guns, with just enough left to make about twenty musket cartridges for each defending soldier. They would have to make do the best they could against the three hundred guns of His Majesty's Royal Navy that would soon be firing ten times that much firepower at their small palmetto fort.

As Moultrie reached a clearing of myrtle trees near the inlet, he squinted against the bright sunlight on the water but immediately noticed a small number of boats carrying British soldiers down Hamlin Creek between the mainland and the western shore of Long Island. As he rode up to where the Patriots were dug in, Colonel Thomson met him with an upraised hand of greeting.

"Good morning, Colonel. What do you make of that flotilla of boats?" Moultrie asked, pointing to the marshy waters on their left flank.

Thomson pulled out his spyglass for a closer look. "Well . . ." he started to say but was interrupted by a warning shout from the sand dunes on their right flank facing the sea.

"British ships at Five Fathom Hole have loosened their topsails!" the sentry called out. "They're inbound on the rising tide!"

Moultrie and Thomson shared quick glances of alarm. "Prepare your men to engage, Colonel! Battle posts, NOW!" Moultrie exclaimed as he quickly turned his horse to gallop the three miles back to Fort Sullivan. The attack was finally at hand.

HMS BRISTOL, JUNE 28, 1776, 10:00 A.M.

The ship's bell finished ringing to bring all hands on deck. Smithy stood next to Tarleton, clearly nervous. He took in a deep breath and puffed out his cheeks as he let it go. "This is it, Ban."

"What perfect weather for a fight!" Tarleton exclaimed, gripping the ship's rails, and squinting against the bright sunlight reflecting off the water. He wasn't nervous. He was ready for action. "Courage, Smithy. The officers think the rebels will only withstand our guns for thirty minutes. It will be quick work."

The sun was already high on this cloudless, gorgeous summer day. The winds had been contrary the past few days, repeatedly delaying the attack. But today conditions were finally right for Sir Peter Parker. At 9:30 a.m. he had raised the signal flag to notify General Clinton that they would weigh anchor within the hour.

"Listen up, men. Understand the types of artillery shells that the rebel guns will fire toward our fleet," Parker began, shouting from the quarterdeck so the men sprawled out across the ship could hear him. "Expect solid iron balls to try to hit us at the waterline to make holes in the hull, chain shot to cut sails and rigging, hot shot balls to set the fleet on fire, and grapeshot to inflict the most damage to personnel."

Smithy gulped and Tarleton stood stoically with his arms crossed over his chest.

"Some of you volunteers have been instructed to remain belowdecks for now and out of the way of seamen manning the guns and climbing rigging," Parker explained. "*Thunder* is already sailing into position to begin the attack, accompanied by *Friendship*. We will sail the *Bristol, Solebay, Active,* and *Experiment* close to the fort so sailors positioned in the masts can fire small arms fire at the platforms where rebels will be manning their guns.

Meanwhile, the *Sphinx, Actaeon,* and *Syren* will sail to our left flank through the channel and attack the vulnerable rear of the fort."

Al hid out of sight back under the steps and covered his ears. He hated hearing about the coming destruction. A small, yellow butterfly found its way over to his hiding spot and landed on his nose, slowly opening and closing its wings. "Pssst. It's me, Al," Clarie whispered. Al looked up, cross-eyed, at the delicate creature. "Thanks for the intelligence, Al. Knowing that Clinton was going to try to attack Haddrell's Point once the *Sphinx, Actaeon,* and *Syren* crossed the bar is exactly what I needed to know to finish my plan."

"At least there's one happy thing to hear," Al whined. "Wait, what plan, lass?"

"I'll be the head harbor pilot to lead the three ships through the channel," she answered. "I'll be on the *Actaeon.*"

"Ye mean, ye're goin' to help them attack the spongy fort from behind?!" Al protested. "What are ye thinkin'?"

"Don't worry, Al," Clarie consoled him. "Trust me. Clinton and Cornwallis won't be able to do anything but try to row their fifteen flat-bottomed boats along Breach Inlet, but they'll look like a trail of anxious ducklings scurrying back to Long Island once Thomson's guns start firing. Clinton and Cornwallis will have to just stand on the beach and watch everything out here unfold through a spyglass."

"I thought I wanted to be here at sea with Tarleton and off that island o' terrible beasties, but now I wish I were back there hidin' in the sand dunes," Al lamented, his lip quivering. "I never should have snuck aboard. It's goin' to get rough here, ain't it, lass?"

"Yes, it's going to get rough, but you can handle it with the Maker. Steady, Al," Clarie encouraged him. "Get down to Cornwallis's cabin and stay there. I'll check in with you later."

"The honor of the Royal Navy is at stake, but I have no doubt that you shall perform admirably this day," Parker encouraged his men who answered back with a round of 'HUZZAH!'s. The commodore smiled and lifted his chin, raising a fist of anticipated triumph. "And I know we shall deliver such a fiery message to these rebels that they will *beg* to return to His Majesty's sovereign rule! Man your battle stations, and Godspeed!"

Parker gave the nod, and a seaman fired the signal gun, instructing the fleet to get underway. Sailors hurriedly climbed the towering masts of the nine warships, looking like a beehive in the rigging as they loosened the topsails. The brisk southwest wind snapped the canvas taut and filled the sails. Sir Peter Parker's fleet caught the strong tide, and off they sailed toward Fort Sullivan.

FORT SULLIVAN, SOUTH CAROLINA, JUNE 28, 1776, 10:00 A.M.

Upon reaching Fort Sullivan, Colonel Moultrie lumbered down from his horse and shouted for the drummer to beat the long roll, calling every man to his post. He rushed from gun to gun, instructing his men, "When the enemy shall come within the reach of your guns, you are to distress them in every shape to the utmost of your powers."

Moultrie looked out at the horizon and saw the bomb ketch *Thunder* positioning itself about a mile and a half from the fort. He saw a single burst of fire and heard the thunderous concussion of the gun firing a mortar. "Incoming!" he shouted as they watched a 13-inch mortar shell hurled into the summer sky, making a perfect arc before it landed with a splash in the ocean.

"It's short!" a soldier exclaimed with a grin. "Why are they positioned so far from us?"

A bombardment of sixty more shells would follow, with some exploding in the air like fireworks, and others landing in the sea, but they soon began to get into closer range as the *Thunder's* gunners added more powder to the charges. Suddenly a shell traced across the blue sky heading directly toward the powder magazine.

"Take cover!" Moultrie shouted.

The men covered their heads and braced for impact, but all that came was a solitary thud. The shell made a direct hit on the entire store of gunpowder, but nothing happened.

"The shell failed to detonate!" a soldier exclaimed. Another incoming shell landed with a thud in the sand, getting completely buried without harm. More shells followed, landing harmlessly until one shell finally made its way through an opening and exploded, sending mortar fragments flying.

"It's not bad!" exclaimed a slightly wounded soldier. "I'm alright."

"But *they* aren't!" another soldier shouted, pointing to a pen where they kept poultry.

"Sir, three ducks, two geese, and a turkey have been slain," a soldier reported to Moultrie.

Moultrie humorously shook his head in disbelief at the only casualties from the opening salvos of the British Royal Navy. "Well, hopefully they'll keep for dinner."

The colonel turned his spyglass to the other ships that seemingly had stopped short and dropped anchor at four hundred yards distant. *Active* was first in line, with *Bristol, Experiment,* and *Solebay* anchored astern, their broadsides open to Fort Sullivan and preparing to fire. Moultrie grinned at the sight and turned to his men. "Okay, men, let them have it!"

The Patriots began firing, but only four guns at a time to conserve powder. They would proceed with slow, steady aim to fire every kind of shot that Peter Parker had told his men to expect. But the Patriot guns *found* their mark, sending English oak splintering in every direction and fiery, tangled rigging crashing down upon British heads. The rebel gunners shed their jackets and wiped black powdery grime and sweat from their faces as they passed fire buckets of grog to quench their parched thirst. They listened for Moultrie's orders of exactly where to take aim, making every round count. "Mind the commodore! Mind the two 50-gun ships!"

The British guns began returning fire at the fort, and just like Archer, their cannonballs bounced off the spongy palmetto trunks, splintering them. Other balls sank into the logs without effect. Other shells simply landed with a thud and got swallowed up by the sand. A few rounds did find their way to the Patriots through open embrasures, killing and wounding a few, but the Americans kept their composure and discipline, staying cool and unafraid. In the coming hours, the fort shook from the impact but remained solid despite the barrage of thousands of rounds now falling on its heroic, humble palmetto logs.

⚜

FIVE FATHOM HOLE, SOUTH CAROLINA, JUNE 28, 1776, NOON

Peter Parker and every ship's captain in the British fleet were in stunned disbelief at the firepower coming from the simple rebel fort. Ship jack-tars (as sailors were known) repeatedly kept up the fight, sponging, loading, and igniting the British guns, sending shock waves over the decks and rippling trousers. But man after man was hit by incoming shells, making the decks slick with blood. The air was filled with smoke and fire, and the screams of wounded men sounded between cannon volleys. Parker gave the signal for the *Actaeon, Sphinx,* and *Syren,* to sail around the fleet and take positions behind Fort Sullivan.

Clarie, now disguised as a local harbor pilot, stood at the railing near the helm of the *Actaeon* and directed Captain Christopher Atkins through the shallow stretch of shoals at the entrance to the Rebellion Road channel. Before leaving England, Atkins had vowed to 'give those fantastic scoundrels a good banging who have dared to treat the mother country with impunity and ingratitude.' She grinned as she studied the emerald waters, taking soundings of the water depth and thinking about Atkin's boast. But little did he or the other humans know that she also was directing a pod of dolphins that hugged the ship on either side.

Rafe stood at the railing of the bow (at the front of the ship), watching the death and destruction unfolding from the cannon duel between the humans. He reveled in it. As he leaned on the railing, grinning at the carnage, the ship suddenly struck a sandbar, almost sending him over the side.

"Ship's run aground!" came the shouts of sailors as they tried to wave off the *Sphinx,* sailing right into the same shoal next to the *Actaeon.* The riggings of the two ships became entangled as they leaned on their sides in a blundering heap. The *Sphinx* kept its distance from the two but also ran aground. Chaos ensued as the crews from all three ships scrambled to free the men-o'-war from the sandbars that had stopped them in their attempt to reach the back side of Fort Sullivan.

Clarie quietly leaned over the side and waved a hand to the dolphins, who swam away, saluting her with their fins by slapping the water. They had pushed the *Actaeon* farther onto the shoal than the other two ships. The humans could try as they might to rock her free, but the *Actaeon* wasn't going anywhere.

⚜

FORT SULLIVAN, SOUTH CAROLINA, JUNE 28, 1776, 3:00 P.M.

Colonel Moultrie ordered the guns silenced at the fort after hearing a report that General Clinton had landed at the north end of Sullivan's Island. Until the report was confirmed, they needed to save their gunpowder, if it came down to a fight with the infantry. Meanwhile, the British ships continued their barrage of cannonballs, which sank or bounced off the palmetto fort.

Suddenly a ball hit the fort's flagstaff and the indigo blue crescent liberty flag fell to the sand. Sergeant William Jasper saw the flag fall and cupped a hand to call over to Colonel Moultrie, "Colonel! Don't let us fight without our flag!"

"What can you do? The staff is broke," Moultrie called back.

"Then, sir," Jasper cried, "I'll fix it to a halbert, and place it on a merlon of the bastion, next to the enemy!" He quickly jumped down from one of the embrasures and ran along the entire length of the fort. When he reached the fallen flag, he detached it from the mast, and looked up to see Captain Horry standing behind one of the merlons, or upright sections of the parapet. "Captain Horry! Throw me a sponge staff!"

Horry immediately threw him the staff and Jasper tied the flag to it with a heavy cord. The men watched in amazement as Jasper ran back through a shower of cannonballs and planted the staff on the merlon. He took off his hat and waved it to the men who started cheering wildly. "God save Liberty and my country forever."

"HUZZAH! HUZZAH! HUZZAH!" the men cheered as Jasper ran back to rejoin his gun crew.

Moultrie raised his fist in victory, joining the cheering men. Then he pulled out his spyglass to search the *Thunder,* whose guns had now fallen silent. The concussion of the ship's overcharged guns had ripped opened the ship's heavy beams, and sailors were busy bailing water. "The *Thunder* is out of action!" He next turned his spyglass over to see the *Actaeon, Sphinx,* and *Syren* now struggling on the shoals. He couldn't believe what he saw. "AND, three ships have run aground on the sandbar!" More HUZZAHS! sounded from the encouraged Patriots. *Heaven be praised!*

Around 4:30 p.m., a messenger came with the good news that not only was the report of Clinton's landing false, but President Rutledge had sent over five hundred pounds of powder.

"Okay, men, have at it, we have powder!" Moultrie exclaimed, spying out the *Bristol.* "Train your guns on the flagship and Commodore Parker! And use chain shot at her masts."

The commander wiped his brow and took out his pipe, relieved, encouraged, and confident. The battle was still raging, but things were shifting in their favor.

At 5:00 p.m. General Lee came walking into the fort, this time without his dogs. "Colonel Moultrie. I decided to come out from Charleston and see how you men are making out."

Colonel Moultrie smiled. "Our fort is holding solid, General. General Clinton's forces have been unable to attack by land. The *Thunder* has burst her seams and is no longer firing." He held his pipe out at the three ships stuck on the sandbar. "And those three were attempting to sail behind our unfinished fort, as you had feared. Had these three ships effected their purpose, they would have enfiladed us in such a manner as to have driven us from our guns."

"But those ships have been *stopped* by the shoals," Lee observed with a grin and a nod of satisfaction, walking around to inspect the guns. "I understand President Rutledge's powder has arrived, and more is on the way. I'm also sending the 8th Virginia up to bolster Thomson's men at Breach Inlet."

"Thank you, General!" Moultrie exclaimed. "I'm sure they will be welcomed reinforcements."

"The real slaughter pen is not this fort, but what's happening aboard those ships," Lee said, gazing out to the fleet that looked to be a sheet of fire and smoke hovering over the water. "I see you are doing very well here, and you have no occasion for me. I will go up to the town again where the people are perched atop every roof, steeple, and high point they can reach to watch the battle. Carry on."

"Thank you, Sir," Colonel Moultrie answered humbly. After Lee walked off, Moultrie watched the general talk to his battle-weary men, infusing them with encouragement and bolstering their fighting spirit. *His coming among us was equal to a reinforcement of one thousand men.*

HMS BRISTOL, JUNE 28, 1776, 5:00 P.M.

"AHHHHHHHH!" Al screamed, his paws covering his flattened ears from the deafening barrage of cannon fire coming from the quarterdeck. He hid under the small set of steps leading to the raised poop deck at the stern of the ship. Peter Parker ran between the six cannons positioned on the quarterdeck, shouting orders as the exhausted sailors toiled at loading the guns on the blood-slick deck. The fearful cat squeezed his eyes shut to block out the scene. "Oh, why did I have to pick this flagship, of the entire fleet, why?"

"You wanted the best food, remember?" came Clarie's voice next to him. She was once again in the form of a yellow butterfly, which was an odd, lovely sight amid such bloodshed and destruction aboard this battered warship. "I came to check on you, Al."

"Clarie?" Al whimpered with big green eyes wide with fear. He tried to grab her with his paw. "Please fly me away from here! I tried stayin' in the cabin, but the windows blew out, so I ran out here! There's no place for a kitty to run!"

"The best place for you is belowdecks, so get out of here! It's not much better down there in terms of carnage, but at least you'll be out of the line of fire," Clarie told him. "You won't have too much longer to endure the shelling, so just hang on, Al." She looked up as she saw an incoming shell heading for the quarterdeck. "Watch out!"

The shell suddenly exploded right next to the commodore, blowing off his britches while shrapnel ripped into everything in sight.

"Well, bust my britches, did ye see that?! Sir Peter Parker's pants jest flew right off!" Al exclaimed in shock. He didn't know whether to laugh or cry from the hilarious, albeit terrifying, scene, so he did both. Two sailors helped the commodore to the broad steps leading to the main deck. "I needed a bit o' comic relief, but I feel bad laughin' at the poor lad with his backside laid bare!"

"His pride is hurt worse than his body. Now make your way below and keep your head down, kitty!" Clarie told him. "Not too much longer." With that she left the frightened cat and fluttered back up into the air and over to the *Actaeon.*

HMS BRISTOL, JUNE 28, 1776, 9:00 P.M.

Governor Campbell sat belowdecks, wincing in pain from the huge, flying splinters that had struck his side. He had tried to be of use on the quarterdeck of this battered ship that was struck seventy times. Three Patriot cannonballs were embedded in the mainmast, and even more in the mizzenmast. Every man who had served on the quarterdeck was either killed or wounded. Commodore Peter Parker suffered not only the humiliation of losing his britches, but contusions and wounds to his knee and thigh from the exploding shell. *Bristol's* Captain John Morris was hit multiple times and died.

"Who remains on deck?" Campbell asked the surgeon tending to him, gritting his teeth.

"Twice the quarterdeck was cleared of every person except Sir Peter," the surgeon numbly answered, hastily extracting the large splinter from Campbell's torso. "Forty dead, and seventy-one wounded on this ship alone. It looks like a slaughterhouse up there."

Campbell clenched his jaw and shook his head, unable to believe what had happened to His Majesty's forces today. The rebels had handed the British fleet their first loss in over a century. The blood-splattered surgeon methodically bandaged up the governor's wound before moving on to the next injured soldier.

One final, defiant cannon blast sounded from Fort Sullivan, followed by the sound of more splintering wood. But the British cannons did not answer—this time they remained silent. The only sounds heard were the cries and moans of the wounded below and frantic shouts above. Peter Parker was ordering the withdrawal of the entire fleet back to Five Fathom Hole, out of range from the deadly Patriot guns that had shredded the royal ships while the spongy palmetto fort remained completely intact.

Bloody, grimy, and unkempt, Governor Campbell lay on the bunk and closed his eyes, holding his throbbing side. Listening to the screams of wounded men who filled the hull, his mind oddly raced back to a quotation Lord Cornwallis had shared with him while aboard *Bristol.* On February 10,1775, the arrogant Earl of Sandwich rose to his feet in the House of Commons and offered his thoughts on handling the American rebels. *Suppose the Colonies do abound with men, what does that signify? They are raw, undisciplined, cowardly men. Believe me, my Lords, the very sound of a cannon would carry them off . . . as fast as their feet could carry them.* Campbell opened his eyes and looked around at the bloody carnage that proved the Earl of Sandwich a presumptive fool. He shook his head in disbelief. *The very sound of a cannon made them stand their ground. WE are the ones now carried off . . . in defeat.*

Across the ship's makeshift hospital cabin stood an unharmed Banastre Tarleton, studying Campbell. He had remained belowdecks as instructed and heard the roar of guns for ten hours. He was in as much shock as every other redcoat in the fleet and thought back on every step of the last few weeks to understand how things had gone so terribly wrong. He knew that Cornwallis was at first consulted at Cape Fear by Clinton and Parker, but ultimately had little say in the final plan of attack. *Clinton never should have landed our troops on Long Island before verifying the hearsay of likely some rebel sympathizer who said we could cross Breach Inlet on foot.* The young officer shook his head. *Communication between the infantry and naval commanders disintegrated into nothing more than signal flags and intermittent messengers. That is no way to execute a battle. And unreliable harbor pilots kept our ships too far from the fort and stranded on the shoals.* He looked around at the dead and the dying and clenched his jaw at the absurd waste of it all. *Delays and bungling have turned victory into a fiasco. Accurate intelligence and clear, decisive, bold action is what is needed going forward.*

"Step aside!" ordered a seaman as he and another seaman carried a dead man to place him alongside the other casualties. It was Smithy.

"Death or glory," Tarleton muttered to himself in anger and disgust. He leaned down and closed Smithy's lifeless eyes with his hand. "This poor chap got death today."

Al's eyes brimmed as he looked from his darkened corner at Smithy and Tarleton. "And the Patriots got glory. But even glory cost them some o' their own Smithy's."

FIVE FATHOM HOLE, SOUTH CAROLINA, JUNE 29, 1776, 8:00 A.M.

It was no use. Despite their efforts, Parker's men were unable to pull the *Actaeon* off the shoal where she had run aground. So, Parker gave Captain Atkins permission to set the stranded ship on fire rather than allow the Patriots to have her. They evacuated most of the men aboard before setting her ablaze. Smoke soon enveloped the *Actaeon*, and the remaining men were coughing and shoving each other along as the ship caught fire. She would explode once the flames reached the barrels of gunpowder stored belowdecks. The men quickly scurried over the side into the last boat that would row them to safety. Strangely, the harbor pilot who had guided the ship calmly stood on the bow, clearly unconcerned and not attempting to escape the doomed ship with the rest of the crew.

As Rafe neared the rope ladder to climb down, he spotted the harbor pilot. "YOU FOOL!" he screamed, pointing an accusing finger. "YOU INCOMPETENT FOOL! This is all *your* fault! YOU were supposed to guide our three ships through the channel to get behind the pathetic rebel fort so we could attack! Because of YOU, we've not only lost the *Actaeon,* but we've lost the entire BATTLE! You deserve to burn to death!"

"GET MOVING, SOLDIER! Before I push you over the side!" an officer ordered.

The fierce grenadier grudgingly complied, swinging his leg over the railing to climb down. He paused as he hung on to the side, snarling at the harbor pilot who turned and glared right at him with striking blue eyes. *Wait—something is not right here. Who is that human?*

The harbor pilot wore a coy smile, lifted his hands, and shrugged his shoulders. "You're absolutely right, this *is* all my fault!" He calmly walked to the ship's railing and tapped it with a chuckle. "What a fitting end for a ship named for a Greek tragedy where the hunter became the hunted and was devoured by a pack of dogs! You of course can appreciate that more than most, can't you?" He saluted Rafe with a big grin and suddenly disappeared while a large brown pelican lifted off the deck and soared above the crippled British fleet.

Rafe was stunned. He took his seat in the boat and furiously looked at the pelican as they pulled away from the burning *Actaeon.* He clinched his fists and threw his head back screaming. "SEVEN!"

"Seven what?" asked a grimy soldier in the boat next to him.

"Seven victors, for *this* battle," Rafe answered through gritted teeth. He squinted out to sea toward the north. "But there's another Long Island where I will personally make sure they suffer a crushing defeat."

19

All London's Afloat

The sultry morning made Daniel McCurtin's sweaty shirt stick to his back. The Maryland rifleman had been standing sentry duty for hours on an elevated hill overlooking the harbor. He yawned, stretched out his back, and wiped the sweat from his brow with his sleeve. He took a drink of water from his canteen and picked up his rifle. "I'll be back in a bit, hey. I need to use the privy," he told his fellow soldiers on duty.

He climbed the stairs of the outhouse that had a window overlooking the harbor. After a few moments he gazed out the window and squinted as he viewed the horizon. "What *is* that?" he muttered to himself. "It looks like . . . a forest of pine trees." He rubbed his eyes and wiped the windowpane with his soggy sleeve. Slowly his eyes widened, and his heart dropped as he stared out at New York Harbor. Over the next ten minutes, he watched the bay fill with white sails that were attached to the 'forest of pine trees'—tall, countless masts rising from the decks of fifty British warships.

The soldier hurriedly stumbled down the stairs and back outside to point a finger at the bay, shouting the alarm, "All London's afloat!"

Colonel Henry Knox reached for the basket of biscuits to fill his breakfast plate for the demanding day ahead. The twenty-six-year-old had a hefty appetite to support his robust frame. He quickly slathered a biscuit with jam and bit into it with delight, eager to eat and get back to the difficult task of preparing artillery positions for the city. "Mmm, delicious."

"It's so beautiful here, even on this overcast day," twenty-year-old Lucy Knox said with a smile as she gazed out the palladium window where she and Henry regularly sat for their morning breakfast. She sighed contentedly to bask in this panoramic view while enjoying being with her husband despite the circumstances. Henry's view was of the northern trek of the river as it snaked its way along the banks of New Jersey and Manhattan. Lucy's view was the direction of New York Harbor spread out below toward the Narrows. "One would hardly know that war was coming."

Henry raised his eyebrows and mumbled, unable to speak with a mouthful of biscuit. He bobbed his head, chewed, and took a sip of coffee to wash it down. "My dear, you must understand that war *is* coming— any day! Now that General Howe's ship arrived yesterday, his fleet will be right behind him. While I am the happiest man on earth to have you and little Lucy here with me, I cannot abide the thought of my family being in danger. I must insist that you make plans to take Lucy and depart for Connecticut."

Lucy furrowed her brow with a pout. "But *Harry*, I feel so lost when I'm not with you! I already had to lose my own family and friends when we fled Boston before the siege. Of course, they had practically disowned me already for marrying a rebel, but I can't lose you, too!"

"Your father worked for General *Gage*, Howe's predecessor as Commander of British forces in North America," Henry reminded her, reaching out to take her hand in his. "I know it came as a shock and disappointment for such a high-ranking Loyalist as your father for his beloved daughter to marry a Patriot rebel. My dear Lucy, you chose a life of uncertainty by marrying me, and I cannot promise you anything but my undying love. But you must realize that you could *never* lose me—my heart will ever be with you regardless of whether we are together or not."

Lucy's heart melted at Henry's words. "Intreat me not to leave thee, or to return from following after thee: for whither thou goest, I will go; and where thou lodgest, I will lodge: thy people shall be my people, and thy God my God."

Henry squeezed Lucy's hand and sighed impatiently. "My love, while I adore your sentiments from the Holy Writ, I am not Naomi, you are not Ruth, and we are *not* in Moab," he started, feeling frustrated that he had been unable to make Lucy understand the seriousness of what was getting ready to happen. She so far had refused to leave his side despite his urging her to depart. He reached out a hand to New York Harbor. "As you can see, we are in *New York.*"

Lucy's gaze followed Henry's outstretched hand, and her eyes widened with fear. She didn't reply but silently lifted a trembling finger toward the bay.

"What is it?" Henry asked in alarm. He quickly turned to see what Lucy was seeing. He shot to his feet, grabbed his spyglass, and peered out the window down into New York Harbor.

There in the distance was the very thing Knox had been dreading. The expected fleet of British ships filled the harbor with white sails pushed along by a brisk northwest wind toward the mouth of the Hudson and East rivers. Henry's heart started racing, and sweat broke out on his brow.

A dozen alarm guns suddenly began to fire, and two cannons sounded their ground-shaking boom from the Grand Battery calling soldiers to battle stations. The windowpanes rattled in the palladium window, and baby Lucy started crying from the other room. Henry Knox collapsed his spyglass and grabbed his terrified wife by the elbow. "NOW DO YOU SEE!? Go pack this instant! No more arguing with me! If you had listened and left as I requested, you and little Lucy would not be in danger now! GO!" he scolded her out of sheer terror for the safety of his young family.

Lucy quickly nodded and began crying as she finally realized their peril. But she was also terrified to leave her husband to fight the British. What if he didn't survive the battle of New York? What would she do then? There was no time to argue, for there was no choice other than to escape New York with the other officers' wives and other reluctant citizens who had put off their departure. She ran to the other room to immediately throw her things and the baby's things together.

Knox opened his spyglass for another look at the harbor filling with white sails before rushing off to headquarters. "The enemy could be on our doorstep within half an hour!"

HMS GREYHOUND, LOWER BAY, NEW YORK, JUNE 29, 1776, 9:30 A.M.

General Howe stood on the quarterdeck of his ship, opened his spyglass, and gazed up at the high ground across from Manhattan over on Long Island. He could see rebels digging in and scurrying about like ants. He frowned, awash once more with the humiliation he had experienced when the rebels took the high ground in Boston and forced him to flee. *This time, I shan't let them keep the high ground,* he thought to himself. He lowered his spyglass to view the vessels in his fleet arriving from Halifax and saw them packed with soldiers eager to get off their transports and onto land. *This time, they will face His Majesty's forces face to face, not from a safe distance to simply lob cannonballs at our ships. And this time, we will CRUSH them once and for all!*

"General Howe, might I say again how *thrilled* I am to have you here to restore things to their proper order," Governor Tryon gushed, coming to stand next to the commander. He had come aboard to meet with Howe on the situation in New York. He pointed to the detachment of marines and sailors making landfall on the small beach at Sandy Hook. "Those spiteful rebels removed the lantern and all the oil from the lighthouse. Can you imagine?

They would rather your fleet crash onto rocks and shoals in darkness! I'm eager for you to exact revenge for how they've destroyed every inch of New York!"

Howe peered through his spyglass to watch the detachment of men carrying casks of whale oil along the beach to climb the seven-story lighthouse. He then looked back to the upper ridge on Long Island. "I, too, am eager to put down this rebellion, Governor, but we must wait for the rest of the royal fleet to arrive. I had planned to make a quick landfall over there on the beaches of Long Island at Gravesend Bay, but our scouts report that the rebels have infested that ridgeline above. Moving prematurely would be ill-advised. But when we land, we shall overwhelm the rebels with a show of force such as they have never seen."

"Indeed, I especially look forward to you unleashing those brutal German Hessians like a pack of wild dogs to hunt down the rebels!" Governor Tryon exclaimed, slapping the ship's railing. "I had planned *quite* the spectacular welcome event for you and your brother Admiral Howe, but *somehow* our plot was discovered and foiled before we could eliminate Washington and his officers and blow up the powder magazines. But I assure you, General Howe, we have an army of Loyalists up in those hills of Long Island at the ready to serve you."

Howe collapsed his spyglass and nodded. "I'm glad to know that, Governor, for I shall certainly enlist them for our campaign."

"Just how many troops are coming to New York, General?" Tryon wanted to know.

"With my fleet, Admiral Howe's fleet from England, and General Clinton's forces rejoining us from South Carolina, we shall have over thirty-thousand soldiers," Howe answered smugly. "This is the greatest expeditionary force ever dispatched in the history of Great Britain."

Tryon's eyes grew wide, envisioning the massive show of force in these waters of New York—*his* waters. He clenched his fists and punched the air. "Huzzah! I have no doubt that the mere sight of this harbor filled with such a show of force will have those rebels buckling at the knees and *begging* for peace. An army of farmers with pitchforks is no match for His Majesty's finest soldiers!"

Howe paused, his mind racing back to the unexpected Patriot resolve and fighting at Bunker Hill that had decimated his forces despite the British 'victory.' He had gained surprising respect for those 'farmers with pitchforks.' He knew they were far more formidable than most Britons understood or cared to admit. "Peace will not be restored in America until the rebel army is defeated. And mark my words, Governor, they will fight."

MORTIER HEADQUARTERS, MANHATTAN, NEW YORK, JUNE 29, 1776, 2:00 P.M.

Martha Washington slipped her quilting basket onto her arm and looked around the bedroom for any items she might have forgotten. She took in a deep breath and slowly let it go, wiping her eyes and then straightening the bedspread with a tender pat. "Now then. Brave face," she whispered to herself before going downstairs to bid her husband farewell.

As she descended the stairs, she could hear the beehive of activity with Washington's staff that had been buzzing ever since sentries standing on the roof first spotted the warning flags hoisted from a hilltop on Staten Island earlier that morning. The three unmistakable red-and-white flags signaled the approach of at least twenty ships from the Atlantic Ocean. They then heard the boom of cannon fire from the battery and saw a flotilla of small American schooners and fishing boats sailing up the Upper Bay to flee to safer waters ahead of the incoming enemy warships. Ferries soon became packed with citizens fleeing Manhattan in a state of panic to reach the Jerseys across the Hudson. Martha scarcely had two words with George before they both realized she had to depart immediately. She hastily packed and tidied things for her husband the best she could, but there was little else she could do other than depart while her husband prepared to meet the enemy.

Reaching the foyer, she walked down to his study where officers and aides stood over the table laden with maps, communiques, and orders. Washington's broad shoulders were the first thing Martha spotted as she reached the door, and the reality of what rested on those shoulders made her catch her breath. She placed a hand over her heart and whispered a silent prayer for her husband. He had done everything he could to assure her that God would continue to protect him. *The all-wise dispenser of events will shield me from such diabolical designs,* he had told her after the terrible Thomas Hickey affair. She knew he had been miraculously protected time and again, but that didn't eliminate her fear for his safety in the coming war. She knew he would not remain here at headquarters once fighting commenced. He would be out in the field with his men, likely out in front if the situation demanded it. She prayed that the bullets certain to fly at him would be divinely pushed away by unseen hands.

"General Washington, Sir! A new report just arrived," Samuel Webb announced, walking hurriedly past Martha, and begging her pardon as he squeezed by her to enter Washington's study. He handed the dispatch over to Washington. "A hundred square-rigged ships have gathered off Sandy Hook."

Washington turned and took the dispatch, reading it with a furrowed brow. He then looked up and saw Martha standing in the doorway. "One moment," he told his officers as he strode over to her. He took her gently by the elbow and led her out of the room. "Are you ready to depart for Philadelphia? Caty Greene and Lucy Knox have already fled with their children, and I am anxious for you to also make haste."

Martha fought back the tears, nodding with a weak smile. "Yes, George. I am ready. I'm grateful those ladies are safely away." They shared a moment of silence as the gravity of this farewell hung in the air. They couldn't know when, or heaven forbid if, they would next see one another.

Finally, Washington enveloped his petite wife in his strong arms, and they shared a tight embrace. "Fear not, Martha. I trust the Almighty to keep us safe until we meet again."

Martha closed her eyes tight and gave her husband a rapid pat on his back. "And so He shall. And so He shall. I will keep you before Him at all times of the day and night."

"General Washington?" called an aide from the other room.

Washington straightened up and lifted his chin, clenching his jaw in a confident nod. He lifted her tiny hand. "Godspeed, Mrs. Washington. Until we meet again."

"Until then, Mr. Washington. Go fight the good fight," Martha answered with a resolute smile before giving him a gentle push. "Go on, now. Get to it."

"Yes, Mrs. Washington," he answered with a sad smile before turning and rejoining his staff.

Martha then noticed Max and Jock sitting there in the foyer. She reached down to give them each a tender petting. "I'm counting on you two to keep him safe," she whispered.

Ye can count on us, lass, Max thought. *I won't let anythin' get near the lad.*

As Martha turned to depart in the awaiting carriage, Jock's lip trembled. "It must be hard being Mrs. Washington, too."

"Aye, the lassies bear a fierce burden in times of war," Max agreed. "Especially the wife of the Commander-in-Chief. Now then, let's see wha' be happenin' in that r-r-room."

The two Scotties slipped under the table and listened in to the plans for further defenses and speculation as to when and where the British would land.

"Washington's sendin' a flurry of letters beggin' for reinforcements from the promised militia that Congress said they'd r-r-recruit," Max whispered. "He's desperate for more men."

"I sure hope they get here in time," Jock whispered back.

THE NARROWS, NEW YORK, JULY 2, 1776, 8:00 A.M.

Big drops of rain slickened the decks and punctuated the water around the *Phoenix*, the *Rose,* and the *Greyhound* as the three men-o'-war carefully navigated around the East Bank sandbar in the Lower Bay and made their way through the Narrows. Rebel riflemen here and there shot at the British ships to no effect, and nine-pound rebel guns fired aimlessly at the passing ships from Denyse's Ferry before the *Asia* opened her broadsides to silence them with a boom.

Smoke filled the gray skies drenched with rain as one transport after another lumbered over the shoals and through the Narrows to reach the Upper Bay. Turning to the upper end of Staten Island, Howe ordered sailors to lower the flat-bottomed boats they brought from Halifax to transport his army to shore. They didn't care that they had to be shuttled about in the pouring rain. They knew what awaited them onshore: fresh water, fresh fruit and vegetables, and ecstatic throngs of Loyalists greeting them with open arms. They now would have everything they could need or want.

Within hours, rows of white tents popped up in the encampment by the Watering Place. As rum rations were distributed to the travel-weary redcoats now entrenched on Staten Island, a cheer of huzzahs drifted into the air as the British Army effortlessly retook the first ground of New York for the Crown.

MORTIER HEADQUARTERS, NEW YORK, JULY 2, 1776, 9:00 P.M.

Washington and Knox stood on the veranda overlooking the harbor, closely observing enemy movements as the sun set behind the clouds. Washington gazed through his spyglass at the British ships now securely anchored at Staten Island. Rain pelted his black hat and clinked off his spyglass, but he paid it no mind.

"The British have easily taken Staten Island," Henry Knox lamented, "but they will find quite a different scenario waiting for them on Long Island, General. Our guns are in place and our men are prepared and waiting for them."

"They are in possession of an island only," Washington answered, clenching his jaw. "This is but a small step toward the conquest of this continent."

"Indeed, General," Knox replied, straightening his three-cornered hat. "I shall take my leave now, Sir, and bring you an early morning report of overnight developments."

"Very well, Colonel Knox," Washington answered, collapsing his spyglass to step back inside.

"And Sir, might I say that your General Orders today will greatly serve to bolster the men's resolve," Knox encouraged him. "The eyes of all America are upon us. As we play our part, posterity will bless us or curse us."

Washington nodded and placed his spyglass down, resting his knuckles on the desk. "May it be the former, Colonel Knox. The fate of unborn millions depends upon how we play our part."

Knox scooped up Jock, and left Washington alone with his thoughts. With Lucy gone, Knox welcomed the company of the wee Scot. "Good night, Sir."

After Knox left, Washington took a seat and picked up the General Orders he had penned by candlelight the night before for distribution to his army today.

The time is now near at hand which must probably determine, whether Americans are to be, Freemen, or Slaves; whether they are to have any property they can call their own; whether their Houses, and Farms, are to be pillaged and destroyed, and they consigned to a State of Wretchedness from which no human efforts will probably deliver them. The fate of unborn Millions will now depend, under God, on the Courage and Conduct of this army—Our cruel and unrelenting Enemy leaves us no choice but a brave resistance, or the most abject submission; this is all we can expect—We have therefore to resolve to conquer or die: Our own Country's Honor, all call upon us for a vigorous and manly exertion, and if we now shamefully fail, we shall become infamous to the whole world—Let us therefore rely upon the goodness of the Cause, and the aid of the supreme Being, in whose hands Victory is, to animate and encourage us to great and noble Actions—The Eyes of all our Countrymen are now upon us, and we shall have their blessings, and praises, if happily we are the instruments of saving them from the Tyranny meditated against them. Let us therefore animate and encourage each other, and shew the whole world, that a Freeman contending for Liberty on his own ground is superior to any slavish mercenary on earth . . .

Washington set the paper down and leaned back in his chair, rubbing his eyes from lack of sleep. Since Martha's departure he had scarcely even set foot in their room, spending countless hours of discussions with his senior officers over maps, orders, and reports. How could he sleep when the fate of unborn millions was resting on every decision he made?

Max frowned, looking at Washington's exhaustion. *The lad needs ta r-r-rest.* He went over to the weary general and nudged his boot. *Come on, lad. Ye're only human. Let's get some r-r-rest.* He growled and nudged again. *Ye said ta encourage one another so that's wha' I'm doin'. Leave things with the Maker tonight.*

Washington yawned and leaned over to pet Max. "I must rest, boy. No doubt tomorrow will be another challenging day." The general stood, blew out the candle, and left the room, with his faithful dog by his side.

20

Epic Days of History

THE IAMISPHERE

"June 28th to June 29th, 1776," Gillamon said softly. "Those two days were quite a pair for the history books, and for the Order of the Seven."

"They were *epic* days, Gillamon," Clarie agreed. "If only every Patriot in the thirteen colonies knew what had happened at the same time for the cause of liberty!"

Gillamon and Claire stood in the IAMISPHERE, viewing multiple panels of time from June 28th and June 29th.

"Philadelphia," Gillamon stated, pointing to a panel of the green table in the Pennsylvania State House where Thomas Jefferson stood, presenting his draft of the Declaration of Independence to the Continental Congress on June 28th. Gillamon chuckled as they peered under the tablecloth to see Nigel dancing and cheering with a fist of victory raised in the air. "Nigel was quite carried out of himself; such was his joy with the Declaration."

Clarie giggled. "I've never seen a mouse so thrilled by words, but there again, those are no ordinary words."

"*That* is self-evident," Gillamon replied with a chuckle. He then pointed to a panel with Liz and MizP, who were equally joyful over Patrick Henry and the Fifth Virginia Convention on June 29th. Liz's eyes glowed as she enthused, "Because Virginia has already declared her independence from Great Britain and written her own Declaration of Rights and Constitution, that makes Patrick Henry the *first* elected governor of a *free* republic under a *written* constitution in the history of the *world!*"

"The Pen of the Revolution in Philadelphia and the Voice of the Revolution in Virginia both made epic history on those days," Clarie declared happily. "But so did the Sword of the Revolution in New York."

"But New York was anything but joyful on June 28th, except for Ketcham's homecoming." He pointed to the panel of Ketcham embracing his children. His smile turned to a somber frown as he pointed to another panel. "Across the river in Manhattan, the hanging of Thomas Hickey was a tragic, heavy moment for the wayward soldier, for Washington, and for the Continental Army."

"What a sad moment. But I'm so proud of how Max and Jock helped to uncover the assassination plot against George Washington," Clarie noted, pointing to the scene of Howe's ship spotted on the horizon. "And just in time! Howe's ship appeared that very afternoon!"

Gillamon nodded, pointing to another panel. "The first fifty ships of the British fleet sailed into New York Harbor the next morning, June 29th, and a total of 130 by the end of the day."

"Meanwhile, I was in South Carolina on June 28th for Battle of Sullivan's Island," Clarie exulted as she pointed to the panel of Peter Parker's britches flying off. "Al withstood the battle as best he could, but I had to give him a lot of encouragement. He mainly lost his appetite."

"Bravo on your handling of this mission," Gillamon complimented her. "I especially applaud you for getting those three ships stuck on the shoals."

"That was rather fun, leading those ships to run aground. Of course, I had help from the local dolphins," Clarie reported. "In all, the greatest blow to our key British humans from the Battle of Sullivan's Island was to their *pride*. Clinton was unharmed, Cornwallis was injured by a flying splinter, and Parker was wounded. Banastre Tarleton was unhurt, but he did witness the dead and dying. He also saw how delay and bungling turned victory into defeat. I think that will make him prone to act swiftly in the coming war."

"I see Kakia, or 'Rafe,' was not pleased to see you there after they set the ship ablaze the following day," Gillamon noted, watching the Grenadier's fury as he was rowed away from the *Actaeon*.

"No, he wasn't," Clarie added with a sly grin. "But look at what happened after Rafe and the British sailed away!" She and Gillamon watched three long-boats rowing toward the burning ship.

A rebel naval officer named Jacob Milligan bravely led three Patriot longboats out to the *Actaeon*. Once aboard, they turned some of the ship's cannons and fired several rounds at the *Bristol*. Having their own abandoned guns hurling cannonballs at them only added insult to injury for the British. The Patriots then took the *Actaeon's* bell and spare sails before rowing off with the captured ship's flag flying upside down. Thirty minutes later, the *Actaeon's* powder magazine exploded, sending oak planks and rigging up into the sky.

Gillamon looked at the scene of a plume of smoke rising from the ship as it burned to the waterline. "That pillar of smoke even looks like the hero of the day—the palmetto tree."

"That's what the Patriots thought! In all, the British lobbed seven thousand rounds over at the Patriots, who only lobbed nine-hundred-sixty balls in return," Claire reported. "But the British suffered two hundred killed and wounded as opposed to thirty-eight for the Patriots. It was a shocking blow to the British but an equally surprising *boost* for the Patriots!"

"The good news of this Patriot victory will help to offset the bad news from Canada. It will also bolster the confidence of those currently making the difficult decision for independence in Philadelphia," Gillamon added. "This victory has subdued the loyalists in the south and proved that the Royal Navy *is* vulnerable. I know that Clinton and Parker are throwing blame on one another, but this defeat will not keep the British from their next target of exacting victory in New York. In fact, it may spur them forward."

"Well, it will take three weeks for this southern fleet to get itself together before it sails north," Clarie informed him. "They'll be licking their wounds on Long Island, burying their dead, and repairing their ships first. So, what's next, Gillamon?"

"I will tend to matters in New York and Philadelphia until the Declaration of Independence is finalized," Gillamon answered. "Liz and Nigel have their hands full with finalizing that historic document and its passage, but I wish to have an Epic War Council for the rest of us in the War Room to make ready for the Battle of New York."

Clarie nodded. "I assume you wish me to go retrieve Al for the meeting?"

Gillamon smiled. "Yes, please bring our fearful feline. I'm sure it will be a welcome respite for him to flee the redcoats for a little while."

"Not to mention the rattlesnakes, the gators, and the mosquitos," Clarie answered with a giggle. A thought suddenly dawned on her. "Gillamon, since Kakia was there in the form of Rafe, I wonder why she hasn't attempted to harm Al?"

"Well, Kakia knows that Al is also immortal," Gillamon reminded her. "The last time she attempted to stop one of our team, it backfired on her."

"Ah, yes, when she locked Nigel in Gage's trunk that sailed to England, he was able to read every document on British intelligence and espionage in the colonies," Clarie answered with a wry grin. "Isn't it fun to watch evil backfire on itself?"

"It's one of my favorite phenomena to observe," Gillamon agreed with a smile.

"What about the rest of Charlatan's evil team?" Clarie asked. "Who besides Kakia has been spotted as of late?"

Gillamon frowned. "I believe Charlatan himself tried to assassinate Washington with poisoned peas, but there are many unanswered questions about that night. It bears further discovery, but the truth always comes out. I suspect that Espion is lurking somewhere in New York, quietly gathering intelligence. When I send you to France to assist Kate and Liz, you can search for Charlatan's suspected headquarters somewhere in Paris."

"Understood, Gillamon," Clarie replied, pointing to a panel of Al begging for more fish from Cornwallis. "It looks like Al's appetite has recovered from June 28th with flying colors. I'll go get him and meet you in the War Room."

"Very well, dear one," Gillamon chuckled, observing Al. He then gazed upon the panel of British sails filling New York Harbor. "Make haste. More epic days of history are coming."

THE FATE OF UNBORN MILLIONS

THE WAR ROOM

"Are we there yet?" Jock asked excitedly, a piece of cloth wrapped around his eyes. Gillamon set him down on one of the leather chairs surrounding the long mahogany table in the center of the circular room with no door. "Are we at the secret hideout?"

Max shared a concerned look with Gillamon, who was in the form of Mr. Atticus, whispering, "Are ye sure it were a good idea ta bring the lad here? After all, he's not . . . one of us. Last time ye said he weren't allowed in our secret r-r-realm."

Gillamon smiled and nodded, covering the single panel of time on the wall with a 'DON'T TREAD ON ME' flag. He leaned over to whisper in Max's ear. "Not to worry, Max. I've changed my mind. He won't realize that he is sitting in an exclusive time portal used by us immortals. Just as Liz transported young Cato through the IAMISPHERE from London to Virginia without harm, young Jock will have no ill effects from being here in the War Room. He needs to understand what we are up against in New York. But we'll wait until the others arrive, so he won't see that part. Trust me."

Max shrugged his shoulders. "Okay, lad, I'll tr-r-rust ye, like always."

Suddenly Clarie and Al entered the War Room. Al's eyes were also covered, but with his chubby paws over them. Clarie was in the form of a British Light Infantryman and held onto the frightened cat.

"Are we there yet?" Al asked, not removing his paws from his eyes.

"Yes, we're there," Clarie answered with a giggle. "And so is everyone else."

Al slowly removed his paws from his eyes and blinked a few times before looking around the room. There he saw Max and Jock. "Somethin's wrong! Help! I've got the double vision!"

"Before ye faint, lad, jest know ye're not seein' double," Max told him. "This here be me gr-r-randlad, Jock."

Al's face lit up with a big smile, and he ran over to envelop the younger Scottie with a big, smothering, furry hug. "Howdy do, little lad! I've heard all aboot ye! Me name's Big Al, but ye can jest call me Al. Are ye afraid to come here, too?"

Max put his paw over Al's mouth before the cat said anything else. "He's come ta our *secret* r-r-room that we have ta keep a *secret*, Big Al."

Jock giggled at the jolly embrace of the chunky feline. "Hi, Al! My grand-sire told me all about you, too." He looked up around him but still had the cloth tied around his head. "Can I take this off now?"

Gillamon smiled and reached over to remove the cloth. "Welcome to our secret War Room, young one."

Jock's draw dropped to see the incredible room lit with wall sconces and filled with books, maps, and spy gear. "Wwwwwhhhoooaaa! This is awesome! How come we've never been here before? We should hang out here all the time!"

"Uh, Gillamon only has us all gather here for, uh, special occasions," Max answered him nervously, not wanting to reveal anything.

"Ayyeeeee, *special* occasions," Al agreed after Max nudged him. "So spe-cial. Very special. So very, very special that I'd be happy to never come here."

Clarie cleared her throat to interrupt Al before he said too much. "Welcome, Jock. I'm glad you could join us here today. It's good to see you again, although I look different than when you saw me last in Boston."

"Hi, Clarie!" Jock enthused. "I don't know how you do it, but it's fun how you and Gillamon can change disguises." He then spotted a massive map lying on the table. It showed the coastline of the thirteen colonies on one edge and Europe on the other, with the vast Atlantic Ocean between them. "That's a big map! What are those little things in the middle of the water?"

"It's not just *any* map," Gillamon told him with a wink. He waved his hand across the map, generating a breeze that lifted its corner. Suddenly the map started to move. It slowly rippled and rose from being a flat piece of parchment to a three-dimensional diorama, as if it were a dry, flat sponge that gradually expanded with water. Whitecaps lazily crested across the deep blue waters of the Atlantic Ocean, and a fleet of tiny ships bearing British flags slowly bobbed along in the direction of New York.

"How are you doing this, Gillamon?" Jock asked with wide eyes and grinning with excited wonder.

Gillamon chuckled and winked. "It's a secret."

Al's face lit up with a goofy grin, and he reached out a paw to tap a wave, unable to resist touching the ocean. "Sure, and it's *wet!*" he exclaimed, shaking his paw, and flinging sea water into Max's eyes.

"Daft kitty!" Max scolded, closing one eye, and shoving Al. "Wha' did ye expect fr-r-rom a water map?"

Al smiled weakly. "Sorry, lad! After livin' on a boat for months with waves so huge they turned me as green as Ireland herself, it feels grand to be bigger than they are then. These look like the wee ripples in me water bowl. This must be how the Maker sees the world all the time."

"A brilliant observation, Al," Gillamon complimented him, drawing a raised chin of affirmation from Al.

"Aye, Big Al," Max laughed, shaking his head at the simple-minded cat who somehow came up with such illuminating insights.

"It's always helpful to get a 'Maker's Eye View' of things when faced with big challenges. It might be helpful to remember the big picture of how the humans got to this moment before we delve into the details of how we are to assist Washington and the Continental Army in New York," Gillamon told them. "Jock, perhaps you could help us."

Jock's eyes widened, looking around the awe-inspiring room. He was feeling quite small and insignificant considering where he was, whom he was with, and what was happening in the world. "Me? I'll try, Gillamon."

"There's a good lad," Max shared, giving the young Scottie a tender nudge, now fluttering his sea-sprayed eye back open.

"Now then, Jock, please remind us of why these thirteen colonies decided to declare independence from Great Britain," Gillamon requested. The colonies on the map lit up with a light blue backdrop as he hovered his hand above them.

Jock grinned broadly at Gillamon's ability to make the map come to life. "Well, first, look how far apart they are from England. It takes a long time to travel back and forth across the ocean. King George and Parliament sit way over there in England and have never been able to give the colonies fast answers to big problems in time to do the people any good. So, when Virginia made their own decisions about taxes to help the farmers, the king overruled them and said they weren't allowed to do that. *Then* the king and parliament started taxing all the colonies without giving them any say about it. When the colonies protested, the Crown only came down harder on them and sent soldiers to make them obey. The colonies tried to talk all of this out, but Great Britain wouldn't listen. Is that about right?"

Al put his paws over his ears. "La-la-la-la-la, we can't hear ye! Trust me, I watched King George and those Lordy Lads not hearin' even though they read what the colonists wrote and wrote and wrote. It weren't for a lack o' tryin' on the part o' the colonies. The king and his men didn't *want* to listen to what their rebellious subjects had to say."

"Aye, there were *no* discussion. 'Jest be quiet an' do as we say,'" Max added. "But the Patriots refused ta tuck their tails an' let the tyr-r-rants have their way. Jest because a few hundred pompous humans in England be tr-r-ryin' ta keep all the power for themselves, the world be headin' ta war."

"It's never been about the *amount* of taxes that King George and Parliament wanted the colonies to pay, but the *principle* behind it—no taxation without representation as the colonists put it," Clarie added.

"Well done, Jock, and everyone. All the colonists wanted was to have a *voice* in Parliament, but they were denied," Gillamon agreed, hovering his hand over England, which lit up with a red backdrop. "Had King George and Parliament agreed to give the colonies a voice, the humans would not be on the eve of war. You see, the British leaders were afraid that if they gave the *American* colonies such a voice, all their other colonies around the world from Canada to the Caribbean to India would want the same thing. And the Crown believed that if they gave a voice to all their colonies, they would lose the ability to control their empire. So, resolving this conflict *politically* failed." He pointed to the bobbing ships. "Now, Jock, why is this huge British fleet sailing toward the coast of America?"

Jock tilted his head, studying the vast armada of ships sailing along the map, their white sails taut with the wind as tiny seagulls trailed behind them. "Well, I think the king thinks he can silence the Patriots by scaring them with lots of ships and soldiers."

Al quickly pointed to Clinton's and Parker's British ships bobbing off the coast of South Carolina. He accidentally dipped his paw again into the water and flicked it onto Max. "But Clarie and me were there to see these king's ships and soldiers beaten by them spongy palmetto trees!"

Clarie smiled and nodded. "That's right, Al, the king's idea to crush the Patriots started with a big fat *failure.*"

Max furrowed his brow and shook the water from his head. "The Patriots done stirred up a hornet's nest by embarrassing them r-r-redcoats first in Boston an' then in Charleston."

Al's eyes grew worried, and he shook his head rapidly. "Aye, they be maaaaaaad!"

"So, having rejected a *political* solution of talking, Great Britain seeks a *military* solution of fighting to bring the colonies in line," Gillamon summarized. "And so, the colonists now must respond. But how many of them will fight back for independence?"

Jock frowned and gazed up and down the colonies. "Well, only a third of them are Patriots who want independence. And a third *want* the British ships to arrive—they're the Loyalists. So, I guess only a third will fight against the king?"

Gillamon closed his eyes and nodded. "Very good, small one. And that leaves a third of the colonists that George Washington must convince to join the glorious cause of liberty." He crossed his arms over his chest. "In a nutshell then, Washington is faced with fighting a *military* war against the British while fighting a *civil* war over the hearts and minds of the Americans."

"That just seems impossible!" Jock lamented. "How can he win both wars?"

"Nothin's impossible when ye're workin' for the Maker," Max shared with an affirmative nod. "It's jest like David an' Goliath. The lad had no business beatin' that powerful giant dressed in all that heavy armor, but he did it with a single r-r-rock."

"Indeed, and Washington is actively seeking the Maker's help to wage war," Gillamon agreed. "But let's look at the strengths and weaknesses of both armies who will soon meet on the field of battle. Let's start with the British army. What are their strengths?"

"Their naval superiority first jumps to mind," Clarie offered, pointing to the fleet sailing toward New York. "All of the major American cities are vulnerable to attack and invasion by water."

"Unless they've got spongy trunks," Al spoke up with a wink and a paw in the air.

"The Patriots have repelled the British from Charleston for *now*, but unfortunately, they'll be back," Clarie answered with a frown, gently squeezing Al's paw. "Clinton and Cornwallis learned important lessons from the Battle of Sullivan's Island. They won't make the same mistakes again. So that means New York, Boston, Philadelphia, Baltimore, Newport, Norfolk, Savannah and eventually Charleston are all in danger, and the Patriots don't have a navy to speak of that can stop them. Aside from a few small ships they are building, the Continental Navy really consists of converted merchant ships and privateers who've been given permission to capture any British ships they can."

"Besides bein' powerful in the sea, them Br-r-ritish R-r-regulars be disciplined fighters who can whip the Patriots on the land, too," Max noted. "They an' them fierce Hessians will outnumber Washington's men, plus they know wha' they're doin'."

"Aye, but look at how far those British ships be from home," Al responded. "I were there when they were loadin' up all them ships with food and stuff. They could only bring so much with them, and lots o' ships didn't even make the journey across, so they'll be runnin' out o' men and supplies at some point. Sure, and it takes a long time to sail back to England with a list o' stuff the army needs, then wait for them to sail back again." He then put his paws up on his fluffy cheeks. "I get seasick thinkin' aboot all that bobbin' back and forth!"

Jock studied the map and cocked his head. "And look at how *big* America is! Those British soldiers can't possibly take over the whole continent! And what about all those rivers and creeks everywhere? Their big ships can't sail into those waters, can they?"

Gillamon clapped. "Bravo! Indeed, a big weakness for the British is their distance from England for reinforcements and supply, and the amount of territory they are expected to capture. You have a good understanding of the lay of the land and the water." He held his hands out over the waters of New York, then acted as if he were pulling a piece of string on both ends. The water map zoomed out until New York and its waterways were the only part showing.

"Me gr-r-randlad gets his smarts from me," Max crowed proudly, patting Jock on the back. He then nodded at the map. "Since the Br-r-ritish can't capture all the colonies, they're goin' ta try an' capture the main area of the r-r-rebellion, New York, an' cut off New England from the south."

"What if I told you that strategy won't work?" Gillamon offered, drawing astonished looks from the team.

"What do you mean, Gillamon?" Clarie asked. *"Both* sides see New York as the 'key to the whole continent.'"

"Aye, this is wha' the humans have thought since the Fr-r-rench an' Indian War," Max protested.

"First, as Jock already observed, the Royal Navy can't possibly be everywhere at once, yet King George expects them to not only capture New York, but *also* blockade up and down the entire east coast of the thirteen colonies, including all the rivers and waterways," Gillamon explained. "They cannot possibly do all of this, and Admiral Howe himself knows it."

"Even *I* can see that," Al offered. "And I'm not even good at math."

"Secondly, King George also believes that most of America so adores him that all he needs to do is show the power of the British Lion, and all his loyal subjects will flock to his side, outnumbering and defeating the tiny band of rebels," Gillamon continued. "And thirdly, because he feels that Loyalists make up most of the citizens, King George doesn't think he needs to offer any concessions to win over the few rebelling colonists. Military power alone will accomplish everything with no political talking. Reconciliation is not in the king's vocabulary."

"So, no discussion then," Max added. "Jest submit or else."

"Then King George's three-pronged strategy is flawed to begin with because none of his assumptions are true," Clarie realized. "Well, his strategy already failed in 1775 with the troops he sent to Boston. That's why he's sending an even greater force this time. But are you saying it will also fail in 1776?"

"1776 and beyond," Gillamon answered. "And as Max said, fewer than four hundred aristocrats ruling Great Britain agree with King George, but they're not about to share their power with lower-class colonial rebels. They will keep supporting the king and this flawed strategy because they think it's the best option they have. But New York will be a red herring for *both sides* throughout the war."

"I love herring!" Al exclaimed, shooting a paw into the air.

Max bonked Al on the head. "Daft kitty."

"What the humans don't yet realize—and what we will be charged with protecting—is the one target the British can destroy to defeat the glorious cause," Gillamon told them. "The strategic target that the British forces must capture is not a piece of ground."

"Ye mean George Washington?" Max surmised.

"Yes, to an extent," Gillamon answered. "But there's more."

"The Continental Army itself?" Jock asked.

Gillamon winked and mussed Jock's head. "Precisely, small one! The British need not capture and destroy land, but only the Continental Army. As vital as George Washington is, there will always be attacks on his life, as the one we've already thwarted. But if his army is destroyed, it won't matter if he lives or dies in the cause of liberty."

"So, we jest need to help the Continental Army survive?" Al asked. He looked around at the five of them gathered there, slowly counting by pointing to each one and then to himself. "But there only be five o' us."

"David picked up five smooth stones, but only ended up usin' one ta slay the giant," Max reminded them. "Plus, we also have Liz, Kate, an' Mousie. But, Gillamon, how are we supposed ta help keep the Continental Army alive?"

"By helping them to escape defeat until they get the guns, men, and ships they need from France. Kate is working on that part of the mission in Paris with Silas Deane and a colorful Frenchman named Beaumarchais. She'll also help the Marquis de Lafayette to escape from France to come fight alongside Washington and serve as a link between the two countries," Gillamon explained. "It will take Washington a while to figure this out, but the Continental Army will not win this war by winning lots of big battles. They will win by repeatedly escaping defeat and living to fight another day, while making the fight costly for the British."

"Wear the British down to the point it is no longer worth the fight," Clarie realized, nodding slowly.

"Ye mean the Patriots will win jest by not givin' up?" Al asked, drawing looks of amazement from everyone.

Gillamon smiled. "Precisely. We are going to help Washington and the Continental Army win by not giving up, even when it looks impossible. We're going to help them to escape every time the British have them backed into a corner. No matter how many soldiers they lose and how small Washington's army becomes, if they don't give up, they will win this war."

"Alr-r-righty then! We can help them do that!" Max declared. "I'll keep the Commander-in-Chief safe an' help lead him ta escape r-r-routes."

"Aye, an' I'll make the weather they need to escape!" Jock enthused, wagging his tail.

"And I'll do me part to wear down the British!" Al exclaimed.

"I know ye'll wear them down with flyin' colors, lad," Max told the big cat with a burly paw on the cat's back and a wink to Jock. "Ye wear *me* out all the time."

"Why, thanks lad!" Al replied with a goofy grin, oblivious to Max's joke.

"Not giving up will equally come down to helping individual humans to press on, not just the army as a whole," Clarie suggested. "As we've seen in helping humans across time, sometimes history pivots on one single individual doing one important thing."

"Indeed," Gillamon agreed. "So, helping the humans to escape will be the key to victory in this war. Now then, let's discuss the situation in New York." He hovered his hand over the watery map of New York, and the land took on the topography of the landscape with the hills and valleys throughout the region. "King George is confident that the Howe Brothers will master New York by the end of September, and then push up the Hudson River Valley to join their forces from Canada. He's expecting full victory over the rebellion by Christmas. Let's get the picture of what Washington is doing to prepare for battle, and what the British might do to make King George's Christmas hopes come true."

"I hate ta say it, but there couldn't be a more perfect place for the Br-r-ritish Navy ta cr-r-rush the Continental Army than in New York City," Max offered with a frown, looking at the waters surrounding Manhattan and Long Island. "After Washington sent him here ta set up the army's defenses, even General Charles Lee reported that whoever controls the sea controls the town. An' I don't think the Patriots can whip up a few hundred warships ta contr-r-rol the sea by the time the r-r-redcoats all ar-r-rive."

"Lee is right, New York is not like Boston," Clarie added. "In Boston, Washington knew *where* the enemy was and *who* they were since the town was not full of Loyalists as it is here. He was able to send Howe's fleet sailing out of Boston by taking the high ground in Dorchester, but that won't be so easy in New York, given the expanse of the bay and the width of its rivers. Here the British will have total control of the waters and can land and strike wherever they choose, whenever they choose. And they'll have the local Loyalists armed, ready, and willing to help them with sabotage."

Jock frowned. "The Patriots have been acting like an army of beavers! They've been cutting down trees, digging trenches, and building stuff all over New York. My human Henry Knox has put his cannons everywhere, but I don't understand what they're trying to do exactly."

"Look here at the map as I summarize Lee's plan," Clarie said, pointing to Long Island. "When Lee was here for a month back in February, he had seventeen hundred men with him. He immediately figured out that the British would easily take the city, but he also determined that they should pay a high price for it. His plan was to put up defenses in key areas of the city, especially the high ground. Just like you helped Knox get those cannons to put on the high ground in Boston at Dorchester, Lee thought setting up guns at Brooklyn Heights on Long Island could make it difficult for British ships to sail up the East River. So, they've built Fort Stirling there." She then pointed to the northwestern side of Manhattan at the Hudson River. "He also planned to do the same thing at this high spot and across on the New Jersey shore, to prevent British ships from sailing up the Hudson."

Jock nodded. "I see, I think."

Al pointed a paw at the narrow tidal straight connecting the East River with Long Island Sound. "What aboot this skinny, swirly place o' water? What's it called?"

"That's called Hell Gate, and Lee's plans included building forts on either side of the East River to close that entrance," Clarie explained.

Al gulped and put his paws up to his mouth. "Ye wouldn't have to build anythin' to keep me out o' a place with a name like that."

"If only the British had more of you in them, Al. But alas, not," Gillamon said with a chuckle. "So, after General Lee left New York to lead things in South Carolina, General Alexander 'Lord Stirling' continued the work. When General Putnam arrived from Boston, he helped Lord Stirling, but both officers became worried about Staten Island over here." Gillamon pointed to the big island in New York Harbor. "Unfortunately, Staten Island is a Loyalist stronghold, so they failed to get much support to build defenses there. But Putnam led a thousand men to storm Governor's Island there off the tip of Manhattan to dig in, as well as build a fort on Red Hook."

"Aye, an' Old Put also sank obstructions in the water there ta slow down ships tryin' ta get by," Max added. "He's got gunners placed there ta get a cr-r-rack at any ships that try ta sail past. So, when Washington arrived ta town, he assigned his men ta build barricades, trenches, redoubts, and forts wherever he could. The city don't look a thing like it did when we arrived then!"

"That's for sure! Manhattan has been torn apart," Jock observed sadly. "All those pretty trees, houses, buildings, and parks had to be sacrificed to dig in."

"That's what war does to places, sadly," Clarie lamented. "It chews up beauty and spits out destruction. Washington's men have been building a fort near King's Bridge plus the two forts on either side of the Hudson River that Lee mapped out."

"But the lad hasn't had time ta finish everythin'!" Max growled. "He didn't have enough men or time ta put up all the defenses before General Howe sailed inta town."

Jock pointed to Sandy Hook where the British ships first arrived from the Atlantic Ocean. "What about this spot? Seems like if you could keep the British from even getting inside the harbor that would be the best thing to do."

"Unfortunately, Washington didn't have enough men, time, or a navy to help him put any defenses there," Clarie told him. "He must helplessly watch as British ships sail right on through into the harbor. And since he couldn't get any support on Staten Island, that area has been taken over by the British as the Loyalists welcome them with open arms."

"Washington has done all he could to dig in before the Howe Brothers arrived, and his army will continue to build defenses as best they can until the British make a move," Gillamon noted. "At least we all know what the theater of war looks like for New York. We won't know exactly what the British will do until they all arrive, so be ready for anything. And remember, always be thinking about escape routes for the humans."

"So, when do you think the British will make a move?" Jock wanted to know.

"That's the number one question that Washington asks as well," Gillamon noted. He pointed to hundreds of British ships bobbing across the Atlantic, and then down to Sir Peter Parker's fleet off of Carolina. "I believe General Howe will wait until all of these white sails are in New York Harbor, so it will be a while until they arrive."

"Can I jest stay here until they do?" Al asked hopefully. "Do I have to go back on Cornwallis's ship?"

"Yes, Al, I'll take you back now in time for lunch, but don't worry," Clarie assured the fearful cat. "You'll be able to eat plenty of fish and take plenty of naps on the journey up to New York."

"True, true," Al agreed, patting his belly. "At least I know what things look like before we arrive."

"Aye, Big Al, ye already know more aboot New York than do them R-r-redcoats," Max encouraged him. "Jest do yer best ta wear them out, so they'll be tired when ye arrive."

"Will do, lad," Al agreed with a determined slap of his paw on the map, sending another spray of water into Max's face. "Sorry, then."

Jock cocked his head. "Wait a minute. How are you getting Al back to Cornwallis's ship by lunch?"

"Uh, well then, we best get back ta General Washington," Max hurriedly suggested, not answering Jock's question. He wiped his face on the cloth that Gillamon held to once more blindfold Jock for departure from the War Room. "Time ta hide yer eyes, lad."

"Are you going to be with us in New York until the rest of the British fleet arrives, Gillamon?" Jock asked worriedly as Gillamon covered the young dog's eyes.

"For the most part, but I will go back and forth between New York and Philadelphia until the Declaration of Independence is secured," Gillamon answered. "The fate of unborn millions depends upon it."

DECIDING INDEPENDENCE

"My dear, I am so happy you arrived in time!" Nigel whispered to Liz. "It would not have been the same without you here for this momentous occasion."

Liz smiled. "I am happy to have made it here as well. I would have come earlier but *mon* Henry appeared not to feel well, and I wanted to make sure he was all right. I still am concerned."

"Well, MizP is there and will most certainly find a way to make sure Patrick is well attended," Nigel assured her.

Liz nodded. *"Oui.* So, *Monsieur* Jefferson and the Committee of Five presented the draft of the Declaration on Friday, the 28th?"

"Yes, Hancock had Secretary Thomson read the draft but then ordered it left on the table above us for delegates to come read at their leisure," Nigel explained, pointing above his head. "Discussion on the draft will not proceed until the vote for independence is accomplished. Delegates are asked to leave written notes regarding edits on the table for Secretary Thomson to read to the assembly at large for discussion."

"Je comprends. Well, since I have not been able to read the full declaration myself, I am anxious to do so as soon as the humans leave this afternoon," Liz replied expectantly.

"Prepare yourself for a long wait, dear girl. It could be this evening, depending on how the debate for independence goes," Nigel told her.

John Hancock pounded his gavel. "Gentlemen, today we return to the vote on the June 7th resolution brought forth by the delegate from Virginia, Mr. Richard Henry Lee, to move for independence." He picked up Lee's resolution to read it aloud:

"Resolved, that these United Colonies are, and of right ought to be, free and independent States, that they are absolved from all allegiance to the British Crown, and that all political connection between them and the State of Great Britain is, and ought to be, totally dissolved.

"That it is expedient forthwith to take the most effectual measures for forming foreign Alliances.

"That a plan of confederation be prepared and transmitted to the respective Colonies for their consideration and approbation." Hancock set the resolution on the table. "We will now enter into a Committee of the Whole for discussion."

Immediately John Dickinson rose to his feet, his face pale and gaunt from exhaustion. "I know how unpopular I have become in this august body," he began, his voice weakened from the toll of these past several weeks. "I know that standing my ground to vote against rushing into independency as a matter of principle will most certainly end my career." He paused and looked over at John Adams and smiled sadly. "My conduct this day, I expect, will give the finishing blow to my once great and now too diminished popularity. But thinking as I do on the subject of debate, silence would be guilt."

"One must admire his zeal to stand upon his principles, unpopular as they are," Nigel whispered to Liz.

"*Oui*, and despite what it might cost him," Liz agreed. "But I feel he will maintain the respect of these men for standing firm despite opposing them."

"Now is not the time, gentlemen," Dickinson continued, shaking his head. A gentle rumble of thunder sounded in the distance. Dickinson lifted a piece of paper. "To proceed with a declaration of independence would be to brave the storm in a skiff made of paper." He tossed the paper on the table and proceeded to recount each and every argument he had made over the course of the past year. The delegates respectfully listened, but the tension in the room continued to build like the heat from the coming summer storm.

After an hour Dickinson finally took his seat just as rain began to fall outside, splattering the window. No one spoke a word as the rain picked up speed and lightning flashed. None rose to speak against this man who was bound and determined to prevent independence because he honestly felt it was the right thing to do.

"The storm inside will soon pick up speed like the storm outside," Liz noted, pointing to John Adams, who gripped the arm of his chair. He leaned forward and looked around the room, drumming his fingers on the table before slowly rising to his feet.

"I wish now as never before that I had been given the gift of oratory possessed by the ancients of Greece and Rome, for I am certain that none of them ever had laid before them a question of greater importance," John Adams began. Lightning flashed in the sky, answered by a clap of thunder that rattled the room. Heavy rain pelted the tall windows as all eyes were trained on him. "The object is great which we have in view, and we must expect a great expense of blood to obtain it." The tireless delegate looked around the room, a lump of emotion in his throat. "But we should always remember that a free constitution of civil government cannot be purchased at too dear a rate, as there is nothing on this side of *Jerusalem* of equal importance to mankind."

"He is quite carried out of himself," Nigel whispered to Liz. John Adams proceeded for the next hour to remind the Congress of the events that had led up to this historic moment in time.

Again, the lightning cracked, and sheets of heavy rain battered the roof of the State House, momentarily diverting the eyes of the delegates from Adams to the windows.

"If I fail to provide a country where my children can live and grow in freedom to pursue all that God in heaven purposes for them, I will see it as a failure also for *their* children and for every future generation of children in America," Adams continued. "I will *gladly* risk everything I have, including laying down my life for those generations to achieve liberty. For without the freedom to live . . . to speak . . . to worship . . . to fail . . . to succeed . . . to pursue hopes and dreams and to do all that one is created and gifted to become, their spirits would be crushed to the core. And that, gentlemen, is not how the Maker intended the human spirit to live on this mortal plane. With life He also gave *liberty*. And no earthly king has the right to take it away." He paused and softly tapped the table in front of him, the rain now softly plinking on the windows. "I urge you, gentlemen, to think not just of yourselves but of the future generations who will look back on this moment and see whether or not we valued them and their freedom enough to fight for it." He then quietly took his seat.

Liz's eyes brimmed with tears. *"Bravo, Monsieur* Adams."

"I daresay no one has fought harder in this Congress than John Adams to declare independence," Nigel whispered, wiping away a tear under his spectacles. "Now to see if his words are enough."

Samuel Adams began tapping his cane on the wooden floor, followed by other delegates around the room who pounded the tables and stood to their feet. After a time, other delegates asked to speak, continuing the discussion for hours on end about independence, foreign alliances, and how thirteen disparate colonies with vastly different constituents, backgrounds, and interests could actually achieve a confederation. Freedom felt very much on the line as much for the individual colonies as it did for individual Americans.

Suddenly the door to the assembly room opened, and an express rider was allowed in to deliver a note to the table of New York delegates. He stood in the back of the room awaiting instructions.

"Mr. Livingston of New York," Hancock announced, nodding to the delegate, who rose to his feet.

"I have just received word that one hundred British ships have been sighted off New York!" Livingston exclaimed, holding up the note. "The Continental Army will soon face the most formidable fighting force in the world in our harbor. How shall we answer them?"

"With *independency* first, Sir," John Adams answered with firm resolution. "And then with guns and blood."

Candles flickered in the now-darkening room. No one spoke a word as the reality of what faced them sank into each and every man present. Independence would not just mean words. It would mean action. And for some, it would mean death.

"Liberty or death," Liz whispered. "That is what they must decide."

"Gentlemen, the hour is late, and we have been in debate for the better part of nine hours," John Hancock announced. "We shall take a preliminary vote and then adjourn for the night. Mr. Thomson, please proceed, beginning with the New England colonies."

Thomson dipped his quill in the silver inkwell and nodded. "The Colony of New Hampshire."

"New Hampshire votes 'Yes,'" delegate Matthew Thornton answered.

Thomson made a notation and lifted his chin. "Massachusetts."

Samuel Adams quickly shot to his feet. "Massachusetts votes 'Yes!'"

"Rhode Island," Thomson called.

Stephen Hopkins rose to his feet. "Rhode Island votes 'Yes.'"

"Connecticut," Thomson called.

"Connecticut votes 'Yes,'" answered Oliver Wolcott.

"New York?" Thomson asked, looking over to where tension ran high among the men whose constituents were soon to feel the next blow from the British lion.

Lewis Morris rose. "New York abstains, as we still require further instructions from our home government."

Thomson made a notation. "New Jersey."

"New Jersey votes 'Yes,'" Richard Stockton answered.

"Pennsylvania?" Thomson asked.

All eyes turned to the seven delegates from Pennsylvania. Benjamin Franklin remained seated, wearing a frown as Robert Morris rose to his feet and declared, "Pennsylvania votes 'No.'"

"Delaware," Thomson called.

Thomas McKean and George Read both stood and simultaneously exclaimed, "Yes" and "No," respectively. They looked at one another and then to Hancock.

"Well, which is it, gentlemen?" Hancock asked.

"Where is Caesar Rodney?" Liz asked Nigel. "I know he is in *favor* of independence."

"I'm afraid he had to return home to attend to an important matter," Nigel answered. "He lives some eighty miles from here."

Liz frowned. "Someone must go get him! His vote could change the entire outcome of independence, no?" She looked over at the express rider. *"He* should go."

"Delaware is divided," McKean finally answered. He locked eyes with John Adams, who mouthed, *Where is Rodney?*

"Maryland?" Thomson continued.

Charles Carroll lifted a hand. "Maryland votes 'Yes.'"

Thomson dipped his quill in the ink, setting it on the page, already knowing the answer to the next colony. "Virginia."

"Virginia votes 'Yes,'" quickly answered Thomas Nelson, Jr.

Thomson nodded. "North Carolina?"

"North Carolina votes 'Yes!'" Joseph Hewes exclaimed.

"South Carolina?" Thomson asked.

The South Carolina delegates huddled together in a feverish discussion and Edward Rutledge held up a finger to request a moment. Finally, he rose to his feet and furrowed his brow. "South Carolina votes 'No.'"

"And Georgia," Thomson called the last colony.

"Georgia votes 'Yes,'" Button Gwinnett answered.

Thomson cleared his throat and announced, "The vote is nine in favor, two against, one abstention, and one undecided."

Rutledge shot to his feet. "South Carolina would like to move that a final vote be postponed until tomorrow."

"Second!" John Adams quickly followed.

"Very well," Hancock announced, slamming the gavel. "Congress is adjourned. We will take the final vote for deciding independence tomorrow."

Immediately the assembly room broke up and McKean rushed over to Adams. They chatted a moment and then immediately walked over to the express rider, instructing him to go get Caesar Rodney from Delaware.

"Well, if Rodney makes it back here in time, that will make it ten votes for independence," Liz noted. "And New York will once again abstain."

"That leaves Pennsylvania and South Carolina to move into our court," Nigel suggested. "City Tavern will no doubt be serving a full menu of intense negotiations tonight."

SECOND CONTINENTAL CONGRESS, PENNSYLVANIA STATE HOUSE, PHILADELPHIA, JULY 2, 1776, 8:30 A.M.

Thomas Jefferson, Benjamin Franklin, and John Adams huddled in the courtyard, waiting to walk into the assembly room. The rain had stopped for now, but dark clouds still lingered overhead. Liz and Nigel had shadowed their every move since last night, following them to City Tavern. In the darkened corners of that bustling establishment, a war of words raged, with pleading and compromising squeezing every last drop of energy from the exhausted men. Once they finally went to their lodgings for the night, no one slept. They were robbed of sleep not only by the late hour of negotiations, but from the anticipation of what the outcome of the war of words would bring this day.

"Well, gentlemen, today is the day," John Adams predicted, looking around them at the other delegates milling about in the courtyard. "All we have strived for, for over a decade, comes down to this single day."

"And if all goes as we hope, the war will next turn its sights on your Declaration, Mr. Jefferson," Benjamin Franklin told him. He leaned over with an impish grin. "Are you prepared for your draft to bleed?"

Jefferson nodded, his arms folded over his chest. "I am, though I shall not relish the process."

Adams gave Jefferson an assuring nod as the delegates began streaming into the State House. "But first, the three men who will determine that outcome are nowhere to be seen."

Franklin pointed his cane to the air and started walking toward the entrance door. "Let us hope that the two we need to remain invisible stay that way."

"But where is the *third?*" Adams asked through gritted teeth with a furrowed brow, following Franklin and Jefferson inside.

Liz peeked at the men streaming into the assembly room, while Nigel anxiously paced back and forth under the table. "Rutledge has thankfully gotten South Carolina on board to vote for independence. If John Dickinson and Robert Morris from Pennsylvania stay home, the remaining five delegates from that colony will split the vote, with the majority of three voting for independence. That only leaves Delaware to determine if independence is declared. But if Caesar Rodney does not make it back in time for the vote . . ."

"Steady, *mon ami,*" Liz told her little friend.

John Hancock sounded his gavel, and guards started to close the heavy doors to maintain the secrecy of this gathered assembly. Just as the latch was about to shut, someone pulled the door open.

"Oh dear, please do not let it be Dickinson!" Nigel exclaimed, gripping his whiskers in suspense. "If so, it is all over!"

In walked a tall, thin, mud-splattered man with a green silk scarf tied awkwardly around his head to hide the skin cancer that ravaged his face. Spurs were still attached to his muddy boots as he clanked over to the Delaware table, escorted by the express rider, who handed a haversack to the strange-looking man.

"Hail, Caesar!" Nigel exclaimed, gripping Liz's arm. "He made it, he made it!"

The express rider bowed respectfully and shot a glance to the floor and the table where Liz and Nigel hid. He put a finger to his dusty three-cornered hat and grinned, giving a wink with his blue eyes.

"I have a sneaking suspicion that the express rider sent to retrieve *Monsieur* Rodney was no ordinary human," Liz surmised, hugging Nigel.

"Good show, Gillamon!" Nigel cheered, saluting the rider.

John Adams clenched his fist and suppressed a smile as he looked back at the doors that were now firmly shut. John Dickinson and Robert Morris from Pennsylvania had not arrived. He looked over at Benjamin Franklin and shared a knowing grin and nod.

"We will resume the motion from last evening and now proceed with a final vote for deciding independence," President John Hancock announced. He lifted a hand to Secretary Charles Thomson. "If you will take the vote, please, Mr. Thomson."

As Thomson once more called out the names of the colonies, one by one they again stood to cast their vote.

"This is it, my pet!" Nigel whispered. "Every word spoken by the Voice of the Revolution, every charge led by the Sword of the Revolution, and every word written by the Pen of the Revolution come down to this moment in history!"

Liz nodded, unable to speak. "Pennsylvania?" Thomson called.

All eyes once more turned to the five delegates representing Pennsylvania. Two chairs remained empty. Benjamin Franklin placed his hands atop his cane and slowly stood to his feet. "Pennsylvania . . . votes *'Yes.'*"

"Delaware," Thomson called.

Caesar Rodney got to his feet, the clank of his spurs sounding before he exclaimed, "Delaware votes *'Yes'!*"

A low murmur of excited anticipation rippled across the room as Thomson proceeded to call the remaining colonies by name.

"South Carolina votes 'Yes,'" Rutledge answered, this time with a broad smile over to John Adams.

"And Georgia," Thomson called the last colony.

"Georgia votes 'Yes,'" Button Gwinnett answered as he had the night before.

A hush fell over the room as Thomson handed John Hancock the official tally. Hancock rose to his feet. "With the delegates of New York abstaining, the vote is twelve to zero." He looked around the room, nodded, and clenched his jaw. "Mr. Lee's resolution for deciding independence passes."

There was no eruption of cheers, but silence. The men looked around the room at one another as if in denial of what had just occurred. Suddenly a gentle rumble of thunder sounded, and rain once more began pelting the windows. No one uttered a word as the gravity of the moment settled in on the men who had just done the unthinkable. They had finally decided for independence.

Now it was time for them to make a public confession of treason.

THE DECLARATION OF INDEPENDENCE

PHILADELPHIA, PENNSYLVANIA, JULY 3, 1776, 7:00 A.M.

John Adams dipped his quill in the inkwell, and smiled, tears of joy filling his eyes as he concluded this letter to his best friend, Abigail.

But on the other hand, the delay of this Declaration to this time, has many great advantages attending it. The hopes of reconciliation, which were fondly entertained by multitudes of honest and well-meaning tho weak and mistaken people, have been gradually and at last totally extinguished. Time has been given for the whole People, maturely to consider the great Question of Independence and to ripen their judgments, dissipate their fears, and allure their hopes, by discussing it in newspapers and pamphlets, by debating it, in Assemblies, Conventions, Committees of Safety and Inspection, in Town and County Meetings, as well as in private conversations, so that the whole People in every Colony of the 13, have now adopted it, as their own Act. This will cement the Union, and avoid those heats and perhaps convulsions which might have been occasioned, by such a Declaration six months ago.

But the day is past. The Second Day of July 1776, will be the most memorable Epocha, in the History of America. I am apt to believe that it will be celebrated, by succeeding generations, as the great anniversary festival. It ought to be commemorated, as the Day of Deliverance by solemn acts of devotion to God Almighty. It ought to be solemnized with pomp and parade, with shews, games, sports, guns, bells, bonfires and illuminations from one end of this Continent to the other from this time forward forever more.

You will think me transported with enthusiasm but I am

not. I am well aware of the toil and blood and treasure, that it will cost us to maintain this Declaration, and support and defend these States. Yet through all the gloom I can see the rays of ravishing Light and Glory. I can see that the End is more than worth all the Means. And that Posterity will tryumph in that Days Transaction, even altho we should rue it, which I trust in God we shall not.

SECOND CONTINENTAL CONGRESS, PENNSYLVANIA STATE HOUSE, PHILADELPHIA, JULY 3, 4:30 P.M.

Thomas Jefferson squirmed in his chair but remained silent as Congress continued to delete from the Declaration chunks of what he had written.

"He is not taking this well, I assure you," Nigel whispered to Liz. "So far, they have toned down Jefferson's explosive words and deleted two of the grievances against King George, reducing the charges from twenty-one to nineteen. Most significantly they removed Jefferson's argument holding King George *personally* responsible for the continuation of the slave trade in the colonies."

"This is wise, no?" Liz said. "These delegates realize that it is not just the King who bears the responsibility for slavery in America. While the southern colonies are guilty of utilizing the most slaves, the northern colonies are equally guilty of participating in their transport." She frowned and slapped her tail on the floor. "But South Carolina and Georgia will not agree to this declaration unless the entire passage on the slave trade is eliminated. It is tragically how it must be for now."

"Quite so. Something as monumental as the abolition of slavery cannot be accomplished with this document but shall need to wait until an independent America can slay that wicked beast." Nigel frowned, shaking his head. "Aside from deleting the slavery issue, Congress has also radically reduced Jefferson's verbose attack on the British people and their lack of assistance to stand up for their American brethren against the long train of abuses from the King and Parliament."

"Well, the revisions large and small have made the Declaration less exaggerated and easier to prove to the watchful world who shall read it," Liz surmised. "But for such an important document written with such haste, I believe this Declaration of Independence to be almost a masterpiece."

"Almost a masterpiece?" Nigel asked, straightening his spectacles. Liz gave a coy grin. "It has yet to receive *our* final edits, *mon ami.*"

PENNSYLVANIA STATE HOUSE, PHILADELPHIA, JULY 3, 8:30 P.M.

After the humans had filed out of the chamber and closed the door, Liz and Nigel jumped up onto the green tablecloth where the draft of the Declaration of Independence sat.

Nigel was preparing to re-light a candle for them to read the document when Liz held up her paw.

"Wait, *mon ami,* we cannot risk light showing in the windows," Liz cautioned him. "No doubt there are spies about who might peer in and see us."

"Right you are, my dear. Spies and no doubt overzealous humans eager to know the contents of this priceless document," Nigel echoed. "Shall we retire under the table? We must take great care to lift the tablecloth for proper ventilation."

"*Bon,*" Liz agreed, picking up the small brass candlestick and gingerly jumping to the chair and then the floor, setting it under the table. She then lifted the green tablecloth to drape it over the chair next to them. "*Voila.*" She then retrieved a quill and ink to have with them.

Nigel delicately took the Declaration of Independence in his mouth and jumped from chair to floor, gently placing it there under the table. He lit the candle, and as the candlelight gleamed off his spectacles, he took in a deep breath, exhaling with delight. "My pet, I am practically speechless to consider that we are sitting alone with the Declaration on the eve of its final approval."

"*Oui,* this moment has an almost *sacred* feel to it," Liz agreed.

The cat and mouse sat in silence for a few moments, slowly, methodically reading the marked-up document, observing all the changes made thus far.

"I must say that was terribly uncomfortable for Mr. Jefferson today," Nigel remarked. "The Committee of Five had already made forty-seven changes to his beloved draft. It is *dreadfully* hard for an author to have his work raked over the coals, scratched out, and reworked by one editor, much less dozens of them."

"*Oui,* you should know as the pen of *Anonymouse,*" Liz answered with a grin. "Although neither you nor I have ever experienced such brutal editing as *Monsieur* Jefferson. But this Declaration of Independence must not be the work of a single author. It is a document by and for the people, so it should have ink splattered across its pages from many pens."

"What a stupendous insight, my dear! You are absolutely right," Nigel agreed, rubbing his tiny paws together and clasping his fingers into a stretch.

"And might I add that the Declaration would not be complete without the pen of Anonymouse and his lovely feline friend?"

Liz giggled. *"Bien sûr!* Let us see what improvements we can add to make the Pen of the Revolution shine."

"They have missed the most important declaration in this Declaration," Liz finally opined, looking at Nigel.

Nigel finished perusing the scribbles all over the document and shared her gaze. "You are absolutely right, my dear."

Liz and Nigel looked back to the document. "If the humans do not submit this work to the Maker, they will miss the very thing they need to infuse American Independence and the entire Revolution with victory!"

She dipped a quill into the inkwell to write an editing note for Secretary Thomson. "We, therefore, the Representatives of the United States of America in General Congress Assembled," Liz read, then added, "APPEALING TO THE SUPREME JUDGE OF THE WORLD FOR THE RECTITUDE OF OUR INTENTIONS."

"That is a brilliant stroke of genius, my pet!" Nigel exclaimed.

"*Merci,* but it still needs something more." Liz looked at Jefferson's last line.

> *acts and things which independant states may of right do. And for the support of this declaration]wi mutually pledge to each other our lives, our fortunes, & our sacred honour.*

Liz looked at Nigel. "*Monsieur* Jefferson needed assistance with the first line of this Declaration of Independence, but he especially needs assistance with the last line. Would you like to do the honors, *mon ami?*"

"I would be utterly delighted!" Nigel exclaimed. "I shall add the most important declaration the humans need betwixt Jefferson's final words."

After he finished writing the note he stood back while Liz read what he had written. The sleek French cat looked at the little mouse with a smile. "*C'est perfect.*"

SECOND CONTINENTAL CONGRESS, PENNSYLVANIA STATE HOUSE, PHILADELPHIA, JULY 4, 11:00 A.M.

Overnight a massive storm had swept through Philadelphia, bringing more pummeling rain, and drenching the stockings of every delegate until their wet feet squished inside their buckled shoes. The storm also caused the temperature to drop ten degrees, bringing a welcome relief to the men confined in the stuffy assembly room.

But as the morning wore on, the heat in the room once more grew unbearable. John Hancock motioned for a clerk to raise the windows. Congress would soon finish its work, and there would soon no longer be a need for secrecy about the Declaration of Independence. In fact, just the opposite would be desired—this Congress would see to it that people and nations around the globe knew of what the United States of America had declared.

As John Hancock got ready to raise his gavel in the air to strike the table and move for a final vote to approve the Declaration of Independence, he halted as Samuel Adams slammed his fist on Massachusetts' table. From across the room Button Gwinnett slammed his fist on Georgia's table, followed by William Hooper of North Carolina and Samuel Huntington of Connecticut.

"Gentlemen, are we to have delegates from each colony to slam their respective tables, or am I still president of this Congress?" Hancock asked with a furrowed brow.

"FLIES, everywhere!" Caesar Rodney shouted, slapping his leg. "They're flying in from the stables nearby."

Jefferson slapped his leg, and next to him Francis Lightfoot Lee slapped the Virginia table, exclaiming, "Surely the edits and final wording are complete by now, Mr. Hancock. Can we please proceed to a vote so we can flee from our tormentors?"

"I am sure Jefferson agrees, but his primary tormentors are his fellow *delegates,* not the flies," Nigel told Liz with a chuckle as Secretary Thomson proceeded to read the final edited draft of the Declaration of Independence.

"If I did not know better, I would think these flies came in here to intentionally harass these humans." Liz's tail curled up and down as she studied the flies. "A fly tormented Jefferson when he was writing the draft in his rooms as well."

Nigel joined Liz in watching the flies buzz around the room and the impatience of the delegates to vacate the premises. "Hmmm, I believe that at least for today they have done a service to Mr. Jefferson in ending his pain with the editing process. In addition to the forty-seven changes the Committee of Five made to his draft, I count thirty-nine additional changes by the Congress."

"Eighty-six changes," Liz noted with a grin as Thomson reached the final line. "Including *ours.*"

"And for the support of this declaration, WITH A FIRM RELIANCE ON THE PROTECTION OF DIVINE PROVIDENCE, we mutually pledge to each other our lives, our fortunes, and our sacred honor," Secretary Thomson concluded.

"*Bravo, cher* Nigel!" Liz cheered, squeezing the little mouse as Hancock moved for an official vote to approve the Declaration of Independence. "I know the Maker is quite pleased with your ten additional words, and the fact that the humans added them to *Monsieur* Jefferson's last sentence, even though the note was left anony*mousely.*"

"I'm sure the Maker doesn't mind *ten* words rather than seven," Nigel quipped, preening his whiskers.

"The Declaration of Independence is approved by unanimous vote," John Hancock finally announced. "I hereby authorize copies to be printed by John Dunlap. Mr. Jefferson, I ask that the Committee of Five take responsibility for superintending and correcting the prepared press. Dunlap's broadsides will be distributed to the Committees of Safety in every colony . . ."

"STATE!" John Adams corrected him.

"Thank you, Mr. Adams, in every *state,* as well as sent to General Washington to be read to the Continental Army in New York," Hancock continued. "In addition, Mr. Thomson, please send a copy to Mr. Silas Deane in Paris immediately. We have no time to waste in sharing this news with our hopeful French allies."

"*Bon!* France will soon have a copy of *la déclaration!*" Liz cheered, putting a paw to her heart. "I cannot wait to hear of their response!"

"We shall have an official, engraved copy prepared for delegates from every *state* to sign within a month's time. For now," Hancock continued, taking a quill and signing his name to the bottom of the draft, "Mr. Thomson, please make a note in the journal of Congress that I have signed the approved Declaration of Independence." He replaced the quill in its holder. "We shall take a short recess and continue with the business of executing the war this afternoon."

As the delegates rose from their chairs to congratulate one another, Benjamin Franklin leaned over to Thomas Jefferson and John Adams and smiled. "We must all hang together or most assuredly we shall all hang separately."

"Good show!" Nigel exclaimed with a fist of victory raised in the air. "It is done, done, and *done!* Now, my dear, whilst these humans print and prepare for the celebratory reading of the Declaration of Independence, shall we away to Williamsburg? I believe we can make your Henry's swearing-in ceremony."

Liz's eyes lit up with joy and she kissed Nigel on the top of his head. "*Oui, merci!* Our work here is finished. Let us go celebrate *Governor* Henry!"

Proclaim Liberty Throughout the Land

WILLIAMSBURG, VIRGINIA, JULY 6, 1776

Patrick Henry's hand shook as he feebly raised it in the air. It was ninety-five degrees, yet he was shivering uncontrollably in his sickbed. Liz and Nigel shared worried looks as did John Page and the four councilors-elect who stood at the foot of the bed. They frowned as they waited on the Voice of the Revolution to repeat the oath of Governor, which they were administering to him.

". . . that th-th-the laws and ordinances of the Commonwealth be duly observed," Patrick repeated, pausing to close his eyes for a moment as he let go a shivering breath, ". . . and that law and j-j-justice, in mercy . . . be executed in all j-j-judgments."

Nigel furrowed his brow and nodded. "I'm afraid Mr. Henry has been stricken with malaria. The Tidewater is notorious for the malady in summer given the horrid mosquitoes and abundant marshlands here."

"He is struggling so!" Liz cried. "I am not used to *mon* Henry having such a weak voice. MizP was right to worry about the mosquitoes. After all the opposition he has faced, how could it be that such a tiny creature could bring down the Voice of the Revolution?"

"So h-h-help me God," Patrick finally gasped, allowing his hand to fall to the bed as he concluded the oath. He closed his eyes and pressed his head into the pillow, pulling the covers up to his quivering chin. He opened his weak, achy eyes and looked up at the men who would now serve at his side as he took the helm of Virginia as their Governor. "Th-th-thank you, gentlemen. Again, I apologize. Pray, allow me . . . to rest now."

The men respectfully bowed and quietly left the room. Patrick rolled over and curled his legs into his chest, violently shivering and moaning softly.

"I cannot bear to see him like this again. It was difficult to watch him suffer when he was recovering from the smallpox inoculation in Philadelphia," Liz lamented. "But I do not see how I can leave him, either. What if he does not recover?!"

Nigel tapped Liz gently on her paw. "There, there, my dear, I'm sure your Henry shall recover *well* once he is back at Scotchtown. For now, his family is here to care for him and see him safely home. It is tragic he has contracted this disease but there is nothing we can do for him that is not already being done. We must entrust Mr. Henry to the Maker and return to Philadelphia. Afterward, you can go to Scotchtown and check on his well-being."

Liz wiped her eyes. *"Oui,* I know we must be there to attend the day of celebration for the liberty that he has helped to accomplish for America. Let me bid him *adieu* and we can be going."

"Of course," Nigel replied softly, squeezing her arm. "We can update MizP on our way out."

Liz nodded, and then jumped up onto the bed, softly tiptoeing over to Patrick. She reached out her paw and gently placed it on his foot so he wouldn't notice her touch. She whispered almost imperceptibly, "Rest now, *cher* Patrick. I will pray you well and see you soon."

As Liz and Nigel quietly left via the open window, another imperceptible voice rose from the corner of the room. "Why settle for 'liberty OR death' when you can have BOTH, Mr. Henry?"

PENNSYLVANIA STATE HOUSE YARD, PHILADELPHIA, JULY 8, NOON

BONG! BONG! BONG! rang the bells all over the city, summoning the citizens to the Pennsylvania State House. Gillamon, Liz, Nigel, and Veritas stood on the roof of the State House, gazing down at the throngs of people surrounding the building below. Fifers fifed and drummers drummed while militiamen marched together, proudly holding various militia standards and Patriotic flags: the Grand Union, DON'T TREAD ON ME, Liberty or Death.

"Just look at this crowd!" Nigel exclaimed, his arms spread out wide. "It has been quite a long time since I've seen such a sea of euphoric humanity gathered in one place!"

"I never thought this happy day would come!" Liz shouted above the celebratory noise below.

Gillamon smiled and nodded. "It took blood, courage, betrayal, persistence, hard work, sacrifice, prayer, diligence, compromise, and unity."

"And miracles," Veritas added.

"Miracles indeed, and the guiding hand of the Maker," Gillamon affirmed him. "But this day has arrived right on time."

"Why aren't they ringing the bell in this steeple?" Veritas asked. "Every other bell in the city is ringing."

"I'm afraid the bell tower is in a dreadful state of disrepair, and quite unstable," Nigel answered. "The humans must feel it too risky to sound the 2,080-pound bronze beauty."

"*Quel dommage,* especially with what is transcribed on the bell, no?" Liz pouted. "If any bell should ring on this day, it is *this* bell."

"What does it say?" Veritas asked.

"Come, let me show you," Gillamon offered with a grin. The eagle and the other animals followed him over to where the silent bell hung in the steeple. "Can you read what it says?"

> PROCLAIM LIBERTY THROUGHOUT ALL THE LAND
> UNTO ALL THE INHABITANTS THEREOF LEV. XXV. V X.
> BY ORDER OF THE ASSEMBLY
> OF THE PROVINCE OF PENSYLVANIA
> FOR THE STATE HOUSE IN PHILADA
> PASS AND STOW
> PHILADA
> MDCCLIII

"It was made in 1753? They misspelled Pennsylvania and Philadelphia," Veritas observed.

"Actually, those are acceptable spellings for both," Liz explained. "This bell was ordered from London in 1751 to commemorate the 50th anniversary of Pennsylvania's original constitution. They chose the inscription of Leviticus 25:10 because the verse before refers to the year of 'Jubilee' when the Israelites were to return property and free slaves every 50 years." She paused and shook her head sadly. "If only this bell were ringing for that purpose today."

"Patience, dear one," Gillamon said. "Sometimes things are *made* broken and need time to be fixed."

"Just like this very bell! It cracked upon its first test ring and was twice recast by Philadelphia metalworkers John Pass and John Stow," Nigel explained.

Gillamon nodded and smiled. "That's right. From its very first 'bong,' this bell was broken. You and Nigel have just seen the creation of Virginia's Constitution. Tell me, was there anything wrong with it?"

"*Bien sûr!* It gives the right to vote primarily to property owners and men of wealth," Liz answered. "It excludes women, the poor, and slaves."

"And the Declaration of Independence?" Gillamon asked.

"All men are created equal and endowed by their Creator with certain inalienable rights," Nigel lamented. "Life, liberty, and the pursuit of happiness, but slaves do not have liberty."

Gillamon held up a finger. "That to secure these rights, Governments are instituted among Men, deriving their just powers from the consent of the governed,—That whenever any Form of Government becomes destructive of these ends, it is the Right of the *People to alter or to abolish it.*" He pointed to the bell. "When this bell was found to be defective, it was completely melted down and recast to correct the crack. But it cracked again, and it will continue to crack. But can it still ring? Have the humans used this bell regardless of the cracks?"

"Indeed, they have, Gillamon. They wisely chose to keep it despite its flaws. It has rung to summon the people for times of celebration as well as alarm: in 1761 for King George III's ascension to the British throne, in 1765 to address the Stamp Act, and just last year to announce the battles of Lexington and Concord."

"The humans are learning as they go—Patrick Henry with his voice, George Washington with his sword, and Thomas Jefferson with his pen. Casting bells and sculpting statues take time to perfect, and so will the founding documents of the United States of America. The humans are learning to take that which is imperfect and to keep refining it; they will do this in how they will govern themselves going forward." Gillamon held up an imaginary chisel and hammer. "Liberty is chiseled one tap at a time, with precision and care. It cannot be hammered into place with one, single blow. Liz, do you remember standing in place for hours on end as the sculptor meticulously carved the image of you and the Roman goddess of liberty long ago? Why did it take time to carve Libertas?"

"The sculptor had to take his time to get it right. At first, he made large cuts in the stone to make the general shape," Liz answered. "He began with just a solid block of marble that looked like nothing. A few substantial blows created the head and the body."

"And the details such as the hands, the robes, the eyes, and the liberty-loving cat at her feet?" Gillamon asked.   ·

"They had to be carefully, delicately carved to ensure the details were just right in order to make the image take the proper form," Liz answered.

Gillamon nodded. "So why can't a sculptor rush?"

"If he rushes, he could destroy the entire work!" Liz declared. "He must take his time, and although the statue does not look ready for display, the day will come when she is in the most beautiful form for all the world to see."

"So, the Fifth Virginia Convention and this new United States of America have made the first blows of the chisel to create, let's call her a 'Statue of Liberty,'"

Gillamon suggested. "These founding documents will not only serve to establish the independence of the United States of America but will serve as a model for other nations in the future. But this vital Declaration of Independence is the starting blow for sculpting Liberty. Finishing the statue will take time."

Liz nodded her head thoughtfully. *"Je comprends.* This is especially so to bring liberty and justice for all, including the slaves, no?"

"And women," Nigel added with a paw on Liz's shoulder, drawing a shy smile from the French cat.

"But the beauty of Lady Liberty will be perfected at the right time in HIStory," Gillamon determined.

"Maybe this bell will be rung when Lady Liberty is complete," Veritas suggested. "Proclaim LIBERTY throughout all the land." The bald eagle reached out the tip of his feather to graze the bronze bell. "You are right, Liz. Of all bells, this one should ring today to celebrate the first blow of the chisel."

"Go ahead, young one," Gillamon told the bald eagle with a smile. "Let freedom ring."

Veritas's eyes widened. "Should I?"

"Yes, of course! How utterly *perfect* since we first met you at the bell tower at Lexington Green!" Nigel exclaimed, already plugging his tiny round ears with his fingers.

"Oui! Please ring it for those who cannot be here with us today," Liz encouraged him. A lump grew in her throat. "Ring it for those who've died so far in this quest for freedom, especially Dr. Warren. And ring it for your father, Cato."

The bald eagle nodded and asked, "How many times should I ring it?" reaching out to take hold of the rope and clinging to it with his beak.

"Seven," Gillamon told him with a knowing grin.

Together Gillamon, Liz, and Nigel beamed as the young bald eagle tugged on the rope seven times, tolling for the remembrance of those lost in the quest for freedom. When he finished, they embraced one another with joy.

"They're starting!" Nigel shouted, hearing a man call the assembly to attention in the courtyard below. The animals ran over to the edge of the roofline to listen.

"I have the honor to read the declaration voted upon four days ago by our Congress," loudly announced John Nixon, a lieutenant colonel in the Philadelphia militia. "In Congress, July 4, 1776. The unanimous Declaration of the thirteen United States of America," Nixon read, looking around and catching the eye of John Adams, who gave him a firm nod and smile of approval. Thomas Jefferson stood next to Adams with his arms folded over his chest, glancing out over the crowd.

"When in the course of human events, it becomes necessary for one people to dissolve the political bands which have connected them with another, and to assume among the powers of the earth, the separate and equal station to which the Laws of Nature and of Nature's God entitle them, a decent respect to the opinions of mankind requires that they should declare the causes which impel them to the separation.

"We hold these truths to be self-evident, that all men are created equal, that they are endowed by their Creator with certain unalienable Rights, that among these are Life, Liberty and the pursuit of Happiness.—That to secure these rights, Governments are instituted among Men, deriving their just powers from the consent of the governed,—That whenever any Form of Government becomes destructive of these ends, it is the Right of the People to alter or to abolish it, and to institute new Government, laying its foundation on such principles and organizing its powers in such form, as to them shall seem most likely to effect their Safety and Happiness. Prudence, indeed, will dictate that Governments long established should not be changed for light and transient causes; and accordingly all experience hath shewn, that mankind are more disposed to suffer, while evils are sufferable, than to right themselves by abolishing the forms to which they are accustomed. But when a long train of abuses and usurpations, pursuing invariably the same Object evinces a design to reduce them under absolute Despotism, it is their right, it is their duty, to throw off such Government, and to provide new Guards for their future security.—Such has been the patient sufferance of these Colonies; and such is now the necessity which constrains them to alter their former Systems of Government. The history of the present King of Great Britain is a history of repeated injuries and usurpations, all having in direct object the establishment of an absolute Tyranny over these States. To prove this, let Facts be submitted to a candid world.

"He has refused his Assent to Laws, the most wholesome and necessary for the public good.

"He has forbidden his Governors to pass Laws of immediate and pressing importance, unless suspended in their operation till his Assent should be obtained; and when so suspended, he has utterly neglected to attend to them.

"He has refused to pass other Laws for the accommodation of large districts of people, unless those people would relinquish the right of Representation in the Legislature, a right inestimable to them and formidable to tyrants only.

"He has called together legislative bodies at places unusual, uncomfortable, and distant from the depository of their public Records, for the sole purpose of fatiguing them into compliance with his measures.

"He has dissolved Representative Houses repeatedly, for opposing with manly firmness his invasions on the rights of the people.

"He has refused for a long time, after such dissolutions, to cause others to be elected; whereby the Legislative powers, incapable of Annihilation, have returned to the People at large for their exercise; the State remaining in the meantime exposed to all the dangers of invasion from without, and convulsions within.

"He has endeavoured to prevent the population of these States; for that purpose obstructing the Laws for Naturalization of Foreigners; refusing to pass others to encourage their migrations hither, and raising the conditions of new Appropriations of Lands.

"He has obstructed the Administration of Justice, by refusing his Assent to Laws for establishing Judiciary powers.

"He has made Judges dependent on his Will alone, for the tenure of their offices, and the amount and payment of their salaries.

"He has erected a multitude of New Offices, and sent hither swarms of Officers to harrass our people, and eat out their substance.

"He has kept among us, in times of peace, Standing Armies without the Consent of our legislatures.

"He has affected to render the Military independent of and superior to the Civil power.

"He has combined with others to subject us to a jurisdiction foreign to our constitution, and unacknowledged by our laws; giving his Assent to their Acts of pretended Legislation:

"For Quartering large bodies of armed troops among us:

"For protecting them, by a mock Trial, from punishment for any Murders which they should commit on the Inhabitants of these States:

"For cutting off our Trade with all parts of the world:

"For imposing Taxes on us without our Consent:

"For depriving us in many cases, of the benefits of Trial by Jury:

"For transporting us beyond Seas to be tried for pretended offences:

"For abolishing the free System of English Laws in a neighbouring Province, establishing therein an Arbitrary government, and enlarging its Boundaries so as to render it at once an example and fit instrument for introducing the same absolute rule into these Colonies:

"For taking away our Charters, abolishing our most valuable Laws, and altering fundamentally the Forms of our Governments:

"For suspending our own Legislatures, and declaring themselves invested with power to legislate for us in all cases whatsoever.

"He has abdicated Government here, by declaring us out of his Protection and waging War against us.

"He has plundered our seas, ravaged our Coasts, burnt our towns, and destroyed the lives of our people.

"He is at this time transporting large Armies of foreign Mercenaries to compleat the works of death, desolation and tyranny, already begun with circumstances of Cruelty & perfidy scarcely paralleled in the most barbarous ages, and totally unworthy the Head of a civilized nation.

"He has constrained our fellow Citizens taken Captive on the high Seas to bear Arms against their Country, to become the executioners of their friends and Brethren, or to fall themselves by their Hands.

"He has excited domestic insurrections amongst us, and has endeavoured to bring on the inhabitants of our frontiers, the merciless Indian Savages, whose known rule of warfare, is an undistinguished destruction of all ages, sexes and conditions.

"In every stage of these Oppressions We have Petitioned for Redress in the most humble terms: Our repeated Petitions have been answered only by repeated injury. A Prince whose character is thus marked by every act which may define a Tyrant, is unfit to be the ruler of a free people.

"Nor have We been wanting in attentions to our British brethren. We have warned them from time to time of attempts by their legislature to extend an unwarrantable jurisdiction over us. We have reminded them of the circumstances of our emigration and settlement here. We have appealed to their native justice and magnanimity, and we have conjured them by the ties of our common kindred to disavow these usurpations, which, would inevitably interrupt our connections and correspondence. They too have been deaf to the voice of justice and of consanguinity. We must, therefore, acquiesce in the necessity, which denounces our Separation, and hold them, as we hold the rest of mankind, Enemies in War, in Peace Friends.

"We, therefore, the Representatives of the united States of America, in General Congress, Assembled, appealing to the Supreme Judge of the world for the rectitude of our intentions, do, in the Name, and by Authority of the good People of these Colonies, solemnly publish and declare, That these United Colonies are, and of Right ought to be Free and Independent States; that they are Absolved from all Allegiance to the British Crown, and that all political connection between them and the State of Great Britain, is and ought to be totally dissolved; and that as Free and Independent States, they have full Power to levy War, conclude Peace, contract Alliances, establish Commerce, and to do all other Acts and Things which Independent States may of right do. And for the support of this Declaration, with a firm reliance on the protection of divine Providence, we mutually pledge to each other our Lives, our Fortunes and our sacred Honor."

Immediately the crowd erupted with three cheers, shouting, "God bless the free states of North America!"

Some Pennsylvania militiamen rushed into the State House and pulled down the king's coat of arms, throwing it into a large bonfire as the fifes and drums sounded and the people hugged, clapped, and cheered.

"Happy Birthday, America!" Nigel cheered.

"Joyeux Anniversaire, aux Etats-Unis d'Amérique!" Liz echoed.

"Speaking of the French, the copy of the Declaration of Independence from Congress is on its way to Silas Deane on one of those ships," Gillamon told them, pointing to the harbor. "You'll be happy to know that Deane safely arrived in Paris a few days ago. Kate has already seen to his lodgings."

"Splendid!" Nigel exclaimed. "Our American in Paris shall soon hear of this glorious Independence Day."

"Oui, this is happy news, and this has been such a happy day," Liz said— but with a frown. "But Gillamon, I am still worried about *mon* Henry."

"Don't worry, little one. Tomorrow you can go to him at Scotchtown," Gillamon told her. "But let's enjoy the celebration and fireworks over Philadelphia tonight."

"And to where shall I go next?" Nigel asked, preening his whiskers. "To Max and Jock in New York?"

"Yes, Veritas can take you," Gillamon agreed, motioning to the bald eagle, who nodded. He then pulled out an ornately carved pipe from his coat pocket. He smiled as he filled the bowl with sweet tobacco before lighting it, sending puffs of aromatic smoke into the air. "And I'll go to Lafayette, after I take care of things in New York."

PORT OF PHILADELPHIA, PENNSYLVANIA,
JULY 8, 9:00 P.M.

The fireworks exploding in the night sky over Philadelphia reflected on the waves of the wake trailing behind a schooner as it sliced through the dark waters of the Delaware River. Its most important cargo was the copy of the Declaration of Independence destined for Silas Deane in Paris. The glow from the fireworks was reflected in a pair of seething, red eyes hidden in the shadows of a thick, coiled rope on the ship's bow. The eyes glanced down at the note scribbled in blood:

THE VOICE IS SILENCED. DECLARATION HEADING TO FRANCE. - V

"At leassssst one of you didn't fail," Charlatan hissed. "But for thisssss task, I trusssssst in no one but mysssssself."

As the men aboard lifted toasts to celebrate the new United States of America, a sailor waved a flag with a coiled snake and DON'T TREAD ON ME. An evil grin crept onto Charlatan's face, as he envisioned the sailor stepping on his tail in the darkness.

"Oh, but I welcome it, so I can ssssstrike again."

FIGHTING WORDS
TO TOPPLE A TYRANT

MORTIER MANSION HEADQUARTERS,
NEW YORK, JULY 8, 1776, 9:00 P.M.

The fleet sailed from Halifax the 10th of June and arrived the 29th. The fleet consists of 120 sail of top-sail vessels... they have on board 10,000 troops received at Halifax, besides some of the Scottish brigade...

Washington's brow was furrowed as he read the urgent report from General Nathanael Greene at his headquarters over on Long Island. Greene had been closely watching the influx of the British fleet, and he along with Washington's officers had tried to estimate how many soldiers Howe had on board. Now they knew. But more were coming. Some of Greene's men had captured four careless British soldiers in the Narrows and gained alarming details of what was headed their way.

Four days before the fleet sailed from Halifax, a packet arrived from England that brought an account of Admiral Howe's sailing with a fleet of 150 sail, on board of which was 20,000 troops...

"They are expected in here every day," Washington read aloud to himself, letting Greene's letter fall to his lap. He leaned his head back on the high-backed chair and closed his tired eyes.

Jock looked worriedly at Max. "I don't know where the humans are going to fit all those ships in New York Harbor! It's already packed with General Howe's ships. Now his brother is going to crowd it even more,

215

followed by the ships coming from the Carolinas. Over 30,000 troops will be here! Washington, Knox, and Greene must be anxious about those numbers."

"Aye, but at least now they *know* wha' they're facin'," Max answered. "Them be big numbers, but when ye know wha' ye be facin', the unknown at least doesn't dr-r-rain yer mind power. Now they can focus on wha' they need ta do ta get r-r-ready."

"I sure hope Washington gets good news soon," Jock added, observing Washington rubbing his eyes.

"Aye, good news be comin', lad," Max told him. "The Declaration of Independence should arrive any day now."

"Just like the British," Jock added heavily. "But I wonder which will arrive first."

MORTIER MANSION HEADQUARTERS, NEW YORK, JULY 9, 1776, 7:00 A.M.

Washington was reading over the day's General Orders before handing them over to his aide for distribution to the troops.

The Honorable Continental Congress having been pleased to allow a Chaplain to each Regiment, with the pay of Thirty-three Dollars and one third per month—The Colonels or commanding officers of each regiment are directed to procure Chaplains accordingly; persons of good Characters and exemplary lives—To see that all inferior officers and soldiers pay them a suitable respect and attend carefully upon religious exercises: The blessing and protection of Heaven are at all times necessary but especially so in times of public distress and danger—The General hopes and trusts, that every officer, and man, will endeavour so to live, and act, as becomes a Christian Soldier defending the dearest Rights and Liberties of his country.

"I thought you could do with a fresh pot, General," Billy Lee announced as he brought in a tray to set on the table by Washington's desk. "I know you haven't been sleeping well. You need lots of strong coffee for the day ahead."

Washington looked up and gave a singular nod and slight smile as Billy poured a steaming cup of coffee. "Thank you, Billy, indeed I do. I've almost completed today's General Orders."

"Very good, Sir," Billy answered, setting the cup on the desk. "You seem pleased."

"I am. Congress has approved a chaplain for each regiment. I believe strongly in having chaplains present with the army," Washington answered, blowing on the cup, and taking a small sip. "They preach that spiritual warfare is just as vital as military warfare in their sermons on biblical heroes who had to use the sword, like David. Soldiers skilled in spiritual warfare have sometimes been some of the most vicious fighters on the battlefield."

Billy nodded, putting the marker of Washington's Bible in place, and closing it from his reading the night before, as was his habit. "The good Lord may grant victory, but He still needs human effort to make it happen."

"We need both earthly *and* heavenly weapons," Washington agreed. "If our army does not possess the Almighty's blessing plus heroic soldiers, we are doomed to failure. Each soldier must choose the path of his own spiritual conduct, but I shall do everything in my power to equip the men's spirits as much as their muskets. Heaven knows they shall need it with the coming battle."

Washington confided many such thoughts to Billy, his personal servant, close companion, and aide. They were inseparable back at Mount Vernon, riding side by side across the estate and on the chase in fox hunts where Billy showcased his masterful riding skills. Billy took care of Washington's every personal need and made certain that the general's uniform was always resplendent. Theirs was an unusual relationship, but one that allowed for honest discussion on such matters.

Billy walked over to raise the window to let in some fresh air. He saw a horse kicking up dust and making its way toward the house. "Looks like a post rider, Sir. Maybe he's from Philadelphia." He turned with an expectant look. "I'll go see."

Max and Jock were sitting in the corner, and shared hopeful glances. "Maybe this is it!" Jock whispered excitedly.

The mud-splattered post rider galloped his horse up the path leading to Washington's Headquarters, out of breath but full of relief to have finally made it to New York. He had ridden ninety miles and crossed five rivers in just three days. He quickly climbed down from the saddle, grabbed his satchel, and hurried up the steps leading to the main entrance. Billy Lee opened the door and the rider stood there with a broad smile.

"I've brought important news from The Continental Congress in Philadelphia to His Excellency, General George Washington," the rider gladly announced, handing over a leather folio.

"Come in and refresh yourself," Billy answered, taking the folio. "I'll take this to the General now, and our stable hands will see to your horse."

Within moments, Washington sat forward in his chair with his arms propped on his desk, reading the letter from John Hancock:

Philadelphia July 6th 1776

Sir,

The Congress, for some Time past, have had their Attention occupied by one of the most interesting and important Subjects, that could possibly come before them, or any other Assembly of Men.

Altho it is not possible to foresee the Consequences of Human Actions, yet it is nevertheless a Duty we owe ourselves and Posterity, in all our public Counsels, to decide in the best Manner we are able, and to leave the Event to that Being who controuls both Causes and Events to bring about his own Determinations.

Impressed with this Sentiment, and at the same Time fully convinced, that our Affairs may take a more favourable Turn, the Congress have judged it necessary to dissolve the Connection between Great Britain and the American Colonies, and to declare them free & independent States; as you will perceive by the enclosed Declaration, which I am directed to transmit to you, and to request you will have it proclaimed at the Head of the Army in the Way, you shall think most proper.

Washington stopped reading the letter and eagerly pulled out one of the freshly minted Dunlap broadsides, holding it with awe. The beleaguered Commander-in-Chief sat in silence and soaked in every one of the 1,300 words.

"I've got ta see if it's the Declaration!" Max told Jock. The two dogs scurried over to sit by Washington's chair. Max put his front paws up on the general's seat and looked up at him, hoping for a glimpse.

Washington's hand went down to rest on Max's head. "Good news, boy. This single piece of paper will change the world."

IN CONGRESS, JULY 4, 1776.

A DECLARATION

BY THE REPRESENTATIVES OF THE

UNITED STATES OF AMERICA,

IN GENERAL CONGRESS ASSEMBLED.

WHEN in the Course of human Events, it becomes necessary for one People to dissolve the Political Bands which have connected them with another, and to assume among the Powers of the Earth, the separate and equal Station to which the Laws of Nature and of Nature's God entitle them, a decent Respect to the Opinions of Mankind requires that they should declare the Causes which impel them to the Separation.

WE hold these Truths to be self-evident, that all Men are created equal, that they are endowed by their Creator with certain unalienable Rights, that among these are Life, Liberty, and the Pursuit of Happiness.— —That to secure these Rights, Governments are instituted among Men, deriving their just Powers from the Consent of the Governed, that whenever any Form of Government becomes destructive of these Ends, it is the Right of the People to alter or to abolish it, and to institute new Government, laying its Foundation on such Principles, and organizing its Powers in such Form, as to them shall seem most likely to effect their Safety and Happiness. Prudence, indeed, will dictate that Governments long established should not be changed for light and transient Causes; and accordingly all Experience hath shewn, that Mankind are more disposed to suffer, while Evils are sufferable, than to right themselves by abolishing the Forms to which they are accustomed. But when a long Train of Abuses and Usurpations, pursuing invariably the same Object, evinces a Design to reduce them under absolute Despotism, it is their Right, it is their Duty, to throw off such Government, and to provide new Guards for their future Security. Such has been the patient Sufferance of these Colonies; and such is now the Necessity which constrains them to alter their former Systems of Government. The History of the present King of Great-Britain is a History of repeated Injuries and Usurpations, all having in direct Object the Establishment of an absolute Tyranny over these States. To prove this, let Facts be submitted to a candid World.

HE has refused his Assent to Laws, the most wholesome and necessary for the public Good.

HE has forbidden his Governors to pass Laws of immediate and pressing Importance, unless suspended in their Operation till his Assent should be obtained; and when so suspended, he has utterly neglected to attend to them.

HE has refused to pass other Laws for the Accommodation of large Districts of People, unless those People would relinquish the Right of Representation in the Legislature, a Right inestimable to them, and formidable to Tyrants only.

HE has called together Legislative Bodies at Places unusual, uncomfortable, and distant from the Depository of their public Records, for the sole Purpose of fatiguing them into Compliance with his Measures.

HE has dissolved Representative Houses repeatedly, for opposing with manly Firmness his Invasions on the Rights of the People.

HE has refused for a long Time, after such Dissolutions, to cause others to be elected; whereby the Legislative Powers, incapable of Annihilation, have returned to the People at large for their Exercise; the State remaining in the mean time exposed to all the Dangers of Invasion from without, and Convulsions within.

HE has endeavoured to prevent the Population of these States; for that Purpose obstructing the Laws for Naturalization of Foreigners; refusing to pass others to encourage their Migrations hither, and raising the Conditions of new Appropriations of Lands.

HE has obstructed the Administration of Justice, by refusing his Assent to Laws for establishing Judiciary Powers.

HE has made Judges dependent on his Will alone, for the Tenure of their Offices, and the Amount and Payment of their Salaries.

HE has erected a Multitude of new Offices, and sent hither Swarms of Officers to harrass our People, and eat out their Substance.

HE has kept among us, in Times of Peace, Standing Armies, without the Consent of our Legislatures.

HE has affected to render the Military independent of and superior to the Civil Power.

HE has combined with others to subject us to a Jurisdiction foreign to our Constitution, and unacknowledged by our Laws; giving his Assent to their Acts of pretended Legislation:

FOR quartering large Bodies of Armed Troops among us:

FOR protecting them, by a mock Trial, from Punishment for any Murders which they should commit on the Inhabitants of these States:

FOR cutting off our Trade with all Parts of the World:

FOR imposing Taxes on us without our Consent:

FOR depriving us, in many Cases, of the Benefits of Trial by Jury:

FOR transporting us beyond Seas to be tried for pretended Offences:

FOR abolishing the free System of English Laws in a neighbouring Province, establishing therein an arbitrary Government, and enlarging its Boundaries, so as to render it at once an Example and fit Instrument for introducing the same absolute Rule into these Colonies:

FOR taking away our Charters, abolishing our most valuable Laws, and altering fundamentally the Forms of our Governments:

FOR suspending our own Legislatures, and declaring themselves invested with Power to legislate for us in all Cases whatsoever:

HE has abdicated Government here, by declaring us out of his Protection and waging War against us.

HE has plundered our Seas, ravaged our Coasts, burnt our Towns, and destroyed the Lives of our People.

HE is, at this Time, transporting large Armies of foreign Mercenaries to compleat the Works of Death, Desolation, and Tyranny, already begun with Circumstances of Cruelty and Perfidy, scarcely parallelled in the most barbarous Ages, and totally unworthy the Head of a civilized Nation.

HE has constrained our fellow Citizens taken Captive on the high Seas to bear Arms against their Country, to become the Executioners of their Friends and Brethren, or to fall themselves by their Hands.

HE has excited domestic Insurrections amongst us, and has endeavoured to bring on the Inhabitants of our Frontiers, the merciless Indian Savages, whose known Rule of Warfare, is an undistinguished Destruction, of all Ages, Sexes and Conditions.

IN every Stage of these Oppressions we have Petitioned for Redress in the most humble Terms: Our repeated Petitions have been answered only by repeated Injury. A Prince, whose Character is thus marked by every Act which may define a Tyrant, is unfit to be the Ruler of a free People.

NOR have we been wanting in Attentions to our British Brethren. We have warned them from Time to Time of Attempts by their Legislature to extend an unwarrantable Jurisdiction over us. We have reminded them of the Circumstances of our Emigration and Settlement here. We have appealed to their native Justice and Magnanimity, and we have conjured them by the Ties of our common Kindred to disavow these Usurpations, which, would inevitably interrupt our Connections and Correspondence. They too have been deaf to the Voice of Justice and of Consanguinity. We must, therefore, acquiesce in the Necessity, which denounces our Separation, and hold them, as we hold the rest of Mankind, Enemies in War, in Peace, Friends.

WE, therefore, the Representatives of the UNITED STATES OF AMERICA, in GENERAL CONGRESS, Assembled, appealing to the Supreme Judge of the World for the Rectitude of our Intentions, do, in the Name, and by Authority of the good People of these Colonies, solemnly Publish and Declare, That these United Colonies are, and of Right ought to be, FREE AND INDEPENDENT STATES; that they are absolved from all Allegiance to the British Crown, and that all political Connection between them and the State of Great-Britain, is and ought to be totally dissolved; and that as FREE AND INDEPENDENT STATES, they have full Power to levy War, conclude Peace, contract Alliances, establish Commerce, and to do all other Acts and Things which INDEPENDENT STATES may of Right do. And for the Support of this Declaration, with a firm Reliance on the Protection of divine Providence, we mutually pledge to each other our Lives, our Fortunes, and our sacred Honor.

Signed by ORDER and in BEHALF of the CONGRESS,

JOHN HANCOCK, PRESIDENT.

ATTEST.
CHARLES THOMSON, SECRETARY.

PHILADELPHIA: PRINTED BY JOHN DUNLAP.

Max smiled and wagged his tale as Washington showed him the Declaration. *Liz an' Mousie did it!* he barked happily. *They got the Declaration of Independence wr-r-ritten!*

Washington chuckled. "If I did not know better, I would think you could read, Max." He set down the document and reached for his quill. "I must add to today's General Orders. This Declaration is going to be read to every soldier in our army this evening."

Max hopped back down by Jock while Washington wrote.

The Honorable the Continental Congress, impelled by the dictates of duty, policy and necessity, having been pleased to dissolve the Connection which subsisted between this Country, and Great Britain, and to declare the United Colonies of North America, free and independent STATES: The several brigades are to be drawn up this evening on their respective Parades, at six OClock, when the declaration of Congress, shewing the grounds & reasons of this measure, is to be read with an audible voice.

The General hopes this important Event will serve as a fresh incentive to every officer, and soldier, to act with Fidelity and Courage, as knowing that now the peace and safety of his Country depends (under God) solely on the success of our arms: And that he is now in the service of a State, possessed of sufficient power to reward his merit, and advance him to the highest Honors of a free Country.

"We'll be headin' back ta the Commons tonight, lad," Max told Jock. "A lot has happened since the army gathered there for Hickey's hangin' jest eleven days ago."

Jock wagged his tail. "Aye, but this time, the army will gather for something happy!"

⚜

THE COMMONS, NEW YORK, JULY 9, 1776, 6:00 P.M.

"Looks like the British are here in full force," Veritas announced, furrowing his brow to see the scores of British ships anchored off Staten Island. The bald eagle circled above the British camp to give Nigel a full view. "All those redcoats milling about look like a swarm of fire ants."

"Indeed, although this is only *half* of the anthill that is coming, I'm afraid," Nigel lamented. The little mouse peered over the side of the bald eagle's wing to see row upon row of tidy, white tents lined up in British disciplined order. "Let's go see how the Patriots have dug in, shall we?"

"Sure thing, Nigel," Veritas answered as he soared over the length of

Manhattan and Long Island to see bare, torn-up ground and newly built fortifications everywhere.

"It appears that the army is assembling at several locales," Nigel told Veritas. He could see troops gathered on Long Island, King's Bridge, Governor's Island, and the Commons. "While they are not *tidy* as the red-coated foe, it does appear that some orderly gathering is taking place. Be a good chap and see if you can locate Max and Jock, will you?"

Veritas used his keen vision to scan the various parade grounds. He suddenly spotted two tiny black dogs trotting along behind a white horse. He smiled and pivoted direction. "Got 'em."

"Splendid! Please take us near their location for a flyover so I can alert them to our presence, but then do find a perch so as not to arouse the humans," Nigel instructed him.

Max and Jock went to sit on a nearby patch of ground as Washington, Knox, and several other staff officers made their way to the center of the Commons where all of those stationed in lower Manhattan were ordered to assemble. The New York and Connecticut regiments formed a hollow square, and Washington slowly rode atop Blueskin into its center, sitting erect and nodding at the men standing at attention on either side. The rank-and-file soldiers looked at one another with expectancy at seeing their Commander-in-Chief among them. His sheer presence was enough to instill confidence in the men.

"This is incredible, Grandsire!" Jock exulted, looking around the parade grounds at the thousands of men assembled. "Look how excited the soldiers are to see Washington!"

"Aye, lad. A str-r-rong leader doesn't have ta even say a word ta inspire his followers," Max answered. Suddenly a shadow flew overhead, and he looked up to see Veritas circling above. He then saw Nigel lean over and wave with his tiny, outstretched paw. "Well, wha' do ye know? Mousie's here, r-r-ridin' on that eagle."

Jock looked up quickly and smiled. He barked, "Hi, Nigel! Hi, Veritas!"

Veritas spotted the scaffold where Hickey had been hanged, and slowly descended to perch on top, shaking out his tail feathers and folding in his wings as he took in the view. Nigel climbed down and gave the bald eagle a grateful petting. "Thank you, dear boy, for your speedy transport from Philadelphia. I do believe we've arrived just in time for the momentous event to hear the reading of the Declaration!"

"You're welcome, Nigel," Veritas answered. "I'm glad we made it in time."

"Now, then, I am sure you are simply *famished* after your long flight," Nigel told him. "As you have recently heard these words, please feel free to go pursue a well-deserved meal of fish while I go join Max and Jock on the ground. Then if you would, please return to this post so we can find you."

"Will do, Nigel," Veritas answered, lifting off. Nigel gave him a salute and scurried down the scaffold as the fifer and drummer beat the call to order.

"ATTENTION!" a uniformed aide suddenly called out in a loud voice with an upraised hand. He held one of the Dunlap broadsides that had been distributed throughout the army regiments with today's General Orders. The crowd of assembled soldiers quieted down and listened as the man began to read:

> "In Congress, July 4, 1776. The unanimous Declaration of the thirteen United States of America. When in the course of human events, it becomes necessary for one people to dissolve the political bands which have connected them with another. . ."

Washington looked around at the assembly of men as they listened intently to the Declaration of Independence. His heart was heavy with the gravity of the moment. His men would finally have a clear and moral purpose and would understand why they were fighting—they were fighting a war of independence that was an *American* Revolution. They were no longer just a handful of disparate colonies, but thirteen *United* States. He prayed their hearts and minds would be cemented together in the resolve of the words they heard.

"These are some fighting words, Grandsire!" Jock enthused, listening to the long train of abuses, and listing of twenty-seven grievances, followed by the bold declaration to break off from Great Britain.

"Aye, lad, but these fightin' words aren't jest worth fightin' for," Max answered with a serious expression. "They be worth *dyin'* for."

"And for the support of this Declaration, with a firm reliance on the protection of divine Providence, we mutually pledge to each other our Lives, our Fortunes, and our sacred Honor," the aide hoarsely cried out, punctuating each word.

Washington immediately nodded at the chaplain, who proceeded to recite Psalm 80. "Turn us again, O God, and cause thy face to shine; and we shall be saved . . ."

Max wore a big grin as he saw Nigel darting among the forested legs of soldiers to reach them. "Glad ye made it, Mousie! Ye an' Liz did a gr-r-rand job gettin' this Declaration written."

"Hi, Nigel! Good job!" Jock added.

Suddenly the assembly of soldiers erupted into wild cheers, their voices echoing across the Commons. Hats went flying into the air, and adjutant general Thomas Mifflin climbed on top of a cannon. He waved his hat and shouted, "My lads, the Rubicon is crossed!"

"Thank you, my good fellows!" Nigel shouted above the din, preening his whiskers, and looking around at the wild celebration. "By the looks of it, the Declaration is an instant hit in Philadelphia *and* New York."

Max, Jock, and Nigel hugged and cheered themselves, watching with joy as the humans allowed the liberty they had just received on paper to become their rallying cry. It would be up to these very soldiers to make this piece of paper a reality.

"My human Henry Knox is smiling a mile wide!" Jock announced, catching the Colonel sitting atop his horse next to Washington, exchanging a handshake of exhilaration with the Commander-in-Chief.

"Aye, so's mine, which be somethin' ye don't see every day," Max added, wagging his tail.

Washington and Knox proceeded to spur their horses on through the crowd, who cheered their commanders on with fists of victory raised in the air. "These are not the same men as the ones who stood here eleven days ago, your Excellency," Knox remarked. "These men have been united in purpose, and not a moment too soon. Congratulations to the Congress!"

Washington nodded, happy to see the desired effect on the men. "Indeed, Colonel Knox. And they appear to be heading to a celebration as one Continental Army. But we have much work to do. Let's leave them with it, and head back to headquarters."

As Washington and Knox trotted along ahead, Max, Jock, and Nigel watched the sea of cheering soldiers making their way south down Broadway.

"I have a feelin' there's gonna be some property destr-r-royed tonight!" Max declared.

"They're heading to Bowling Green!" Jock added.

"The statue! I do believe I know exactly where these jolly throngs are headed. I shall go catch a ride on Veritas and soar above the mayhem to observe from the air," Nigel told them as he scurried off to find the bald eagle.

BOWLING GREEN, MANHATTAN, NEW YORK,
JULY 9, 1776, 9:00 P.M.

The sun had dipped below the horizon, leaving a panoramic sky painted with red, orange, pink, and yellow. From the air, Nigel and Veritas could see tiny lantern lights bobbing along toward Bowling Green as citizens poured into the streets to meld with the exuberant soldiers.

"They're heading for the statue, alright," Veritas confirmed, spotting a group of men carrying huge coils of rope over their shoulders.

"By Jove, they're going to pull it down!" Nigel exclaimed. A wry grin appeared on his face and his whiskers quivered as he let out a jolly chuckle. "My boy, I have had quite the naughty thought."

"What's that, Nigel?" Veritas asked.

"Once upon a memory, I soared above the detestable statue of another king, but on a pigeon," Nigel relayed. "I just could not *resist* the urge to leave a mark of disapproval on the statue of King Nebuchadnezzar, as it had caused three young men to be thrown into a fiery furnace, despite the fact that they were unharmed, with the Maker's help. But I digress. I don't suppose . . ."

"Say no more," Veritas laughed. "Coming right up."

With that, Veritas circled the statue of King George III. Nigel held on to the eagle's feathers and leaned over the side until they were situated perfectly. "On my mark!" he exclaimed. Veritas swooshed in closer, heading straight for the statue. The crowds below were armed with tools and a handful of them began breaking into the iron fence surrounding the statue. When they were almost right on top of the statue, Nigel shouted, "FIRE!"

A plop of poop hit King George in the face, and Nigel erupted in cheers, patting the bald eagle excitedly. "HUZZAH! Direct hit on the gilded tyrant, old boy!"

"Happy to offer my sentiments as well, Nigel," Veritas answered coyly.

A roar of cheers sounded as the fence was opened and a mass of people rushed inside to surround King George III. Men climbed up onto the marble pedestal where the statue sat and threw ropes around it from every angle. Exclamations from the Sons of Liberty punctuated the revelry and spurred on the crowd. It wasn't just soldiers in the crowd, but women, distinguished gentlemen, and even children.

"Down with the tyrant!"

"The Declaration of Independence says he's unfit to be the ruler of a free people, and I say he's unfit to stay on his perch!"

"Let's melt him down for lead musket balls to fire back into the tyrant's army!"

Max and Jock sat by with their jaws hanging open as the crowd pulled and pulled and pulled until the statue came crashing down to the ground. Immediately, the crowd knocked off the head, cut off its crowning laurels, and whacked off its nose. A few soldiers then fired their guns, sinking lead musket balls into the head and torso.

"Them fightin' words have toppled the tyrant," Max said with a grin.

"Looks like they're scraping the gold off the statue and the horse!" Jock exclaimed.

"Aye, waste not, want not," Max answered with a chuckle. "Now they're tearin' the statue apart."

"I say, this is quite the celebration, filled with jocularity!" Nigel shouted as he and Veritas came in for a landing next to the two Scotties.

"Jock-u-what?" Jock asked. "Are you talking about me?"

Nigel chuckled and patted the little Scottish terrier. "Jocularity, meaning humorousness, playfulness, cheerfulness, sportiveness, and dare I say *roguishness!*"

Suddenly the fifes and drums struck up a cadence and started playing "The Rogue's March."

Nigel's eyes lit up. "What perfect timing! They are playing quite the fitting tune!"

Some men put the head of King George in a wheelbarrow and started making their way north on Broadway. "Let's take it to the Mortier House!'

"Knowin' him, I don't think Washington's gonna like this," Max cautioned. "He an' those in charge fr-r-rown on destruction of property, jest like they did when the Sons of Liberty tossed the tea inta Boston Harbor. We best follow them back ta the Mortier House."

"Indeed, I am sure that His Excellency will dictate a reproach of sorts," Nigel agreed. "But for now, let these jolly fellows have their fun to celebrate the Declaration of Independence!"

"With jocularity!" Jock exclaimed. "I like that new word!"

With that, Max and Jock fell in behind the jubilant crowd, and Nigel took flight atop Veritas to observe the festivities all over the area. As they soared above Long Island, they saw people with torches.

"Since they don't have a statue, I guess they needed to make their own King George III to topple," Veritas said. "Look below in that village."

The soldiers on Long Island had made an effigy of King George wearing a wooden crown and feathers. They wrapped it in a Union Jack flag and packed it with gunpowder.

"They are hanging that effigy on a gallows," Nigel noted, adjusting his spectacles as he strained to see the crowd of people hurriedly backing away from it. "I dare say, they are going to light it!"

Suddenly a soldier lit a fuse and ran away from the hanging powder-keg effigy. Within moments, wooden King George III exploded in spectacular fashion, sending pieces flying into the night sky like fireworks.

"New York has their own fireworks tonight after the reading of the Declaration," Veritas exclaimed.

"Indeed, and General Howe is most assuredly watching this celebration with great interest," Nigel added. "He will no doubt give a prompt reply to all the . . . jocularity."

26

OUR MAN IN PARIS

HÔTEL DU GRAND VILLARS, PARIS, FRANCE, JULY 8, 1776

E dward Bancroft stepped out of the carriage and down into a deep puddle as driving rain pummeled him from every direction in the busy Parisian Street. The thirty-one-year-old American squinted against a gust that hit him in the face as he tried to read the hotel sign, checking to make sure he was at the right place. He pulled a few coins from his pocket and handed them to the driver, who handed him his soaked leather valise. *"Merci,"* he muttered as he quickly darted under the etched stone edifice, grabbed the brass handle to open the wooden door leading into the hotel, and slipped inside.

Several moments later, Silas Deane opened his suite door, surprised to see his former pupil standing there, a soggy, dripping mess. "My dear Mr. Bancroft! Or I should say *Dr.* Bancroft, come in, come in!" he exclaimed, taking the man by the elbow. "I'm terribly sorry you had to battle the elements this morning, but I am delighted to see you!"

"Good day, Mr. Deane," Bancroft replied with a chagrined expression, removing his black hat and bowing humbly. He was somewhat embarrassed to feel like a young teenager before his tutor again, wiping his hands onto his coat as best he could. "Forgive my, uh, rather damp entry into your chambers." He pulled out a kerchief and dabbed the sides of his face where the powder from his wig dripped in white streaks. "I had hoped for a more pleasant first reunion."

"Nonsense, it is indeed a pleasure to see you regardless of your appearance! Permit me to retrieve for you a drying cloth," Deane offered as he turned on his heels to go into another room.

Kate stood nearby unseen and unheard, and observed the man she had looked forward to joining Silas Deane, who had just arrived in Paris as well. Bancroft had a rather round face, thick eyebrows that angled up over his deep-set brown eyes, and a slight dimple in his full chin. He wore a black coat and breeches, cream-colored shirt, and green silk stockings that slid inside his wet buckled shoes. Bancroft looked around the ornately decorated room and set his valise on the floor, careful not to touch the furniture.

"Here you are," Deane said, returning with a long, white, cotton cloth. "I must say that I am impressed by the quality of linens in this establishment. The French appear to appreciate the finer details of comfort."

"Thank you, sir," Bancroft answered, gratefully taking the towel in hand, and drying his face, neck, and hands. "Indeed, the French do place great value in creature comforts." He pointed to the light blue velvet settee. "I dare not sit down on that in my current state."

"You obviously must stay for a few days in Paris," Deane assumed. "Have you made arrangements to lodge here?"

"No, sir, I first wanted to come straight to see you and determine what would be most convenient," Bancroft replied.

"Well, might I suggest that you proceed to rent your room and change so we can *sit* and talk in comfort?" Deane jested. "I shall arrange for breakfast to be delivered. Or as I am learning, *petit . . .*" he stopped short, reaching for his English-French dictionary.

"Petit déjeuner, I believe is what you are looking for, French for breakfast," Bancroft offered with a smile.

Deane closed his eyes and laughed. "Indeed, my friend! How glad I am to have you here to help me with this difficult language. You always were a quick learner. Are you fluent in French?"

"Oui, I am. Why don't I order our breakfast when I go obtain my room?" Bancroft suggested.

"Thank you, yes! You shall be far speedier than I," Deane lamented. "Very well, I shall see you shortly after you get settled in."

Don't forget the madeleines! Kate thought hopefully.

An hour later the two men sat eating their French bread with butter and cherry jam, boiled eggs, various cheeses, pastries, and madeleines, and sipping hot *chocolat.* They were enjoying getting caught up with one another after fifteen years apart. Deane was twenty-two as tutor and Bancroft fifteen as pupil in Connecticut, but the age difference mattered little especially now that they were grown men. Deane filled Bancroft in on his years in America. Now it was his pupil's turn.

"So, you ran away to sea at eighteen to pursue adventure after briefly apprenticing as a doctor?" Deane asked.

Bancroft swallowed with a nod. "Indeed, yes, I sailed to Barbados and then South America before settling in Dutch Guiana. I worked on a planta-tion as a surgeon, caring for two hundred slaves. By the age of twenty, I was physician to *four* plantations but I soon quit that work to pursue the study of animal and plant life. I found it extremely fascinating. I love researching, discovering, and sharing new things, so I wrote a book, *The Natural History of Guiana.* I must admit that after its 1769 release in London, where I had moved in 1767, I enjoyed some scholarly celebrity."

"Impressive! You certainly have the ability to quickly gain the confidence of men of wealth and importance," Deane noted. "And you certainly move around a great deal. You were always a voracious reader. So, medicine, science, travel, history. Tell me about your book."

"You are most gracious, sir. Well, the first part of the book provides the history, topography, and geography of the region," Bancroft explained, growing animated. "The second part is devoted to animals, particularly my four favorite species: insects, snakes, bats, and eels. I collected more than three hundred snakes in my studies!"

Kate wrinkled her brow and frowned. *So he's more a lover of the slimy species than the furry kind.*

"My most thrilling discovery was the torporific eel," Bancroft shared excitedly. "It actually gives off an electric shock! Other scientists have been inspired by my findings of animal physiology and electricity."

Deane raised his eyebrows. "Fascinating. No doubt, you and Dr. Franklin enjoyed many such discussions while you were together in London. He drew electricity from the sky, and you from the water! No wonder he thinks so highly of you."

"Yes, Dr. Franklin took me under his wing as a protégé of sorts, and we indeed bonded over electricity," Bancroft chuckled. "The third section of my book focuses on the eating habits of the natives and natural treatments for a variety of health issues, including snake bites, of course. I dedicated thirty pages alone to the study of poison and how the natives use it on their arrows."

"What a totally different world you experienced in that mystical, exotic place," Deane noted, filling their cups with more *chocolat.* "You gained a broad range of knowledge of good and bad medicine in that country."

Bancroft lifted the cup. "Good and evil are indiscriminately mingled in every cup." He took a sip and set the cup in the saucer. "But all this to say that my book opened the door to many acquaintances in London, such as Dr. Franklin. Why, New Hampshire's colonial agent in London, Mr. Paul Wentworth, even asked me to travel back to the Dutch Netherlands to find ways for improving the production of coffee on his three plantations."

Deane smiled and shook his head good naturedly. "My dear sir, you are certainly a *boundless* explorer of every field, and a man of the world! Tell me, when did you find time to get a medical degree? Have you had time to have a family?"

"After traveling between London, Ireland, and briefly to America for land speculation with Dr. Franklin and others, I began an import business with my brother for bark used to make dyes for cloth. With my studies upon the subject, I wrote a paper on black ink that led to my nomination in the Royal Society in London with Dr. Franklin's gracious endorsement. I continue to write publications on dyes and inks. I joined the Medical Society of London and became its secretary just last year," Bancroft rattled off. "But to answer your questions, *yes,* I got my medical degree from the University of Aberdeen and married a lovely Catholic girl named Penelope. Sadly, her parents were none too thrilled with her marrying an anti-Catholic Puritan Deist, but we are happily married and have two children. I now practice medicine on Downing Street in London. And I still love to research and write reports on my findings. I don't think I shall ever lose my wanderlust for discovery."

Deane dabbed the corners of his mouth with his napkin and sat back in his chair, raising his hands in stunned appreciation for all his pupil had accomplished. "Dr. Bancroft, I am truly amazed and extremely proud of all you have achieved. And to be a respectable physician sharing a street address with no less than the Prime Minister, Lord North? Well done!" He leaned in with a knowing grin. "Your locale could prove to be quite invaluable, having neighbors at the ruling epicenter of the British Empire." He patted his stomach. "Now, shall we retire to the parlor to sit on the comfortable furniture and digest our *petit déjeuner?*"

"Thank you, yes, and you can tell me what has brought you to Paris," Bancroft suggested with a smile. "Something tells me it is not about South America, but about *North* America."

Kate jumped up on a chair to grab a couple of madeleines for breakfast and to save some in her pouch after the gentlemen went to the other room. *This meetin' is shapin' up rather nicely for all of us!*

"I'm sure my letter of invitation to join me in Paris was rather vague, but I needed of course to omit any political affair business should the British post office intercept it," Deane explained.

Bancroft pulled from his folio a stack of pamphlets and newspapers. "I assumed your visit must have something to do with colonial affairs, so I took the liberty of bringing information for you on the latest news from London."

Deane smiled broadly, taking the papers in hand. "Excellent! Thank you, sir. I look forward to reading these." He set them on the table and picked up his letter of credence to show Bancroft. "I am indeed here on secret business on behalf of the Secret Committee of Congress, posing as a merchant sent to acquire goods for gifts and trade with the Native Americans. But my *true* mission is to acquire French aid in the form of artillery, arms, uniforms, and equipment for an army of 25,000 men. I also am to assess if France would ally themselves with the Patriots for trade and support of our independency."

Bancroft slowly nodded as he read Benjamin Franklin's penned instructions. "I see. You know I have always supported the Patriot cause, but I had hoped that such a drastic step of independency could be avoided. I suppose a decade of remonstrances to the King and Parliament have left the colonies no other choice. Do you expect such a declaration soon?"

Aye, four days ago! Kate thought to herself, frustrated that she knew far more than the humans on this side of the Atlantic. *News of the Declaration of Independence be on its way ta France right now!*

"I certainly hope and *expect* so," Deane answered, sitting back on the settee and crossing his legs. "I am anxious for official word, as you can imagine. The Congress was determined that such a monumental decision be made only through unanimous vote among the delegates. When I left Philadelphia in March, I believe those sharing your longstanding hope of restoring relations with the Crown like Mr. Dickinson were finally becoming aware of the futility of such hope. Nonetheless, I am to seek an audience with Comte de Vergennes as soon as possible." He leaned forward. "I would ask that you accompany me to Versailles for such a momentous meeting and serve as my translator and assistant."

Bancroft became pensive, then nodded somberly. "I am honored by the confidence you and the Secret Committee have placed in me for such an historic purpose. I will gladly accompany you to Versailles. Should Vergennes provide his own translator, I shall respectfully wait while you converse in confidence."

Deane slapped his knees. "Splendid! Then we shall prepare for that important meeting which may very well chart a new course for our new nation!"

"I am your humble servant to command, sir," Bancroft replied, hands held wide, and head slightly bowed in respect.

HUZZAH! Kate cheered silently with her perky grin. *Next stop, Versailles! An' I won't even have ta worry aboot bein' seen even if that British Lord Stormont himself struts by.* A concerned look came over her invisible face. *Aye, but wha' if Stormont sees Deane an' Bancroft?*

27

AN OFFICIAL SECRET

CHÂTEAU DE VERSAILLES, FRANCE, JULY 10, 1776

Silas Deane's teeth involuntarily chattered as the carriage wheels met the bumpy brick pavement of the long causeway leading to the imposing gilded gates of Versailles. He peered out the window, and his eyes widened to see the grandeur of Europe's largest château, which was also the seat of power and government for France. This son of a simple blacksmith from Connecticut had never laid eyes on anything like this, and he gaped in awe as the bouncy carriage traipsed onto the grounds of French splendor.

What King Louis XIII had used as a quaint hunting lodge in the French countryside fourteen miles from Paris, his son, King Louis XIV, began transforming into a lavish display of wealth, fashion, and power in 1666. A new day dawned as "the Sun King" constructed numerous buildings and stables and spared no expense on manicured grounds with topiary gardens, exquisite pools and fountains, a royal chapel, and ornate décor dotted with statues of himself in various godlike visages. Versailles housed not only the royal family, but the French court and all the government departments, with ten thousand inhabitants milling about the expansive grounds.

Official state guests to Versailles would first enter the War Room, which oozed the glory of wartime victories from France's military supremacy and featured a huge, sculpted relief of King Louis XIV on horseback crowned by victory. This room overlooked the splendid gardens and celebrated the "Sun King's" civil and military victories. Louis XIV's acquired titles of "King of War" and "King of Glory" were shown through art to awe visitors by communicating to them exactly who they were privileged to approach. Louis XIV displayed busts of the first twelve Roman Emperors, from Julius Caesar to Domitian. As they were responsible for the establishment of Rome's imperial power, the King of France assumed that he inherited that same power.

The War Room opened to the long Hall of Mirrors, which ultimately led to the Peace Room on the far side of the hall. The entire length of the Hall of Mirrors paid tribute to the political, economic, and artistic success of France. The soaring, vaulted ceiling was covered with thirty exquisite paintings by Le Brun, illustrating the political successes and glorious history of Louis XIV during the first eighteen years of his reign. Figures of "Fame" and "Victory" also lined the ceiling to show the brilliance of French victories. The Hall of Mirrors was the corridor that courtiers and visitors traversed daily to reach the king or the queen. It served as a place for waiting, meeting, ceremonies, balls, and royal weddings or diplomatic receptions. When foreign diplomats were received by the king, his throne was placed on a platform at the end of the hall near the Peace Room. Subtly anchoring the corners of the Hall of Mirrors were four dark figures representing envy, anger, ambition, and discord.

At the opposite end of the Hall of Mirrors was the Peace Room. This room was symmetrical in shape and design to the War Room, but instead of war, the cupola and arches expressed the benefits of peace brought to Europe by France. Foreign guests were subtly reminded of the pleasures of peace contrasted with the pain of war—which path they experienced would be determined by the decisions and actions of their countries.

King Louis XV continued the glorious transformation begun by the Sun King with the addition of an exquisite opera house and apartments of convenience and luxury for courtiers who visited and waited upon the French court. Opulence reigned in Versailles with endless parties, balls, plays, and entertainment coupled with intrigue, scheming, and gossip. When the young newlyweds King Louis XVI and his Queen Marie Antoinette assumed the throne in Versailles, she thrived on the energy of taking merriment, lavishness, and spending to a whole new level with her dinners, masquerade balls, and fireworks, while he was content to sit with a good book by the fire or study his maps in quiet solitude.

"Perhaps someday you will be presented to the King in *La galerie des Glaces,*" Dubourg suggested to Deane, who turned to look at him quizzically.

"He means The Hall of Mirrors, which is reserved for *official* guests of the king and his government," Bancroft explained as the three men were jostled about in the carriage when it turned away from the front gate.

"But many things must first take place before that day. So today, you will meet with Comte de Vergennes in the administrative wing of the palace," Dubourg added, pointing to the impressive building. "The Ministry of Foreign Affairs."

Deane nodded with relief yet curious disappointment, as he wished to see for himself the wonder that was inside the main palace of Versailles. "I would not be ready to enter those halls even if it were in my instructions to do so. I fear I would most assuredly make more than one *faux pas.*"

"Learning the French language is one thing, but learning the protocols for presentation at court is another thing in and of itself," Dubourg offered with a knowing grin. "Besides, this will be an *unofficial* visit with the French government. A first conversation with America in France."

"Making it an official *secret,*" Bancroft followed with a smile of reassurance.

The horses' hoofs clip-clopped to a stop, and a footman quickly unfolded the hinged steps for the men to exit the carriage. Deane, Dubourg, and Bancroft stepped out and were greeted by a servant dressed in blue silk finery and a powdered wig. Once Dubourg explained the reason for their visit, they followed the servant up the steps and entered the esteemed halls representing the one ancient European power that the thirteen young colonies hoped would soon become their first ally.

Kate jumped off the carriage and followed unseen closely behind the men, stepping lightly so as not to be heard as they walked the tiled floors leading to the office of the one man who could make that happen.

Charles Gravier, Comte de Vergennes kept his gaze on the papers in front of him as the soft knock sounded on his door. *"Oui?"*

Vergennes's *premier commis,* or chief secretary, Conrad Alexandre Gérard de Rayneval opened the door and came over to whisper in his ear.

The fifty-seven-year-old, distinguished gentleman raised his eyebrows. *"Monsieur* Deane is here, now? I wondered when he would approach me."

"Oui, Monsieur. He is accompanied by *Messieurs* Dubourg and Bancroft," Gérard reported. "Shall I show them in?"

"Juste Monsieur Deane," Vergennes instructed as he put his quill back into the red crystal ink well. *"Un moment."* Gérard bowed in understanding and turned to go get Deane, allowing Vergennes time to collect his thoughts.

Vergennes placed his hands atop the ornate walnut desk trimmed in gold filigree, his mind racing. Of course, he knew from his spies that Silas Deane had landed in Bordeaux weeks ago. He also knew the hotel where Deane was staying in Paris, and that Bancroft had recently joined him there. The British ambassador Lord Stormont also knew Deane was in France from his *own* spies in Bordeaux, and in fact had known that Deane was due to arrive from sources in Philadelphia. The web of espionage stretched from one continent to another.

Stormont had already questioned Vergennes about the arrival of the American, keeping the heat on the French minister at the first whiff of France helping the rebels. Vergennes was able to honestly feign no personal knowledge of Deane nor why he was in France, but that would not be the case after this meeting. He paid close attention to business and remained clear-headed and forthright in all his affairs, making him the king's most trusted official.

In matters of international secrecy and diplomacy, Vergennes needed to play his part with perfection.

This was the meeting that Vergennes had long anticipated would eventually come. He was the one who had set it in motion when he instructed his spy Bonvouloir to meet secretly with Benjamin Franklin in Philadelphia seven months ago, gently feeling out the Americans about their growing rebellion. Bonvouloir suggested that the Americans send a representative to France, and Deane was the man chosen for the task. For months Vergennes had been laying the groundwork for a Franco-American alliance, using the utmost secrecy as he quietly maneuvered to convince the king to begin sending aid to the rebels. Vergennes had to keep up appearances with the British that France wanted peace while preparing for war. This was easier to do behind the scenes, but now an American was standing outside his door, which would change everything. Vergennes gave a singular laugh, wondering not how many days, but how many *hours* it would be before Stormont knew of this meeting. Then it would only be a matter of days before King George III himself knew of it in London.

Vergennes stood and straightened his white- and silver-trimmed waistcoat and coat. The modest, dignified gentleman walked from around his desk carved with the images of *Victoire* over to glance in the mirror to make sure his wig was not out of place. He breathed in deeply through his nose, exhaled, and thought, *Alors ça commence.* So it begins.

Gérard tapped again softly on the door before opening it to usher in Silas Deane. Vergennes raised his chin and stood with his hands clasped behind his back in a stately posture.

"Je vous présente Monsieur Silas Deane," Gérard said, his hand outstretched to introduce Deane, then gesturing to the French Minister, "and I am pleased to present *Monsieur* Charles Gravier, Comte de Vergennes."

Vergennes and Deane bowed as they greeted one another, each with a foot placed forward and arms outstretched in the respectful posture of gentlemen.

"S'il vous plaît." Vergennes gestured for the men to sit on the ornately upholstered French chairs as he also took a seat.

"I will act as translator, *Monsieur* Deane," Gérard assured the American.

Deane nodded. *"Merci, Monsieur* Gérard. I am grateful for your assistance. Please tell *Monsieur le Comte* that it is my highest honor to meet him and express my gratitude for his willingness to see me today."

Kate took her seat on the rug next to the men, excited to hear what they would discuss. After a few moments of exchanged niceties, Deane began to explain the reason for his visit.

Nearly three hours passed, and both Vergennes and Deane were delightfully surprised at how well their discussion proceeded.

"The people and their cause are very respectable in the eyes of all disinterested persons," Gérard assured Deane with a gracious bow of his head.

The men stood and bowed respectfully to one another, as the meeting was clearly at an end.

"*Merci, Monsieur le Comte,*" Deane said with gratitude, his hand on his heart.

At least he said 'thank ye' on his own then, Kate thought with a smile.

As Gérard held out his hand to direct Deane to the door, Vergennes lifted his hand for a final word. "*Monsieur* Deane, *une chose de plus.*"

"One more thing, Mr. Deane," Gérard translated.

Deane stopped and turned to the French Minister, who came up to him wearing a serious expression. He pointed a finger at Deane and then to himself. "*Comme vous êtes un simple citoyen, vous êtes sous la protection du roi. Si vous avez des problèmes avec les représentants du gouvernement, informez-moi.*"

"As you are a *private citizen,* you are under the protection of the king," Gérard relayed as Deane looked between the two men. "If you have any trouble with government officials, I want you to report it to *me.*"

Deane tightened his lips and nodded with sober understanding. "Please tell *Monsieur* Vergennes that I humbly appreciate his word of caution and protection, and I shall do as he directs."

Vergennes nodded once in satisfaction as Gérard translated Deane's words. "*Bonne journée, Monsieur* Deane."

The men shared a final bow and Vergennes returned to his desk while Gérard escorted Deane back out into the antechamber where Bancroft and Dubourg waited. Kate slipped out the door, but not before she saw Vergennes grin broadly and wave his fists in the air with great satisfaction, as if he had just won a great victory.

Bancroft and Dubourg stood up, and Deane lifted his chin with a confident smile. "It went well, I think," Deane offered with a hand on his chest. "Do you agree, *Monsieur Gérard?*"

Gérard clasped his hands behind his back and bowed with a smile. "Indeed, *Monsieur.* For both parties. Now, please allow me to escort you out."

Kate took notice of all the humans milling about, wondering which of them would be reporting to Lord Stormont about what had taken place. *I know one of ye will snitch any minute now.*

HÔTEL DU GRAND VILLARS, PARIS, FRANCE, JULY 10, 1776

The three men waited until they were behind closed doors in Deane's hotel suite before they discussed the meeting. Vergennes had put a healthy fear in Deane about the fact that he was being watched by spies everywhere, including by his hotel landlady, who was suspected of being a British spy! He even suggested that Deane change hotels, which the American agreed would be a prudent thing to do. The French Minister also instructed Deane to go through Gérard for all future meetings, gathering privately at Gérard's home away from the prying eyes of Stormont and his spies at Versailles.

"This will no doubt be a game of cat and mouse with Stormont," Deane explained. "Vergennes will relay that I presented myself as a merchant traveling from Bermuda, which can be shown by the captain who transported me here." He dabbed his brow. It was a hot July day in Paris, and the high ceilings offered little relief from the stuffy heat. But Deane also felt the heat of all the hidden eyes trained upon him.

"What was the gist of your talking points?" Bancroft wanted to know.

"Yes, yours and Vergennes's?" Dubourg added.

"Well, I emphasized the importance of American commerce, and how Great Britain has had a monopoly on all we produce," Deane began. "I told Vergennes that with the breaking away of the colonies from Great Britain and the halt of trade, we naturally wonder what we can do with the overabundance of our raw resources, and how we can receive the manufactured goods we desire. I assured him that we look to France as the best country in Europe for trade. I told him that I was here to buy a large quantity of goods for the Indian trade, but that what I really needed was military supplies for twenty-five thousand soldiers."

Deane reached for his glass of water. Kate helped herself to a madeleine as she listened in, realizing she'd have to stay thirsty for a while longer.

"I told him that a Declaration of Independence would be forthcoming, and that I shall have further instructions when that news arrives," Deane continued. "Meanwhile, the Congress is anxious to know how such a declaration will be received by the powers of Europe, especially France. Would they enter into trade and form an alliance with an independent America, and would France receive an American ambassador?"

"An *official* ambassador," Bancroft emphasized with a raised finger.

Deane nodded. "Yes, an *official* ambassador, for I am an unofficial, *private citizen* doing business in France in the eyes of the court. Vergennes expressed France's knowledge of the importance of American commerce, and that no country could better supply the colonies with manufactured goods than France. Therefore, it is in the interests of both countries to have free and uninterrupted trade. Vergennes said that French ports are open and free to American and British merchants, so I am free to conduct business at will for goods as well as military supplies."

"France can say that they cannot regulate who comes in and out of their ports for trade," Dubourg offered, shrugging his shoulders with a broad smile.

"Exactly," Deane agreed with a grin. "Vergennes will explain to Stormont that I am simply here to conduct trade as a merchant, which of course is beyond his control." His face grew serious. "But Vergennes made it very clear that France cannot openly encourage the trade of military supplies. It would be seen as an act of war with England."

"So, what did Vergennes say about an American Declaration of Independence?" Bancroft wanted to know.

"He said that as it was still 'in the womb of time' it would be improper for him as the Minister of France to say anything on the subject until it takes place," Deane answered. "France cannot openly aid the colonies until such a formal declaration is made and the colonies prove that they will defend it. Vergennes would then need to confer with the king and his ministers. But he added, in his own *private* opinion, that if the colonies were finally determined to reject the sovereignty of his Britannic Majesty, it would not be in the interest of France to see them reduced by force. He believes our cause is deserving of the support of every friend to justice and assured me that the colonies might be certain of them having the unanimous good wishes of the government and people of France."

"I'm sure that was a tremendous encouragement to you on this mission," Bancroft offered. "So, where do you go from here?"

"King Louis's public decision to modernize and reequip his army and navy will be our cover story for purchasing France's older weapons and supplies," Deane explained. He turned to Dubourg. "We will need the names of some skilled French engineers to help us with this old French equipment. It won't help our army if we get the guns to them without the knowledge of how to use them."

Deane turned to Bancroft. "I shall need your help to translate in meetings with two men that Vergennes recommends for securing our needed supplies. One of the wealthiest businessmen in France who can supply the items our soldiers need such as uniforms and tents is a *Monsieur* Jacques-Donatien Leray de Chaumont."

"Of course," Bancroft assured him. "And who is the other man?"

Deane furrowed his brow. "I am not certain about him, as *Monsieur*

Vergennes's recommendation does not make sense to me. He is not what I would consider a man of business. He is a flamboyant playwright of all things! A *Monsieur* Pierre-Augustin Carson de Beaumarchais."

Figaro! Kate thought to herself. *Who could be better at pullin' off the greatest act of spyin' right under the nose of Stormont an' the British than a lad who acts on stage for a livin'? Ye'll see. Beaumarchais may seem like a colorful, unlikely partner, but he's already got money in the bank an' arms, ammunition, an' equipment headin' ta French ports ta ship ta America.* The invisible white Westie grinned about what she knew that Vergennes couldn't officially tell Deane of Beaumarchais and everything they had already mapped out to help the Americans. *Mr. Deane, ye're officially now in the middle of the greatest performance ever acted out on the world's stage. An' me an' Bancroft have front row seats.*

HOWE, EXACTLY

HEADQUARTERS OF GENERAL WILLIAM HOWE,
ROSE AND CROWN TAVERN, STATEN ISLAND, NEW YORK,
JULY 12, 1776, 3:00 P.M.

B ritish Admiral Shuldham squinted up into the sunshine to observe the flags blowing from the top of British ships anchored off Staten Island. "We have a favorable southerly wind," he remarked. "And a strong incoming tidal current. Are you determined that the *Phoenix* and the *Rose* should proceed, General Howe?" He remained hesitant to risk two of his men-o'-war and their crews on such a risky venture.

General Howe stared through his spyglass over at Manhattan. "Yes, Admiral. Not only do I intend to send my *clear* answer to the Americans' Declaration of Independence, but I also need to see just how strong their defenses are."

"Very well, two of my best captains will make the run up the Hudson to Haverstraw Bay to find out, Sir," Shuldham answered, turning to give the signaling order for the ships to proceed.

Haverstraw Bay was thirty-five miles north of Manhattan and was five miles long and three and a half miles wide, making it the widest part of the Hudson River. General Howe believed that British warships could anchor there in safety from rebel attacks and block any movement of supplies to Washington's forces from the northern colonies. Howe knew that Washington was erecting two forts facing each other across the river, Fort Constitution on the New Jersey side and Fort Washington on Manhattan's highest point. The rebels had begun to sink large obstructions between the forts to slow ships attempting to sail between them, and which would allow rebel gunners to have a good shot at them. But were the rebel defenses fully operational, and could they stop the British fleet? Howe needed to know before his brother, Lord Admiral Richard Howe, sailed into these waters.

At 3:20 p.m., Captain Hyde Parker of the forty-four-gun *Phoenix* and Captain James Wallace of the twenty-gun *Rose* sounded the orders for their ships to weigh anchor, loosen and sheet their sails, and get underway, followed by the three tenders *Tryal, Shuldham,* and *Charlotta.* As they reached the lower tip of Manhattan, the squadron opened fire, sending cannonballs through houses, and filling the air with a thick screen of smoke.

Immediately the city flew into a panic, with women and children shrieking cries of distress and citizens running for cover as cannonballs came bounding down the busy streets. Was this the beginning of the major assault they had long expected?! Alarm guns sounded all over the city, and soldiers hastened to their battle stations. American gunners in batteries at Red Hook, Governors Island, Paulus Hook, and in the city peppered the passing ships, but they kept moving. The air soon reeked of gunpowder.

"Do hurry, dear boy!" Nigel shouted, coughing, and waving a paw in front of his face as Veritas lifted off from Washington's headquarters. The eagle soared up through the smoke-filled air so they could see exactly what was going on and report back to Max and Jock.

"Looks like two big ships and three small vessels are attempting to get past the defenses," Veritas observed. "None of the American gunfire seems to be having any effect."

"Indeed, *nothing* is stopping those ships from racing up the Hudson," Nigel added. "They are hugging the New Jersey shoreline."

"And spectators are hugging the Manhattan shoreline," Veritas added. "But it isn't just civilians. *Soldiers* are just standing there watching the ships sailing past, like they're stunned."

"This will *not* set well with General Washington or Colonel Knox," Nigel fumed.

Suddenly they heard a huge explosion and looked back to see that it came from the Grand Battery down from Fort George near Knox's headquarters at No. 1 Broadway.

"Oh, dear! It appears that Patriot gunners just blew up their own gun!" Nigel shouted. "I do believe Colonel Knox placed a young nineteen-year-old captain of the New York artillery in charge there. I pray the young boy is alright."

"What's his name?" Veritas asked.

"His name is Alexander Hamilton," Nigel answered.

"When inexperienced humans don't know how to properly load cannons, they throw away their shot," Veritas lamented, sad to see several men dead on the ground. The eagle looked upriver as the ships continued their northern trek. "It won't take long for these ships to pass all the forts."

After the squadron sailed unharmed by Fort Washington, the batteries on the heights of Westchester County continued to fire on them for eleven miles, but again without effect. They finally came to anchor at the Tappan Zee at Tarrytown before they would move further north to Haverstraw.

Nigel and Veritas could see men aboard popping corks to celebrate their easy sail past rebel defenses powerless to stop them.

"Looks like the *Phoenix* has some perforations in her sails and rigging, and the *Rose* took a hit to its foremast," Veritas reported, circling over the celebrating British ships. "But that's about all the damage from the two hundred American cannonballs slung at them."

"We best get back to headquarters and report," Nigel offered with a furrowed brow. "This is not good."

MORTIER MANSION HEADQUARTERS, NEW YORK, JULY 12, 1776, 6:00 P.M.

"They broke through our defenses like cobwebs," Washington bristled as reports flooded his office from all over Manhattan. He, Knox, and other officers pored over maps of forts, entrenchments, and artillery.

Knox furrowed his brow. "We rained balls all around their ships, your Excellency, and I believe we did inflict much damage. This proves to me beyond a doubt that their ships cannot lay before our batteries."

"But those ships are now safely anchored out of reach of our guns," Washington countered, pointing to Tarrytown. "Now they can disrupt our northern source of supply and communication by sea." He shook his head. "And the unsoldierly conduct of our men lining the shore and just standing by is mortifying. Such behavior makes us a laughingstock to the enemy."

"Washington's not happy. This be a bad day," Max whispered to Jock and Nigel, who had just arrived. They sat in the corner, listening to the humans. Nigel had reported everything he and Veritas saw from the air.

"Neither is Knox. He lost six men from our own guns!" Jock added glumly. "Some more were wounded, too. They're burying the poor lads on Bowling Green. It's sad to think those soldiers were celebrating there just three nights ago."

"What a travesty!" Nigel lamented. "We saw the explosion from above. What happened exactly?"

"Well, the sad fact be that some of those lads on duty had been drinkin' so were 'in their cups' as the humans say," Max reported with a frown. "They were sloppy an' didn't sponge the cannon in between shots ta clean before reloadin'. So, the sparks ignited the powder too early when they lit the fuse, blowin' up the cannon an' killin' those lads."

Nigel pulled on his whiskers. "Blast it all! This needless loss is a shocking display of inadequate training and discipline!"

"Not the best choice of words, Mousie," Max told the angry mouse, referring to his use of "blast." "Aye, but senseless death makes everyone angry. This army needs a swift kick in its discipline as much as it needs supplies."

"It really upset Washington to hear all the women and children crying out today," Jock offered. "But one bright spot for Knox at least is that Lucy and the baby weren't here."

"Sir, might I make a request?" Knox asked. "The loss of those six men today convinces me that we need a battalion of men assigned specifically to a dedicated artillery corps where I can better train and discipline them under closer supervision."

"Agreed. Draft a plan, Colonel Knox, and I will present it to the Congress," Washington instructed him.

Suddenly in the distance they heard more cannon blasts coming from the harbor with a window-rattling boom. Sentries on the roof trained their spyglasses on the source of the blasts. As the smoke cleared, they watched as a newly arrived sixty-four-gun British man-o'-war sailed into view. The Royal Navy continued its booming salute as the flag of St. George on the foretop masthead appeared, signifying who was on board. Soldiers and sailors on the decks of every British ship in the harbor and on the shore at Staten Island were waving and cheering as the salute continued.

"This isn't good," one sentry told the other, lowering his spyglass. "It's the flagship." He hurriedly made his way inside and down the steps to urgently knock on Washington's door.

"Now what?" Washington asked sternly.

"Sir, I need to report that Admiral Lord Howe has just arrived," the sentry reported. "His flagship, the *HMS Eagle* just anchored off Staten Island."

Washington shot a glance of alarm at Knox. "That means the rest of the fleet from England isn't far behind."

Max, Jock, and Nigel quickly bolted out of the room and upstairs to the roof to see for themselves. They watched as one ship after another sailed unopposed into the harbor with sails full of wind and sailors full of eagerness to get onshore after the long voyage from England.

"This day jest got a whole lot worse," Max growled.

"Indeed. There shall soon be one hundred-fifty more ships arriving behind Admiral Howe," Nigel reminded them.

"Plus, the forty ships coming with General Clinton from South Carolina," Jock added.

Max frowned. "But when will them Howe br-r-rothers make their *real* move? Today were jest a test with them two warships sailin' up the Hudson."

"Not just when but *how?*" Nigel retorted. "The Howe Brothers now have full command of the sea in New York and shall next turn their aim to the land."

Max put a burly paw on the little mouse's shoulder. "Mousie, see if ye kin go find out jest *Howe* exactly."

ABOARD *HMS EAGLE,* NEW YORK, JULY 12, 1776, 9:00 P.M.

"Welcome to New York, Brother!" General Howe exclaimed with an upraised glass. "The timing of your arrival couldn't have been more perfect with our booming salute to punctuate this excellent day! No doubt Washington and every single rebel knows you're here."

General Howe, Admiral Shuldham, other British officers, and Governor Tryon had come aboard to dine in Admiral Lord Richard Howe's well-appointed chambers illuminated by ornate brass chandeliers and furnished with the finest mahogany table and carved, upholstered chairs. Admiral Howe's secretary, Ambrose Serle, was pleased to join them as they relayed the exciting events of the day. Admiral Shuldham would now formally turn over full command to Admiral Howe but did so with the relief that his warships had brilliantly passed the rebel defenses with barely a scratch, and with only three men wounded. There was much to celebrate. A sumptuous meal was spread before them on plates of fine china, and servants filled crystal goblets with expensive wine.

"Thank you for the *booming* welcome, Brother," Admiral Howe smiled and said with his upraised glass. "With your daring run up the Hudson, you have prepared the rebels for my first order of business here in New York. I'm happy to tell you that the King has seen fit to make us peace commissioners in an attempt to avoid war. Tomorrow I shall send out a Declaration to circulate among the governors and the citizens granting pardons to those who will cease this belligerent nonsense and return their loyalty to the Crown." He lifted a glass with a hopeful smile. "To pardons and peace."

"I'm afraid you've arrived too late, my Lord," Governor Tryon lamented with a spiteful tone as he lifted his glass.

Admiral Howe wore a puzzled expression, his brow furrowed, lowering his glass. "What do you mean?"

"Their Congress passed a Declaration of Independence on July 4th, announcing the colonies to be independent *states,*" General Howe explained, taking a sip from his glass, and setting it down. He reached into the folds of his jacket and pulled out one of the Dunlap broadsides that one of his agents had acquired, handing it over to his brother. "It was read publicly here to Washington's troops three days ago. I read it to my officers as well."

"This is *madness!*" Serle exclaimed with disdain, slapping the arm of his chair. "Such deluded people!"

"Yes, and a mob of nasty rebels *dared* to pull down King George III's glorious statue at Bowling Green! They had the *gall* to tear it asunder," Tryon scoffed. "*Then* they blew up an effigy of our Sovereign over on Long Island! These are *despicable* people who do not deserve a pardon if I may be so bold."

"Is that so? How unfortunate," Lord Howe answered somberly with a wrinkled brow, looking over the Declaration of Independence. He handed his brother a copy of the document he would send out tomorrow to Loyalist sympathizers for posting in towns throughout the region. "Well, here is our *British* Declaration."

General Howe took the Declaration of pardon in hand to read. ". . . a free and general pardon to all who in the tumult and disorder of the times may have deviated from just allegiance and are willing by a speedy return to their duty to reap the benefits of the royal favor." He shook his head and set it aside. "I know you have an undying hope of peace with the rebel colonies, Brother, but I do not believe you will be able to reverse what has happened with this paper. Their Declaration of Independence clearly indicates a determination to *fight* rather than negotiate. The rebels are heavily entrenched over on Manhattan and Long Island. We believe they have as many as thirty-five thousand men and over one hundred pieces of artillery."

Lord Howe frowned and took a sip of wine, setting his glass thoughtfully on the table. "Then perhaps I must attempt to reverse what has happened instead with a *parler.* I will write to the one man who might be able to divert military action—George Washington himself."

"And how do you propose to address this letter?" General Howe quipped. "You certainly can't acknowledge his status as the Generalissimo of a sovereign country!"

"Indeed, Admiral," Ambrose Serle agreed. "It would appear that this Declaration of Independence has given your task a bit of a fly in the ointment."

"Such *terribly* inconvenient timing," Governor Tryon retorted, clucking his tongue.

"I shall address it to the only title that the Crown acknowledges," Admiral Howe decided, his nose lifted in the air. "George Washington, Esquire."

Nigel raised his eyebrows in surprise and folded his arms over his chest. He tapped his elbow as he stood on the ledge of a window looking down at the Howe Brothers and their dinner guests. "Well, well, well, I believe I know exactly *Howe* this shall go. Lord Howe does not realize that his pen is not mightier than the Sword."

No One
by That Name

"I predict that aboard this ship bearing the white flag of truce shall come a letter for General Washington," Nigel announced as he stood with Max and Jock on the seawall at the Hudson River behind the Mortier House.

Jock's eyes widened. "How do you know *that?!*"

"Curse not the king, no not in thy thought; and curse not the rich in thy bedchamber: for a bird of the air shall carry the voice, and that which hath wings shall tell the matter," Nigel quoted with a chuckle, twirling a whisker. "Of course, that is taken from Ecclesiastes 10:20."

Max nudged Jock. "Mousie knows the Holy Wr-r-rit better than me, but the short version be a little bird told him."

"Actually, *Lord Howe* told me, but Veritas was the proverbial bird as it were, carrying the admiral's voice on his wings to tell the matter through your humble servant," Nigel corrected him, bowing with a paw draped across his chest.

Max stared blankly at Nigel before turning to Jock. "Mousie loves ta be poetic aboot everything an' talk fancy. But I'll translate. Veritas flew him ta Howe's ship an' he overheard wha' he said."

"So, a little *mouse* told us," Jock giggled. "I like your delivery, Nigel. So, what about this letter?"

Nigel preened his whiskers. "Right. Well, the Howe brothers have been appointed as peace commissioners by King George. Lord Howe was shocked to learn of the Declaration of Independence and upset that he arrived too late to prevent its passage. But he intends to push on with his assignment, beginning with a letter written to 'George Washington, Esquire.'"

"What's an esquire?" Jock asked.

"It be Washington's fancy civilian title, not his military one," Max explained. He wrinkled his brow. "Why won't Howe write ta him as *General* Washington then?"

"Because to do so would mean that he and the Crown *acknowledge* Washington as the military leader of an independent nation," Nigel explained, clucking his tongue and shaking his head. "Of course, they can't have *that* now, can they?"

"Why is a letter addressed like that such a big deal?" Jock wanted to know.

"My dear boy, this is an extremely delicate situation!" Nigel exclaimed. "Words mean things, and the use of titles and such determines the atmosphere of how those words will be received or rejected. Respect and decorum always set the mood for discussion and negotiations."

"Because King George not only doesn't want ta r-r-recognize the United States of America, he wants ta r-r-rip it apart," Max interjected with a growl. "Here comes a *big* bird now—another *Eagle!*"

"So, what's going to happen?" Jock asked.

"We shall soon see," Nigel answered, pointing to Henry Knox, Joseph Reed, and Samuel Webb, who hurried down the path toward the water from the house, sent by George Washington. He quickly looked over at the small barge making its way over to pick up the men. "I shall stowaway on this vessel that I assume shall take Washington's representatives to intercept said letter."

"We'll wait for ye here, Mousie," Max shouted after him.

Knox came over and bent down to give Max and Jock a scratch behind the ears. "I'm happy to see the two finest Scotties in America keeping watch for His Excellency's headquarters. Stay here while I go see what's what."

It's a letter! Jock barked happily, wagging his tail as Knox and the other men stepped foot into the vessel.

Max and Jock watched as they sailed out to meet the *Eagle.* "This should be interestin'."

As the American barge came alongside the barge sent from the *Eagle,* British Lieutenant Philip Brown rose, bowed, and removed his hat. "I have a letter, Sir, from Lord Howe to Mr. Washington."

"Sir, we have no person in our army with that address," Colonel Reed quickly offered.

"Sir, will you look at the address?" Brown answered, removing from his pocket a sealed letter, and handed it to Reed.

Reed, Knox, and Webb read the address:

George Washington, Esq., New York. Howe.

The three men looked at one another and shook their heads. Reed handed the letter back to Brown. "No, Sir, I cannot receive that letter."

"I am very sorry, and so will be Lord Howe, that any error in the superscription prevent the letter being received by *General* Washington," Brown lamented with a frown.

"Why, Sir, I must obey orders," Reed countered confidently.

Brown quickly nodded. "Oh yes, Sir, you must obey orders, to be sure."

"But we do have some letters for your officers," Knox added, handing Brown a packet of letters from Colonel Campbell to General Howe and other letters from prisoners to their friends.

Brown gave a singular nod, and with that the men all stood off, saluted, and bowed to each other. After the barge had taken the Americans a little way off, they heard Brown call out to them, having turned his barge around.

"Sirs, by what particular title would he choose to be addressed?" Brown asked.

"You are sensible, Sir, of the rank of General Washington in our army?" Colonel Reed quickly replied.

"Yes, Sir, we are. I am sure Lord Howe will lament exceedingly this affair, as the letter is quite of a civil nature, and not a military one. He laments exceedingly that he was not here a little sooner."

"He means that he didn't arrive before the Declaration of Independence," Webb muttered under his breath.

"Indeed, that's *exactly* what he means," Knox agreed.

After the barge of Americans returned to the Mortier house, the three men hurried inside to report to General Washington what had taken place. Nigel jumped onto the seawall and raced over to Max and Jock.

"They were utterly brilliant!" Nigel exclaimed with two fists up in the air. "They told Lord Howe's little bird that there was no one here by that name!"

"Huzzah!" Jock cheered.

Max grinned broadly. "I wonder wha' those pompous Br-r-rits will tr-r-ry next."

"I know how to find out, old boy!" Nigel exclaimed, waving as Veritas circled overhead.

NO. 1 BROADWAY, MANHATTAN, NEW YORK, JULY 20, 1776

Over the course of the next three days Howe tried again to deliver the letter, addressed now as:

George Washington, Esq., Etc., Etc.

Brown was emphatically rejected the second time, so Lord Howe sent a different messenger with a different message the third time. Captain Nisbet Balfour came to inquire if Washington would meet with General Howe's

Adjutant General, Colonel James Paterson. To this request, the Howe Brothers finally received a 'Yes.' The meeting would take place at Knox's headquarters. By now, Lord Howe's Declaration of pardon had been distributed throughout the region, and Washington and his officers had discussed it at length.

"Just set me down on the roof and I shall wend my way to the inner meeting room," Nigel instructed Veritas. "There's a good chap."

"I'll wait for you nearby, Nigel," Veritas told him as the little mouse hopped off.

Nigel scurried in through a window and down to the meeting room and found a perch on the ledge. "I simply cannot wait for this scene to unfold!" he whispered to himself.

Colonel Paterson was escorted into the room and shown a seat on one side of the table. Washington's Life Guards stood at the entrance, and they allowed the British representative a few moments alone. Nigel watched as Paterson squirmed in his seat and looked around the quiet room, strumming his fingers in anxious anticipation of this crucial meeting. *Brilliant. Let the chap sweat a bit, what?* the little mouse thought.

Suddenly the doors opened and in walked Knox, Reed, and a few others who cordially greeted Paterson in formal, one-worded hellos. "Sir." "Sir." The men took their seats and softly murmured among themselves.

After another moment, they heard the unmistakable sound of Washington's heavy footsteps on the wood floors. When he appeared and stopped in the doorway, his commanding appearance swept over the room. He was impeccably dressed, with perfectly groomed hair and a freshly pressed uniform. His blue sash draped across his chest and his dress sword at his side, Washington strode to the chair in the center of the table opposite Paterson, as everyone rose to their feet.

He looks resplendent! Nigel cheered to himself. *He simply enters the room and immediately takes charge without uttering a word!*

"Gentlemen," Washington greeted them. Then looking across at Paterson, he gave a slight bow of courtesy. "Sir, we extend to you our most sincere welcome." He extended a hand. "Please, have a seat."

"Thank you, your Excellency, it is an honor, your Excellency," Paterson gushed as he eagerly did as Washington instructed, clearly awed by the general's presence. "If it please your Excellency, may I express that Lord Howe by *no means* intended to derogate from the respect or rank of General Washington."

Every other word is 'your Excellency,' Nigel noted. *This fellow is oozing politeness and respect, as well he should.*

Washington kept his gaze locked on Paterson but did not react or respond as the eager agent continued.

"Your Excellency, both General Howe and Lord Howe hold the person and character of General Washington in high esteem," Paterson gushed, lifting from his pocket the same letter that had already been rejected. He set it on the table and slowly pushed it toward Washington.

Nigel put his face in his palm and shook his head. "Well that just blew any bit of respect and decorum straight out the window!" he blurted out. "Paterson, old boy, you clearly do *not* know who you are dealing with! *General* Washington does not care about your flattery, but he does care about formal recognition of his country and his *station.*" He then clamped a paw over his mouth so he wouldn't be heard squeaking.

Washington didn't bat an eye but kept his gaze on Paterson, leaving the letter sitting there on the table, untouched. As the moments ticked on, the weight of that single piece of parchment grew greater and greater.

Beads of sweat began to appear on Paterson's forehead, and he reached out his hand to tap the letter. "If I may explain, your Excellency, the use of 'etc., etc.' implies everything that ought to follow," he said with an awkward smile.

"It does so," Washington replied coolly, "and *anything.*"

Paterson withdrew his hand and sat back uncomfortably in his chair.

"A letter addressed to one in a position of public service must by necessity indicate that station, otherwise it is merely private correspondence," Washington told him, giving him an elementary lesson on etiquette. "I cannot accept such a letter."

"Your Excellency, again, I must apologize for any unintended slight," Paterson groveled again. "The goodness and benevolence of the King moved him to appoint Lord and General Howe as peace commissioners to accommodate this unhappy dispute. They have come with great powers to negotiate a peace settlement."

"*Goodness? Benevolence?*" Nigel fumed, now pacing back and forth. "Poppycock!"

"Colonel Paterson, I am not vested with any powers on this subject by those from whom I derive my authority and power," Washington said plainly. "I have heard that Lord Howe has the power to grant pardons, but he has come to the wrong place. Those who have committed no fault want no pardon. We are only defending what we deem our indisputable rights."

"Brilliant!" Nigel cheered with a fist of victory in the air. "Give him what for and all that, General!"

Paterson sat there in utter awe, dumbstruck by Washington's resolute words and calm demeanor. After a moment he stirred himself back to reality.

"Uh, your Excellency, I exceedingly lament that an adherence to forms might obstruct business of the greatest moment and concern."

Silence.

"Has your Excellency no particular commands with which you would please to honor me to Lord and General Howe?" Paterson asked.

"Nothing, Sir, but my particular compliments to both," Washington answered respectfully. With that he scooted back his chair and nodded to Paterson. "Sir, you may take your leave. My officers will escort you back to your vessel."

With that, General George Washington, Commander-in-Chief of the Continental Army of the United States of America, strode confidently out of the room.

ABOARD *HMS EAGLE*, NEW YORK, JULY 20, 1776, 6:00 P.M.

"We strove as far as decency and honor could permit, to avert all bloodshed!" Ambrose Serle scoffed in a thick British accent with disdain. "And yet it seems to be beneath a little paltry colonel of banditi rebels to treat with a representative of his lawful sovereign because it is impossible to give all the titles which the poor creature requires."

"Why you CHEEKY. . .!" Nigel had to clamp both paws over his mouth to keep from screaming at the top of his little mouse lungs.

"It would appear that our attempts at peace were as ineffective as the Patriot guns that fired upon our ships," General Howe noted. "So will you now relinquish this futile quest for peace with the rebels?"

Lord Howe strummed his fingers on the table, thinking. He was shocked and disappointed, of course, with Paterson's report of the interview with Washington. But he held fast to his faith that peace could be achieved. "I came here as both peace commissioner and admiral of war, and I intend to see my dual appointment through its course. Let us see if military action will bring the Americans to the negotiating table."

"Not yet, Brother," General Howe insisted. "We must wait for all our reinforcements—Clinton's fleet as well as the Hessians. Then we will overpower the rebels with such force that they will *run* to the negotiating table."

Jolly good. I shall report that the Americans have more time to prepare, Nigel thought. He gazed out the window of Howe's quarters at the fleet of British ships that stretched out for more than a mile. They were so thick and close together that he could jump from one ship to the next without Veritas's transport. *Let us pray that their preparations will be enough, for this shall be a terribly bloody clash.*

PHILADELPHIA, PENNSYLVANIA, JULY 20, 1776

The Official Dispatches to which you refer me, contain nothing more than what we had seen in the Act of Parliament, viz. Offers of Pardon upon Submission; which I was sorry to find, as it must give your Lordship Pain to be sent so far on so hopeless a Business.

Benjamin Franklin rubbed his eyes under his spectacles, taking a break from responding to Lord Howe's letter of July 12th. The Admiral had sent it under a white flag immediately to his longtime friend upon anchoring off Staten Island. He included his Declaration of pardon and a personal note regarding his designated role from the king as peace commissioner. Franklin had both documents publicly read in Congress, who would proceed to publish every word of Howe's offer of "pardon" so every American could read for themselves "how the insidious court of Britain has endeavoured to amuse and disarm them." Congress also wanted to show Americans that their representatives could not be bought with the reward offered to those who would promote a peace settlement. But they would also publish Howe's private letter to Benjamin Franklin and Franklin's response:

These atrocious Injuries have extinguished every remaining Spark of Affection for that Parent Country we once held so dear: But were it possible for us to forget and forgive them, it is not possible for you (I mean the British Nation) to forgive the People you have so heavily injured; you can never confide again in those as Fellow Subjects, and permit them to enjoy equal Freedom, to whom you know you have given such just Cause of lasting Enmity. And this must impel you, were we again under your Government, to endeavour the breaking our Sprit by the severest Tyranny, and obstructing by every means in your Power our growing Strength and Prosperity.

Franklin paused and sighed, remembering fondly his time of playing chess in London with Lord Howe and his sister while he lived there representing colonial interests before the Crown. He wore a sad smile as he penned sentiments from those days.

Long did I endeavour with unfeigned and unwearied Zeal, to preserve from breaking, that fine and noble China Vase the British Empire: for I knew that being once broken, the separate Parts could not retain even their Share of the Strength or Value that existed in the Whole, and that a perfect Re-Union of those Parts could scarce even be hoped for. Your Lordship may possibly remember the Tears of Joy that wet my Cheek, when, at your good Sister's in London, you once gave me Expectations that a Reconciliation might soon take place.

Franklin never wanted to sever ties with the Mother Country. But his hopes and expectations sadly were not met, and in 1774 he found himself publicly ridiculed before Lord North and the Privy Council as a scapegoat for conflicts with Boston. He stood there silently in the "Cockpit" wearing his blue Manchester velvet suit and enduring the mocking diatribe of Solicitor General Wedderburn as the lords looked on with scorn and laughter. He decided he would not wear that blue velvet suit again until a day of reckoning came for the ill treatment he silently endured that day. He had walked into that room as an Englishman. He walked out of that room an American. From that moment, there was no turning back in Franklin's commitment to the cause of American Independence, despite his personal feelings of affection for the Howe family.

I know your great Motive in coming hither was the Hope of being instrumental in a Reconciliation; and I believe when you find that impossible on any Terms given you to propose, you will relinquish so odious a Command, and return to a more honourable private Station. With the greatest and most sincere Respect I have the honour to be, My Lord your Lordships most obedient humble Servant

B Franklin

Franklin put his quill back in the inkwell and sat back in his chair. He glanced over at his chessboard with an ongoing solo game in place. He got up and went over to move the queen. "Check, Admiral Howe," he said to himself. "Your move, my friend."

A Newsworthy
Recovery

SCOTCHTOWN, VIRGINIA, JULY 10, 1776

"I'm more pleased than a June bug in *July* that you're here, Liz! Pahtrick will be so happy tuh see his favorite cat again," MizP exulted. The black horse shook her black mane happily as Liz sat on the fence railing, yawning. "But you look about as tired as Pahtrick."

Liz yawned wide, showing her sharp teeth. *"Pardon, mon amie,* but *oui,* I *am* very tired. The past month has been quite exhausting, no? It is hard to believe all that happened in Williamsburg and Philadelphia! Between sitting with the Fifth Virginia Convention and the founding of a new government in Virginia, getting *mon* Henry elected and sworn in as governor, helping *Monsieur* Jefferson to write the Declaration of Independence and making the necessary edits for the Continental Congress, attending the historic vote for independence, and attending the reading and celebration of the Declaration in Philadelphia, I am how do you say, dog-tired?" Liz recounted, yawning again.

"I'd say you've earned a long catnap," MizP told her. "You can snuggle up next tuh Pahtrick and be a great comfort tuh him. He's not doing anything but sleeping. Poor man is weak as a kitten."

"My emotions have been especially exhausted from worry over *mon* Henry's condition," Liz replied with a furrowed brow. "Leaving him in Williamsburg was very difficult. But you say he has made a small bit of progress from his bout with malaria?"

"Yes, I heard the humans say that his fever finally broke. But he's as wiped out as dust from a dry stream bed after a *flood,*" MizP explained. "But between his sister Elizabeth and his daughter Patsy, he's been in good human hands, so you can stop worrying and get some rest *yourself.*"

Liz closed her eyes and smiled. "Hmmm, that sounds heavenly, MizP. *Merci* for this good news!"

"There's also some bad news, though. A rumor is spreading that Pahtrick has *died* from this sickness," MizP told her, stomping the ground with her hoof. "Those men who swore Pahtrick in as the new Governor of Virginia didn't know if they'd even see him alive again, so when he came back here tuh recover, word spread like wildfire that the new Governor had died."

"But this is *fake* news, *mon amie!* I must see about publishing the truth of *mon* Henry's condition to dispel such lies. I shall pen a note to Alexander Purdie myself to print in the *Virginia Gazette* before such rumors go too far," Liz said excitedly. She frowned and slapped her tail on the fence rail.

"I knew you'd help set the news right, Liz," MizP said happily.

"MizP, I have wondered if the Enemy somehow caused this sudden, mysterious attack on Patrick just as he stepped into this historic moment," Liz offered. "Such lies to stir up panic only add to my suspicions."

"Hmmm, you may be right," MizP agreed. "Fingerprints have a way of showing up, or in this case, some other kind of prints. I don't know what kind of prints a mosquito might leave, but that's the only critter I know that spreads malaria."

"*Oui, c'est vrai.* The truth always comes out, no?" Liz replied, thinking. "Since mosquitos draw blood, it is possible that one could leave a trace of blood somewhere. I shall explore this further."

"Well, I can't *wait* until Pahtrick recovers so we can move intuh the Governor's Palace in Williamsburg!" MizP cheered. "I chuckle every time I think how that mean Governor Dunmore who declared Pahtrick an 'outlaw' is *himself* on the run while the outlaw takes over his house and title! If that ain't taking the spoils of wahr, I don't know what is."

Liz smiled and stretched out. "*Oui,* it is such poetic justice after *mon* Henry's hard-won fight for liberty here in Virginia! That will be a happy day when he moves into the palace. After General Lee and his forces stayed there on their way to the Carolinas, it required cleaning and repairs, so it is good that Patrick is here at Scotchtown. For now, I am relieved that John Page is serving as Lieutenant Governor to take care of things until *mon* Henry can get back on his feet. The Virginia Assembly won't meet again until October, so he has plenty of time to recover his voice and move in."

"I'm only sorry that Pahtrick won't get tuh attend one of the happy public readings of the Declaration of Independence," MizP lamented.

"*Oui,* nor will Patrick Henry get to *sign* the Declaration of Independence in August when the delegates in Philadelphia return to do so," Liz added. "Now that he is Governor of Virginia, he is not eligible."

"Knowing Pahtrick, he'd prefer tuh be serving the citizens of Virginia than make sure his name is on some document, no matter how much he had tuh do with it or how important it is," MizP suggested. "Pahtrick knows it's not about *him.*"

"*Oui, mon* Henry's humility is one of the things I admire most about him," Liz agreed. "Now, I shall go tend to him and curl up for a nap."

"You do that, nurse Liz," MizP said, giving her a tender nudge. "You're good medicine, sugah."

Light poured in through the window next to Patrick's bed. He could feel the warmth of the sun's rays across his face, but he didn't open his eyes. His head ached, and he was too tired, even after having slept for hours. He then noticed warmth next to his leg and reached out a hand to feel soft, silky fur. He lifted his head slightly and cracked open an eye to see Liz lying there next to him. She was basking in the sunshine with her head upside down and her front paws cutely curled into her chest. Patrick smiled and softly started petting her. "Hello, Liz," his weak voice whispered. He immediately felt her start to purr. "I'm glad you are here."

Liz half-opened her sleepy eyes, surprised to hear how weak Patrick sounded. *I will not leave your side until you are completely well,* cher *Patrick,* she meowed. She draped a paw over him and squeezed to give him a hug of affection. *Keep resting, and we shall talk more later.*

Liz's soft purr soothed Patrick. He took in a deep breath and exhaled through his nostrils, leaving his hand on the petite cat as he drifted back to sleep.

"Papa?" Martha, or 'Patsy,' as Patrick called her, whispered as she slowly cracked open the door and stepped inside the bedroom. She carried a tray with a teapot painted in black letters with "No Stamp Act" on one side and "America, Liberty Restored" on the other. Made in England after the repeal of the Stamp Act (in large part due to Patrick Henry's famous Stamp Act Speech), this teapot was sold in the colonies and became a favorite of the Henry girls. Of course, they preferred not to serve tea these days, but nevertheless used the pitcher for other beverages. She set the tray down on the bedside table and smiled to see Liz there.

Patrick stirred, and his eyes fluttered open. He smiled at his daughter. "Hello, little girl."

"Good evening, Papa. I'm glad to see you resting so well," Patsy replied, pouring a glass. "You have a little nurse with you, I see. I've brought you some cool lemonade and a little bread. Please try to nibble a few bites. You need to regain your strength."

Patrick nodded and raised up to scoot back and sit with his head against the headboard. "Yes, Liz has reappeared. I never know where she goes for periods of time, but she always returns to me." He took the glass in hand, as well as the piece of bread. "Thank you, my dear."

"Do you think you're up for some news?" Patsy asked. "I've held onto the *Virginia Gazette* from July 5th, and I can't wait for you to read it, Papa. *Governor* Henry is featured quite a bit!"

Patrick slowly sipped the cool drink and rested his head on the headboard. "Is he now? What does it say about his *Excellency*? I'm not quite up to reading yet. Perhaps you could give me the highlights."

"Of course, Papa," Patsy replied, taking a seat on the foot of the bed and opening the paper. "'High Heaven to Gracious Ends directs the Storm!' is the banner. It opens with the news of the Fifth Virginia Convention and procedures for the General Court, magistrates, and electing senators."

JULY 5, 1776.   T H E   NUMBER 75.

VIRGINIA GAZETTE.

ALWAYS FOR LIBERTY,   AND THE PUBLICK GOOD.

DON'T TREAD ON ME

High HEAVEN *to* GRACIOUS ENDS *directs the* STORM!

IN CONVENTION.
SATURDAY, March 25, 1775.

RESOLVED, as the opinion of this Convention, that on account of the unhappy difputes betweeu Great Britain and the colonies and the unfettled ftate of this country, the lawyers, fuitors, and witneffes, ought not to attend the profecution or defence of civil fuits at the next General Court; and it is recommended to the feveral courts of juftice not to proceed to the hearing or determination of fuits on their dockets, except attachments, nor to give judgments but in the cafe of fheriffs or other collectors for money or tobacco received by them; in other cafes, where fuch judgment fhall be voluntarily confeffed, or upon fuch amicable proceedings as may become neceffary for the fettlement, divifion, or diftribution of eftates. And during this fufpenfion of the adminiftration of juftice, it is earneftly recommended to the people to obferve a peaceable and orderly behaviour, to all creditors to be as indulgent to their debtors as may be, and to all debtors to pay as far as they are able; and where differences may arife which cannot be adjufted between the parties, that they refer the decifion thereof to judicious

power to execute the office of a juftice of peace, as well within his county court as without, in all things, according to law.

And be it farther ordained, that where it fhall happen that there is not a fufficient number of magiftrates for holding a court in any county already appointed, the Governour may, with the advice of the Privy Council, appoint fuch and fo many magiftrates in fuch county as may be judged proper and neceffary.

And whereas courts in the diftrict of *Weft Augufta* have been hitherto held by writs of adjournment, which writs cannot now be obtained: *Be it therefore ordained*, that the juftices refiding in the faid diftrict, on taking the fame oath aforefaid, fhall have the power and authority to hold a court within the faid diftrict, on the third *Tuefday* in every month, at fuch place as they may appoint, and fhall exercife their office, both in court and without, in the fame manner as the juftices of the feveral counties are by this ordinance empowered to do.

Provided always, that upon complaint made to the Governour and Privy Council againft any juftice of peace, now in commiffion, of misfeazance in office, or

miffion from the late Governour, upon taking the oath before prefcribed in the court of their county, fhall continue to act, and have all the powers and authorities of fheriff, according to law, until the 25th day of *October* next.

An ORDINANCE to arrange the counties in diftricts, for electing Senators, and to afcertain their wages.

FOR the regular election of Senators to this Convention, at the time the fame fhall be adjourned to, and that the people may be more equally reprefented in that branch of the legiflature:

Be it ordained, by the delegates of the counties and corporations of Virginia *now met in Convention, and it is hereby ordained by the authority thereof*, that the counties of *Accomack* and *Northampton* fhall be one diftrict; the counties of *Princefs Anne*, *Norfolk*, and *Nanfemond*, one other diftrict; the counties of *Ifle of Wight*, *Surry*, and *Prince George*, one other diftrict; the counties of *Dinwiddie*, *Southampton*, and *Suffex*, one other diftrict; the counties of *Brunfwick*, *Lunenburg*, and *Mecklenburg*, one other diftrict; the counties of *Charlotte*, *Halifax*, and *Prince Edward*, one other diftrict; the counties of *Chefterfield*

Liz sat up, stretched, and walked over to glance at the paper. Patsy turned the page and scanned the contents. She raised her eyebrows as she caught a headline. "News from New York via John Hancock in Philadelphia. They have word that General Howe is soon to make an attack on the city! He is urging the Congress to call forth its militia to send to New York immediately. He says, 'The important day is at hand that will decide not only the fate of the city of New York, but, in all probability, of the whole province. On such an occasion, there is no necessity to use arguments with Americans. Their feeling, I well know, will prompt them to their duty; and the sacredness of the cause will urge them to the field.'"

"Americans," Patrick said softly, his eyes closed.

You were the first to use the term in the First Continental Congress to inspire unity among the arguing colonies, Liz meowed. *'I am not a Virginian, but an American.' Your words of unity are finally being realized,* cher *Patrick!*

"I pray General Washington shall get the men he needs," Patrick uttered with concern. "This battle in New York will be fierce."

"Amen," Patsy answered, her brow furrowed. Her eyes then brightened. "Now here we have the acceptance letter of the newly elected Governor, his *Excellency* Patrick Henry!"

'Upon col. HENRY's being chofen our Governour by the Hon. Convention, a committee of the Houfe was directed to wait upon his Excellency, to notify to him his appointment, to whom he delivered the following letter.

To the Honourable the PRESIDENT *and* HOUSE *of* CONVENTION.

Gentlemen,

THE vote of this day appointing me governour of this commonwealth has been notified to me in the moft polite and obliging manner, by George Mafon, Henry Lee, Dudley Dgges, John Blair, and Bartholomew Dandridge, efquires.

A fenfe of the high and unmerited honour conferred upon me by the Convention fills my heart· with gratitude, which I truft my whole life will manifeft. I take this earlieft opportunity to exprefs my thanks, which I wifh to convey to you, gentlemen, in the ftrongeft terms of acknowledgment.

When I reflect that the tyranny of the Britifh king and parliament hath kindled a formidable war, now raging throughout this wide-extended continent, and in the operations of which this commonwealth muft bear fo great a part, and that, from the events of this war, the lafting happinefs or mifery of a great proportion of the human fpecies will finally refult; that, in order to preferve this commonwealth from anarchy, and its attendant ruin, and to give vigour to our councils, and effect to all our meafures, government hath been neceffarily affumed, and new modelled; that it is expofed to numberlefs hazards, and perils, in its infantine ftate; that it can never attain to maturity, or ripen into firmnefs, unlefs it is guarded by affectionate affiduity, and managed by great abilities; I lament my want of talents, I feel my mind filled with anxiety and uneafinefs, to find myfelf fo unequal to the duties of that important ftation to which I am called by the favour of my fellow citizens, at this truly critical conjuncture. The errours of my conduct fhall be atoned for, fo far as I am able, by unwearied endeavours to fecure the freedom and happinefs of our common country.

I fhall enter upon the duties of my office, whenever you, gentlemen, fhall be pleafed to direct; relying upon the known wifdom and virtue of your Honourable Houfe to fupply my defects, and to give permanency and fuccefs to that fyftem of government which you have formed; and which is fo wifely calculated to fecure equal liberty, and advance human happinefs. I have the honour to be, gentlemen, your moft obedient and very humble fervant,

      P. HENRY, junior.

To his Excellency PATRICK HENRY, jun.
efq; Governour of the Commonwealth of
VIRGINIA :
The humble addrefs of the firft and fecond
Virginia regiments.

May it pleafe your Excellency,

PERMIT us, with the fincereft fentiments of refpect and joy, to congratulate your Excellency upon your unfolicited promotion to the higheft honours a grateful people can beftow.

Uninfluenced by private ambition, regardlefs of fordid intereft, you have uniformly purfued the general good of your country ; and have taught the world, that an ingenuous love of the rights of mankind, an inflexible refolution, and a fteady perfeverance in the practice of every private and publick virtue, lead directly to preferment, and give the beft title to the honours of an uncorrupted and vigorous ftate.

Once happy under your military command, we hope for more extenfive bleffings from your civil adminiftration. Interefted as your Excellency is in fome meafure with the fupport of a young empire, our hearts are willing, and arms ready, to maintain your authority as chief magiftrate ; happy that we have lived to fee the day when freedom and equal right, eftablifhed by the voice of the people, fhall prevail through the land.

We are, may it pleafe your Excellency,
    Your excellency's moft devoted
      And moft obedient fervants.

To which his EXCELLENCY was pleafed
to return the following anfwer :
Gentlemen of the firft and fecond Virginia

danger. Be affured, gentlemen, I fhall feel the higheft pleafure in embracing every opportunity to contribute to your happinefs and welfare; and I truft the day will come, when I fhall make one of thofe that hail you among the triumphant deliverers of America.

I have the honour to be,
    Gentlemen,
      Your moft obedient
        And very humble fervant,
          P. HENRY, jun.

Extract from the ordinance for erecting
SALT WORKS *in this colony, and for*
encouraging the making of SALT.

AND whereas it may contribute greatly towards procuring a fpeedy fupply of fo neceffary an article to allow a bounty to private adventurers,

Be it therefore ordained, by the authority aforefaid, that there fhall be allowed and paid by the treafurer a bounty upon the feveral quantities of falt herein after mentioned, to each perfon producing a certificate of his having made the fame within fix months after the paffing of this ordinance, except mr. James Tait, who hath already received fufficient encouragement, that is to fay: For fifty bufhels, the fum of fifty fhillings; for one hundred bufhels, the fum of feven pounds ten fhillings; for two hundred bufhels, the fum of twenty pounds; and for five hundred bufhels, the fum of fixty two pounds ten fhillings. The faid certificates to be granted by the court of the county wherein fuch falt fhall be made, on proof thereof appearing to them.

And be it farther ordained, that the feveral lands whereon it fhall be found neceffary to erect publick falt works fhall, previous to the erecting the fame, be valued by three difinterefted freeholders on oath, and the amount of fuch valuation, upon a certificate from the managers of the faid works, be paid by the treafurer to the owner or owners of fuch lands, which fhall from thenceforth be vefted in the publick, to revert to the proprietor when fuch works fhall be difcontinued.

And be it farther ordained, that all appointments and powers heretofore given to commiffioners for erecting falt works, by virtue of any refolutions of Convention, fhall henceforth ceafe.

Provided neverthelefs, that the faid managers fhall, and they are hereby authorifed and required to ftate and fettle the accounts of the faid commiffioners, and to take the hands by them employed for the purpofes aforefaid, and alfo all fuch materials as may have been contracted for or

"No need to read this to you since you wrote it. Next there is the fond letter from the First and Second Virginia regiments congratulating you on your election, followed by your response to them," Patsy continued.

'Uninfluenced by private ambition,' Liz read as she peered over the column and beamed with pride to see her Henry so honored by the men who followed him as their Colonel for a brief period. *They love you still and would follow you into battle today if you asked,* mon *Henry. But you were needed more in politics rather than in the field.*

Patsy set the folded paper aside and pulled from it two additional sheets included in the special edition. "Ah, but here we have a special *Supplement* with Virginia's new Constitution!"

FRIDAY,
July 5, 1776.   # SUPPLEMENT.

IN A GENERAL CONVENTION Begun and holden at the CAPITOL, in the city of WILLIAMSBURG, on MONDAY the fixth day of MAY, one thoufand feven hundred and feventy-fix, and continued, by adjournment, to the day of JULY following.

The CONSTITUTION, *or FORM of* GOVERNMENT, *agreed to and refolved upon by the Delegates and Reprefentatives of the feveral counties and corporations of* VIRGINIA.

WHEREAS *George* the third, king of *Great Britain* and *Ireland*, and elector of *Hanover*, heretofore intrufted with the exercife of the kingly office in this government, hath endeavoured to pervert the fame into a deteftable and infupportable tyranny, by putting his negative on laws the moft wholefome and neceffary for the publick good:

By denying his governours permiffion to pafs laws of immediate and preffing importance, unlefs fufpended in their operation for his affent, and, when fo fufpended, neglecting to attend to them for many years:

By refufing to pafs certain other laws, unlefs the perfons to be benefited by them would relinquifh the ineftimable right of reprefentation in the legiflature:

By diffolving legiflative affemblies repeatedly and continually, for oppofing with manly firmnefs his invafions of the rights of the people:

When diffolved, by refufing to call others for a long fpace of time, thereby leaving the political fyftem without any legiflative head:

By endeavouring to prevent the population of our country, and, for that purpofe, obftructing the laws for the naturalization of forcigners:

By keeping among us, in times of peace, ftanding armies and fhips of war:

By affecting to render the military independent of, and fuperiour to, the civil power:

By combining with others to fubject us to a foreign jurifdiction, giving his affent to their pretended acts of legiflation:

For quartering large bodies of armed troops among us:

For cutting off our trade with all parts of the world:

For impofing taxes on us without our confent:

For depriving us of the benefits of trial by jury:

For tranfporting us beyond feas, to be tried for pretended offences:

By which feveral acts of mifrule, the government of this country, as formerly exercifed under the crown of *Great Britain*, is TOTALLY DISSOLVED:

We therefore, the delegates and reprefentatives of the good people of *Virginia*, having maturely confidered the premifes, and viewing with great concern the deplorable condition to which this once happy country muft be reduced, unlefs fome regular adequate mode of civil polity is fpeedily adopted, and in compliance with a recommendation of the General Congrefs, do ordain and declare the future form of government of *Virginia* to be as followeth:

The legiflative, executive, and judiciary departments, fhall be feparate and diftinct, fo that neither exercife the powers properly belonging to the other; nor fhall any perfon exercife the powers of more than one of them at the fame time, except that the juftices of the county courts fhall be eligible to either Houfe of Affembly.

The legiflative fhall be formed of two diftinct branches, who, together, fhall be a complete legiflature. They fhall meet once, or oftener, every year, and fhall be called the GENERAL ASSEMBLY OF VIRGINIA.

One of thefe fhall be called the HOUSE OF DELEGATES, and confift of two reprefentatives to be chofen for each county, and for the diftrict of *Weft Augufta*, annually, of fuch men as actually refide in and are freeholders of the fame, or duly qualified according to law, and alfo of one delegate or reprefentative to be chofen annually for the city of *Williamsburg*, and one for the borough of *Norfolk*, and a reprefentative for each of fuch other cities and boroughs as may hereafter be allowed particular reprefentation by the legiflature; but when any city or borough fhall fo decreafe as that the number of perfons having right of fuffrage therein fhall have been for the fpace of feven years fucceffively lefs than half the number of voters in fome one county in *Virginia*, fuch city or borough thenceforward fhall ceafe to fend a delegate or reprefentative to the Affembly.

The other fhall be called the SENATE, and confift of twenty four members, of whom thirteen fhall conftitute a Houfe to proceed on bufinefs, for whofe election the different counties fhall be divided into twenty four diftricts, and each county of the refpective diftrict, at the time of the election of its delegates, fhall vote for one

All laws fhall originate Delegates, to be approv the Senate, or to be ar confent of the Houfe of L money bills, which in no altered by the Senate, but or rejected.

A Governour, or chief be chofen annually, by joi Houfes, to be taken in ea tively, depofited in the boxes examined jointly of each Houfe, and the n reported to them, that t may be entered (which fl of taking the joint ballot in all cafes) who fhall not office longer than three ye nor be eligible until the e years after he fhall have b office. An adequate, bu ry, fhall be fettled on him tinuance in office; and he advice of a Council of Sta executive powers of go ding to the laws of this and fhall not, under any cife any power or prerog of any law, ftatute, or cuft But he fhall, with the adv cil of State, have the po reprieves or pardons, exc profecution fhall have bee the Houfe of Delegates, otherwife particularly di cafes, no reprieve or pardo ed but by refolve of the gates.

Either Houfe of the Gener adjourn themfelves refpe Governour fhall not proro the Affembly during their folve them at any time; bu ceffary, either by advice c State, or on application c the Houfe of Delegates, c the time to which they fl rogued or adjourned.

A Privy Council, or C confifting of eight member fen by joint ballot of both F bly, either from their ov the people at large, to af niftration of government. nually choofe out of their prefident, who, in cafe of ability, or neceffary abfenc nour from the governmen Lieutenant-Governour. fhall be fufficient to act, a

---

Patrick smiled. "Good, I want the people to read every word."

Patsy then turned the page over and tapped it, proudly holding it over her heart. "And will you look at the brilliant new plan of Government, with *my* Papa at the top!"

The following are the appointments under the above PLAN *of* GOVERNMENT.

PATRICK HENRY, junior, efq; Governour.

JOHN PAGE, DUDLEY DIGGES, JOHN TAYLOE, JOHN BLAIR, BENJAMIN HARRISON of Berkeley, BARTHOLOMEW DANDRIDGE, CHARLES CARTER of Shirley, and BENJAMIN HARRISON of Brandon, Counfellors of State.

THOMAS WHITING, JOHN HUTCHINGS, CHAMPION TRAVIS, THOMAS NEWTON, jun. and GEORGE WEBB, efquires, Commiffioners of Admiralty.

EDMUND RANDOLPH, efq; Attorney-General.

THOMAS EVERARD, and JAMES COCKE, efquires, Commiffioners for fettling accounts.

GOD fave the COMMONWEALTH.

Mon Henry, you are so very special, Liz meowed, looking at her beloved human with deep affection. *You are not just Virginia's first elected governor. You are the first elected governor of a free republic under a written constitution in the history of the world. But you are too humble to think in such terms, so I shall think them for you, no?*

"Like Washington when he was made Commander-in-Chief, I find myself unequal to the duties of this important station," Patrick whispered.

And just like General Washington, you were handpicked for that station for such a time as this! Liz thought. *The Maker will equip you with everything you need.*

"There's also a PostScript here that lists all that was accomplished in the Virginia Convention, including the Declaration of Rights," Patsy told him, scanning the page. "And the Convention's adjournment until October. Also, Mr. Pendleton lists the revisions to sentences in the morning and evening service prayers, and the prayers in the communion service that acknowledge the authority of the king. They have modified words to ask for blessings of grace, wisdom, and understanding upon the magistrates, meaning *you,* Papa."

"Please read me the prayer," Patrick requested, softly petting Liz, who purred.

"Of course," Patsy answered, holding up the paper. "*'O Lord, our heavenly father, high and mighty, king of kings, Lord of Lords, the only ruler of the universe, who dost from thy throne behold all the dwellers upon the earth, most heartily we beseech thee with thy favour to behold the magistrates of this commonwealth, and so replenish them with the grace of thy holy Spirit, that they may always incline to thy will, and walk in thy way; endue them plenteously with heavenly gifts; strengthen them, that they may vanquish and overcome all their enemies; and finally, after this life, they may obtain everlasting joy and felicity, through Jesus Christ, our Lord. Amen.'*"

"Amen. I need replenishment, strength, and wisdom," Patrick admitted. "Of course, my political opponents no doubt wished for the 'after this life' portion of that prayer for me with their hopeful rumors of my recent death. I am happy to disappoint them for now." He chuckled and handed his glass to Patsy. "Thank you for reading to me, daughter. I shall read the paper for myself in greater detail when I am up to it. Just leave it here while I rest."

"Of course, Papa. I will leave the paper here with you and Liz," Patsy answered with a smile to see Liz looking over the paper. "It looks as if she is reading!"

Patrick softly chuckled, scooting down to rest his head on the pillow. "She has always had a fascination with the written word. She plays with my quill pens, too. Perhaps the feathers and ink fascinate her."

Liz rolled her eyes. *If you only knew, Monsieur. Just wait until you read the Declaration of Independence.*

An ordinance to enable the prefent magiftrates and officers to continue the adminiftration of juftice, and for fettling the general mode of proceedings in criminal and other cafes, till the fame can be more amply provided for.

An ordinance to amend an ordinance entitled An ordinance to provide for paying the expenfes of the delegates from this colony to the General Congrefs.

An ordinance to arrange the counties in diftricts for electing Senators, and to afcertain their wages.

An ordinance prefcribing the oaths of office to be taken by the Governour and Privy Council, and other officers of the commonwealth of Virginia, and for other purpofes therein mentioned.

An ordinance for amending an ordinance entitled An ordinance for raifing and embodying a fufficient force for the defence and protection of this colony, and for other purpofes therein mentioned.

An ordinance making it felony to counterfeit the continental paper currency, and for other purpofes therein mentioned.

By a gentleman from Halifax, in North Carolina, we are informed that general Clinton, in attempting to come into Charleftown harbour, the 17th of laft month, was overtaken by a violent ftorm, which drove afhore a 36 gun frigate, and 8 tranfports with foldiers, who it is faid were chiefly loft. He had this intelligence from an officer from Cape Fear, who faid that general Moore had received it by exprefs; in confequence of which, four regiments under marching orders for Charleftown, and col. Muhlenburg's Virginia battalion, had been countermanded.

Lord Dunmore fent a flag of truce fome few days ago to Gwyn's ifland, with a letter for general Lewis, wherein he propofes an exchange of prifoners, and tells the general, that if he has not a fufficient number of our people, that he fhall give him credit for the overplus, and pay him as foon as he can. General Lewis, we hear, anfwered his lordfhip's very *witty* and *ingenious* propofal as it deferved.

IN CONVENTION,
July 5, 1776.

RESOLVED, that the plan of government for this country, and the ordinance to arrange the counties in diftricts for electing Senators, and to afcertain their wages, be publifhed in the refpective parifh churches and meeting-houfes, for two Sundays fuccefsively, immediately after divine fervice.

EDMUND PENDLETON, prefident.
(*A copy*)
John Tazewell, clerk of the Convention.

of the prayer for the church militant as declares the fame authority, fhall be omitted, and this alteration made in one of the above prayers in the communion fervice : *Almighty and everlafting God, we are taught by thy holy word that the hearts of all rulers are in thy governance, and that thou doft difpofe and turn them as it feemeth beft to thy godly wifdom, we humbly befeech thee fo to difpofe and govern the hearts of allthe magiftrates of this commonwealth, that in all their thoughts, words, and works they may evermore feek thy honour and glory, and ftudy to preferve thy people committed to their charge, in wealth, peace, and godlinefs. Grant this, O merciful father, for thy dear fon'sfake, Jefus Chrift, our Lord. Amen.*

That the following prayer fhall be ufed, inftead of the prayer for the king's majefty, in the morning and evening fervice : *O Lord, our heavenly father, high and mighty, king of kings, Lord of Lords, the only ruler of the univerfe, who doft from thy throne behold all the dwellers upon earth, moft heartily we befeech thee with thy favour to behold the magiftrates of this commonwealth, and fo replenifh them with the grace of thy holy fpirit, that they may alway incline to thy will, and walk in thy way ; endue them plenteoufly with heavenly gifts ; ftrengthen them, that they may vanquifh and overcome all their enemies ; and finally, after this life, they may obtain everlafting joy and felicity, through Jefus Chrift, our Lord. Amen.*

In the 20th fentence of the litany ufe thefe words : *That it may pleafe thee to endue the magiftrates of this commonwealth with grace, wifdom, and underftanding.*

In the fucceeding one, ufe thefe words : *That it may pleafe thee to blefs and keep them, giving them grace to execute juftice, and to maintain truth.*

Let every other fentence of the litany be retained, without any alteration, except the above fentences recited.

EDMUND PENDLETON, prefident.
(*A copy*)
J. Tazewell, clerk of the Convention.

An ORDINANCE *making it felony to*

SCOTCHTOWN, VIRGINIA, JULY 22, 1776

Patrick slowly began to regain strength, eating a little more each day, and walking back and forth in the long foyer of the house, with the doors opened on either end to allow a breeze of fresh air to circulate. The children were so happy to see their father up and about, but knew he wasn't up for wrestling with them on the floor as he loved to do. They played outside and tried to be as quiet as possible when he rested. Having lost their mother just a year and a half before, they were especially anxious for their only parent to recover. While they were excited that their father was the new governor, they were mainly excited that their father was simply getting better.

Letters of congratulations for his new post as Governor poured into the house from all corners of Virginia as well as other colonies. The religious dissenters and soldiers especially expressed their confidence and trust in Patrick Henry's leadership. Liz most looked forward to each paper that arrived, eager for him to see the news from Philadelphia, New York, and South Carolina.

"Would you look at that? General Lee reports that the Patriots routed the British at Sullivan's Island!" Patrick exclaimed as he and Liz sat on the bed reading the latest paper. "Huzzah, that is good news!"

Oui, mon *Albert was there,* Liz meowed, happy to see the report.

JULY 19, 1776.   T H E   NUMBER 77.

VIRGINIA GAZETTE.

ALWAYS FOR LIBERTY,   AND THE PUBLICK GOOD.

High HEAVEN *to* GRACIOUS ENDS *directs the* STORM!

Extract of a letter from his Excellency Major-General LEE, *to the Hon.* EDMUND PENDLETON, *esq; President of the Convention, dated* Charlestown, *June* 29, 1776.

YESTERDAY, about 11 o'clock, the enemy's squadron, consisting of one 50 and one 40 gun ship, and six frigates, came to anchor before fort Sullivan, and began one of the most furious cannonades I ever heard or saw. Their project was apparently, at the same time, to land their troops on the east end of the island. Twice they attempted it, and as often were gallantly repulsed. The ships continued their fire on the fort till 11 at night. The behaviour of the garrison, both men and officers, with col. Moutrie at their head, I confess, astonished me. It was brave to the last degree. I had no idea that so much coolness and intrepidity could be displayed, by a collection of raw recruits, as I was witness of in this garrison. Had we been better supplied with ammunition, it is most probable this squadron would have been utterly destroyed. However, they have no reason to triumph. One of their frigates is now in flames; another lost her boltsprit. The commodore and a 40 gun ship had their mizzens shot away, and

Colonel St. Paul is appointed minister plenipotentiary to the court of France.

Orders are said to be given from the war-office, and also from the victualling-office, to stop all provisions from being put on board the transport ships, and for the soldiers lying at Portsmouth, Chatham, &c. from embarking, and to stop all other proceedings for 20 days.

Yesterday morning four waggons laden with money were sent off from the Bank, under a proper escort, to Portsmouth, for the payment of his majesty's ships and the transports lying there bound to America.

March 30. Previous to the departure of the foreign mercenaries to America, the sums stipulated for their hire and pay are to be advanced by Great Britain. The prince of Waldeck, and several of the German princes who have engaged to furnish troops, are expected in England. These princes have a juster notion of the finances of England than to permit their subjects to embark before they are paid for their hire.

It is astonishing how any man could even dream of sending cavalry to America. Only let us for a moment conceive a dragoon with his bags, his bucket, his boots,

Extract of a letter from Madrid, *March* 17.

" Our court seems to have quite given up the proposed attempt of a second expedition against Algiers. All the preparations for that expedition have now another destination, and are said to be intended to watch over our settlements in America; as the war between England and its colonies renders it necessary for all powers, who have any settlements in those parts, to put them in so secure a situation that they may be in no danger of suffering from the above-mentioned disputes."

Extract of a letter from Bristol, *April* 13.

" This morning arrived here the Hibernia, Knethell, from Corke, who sailed from thence the 9th instant, and informs, that the men of war, with upwards of 40 sail of transports under their convoy, sailed the 8th from the Cove; and as the wind blew fresh at N. E. and continued so for many days, it is imagined they must be got quite clear. The Tartar, capt. Ruffell, and the Friendly Trader, with several volunteers on board, sailed from this place for Corke and America."

April 16. Letters from Stockholm advise, that the great activity shewn in putting the army, fleet, and fortresses, in the best state of defence, causes much talk:

Patrick's brow was furrowed and he mumbled as he read various news nuggets. "Hmmm, the German princes who are supplying the Hessian fighters to the British insisted on payment *before* the mercenaries sailed to America. Smart of them, since the British have already underestimated the costs of this war . . . General Burgoyne transported twelve-hundred flat-bottomed boats to carry soldiers across the lakes in New England . . ." He turned the page.

"Ah, New York. One of Washington's guards was hanged for attempting to aid the enemy," Patrick read, shocked, and saddened to see such traitorous behavior. "Such Judases will ever be among us . . . July 4. Last Saturday arrived at the Hook (like a swarm of locusts escaped from the bottomless pit) a fleet said to be one hundred-thirty sail of ships and vessels from Halifax, having on board General Howe, etc., sent out by the tyrants of Great Britain," Patrick read, smiling at the descriptions given to them.

Max and Jock were instrumental in that terrible Hickey affair, Liz thought, her brow furrowed. *I know they are very busy protecting General Washington as the British arrive.*

Patrick scanned down and rapidly tapped his finger. "Philadelphia! July 8th, the Declaration of Independence was read at the State House! They have an excerpt of it here, and it will be printed in full in next week's *Gazette!*"

Oui, I was there, mon *Henry,* Liz meowed with a coy grin. *I, of course, could recite it for you now.*

"Oh, my, Admiral Howe is not yet arrived, but is expected with 150 ships and 20,000 men," Patrick reported. "That means the Continental Army will face 30,000 enemy forces. They are going to require tremendous provisions. And prayer."

Liz scanned down and saw the news of the rout of Lord Dunmore at Gwyn's Island. *Look,* mon *Henry! Your nemesis predecessor has finally been driven away from Virginia for good!*

She and Patrick reveled in the tremendous news of Andrew Lewis and his brave, persistent Virginia forces, who pursued Dunmore. "The former royal governor received a splinter in the leg and had 'all his valuable china smashed about his ears,'" Patrick read with a grin, imagining the arrogant former royal governor sitting among the shattered pieces of his precious china.

"Ever since the Battle of Point Pleasant in October 1774, Andrew Lewis felt that Lord Dunmore acted treacherously," Patrick Henry recalled. "General Lewis holds to the belief that the royal governor hired those hostile Indian forces as mercenaries to wipe out the Virginia forces to eliminate military threats against him."

Which would make that battle the true *beginning of the American Revolution, no?* Liz thought. *Even before Lexington and Concord. And the first Patriot to die in that battle was, of course, Samuel Crowley.*

"I wonder how my widowed childhood friend Elizabeth Crowley is faring with her seven children," Patrick muttered with a sigh. "I hope she feels some satisfaction knowing that her husband's death there has been answered by driving Dunmore from Virginia. I know that the Virginia House of Burgesses awarded her a wartime pension. But now that I am Governor, I wish to assist her and other such war widows as much as I am able."

Bon, I am happy to hear this, as Gillamon said that one of those Crowley children named 'Littleberry' will do something crucial for the Order of the Seven team someday, Liz thought. *I wonder what it could be.*

SCOTCHTOWN, VIRGINIA, JULY 30, 1776

"Finally, the full Declaration of Independence!" Patrick exclaimed happily, unfolding the crisp copy of the July 26th *Virginia Gazette.* "When, in the course of human events . . ."

Liz sat there, smiling. *I gave* Monsieur *Jefferson those first seven words.* She closed her eyes contentedly and listened as he continued to read aloud every one of the 1,300 words.

". . . appealing to the Supreme Judge of the world for the rectitude of our intentions . . .

That, too, was my line, Liz meowed, licking her paw, and wiping her whiskers.

". . . with a firm reliance on the protection of Divine Providence . . ."

But Nigel added that line, Liz meowed. *Edits required teamwork, no?*

". . . we mutually pledge to each other our lives, our fortunes, and our sacred honor," Patrick finished, a broad smile on his face. "Well done, gentlemen."

And lady, Liz protested with a grin.

"The Declaration was read in Trenton, Williamsburg, New York," Patrick read, then leaned forward to hurriedly read about the fallout after it was read before Washington's troops. "They pulled down the statue of King George at Bowling Green! The Patriots will melt it for bullets, huzzah!"

Patrick Henry let the paper fall to his lap, and he reached out a hand to pet Liz while he rubbed his tired eyes with the other. "It is done now. There is no turning back. America has declared her independence, and now France will soon learn of it. *Then* they will come to our aid, as I have predicted all along."

We shall not fight our battles alone, Liz meowed, quoting from Patrick's Liberty or Death Speech. *Kate is already in France to set things in motion, and I will join her there soon to make sure your words come true,* cher *Patrick.*

Patrick yawned and laid his head back on the pillow, ready for another nap. He could rest easy and contentedly, seeing how magnificently independence had been declared. He knew he had much work ahead to support the cause and was already thinking of how he would lend aid to the Continental Army and to his dear friend, General George Washington.

JULY 26, 1776.   THE   NUMBER 78.

VIRGINIA GAZETTE.

ALWAYS FOR LIBERTY,   AND THE PUBLICK GOOD.

High HEAVEN *to* GRACIOUS ENDS *directs the* STORM!

IN COUNCIL, *July* 20, 1776. Ordered, THAT *the printers publish in their respective Gazettes the DECLARATION of INDEPENDENCE made by the Honourable the Continental Congress, and that the sheriff of each county in this commonwealth proclaim the same at the door of his courthouse the first court day after he shall have received the same.*

ARCHIBALD BLAIR, *Cl. Con.*

IN CONGRESS, July 4, 1776.

A DECLARATION *by the representatives of the* UNITED STATES *of* AMERICA, *in* GENERAL CONGRESS *assembled.*

WHEN, in the course of human events, it becomes necessary for one people to dissolve the political bands which have connected them with another, and to assume, among the powers of the earth, the separate and equal station to which the laws of nature and of nature's God entitle them, a decent respect to the opinions of mankind requires that they should declare the causes which impel them to the separation.

tance, unless suspended in their operation till his assent should be obtained; and, when so suspended, he has utterly neglected to attend to them.

He has refused to pass other laws for the accommodation of large districts of people, unless those people would relinquish the right of representation in the legislature; a right inestimable to them, and formidable to tyrants only.

He has called together legislative bodies at places unusual, uncomfortable, and distant from the depository of their publick records, for the sole purpose of fatiguing them into compliance with his measures.

He has dissolved Representative Houses repeatedly, for opposing, with manly firmness, his invasions on the rights of the people.

He has refused, for a long time, after such dissolutions, to cause others to be elected; whereby the legislative powers, incapable of annihilation, have returned to the people at large for their exercise, the state remaining in the mean time exposed to all the dangers of invasion from without and convulsions within.

He has endeavoured to prevent the population of these states, for that purpose

der it at once an example and fit instrument for introducing the same absolute rule into these colonies:

For taking away our charters, abolishing our most valuable laws, and altering fundamentally the forms of our governments:

For suspending our own legislatures, and declaring themselves invested with power to legislate for us in all cases whatsoever.

He has abdicated government here, by declaring us out of his protection, and waging war against us.

He has plundered our seas, ravaged our coasts, burnt our towns, and destroyed the lives of our people.

He is, at this time, transporting large armies of foreign mercenaries to complete the works of death, desolation, and tyranny, already begun with circumstances of cruelty and perfidy scarcely parallelled in the most barbarous ages, and totally unworthy the head of a civilized nation.

He has constrained our fellow citizens taken captive on the high seas to bear arms against their country, to become the executioners of their friends and brethren,

Liz sighed contentedly, closed her eyes, and curled up in the sunshine next to the Voice of the Revolution. She immediately began to dream of returning to her beloved homeland of France, and of the day when the headlines of a French Alliance would be printed in big, bold letters for all the world to see.

The Place of the Skull

K akia felt the warm rays of sunshine that slowly prodded her to consciousness as she lay curled up next to a gravestone. She didn't want to wake up. She was having the 'good dream' again. It came to her periodically, and she was so drawn to the light filling her dream that she never wanted it to end. In her dream she felt safe and loved. She felt new, green grass under her feet, and she could hear happy, good laughter . . . but who was laughing? She always woke up before she could find out.

The stench of death filled her nostrils as she took a deep breath. Her eyes quickly opened, bringing her cruelly back to reality. Here she didn't feel safe or loved. The cat shook off her dream and looked around. She was in the oldest cemetery in Paris, located next to *Les Halles* market at *Rue D'Enfer*—Hell Street. She looked up to see the macabre marker carved with the skull and crossbones and the Latin words MEMENTO MORI etched into the blackened stone. "Remember that you die," the gray striped, forlorn-looking tabby cat muttered, translating the words. It was her master's favorite motto, and he used it frequently to remind her and other members of their growing team that he had the power to take back their immortality and send them down into the abyss.

Charlatan laughed at the humans' use of the phrase in sermons, or for adorning gravestones, jewelry, paintings, or even with celebrations. *I don't care how the humans use 'memento mori,' as long as it reminds them of death,* he stated emphatically. *Death is my specialty, my passion, my* raison d'être, *as the French call it. My reason for being.*

She looked over at the huge medieval carved mural from 1424 on the wall of the cemetery, depicting the *Danse Macabre,* or the Dance of Death. It portrayed the personification of death summoning humans from all walks of life to dance along to the grave with a pope, a king, a child, and a common laborer. The scene was meant as a sobering reminder to humans that their lives were fragile, the glories of earthly life were fleeting, and all possessions were gathered in vain. Death was common to all, no matter their age or station in life. It would come to every life eventually, and it was Charlatan's unquenchable desire to bring it to pass for humans, ever since his first assignment with the very first humans in the Garden.

The humans mainly used four symbols for mortality: the hourglass, the bell, the skull, and the coffin. Charlatan decided to incorporate these symbols into his team's methods as they glorified his master, the Evil One, who had chosen the Place of the Skull for his finest work over seventeen hundred years ago. Kakia's brow furrowed as she thought of that place where innocent blood had been shed on a cruel Roman cross. It seemed as if it were a place of victory at the time. But some humans had since claimed that their one true God had turned that place of pain into a place of *joy*. They dared to claim victory at the site of a garden tomb just a few yards away. The followers of the crucified man had taken the symbol of the most horrific way to die ever conceived by man and turned it into a symbol of hope! "How? Why?" Kakia spat, spotting gravestones carved in the shape of crosses. The humans put their transformed symbol of death everywhere. They even proudly wore the symbol of the torture device around their necks! "How could a device of such horrific death become so beloved by the pathetic creatures?" She just didn't understand it. That enigmatic symbol of a cross held an uncomfortable yet magnetic attraction for her. She bristled whenever she thought of the bloody scene that came before the cross. The innocent man was scourged beyond recognition, and the image of his red stripes was forever burned into her memory. "I hate stripes," she snarled. She was ever eager to convert to another form to get away from her own stripes.

Charlatan used the macabre symbols of death in his coded messages and enabled his team of immortal minions to transport to this place from anywhere in the world by uttering the phrase *memento mori* and then licking a gravestone, breaking an hourglass, or striking a bell. Any geographic place that referenced death could also be used as a transport portal when the words were spoken. Kakia had taken the form of the fierce British grenadier soldier Rafe for so long that she was knocked out for a while when converting and transporting here after clanging the ship's bell in South Carolina.

The cat got up from the slab next to the gravestone and made her way to the entrance of a tunnel that would lead her to Charlatan's current headquarters, which he called "The Place of the Skull"—in honor of the Evil One's favorite place on Earth—no matter where it was located. Kakia preferred the old headquarters in the catacombs of Rome, but she had no say. She left the bright sunshine and entered the cold darkness. Her eyes quickly adjusted, and she began walking along the smelly, dark tunnel. The echo of dripping water was all she heard as she wound through the endless maze of tunnels. After a while, she heard a low, sinister laugh, and a chill ran down her spine. On the bottom of the tunnel wall near the floor was etched a skull. She pressed the skull, which cracked open a hidden door. She took a breath and slipped through the narrow opening behind the tunnel wall.

"There you are," Charlatan greeted her in his usual form of a massive snake. "You're LATE!"

Kakia bowed low. "Forgive me, my Master. My conversion must have left me knocked out a bit longer than usual for some reason." She looked around the darkened room illuminated by the burning flame of an oil lamp made from a human skull. But it wasn't just any human skull. It belonged to Abel—the first human to die a physical death. After Cain buried it, the Evil One gave it to Charlatan as a trophy to reward him for his great accomplishment in the fall of man. It was the snake's most prized possession, and he took it wherever he moved his headquarters.

A massive, wet wolf sat there in a puddle with glowing eyes that reflected the fire. Kakia looked at him with curiosity. "Espion. I'm anxious to hear of your progress in New York. Why are you wet?"

"I transferred through the Hell Gate portal in New York," the wolf explained.

An insect scurried across the wall behind Charlatan and whispered in his ear. "My newest team member says he is anxious to hear about your *failure* in Charleston, Kakia. Oh, but there are sssssssso many more to recount, for both of you."

Kakia and Espion sat with their heads lowered and braced themselves for the diatribe that was coming.

"Beginning with BOSSSSSSTON," Charlatan began, "Kakia, *you* failed to kill Henry Knox, and Espion, *you* allowed Jock to live, which in turn helped Knox and the rest of the Patriots to achieve victory. Kakia, *you* then thought it would be *so* brilliant to lock that pipsqueak mouse Nigel in Gage's trunk. But that trunk contained every document of British intelligence in North America, so now the enemy knows how to combat British espionage!"

"But we started the war at Lexington and Concord with the wolf gun!" Espion desperately protested.

"And I killed countless humans there and at Bunker Hill with that gun," Kakia quickly added, "including the rebel leader Dr. Joseph Warren."

Charlatan slithered around them. "Yesssssss, so because of that you offset your previous failures. That's why I decided to give you another chance." He came right behind Kakia's ear and tickled it with his forked tongue. "But what about Sullivan's Island? You failed to reach that pathetic fort and its defenders, which prevented Charleston and the South from being taken. At the least you should have killed General Lee! But the British have been humiliated

in Boston *and* Sssssssouth Carolina and ssssssent packing! WE CANNOT
ALLOW THISSSSSS TO CONTINUE!"

Kakia's fur stood on end as a wave of evil swept over her. Espion shivered
from fear as Charlatan came over to his ear and whispered, "Do you realize
what will happen if America becomes free?"

"Wh-what, Master?" Espion timidly asked.

"EVERYTHING CHANGES, OF COURSSSSSSSSE!" the snake hissed.
"The Enemy's plans to sssssspread His 'good news' of freedom will lead to
free thought and free will. They will be able to worship the Enemy *freely*, just
like He wants. It will open the door for free expression and opportunities
for humans to do things they never dreamed they could do, as the Enemy
intended. It will lead to *joy* and *happinessssss* and GOODNESSSSSS!" The
snake closed his eyes and shuddered. "Freedom stands opposed to all that my
Master stands for. He first chose ME in the animal kingdom to fight against
such unimaginable light. WE are charged with death. We kill human *bodies*
as our first priority, and if we can't kill their bodies, then we'll kill their *minds,*
or their *spirits.*" The snake slithered in front of them, held them in his gaze,
and wore a malicious grin. "Killing their will to be free leads to the death of
everything else."

The insect scribbled something on the wall, and Charlatan slithered over
to read it. The snake chuckled. "Oh, how right you are, my parasitic friend.
Vector says that killing the hope in humans through prolonged illness is *his*
favorite. And he does it *so* well!" He turned to glare at Kakia and Espion.
"While you two have repeatedly failed in your missions, Vector has succeeded
brilliantly in his."

Suddenly Charlatan morphed into a human with smallpox. "I especially love this one. It's so *grotesque!* Kakia, your failure to administer a strong
enough exposure of smallpox to George Washington convinced me to enlist
an assassin bug for all human disease assignments. I've given Vector the power
to convert from an assassin bug to any form of insect or pathogen that will
accomplish our purposes, and he can enlist as many of his kind as he needs.
So far, he's spread smallpox with flying colors, especially in Canada. He's been
a fly to live among filth and garbage in the soldier camps of both armies to
carry the pathogens for dysentery and typhoid fever."

Vector hopped onto Charlatan's shoulder and whispered in his ear.

"Ah yes, and just for fun he and his team of flies harassed Thomas Jefferson
and the Continental Congress, so they'd become irritated and rush through
their little independence exercise," Charlatan told them. "He's also been lice
to spread typhus and trench fever. But I'm particularly partial to his skills as a
mosquito." He pulled from his pocket Vector's note written in blood:

THE VOICE IS SILENCED. DECLARATION HEADING TO FRANCE.
- V

"Malaria worked like a charm for the Voice of the Revolution," Charlatan boasted. "Of course, we all remember how Kakia had previously *failed* to poison Patrick Henry with the letter opener. I predict that Vector will be my most efficient soldier and will maim and kill more humans in this war than any bullets you might shoot from your wolf gun, '*Rafe*.'"

Kakia's ears burned hot with anger and jealousy. She knew her embodiment as Rafe had created a cruel, smart, fierce, manipulative, deadly soldier. She was proud of how she had sculpted him. But she needed to do more. She needed to prove herself to Charlatan. "So, the humans have sent the Declaration of Independence here to France?" she asked, trying to deflect from Charlatan's doting on his new favorite minion.

Charlatan laughed, pulling from his other pocket the copy of the Declaration of Independence that had been sent to Silas Deane. He proceeded to tear it into pieces and threw it up into the air. The tattered pieces drifted to the floor. "The ship of humans bringing this rag tragically met with a leak in its hull in the middle of the ocean, so NO! It never arrived. *Poor drowned humans,*" he mocked with a smug laugh. "I'll keep Silas Deane guessing about if his friends are going through with independence, and I'll make the French confused and hesitant to do anything to help the Americans. The French will NOT help the Americans if the Patriots either stop fighting or never win any sort of major battle. The human spies are working perfectly in England and France, and I'm supplying them with intelligence at every turn to prevent French aid." He paused and took a deep breath. "So. Now that we've had this friendly chat to remember what is at *stake,* let's get to the matter at hand. Everything is heading to New York."

"Master, how did the assassination attempt of George Washington fail?" Espion wanted to know. "I thought since you got rid of the housekeeper and delivered the poisoned peas that everything would go according to plan. And weren't you going to kill Jock?"

Charlatan reverted to a snake and grew to a massive size, hissing and swaying back and forth. "HOW DARE YOU IMPLY THAT I FAILED! If YOU hadn't failed in your second chance assignment, that whelp would be dead. I had to choose where to put my venom, and Washington was the greater target. Unfortunately, that other mangy canine stopped the delivery of the poisoned peas." He slithered over to Espion and got right in his face to quickly change the subject. "And if you hadn't failed in your *first* assignment, Lafayette wouldn't be posing a threat to us now. I must clean up *your* mess with that, too. I'll put enough obstacles in his way so the Marquis can't escape from France. But perhaps I made a mistake by allowing *you* to escape death in that bog."

Charlatan doesn't like it when HIS *failures are thrown into his face*, Kakia thought with a frown. *All he does is accuse us of failing. There's one standard for him, and one for the rest of us.*

"I'm sorry for my failures, Master," Espion groveled. "But I've done as you said and been all over New York. The city has been torn up block by block with preparations for war. The humans are divided and fearful. Families have been broken apart and are losing hope. Widows and children are suffering, as husbands and sons are gone off to fight or have died from disease or accidents. The Holy Ground is thriving with debauchery and disease. Lying, stealing, cheating, drunkenness, and filthiness are rampant. Counterfeiters and con artists are increasing in number. Meanwhile, more and more British forces arrive each day. I can report that the Patriots are digging in all over, but their fortifications are very crude and no match for the coming British attack. But still they celebrated after the Declaration of Independence was read. They even tore down King George's statue and are melting it down to make bullets to fire back at the British."

"Let them celebrate," Charlatan hissed. "Their jubilant voices will soon be choked silent when thirty-two thousand troops arrive in New York Harbor. The British humans will have all they need to crush this rebellion once and for all. BUT, just in case, we need to step it up in New York. Look for weaknesses in the Patriots and find a way to break them. WE must do everything to thwart the Enemy's plan for America to be some 'shining city on a hill, filled with light and hope for the world,'" he gushed in a falsetto, mocking tone. He then got right in their faces.

"Kakia and Espion, if you do not deliver me a Patriot defeat in New York, I will be forced to put you away, permanently," Charlatan threatened.

"We will defeat them," Kakia boldly asserted. "I'll stake my immortality on it."

Charlatan raised his brow, delighted with such a self-sacrificing declaration. "I can look forward to either outcome then, can't I?"

"Master, I can report that the British seek to attack the Patriots first over on Long Island," Espion reported. "So, I will look for weaknesses in their defenses there and tell Rafe when he arrives."

Kakia nodded. "I'll then notify the British commanders."

Vector quickly transformed into a fly and buzzed over to land on Espion's nose. "Who is the human commander over on Long Island?" he buzzed in a barely perceptible, high-pitched voice.

Espion thought a moment. "Greene. General Nathanael Greene commands Washington's forces there, so he'll be there when the British attack."

Vector laughed and buzzed around the room.

"Something tells me Greene will *not* be the commander by then," Charlatan predicted with a sinister laugh. "Very well, my little minions. Go see that your worst harm is inflicted, and that death in every form is accomplished."

"What of the Order of the Seven?" Kakia asked.

"What *of* them?" Charlatan snapped. "You obviously can't control them, so you must outsmart them, unless that is too difficult for you." He got right in Kakia's face. "YESSSSSS OR NO?"

Kakia swallowed. "No, my Master."

"I'm glad to hear it. Now be gone, all of you," Charlatan ordered. "On my mark."

The evil team gathered around Abel's skull, touched it, and shouted, "MEMENTO MORI!"

Instantly the light was snuffed out, and they vanished from the dark room. But the force of their exit briefly cracked open the door, sending a slip of the torn Declaration of Independence out into the tunnel.

PART THREE

LIVE TO FIGHT ANOTHER DAY

August 1776 – November 1776

THE FOX AND THE GREYHOUND

"George Washington, Esquire, etc., etc., is how Lord Howe *then* addressed the note," Ambrose Serle explained to the British officers gathered for dinner at General Howe's headquarters. He was recounting their attempt to arrange a peace negotiation. "But still, he wouldn't even *touch* the letter, the obstinate, pompous rebel!"

"It sounds as if *General* Washington knows a thing or two about not getting caught by such details," General Clinton suggested with a smirk. "Like a fish avoiding the hook."

"Or like a *fox* avoiding the hounds," Admiral Howe jested. "After all, General Howe's flagship *Greyhound* is named for a hound that chases foxes by *sight.*"

"I say, chasing Washington *shall* be a bit like a fox hunt, what?" General Cornwallis offered with a chuckle. He lifted one hand out to the uniformed men in their splendid red coats gathered around the table and tugged his lapel with the other hand. "We gentlemen officers shall wear our proper red-coated attire and release our hounds into the coverts of Long Island to hunt until the old Fox is overtaken!"

"Or until the Fox *evades* the hounds," General Clinton interjected with a slight shake of his head, unable to mask his emotions. He was irritated that General Howe had just rejected his strategic advice for attacking New York. He advised Howe to surround Manhattan and land above the rebels to cut off the land bridge from the island to the mainland at King's Bridge. But Howe refused to listen. It was no secret he did not like General Clinton.

Howe had previously rejected Clinton's advice on continuing the chase of the rebels after Bunker Hill, and of taking Dorchester Heights in Boston before the rebels got to the high ground to drive the British out of the city. In South Carolina, Clinton had deferred from his own plan and instead agreed to Sir Peter Parker's vague strategy to capture Charleston, which ended in disaster. His fleet of three thousand men and forty ships had come limping into New York Harbor a week earlier, much to his superior officers' displeasure. Clinton was equally chagrined that his first independent command in North America ended in failure because he deferred to another's strategy. General Clinton may have been unliked and irritating to his superior and fellow officers, but so far, his strategic thinking for America had been spot on. He had an innate ability to pick up the scent of the rebels and how they would act.

General Howe was under orders from Minister of War Lord Germain to wait to attack New York until all British forces and support vessels had arrived. These included British regulars, Irish regiments, the Royal Scottish Highlanders, the mercenary German Hessians, a few black regiments from the West Indies, and even the bedraggled remnant of Lord Dunmore's Ethiopian Regiment—slaves from Virginia who had been promised their freedom in return for fighting for the Crown. In all, Howe would have thirty-two thousand men plus ten thousand sailors, thirty warships, and four hundred transports. He would also have a train of artillery with more than two hundred field guns and forty-six mortars. It was the largest and best-equipped expeditionary force in the history of British warfare.

Germain's strategy was to draw American forces from all the colonies to New York, where the overpowering British juggernaut could defeat them in one swift blow. His fear was that without a decisive win, escaping rebels would retreat into the colonies, where fighting the war would become too spread out and lengthy to win. Germain and Howe knew that even their large number of forces wouldn't be enough to conquer and hold the vast expanse of territory in America if the war dragged on. They knew they would need to recruit a great number of colonial Loyalists to come fight for their king—unless they could make one, decisive blow and destroy Washington's forces in New York.

But as Howe gazed up at the heights of Brooklyn on Long Island and saw the rebel fortifications looking down on the city, he had sobering reminders of his costly, bloody "victory" at Bunker Hill and the rebels' miraculous overnight fortifications built on Breed's Hill and later up on Dorchester Heights. Adding to that sting of British defeat was the rout of Clinton in South Carolina by a few hundred rebels behind an incomplete fort built with spongy palmetto logs. Howe knew what the rebels were capable of, and they had gained his respect. Originally, Germain had hoped for an attack in May or June, but it was now August, and their full force was yet to arrive. Some seasick Hessians had slipped in through the Narrows today, but the bulk of that fleet from landlocked Hesse-Cassel was still expected. So, they would continue to wait. The king's Christmas wish of one decisive blow to end this war by the end of 1776 now seemed unrealistic to General Howe, who had reluctantly agreed to come fight this war.

Howe wanted to seize New York City, but he believed that it would require invading Long Island, driving the rebels from their fortifications and then turning their artillery from Brooklyn Heights down on the city. Long Island was a Loyalist hotbed, so Howe predicted they would be aided by eager colonists. But to minimize casualties, instead of entrapping and fighting the rebels to the death, Howe hoped that the rebellion would just evaporate in the face of the massive British invasion. Knowing the stubborn determination of the rebels thus far, he felt it would realistically require one more campaign in the spring to end the war. He would need to establish outposts on any newly conquered territory and defend those posts through the winter. That meant he needed food and supplies to sustain his army—a thousand tons of food per month, sixty-four thousand cords of firewood, and seventy tons of candles. Not to mention supplies to sustain their four thousand horses with twenty-four thousand tons of hay and oats, twenty thousand horseshoes, and eleven hundred harnesses. And where would he find such an ample supply of food and resources for his army? On Long Island, New York. But Howe decided not to communicate his change of plans to Lord Germain just yet. He wanted to wait and see the outcome of the coming battle of New York.

"Or until the Fox goes to *ground,*" General Howe added with a perturbed snap at Clinton. "In which case we would need to send 'terriers' to dig them out."

"Let the mercenary Hessians do such dirty work," Clinton suggested, lifting a glass. *"Prost, zu den Hunden!"* He looked around the table at the blank faces staring back at him after his German toast. "Cheers, to the dogs." General Clinton had a way of grating on everyone's nerves.

"Right," Cornwallis said with an awkward smile, clearing his throat. "Other than the meeting under the white flag, has the *Greyhound* yet spotted the Fox 'in the wild,' so to speak?"

"No, but Washington's defenses were unable to stop the *Phoenix* and the *Rose* from sailing up the Hudson," Howe reported proudly. He pointed to his chest. "But *this* Greyhound looks forward to *seeing* the Old Fox himself on the battlefield when he surrenders his rusty sword."

The group of officers lifted their glasses and laughed at the reference to General Burgoyne's play that was staged back in Boston, depicting a confused Washington dragging an oversized, rusty sword.

"Scent hounds are used far more than sight hounds in fox hunts," Clinton obtusely offered, implying his instinct to pick up the scent of how the rebels would move. "Especially when the fox moves at night."

General Howe waved him off. "Well, in order to bag *this* Fox, it shall require seeing as well as scenting him out." He looked at Clinton. "And remember, *I* am the Master of Foxhounds, and I have the final say over all matters in the field. And that field will be Long Island."

Clinton gave a sly grin. "As you say, General."

Cornwallis quickly lifted his glass. "To the hunt!"

"To the hunt!" the officers echoed.

From an opened window, a pair of brown eyes narrowed at hearing their discussion.

STATEN ISLAND, NEW YORK, AUGUST 9, 1776

"Come to me, me precious!" Al cried, embracing a blackberry bush. He pulled off one berry after another and stuffed them into his mouth, mumbling as tears of joy filled his eyes. As soon as Clinton's fleet arrived and disembarked on Staten Island, Al took off running into the countryside. He followed the intoxicating aromas of peaches, apples, pears, grapes, chestnuts, and other fresh produce growing in abundance on this beautiful, hilly island. He had gorged himself for a week after enduring the poor rations aboard Cornwallis's ship. "But where be the bananas?" he lamented. "Aye, but this kitty's glad to have fresh fruit o' any kind. It's a wonder I didn't get the scurvy then."

As Al pulled back a branch to reach a cluster of berries, he jumped as he heard a strange bark-like scream and saw a pair of brown eyes staring at him. "Ahhh!" he yelled, startled, and falling onto his back.

"*Guten tag,*" said the creature with the brown eyes.

The plump cat looked around him on the ground. "I'm not a gooten tock. I'm an Irish kitty."

Suddenly a beautiful red fox cautiously poked its head out from the bush and looked both ways. "I said, 'Good morning.'"

Al's eyes widened with a goofy grin. "And ye're a fox! Where'd ye come from?"

"Büdingen," the fox answered, stepping out from the bush to reveal her petite form with shiny red fur. She was no more than seven pounds, with a slender face and beautiful smile. Her cheeks, neck, and chest were white, and her small, black nose was surrounded by black whiskers. The backs of her pointy ears were black, and she appeared to be wearing velvety, black socks. The tip of her long, bushy tail looked as if she had dipped it in white paint, and she curled it daintily around her feet.

"Well, ye ain't in booding-hen anymore, little lass," Al told her, scratching his head. "Ye sure talk funny. I once knew a *brooding* hen named Henriette. She were the bossiest hen I ever knew. Where's booding-hen anyway?"

"How I vould *love* to find some hens," the fox answered, picking off a berry to eat. "It's in the Hesse-Cassel region of Germany."

"Ain't that across the ocean?" Al pulled off a berry and juice squirted down his chin. "How'd ye get here?"

"*Ja,* I vas running for my life *und* jumped in a barrel that vas suddenly closed *und* loaded onto a cart. The cart vas driven a long vay to a ship," the fox explained. "After the barrel vas loaded onto the ship, I vas stuck inside until the barrel fell over *und* the lid popped off. I didn't realize the ship had set sail, but by then it vas too late. Ve vere at sea." The fox frowned as she looked around. "I did not mean to come here. I don't even know vhere 'here' is."

Al pouted his lower lip in sympathy and put a fluffy paw on the fox's back. "There, there, little lass, I know how ye feel, gettin' chased and stuck in places ye don't belong and goin' where ye don't want to go. Happens to me alllllllll the time." He stretched out a paw. "Ye're not in booding-hen anymore. Ye be in America! New York to be exactly. I'll be yer friend. Me name's Al. What's yers, lass?"

"Elsa," the fox answered, growing a slight smile. "*Danke,* Al. I'm glad to have a friend."

Suddenly Al's eyes widened and he put a chubby finger under his nose. "Ye must have sailed over with them Hessian soldiers that have them long, funny black mustaches and pointy hats!"

"*Ja,* ve arrived yesterday," Elsa explained. "Only they are so very sick from the fourteen-veek voyage. I had to hide from them *und* steal their food to survive. But it vasn't a problem as many of them didn't *vant* to eat, from getting sick at both ends. Those poor soldiers had to sleep six to a bunk that usually held four. The drinking vater vas so bad that the humans had to strain it to drink it!"

Al's face started to turn green, and he put a paw to his mouth. "I think *I'm* gonna be sick."

"*Und* their main food of hardtack vas so hard that they had to pound it soft vith a cannonball," Elsa relayed.

"The horror!" Al gasped.

"*Ja,* but I suppose I am stuck here now, *und* from vhat I heard last night I am no better off than vhen I vas running," Elsa sighed.

"Why were ye runnin' in the first place?" Al wanted to know.

"A fat Hessian prince vas chasing me with his hound dogs," Elsa told him, her brow furrowed. "They vere on the hunt to kill me."

Al put both paws up to his mouth. "Oh, no! Did ye get away?"

Elsa gave Al a confused look since she was sitting there in front of him. "Uh, *ja* . . . I ran through the forest into town just as the cart vas leaving the Jerusalem Gate at the castle. That's vhere I jumped to hide, but now I'm here."

"I've been to Jerusalem!" Al exclaimed, drawing another cocked head of confusion from Elsa. "Wait, lass, what exactly did ye hear last night?"

"The soldiers who vear red said they vere going on a fox hunt over on Long Island," Elsa told him.

"Ye better stay away from there then," Al told her. "They're goin' to be fightin' there, too. I'm here with them, not that I want to be, but that's my assignment."

Elsa looked around the harbor. "Vhere is the island that is long?"

Al pointed across the harbor to Long Island. "Right over there, little fox lass." He then pointed over to Manhattan. "Now over on *that* island is where the good humans are. Me friends Max, Jock, and Nigel be there on assignment with General Washington."

"Your friends are vith a fox?" Elsa asked.

Now it was Al who cocked his head in confusion. "No, they be with a *human* named George Washington. Why did ye think he's a bushy-tailed fox beastie?"

"Because this is vhat the redcoat humans called him last night," Elsa explained. Then she closed her eyes and smiled in understanding. "Ah, now I see. The humans must have been making a comparison of a fox hunt *und* capturing this human named George Vashington."

Al shrugged his shoulders. "Humans say weird stuff all the time, lass. All I can tell ye is that the redcoat humans be the *British,* and the blue coat and hodge-podge dressed humans be the *Americans.* They be fightin' a war."

Elsa looked confused again. "Vat kind of var?"

"The Americans be fightin' to win their freedom from England and the mean king," Al explained.

"I admire any creature that vants to be free, *ja?*" Elsa stated with an affirmative nod. *"Und* vhat is this assignment you *und* your friends have?"

"Can ye keep a secret?" Al asked, looking both ways. "We're on mission from the Maker to help the humans."

Elsa's eyes widened. "The Maker? Vhat an important responsibility! But vhy are you helping the bad redcoat humans in this var?"

Al vigorously shook his head and gave a goofy smile. "I'm not *helpin'* them, lass, but I'm gatherin' *intelligence* on 'em."

Elsa looked at Al's simple face and stifled a laugh. "Uh . . . *ja,* okay, if you say so."

"Been doin' this job for *years,* lass," Al explained with the understatement of the millenium. "I always get stuck with the bad laddies: pharaohs, kings, princes, generals. It's me lot in life, but the good food makes up for it. I suggestionize stuff based on what I hear."

"So, if this Fox Vashington is the leader of the American army, I vould think he has a nice house vhere he stays, *ja?*" Elsa asked, unable to stop thinking about hens and eggs. "One vith perhaps a chicken house?"

"Aye, they stay at a nice place a couple of miles north overlookin' the river," Al said. "Some mortar house."

"*Danke*, Al!" Elsa said with a grin. She started walking away but Al stopped her.

"How are ye goin' to get there, lass?" Al asked.

"I'm going to svim!" Elsa explained. *"Auf wiedersehen!"*

Al scratched his head. "Whatever that means. Bye, and tell me friends I sent ye!" he called after her.

With that the petite fox went hurriedly trotting off, lightly bouncing on her feet as she quickly made her way to the water. It wasn't long before her slender form sliced through the bay toward Manhattan. All that was visible was her slender head and her bushy tail operating like a rudder as she navigated through the forest of anchored British ships. She soon passed General Howe's ship and glanced up to see the name, the *Greyhound*. She couldn't resist slapping it with her tail as she glided past. "Humph! I vill go be vith your American Fox vhere I vill be safe from your hounds."

Little did Elsa know that George Washington not only had a chicken house with dogs, but also a fast horse named Blueskin that made "Vashington" the best fox hunter in Virginia.

A Fox in
the Henhouse

Veritas soared above lower Manhattan, scanning the water for fish. The glint of sunshine sparkled off the bay, hiding fish under the surface. Suddenly the bald eagle spotted something swimming near the shoreline. He pivoted and flew in for a closer look. "A fox?" Veritas grinned to himself and rapidly descended right toward the beach.

Elsa struggled to hold onto the large, flopping fish as she stepped onto the beach. She dropped the fish for a moment to shake the water off her fur down to her bushy tail that was now twice as heavy as when dry. "Now then, to enjoy my lunch in a quiet picnic spot." She picked up the fish and looked around. She began trotting toward a shady cluster of trees, the fish flopping around in her jaws.

Suddenly her ears perked up as she heard the unmistakable sound of large wings flapping behind her. It was an eagle! She picked up her pace but within seconds, Veritas came toward her with his sharp, yellow talons thrust forward. Elsa's heart was beating rapidly but in an instant the eagle grabbed the fish from her jaws and took off soaring back into the sky.

Elsa stopped in her tracks, stunned yet relieved that the eagle took only the fish. *"Guten Appetit!"* she called after him in her high-pitched fox scream. "At least *I* vas not on *his* lunch menu." She frowned, her stomach growling. "Humph. I suppose I vill go find that henhouse now."

". . . the whole world seems against us. Enemies on every side, and no new friends arise. But our cause is just, and there is a Providence which directs and governs all things," Nigel read from Colonel Reed's journal, sipping a thimble of tea. "Quite right. But give it time, old boy. The French are coming."

"Mousie, are ye finished up there?" Max wanted to know. "Me an' Jock want ta get outside."

"Right, coming old boy," Nigel answered, draining his thimble with a final gulp. He jumped from the desk to the chair and tucked his thimble out of the way for later use. He jumped onto Max's back and together they trotted past the Life Guard and out the back door.

"Any news to report, Nigel?" Jock asked as they trotted down the path to the banks of the Hudson.

"Well, General Washington wrote to Congress of having seventeen thousand men as of the latest count, but I'm afraid that nearly a quarter of them are sick," Nigel answered with a frown. "He is urgently requesting militia to pour into New York from every surrounding state. Still, he and Reed are keeping the old chin up and all that, trusting the Maker at every step."

"That's good at least," Max said. "It be dr-r-rivin' him nuts that the Br-r-ritish jest keep sittin' in the harbor *not* attackin'. He can't figure out wha' they be doin'. But he's startin' ta pack up all his important papers ta send ta Philadelphia for safekeepin'. He knows they'll be attackin' soon."

"Indeed, I know Washington was terribly alarmed at the sight of Clinton's forces arriving from South Carolina last week, albeit in their battered condition," Nigel replied. "I believe that General Howe must be stalling for time. Perhaps he hasn't yet decided what his strategy shall be."

"Isn't Al with Cornwallis?" Jock asked. "He's here now, so he should know what's going on."

"Right you are, dear boy," Nigel said with a pat to the young Scottie. "I think I shall pay a visit to our undercover feline on Staten Island to see what's what, what?"

"Perfect timin', Mousie," Max agreed, spotting Veritas coming in for a landing. "Here's yer r-r-ride."

"Ah, splendid!" Nigel exclaimed with a clap.

Veritas swooped in for a landing next to them and shook his tail feathers. "Boys." He then belched right in Nigel's face. "Sorry, just finished lunch."

"I assume fish was on the menu today," Nigel replied, waving a paw in front of his nose.

"Yep, and I didn't even have to catch it," Veritas boasted. "A red fox was on the beach with a fish in its mouth. Always easier to snatch fish that have already been caught."

Nigel frowned and put his paws on his hips. "How very *ungentlemanly* of you, stealing that poor fox's lunch."

"I'm an *eagle*, Nigel. It's what we do," Veritas retorted.

"I bet ye wouldn't mind it if Veritas snatched ye fr-r-rom the jaws of that fox if it caught *ye* for dinner!" Max jested.

Nigel contorted his mouth. "Quite. Well, anyway, I was wondering if you would fly me over to Staten Island now that your stomach is full."

"Sure thing, Nigel," Veritas answered. "And if that fox tries to catch you, I'll have your back."

Nigel climbed onto the eagle. "I prefer not to think of such a predicament but thank you all the same. Cheerio, Max and Jock. We shall return."

"Tell Big Al hello," Jock said, wagging his tail. He turned to Max and smiled. "He sure is an unusual mouse, isn't he? I bet creatures try to eat him all the time."

"Aye, Big Al were attemptin' ta eat Mousie the day we met, way back in Egypt," Max remembered with a chuckle. "Wha' happened was . . ." Max stopped mid-sentence when they suddenly heard a ruckus from the henhouse.

"Do foxes like chickens?" Jock asked.

"AYE!" Max shouted as they took off running back to the house.

In the courtyard chickens were running around like mad, and their feathers were flying everywhere. Max and Jock ran right into the henhouse and there sitting on one of the upper nests was a fox with an egg in her mouth.

"STOP IT R-R-RIGHT THERE, YE R-R-RED MENACE!" Max growled.

The fox mumbled but with the egg in her mouth, they couldn't hear what she said.

Jock smiled. "She sure is pretty."

"She's a r-r-redcoated beastie. She's probably workin' for the Br-r-ritish!" Max surmised with a grumbling snarl. "Never be taken in by a pr-r-retty face, lad." He looked up at the fox, well out of his reach. "Ye come down here r-r-right this instant!"

The fox laughed, shook her head 'No', and then bit into the egg, ignoring Max's demand. She lapped up the yellow yoke and licked her chops. "Hmmmm. Now, vhich vone of you is Max?" She looked at Jock. "Are you Jock?" She winked at the younger Scottie. "I don't think you look like a 'Nigel.'"

Max and Jock looked at one another in confusion. Jock smiled and wagged his tail. "Aye, I'm Jock! How did you know our names?"

"I met a friend of yours who said to tell you that he sent me," Elsa answered, walking along the top railing to the next hen nest, out of reach of the Scotties. She poked her head into the nest and helped herself to another egg.

"Was it Veritas the eagle?" Jock asked. "He just told us he saw a fox."

"Aye, he said he snatched a fish fr-r-rom it then," Max added with a grin. "It didn't sound like a fr-r-riendly chat, though."

Elsa frowned and bit into the second egg, taking her time to lap it up with pleasure. She swallowed and wiped back her whiskers. "Vell, if this Veritas is *your* friend, then you vill not mind me taking a few eggs to make up for the lunch he stole from me, *ja?*" She batted her eyes at the dogs.

"She's got you there, Grandsire," Jock chided with a smile. "I like her."

Max frowned. "Fine."

"I like you too, *mein Hundebaby,*" Elsa told Jock with a grin, walking to another nest.

Jock cocked his head, not understanding her.

"I like you too, my puppy," Elsa translated before grabbing another egg.

Jock grinned, blushing. "I'm a hunda-baby!" It suddenly dawned on him. "Wait, you were swimming? Did you swim over from Staten Island?"

"Vhy are there *so* many islands in this place?" Elsa asked. "I am from the forest, not the sea, so I am not used to all of this vater. But *ja,* I did svim from the island across the bay, but I do not know its name."

"Staten Island's where Big Al our orange kitty fr-r-riend be," Max explained. "Were he the one who sent ye?"

Elsa swallowed her last egg and licked her chops. "*Ja,* it vas Al." She daintily jumped down next to the two dogs, looking them in the face. "*Und* I am Elsa. I accidentally sailed vith the Hessians *und* am stuck here now. Al told me about this var, *und* I vish to be on the right side vith General Vashington, the Fox."

"Nice to meet you, Elsa," Jock said with a big smile, clearly smitten with the fox. "You can stay with us!"

"Not so fast, lad," Max interjected with a frown. "If Washington knew there was a fox in his henhouse, he'd be madder than a hornet. I'm the Scottie in charge of keepin' his house fr-r-ree from pests. Plus, how do we know she ain't a fox in a henhouse?"

Elsa and Jock looked at each other and then at Max.

Max grumbled and rolled his eyes. "I meant the *figure of speech* for 'a fox in a henhouse,' meanin' that ye don't put a hunter in charge of where the prey be. In other words, ye don't allow a creature ta be put somewhere where it kin jest take advantage of everythin' for its own benefit while hurtin' others."

Elsa raised her eyebrows and got right in his face with her beautiful eyes. "Vell, I am literally a fox in a henhouse, but am I a *pest,* Max?"

"NO!" Jock protested, answering for him. "You're not a pest! I think you're neat, and you could be a great member of our team!" He turned to Max. "Then she'd just be earning her eggs, so it wouldn't be stealing, right, Grandsire?"

Max frowned. "Hmmm, maybe. Wha' did ye have in mind, lad?"

"Um, well," Jock stammered, uncertain. "Well, I'm not sure. Elsa, what can you do?"

"Besides *stealin'*," Max quickly added.

Elsa ignored his jab and sauntered around the henhouse. "Vell, I can hear anything from forty yards avay, *und* I am light on my feet, so I can escape easily. I can quietly sneak into enemy territory *und* figure out their plans. Like how I overheard the redcoat humans talking about their battle plans on the island that is long."

"Long Island?" Jock asked.

Elsa rolled her eyes. *"So* many islands. *Ja."*

"They're goin' ta attack Long Island for sure, lass?" Max wanted to know. "Wait a minute, why did ye call Washington a fox a minute ago?"

"Because the human General Howe known as the Greyhound said he vill hunt down Vashington like a fox," Elsa explained. "All of the redcoat humans said it vould be like a fox hunt vhen they attack on the island that is long. The human General Cornwallis called Vashington the 'Old Fox.'"

Max started laughing. "Well, if they think Washington's goin' ta be the fox, they got another think comin'! He's the best fox hunter in all of Virginia."

Elsa's eyes widened, and Jock's face fell. "But your friend Al told me that Vashington is fighting for freedom so I vish to help him. Do you mean to tell me I have come to help a . . . a *fox hunter?!*"

"Aye, but Washington enjoys the chase more than anythin'. He doesn't always want or need ta catch the fox," Max explained. "His horse Blueskin be the best fox huntin' horse in the state."

"Yep, Blueskin's pretty proud about it, too," Jock added with a frown. "But I'm sure Washington won't be fox hunting now. He's pretty busy with the war. And Al is right, Elsa. General Washington is a good human, and he's sacrificing everything to help the Americans win their freedom from the king who is taking away their rights."

"So, these Americans vish to escape a tyrant?" Elsa asked.

"Aye, an' the Maker has us helpin' Washington ta make it happen," Max added. "This new country is goin' ta be important ta the whole earth for helpin' humans escape tyranny everywhere, lass."

Elsa thought a moment, then let go a deep breath. "Vhere is this horse vith skin that is blue?"

"Washington's out riding him now, inspecting forts and stuff," Jock told her.

"Danke, mein Hundebaby," Elsa said with a kiss to Jock's head. "He vill be easy to find, *ja?"* she noted, giving him a wink. "Very vell, this fox vill prove

to you that I am not just a fox in a henhouse by escaping the best fox hunter in Virginia. *Und* vhen I do, you vill let me help you vith keeping the redcoat humans from catching *your* Fox."

With that, Elsa took off running away from the house, leaving Max and Jock sitting there in the henhouse, surrounded by feathers and broken eggshells.

George Washington rode along slowly atop Blueskin, with Henry Knox next to him and a mounted Life Guard behind them. They were heading north to the Mortier Mansion from headquarters at No. 1 Broadway after surveying the latest arrival of British ships.

"Although we are receiving new recruits daily, we also are losing men to desertion," Washington lamented with a frown. "This summer there has been a bumper crop, and farms are full of fields that need to be harvested. Some women are at home with young children and no one to help them. Others are sick with fever, and the fields of grass, grain, or corn grow high. I understand the need for these men to tend to their farms to support their families. I also know full well that the army will need grain from these farms. It is a difficult dilemma. We must rob Peter to pay Paul."

"Indeed, Sir," Knox agreed. "Summer fever not only ravishes the home-steads but also our camp here in New York. General Heath reports that in every barn, stable, shed, and even under the fences and bushes are sick men."

Washington sighed and nodded. "Although sickness is afflicting the army, I am encouraged by the positive attitudes of the men. The sight of the supe-rior numbers of the enemy and the expected attack have not depressed their spirits."

Knox smiled with an affirmative nod. "The men are eager for the fight. It's been four long months of waiting for it to come, and they are ready to get on with it."

Blueskin listened to the men as they talked. He kept his gaze up ahead and clip-clopped along. Suddenly he saw a flash of red and snorted as he smelled a familiar scent. *Why, that's a fox!* he whinnied. *I'm no hound dog but I've smelled enough of them to know.*

Knox's horse suddenly saw the fox up ahead. *You're right, Blue! There he is!*

"What is it, boy?" Washington asked Blueskin, hearing his whinny and snorts. He looked up ahead and spotted Elsa. "It's a fox!" In that moment, Washington simply wanted to have a few moments of respite from the war and just be on the chase as he loved to do back home at Mt. Vernon. "I'll see you back at the Mortier House!" He suddenly snapped the reins and squeezed his heels into Blueskin. "Let's get her, Blueskin!" Washington took off, leaving Knox and the Life Guard in the dust.

Elsa grinned and waited for Blueskin to close the gap a bit before she started running. "Come on, Fox Vashington on your horse that is blue. Catch me if you can!" She suddenly bolted, running at her top speed of thirty miles per hour, staying on the main road that stretched into the countryside. She didn't even try to hide by running into the thick forest.

Washington leaned forward in the saddle and felt the exhilaration of the wind in his face with the thrill of the chase. He didn't have a slew of barking hunting dogs ahead of him as in a normal fox hunt, but he didn't care. "She's *fast!*"

Blueskin ran as fast as he could, but at twenty-five miles per hour, the horse couldn't catch her. As they neared the Mortier Mansion, Elsa finally veered off into the forest and Washington chased her as far as he could. But she disappeared into the thick brush. Washington sat in the saddle and slowly turned Blueskin in a circle, trying to spot the fox. A big grin appeared on his face, and he patted the sweaty horse on the neck. "That was fun, huh, boy?"

Blueskin rolled his eyes and snorted. *For you, maybe.*

"I hope we see her again," Washington stated before turning Blueskin to head back to the house.

Elsa sat hiding in a hollow log, watching them. She grinned and caught her breath. "You vill, *mein* Fox Vashington."

"Vhy the long face?" Elsa quipped, jumping up on the fence post where Blueskin stood. He was still cooling down from the exhausting run. "Do not be angry, horse that is blue, for I come in peace, *ja?*"

The horse's skin bristled, and he snorted. "Why, you've got a lot of nerve showing up here! I've never been so humiliated in my life!"

"Settle down, lad," Max said, trotting up next to them. "She's with us."

"Yeah, she's going to help with the coming battle, fighting on our side," Jock added. "She's a *good* fox. Her name is Elsa."

Blueskin snorted and narrowed his eyes at the fox. "Why, I've never known a fox to be anything but *wily*. How do you know this vixen isn't just another fox in the henhouse?"

Elsa rolled her eyes and held out a paw. "Max *und* Jock, explain to this horse that is blue who I am, *bitte.*"

"Aye, we've been through all that, lad," Max explained. "Elsa here accidentally got stuck on a ship with Hessians an' landed on Staten Island with the Br-r-ritish. She met Big Al, an' overheard their generals talkin' aboot how they're goin' ta attack Long Island."

"And they were joking about how hunting General Washington will be like a fox hunt!" Jock quickly added.

Blueskin's eyes grew wide with shock. "Why, how dare they say such a thing!"

"I can attest that the lady's story is quite true," Nigel said, scurrying up to join Elsa on the fence post. "My name is Nigel P. Monaco, another member of the team, so consumption of my person is quite out of the question, my dear."

"Aye, no one eats Mousie, lass," Max told her.

Elsa bit her lip. "Very vell, I am happy to meet you *und* will not eat you, Nigel."

"Enchanted," Nigel said, bowing and kissing her paw. "Your humble servant. Right, I have just returned from Staten Island and can report that the British indeed shall be attacking Long Island, and quip of bagging 'The Old Fox' Washington."

"Kinda makes you feel bad for all the foxes you've chased up 'til now, huh?" Jock asked Blueskin.

The horse lifted his chin. "Why, I serve at the pleasure of General Washington and will make sure he is *not* caught."

"Perhaps I can teach you to think like a fox?" Elsa suggested with a wink, drawing a slight smile from the horse.

"Veritas sends his most sincere apology for having stolen your lunch and promises to return a fish to you in short order," Nigel told her.

Suddenly a fish fell from the sky and landed with a thud on the ground in front of them. They all looked up as Veritas circled above them. *"Guten Appetit!"* he called out to her.

"Danke!" Elsa called back, waving to the eagle.

"By Jove that timing jolly well takes the biscuit!" Nigel enthused. "Or rather the *fish*, as it were."

"Welcome to America, Elsa," Jock told the fox with a big grin. "I'm glad you're on our side."

"Aye, ye kin be our resident fox in the henhouse," Max added. "Jest don't let the humans catch ye."

"Do not vorry. I vill not stay here, *und* vill only come for eggs vhen the humans are not around," Elsa agreed, yawning. "I found a cozy log to be my den for now. After this long day, I vill take *mein* fish *und* go eat it before I sleep. I vill see you later, *ja? Gute Nacht!*"

"Why, I never thought I'd be outrun by a fox," Blueskin marveled after Elsa trotted off.

"That's okay, I'm sure she never thought she'd sail to America with a ship full of Hessian soldiers, overhear British invasion plans, swim across New York Harbor, have a fish snatched from her jaws by a bald eagle, and then be chased by the Commander-in-Chief of the Continental Army to prove she's not just another fox in a henhouse," Jock posed with a grin.

"Indeed, so no need to be so *blue*, old boy," Nigel quipped with a jolly chuckle.

Blueskin snorted and nodded his head. "Why, I suppose you're right. Maybe this fox in a henhouse will end up teaching me a thing or two."

LAFAYETTE ET LIBERTAS

THE HALL OF MIRRORS, *CHÂTEAU DE VERSAILLES,* FRANCE, AUGUST 15, 1776

"*La perruque de la reine tient un bateau?*" asked a shocked courtier dressed in a dark blue gown. She almost dropped the gold-sequined mask she held in her hand on a stick embellished with ribbons.

"*Oui!* I heard it is *three* feet high with *eighteen* yards of ribbon!" exclaimed a plump woman behind a bright pink mask adorned with black feathers, holding her arm high above her head.

The circle of gossipy courtiers giggled with excitement over the much-anticipated debut of Marie Antoinette's latest wig designed by *coiffeur* Léonard Autié in Paris.

Lafayette stared up at the ceiling and clenched his jaw at the endless absurdity of court life at Versailles. The Queen of France would soon appear and grace them all with a wig that towered three feet above her head and held a ship. *Un bateau?!* he thought to himself. *If only I could sail away from here on a ship.* He had to escape this conversation, but even more so, he had to escape this life at court. Recent changes in France's military structure had closed doors for him that would have allowed him to actively serve and pursue his dream for a command.

"*Excusez-moi, Mesdames,*" Lafayette said with a bow. "*Je vais prendre l'air.*" He turned to reach the closest open door leading to the balcony outside. He needed some fresh air.

The eighteen-year-old Frenchman gripped the edge of the wall and gazed out at the illuminated gardens stretching out before the palace as far as the eye could see. Torches were placed amidst the exquisite fountains and beautifully landscaped topiaries. Lovers walked slowly down the garden paths to steal moments of romance.

"*Bonsoir, Monsieur,*" greeted a masked man, walking up behind Lafayette. He was dressed in a red mask and a black hat with a large ostrich feather. In his hand was an ornately carved pipe. "I much prefer the outdoors where I can enjoy my pipe."

"Ah, *bonsoir Monsieur,* how splendid to see you again!" Lafayette remarked with a broad smile and a courteous bow. "I do not believe I have seen you at one of the queen's balls since last year. I recall we had an engaging discussion about Shakespeare."

"*Oui,* also about Vercingetorix," the man reminded him with a grin, leaning in to stare at Lafayette with blue eyes from behind his mask, "and glory."

Lafayette tightened his mouth, reminded of the present state of affairs and his meaningless existence at court. "With the recent military reforms, I feel that the type of glory achieved by Vercingetorix will never be part of my story." He clenched his jaw at the sound of laughter coming from inside the Hall of Mirrors.

"I have some news from America that I think might interest you, *Monsieur le Marquis,*" he said, handing Lafayette a piece of paper.

Lafayette's eyes brightened behind his mask as he took the paper in hand. "What news from America?"

Looking around at other guests passing by, the masked man put a cautionary hand on the young Frenchman's arm and drew him close to whisper in his ear. "Do not read it here, but when you return to your home. And remember—to thine own self be true."

"Gilbert? Where are you?" called Adrienne. The petite, beautiful girl sauntered up to him dressed in her silk finery, emitting an air of rose water.

Lafayette turned to his young bride and smiled, holding up his hand. "*Je suis ici, mon amour.* Come, I wish to introduce you to my friend, *Monsieur . . .*" He turned to see that the masked man was gone. He spun around. "Where did he go?"

"Who, Gilbert?" Adrienne asked, placing her arm in his.

Lafayette slipped the paper into his pocket and placed his hand atop hers. "I did not get his name, but he is a very kind man. A mysterious man."

"As are you, *mon cher,*" Adrienne joked playfully, her dimples showing. "Especially behind that mask. Come back inside with me, Gilbert. Marie Antoinette has arrived! You must see her wig! Can you imagine? *Un bateau!*"

Lafayette smiled and kissed Adrienne on the cheek. "Very well, *ma chérie.* Let us go see." He patted the paper in his pocket, eager to read its contents. But he would wait until he returned home with his bride. For now, he had something to look forward to besides the nautical headdress of his queen.

CHÂTEAU DE NOAILLES, FRANCE, AUGUST 16, 1776

The first rays of sunlight crept into the bedroom, softly drifting over Lafayette's face. He suddenly opened his eyes, remembering the paper from the masked man. He looked over at Adrienne, who still slept soundly. They had returned home from the palace in the wee hours of the morning, and he had forgotten the note for the time being. He quietly got up, pulled on his military uniform, boots, hat, and dress sword. Lafayette always preferred his military attire to the latest Parisian fashion when walking the grounds of Versailles. He slipped out the door and made his way to the courtyard.

There, surrounded by ornate flowering shrubs, stood the statue of Libertas that had once graced the garden of his childhood home of Chavaniac in the south of France. He was delightfully surprised the day it arrived here along with other items sent from his beloved estate. Since boyhood he had loved this statue with her upraised hand bearing a torch and the liberty-loving cat carved at her feet. This statue had been in his family for centuries, and was among his most precious possessions, for it not only reminded him of home. It reminded him of his love of freedom.

Kate came bounding up to Lafayette, barking, *"Bonjour!"*

"Bonjour, Bibi," Lafayette greeted her, picking up the little dog with a kiss and setting her down on the bench next to him. He was doubly happy when this little Westie appeared in this courtyard on the same day the Libertas statue arrived. She was yet another remembrance from his childhood at Chavaniac, although he knew she couldn't possibly be the same dog. He had decided to name this stray after the dog of his childhood. She looked just like the beloved dog that never left his side as a boy. "I have received news from America! I shall read it to you, Bibi."

Aye, I think ye'll like wha' ye read, lad, Kate thought, wagging her tail.

Lafayette unfolded the paper, and his eyes widened when he read the first line at the top of the page.

"Déclaration unanime des 13 États unis d'Amérique réunis en Congrès le 4 juillet 1776

"Lorsque, dans le cours des événements humains, il devient nécessaire pour un peuple de dissoudre les liens politiques qui l'ont attaché à un autre et de prendre, parmi les puissances de la Terre, la place séparée et égale à laquelle les lois de la nature et du Dieu de la nature lui donnent droit, le respect dû à l'opinion de l'humanité oblige à déclarer les causes qui le déterminent à la séparation.

"En fin! They have declared their independence!" Lafayette excitedly scratched Kate's back as he continued reading the rest of the translated document. When he reached the final paragraph, he stood and paced around the Libertas statue, growing more animated with each and every word.

"*Et pleins d'une ferme confiance dans la protection de la divine Providence, nous engageons mutuellement au soutien de cette Déclaration, nos vies, nos fortunes et notre bien le plus sacré, l'honneur.*"

Lafayette dropped the paper to his side, his mind racing with excitement. This is what he had been waiting for. He had heard the secret murmurings in the salons of Versailles, especially after the arrival last month of the American "businessman" at court, Silas Deane. Everyone suspected that there was more to this merchant than he let on. There was plenty of speculation, but nothing definitive. Everyone knew that France wanted to reclaim her honor, and the best way to do that was to take up arms with the Americans to fight the British. Lafayette knew that France was not ready to start another war openly. But what if she was ready to start a war *secretly?*

The young Marquis looked down at the Declaration of Independence and smiled. It was easy to read between the lines of this beautiful document. America now looked to France for aid. America looked to France not only for gunpowder and arms, but for *soldiers* to help them fight. And America had done what France was waiting for her to do—she had finally declared her independence. Lafayette suddenly remembered the dinner in Metz and how his heart instantly burned with passion for America the first moment he learned of her struggle for liberty.

"*Liberté,*" Lafayette spoke softly, looking up at the statue. He gave the Declaration an exuberant kiss and set it on the bench next to Kate, his heart pounding almost out of his chest with the realization of how he could finally be free himself. Free to escape his meaningless existence at court. Free to bring honor to his family name by adding to its long history of military heroes. Free to pursue his dream of glory on the battlefield as did Vercingetorix. Free to do what he was born to do. The words of the masked man were repeated in his heart and mind. *To thine own self be true.*

Lafayette gripped the hilt of his sword and drew it from its sheath, holding it up high in the air, pointing to Libertas and toward the west.

"*Je viens à vous, Amérique!*"

The Storm
Before the Storm

Max, Jock, and Elsa sat hidden in front of a clump of reeds on the banks of the Hudson River, watching as Veritas slowly descended in wide, swooping circles toward them. They could see Nigel waving at them from atop the bald eagle.

"Nigel loves flying on that eagle," Jock observed with a grin.

"Aye, I can't decide wha' Mousie loves more—flyin', music, or books," Max agreed with a chuckle.

Elsa's eyes widened. "That mouse loves music *und* books?"

"He ain't yer usual r-r-rodent, lass," Max answered with a wink.

"General Nathanael Greene is *deathly* ill with a raging fever!" Nigel reported upon landing and jumping from Veritas's wings. He ran over to them, and genteelly kissed Elsa's paw in greeting. "Hello, my dear." Turning to Max and Jock, he continued, "They're taking Greene away from Long Island to a house here in Manhattan."

"Aye, we heard. Washington has jest replaced him with General John Sullivan," Max told the mouse with a frown. "He had ta scr-r-ramble ta find someone ta figure out wha' ta do aboot the army's left wing."

"Left wing?" Jock asked, looking at the bald eagle.

"Allow me to explain, dear boy," Nigel answered, pointing as Veritas lifted his left wing.

Elsa smiled and whispered to Max as Nigel proceeded to give an object lesson. "*Ja,* he is vone unusual mouse. It vould be a shame to eat him."

"See here, Veritas's left wing represents Long Island." The little mouse stood in front of the bald eagle's belly and swiped his paws along the soft brown feathers. "Veritas's mid-section represents the East River, and his right wing represents Manhattan. Hence, Washington's army is split betwixt his *left* wing on Long Island and his *right* wing here on Manhattan."

Veritas spread out his vast wings. "I never thought these babies could be used for a geography lesson."

"After the *Phoenix* an' *R-r-rose* sailed up the Hudson R-r-river, Washington grew even more worried aboot thr-r-reats ta his r-r-right wing," Max offered. "That's why he's had new fortifications built at Fort Washington on this side of the Hudson, an' over on the New Jersey side at that new Fort Constitution."

"In addition to these fortifications, some brave Patriots just attempted using fire ships on the *Phoenix* and *Rose,* but unfortunately it did little good," Nigel added. "Despite their valiant efforts, the British ships sailed once more past eleven Patriot batteries along the Hudson and have now rejoined Howe's fleet off Staten Island."

"That was quite a sight flying above that fiery skirmish at night," Veritas added.

"Seems like it'd be hard to fly with just one of those wings," Jock surmised. "Wouldn't that be the same for Washington's 'wings' of his army?"

"Aye, me br-r-rilliant grand-lad," Max answered. "Since Washington's not sure where Howe's army will str-r-rike, he's split it inta two 'wings,' which ain't the wisest thing ta do. But aye, it will be hard for his army ta 'fly' against the Br-r-ritish with them two wings not workin' together. Now it'll be even harder with his left-wing commander str-r-ruck down with sickness."

"This is simply dreadful, not only for Greene but for the Continental Army on the eve of battle!" Nigel lamented. "It's almost as if Greene was specifically *targeted* to weaken the Patriot's position. Greene has extensive knowledge of the terrain and fortifications he designed to defend Long Island these past four months."

"Won't General Sullivan know what to do?" Jock asked.

"Military commanders have different styles and strategic approaches to things," Nigel explained. "But no substitute commander will have the detailed knowledge that Greene possesses to provide the best defense and response to the British attack."

"Aye, plus Sullivan jest r-r-returned from bein' defeated in Canada," Max added. "Washington has concerns aboot the man's wants an' foibles. Sullivan wants ta be popular a wee bit too much."

"Sounds like Washington's left wing is sorta broken," Jock suggested with a frown.

"I fear you may be right, young one," Nigel agreed. "Still, Washington decided to send out a proclamation to tell citizens to leave and prepare for an imminent attack."

"So vhat vill Vashington do with a broken left ving?" Elsa wanted to know.

"He'll have to fly the best he can," came Gillamon's voice, walking up to them in the form of Mr. Atticus. "Hello, little ones."

"Gillamon! Where'd ye come fr-r-rom?" Max asked, wagging his tail.

"I've just come from seeing Lafayette in France," Gillamon answered. "Our young Frenchman is eager to come fight for America, so the French connection has been secured. Kate sends her love to you both, Max and Jock."

"Hi, Gillamon! I'm glad you're back here with us!" Jock enthused. "We were just talking about the British invasion."

"It must be gettin' r-r-ready ta happen with ye here, Gillamon," Max surmised.

"Indeed, we are on the eve of the opening moves of the British, but the Maker will bring his own opening moves tomorrow tonight," Gillamon told them. He turned to Jock. "It will be an unusual storm. No need for *you* to do any weather making, Jock. Just observe. The Maker's storm will help to send the Long Island residents fleeing away from the dangerous war zone. But it will also serve as a sober warning to both sides that the Maker is sovereign over the affairs of men and nature."

Gillamon paused and saw Elsa hiding behind Max and Jock, wary of his human form. He smiled warmly and knelt on one knee. "And you must be Elsa. I'm glad to have your help with our animal team."

"Gillamon is our leader, Elsa," Jock told her. "No need to fear! He's really a mountain goat when he doesn't look like a human."

Elsa furrowed her brow. "A mouse that flies, a dog that makes veather, *und* a mountain goat that becomes a human? I cannot do such extraordinary things, being just a simple fox, *ja?*"

Gillamon chuckled softly and looked at the beautiful, petite fox. "*Ja.* But you've already made Washington think about fox hunting. When *he* becomes the fox, those thoughts will come quickly to mind. Keep making appearances as he rides on Blueskin but elude him each time."

Elsa smiled. "I vill do my best, Gillamon. I am growing quite fond of the horse that is blue."

Gillamon gently tickled Elsa behind the ears. "Meanwhile, use those fine-tuned ears of yours to listen and bring any word of British plans after they land on Long Island. Al will be glad to see a friendly face and can tell you what he knows."

"I say, I've been curious as to Clarie's status during all this activity in New York," Nigel said. "Will she be assisting us as we fight the dreaded foe on the field of battle?"

"Clarie is currently on assignment in upstate New York assisting Benedict

Arnold," Gillamon answered. "But she will be here to help as the coming battle of Brooklyn unfolds."

"Clarie is another member of the team, Elsa," Jock explained. "She's really a lamb but can take any form."

"Indeed, right now her underwater aquatic skills are needed to keep Arnold's small American fleet afloat through a horrific storm on Lake Champlain," Gillamon added.

"*Und* a lamb that svims?" Elsa marveled. "I had no idea vhat kind of team I vas getting involved vith."

"The epic kind, lass," Max said with a wink. "Jest wait."

HMS EAGLE, NEW YORK HARBOR, AUGUST 21, 1776

The last orange ribbons of sunset quickly faded to black as a dark, circular cloud formed over the skies of New York, spreading out like a menacing wheel turned by unseen hands. Waves crested with whitecaps as the wind picked up speed, lashing the hull of Lord Howe's flagship.

"A toast to His Majesty's forces!" Cornwallis exclaimed, holding up his goblet. "May these long months of planning and assembly bring us rapid success in defeating the rebels with one swift blow!"

General Howe and his senior staff assembled for dinner on the eve before embarking over onto Long Island. It had taken a Herculean effort to plan logistics in England, Ireland, Germany, and here in America to amass thirty-two thousand soldiers, including eight thousand Hessians and ten thousand sailors. Their forces boasted seventy warships, hundreds of transport vessels, and twelve hundred cannons. The combined British army and navy was the largest invasion force ever assembled in history, and they were eager to launch their assault after months of endless waiting. Not to mention the men's thirst to exact revenge and reclaim their honor from the humiliation at Boston and Charleston. But General Howe had obeyed orders to bide his time and wait for the full force to assemble before making his first move. Everything was now firmly in place, and their plans for the invasion of New York were set.

"One, swift blow!" came the responsive toast from the group of officers around the table. As they clinked their goblets, there came a deafening clash of thunder that rattled the ship.

"What the devil?" Lord Howe asked in alarm, quickly scooting back his chair to peer out the window. The rest of the officers gathered around him to watch the spectacle of gathering darkness.

"Those thunderheads look like they are made of marble," Sir Peter Parker observed.

Suddenly, lightning flashed sporadically across the sky in every direction, while the thunder continued to roar and boom, rattling the goblets and dishes around the table.

"It looks like *sheets* of fire, not just individual lightning bolts," General Howe shouted in awe above howling winds and the violent storm enveloping them.

Heavy rain pelted against the windows, making it hard to see through the streaked glass. But the lightning strikes continued in the distance on Manhattan and Long Island, with peals of thunder that echoed in a continual strain.

General Grant smiled and lifted his goblet. "It sounds as if our cannons are already blasting away! The rebels will think we've started our invasion."

The officers laughed. "Hear, hear!"

"If there is a God, he must be on our side to give such a display of force," Clinton offered. "A prelude of things to come."

Sure, there be a God, laddie, Al thought fearfully from under the table, his paws clasped over his head. *Ye'll soon see which side He's on . . . if we survive this tempest! Maker, please help this frightened kitty!*

For three hours the violent storm raged. Houses burst into flame from lightning, and people panicked in fear and confusion across the region. Just as Gillamon predicted, the citizens of Long Island heard the thunder and indeed thought the invasion had begun. They immediately began to flee their homes to head north and east, getting away from what would soon become a killing field of redcoats spreading out over the countryside.

Several of Washington's soldiers were struck and killed, the coins in their pockets and the tips of their swords melted. One man was struck deaf, mute, and blind. It was as if God were warning the people of what was to come. War was coming. Death was coming. It was time to prepare themselves . . . and their souls.

36

A Broken Wing and a Prayer

STATEN ISLAND, NEW YORK, AUGUST 22, 1776, 6:00 A.M.

Banastre Tarleton stepped out of his dripping wet tent and hurriedly stomped through puddles left from the violent storm, exhilarated by the rousing music of the fife and drum sounding the command to assemble at the staging area. His eyes were trained on finding Lord Cornwallis as the first wave of British forces gathered on the shores of Staten Island. He was determined to get to the head of the line of men of the King's elite troops led by Generals Clinton and Cornwallis and gain an audience with the commanding officer. General Howe had given Cornwallis command of his reserve comprised of light infantry battalions plus a force of Hessian *Jägers* and grenadiers under the command of Colonel Emil Kurt von Donop.

The first pink streaks of an almost tropical sunrise appeared on the horizon as the *Greyhound, Phoenix, Rose,* and the two bomb ketches *Carcass* and *Thunder* weighed anchor. A gentle breeze filled and dried their saturated sails as they moved into position in the Narrows next to the frigate *Rainbow.* Lord Howe had moved to the *Phoenix* as his flagship to be closer to the coming action.

On shore, men gathered their equipment of blanket, haversack with an extra shirt, three days' cooked pork provisions and canteens filled with a cup of rum. A sea of red-coated foot regiments assembled with lapels trimmed in either royal blue, green, black, buff, or yellow. The rank-and-file line infantry "hatmen" wore three-cornered hats and bore the brunt of the fighting with their Brown Bess muskets with fixed bayonets. The Light Infantrymen were agile scouts or flankers who ranged ahead of the main body of fighters, climbing trees or fences, and firing from hidden positions, as did the Americans. They wore short jackets and skullcaps. But it was the tall, fierce Grenadiers marching through the smoke of battle that evoked the most fear with their deadly bayonet charge. The largest men in the army, these physically imposing soldiers towered over the rest with their tall bearskin hats with engraved plates of the royal motto, *Nec aspera terrent,* meaning 'No fear on Earth.'

The 17th Light Dragoons' red coats were lined and trimmed in white. Known as "Death or Glory Boys" for their motto, this British cavalry regiment wore brass helmets with red horsehair crests ornamented by a white metal skull (death's head) and the words 'or glory' engraved on a scroll. Scottish highlanders wore short red jackets and kilts and were accompanied by bagpipers. Hessians donned eight-inch brass conical miter caps etched with such images as lions and wore dark blue, except for the huntsman *Jägers,* who were dressed in green. Having been warned about how sharpshooting American riflemen targeted officers, Hessian officers took care to remove their rank insignias. The Hessians had also been warned that Americans would give them no quarter should they be captured; the alarmed Germans therefore determined that neither would *they* show mercy to any Americans who fell into their hands. Each fully uniformed soldier was equipped with a Brown Bess musket and deadly three-sided bayonet, certain to terrify Americans not yet equipped or trained to use them.

Tarleton glanced over at the spectacle of seventy-five flatboats, eleven bateaux, and two galleys that would soon transport fifteen thousand men across the Narrows to Long Island while the British ships opened their gun ports to provide covering fire. The rain-drenched, lush green countryside above the beach on the far shore glistened against the early rays of sunshine, offering a welcoming landscape of beauty to the British war machine. The young cornet smiled with pride at how everything was unfolding with perfect British precision: each boat had a number painted on the bow and a flag flying to indicate the landing division. Field guns with grey carriages were wheeled onto the waiting vessels via long gangplanks or through the hinged fronts of the landing craft designed by Lord Howe himself to drop onto the beach for swift unloading of men and materiel. The seasoned admiral had perfected British large-scale amphibious landings after gaining experience in fighting along the French coast in the Seven Years' War. Horses of the 17th Light Dragoons neighed and clip-clopped across the gangplanks to fill flatboats that would follow later with the baggage.

Cornwallis stood in his handsome scarlet and gold-trimmed coat with his hands clasped behind his back, one shiny, black boot forward as he watched the orderly assembly of forces at the water's edge. Tarleton came up behind the senior officer and took in a quick breath to gather his nerve.

"Good morning, Sir," Tarleton began with a crisp salute, standing tall and erect. "Cornet Banastre Tarleton. Might I have a word, General?"

Cornwallis slowly turned his head and gazed at the young soldier through his oddly malformed eye, the result of an old sports injury. His double chin shook slightly as he returned the salute. "Cornet Tarleton. It is a glorious morning for an invasion, is it not?"

"Indeed, it is, my Lord!" Tarleton quickly answered. "I am eager to reach Long Island but wished to find you before we crossed. I would like to volunteer as an advance guard or for whatever post may be of service to you, General."

A vague look of familiarity crossed Cornwallis's face. "Long Island. Long Island, *South Carolina?* You also volunteered there, did you not?"

"Yes, my Lord," Tarleton answered with a proud expression of confidence. "I came to your headquarters there on Long Island to volunteer to be among the first fifty men to serve aboard the ships for the Battle at Sullivan's Island. I was on the *Bristol,* Sir."

Cornwallis tightened his mouth and nodded. "Brave lad. What a terrible day that was." The general lifted his chin and breathed in through his nostrils with confidence. "However, *this* is a different Long Island, and I have no doubt we shall rout the rebels *here.*"

"Undoubtedly, my Lord!" Tarleton heartily agreed.

Cornwallis looked the eager soldier up and down with approval. "I admire your zeal, Cornet Tarleton. I, too, was eager for battle as a young soldier when I volunteered to serve the King in the Seven Years' War."

"And you served with distinction, did you not, my Lord?" Tarleton quickly followed. "You were noted for your gallantry in battle, and the men admired how you led from the front. I understand you had several horses shot out from under you. I admire your bravery."

"Sometimes *reckless* bravery," Cornwallis admitted with a chuckle. He raised his eyebrows in delight to hear this son of England laud his previous service. "My regimental motto is *Virtutis fortuna comes.* 'Fortune is the companion of courage.' Mottos are not worth much unless they are put into *action,* what?" The older officer studied Tarleton's face, seeing much of himself in the young soldier. "Very well, Cornet Tarleton, I shall grant your request and place you accordingly for your *next* Long Island assignment."

"Thank you, Sir!" Tarleton exulted. "I am to serve with the 16th Light Dragoons, who have not yet arrived in America, so I would be pleased to serve as an escort or courier."

Cornwallis nodded approvingly. "Ah, a horseman. Fancy a good fox hunt?"

Tarleton smiled. "Doesn't every British gentleman, my Lord?"

Cornwallis smiled. "We shall have a fine fox chase to catch our rebel Fox Washington. Once the horses are transported to Long Island and our field headquarters established, come see me there."

"Yes, Sir! Thank you, Sir!" Tarleton exclaimed.

Cornwallis nodded, saluted, and dismissed the young soldier, as an aide came up needing the general's direction. Tarleton clenched his fists excitedly and grinned from ear to ear as he walked off to the assembly area. *This Long Island will undoubtedly be different. I shall make sure of it!*

STATEN ISLAND, NEW YORK, AUGUST 22, 1776, 8:00 A.M.

The blue-and-white-striped signal flag flapped in the breeze as it was briskly hoisted up the mizen topmast of the *Phoenix*. Immediately a signal gun fired, officially launching the invasion flotilla of ten divisions of flatboats. Each boat was packed with fifty soldiers sitting close together and clutching their upright, loaded muskets with fixed, gleaming bayonets as twenty oarsmen rowed in unison the mile plus across to Long Island. An orderly procession of boats filled the Narrows until reaching the unoccupied beaches of Long Island at Denyse's Ferry. By 8:30 a.m., a red flag from the lead boat gave the signal for the first wave to make their landing. Sailors spilled overboard to steady the boats in the surf as the British and Hessian forces stepped foot onto the beach. Once empty, the boats peeled away to make room for the next wave incoming and to make another run to retrieve more soldiers. Landings at Gravesend Bay followed.

The entire operation ran smoothly because the forces landed virtually unopposed. Washington had positioned Colonel Edward Hand and his two hundred Pennsylvania riflemen on the heights overlooking the Narrows. They fired off a few shots before retreating to Brooklyn Heights, burning supplies and forage crops as they withdrew, to deprive the British of their use. But the brief skirmish amounted to nothing.

By noon, fifteen-thousand British and Hessian men were on Long Island, along with forty pieces of artillery and one hundred twenty cavalry. They took control of the roads and the Dutch villages of Utrecht, Gravesend, and Flatbush. General Howe set up his headquarters a mile inland at Gravesend, while he sent General Cornwallis and his advance guard pressing onward six miles to Flatbush.

"Gravesend. I like the sound of that," Rafe exclaimed as he planted his feet on the sandy beach. He gazed up to the American fortifications in the distance and lifted his wolf gun to his shoulder, taking them in his sights. He grinned. "I can't wait to send as many rebels as I can to *their* grave's end." He looked down to see massive paw prints forming in the sand leading off to a clearing of trees. "I'll be back," he told some other grenadiers gathered next to him, pointing to the woods as if he needed to go.

Rafe soon was under the trees where the massive invisible wolf sat waiting. "Talk to me."

"Vector accomplished the task of targeting General Greene with fever," Espion told him. "Greene has been removed from the field of battle, and chaos is already running through the Patriot lines."

Al flattened his ears and lay as still as possible. He was on the other side of a bush after scrambling ashore from a transport of horses. He was a soggy, wet, sandy mess. *Victor?* he thought. *Oh, no! Sounds like they got a new evil beastie helpin' Charlatan. But how could he give Greene a fever?*

"Good, good!" Rafe enthused with a closed fist. "What else?"

"The Patriots have left a gaping hole in their defenses at Jamaica Pass," Espion reported. "Make sure the humans know about this weakness so they can break through and get behind their left flank."

"I'll make sure I'm part of a reconnaissance team for General Clinton." Rafe clapped his hands once. "This is excellent! Our easy landing and massive show of force coupled with confusion and gaps in the Patriot lines make this mission look promising."

"Perhaps it will be enough to gain our Lord's favor," Espion hoped.

"Nothing short of annihilation of the Americans will gain his favor!" Rafe shot back brusquely. "Get back out there and report any further intelligence to me. When it comes time for battle, I'll tell you where to be."

"Understood," came Espion's reply as Rafe walked off, leaving him in the shadows.

Al's heart was beating fast. He didn't want to move until he knew it was safe. *Why do I always get stuck with the bad lads? I'd be worried if I didn't have more than nine lives.*

MORTIER MANSION, MANHATTAN, NEW YORK, AUGUST 23, 1776, 5:00 A.M.

Washington rubbed his eyes and reached for his quill to pen the general orders of the day before he crossed over to Long Island to inspect the fortifications. Reports had flooded into his office all afternoon and evening following the British landings. While a previous report from a spy on Staten Island indicated that a full force of twenty thousand troops would soon land on Long Island, most of the new reports estimated only nine thousand had landed. *If these new reports are true, then General Howe must be retaining the bulk of his force to invade Manhattan. I simply cannot risk sending all my troops to Long Island, as it may be a feint to trick us.* Still, he needed to prepare his men as best he could. The Commander-in-Chief dipped his quill in the ink and began to write:

The Enemy have now landed on Long Island, and the hour is fast approaching, on which the Honor and Success of this army, and the safety of our bleeding Country depend. Remember officers and Soldiers, that you are Freemen, fighting for the blessings of Liberty—that slavery will be your portion, and that of your posterity, if you do not acquit yourselves like men: Remember how your Courage and Spirit have been despised, and traduced by your cruel invaders; though they have found by dear experience at Boston, Charlestown and other places, what a few brave men contending in their own land, and in the best of causes can do, against base hirelings and mercenaries—

Washington paused and frowned, knowing full well that most of his men had never tasted battle or seen the carnage that war brings. He needed to give them a sobering understanding of the consequences of *not* acting in the face of an enemy determined to freeze with them fear.

Be cool, but determined; do not fire at a distance, but wait for orders from your officers—It is the General's express orders that if any man attempt to skulk, lay down, or retreat without Orders he be instantly shot down as an example, he hopes no such Scoundrel will be found in this army; but on the contrary, every one for himself resolving to conquer, or die, and trusting to the smiles of heaven upon so just a cause, will behave with Bravery and Resolution: Those who are distinguished for their Gallantry, and good Conduct, may depend upon being honorably noticed, and suitably rewarded: And if this Army will but emulate, and imitate their brave Countrymen, in other parts of America, he has no doubt they will, by a glorious Victory, save their Country, and acquire to themselves immortal Honor.

MORTIER MANSION, MANHATTAN, NEW YORK, AUGUST 26, 1776

"I have completed my aerial reconnaissance of the field of battle," Nigel offered, swiping back his whiskers. He took a stick and began drawing in the dirt. "Permit me to show you the situation on the ground with a rather crude map."

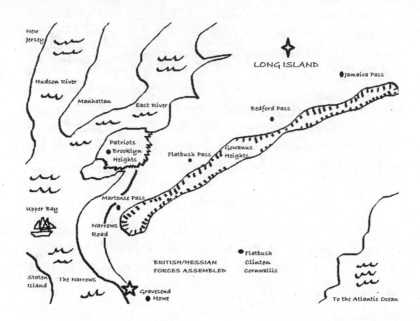

Jock and Max smiled as Nigel scurried back and forth across the floor of the henhouse, putting details on his map, including a ship, little waves to indicate water, and lines on the Gowanus Heights to indicate elevated land.

"Right," Nigel said, adjusting his spectacles. "As you know, the British landed fifteen thousand men around Gravesend on the 20th and advanced six miles north to set up camp in the village of Flatbush. Three days later, five thousand additional troops landed, bringing their total to roughly twenty thousand British and Hessian forces now on Long Island. They've met with only token resistance given the heavy Loyalist population there. Meanwhile, Washington's forces have withdrawn to Brooklyn Heights."

"It's not as fancy as Gillamon's water map, but this helps me understand what you see from the air while riding on Veritas," Jock told him.

"Ye can clearly see the Patriot's main defenses in the head of wha' looks like a seahorse," Max added with a grin, pointing to Brooklyn Heights, and drawing a frown from Nigel. "What's the worm stickin' out of the seahorsey's back then?"

Nigel cleared his throat and pointed his drawing stick to the map. "This long, worm-like object betwixt Washington and the British is *meant* to depict the natural, high stone ridge of the Gowanus Heights, no doubt carved by a glacier eons ago. It runs four to five miles through the middle of the impending battlefield and is quite thick with woods and other foliage. Its steep sides reach up some eighty to even one hundred fifty feet, providing a natural defense barrier for Washington's forces, as it presents a *devil* of an obstacle for the British."

"So, the British will have to either go around the Gowanus Heights by the Narrows Road, or march up one of the passes to cross through the ridge to reach Washington's forces, right?" Jock reasoned, studying the map.

"Quite right, my young cartography novice," Nigel quipped. "There are four major roads that cut through the Gowanus Heights leading to Brooklyn. The quickest route of course is the Narrows Road at the western end of this ridge beginning at Gravesend and running along the shoreline toward Brooklyn by Martense Pass. The other three roads cut through the ridge at Flatbush Pass, Bedford Pass, and Jamaica Pass. During Sullivan's brief four-day tenure, he had the Patriots construct defenses at three of these key areas: Martense Pass, Flatbush Pass, and Bedford Pass, but it appears he left the Jamaica Pass unguarded."

"Aye, after Washington inspected all the fortifications in Brooklyn today, he noticed that weak spot at Jamaica Pass that weren't defended," Max offered with a frown. "He ordered Colonel Samuel Miles an' aboot five hundred riflemen ta patr-r-rol the area, but that's a lot of gr-r-round ta cover. Seems kinda late ta do anything aboot it now."

"The Patriots have spent all this time digging and building eight forts across this whole area," Jock added, looking at the map. "My human Henry Knox is in charge of the artillery and put a bunch of cannons everywhere. He told Washington he has thirty-five cannons facing the water and twenty-eight cannons for the inner line. The soldiers cut down trees and underbrush for a hundred yards in front of each defense line so they could see the British coming at them. Then they piled up all that brushwood to make it hard for the enemy to reach them. The Patriots are supposed to hold their fire until the enemy crosses the brushwood pile fifty yards away." Jock cocked his head. "I wonder why they would go through all that trouble to build such good defenses for each pass area but leave the Jamaica Pass wide open."

"Well, if you recall, a week ago, Washington had believed that these British landings were a ruse and so split his army betwixt Manhattan and Brooklyn," Nigel reminded them. "Just as they were unable to complete fortifications for the approach of British ships to the harbor back in the spring, perhaps they simply ran out of time and men to address that far left flank. Or perhaps Sullivan felt it would be too far out of the way for an assault."

"Or maybe they jest made a big fat mistake!" Max growled. "Well, Washington now knows it ain't a r-r-ruse with all these r-r-redcoats marchin' around Long Island like fire ants swarmin' an anthill! Wha' do our soldier numbers look like now, Mousie? Washington an' his generals don't even know how many men they have. Countin' them be like herdin' cats."

"Right, herding cats is indeed the perfect metaphor old boy, for it is simply *impossible* to get an accurate headcount between incoming soldiers, sick soldiers, injured soldiers, and deserting soldiers," Nigel relayed. "But from the latest tallies, Washington's entire army has roughly twenty thousand troops from ten states, half of which are Continentals and half of which are Militia or provincial forces. He is finally sending more reinforcements over from Manhattan, and thus shall have ten thousand or so on Brooklyn to defend the high ground. He is essentially cutting his army in two."

"So, Washington's forces will be outnumbered two to one," Jock realized. "And now General Putnam is in overall command since Washington only let General Sullivan command for four days before replacing him. That can't be good to change up things so fast."

"Aye, Old Put will be supported by Br-r-rigadier General Alexander (Lord Stirling) on the Patriot right flank, an' Major General John Sullivan in the Patriot center," Max added. "But Old Put hasn't made any attempt ta learn much aboot Long Island."

"Oh, dear, musical commanders do *not* a secure battle command make," Nigel sighed. "General Putnam may be a hard fighter, but he is utterly incapable of managing such a large-scale field of battle as Long Island! He knows even less about the terrain than General Sullivan! At the Battle of Bunker Hill, he rode to and fro to rally the men, but offered very little by way of command."

"What about horses?" Jock asked. "I don't see many on our side like the British seem to have."

Nigel frowned and shook his head. "I fear that Washington has also weakened his position by turning down offers of *three* cavalry regiments from Connecticut. He evidently believes that the feeding requirement of horses outweighs the benefits of having them. So, besides officers on horseback, the only sizable, mounted troops belong to the Long Island Militia under the command of Nathaniel Woodhull. But that small cavalry element is only being used to round up livestock and drive them out of the reach of the British."

Max frowned. "That don't sound good. I wish Washington had at least some scouts r-r-ridin' aboot the island ta send information back an' forth."

"I can report that before General Putnam assumed command, General Sullivan placed five men on horseback to guard the Jamaica Pass," Nigel answered. "I saw them this afternoon."

"Five? Only *five* lads ta guard one of the main cut-thr-r-rough r-r-roads?" Max asked in alarm.

Together they looked at Nigel's map. Suddenly Nigel's face fell, and he put a paw to his forehead. "Dare I say it? What if that's *precisely* where the British choose to march—on the Patriots' far left flank?"

"You mean march through the undefended gap at the Jamaica Pass?" Jock offered.

"This is precisely vhat the British vill do, *mein Hundebaby,*" Elsa reported with labored breath, joining them in the henhouse. She was sopping wet from having swum across the East River. "Al *und* I just listened in on the officers reviewing their plan."

"Wha' did ye hear then, lass?" Max asked eagerly.

"The British have many Loyalists *und* spies bringing them information," Elsa reported. "But Al *und* I overheard a grenadier named Rafe tell General Clinton that the Jamaica Pass is not defended. Clinton then rode out to inspect the Patriot defenses for himself. He wrote up a plan but had another officer present it to General Howe."

Nigel shot Max a look of alarm. "Oh, dear! Rafe is here!"

"He's a bad guy on the enemy's team," Jock explained to Elsa.

"*Ja, und* Al said they've got a new bad guy, somevone named Victor that gave General Greene the fever," Elsa relayed.

"I KNEW IT! I just *knew* it!" Nigel fumed. "I knew Greene was intentionally taken out. But Victor? What an odd name for a creature that spreads disease. *Vector* would be the more appropriate name for an agent that carries and transmits disease."

"Well, ye know how Big Al messes up his words," Max offered.

"Vector has managed to wipe out one quarter of Washington's army with sickness, so that might make him a Victor, too," Jock worried.

"Quite right. Silent, invisible yet deadly, disease has the potential to kill more soldiers than bullets," Nigel noted with a frown.

"Well, let's talk aboot the bad guys we *can* see," Max suggested. "Elsa, wha' happened when Howe heard Clinton's plan?"

"Thus far, Clinton's strategic instincts have been correct, but Howe hasn't wanted to listen to his irritating subordinate," Nigel added.

"Vell, it looks like Howe didn't have a choice this time," Elsa explained. "Clinton had the best plan of anyvone."

"So, the Br-r-ritish will sneak through Jamaica Pass, snatch up them five lone guards, an' get behind all the Patriot defenses," Max offered with a growl. "All they need ta do is distr-r-ract Stirling an' Sullivan ta make the Patriots *think* that all the fightin' will take place on the r-r-right flank."

Elsa looked at Max with a look of surprise. "*Ja!* This is exactly vhat they plan to do, starting tomorrow night. How did you know?"

"I've been ar-r-r-ound a war or two meself, lass," Max answered with a frown.

"I guess the left flank of Washington's left wing is broken, too!" Jock realized. "What should we do?"

"I, for one, shall mount upon the wings of Veritas and provide ongoing aerial support and intelligence," Nigel asserted. "Elsa, my dear, please return to Al and let us know of further developments as they unfold."

"*Ja,* I vill," Elsa assured him. "Al said ve should hide from Rafe but vatch vhat he does."

"Washington won't want us ta be underfoot, lad, so we'll have ta sneak onta a ferry when fightin' begins over on Long Island," Max decided. "I'm not aboot ta let the general out of me sight. Gillamon will find us with further instructions. In the meantime, pr-r-ray. The Patr-r-riots are goin' ta need all the help they can get."

"Aye, with a broken wing and a prayer," Jock answered.

37

A Devilish Shot of Watermelon and Rum

"How is this melon made with vater?" Elsa whispered as she and Al crept toward the watermelon patch near the Red Lion Inn where Martense Lane, Narrows Road, and Gowanus Road met.

Al wrinkled his brow. "I'm not sure, lass. But it must be called watermelon for a reason. I'm dyin' ta get me paws on one. We can enjoy a tasty treat while we keep our eyes on Rafe. I love combinin' work with pleasure, which for me always involves food."

Elsa kept her gaze on Rafe walking along the road as he met two British scouts from General James Grant's division at the watermelon patch. Her ears perked up at their conversation. "It vould seem that a smart human planted this patch of melons made of vater next to a tourist attraction so he could sell them."

"Blimey, the devil's footprint, ye say?" one of the soldiers asked. "I've got to see that, hey?"

"Aye. The devil himself stomped on that rock after he lost a fiddling contest to a man named Joost," Rafe explained with a wry grin, pointing to a large boulder.

The other British soldier leaned over and put his hand into what looked like a hoofprint in the boulder. "I wouldn't have believed it if I hadn't seen it for meself!"

"People come from miles around to see this rock," Rafe explained. He leaned over and broke off an oblong watermelon from the vine. "But this is what you *really* came for—the American delicacy of watermelon." He held up the fruit to the British soldiers.

Elsa frowned and stepped back. "The Devil *und* fruit caused trouble in a garden once before, *ja?*"

Just as Al opened his mouth to speak, sputtering gunfire erupted from the hillside above, blasting the watermelon in Rafe's hand and sending pink fruit and seeds splattering over the men and Al, who was crouched down near them. The two soldiers immediately returned fire, then quickly fled back to Grant's lines.

Rafe grinned and shot his wolf gun at the American pickets under Colonel Hand's First Continentals who had spotted the three men in the watermelon patch. "Go on now, send word to Washington to send reinforcements," he called mockingly with a chuckle, licking the sticky watermelon remnants from his fingers. "Bring them all over here. The more the merrier! Just keep your American eyes on the fruit." He then took off running into the darkness, laughing.

"I never knew watermelons were so deadly!" Al gasped in horror, pulling seeds and chunks of watermelon from his fur.

"This must be part of the plan to trick the Americans!" Elsa realized. "They only have a few hundred men posted out here on the Govanus Heights. The rest are behind the lines at Brooklyn Heights. But vhen they hear that the British are coming up this hill, they vill send more forces out to face them."

"Aye, then they won't see them other ten thousand redcoats sneakin' up from behind on the Jamaica Pass," Al worried, looking around the sloping hillside. "Grant will have five thousand redcoats and marines ready to pounce here on the right, and thousands more Hessians and Highlanders under General von Heister pouncin' from the center to keep the Americans busy. But the real action be comin' wayyy over on the left where me humans Cornwallis and Tarleton be headed."

"Vhich vay should we go, *und* vhat should ve do?" Elsa asked anxiously.

Al thought a moment, polka dotted with black seeds stuck to his fur. "Usually, I jest do whatever comes natural to help humans." He shook his head at himself. "I don't believe I'm sayin' this, but I suppose we best head to where they'll need us the most."

"To the left flank?" Elsa asked.

Al looked up at the imposing hillside thick with trees under an almost full moon. "Aye, lass. We'll head left, right into the hottest action."

"This is very brave of you, Al! I think even you vould retrieve Edelveiss," Elsa said with a smile. "No vonder Liz calls you her noble, famous varrior, *ja?*"

"Been there, done that, lass." Al thought back to that long ago, moonlit night when he retrieved Edelweiss for Liz on a high mountain ridge. Only the bravest warriors ventured to the heights. "Bein' noble comes easy, lass. It's the fame that's hard," Al admitted, playfully wiping back the fur on his head. "Jest watch out for that dragon named Tarleton. Cornwallis gave him a horse and a huntin' horn to blow when he rides ahead of the troops. I don't want them redcoats to spot ye and think they're on a fox hunt."

KING'S HIGHWAY, LONG ISLAND, NEW YORK, AUGUST 27, 1776, 1:00 A.M.

"Elsa indicated that the invasion was to begin tonight. Can you make out anything?" Nigel asked Veritas as they flew above lower Long Island. He squinted to make out hundreds of white tents lined up in orderly rows throughout the British camp at Flatbush.

The bald eagle scanned the encampment and observed campfires still lit, but with little sign of movement. "Things are quiet. Too quiet." He flew in for a closer look. "There's only a handful of humans down there, and certainly not as many tents as there were before."

"By Jove, they've kept their fires burning to make it *appear* they are all asleep and snug in their tents," Nigel surmised.

"Let's see where they *really* are," Veritas suggested, turning to fly northeast above the King's Highway. It didn't take long before he made out the movement of dark shadows stretching for two miles down the road. "Got 'em, Nigel. Looks like a column of soldiers heading toward the Jamaica Pass."

Nigel squinted to try to make out the movement of the British soldiers. Suddenly he saw moonlight gleaming off thousands of bayonets. "Oh, dear! I see them! Please land at the front of the column so we can determine what's what."

Veritas flew ahead of the column and landed in a tall pine tree not far from the Rising Sun Tavern. "They're awfully quiet for an army."

Below them, the column moved slowly as they had since they broke camp at 9:00 p.m., making only a mile every hour. They were led by a few mounted officers and three local farmers who knew the terrain. They moved along the edge of the woods and marshes toward the village of New Lots to avoid Washington's roaming foot patrol under Colonel Samuel Miles. Scouting parties fanned out to make sure they found any rebels before the rebels spotted them. But there was none to be found.

General Clinton was at the head of the column with a brigade of light infantry. They cleared the way for the entire column, quietly sawing fallen trees in the road instead of using noisy axes. Any farmers who were on the road transporting their goods to the dawn ferry to sell in the city were detained and not allowed to journey further. General Cornwallis followed Clinton with eight reserve battalions and fourteen cannons. At the rear of the column rode Generals Howe and Percy with six more battalions, artillery, and the baggage train. Only the commanders knew where they were going. The sleep-deprived soldiers marched along the nine-mile trek through the unseasonably cool darkness, stopping for a few minutes at a time to shut their eyes only to abruptly reopen them to move again when obstacles were cleared from the road. The anxiety among the men was high as they maintained strict silence, fearing that the slightest sound would cause rebel snipers to unload volleys of shot into them at any moment.

Suddenly Nigel spotted a forward patrol of mounted cavalry led by Captain Glanville Evelyn, who spoke with Clinton before trotting off ahead of the column. "Let's see where those chaps are going."

Veritas lifted off, and they followed the mounted patrol as they quietly made their way to the head of Jamaica Pass. The eagle then spotted the five lone Patriot patrolmen that General Sullivan had placed there. "Uh-oh, Nigel."

"Blast it all, *run!*" Nigel fumed at the five Americans, pulling on his whiskers. He and Veritas watched helplessly as the Americans mistook the British patrol slowly riding up to them for other Patriot defenders. Not a shot was fired as the British encircled the men, easily taking their firearms in hand.

"You are hereby in the custody of His Majesty's forces. I suggest you cooperate fully," Captain Evelyn told them, confiscating their horses. Within a few minutes, the five Patriots were escorted back to General Clinton, with Veritas following them from above.

General Clinton walked in front of the five Americans. "I am told you alone were guarding the pass. How many others are there?"

"None," one Patriot answered boldly. "We are the only five men guarding the Jamaica Pass."

"What an *auspicious* number to guard so vast an area," Clinton remarked with a low chuckle of disbelief. He got face-to-face with a young twenty-two-year-old graduate of King's College named Lieutenant Edward Dunscomb. "How many rebels are at Brooklyn? Tell me how many forces Washington has positioned here."

Dunscomb merely glared at Clinton with a defiant smile. "Under different circumstances, you wouldn't insult us in such a manner."

"Impudent rebel!" Clinton spat. "I should hang you on the spot."

"General Washington will respond in kind and hang man for man," Dunscomb shot back.

Nigel's eyes widened. "Good show of bravery, young chap!"

"We'll see how defiant you remain in a British prison," Clinton threatened. "Take them away."

Clinton mounted his horse and once more the advance guard moved ahead as the five Patriots were dragged off. Meanwhile, Clinton sent out patrols ahead to the Bedford and Newtown Roads to ensure that no rebel guards or scouts remained in the area.

As they came upon the Rising Sun Tavern they watched from the shadows until the lights in the tavern were snuffed out. Clinton then had the tavern and nearby buildings surrounded by soldiers. Here they waited in the darkness until Generals Cornwallis, Percy, and Howe rode forward to join them.

RISING SUN TAVERN, LONG ISLAND, NEW YORK, AUGUST 27, 1776, 2:00 A.M.

Banastre Tarleton rode back to General Cornwallis with a report. "Sir, General Clinton sends word that they've captured five rebels who alone were guarding Jamaica Pass. He has sent several scouting parties ahead of the column but waits for you and General Howe at a tavern where he'll secure guides who know the terrain well."

"Very well, Cornet," Cornwallis answered. "Go deliver this word to Generals Howe and Percy."

"Right away, Sir!" Tarleton answered, riding to the back of the column to inform the other commanding officers. He was wide awake with the exhilaration of communicating with leaders of the British army. His volunteering had placed him right where he wanted to be—in the center of the action.

Clinton soon gave the command for his soldiers surrounding the tavern to storm through the front door and rouse the tavern owner William Howard, his wife, and their son. His men re-lit the lanterns in the tavern and stood at attention, guarding the premises. It wasn't long before Generals Howe, Cornwallis, and Percy entered the tavern. Tarleton stood at the entrance, eager to watch things unfold.

Howard was escorted into the bar room at the point of a bayonet pressed against his nightshirt. General Howe leaned casually against the bar as if he were a paying customer, a woven cloak over his uniform, surrounded by his other generals. He smiled and lifted a hand as Howard was shoved behind the bar. "A glass of rum, please, Mr . . .?"

"H-h-howard," the tavern keeper nervously answered, pulling a bottle from the shelf, and clinking the rim of the glass, his hand shaking as he poured. He swallowed hard, sliding the glass over to General Howe.

"Thank you, Mr. Howard," Howe responded politely, calmly taking a sip of rum. "Now then. I must have some of you show me over the Rockaway Path around the Pass."

Howard shot a glance over at his wife, who fearfully held on to their son's shoulders. "We belong to the other side, General, and can't serve you against our duty."

"That is all right. Stick to your country or stick to your principles when you're free to do so, but, Mr. Howard," Howe replied, casually taking another sip, "tonight you are my prisoner, and must guide my men over the hill."

"But General . . ." Howard started to protest.

"BUT!" Howe exclaimed, slamming his fist on the bar and making Howard jump back. He locked eyes with the tavern keeper's. "You have no alternative," the commander stated in a matter-of-fact tone. "If you refuse, I shall have you shot through the head."

Tarleton raised his eyebrows in delight to hear his supreme commander easily handle this defiant rebel with such power and cool authority.

Howard shared a fearful look with his wife and then returned his gaze to General Howe. He lowered his head and nodded in defeat. "My son and I will guide you through."

"Splendid!" Howe exclaimed, finishing off his rum and calmly setting the glass on the bar. He held out a hand toward the door with a smile. "Shall we be going, Mr. Howard? After you retrieve your britches and boots, of course."

Nigel scurried out of the tavern and back up the tree where Veritas waited. "Nothing shall stop the British juggernaut from creeping up behind Washington's forces now! All Patriot scouts have been removed, and General Howe has *enlisted* Mr. Howard and his son to guide the column through the pass. *And,* that scoundrel Banastre Tarleton has managed to weasel his way to the front of the line of command. He appears to be a scout or escort for Cornwallis."

Veritas frowned. "I'm sorry to hear it. So, when do you think the Battle of Brooklyn will begin?"

The little mouse climbed aboard the eagle's broad shoulders and grabbed a feather in either paw. Suddenly they heard the roar of guns in the distance. "The diversion! The Battle of Brooklyn has already begun!"

38

WHAT BRAVE FELLOWS

MANHATTAN FERRY, NEW YORK,
AUGUST 27, 1776, 8:00 A.M.

"Keep yer paws tucked in, lad," Max whispered to Jock as they hid under a tarp on the ferry bateau filling with reinforcements heading to Long Island. "Ye don't want the lads ta see us."

"Sorry, grandsire!" Jock whispered back, pulling his paw under the canvas so he wouldn't be seen.

"Well, Joseph Plumb Martin, how many of those biscuits did you take?" a soldier named Sam asked with a laugh.

"Only a dozen or so," mumbled Joseph, a biscuit stuck between his teeth. "They told us to grab as many as we wanted from the baskets." The fifteen-year-old recruit from Connecticut plopped onto the deck right next to the tarp where Max and Jock were hiding. He emptied a load of biscuits from his shirt and stuck them down in his knapsack. "My grandsire taught me to always be prepared. When he found out I was going a soldiering, he and my grandmum fitted me out with cake, cheese, and this," he explained, taking out a small pocket Bible as he situated the biscuits.

Jock looked at Max with a grin. "He has a wise grandsire, too."

Sam laughed. "Well, those biscuits are about as hard as that Bible. Don't break your teeth on 'em."

"They may be hard enough to break the teeth of a rat, but like Jesus said, 'Man shall not live by bread alone, but by every word that proceedeth out of the mouth of God,'" Joseph answered with a wink. "At least my belly won't be empty."

Max smiled. "I were with another Joseph who ate hard biscuits in prison. Like this Joseph, he looked on the br-r-right side of things an' tr-r-rusted the Maker. Somethin' tells me I should watch over this Joseph like I did the other Joseph."

Suddenly three cheers rose from the soldiers as they left the pier, answered by spectators on the wharf, shouting, "Good luck, lads!"

"We're going to need it," Sam said, now looking somberly over at the smoke rising from Long Island.

Joseph swallowed a bite of hard biscuit and looked at the scene of battle currently underway. They could hear cannon fire and see the green hillside covered in redcoats marching toward the Patriot defenses. "Well, I will endeavor to do my duty as well as I am able and leave the event with Providence."

Jock turned to Max. "You can be his four-legged grandsire right now."

Max grinned. "Aye, I like the lad. After I make sure Washington's secure, we'll keep watch over Joseph Plumb Martin today."

It wasn't long before they arrived at the Brooklyn Ferry. Max and Jock darted out from the tarp and off the boat after the soldiers. As the young men ascended the steps they were immediately met by wounded men. Joseph's face filled with horror at seeing men with broken legs, broken arms, and broken heads. He shut his eyes briefly and thought of home, but quickly snapped out of it as the men were ordered to march on.

"I think I know how Joseph feels to see sights like this for the first time," Jock lamented with tearful eyes, saddened to see the men crying out in pain.

Max placed his burly paw on Jock's shoulder with a frown. "Steady, Jock. It's goin' ta get worse before the day's done."

CORNELL HOUSE, BROOKLYN HEIGHTS, NEW YORK, AUGUST 27, 1776, 8:45 A.M.

"Report, General Putnam," Washington demanded as he swept into the room, not wasting any time. His Brooklyn Heights command headquarters sat atop a bluff overlooking the harbor and the East River. The general had devised a system of communication signals to report on British troop movements with his Manhattan headquarters by using a tall pole affixed to the roof that flew flags by day and lanterns by night. He immediately ferried over upon receiving word of British activity in the early morning hours. Washington also ordered reinforcements from Manhattan to ferry over to Long Island.

Old Put scratched his round balding head and pressed the knuckles of his left hand into a map of Brooklyn that was spread out across the table. His right hand pointed to the spot where hostilities had begun. "General Washington, I was awakened at 3:00 a.m. with word that a skirmish broke out at midnight in a watermelon patch by the Red Lion Inn with Colonel Hand's riflemen on our right flank. After Hand's men were relieved by our new militia levies, three hundred British troops stormed their position at 2:00 a.m., sending the militia fleeing."

Washington clenched his jaw and slapped his leather riding gloves on the table. "Inexcusable! I have little faith in this green militia! Continue."

"I first rode to Lord Stirling's headquarters by the Old Cortelyou House and ordered him to move out and repulse the enemy with sixteen-hundred men," Putnam reported. "They're the best men we've got, from Connecticut, Delaware, and Pennsylvania, plus the elite First Maryland Regiment. I then rode to General Sullivan's location at Battle Pass, and he sent four-hundred more men to support Stirling, leaving him with eight-hundred men to guard the center. An artillery company joined the right flank and trained two guns on British General Grant's forces. They are lined up for battle now."

"The same General Grant who boasted before the House of Commons that with five-thousand men he could march from one end of America to another," Washington noted, grabbing his spyglass, and heading to view the battle from the rooftop observation post. "Let us see if he can accomplish his boast this day."

Sunlight pulled back the curtain of darkness to reveal a menacing red sea of thousands of British troops lined up in traditional European formation, flags flying and drummers beating out the battle cadence. As Stirling marched his men over a mile to confront Grant's forces, he positioned them in an inverted V to try to envelop the enemy as they advanced. Grant lobbed artillery shells at Stirling's men while British ships bombarded the Patriot lines with cannon fire.

"Our men are standing their ground despite the hail of artillery," Washington noted proudly. "The British have advanced to within two hundred yards." Suddenly British muskets let loose a volley of gunfire.

"The men are not to fire until the enemy comes within fifty yards," Putnam stated. "But our cannons are answering theirs."

"Stirling's men are not flinching, and Grant's men are pulling back slightly," Washington observed, nodding with satisfaction. "This must be the main thrust of the British attack. What about our center lines, General Putnam?"

"General Sullivan's forces up on the ridge at Flatbush Pass have been under cannon fire from Hessian artillery since daybreak," Putnam answered. "General von Heister has command of both Hessian and Highlander forces, and they've taken positions on either side of Flatbush Road facing the pass."

"I see them drawn up for approximately a mile, but they show no signs of moving," Washington observed. He removed his spyglass and looked with the naked eye down to the southern plain of Brooklyn. "What are they waiting for?"

Suddenly they heard the boom of two signal guns coming from Bedford Pass. It was 9:00 a.m. Instantly, both the right and center lines braced as British forces unleashed an attack of musket and cannon fire, their troops advancing toward the Patriot defenses. A wave of dread came over Washington, Putnam, and the other officers.

"Unless . . . those two columns were just . . . a ruse!" Washington exclaimed, collapsing his spyglass, and rushing downstairs to head out to the Patriot lines.

"Here we go, lad," Max told Jock. "Look sharp!"

"Blast it all, it's working just as Clinton planned!" Nigel shouted as he and Veritas flew above the battlefield. They could see the three British columns now advancing to encircle the American lines with Grant on the right, von Heister in the center, and Howe, Clinton, and Cornwallis launching their surprise attack from the left. "It shall be a bloodbath for both sides, I fear!"

Colonel Miles and his five hundred men advancing from Bedford near the Jamaica Road were the first to encounter Howe's ten thousand redcoats. Although he immediately sent word to General Putnam about the column, it was too late. Miles and half of his men were captured, while the other half fled to the safety of Brooklyn Heights.

When General Sullivan heard the 9:00 a.m. guns, he knew immediately that his men would soon be surrounded. He ordered his advance guard in the center to fight as best they could against the Hessians while swinging his main force around to face Howe's surprise troops advancing behind him. Because of the lack of uniformity in dress, he had ordered all his troops to put a green sprig or branch in their hats to identify who they were.

"Looks like Sullivan's riflemen are giving the British a surprising response themselves," Veritas noted, watching the Americans unleash a hail of musket fire, the green sprigs in their three-cornered hats visible to his keen eye. Scores of British redcoats were cut down and many fled for the forests as Patriot fire came from every direction.

"Despite their bravery, I'm afraid retreat is their only option at this point," Nigel pointed out, watching Sullivan try to hold his men together while leading them on a fighting retreat to the Brooklyn lines. "The Americans are too outnumbered to sustain the fight!"

Veritas spotted the Hessians overrunning Sullivan's men who had stayed to hold the ridge. He could see the blue and green coats making their way up through the forests, their seventeen-inch bayonets catching the gleam of sunlight as they advanced and surrounded the Americans. "Some of the Patriots are fighting, but most are fearfully falling to their knees in surrender. But still the Hessians are bayoneting them through!"

"They are giving the Americans no quarter! Oh, the humanity!" Nigel cried, watching the carnage below. The American left was collapsing and melting into the cornfields and forests in a chaotic retreat. It was now 11:00 a.m., and Washington's entire army had been outflanked. "Only Lord Stirling's forces are keeping up the fight against Grant on the right!"

"But I think they've stayed too long," Veritas observed darkly. "Grant's column is crushing through the center, and now Hessians are pouring in from the left. Stirling is trying to pull back but it's too late. Now more redcoats are coming at him from behind!"

"Cornwallis and a full division stand between Stirling and the safety of Brooklyn Heights!" Nigel shouted, pointing to the scene. "The only way the Americans can escape is through the marshes and creeks of Gowanus Bay, but it's now high tide!"

"Those poor boys are going to have to swim eighty yards to make it," Veritas pointed out. "And they'll have to do it while under enemy fire."

Nigel and Veritas helplessly watched the retreating Patriots desperately making their way through the Gowanus Creek. Some fell to enemy fire, some were captured, and some drowned. "'Brooklyn' comes from the original Dutch term *Breukelen,* which means 'marshland.' These poor lads are indeed now fighting a battle of marshlands."

"Looks like things are converging at the Old Stone House," Veritas observed, circling above the spot where Cornwallis's forces were positioned. "Stirling's men are heading right into Cornwallis's trap."

Elsa squeezed her eyes shut and flattened her ears at the sound of the fox horn, awash in fear from her hiding spot in a hollow log. Memories of being chased through the forest near her home in Germany filled her mind as Banastre Tarleton sat atop his horse, using a short, copper horn to sound the short staccato hunting signal, "Blowing Away." That signal was usually used to communicate a sense of urgency to the hounds, letting the Field Master know that the time had come to move on swiftly, following the hounds.

"Are ye alright, little lass?" Al asked Elsa.

Elsa opened her eyes and nodded her head. *"Ja,* I am okay. The sound of the horn got to me. Bad memories of being chased."

Al frowned. "I know how that must feel. I were chased by a bull once. It weren't a pretty sight." The plump Irish cat didn't mean to do so but thinking of that image of Al and the bull made Elsa smile from comic relief.

"But I know that today, I am not the fox they are after," Elsa realized, watching the scene. "Today the 'fox' is Vashington *und* his army, *und* the hounds are British *und* Hessian soldiers. Many Patriot foxes are running back to their fort, but some have chosen to stay *und* fight."

"Aye, it looks like that Lordy Stirling has aboot four hundred brave Marylanders with him to hold off the British while most of the Patriot lads retreat," Al noted, his eyes welling up at their bravery. "Now *that's* noble."

Inside the two-story fieldstone farmhouse, Cornwallis stationed men at windows with muskets trained on the approaching Patriots. Outside the farmhouse and in the surrounding orchard, thousands of British troops stood ready with muskets and cannons to wipe out the opposition.

Suddenly a group of Marylanders charged the Old Stone House and were cut down under withering fire. Some young men screamed and fell to the ground, their blood seeping red through the buff color of their uniforms. Others fell back, and Stirling regrouped his men in the screen of smoke. Again, they charged the house, firing their muskets as they ran headlong at the British forces.

"What madness!" Cornwallis exclaimed, taken aback by their boldness. "Bring those two fieldpieces forward and fill them with cannister shot!"

Immediately, British gunners rushed up with the guns and let loose a barrage against Stirling's position, sending a shower of deadly iron into young men along the nearby fence.

Al and Elsa watched helplessly as the Americans charged and fell back five times, giving their all as they were cut to pieces.

Elsa's eyes filled with tears at the bloody scene. "These brave foxes are outnumbered ten to vone. How can ve help them?"

"There's only two things we can do," Al told her, his lip quivering. "We can help the dyin' lads go on home by givin' them comfort. And we can help those escapin' through the creek somehow to keep their heads above water."

Elsa wiped her eyes. "I can svim, so that is vhat I vill do."

Al put his paw on her shoulder. "That's a good lass. And I can give comfort, so that is what I'll do."

Across the creek from the Old Stone House, Joseph Plumb Martin marched with his unit toward the sounds of the carnage, passing a small party of Patriot men struggling to pull a twelve-pound cannon on a field carriage through the sandy soil.

"Help us, please!" the struggling artillerymen pleaded as Joseph's men marched past.

"Onward, men!" Joseph's officers instructed, paying no mind to the men and their cannon. It was as if the men and the cannon were invisible to them as they marched on.

"Why won't they help our boys with the cannon?" Jock asked with a frown. "Aren't they on the same side?" He and Max had followed Joseph after Washington, Putnam, and other officers decided to stay behind the lines and observe the battle at a distance.

Max growled. "Joseph's officers be tr-r-r-yin' ta get their men ta another spot ta fight, but aye, since Washington ordered that cannon ta help Stirling's men at the Old Stone House, they *should* have given them a push."

Suddenly Max felt a hand on his back. It was Clarie, in the form of a militiaman. "I'll give them a hand. Then you two follow me to the creek."

"Good on ye, lass!" Max cheered. Together, he and Jock watched Clarie get behind the carriage and push it out of the deep sand. Once they got it up and over the crest of the hill, the artillerymen cheered as they were able to easily maneuver the gun to fire on Cornwallis's position. Within moments they fired on the Old Stone House, sending Cornwallis's forces scattering. But the British quickly regrouped, now supported by Hessians and grenadiers coming to reinforce them.

Stirling knew it was over. But the Marylanders had bought the retreating Patriots one precious hour. He gave the order for the remaining men to run and get to safety as best they could. Sputtering gunfire sounded after the retreating Patriots, while groans of the dying men could be heard around the Old Stone House.

Banastre Tarleton rode up to Cornwallis, who sat atop his horse surveying the field of battle with his spyglass. "Shall I play 'The Kill' to congratulate our men, General?" he coarsely asked, referring to the victorious signal given at the end of a foxhunt when the fox was caught.

"Mmmm," Cornwallis mumbled, watching as Stirling surrendered in the distance to the Hessian commander. "Stirling fought like a wolf." He collapsed his spyglass. "I didn't know the pompous glutton had it in him, what?" The general looked at Tarleton. "Battle is always full of unexpected turns. This isn't over yet, Cornet. You may blow 'The Kill' when we've bagged Washington himself."

"Gladly, my Lord!" Tarleton answered.

"Now, to see to the end of the matter," Cornwallis declared with a nod of confidence. "We must continue the hunt and fall in with Generals Clinton and Howe to bring our entire force to bear on the Patriot lines."

As Cornwallis and Tarleton rode off with their regiments, Al wandered up to the wounded men scattered across the battlefield, left to die in pools of blood. He went from one young lad to the next, wiping sweat and blood from their faces and whispering words of comfort in their ears. He told them how much their sacrifice meant. "Ye done saved liberty, lad."

The dying men paid no heed to the fact that a cat spoke to them as they entered the twilight of death. Everything was surreal at the end of life. Some of them didn't even see Al, but only heard him. Somehow, Al's words gave them a bit of grace as they slipped way.

"In jest a minute, ye'll be with the Maker," Al told a young man blinded by shock and clutching a pocket Bible. "It won't hurt anymore, and ye'll be happy forever."

The young man shivered from blood loss and shakily lifted a piece of paper from his Bible. "S-s-sing?" was all he could say.

Al opened the paper smeared with the soldier's blood and saw that it was the words of an old hymn, *Soldiers of Christ, Arise.*

> Soldiers of Christ, Arise, and put your armour on,
> Strong in the strength which God supplies
> through His eternal Son.
> Strong in the Lord of hosts, and in His Mighty Power,
> Who in the strength of Jesus is more than conqueror.
> Send then in His great might, with all His strength endued,
> But take, to arm you for the fight, the panoply of God;
> That, having all things done, and all your conflicts passed,
> Ye may o'ercome through Christ alone and stand entire at last.

"It would be me honor, lad." As Al sang the words, a sense of peace poured over the young man. He closed his eyes, and his breathing slowed. Al blinked back the tears and cleared his throat to see the young man slip away. "What ye did here will be remembered and told to future generations." He looked around at the brave Marylanders who had died so others could live. "Ye'll be known as The Immortals, aye. Ye be the real noble, famous warriors."

"Many of these boys can't swim, or they're wounded or too scared to try," Clarie told Max, Jock, and now Elsa, who found them when she reached the Gowanus Creek behind the Old Stone House. "Grab anything to help them float until they can reach the other side. Go!"

Immediately, the team scattered in all directions, diving into the water as they spotted Patriots who struggled to keep their heads above water. Max and Jock worked as a team to grab logs and push them toward the panicked men. Elsa did the same, grabbing large floating tree branches shot into the water from musket fire and pushing them toward the soldiers. Clarie sought out the wounded who were attempting to swim to safety. "I've got you," she told them, swimming them to the far bank, one by one.

Joseph Plumb Martin stood on the bank of the creek as men emerged from the marshy ponds, covered in mud. He grabbed Sam by the arm. "They look like water rats. Let's give them a hand!" Together he and Sam helped the men out of the water, lifting their guns or bags and helping however else they could.

Max suddenly whiffed a foul odor as he reached the bank. "Speakin' of r-r-rats, I smell one!" He looked up and saw Rafe on the far bank shoot a retreating soldier in the back. The man fell face first into the creek and floated with the current as the tide started to recede.

Jock's eyes widened in horror as Rafe then stomped over to another panicked young man who dropped to his knees, pleading for mercy to surrender. "He's going to kill that poor lad!" The mean grenadier smiled wickedly and thrust his bayonet into the soldier, killing him instantly. He then turned and spotted Elsa swimming through the creek.

"NO!!!!!!" Jock cried, seeing what was happening. "We've got to save Elsa!"

Max held him back. "We can't r-r-reach her in time!"

Rafe held his wolf gun up to his shoulder and trained his aim on the swimming fox.

"Elsa! Elsa! Get out of there!" Jock shouted furiously.

The fox heard Jock barking and turned to see the wicked soldier with his gun pointed right at her. She took a deep breath and dove under the water just as Rafe fired, a cloud of smoke covering his face. He laughed and then ran off to join the advancing British column.

"He shot Elsa!" Jock cried, running along the bank in her direction.

"He shot *at* Elsa, lad," Max told Jock, following him. "It don't mean he got her." As they ran along the bank, Max spotted another soldier struggling to make it to shore. He jumped in the water and shoved a log to the man who latched on to it with relief. "Steady, lad," Max sputtered, nudging the log to shore.

"Elsa?! Elsa?! Where are you?" Jock frantically shouted, running through the mud at the water's edge, looking all around the swirling waters of the creek for his friend.

Suddenly Jock stepped into a massive paw print left in the mud, one he had seen before. Fear gripped him as he heard a menacing voice behind him. "Looking for someone?"

Jock spun around, his heart beating out of his chest. Tears of anger and fear burned his eyes. He knew who the voice belonged to, even though he didn't see the massive wolf. "Espion!"

"I'm delighted to see you again, whelp," Espion answered. "We have some unfinished business."

Jock looked down and saw pawprints forming in the mud toward him. He opened his mouth to scream but nothing came out.

Max reached the bank, shook the mud off his head, and saw what was happening. "No, no, NO!" he screamed, running toward Jock.

Just then they heard the screech of an eagle and saw a shadow pass overhead. They looked up and down fell a cannon ball hurtling toward the unseen beast. It landed with a thud as Espion grunted and the impression of his body sank into the mud.

"Direct hit!" Nigel exclaimed, patting Veritas's neck. "HUZZAH!"

"HUZZAH!" Veritas screeched in victory. "Let's do that again!"

"I say, I'm quite impressed with your precision, especially at an invisible target!" Nigel cheered. He waved at Max and Jock. "Onward to rout the dreaded foe with a reload!" With that, Veritas flew back toward the Patriot lines.

Max reached Jock, and the little Scottie fell into his shoulder sobbing with a mixture of fear, relief, and grief. "Grandsire!"

"Come on, lad, let's get ye out of here," Max told him, closing his eyes in relief. *Thank ye, Maker. An' thank ye, Mousie.* He nudged the little Scottie through the mud and up the bank, leaving the Gowanus Creek and the horrific scene behind.

Washington stood on a redoubt at Cobble Hill with his spyglass, watching as the brave Marylanders were decimated. Tears stung his eyes, and a lump filled his throat. "What brave fellows I must this day lose!"

Max and Jock stood off in the distance as Gillamon came up behind them in the form of Mr. Atticus. "Greater love hath no man than this, that a man lay down his life for his friends," he said reverently, quoting Jesus in the Gospel of John. "We are witness again to sacrificial blood being spilled for others."

"It took the Americans four months ta dig in, but only aboot four hours for the British ta completely cr-r-rush Washington's army," Max growled in anger and anguish.

Jock's lip trembled, and he cried profusely, tears blinding him. "H-h-how can humans kill one another like this? Especially English and American brothers like these?"

Gillamon swept up Jock in his arms. "They've killed one another since the very first pair of brothers walked the earth. War has always been and will always be part of the human experience in this fallen sin-filled world. Some wars are unjust, and some are just like this one. But despite the horrors of war, somehow the valor and goodness of men can shine through, spurring others on to fight the good fight."

"Aye, it's hard ta watch the tr-r-ragedy of war," Max added. "But there always be heroes willin' ta make the ultimate sacr-r-rifice for fr-r-reedom."

Tears rolled down Jock's face and his little body shook with sobs. "Including Elsa."

Max shared a mournful look with Gillamon. "She's missin', Gillamon. R-r-rafe shot at her in the cr-r-reek, but then his evil comr-r-rade Espion thr-r-reatened Jock on the bank. Mousie an' Veritas saved the day by dr-r-roppin' a six-pound ball on the beastie, but I got the lad out of there before anythin' else happened."

"We haven't seen her since," Jock reported with a sniff.

"Losing our brave friends either through death or missing in action brings equal grief," Gillamon said, nodding. "But take heart that her and your efforts saved many men who would have drowned. Only seven soldiers were lost to drowning in the Gowanus Creek. But nearly all the Marylanders are lost from the battle at the Old Stone House—two hundred fifty-six of them. Some are missing, just like Elsa. Soldiers go missing in battle, but some will make it back. Things are uncertain until the fog of war lifts."

Jock looked up at Gillamon and blinked back the tears. "Then there's hope?"

"There's always hope," Gillamon answered, giving the little dog a gentle hug.

"So wha's the status of the humans now that the r-r-redcoats have chased the Patr-r-riots all the way back ta Br-r-rooklyn Heights?" Max asked.

"Among a slew of colonels, majors, and other officers taken prisoner, General Sullivan was captured, as was General Stirling, who surrendered to Hessian General von Heister to deprive British General Grant of such a prize. Washington has lost three hundred killed, seven hundred wounded and a thousand taken prisoner," Gillamon answered. "The British and Hessian casualties number less than four hundred, with sixty-one regulars and only two Hessians killed."

"The enemy done slaughtered us! Aye, an' now that the Br-r-ritish have Washington's army pinned with their backs against the East R-r-river, it's only a matter of time before they'll have ta surrender anyway, ain't it?" Max lamented, lowering and shaking his head. "I hate ta say it, but it looks hopeless for the Americans an' their independence."

"It does look hopeless, doesn't it?" Gillamon agreed. "But that's when the Maker does his finest work. And that's when we must soldier on."

"What do you mean, Gillamon?" Jock sniffed, still crying. "Now, what?"

Gillamon smiled and looked at the tears spilling from Jock's eyes. "Let's see if we can put those tears to good use. What Washington's army needs is a strong northeast wind and a good, drenching rain."

FIELD OUTSIDE BROOKLYN HEIGHTS, NEW YORK, AUGUST 27, 1776, 3:00 P.M.

"If a good bleeding can bring those Bible-faced Yankees to their senses, the fever of independence should soon abate!" boasted General Grant, laughing with a slap on the back of General Clinton.

A Hessian captain piped up, adding, "*Ja, und* after this day, I think ve shall hear no more of the riflemen. They have been exterminated from the face of the earth!"

The British and Hessian command slowly gathered to regroup two thousand yards outside the Patriot inner line. After Washington's outer lines collapsed and the rebels retreated behind their defenses, the commanders awaited their orders to finish them off.

"Congratulations, General Howe!" Cornwallis exulted. "You have routed the rebels and cornered the Fox!"

Clinton beamed with pride, knowing it was his plan that had destroyed Washington's left flank, leading to the fall of the rest of his army. Tarleton stood behind at a distance, reveling in the British rout and listening to the boasts of his superior officers.

"I'm ordering a halt to all forward movement," General Howe announced, drawing shocked looks of disbelief and disappointment from his officers. "All that's left is to tighten the noose around Washington's defeated army. There is no need to press our men further today and suffer unnecessary casualties." The last thing Howe wanted was another Bunker Hill.

"But, Sir, we only need to push on a bit further, and this rebellion will be over!" Clinton objected, raising a hand toward Washington's line.

Howe shot Clinton a heated glance and raised a finger in the air. "The troops have for this day done handsomely enough! Mounting a frontal assault right now could cost us upward of fifteen-hundred casualties, and that is not something I am willing to risk, General Clinton. Such a move would be inconsiderate, and even criminal!"

"I'm sure my Lord feels confident that the Fox Washington is indeed securely trapped," Cornwallis followed. "General Howe's assessment is valid.

Our men have been on the march since last night and need to rest and gain sustenance."

Clinton shook his head and glanced up at the sky, clenching his jaw in anger. Once again, General Howe refused to push just a little farther to finish off the rebels, just as he had done at Bunker Hill when Clinton urged him to pursue them on to Cambridge. But Howe allowed the rebels to escape and fight another day, which led to Dorchester Heights, and now to this day in New York. *How many more days will he let the rebels live?*

"We will begin siege works immediately to bag the Fox," Howe declared. "See to your men to make it so."

Soon the sounds of picks and shovels could be heard. A siege trench stretching a thousand feet long formed as the Patriots watched the British dig in. It would only take a day or two to reach them, and then it would all be over.

But suddenly, a brisk northeast wind kicked up.

39

A Long Island Shot

BROOKLYN, NEW YORK, AUGUST 28, 1776, NOON

The soaking rain pinged off Blueskin's harness as Washington rode along the three miles of the Patriot lines, inspecting conditions and assessing the desperate situation of his troops. He silently ruminated about every decision and mistake he had made over the past few weeks and days leading up to the Battle of Brooklyn. *How could I have thought the attack on Brooklyn was only a feint and not the real invasion?* He didn't know how many yet, but hundreds of his men were now prisoners, wounded, or dead. *Oh, my brave fellows!* Washington thought, a lump in his throat, and tears stinging his eyes. The Marylanders were virtually wiped out as those fallen Patriots were either cut down by fire, slaughtered by the merciless British and Hessian soldiers, or drowned in the Gowanus Creek as they tried to retreat. But they had held off Cornwallis and the British forces long enough to allow hundreds of their countrymen to escape to safety.

Washington paid no mind to the rain that dripped from his three-cornered hat as he lifted a hand here and there with the confidence that he ever sought to portray for his men. Inside, his emotions were as tumultuous as the storm that had suddenly descended on Brooklyn, but outwardly the Commander-in-Chief exuded calm and control. His men were suffering mightily. They had been crushed by the British juggernaut, leaving them traumatized by the horrors of war and grief-stricken from having seen their friends slaughtered right next to them. Aside from the mental and emotional anguish, they were physically beaten. Some men had no tents and little or no food. They were hungry and soaked to the skin with this chilling rain that had brought with it a ten-degree drop in temperature. Washington observed exhausted men sitting in the mud, and some standing waist-deep in water that filled the trenches. One man was even asleep standing up, such was his fatigue. He didn't seem bothered by the heavy rain that splattered around his mud-soaked feet as he leaned on his gun. It was impossible to keep guns and powder dry in these conditions. Washington clenched his jaw to stifle a yawn, having had scarcely any sleep himself when suddenly he got a whiff of cherry tobacco. He looked over and saw to his surprise a familiar face belonging to an old soldier who sat under a tree, smoking his intricately carved pipe, and calmly carving a powder horn.

Washington dismounted from Blueskin to go greet the older man under the tree. "Why, Mr. Atticus, I didn't realize you were with us here in Brooklyn. I'm glad to see you've endured the battle."

Mr. Atticus stood and saluted him. "Good-day, General Washington. I'm always with you, Sir, even though I'm too old to wield a gun. But I can still wield a helpful hand or an encouraging word for the cause of liberty." He paused and stared into Washington's face with his piercing blue eyes. "I know the battle didn't go as you had hoped, Your Excellency."

For some reason, Mr. Atticus always seemed to appear right when Washington needed a confidential ear, some solid wisdom, or a word of encouragement. Stoic and private as he was in his emotions and words, especially to someone of Mr. Atticus's station, Washington had an unusual, comfortable trust with this veteran militia soldier who had first appeared when the inexperienced Commander-in-Chief assumed command in Cambridge. The old soldier had found and delivered Max when the dog had miraculously followed Washington to Boston. Mr. Atticus liked to carve powder horns with amazing scenes and words from the Holy Writ. He carved one for Colonel Knox just as the ambitious young man returned from bringing the cannons from Fort Ticonderoga. Knox used that powder horn to prime the first cannon fired on the British as they positioned those guns up on Dorchester Heights.

"It was a difficult day for our army," Washington confessed. He tightened his lips, needing to simply state the truth. "Errors in judgment, indecision, unexpected moves of the enemy."

"'A double-minded man is unstable in all his ways,'" Mr. Atticus quoted from the book of James, delivering an unspoken emotional slap to Washington, almost to shake him from his gloom. "James didn't mince words, did he? But I must admit that he was right. It's always best to decide upon one firm, clear plan and then confidently see it through, come what may. Experience is a harsh, unapologetic teacher, especially for a leader. But greatness requires it, and strong leaders put it to good use."

Washington felt personal conviction and regret for his indecision and errors, but he didn't sense condemnation from this wise old sage—only an unspoken admonition to learn from his mistakes and press on. The inexperienced general knew he had made a series of missteps. He had failed to get the intelligence he needed about what the British were going to do, and his delay and indecision trickled down through every move he made. He had replaced Nathanael Greene with not one but *two* generals who were completely unfamiliar with the terrain of Long Island. And he had changed that command structure twice in four days, causing confusion. *He* should have taken personal charge from the beginning but arrived at Long Island after the British had begun their attack and then did nothing but observe from afar. He split his force, leaving the troops on Long Island vastly outnumbered. Oh, and leaving the Jamaica Pass completely undefended! That error alone was enough to seal their fate. *How could I have allowed such a thing?!* Washington lamented in his mind.

Mr. Atticus pointed to the distance. "I was over on the left flank, where the surprise came from Howe's forces. When I heard the British cavalry galloping toward us from behind, I must admit that my heart fell mighty hard. Hearing them blow that hunting horn, I thought I was back in Virginia at a fox hunt for a moment."

Washington clenched his jaw, his brow furrowed, gripping his riding crop in hand. "I regret that we had no cavalry with which to answer them. The few mounted patrol we had at Jamaica Pass were easily taken. Perhaps if we—if *I*—had utilized the horses offered us by Connecticut, things would have been different. Perhaps if we had had more advance warning as to the movement of the enemy . . ." *Another error in judgment.*

"The old psalmist wrote that no king is saved by the size of his army, and no warrior *escapes* by his great strength," Mr. Atticus interjected, paraphrasing the thirty-third Psalm. He held up his powder horn in progress. "A horse is a vain hope for deliverance; despite all its great strength, it cannot save." He pointed a finger to his eyes. "But the eyes of the Lord are on those who fear him, on those whose hope is in his unfailing love, to deliver them from death and keep them alive in famine."

Washington leaned over to study the powder horn. It depicted a horse and rider chasing a fox with the verse Mr. Atticus had just quoted: *No warrior escapes by his great strength.* He raised his eyebrows to see such exquisite carving of the exact thing they discussed. "For once, I know how the fox must feel in its need to escape." Blueskin snorted and stomped a hoof in the mud.

"Do you recall our conversation back in Cambridge about Gideon and his three hundred dog-lapping men?" Mr. Atticus asked.

Washington nodded. "Indeed, I remember."

"The reason God wanted to strip General Gideon of men and weapons was so that the nation of Israel would know that it was not their might but the power of God that brought them an impossible victory against the Midianites," Mr. Atticus reminded him. "Like Gideon, the psalmist understood that human effort alone doesn't determine the outcome of events. God accomplishes His purposes, sometimes *with*—but sometimes *despite*—human effort, regardless of the circumstances. History bears out that the strongest armies melt like snowflakes when God is against them. Remember what happened to the Egyptians?"

"You mean when Pharaoh's army came after the Israelites after he had told Moses to take the people and go?" Washington asked.

Mr. Atticus slowly nodded. "That Egyptian king wasn't about to let those people up and walk away from him without a fight. And King George isn't about to let his colonies walk away from him without a fight either, is he?"

"Hardly," Washington answered with a frown. "But I don't recall the Israelites having to fight against the Egyptians."

"That's true, General. At that point, God told Moses exactly what to do, and all the people had to do was listen and do as their leader instructed," Mr. Atticus answered. "God divided the sea, and they just walked on through to escape the Egyptian army. He used weather to *guide* them and then to *save* them. A pillar of fire by night, and a pillar of cloud by day."

"We also have been the beneficiaries of divine Providence with weather thus far," Washington realized, nodding. "Colonel Knox received snow just as he needed it to transport the cannons, we received fog just as we needed it to mount those guns in a single night up on Dorchester Heights, a sudden squall of a storm prevented General Howe from attacking us in Boston, and even this storm now has its benefits, despite the misery it brings." He pointed to the British siege line six hundred yards away. "This rain has bought us time."

"And that wind blowing from the northeast is keeping British ships anchored in place," Mr. Atticus added. He grinned, thinking of Jock's good work as weather agent for each of those occasions. "The Maker can do anything He wishes with weather. And as you've recounted, Your Excellency, He can do it in a single night."

Washington peered out over the East River to gaze at the British warships being held in place by the unfavorable northeast winds. As miserable as this storm of rain and wind was, it was a blessing in disguise, as it kept Lord Howe's ships from advancing up the East River to surround them from behind. General Howe's troops had dug siege trenches and were now only six hundred yards away from the Patriot front lines. As things stood right now, Washington's army was hemmed in with their backs to the East River. It was only a matter of time before the Howe Brothers would move in for the kill by land and sea to force Washington's surrender. King George III, Parliament, and His Majesty's mighty forces would claim victory, and any hope for American Independence would melt like snowflakes. The Revolution would be over with the first official battle of Washington's Continental Army.

But one short mile across the East River was Manhattan . . . and escape from annihilation.

"You may have lost a battle, General, but you can still save an army," Mr. Atticus stated, as if reading Washington's thoughts. He pointed to Manhattan. "Allowing His people to escape across seas and rivers seems to be the Maker's specialty. He kept the winds blowing all night for Moses to allow the Israelites to cross through the Red Sea while he kept the Egyptian army at bay with a pillar of fire."

"Fire." Washington nodded slowly. He didn't say anything for a moment. *Fires. The British left their fires burning while they came behind our left flank, fooling us into thinking they hadn't moved,* he thought. He glanced at the powder horn in Mr. Atticus's hand. *Foxes. Even weather can help a fox to escape. Scenting on the fox hunt can be affected by temperature, and humidity. Foxes can evade hounds by running up or down streams, running along the tops of fences, and using other tactics to throw the hounds off the scent. I need to think like a fox.*

"Thank you, Mr. Atticus. I must get back to headquarters." Washington suddenly felt a surge of resolve and solid determination of how he needed to proceed as the Commander-in-Chief. He led his army into this predicament, and he would now lead them out of it. Washington turned and mounted Blueskin. "The same Providence that ruled yesterday rules today and will rule tomorrow. Godspeed, Mr. Atticus."

"Godspeed, General Washington," Mr. Atticus replied with a salute. As he watched Washington ride away, he smiled. "Now to get Jock ready for tonight."

⚜

LIVINGSTON HOUSE, BROOKLYN, NEW YORK, AUGUST 29, 1776, 4:00 P.M.

Nigel, Max, and Jock kept out of sight as Washington called his War Council to meet in the country house of Philip Livingston, a signer of the Declaration of Independence.

"I count *seven* generals at this War Council," Nigel whispered. "That certainly bodes well."

"It's unanimous, then," Washington asserted. "We will evacuate Long Island tonight, beginning at 9:00 p.m. I have taken the liberty of sending word to General Heath at King's Bridge to acquire every boat, vessel, or watercraft available without delay, giving the reason that we have many battalions from New Jersey which are coming over to relieve others here. We must keep this operation *secret,* even from our own men. It would only take *one traitor* to expose our true intentions of escape and doom the entire operation. Orders are not to be given until 7:00 p.m., for the men to be under arms with packs for a night attack on the enemy." He nodded to General Thomas Mifflin.

"As I and my Pennsylvania brigades have freshly arrived today, we will serve as the rear guard in the outermost defenses and hold the line until the army has safely departed," Mifflin explained.

"Campfires are to be kept burning to make the enemy believe that our troops remain in place," Washington added. "The sick, wounded, and the troops with the least experience are to start for the Brooklyn ferry landing first, with the understanding that they are being relieved by reinforcements."

"We shall also transport our artillery, ammunition, supplies, and horses," Colonel Knox added. "The wheels of the carts must be wrapped and muffled, as well as the oars of all the vessels."

"Silence and secrecy are *crucial*, gentlemen," Washington told them. "General McDougall will oversee the embarkation, and I will be present at all times until the final boat has pushed off the shore of Long Island."

"Well, a year ago, Washington caught Howe by surpr-r-rise in one night in Boston with puttin' guns up on Dorchester Heights," Max whispered. "Then Howe surpr-r-rised Washington here on Long Island by puttin' ten thousand troops behind his lines in one night."

"Now it's Washington's turn again to surprise Howe in one night!" Jock added excitedly. "I better go make sure the wind is still working."

BROOKLYN FERRY LANDING, NEW YORK,
AUGUST 29, 1776, 9:00 P.M.

"At least the rain has stopped," chattered a shivering soldier with a bloodied bandage wrapped around his head.

"But the ebb tide is in, and that northeast wind is going to make it impossible for the sailing vessels to cross this river," another wounded soldier added, pointing to the waves lashing against the shore. "It's far too rough even for the rowing vessels not to get swamped."

The first wave of sick and wounded soldiers stood there in the dark, longing to escape Long Island, but fearing that attempting to cross would be no escape at all. General McDougall quickly scribbled a message to Washington: *Given these conditions, there can be no retreat tonight.*

"I fear I, too, am grounded until the winds abate," Nigel said. "Veritas is standing by until we can once more be airborne."

Gillamon (as Mr. Atticus), Clarie, Max, Jock, and Nigel stood on a darkened bank to watch what was happening. "Expect opposition at every turn here tonight. Be alert and ready to act on a moment's notice." Gillamon knelt and looked Jock in the eye. "Jock, we need you to reduce the wind so the boats can cross the East River. You'll need to stay here with me for weather updates as needed."

"Aye, aye, Gillamon," Jock answered.

"Good boy," Gillamon said, giving Jock an affectionate scratch behind an ear.

"Clarie, I need for you to run interference with McDougall's message to Washington, so he does *not* receive it," Gillamon told her. "He doesn't need to halt anything, as Jock will calm the wind. The last thing Washington needs is to doubt his plans. Then provide underwater support as needed to keep the boats from swamping. Those brave seamen could benefit from a push here and there as they are in for an exhausting night."

"Understood," Clarie answered with a grin. "I'll be a busy courier and dolphin tonight."

"Max, you are to guard Washington from anyone—or anything—that might try to get to him tonight," Gillamon instructed. "No doubt Rafe and Espion are present."

"Aye, Gillamon! I've got me smeller on high alert." Max growled and sniffed the air. "Mousie, feel free ta stop them evil minions with more cannonballs."

"We'd be more than happy to, old boy! By my calculations, our six-pound cannonball delivered six hundred pounds of force when dropped from one hundred feet," Nigel relayed. "Quite the smashing delivery at more than fifty miles-per-hour, huzzah! It may not be able to extinguish the immortal beast, but it can certainly knock it out cold!"

"Well done, Nigel. Keep monitoring things from the air and let any of us know about matters of urgency," Gillamon told the mouse.

"Right! You shall have our eagle eyes in the sky," Nigel asserted with a salute.

"And please keep an eye out for Elsa," Jock asked Nigel hopefully.

"I shall, my boy," Nigel told him with a tender pat.

"Very well, team. It's time to help the humans with their great escape," Gillamon told them. He paused and then punctuated the importance of what lay before them. "The future of American Independence will be determined tonight. If we fail in our mission, all will be lost, including everything we and the humans have striven for over the years. This escape is a final Long Island shot for Washington to keep liberty alive."

A Pillar of Cloud

BROOKLYN, NEW YORK, AUGUST 30, 1776, 2:00 A.M.

"Shhhh! You heard Colonel Knox's orders. Muffle those wheels!" a Patriot captain hoarsely commanded a team of artillerymen. The soldiers quickly wrapped the wheels of a cart loaded with crates of musket balls and powder, moving as silently as they could to transport the cache of ammunition and guns to the ferry landing.

While Knox's men pulled the cart down the path away from the cannon that they would next move, massive paw prints quietly formed in the mud behind the gun's huge carriage. The prints stopped for a moment and then formed again in a line to a nearby campfire.

As the paw prints neared the fire, Espion's eyes glowed in the darkness, reflecting the red and orange flames. Washington had ordered all campfires to remain stoked through the night to convince the enemy that the Continental Army remained entrenched in Brooklyn while they were actually escaping across the East River. The invisible wolf grinned and picked up a burning stick with his mouth before smothering the fire by kicking dirt into the flames. He walked over to the cannon sitting there in the darkness, knowing it was loaded.

Espion lit the cannon's fuse and dropped the burning stick on the ground by the gun carriage. "BOOM," he muttered with a laugh before running off into the darkness.

Within moments the cannon blast sounded, and panic rippled through the Patriot lines. Such a blast could easily invite a British response, rousing the entire British army to wake and discover that Washington's forces were attempting an escape. The Patriots feverishly whispered among themselves to determine what had happened, but no one had an answer. Miraculously, the British lines did not respond. Whether it was exhaustion, apathy, or a decision to wait and see if more blasts followed, British guns remained silent.

"By Jove, did you see that?" Nigel asked Veritas, pointing to the arc of the red-hot cannon ball as it sailed in the air. "Who in their right mind would fire a cannon tonight?!"

Veritas peered down at the cannon that sat motionless in the darkness, a

337

lingering cloud of smoke rising into the air above its barrel. "Who, or *what?*" he countered. "The Patriots didn't fire that gun. Plus, their campfire is out."

"Oh, dear, I suspect something evil afoot," Nigel grumbled. "Let us land to relight that fire, old boy. How are you at gripping a torch with those mighty talons?"

Veritas wriggled his talons, as if preparing them for landing. "No problem, unless there's some gunpowder residue from the last ball we dropped."

"Right!" Nigel answered. He swallowed and patted the bald eagle with a nervous chuckle. "What do you say we first give your feet a good rinse with a dip in the river? It may be up to us to keep the fires burning all night if the enemy seeks to extinguish them, but I do not relish serving the British roasted eagle topped with charred mouse for breakfast."

BROOKLYN, NEW YORK, AUGUST 30, 1776, 3:00 A.M.

Major Alexander Scammell plodded his horse through the mud to make his way to General Mifflin. "Sir," he whispered hoarsely, "the boats are waiting, and the Commander-in-Chief is anxious for the arrival of your troops at the ferry."

Mifflin looked at Scammell with a look of doubt. "You must be mistaken, Major. You cannot mean the troops here under my command."

"Respectfully, I am not mistaken, General Mifflin," Scammell answered insistently yet quietly. "I came from the extreme left flank and have ordered all the troops I've met on the march which are now in motion. I will go on and give the same orders from here."

Mifflin shook his head and sighed. "Very well." He reluctantly made his way over to Colonel Edward Hand and ordered him to call his advance pickets and sentinels to march immediately.

Not long after Colonel Hand's men began to move, General Washington encountered his line of men as he rode along on Blueskin. "Is that you, Colonel Hand?" he called quietly.

"Yes, Your Excellency, it is I," Colonel Hand whispered back.

Washington frowned. "I am surprised to find you abandoning your post."

"But Sir, I have not abandoned my post," Hand hoarsely protested. "I have marched by order of my immediate commanding officer."

Washington clenched his teeth. "Impossible!"

"Sir, I assure you that I have the orders of General Mifflin. I pray you will not think me particularly to blame," Hand anxiously answered.

"I undoubtedly would not blame you if that were the case, Colonel," Washington assured him.

Just then, General Mifflin came riding up to the men. "Sir, is there something the matter?"

"General Mifflin, I am afraid you have ruined us by so unseasonably withdrawing troops from the lines!" Washington blurted out in a raspy voice.

"But Sir, I did it by *your* order," Mifflin protested with a forced whisper.

Washington adamantly shook his head. "That *cannot* be!"

"But I did!" Mifflin countered. "Does Scammell act as an aide-de-camp for the day, or does he not?"

"He does indeed," Washington answered haltingly.

"Then, I had orders through him," Mifflin explained. "He came to me directly and told me to retreat."

Washington looked up at the darkened sky in exasperation. "First that cannon blast, *now,* this dreadful mistake! Matters at the ferry are in much confusion, and unless you and your men can hurriedly resume your posts before the enemy discovers you have left them, we shall soon be found out!" Washington pointed his riding crop. "Now, General, turn this line around and make haste back to your positions!"

"Yes, Sir!" Mifflin answered as he and Colonel Hand gave the orders to turn the men around.

Max watched from the shadows as an anxious Washington observed the men return to their positions. "Someone must have given that fake order ta Scammell ta r-r-ruin this entire operation. The Patriots done been *scammed.*"

BROOKLYN, NEW YORK, AUGUST 30, 1776, 5:00 A.M.

Washington peered down the East River with his spyglass toward New York Harbor. Admiral Howe's warships remained in place as silent, menacing beasts. The northeast wind had seen to that. But what about Howe's smaller craft armed with swivel guns? Why were they not patrolling the East River? All it would take was one small British vessel's crew to spot the retreating Patriots, and the British giant would quickly be awakened from slumber to descend upon them. But night was nearly over, and the giant would soon awake on its own as daylight approached.

Washington let go a worried breath and surveyed the men still piling up at the wharf, eager to board the transports. While they had successfully transported several thousand men across to Manhattan, they were far from completing their stealthy retreat. They soon would not have the cover of darkness to mask their operation. Daylight would come within the hour. What they needed was a miracle. *What was it Mr. Atticus said had saved the retreating Israelites? A pillar of fire by night, and a pillar of cloud by day.* The weary general looked up to the heavens and scanned the skies, which had a faint tinge of grey. His heart raced at the thought of his army being exposed by the rising sun. He briefly closed his eyes and breathed a silent prayer. *Dear God in Heaven, please do the same for us.*

Max and Gillamon (in the form of Mr. Atticus) heard the flutter of wings as Veritas came in for a landing where they stood in the distance behind Washington.

"I fear the game will soon be up, along with the sun!" Nigel gushed worriedly, his spectacles askew and his disheveled fur covered in soot.

"Mornin', Mousie," Max answered calmly. "Glad ye could finally land, eagle lad."

Nigel pulled on his whiskers and pointed an exasperated paw down to the ferry. "My dear boy, do you not *realize* that whilst Washington and his men hurry to make their great escape, the sun will soon crest over the horizon, exposing them to the British war machine?! They have run out of *time!* We have done our best to relight fires extinguished by the enemy all night, but it is over!" the little mouse wailed, throwing his paws into the air. He plopped down on the ground to sit in a heap of despair. "Independence, liberty, America! It's all over! Oh, the humanity! I had such grand hopes for this new nation!"

Max and Gillamon shared a sympathetic look. "I think someone needs a nap," observed Max as he walked over and nudged Nigel with his nose. "Don't worry, Mousie. Jock had a big breakfast."

Nigel looked at Max with wide eyes and slowly shook his head in disbelief. "Have you gone *completely* insane?!"

Veritas cocked his head in question. "What did Jock eat?"

Nigel turned to stare at the bald eagle, his jaw hanging open. "You've all gone mad! Oh, dear. The strain of war has been too much for you."

"Peas," Gillamon answered Veritas with a wink. "A whole bowl full of them."

Suddenly a cool mist swept over the group and enveloped them with a fog so thick they could scarcely see one another. Nigel's spectacles also fogged up, and he put his paws out in front of him, reaching into the air. "I cannot see a thing!"

Max grinned. "Exactly."

"And neither will the British," Veritas realized with a chuckle.

"Only six feet in front of them, to be exact," Gillamon told him. "That's all they'll be able to see."

A flock of honking geese flew low past them, disappearing into the dense fog just as two black, pointy ears emerged.

"Will this do?" Jock asked, stepping out from the thick mist with a wide smile.

Gillamon clapped his hands and chuckled warmly. "Bravo, our young weathermaker!"

"Well, I'll be a Scottie's uncle," Nigel muttered in shock, hastily wiping his spectacles on Gillamon's trousers and replacing them on his nose.

"Aye, ye done made the fog as thick as pea soup then!" Max exclaimed.

"Aye, grandsire! I had lots of gas just like when I ate Washington's poisoned peas!" Jock cheered, wagging his tail.

The young Scottie suddenly heard a voice behind him. "Vhy vould mein *Hundebaby* eat poisoned peas?"

Jock whipped around but didn't see who had spoken those words. His voice cracked with emotion as he dared to hope. "El . . . Elsa?" But there was nothing but fog swirling in front of him. He squinted, and a lump formed in his throat as two pointy ears and a beautiful red and white face emerged from the fog. Tears stung his eyes, and he could barely exclaim, "Elsa! Oh, Elsa! You're alive!"

Jock rushed over to the fox, and she cupped her soft paw under his chin. "*Ja*, very much so, vhich I could not say if I ate peas that vere poisoned. Vhat is this crazy talk?"

"It's a long story, lass!" Max explained, trotting up to them with a wide grin. "I'm glad ta see ye, lass! We thought ye were done for."

"But we never gave up hope!" Jock quickly added, now crying tears of joy.

"Aye, lad," Max agreed. "Wha' happened back at the mill pond, lass?"

"Vhen that evil soldier Rafe shot at me, I dove down deep into the vater, *und* suddenly vas svept under the mill vheel," the fox explained. "Vhen the tide is high, the dam shuts vater in the pond, but vhen the tide is low, the dam opens, *und* the falling vater turns the mill vheel."

Jock's eyes widened. "How terrible! You could have drowned! I know what that feels like!"

Elsa nodded her head. "*Ja*, it *vas* terrible! I passed out but somehow vas pushed to the surface of the vater. I drifted vith the current a long vay. Vhen I voke I didn't know vhere I vas!"

"Where were ye then?" Max wanted to know, his brow furrowed.

"I drifted all the vay to New York Harbor *und* vay up the East River along the banks of Long Island," Elsa explained. "I floated into a clump of reeds *und* lay there a long time to rest. I vas unsure vhere I vas, so I just started valking. I kept valking south until I finally made it back here to Brooklyn a few hours ago." She paused and wrinkled her brow. "But I saw something very strange on my vay to find Al. I saw a human that looked like Vashington vhispering vith an aide named Scammell, but there vas something not right about him."

Max stiffened his spine. "How do ye mean 'str-r-range,' lass?"

"For vone thing, Vashington vas not riding his horse that is blue. *Und* he smelled very bad," Elsa reported. "I know the humans have not bathed in days vith everything going on, but this vas vorse than a normal dirty human."

"I knew it! I knew that Scammell didn't get those orders fr-r-rom Washington hisself!" Max growled. "I were with the general at all times, an' I didn't hear him give them orders that aboot r-r-ruined the entire escape!"

Jock turned to Elsa. "The bad guys usually have this terrible smell of death about them." He swallowed hard. "Do you think it was *Rafe* that took the form of . . . Washington?"

"Or Charlatan," Max grumbled. "He's all aboot twistin' things an' words. But whoever it were, it were a scam!"

"I do not understand this term of 'scam,'" Elsa interjected, tilting her head. "But there vas also another thing that happened. Vhen I found Al, he had just led a young slave boy right to a group of Hessians." She giggled. "That Irish kitty is smarter than he lets on."

Max grinned. "Aye, but sometimes that kitty don't *plan* on doin' smart things. He jest stumbles inta smartness."

"I say, what exactly did Al do that was so smart?" Nigel wanted to know.

Elsa giggled. "The young slave boy vas trying to tell the Hessians that the Patriots vere escaping, but the German soldiers did not understand him. Al just sat there *und* grinned as they tried to communicate. The Hessians decided to keep the boy vith them until daylight."

Jock laughed. "Who sent that young boy to inform the British?"

"He kept saying a lady's name who is a Tory *und* lives by the ferry," Elsa told them. "She sent him to varn the British, but for vonce, it vas a good thing to have a language barrier, *ja?*"

"*Ja!*" they all exclaimed in unison.

"Al decided I should come tell you these things while he kept vatch for any messages coming to the officers' tent," Elsa explained. "About an hour ago, a message came from Captain Montressor who got suspicious of the Patriots *und* found an abandoned redoubt. He varned Howe *und* took a combat patrol, but all they found vas a few cows, horses, *und* three Patriot soldiers who foolishly stayed behind to plunder. They vere the only Americans to get caught."

"Serves 'em r-r-right," Max growled. "Those lads made a stupid choice ta stay behind. But at least they were the only lads lost from Washington's army."

"The enemy was active all night trying to thwart this escape," Gillamon told them. "Between setting off the cannon, confusing the humans with false orders, sending messengers to warn the British, and extinguishing the Patriot fires, any one of those things could have sabotaged Washington's escape. I'm very proud of the part each of our team played to aid his efforts." He paused and lifted a hand to point to the ferry. "Now see for yourself how the Maker has once more delivered his people with a pillar of cloud."

The animals turned to see Washington looking around the now deserted wharf after a final group of Marylanders cast off from the dock. They watched in awe as he made sure that he alone remained. After leading Blueskin aboard, Washington set foot onto the last barge to depart Brooklyn and shoved off into the East River. Washington stood calm and erect as he soon disappeared into the fog.

"He did it! And we did it!" Jock exulted. "The Continental Army has escaped!"

"The Fox has escaped through your fog, along vith his horse that is blue," Elsa added with a kiss to Jock's head.

"Aye, the Sword of the R-r-revolution cut thr-r-rough the fog of war!" Max cheered. "Thank the Maker!"

"I shall *never* forget this scene," Nigel softly said, emotion in his voice. "Independence, liberty, and America are *not* over."

Gillamon nodded. "The Commander-in-Chief was determined to save his army and live to fight another day. He personally took the responsibility for his actions that led to the debacle of Brooklyn by making sure his men were safely away. He has much to learn, but one thing is clear. When this fog lifts, George Washington will emerge wiser than before."

"And the enemy will emerge angrier than before," Veritas noted, pointing to the redcoats spilling into the abandoned redoubts and campfires.

Some British light horsemen galloped over the crest of the hill and rode down to the water's edge. They fired their carbines into the river, trying to hit the last boat of departing Marylanders rowing ahead of Washington, but only hit fog.

Banastre Tarleton fumed and gripped his fox horn in anger. "No need for this now! The Fox has escaped," he scoffed. He tucked the horn back into his satchel and buckled it with a huff.

British officer Charles Stedman sat atop his horse and marveled at what they saw as the fog began to lift. He couldn't help but admire what the Americans had done. "Driven to the corner of an island, hemmed in within a narrow space of two square miles, in their front near twenty thousand men, in their rear an arm of the sea a mile wide, and yet they secured a retreat without the loss of a man. Extraordinary."

Tarleton narrowed his eyes and clenched his jaw in anger. *Extraordinary failure on our part. When I am put in command, I will not allow such an escape.*

GENTLEMEN MAY CRY PEACE

"*Now to make peace!*' That's what sailor Howe cried when he heard aboot how his brother beat the Americans in Brooklyn," Al explained to Nigel. "Both brothers were so sure o' themselves that while army Howe dug a siege trench, sailor Howe didn't even bother protectin' the East River. Instead, sailor Howe started workin' on bein' a peace conditioner."

Nigel wrinkled his brow as he listened to Al's report of the British response following the Battle of Brooklyn. "Peace conditioner? Ah, you must mean peace *commissioner,* old boy."

Al scratched his head. "Ain't they the same thing? Anyhoo, before then while the fightin' were still happenin' in Brooklyn, sailor Howe invited those captured American Generals Stirling and Sullivan to some dinners aboard his *Eagle* ship." Al's stomach rumbled, and he wore a goofy grin. "Those were some tasty vittles."

"Yes, I'm sure they were, but please stay focused on the story of what happened at the dinners," Nigel pressed, eager for news of next steps.

"Sailor Howe convinced General Sullivan to go talk to the Congress in Philadelphia while on parade," Al continued.

"On *parole,*" Nigel surmised. "Yes, Sullivan came to get permission from General Washington to go speak to Congress. The Commander-in-Chief believed that Sullivan was naïve to think that Admiral Howe could truly offer anything to the Americans but decided that Congress should be the one to decide. What happened then?"

"Well, Congress decided to send John Adams, Benjamin Franklin, and Edward Rutledge to talk with sailor Howe, so they've got a big meetin' tomorrow," Al told him. "Sailor Howe is plannin' another meal to meet them at the Billopp House, so I figured I'd best go along and, um, gather intelligence."

"And more vittles, no doubt," Nigel guessed with a chuckle as he twirled a whisker, thinking this through. "Congress wisely selected a delegate to represent the northern, middle, and southern states to chat with the king's liaison. Even though Admiral Howe thought that his job to negotiate a peace would be easy with the assumed surrender of Washington, things undoubtedly changed when the Americans escaped to Manhattan. Does Admiral Howe still believe he can arrange a peace settlement?"

Al shrugged his shoulders. "I dunno, but he told Sullivan to let Congress know that the king won't let him call them a Congress, jest like he can't call Washington a General. King George thinks the Americans are playing make-believe in bein' a real country with a real army. But sailor Howe still wants to talk aboot peace, jest for thirty minutes. He's hopin' that Congress will change their minds aboot independence since the British whipped the Americans in Brooklyn."

"What exactly did King George say the Howe brothers could do at such a peace meeting?" Nigel asked.

"Not much 'til the rebels break up Congress and every state assembly, get rid o' their army, surrender all the forts, promise to pay all the injured loyalists, and agree to not tax any stuff sent over from Britain," Al answered. He lifted a paw, "Oh yeah, and anythin' they decide aboot peace can't happen 'til King George and his Lordy lads approve it."

"Right. This does not sound promising despite Admiral Howe's seemingly sincere cry for peace," Nigel lamented with a frown. "I suppose we shall both be in attendance to see what happens at the peace table tomorrow."

"And especially at the *dinner* table," Al added with a goofy grin. "I like sailor Howe's dinners. He serves lots o' fish and sometimes even turtle soup."

"Well, I'm glad you weren't aboard the *Eagle* when the Patriots sent the *Turtle* to blow it to smithereens a few days ago," Nigel told Al, tapping the chubby cat's paw.

Al's eyes widened in terror. "Ye mean to tell me that they sent a *turtle* to blow up sailor Howe's ship?! I see turtles in the water all the time, but I didn't know they were such deadly beasties!"

Nigel chuckled. "Forgive me, dear boy! *This Turtle* was not of the amphibious animal species, but a man-made submersible barrel operated by a human sitting inside. Utterly fascinating! It was designed to tow and affix an egg-shaped powder keg with a clock to the hull of Admiral Howe's ship. Unfortunately, things didn't quite work as planned, and the bomb exploded harmlessly in the East River, sending water and pieces of wood flying into the air. Alas, the dawn of submarine warfare began with failure, but I expect the humans shall figure it out in due time."

"Well, until they do, I'm stayin' away from explodin' turtles . . . or explodin' beavers, or explodin' fish, for that matter." The scaredy cat suddenly put his paws up to his mouth, and his eyes filled with tears. "Oh, no! How will I know if sailor Howe's fish have bombs inside? I best not eat them anymore. I'm gonna *starve!*"

"I should have never brought up the *Turtle,*" Nigel muttered under his breath.

"I'm not goin' anywhere near that peace meetin' tomorrow if it's goin' to be so deadly!" Al wailed in despair as he ran off.

"'How does a man *feel* when he is frightened? I need not ask how he *looks,*" Nigel quipped, quoting what Admiral Howe famously once said to a young lieutenant reporting a fire aboard ship. "But I know how an Irish cat does both."

BILLOPP HOUSE, STATEN ISLAND, NEW YORK, SEPTEMBER 11, 1776, 2:00 P.M.

Resplendently dressed, fifty-five-year-old Admiral Richard Howe stood on the beach and gazed with large, sad eyes into the rippling waters of the Arthur Kill tidal straight that emptied into the Raritan Bay at the southern tip of Staten Island. The beauty of this seascape was striking, and emitted peaceful overtones as opposed to the backdrop of the scarred, smoking landscape on Long Island back across New York Harbor. He hoped his soon-to-arrive guests would not see the very visible aftermath of war behind where he stood, and the preparations for more fighting to come.

Over on Long Island, his brother General William Howe prepared British troops to return to the field of battle, keeping Washington's army guessing as to where they would make landfall to attack Manhattan. General Howe's redcoats stretched from Red Hook to Hell Gate, but ever since Washington's miraculous escape, they made no attempt to cross the East River after them. General Howe's motive wasn't solely psychological warfare but a temporary ceasefire while his brother made one final attempt to end the conflict peacefully. But the break in fighting gave Washington and the Continental Army desperately needed time to regroup.

Perhaps this will all end today, Admiral Howe thought hopefully as he turned his gaze to see the barge trimmed in red and gold approaching from Perth Amboy a quarter mile across on the Jersey shore. With his brother occupied on Long Island, Richard would alone make one final attempt at peace with the Americans. He brushed off his knee-length blue uniform coat trimmed in white lapels and cuffs; the buttonholes were stitched with gold thread to match the shiny gold buttons. He pulled at the white lace cuffs of his shirt before straightening his black cocked hat, also trimmed in gold and bearing a black silk cockade. He rested a hand on the gold-hilted dress sword at his side and breathed in a deep breath of salt air through his prominent nose. It was then he spotted the bespectacled form of his longtime friend, Benjamin Franklin. A sad smile came upon the Admiral's face, remembering the fond times he had shared with his widowed sister and Dr. Franklin around a chess table in London. The last time he had seen the seventy-year-old diplomat they were friends and fellow Britons. Now they were enemies, separated by a piece of paper declaring independency of Great Britain's thirteen colonies now referred to by themselves as "states." *If only I had arrived sooner,* Howe lamented, *before Dr. Franklin committed treason by signing his name to that destructive parchment!*

The elder Franklin held up his walking cane in greeting as the barge approached. Howe returned a hand in greeting to Franklin and to the youthful twenty-seven-year-old South Carolinian Edward Rutledge. But the weathered Admiral frowned when he spotted the grumpy-looking forty-year-old John Adams. Before leaving London, Howe received a list of American rebels who would receive a pardon should peace be achieved. Dr. Franklin of course was on that list. John Adams was not. John Adams would be hanged for his treason, but not today. Little did Howe realize it, but Congress had wisely sent Adams to accompany Franklin to this meeting, knowing full-well that the peace-loving Franklin would so desire reconciliation with his old friend and beloved Mother Country that he might be swayed away from independence.

As the American delegation stepped off the barge, Howe was surprised to see that the officer he had sent over to retrieve the men had not stayed at Perth Amboy as a volunteer hostage. Howe sent him to guarantee that the delegates would not be seized as prisoners and would return safely back to New Jersey once the conference was over.

"Good-day, your Lordship," Franklin greeted Howe with a tip of his hat and bowing with a foot forward. "May I present my esteemed colleagues, Mr. John Adams of Massachusetts and Mr. Edward Rutledge of South Carolina." The men exchanged bows of courtesy.

"Welcome to Staten Island, gentlemen," Howe told them. "I am surprised to see my officer has returned with you."

"It was an absurd idea, sending a hostage," Adams noted brusquely, dabbing the sweat from his furrowed brow. "Your word of honor as a *gentleman* sending a craft with a white flag of truce was quite sufficient, Sir."

"I agreed, so we insisted your officer return with us," Franklin quickly added.

Howe nodded with a surprised smile. "Gentlemen, you make me a very high compliment, and you may depend upon it, I will consider it as the most sacred of things." He held out a hand leading up the path to the two-story, rubblestone masonry manor house. "Shall we?"

The path was lined by two rows of Hessian grenadiers wearing tall brass caps. As the men walked along between them, the Hessians grimaced and heralded the delegation by holding muskets with fixed bayonets in some sort of formal military salute that the Americans neither understood nor appreciated. Adams leaned over to Franklin and muttered, "They look as fierce as ten furies."

As they reached the hundred-year-old mansion built by Captain Christopher Billopp, it was clear that the house was currently being used as a barracks for the fierce Hessians lining the path and was therefore quite filthy. The entrance hall and parlor had been hastily prepared to make the two meeting rooms more appealing with fresh moss and flowering sprigs scattered across the oak floors.

"What splendid camouflage!" Nigel exclaimed, scampering in behind the men and taking cover under a patch of aromatic moss. "Jolly good for a mouse under cover. Now to see what shall become of this meeting of minds separated by an ocean and a declaration."

A gentle breeze and light poured in through the opened, blue-trimmed windows with window seats below. On another wall was a massive fireplace also trimmed in blue but covered by an ornately painted screen for the warm season. A large grandfather clock sat in the corner and rhythmically ticked off the seconds, and in the center of the room was a covered table set with a cold meal of ham, mutton, and glasses of claret wine.

As the men small-talked and the clock tick-tocked, Nigel was impatient for the pleasantries to give way to the discussion. "At least Al didn't miss dining on fish," he chuckled. After thirty minutes, Howe ordered the table cleared so they could get down to business. The Admiral made a few opening remarks and then got to the heart of the matter.

"As you know, my brother General Howe and I hold deep affection for America for the honor paid to our brother George who fell at Fort Ticonderoga in the war with the French. We especially appreciate the Massachusetts Assembly placing the marble memorial in Westminster Abbey in tribute to George. It is an honor I esteem above all," Howe began, holding a hand to John Adams, who gave a nod of recognition. "I feel for America as a brother. If America should fail, I should feel and lament it like the loss of a brother."

Benjamin Franklin leaned over and smiled through his spectacles. "My Lord, we will do our utmost endeavors to save your Lordship that mortification."

Howe tightened his lips, and his brow became furrowed. "I regret that I did not arrive sooner."

"You mean before the Declaration of Independence was signed?" Rutledge surmised.

"This Declaration has changed the ground," Howe explained with a nod. "If it were given up, however, I might possibly affect the king's purposes to restore peace and grant pardons. Our discussions could lead to a reunion upon terms honorable and advantageous to the colonies as well as to Great Britain. Is there no way of treading back this step of independency?"

Adams drummed the table with his fingers and shook his head before looking at Rutledge and Franklin.

"This declaration of independency has complicated my task, as I have no authority to consider the colonies in the light of independent states," Howe told them. "Nor can I acknowledge Congress as a legitimate body; therefore, I must negotiate with you not as *congressmen* but merely as gentlemen of ability and influence whom I hope will help put a stop to the calamities of war."

Franklin tapped the table and wore a congenial smile. "Indeed, this conversation might be held as amongst friends."

Adams looked straight at Howe with a wry smile. "Your Lordship may consider me in what light you please, and indeed, I should be willing to consider myself, for a few minutes, in any character which would be agreeable to your Lordship . . . except that of a British subject."

All that was heard was the tick-tock of the clock as the room fell silent for a moment.

"I would add that nothing shall make me depart from the idea of independency," Adams defiantly warned.

"Mr. Adams is a *decided* character," Howe retorted gravely, looking at Franklin and Rutledge. He straightened in his chair and cleared his throat to press on. "As the king's representative, let me assure you that his most earnest desire is to make his American subjects happy, but to do so, it requires renouncing independence. If America returns her allegiance and obedience to the government of Great Britain, it may be possible for her to control her own legislation and taxes. Indeed, America might once more provide solid advantages to the empire, in commerce and manpower."

Franklin gave a jolly chuckle and rested his hands atop his walking stick. "Aye, my Lord, we have a pretty considerable manufactory of men."

"In regard to the Olive Branch Petition which we made to the king, it contained all that we thought proper to be addressed to His Majesty," Rutledge interjected.

"Which the king did not even *bother* to read," Nigel scoffed.

"The other matters which could not come under the head of a petition and therefore could not with propriety be inserted were put into the address to the People," Rutledge continued. "The Declaration of Independence was meant to show them the importance of America to Great Britain. The Petition to the king was meant to be respectful."

The conversation proceeded in a circular pattern, going over the same points but getting nowhere. For the next two and a half hours, Howe did most of the talking.

"Lord Howe has no power whatsoever, but to grant pardons upon submission and discuss the issues with persons he thinks proper," Nigel observed, shaking his head. "What a pity! Nothing shall come of this meeting. Alas, we've all come here for nothing but a cold meal with no fish and not even a cube of cheese for a hungry mouse."

"I must urge you to put a stop to these ruinous extremities," Howe finally insisted.

"Remember the cockpit in London, Dr. Franklin!" Nigel quietly urged the aging statesman, willing him to remember how he had been humiliated by these same men who insisted that America lay down her arms and submit. "You became an American that day. Stick to your independent guns!"

"Forces have been sent out, and towns have been burnt. We cannot now expect happiness under the domination of Great Britain. All former attachments have been obliterated," Franklin shot back.

"Good show, my old kite-flying colleague!" Nigel cheered, raising a fist in the air.

"Each state has gone through a revolution, thereby stripping authority from the Crown and empowering the Congress and the local assemblies," Adams added. "There cannot and *will* not be a return to the old imperial ways of conduct between our countries."

"Might I add that perhaps Britain should seek alliances with the independent states before anything is settled with other foreign powers?" Rutledge suggested.

"*Vive la France!*" Nigel cheered, putting both paws in the air in response to Rutledge's veiled reference to France. The little mouse chuckled with a paw up to his mouth. "I cannot *believe* those words just came from my mouth! Liz would be quite proud of me."

Finally, Lord Howe frowned, and shrugged his shoulders. "I regret that you gentlemen had the trouble of coming so far for so little purpose."

The clock's tick-tock seemed to punctuate the loss of time.

"Well, my Lord, as America is to expect nothing but upon total, unconditional submission . . ."

"Britain did *not* require unconditional submission," Howe objected with a raised hand, interrupting Franklin. "I thought what we had already discussed proved the contrary. You gentlemen must not go away with such an idea."

Tick-tock. Tick-tock. Tick-tock.

"Well, the Declaration of Independence has happily passed its first test," Nigel noted. "Nothing remains now but to fight it out."

Admiral Howe rose to his feet. "I'm sorry to find no accommodation today. I shall escort you back to the barge."

As the men gathered their hats and left the house to walk back down the pathway, Nigel scurried out to follow them. Franklin, Adams, and Rutledge would travel back to Philadelphia. Admiral Howe would return to his flagship *Eagle*. And they would all write to their superiors about the stalemate of the Staten Island conference.

"Well, gentlemen, as our esteemed colleague Patrick Henry noted when he sounded the alarm last year in Virginia, 'Gentlemen may cry, "Peace, Peace!"—but there is no peace,'" John Adams quoted as the barge pulled away from the dock to head back to Perth Amboy.

Benjamin Franklin nodded and scanned New York Harbor, taking mental notes of the number of French ships that would be needed to destroy the British armada. "The war is actually begun! The next gale that sweeps from the north will bring to our ears the clash of resounding arms!" he continued, quoting Henry. "May Governor Henry's prophecies continue to unfold. Namely, the one about 'a just God who will raise up friends to fight our battles for us.' I'm suddenly inspired to pick up a new book when we return to Philadelphia."

"Which book would that be, Dr. Franklin?" Rutledge asked.

Franklin winked at the young statesman. "A French dictionary."

FROM OUTLAW TO OVID,
VOICE TO SWORD

GOVERNOR'S PALACE, WILLIAMSBURG, VIRGINIA,
SEPTEMBER 14, 1776

Forty-year-old Patrick Henry squinted against the bright sunshine as he opened the front door of the handsome brick Governor's Palace and stepped outside. He took in a deep breath and smiled as he gazed out across the long Palace Green stretched in front of him down to the distant Duke of Gloucester Street. He was happy to finally be well enough to return to his duties in Williamsburg following his recovery from malaria at Scotchtown. During his absence, the Virginia State Council ordered the Palace cleaned and prepared for the new governor to move in. The magnificent building and grounds were in poor condition following use as a military post for the newly formed Virginia army after Lord Dunmore's departure. The building and grounds were now a beehive of activity with workers making repairs to windows, doors, furniture, and outbuildings. New barracks and stables were also under construction to house six troops of dragoons after Governor Henry gladly gave up two hundred acres of park land at the Palace.

In his haste to depart the Palace and flee to the *HMS Fowey* in June 1775, previous royal governor Lord Dunmore left behind numerous personal items. Patrick decided they should be put up for public sale, with proceeds going to pay for Palace repairs. Patrick made his way down the front entrance steps and through the gate to where people surrounded items displayed there on Palace Green. He slowly walked along looking at the odd pieces of ornate furniture, pictures, books, and dishes stacked on wooden crates. Liz sauntered behind him with her curlycue tail high in the air as she also surveyed the items.

What a perfect day for a yard sale, no? Liz meowed. She jumped up on a crate where sat a stack of books. She read the spines and smiled as a volume of the ancient Roman poet Ovid caught her eye. She lifted the cover and saw that it was signed by Lord Dunmore himself. *How appropriate for you to purchase this book* mon *Henry,* she meowed.

"What do you have there, Liz?" Patrick asked as he leaned over to see what Liz was fiddling with. "Ah, Ovid. Father had us read the ancient classics of Greece and Rome—Ovid, Livy, Plutarch. I have always enjoyed studying great characters of antiquity." He chuckled and scratched her under the chin. "Of course, you wouldn't understand, little cat."

Liz rolled her eyes. *Like Cato, your favorite? If you only knew,* Monsieur. *I sat on Plutarch's desk and arranged for him to write about Cato. But of course, you would not understand,* mon ami.

Patrick raised his eyebrows when he noticed Dunmore's signature as he thumbed through the book. "Now *this* would be a fitting souvenir from the previous occupant of the Palace."

A book owned by the last royal governor of the colony of Virginia now in the possession of the first elected governor of the state of Virginia? Liz meowed with a coy grin. *But of course, it is perfect! Especially since Dunmore declared you an outlaw, and now you have moved into not only his mansion, but into his position as governor. From Outlaw to Ovid.* C'est magnifique!

Patrick reached into his pocket and lifted a few coins to pay for the book, which he tucked under his arm. He smiled and walked back toward the Palace, stopping at the front entrance to gaze up at the imposing iron gate that bore the royal crest of the king of England. A stone lion and a stone unicorn each sat atop the two brick gate piers, proud symbols of the British Empire. A memory flashed in his mind of standing at this very spot on April 1, 1760. He had ridden to Williamsburg on MizP to obtain a license to practice law. At the time he was living in a tiny cabin behind Hanover Tavern with his wife and small children after their house had burned to the ground. He had failed at everything he tried, and a law career was his last hope to make something of himself. Patrick smiled as he recalled his thoughts that day. *I can't imagine living in a place this grand.* The governor shook his head in grateful humility of all that God had done for him over the past sixteen years. He could scarcely believe that not only was he the most popular lawyer in Virginia with a wildly successful career, but he had soared to the heights of national politics representing Virginia at the Continental Congress, and now was the first elected governor of the largest state in America. He was a wartime governor, with the heavy responsibility of not only managing the affairs of his state, but also of supporting his longtime friend General Washington and the Continental Army in this war for independence. Patrick's oldest son, John, had just been made cornet for the 1st Virginia Cavalry, so he also had a personal stake in supporting the army.

Suddenly twelve-year-old William and nine-year-old Anne came bounding out of the Palace, running down the stairs toward Patrick. "Father! Do you want to go exploring in the maze with us?" Anne asked excitedly, gripping his arm.

Patrick smiled and fondly cupped Anne under the chin. "Later, perhaps, little girl. I have much work to do. But you two explore and let me know what you discover. William, take care of your sister. Don't get lost in the maze."

"I shall not get lost, Father! We're going to get some gingerbread cookies and leave some crumbs, so we don't get lost," William exclaimed, taking Anne by the hand. "Come on, Anne."

Patrick watched his children hurry down the path of crushed oyster shells toward the side of the Palace to the kitchen outbuilding. He was happy to see them excited to live here at the Palace. There were plenty of outdoor spaces to occupy them, including the intricate green maze of tall hedges, a lush garden with ornately designed topiary plants, flowers, vine-covered arbors, and oyster-shell paths leading to a beautiful canal graced by lily pads. Delicate weeping willow branches kissed the water as swans glided across the surface.

Governor Henry was a widower with six children, so his sisters Anne and Elizabeth moved in with him to serve as temporary hostesses. Twenty-one-year-old Martha also followed to take charge of her father's household, just as she had done at Scotchtown when her mother Sallie died. "Patsey" would care for the children, along with her own infant son, Patrick Henry Fontaine. For now, it was thought best to leave Patrick's two youngest children (five-year-old Neddy and seven-year-old Betsey) with their grandmother back in Hanover.

"Oh, Sallie, how I wish you could see where we live now," Patrick whispered softly as he headed back inside to reach his study.

Liz frowned with a sad lump in her throat. "We must find you another wife, *mon* Henry. It is not good for man to be alone, no? But, first things first." The petite black cat walked off to go see MizP in the stables behind the Palace.

MizP happily trotted over to the edge of the pasture under a shady tree and shook her mane contentedly in the refreshing breeze. Yellow buttercups and green grass filled the pasture, and butterflies darted about, landing gracefully on the flowers. Everywhere she looked was beauty.

"How do you like your new accommodations, *mon amie?*" Liz asked, jumping up on the fence railing. "Is the Palace all you had hoped it would be?"

"Does a one-legged duck swim in circles?" quipped MizP. "Pahtrick has landed all of us in heavenly quarters! Of course, seeing how the Palace was turned intuh an army barracks, I'm glad we didn't see how messy it was before our arrival. But the stables are spacious and filled with fresh hay and water, and the pasture gives me lots of room tuh run. I love it here, Liz!"

Liz curled her tail around her feet and grinned. "I am so very happy to hear it, MizP. The children are quite happy, too. I heard Patrick softly wishing Sallie were here with him. He never speaks of her to others, but I know he is lonely for a companion."

"Those children need a mother, too. Maybe Pahtrick will meet a young filly here in Williamsburg tuh marry," MizP suggested.

"*Oui,* I agree. We shall keep our eyes out for prospects, no?" Liz answered. "But Patrick's hands are quite full now as he settles into his governorship. I know that Lieutenant Governor John Page is relieved to have him back at the helm after managing things here since July."

"Governors must push a lot of paper around, and I know Pahtrick won't enjoy that part of his job," MizP added. "But he was still plenty busy with important business in Scotchtown last month with them Baptists visiting him and that George Rogers Clark business."

Liz nodded. "*Mon* Henry was more than happy to further the cause of religious freedom for Baptists and all dissenters, as has been his passion for many years. He promised to guard their rights to worship and operate freely, and in turn gained their support to join the war effort."

"Pahtrick learned from his mentor Reverend Samuel Davies how tuh use the power of the pulpit in the last war," MizP added. "'May God crown our arms with success!' he told them Baptists. We're surely going tuh need it, given the bad news from New York."

Liz wrinkled her brow. "*Oui,* the *Gazette* reported Washington's safe retreat following the defeat on Long Island. I do hope Clarie comes to update us on things soon. I desire to know more details. And Patrick, of course, needs more details on whether the British will threaten Virginia's waters by sending ships here."

"Well, at least Pahtrick sent that red-haired, shaggy George Rogers Clark fella tuh get the Kentucky frontier secure from the hostile Indians *and* from the British," MizP offered. "Virginia has a lot of land tuh protect."

"*Oui,* Clark was wise to let Patrick know about the Kentuckians' fear that Dunmore's 1774 treaty with Indian tribes northwest of the Ohio could collapse," Liz asserted with a furrowed brow. "British agents are stirring things up with those neutral Indian tribes, and if they band together, they could attack Virginia from the west."

"Not to mention the angry Cherokee to the south," MizP added, pawing the ground with her hoof. "Things are testy every which way for Virginia."

"We shall pray that the five hundred pounds of gunpowder that Patrick authorized for Clark will go far in aiding Kentucky's defense," Liz said. "Clark will organize that defense, and Virginia will organize a government in Kentucky to secure that land. Patrick is so very wise, no?"

"Does a fish get wet?" MizP answered with a snort. "He's got a Scotsman's nose for wise land deals. And something tells me that Kentucky will make for good horse country as well."

"Undoubtedly it will, MizP," came the voice of Clarie, now in the form of a lamb walking up to them in the meadow.

"Clarie! How lovely to see you in your sweet form," Liz exclaimed, jumping down to kiss her on the cheek.

"And *surprising,* little lamb," MizP added with a wink.

"Sometimes I get tired of being a human, especially in the middle of a war," Clarie told them. "It feels good to just be myself for a change! I have lots of news from New York."

"We heard about the defeat at Long Island yesterday in the *Gazette,*" Liz offered. "Did Jock have anything to do with the fog that helped Washington to escape?"

Clarie nodded and smiled. "Yes! Jock *made* the fog. He's been a busy weather-dog in this war so far. The Maker was wise to add him to our team's efforts to help the humans with weather miracles."

"*C'est bon!* I know Max is quite proud of his grandlad," Liz cheered. "Tell us what has happened since, *s'il vous plaît.*"

"Nigel attended a failed peace attempt at Staten Island between Admiral Howe and John Adams, Benjamin Franklin, and Edward Rutledge," Clarie reported. "While the meeting went nowhere, it bought Washington and the army some much needed time to plan their further retreat from Manhattan."

"I see. So, New York cannot be defended," Liz realized with a frown. "It was too much to ask to defend such a place with so much water, especially without a navy."

"I bet General Washington has learned a thing or two so far," MizP assumed.

"Indeed, he has, MizP," Clarie answered. "He quickly learned that the Continental Army will not win this war by fighting the British Army head-to-head on the field of battle, but by fighting a defensive war with limited engagements. He also now knows he needs soldiers with lengthier enlistments to secure a reliable army. He can't run a war with militias and troops coming and going in such short periods of time. And, Washington has learned that he needs better intelligence to understand the enemy's plans and movements."

"You mean he's learning how tuh live tuh fight another day?" MizP suggested.

"That's right," Clarie agreed. "And I need to get back to New York to help them do just that. We're expecting General Howe to strike at any time. I'll be back soon to serve as an express courier between Patrick Henry and Washington, and will tell you more then."

"*Bonne chance, mon amie,*" Liz told her. "But before you go, tell me, does Washington have any spies at his disposal?"

"He just sent a spy to Long Island acting like a schoolteacher looking for work," Clarie answered. "A young man by the name of Nathan Hale."

"His Excellency" Governor Patrick Henry hit the ground running in Williamsburg, sitting in at his first council meeting on September 17th, 1776. He sat at the head of the same oval table on the second floor of the Capitol Building where previous royal governors had dissolved the House of Burgesses, sending them to reconvene at the Raleigh Tavern. The irony of places and the turning of events continued to unfold. Although Patrick was governor, his powers were limited in scope, and he was obligated to heed the advice of a five-man council consisting of Tidewater planters who lived close to Williamsburg: John Page, Dudley Digges, John Blair, Bartholomew Dandridge, and Benjamin Harrison of Brandon. The new Virginia Constitution made sure that as authority shifted from the Crown to the people, the governing power now rested in the hands of the Virginia Assembly, not the governor. Patrick couldn't call or dissolve the legislature or veto their actions. While frustrated with having his hands tied on some things, Patrick vowed to govern as best he could to fight three wars: the general cause, Virginia's frontier, and defense of the eastern seaboard from British attack.

His daily routine consisted of handling the infinite details of managing the war with men and supplies, endless paperwork of bills, proclamations, council orders, and writing letters. From dawn until dusk, Patrick Henry was consumed with business. There was no time for playing in the maze with his children. He realized he needed wisdom to fulfill his obligations well, and his thoughts turned to his friend, the Commander-in-Chief.

TO: General George Washington,
Commander-in-Chief of the Continental Army
Williamsburgh Sept. 20th 1776

Dear Sir.
After a long & Severe Illness, I am now but just able

to come hither in Order to discharge as I may be able, the Dutys of my public Station. Will you pardon me for asking the Favor of a Correspondence with you? Besides the pleasure it will give me, I shall be taught by your Ideas, to form more correct Opinions, of those Movements that may be proposed for the general Defence in this Quarter.

Liz smiled, thinking of the long friendship that Patrick shared with George Washington. They had ridden together to attend the Continental Congress in Philadelphia. And it was to Patrick Henry that Washington tearfully confided his anxious fears after being appointed Commander-in-Chief: *Remember, Mr. Henry, what I now tell you. From the day I enter upon the command of the American armies, I date my fall, and the ruin of my reputation.* The Voice of the Revolution then sharpened the blade of the Sword of the Revolution with words of encouragement and affirmation of Washington's calling for such a time as this in America. Henry promised to pray for Washington, and Liz knew that he had kept his word. Now Governor Henry sought General Washington's advice for the defense of Virginia against British forces that might invade her waters following the New York campaign.

We have heard of the Affair at Long Island. I trust every virtuous man will be stimulated by it to fresh Exertions. My poor friend Sullivan I hear is a prisoner, & Report says at Congress to offer Terms of peace. I should not think he would be the Bearer of disadvantageous Offers.

I can readily guess the infinite Variety of Affairs with which you are worried. God grant you may end the glorious Work in which you are so nobly engaged & be crown'd with Success. With Sentiments of the most perfect Esteem I am Dear sir yr most obt Servt

P. Henry Jr.

Liz of course already knew that Sullivan's message to Congress resulted in the failed peace meeting on Staten Island. It was frustrating for her to know much more than her human assignees, at times. Still, she was glad that she knew the results before they did. She wrinkled her brow, remembering Henry's words to Washington in that private conversation in Philadelphia: *Always be as sly as a fox among wolves, for they will ever be out for your blood.*

GOVERNOR'S PALACE, WILLIAMSBURG, VIRGINIA, OCTOBER 14, 1776

MizP's jet black coat bristled against the chilly morning, and her steamy breath rose in the air as she stepped outside the stable. She looked up at the vibrant blue Virginia sky and knew the day would warm up as the sun rose above the trees.

"*Bonjour*, MizP," Liz greeted her. "It looks to be a beautiful day, no?"

"There's enough blue sky tuh knit a cat a pair of britches, so yes," MizP answered, flipping aside her black mane. She had a tiny white star on her forehead, just beneath the forelock of hair between her large brown eyes. "These fall Virginia mornings give way tuh sunshine that warms this old mare's hide."

"And it warms my black fur as well," Liz added with a grin, stretching out next to the fence.

"Good morning, ladies," came the voice of Clarie, now in the form of a courier.

"I am so happy to see you, *mon amie*," Liz replied. "What news do you have for us?"

"And is it *good* news?" MizP asked.

"I have plenty of news, but unfortunately it is not good." Clarie frowned and leaned against the fence, shaking her head. "It's hard to know where to start. So much has happened in New York."

"The beginning is usually a good place tuh start," MizP suggested.

"Well, I last told you of the failed peace meeting on Staten Island on September 11th," Clarie began. "After going back and forth on the matter, on September 12th Washington and his officers decided to abandon the city. He had reconfigured his army into three divisions that stretched over fourteen miles, but they had to try to figure out where the British were going to land and attack while retreating."

"So that is why Washington needed to send a spy to Long Island, no?" Liz asked.

"What happened tuh that young spy fella he sent, Nathan Hale?" MizP interjected.

"*Oui*, did he accomplish his mission?" Liz followed.

Clarie looked at the ground. "Sadly, no. But I'll get to that in a moment. So, the Continental Army moved up to Harlem Heights, but about three to four thousand men remained in New York City with Old Put. Meanwhile, according to Al, General Howe and General Clinton argued about where to attack. Once again, Howe ignored Clinton's advice to seize King's Bridge north of them and trap the Americans once and for all on Manhattan. Howe instead decided to land at Kip's Bay on the west bank of the East River, across from Long Island."

"*Mon* Albert provides the best intelligence," Liz noted proudly.

"That continual bickering between the British commanders will only help our cause!" MizP said with a nod. "What happened next?"

"On September 15th, the British positioned battleships with eighty cannons offshore and unloaded nine thousand British and Hessian troops," Clarie told them. "When Washington heard the guns roaring, he took off on Blueskin from his new headquarters in Harlem Heights and galloped four miles on the Post Road to reach Kip's Bay."

"Those young American soldiers must have been terrified!" Liz exclaimed with a paw to her mouth.

"They were, Liz. And they started running," Clarie told her. "General Washington arrived at the battle and saw the militia and regiments fleeing in the face of the enemy. He was most furious to see officers running and their men following their example. Washington threw his hat on the ground and exclaimed, 'Are these the men with which I am to defend America?' The enemy was only eighty yards away, but the general was so furious at the conduct of his troops that he continued to wildly ride into the fray, trying to stop them. Max was beside himself, barking the alarm, so I ran over. Washington was in such danger that I had to seize Blueskin's reins and move the General in a different direction."

"That man must have been as mad as a hornet's nest knocked down by a bear tuh do that," MizP opined.

"Meanwhile, Old Put acted fast to lead the remaining soldiers out of the city to escape to Harlem Heights before they became trapped by the redcoats," Clarie added. "He left Colonels Knox and Silliman in charge of the city at the bottom of the island, but Old Put's aide Major Aaron Burr soon arrived with orders for them to abandon their cannons and leave. They barely escaped with their lives."

Liz's face showed her concern. "I am sure that Max and Jock were in the thick of things at all times, especially with their humans in harm's way."

"They were indeed!" Clarie answered. "Even though the Americans' pride was hurt by having to retreat, they lived to fight another day. And those fleeing militiamen at Kip's Bay actually sped up the retreat that Washington's generals had decided they needed to carry out anyway."

"Running away is not always a bad thing, if it's the smart thing," MizP philosophized.

"Well, on the next day, September 16th, the British advanced again, and that Banastre Tarleton sounded the fox horn as if they were on a fox hunt. It was such an insult that a small American reconnaissance force under Colonel William Knowlton, the hero of Bunker Hill, rallied and were able to drive back a detachment of British light infantry. They soon had eighteen hundred Americans from every state fighting for two hours until the British ran low on ammunition and retreated. Washington's army had a small but needed victory at the Battle of Harlem Heights. For once, they finally saw the *British* turn and run."

"Well, HUZZAH for *that!*" MizP snorted. "Sometimes we all just need the tiniest of victories tuh keep us going."

"*Oui,* I am happy they were able to have a small success," Liz agreed. "What happened next, *mon amie?*"

"Yes, that small victory gave Washington's army a morale boost, and it caused Howe to pause his forward movement," Clarie relayed, suddenly frowning. "Sadly, fearless Colonel Knowlton died that day when a musket ball hit him in the back. He was a simple thirty-seven-year-old farmer from Connecticut, but I heard one of his grieving men say that Knowlton never said, 'Go on, boys!' but always, 'Come on, boys!' When they helped him off the field gasping in agony, the only thing he wanted to know is if they had driven the enemy back."

"That's the way heroes lead," MizP observed somberly. "He gave his all that day."

"*Quel dommage!*" Liz lamented. "Such is the price of liberty."

"Well, the British then suffered another setback," Clarie continued. "Someone set the city on fire just after midnight on September 21st and strong winds drove the flames north a mile wide to consume one thousand buildings. The fire essentially destroyed a quarter of the city, including Trinity Church."

"Oh, no!" Liz exclaimed. "But who set the fire?"

"Although General Nathanael Greene a while ago had first suggested that they do just that, Congress wouldn't allow it, so it wasn't the Americans," Clarie reported. "Washington wrote his cousin that, *Providence, or some good, honest fellow has done more for us than we were disposed of to do for ourselves.* The fire deprived the British of much needed barracks and provisions for the coming winter, plus it made them paranoid. General Howe, of course, blamed the Americans, and ordered the roundup of two hundred suspects. No one was convicted, and all were released, but this is where Nathan Hale's story reaches its sad end." Clarie teared up.

Liz and MizP shared a somber look. "Go on, sugah. Tell us what happened," MizP encouraged her.

"Well, as I shared with you before, on September 12th General Washington had asked for someone to step up and try to find out where the British would land on Manhattan," Clarie reminded them. "Twenty-one-year-old Hale volunteered and disguised himself as a Dutch schoolmaster. He slipped behind enemy lines on Long Island and over the next few days gathered information about British troop movements. Of course, while he was over there, the British landed at Kip's Bay and took control of the city. When the fire broke out, Howe put his soldiers on high alert for Patriot movements. Hale tried to sneak back to Manhattan by crossing Long Island Sound, but the British caught him on September 21st."

"Oh, my!" Liz exclaimed fearfully. "What did they do to him?"

"They searched Hale and discovered he was carrying incriminating sketches and notes, so General Howe ordered his execution for spying," Clarie answered. "The next morning, he was led to the gallows, and when asked if he had any last words, he replied, 'I only regret that I have but one life to lose for my country.'"

Liz's eyes filled with tears. "He was quoting the line from Addison's play, *Cato.*"

"The same play where Pahtrick got his 'liberty or death' line," MizP followed.

Clarie nodded and wiped away a tear. "Captain Nathan Hale was following the brave, bold leadership of his commander, Colonel Knowlton."

"Bravery begets bravery," MizP offered quietly.

"Washington also learned the hard lesson that they must conduct espionage with far greater planning," Clarie noted. "Hale was not given any training, money, or safe contacts to turn to for help on Long Island. He also had no means of communication with headquarters."

"Hale's mission was obviously poorly planned," Liz suggested with a frown. "The poor boy did not even have invisible ink to write down what he discovered, which could have saved his life!"

"He was also too honest for spy work," Clarie added. "He was not a good liar, plus he had scars on his face from a gunpowder explosion that made him easy to remember. And his cousin, Samuel Hale, is the British army's deputy commissioner of prisoners, so could easily identify him."

"Did anyone try tuh stop the boy from going in the first place?" MizP wanted to know.

"Yes, but even when his friend told him that espionage carried a stigma of dishonor and deceit, Hale replied, 'Every kind of service, necessary to the public good, becomes honorable by being necessary,'" Clarie relayed. She frowned and slapped her thigh. "Hale was denied his two last requests for a Bible and for a clergyman to be present."

MizP stomped the ground angrily. "Why, those hateful redcoats! How dare they deny that boy the spiritual comfort he deserved!"

"C'est tragique!" Liz added, slapping her tail on the ground. "I am sure the British took out their anger from the fire on that dear boy."

Clarie nodded. "They left him hanging for several days as a warning to other rebels. Some British soldiers even hung a wooden painted figure of a gentleman next to Hale with a sign that read, 'George Washington.'"

"So, what now?" MizP asked.

"The British army is at a standstill for the moment, so Washington continues to pull back north of the city," Clarie answered, reaching in her satchel to retrieve a letter. "I've brought Washington's reply to Patrick Henry's letter." She squatted down next to Liz. "But it's time for you to bid Patrick farewell for a time. It's time for you to go join Kate in France to help her with the Lafayette part of our mission."

Liz sighed and nodded, looking up at the Governor's Palace. "While I very much look forward to returning to my beloved France and assisting Kate, I shall miss *mon* Henry. But at least he is safe and secure here for now."

"I'll be sure tuh keep an eye on things, Liz," MizP assured her, lowering her head to nudge the petite cat. "And if the enemy comes knocking on that Palace door, I'll gallop up the steps and knock them redcoats back myself."

Liz smiled and kissed MizP on the cheek. "I know you will, *mon amie.* Very well, I shall spend a few minutes with *mon* Henry, and then be on my way to France. I shall leave *mon* Albert a note in the War Room," she said with a warm smile. "I could do with his humor right now."

Clarie giggled. "Well, I'll tell you that after the Americans retreated after having beat the British at Harlem Heights, Al said, 'It sounds like the laddies failed well!'"

Liz giggled. *"Merci, mon amie.* I needed this, no? Very well, I shall go bid *mon* Henry *adieu."*

"You'll be glad to know that Congress decided to send Benjamin Franklin to join Silas Deane in Paris to secure a French alliance," Clarie added. "He is already on his way to France, so you will see him there. And I will see you in France at some point as well."

"C'est bon," Liz replied. She nudged MizP. *"Adieu,* MizP."

"Bone voyagee, Liz," MizP said in a very southern accent, butchering her French.

To Governor Patrick Henry, Jr., ESQ

Head Quarters Heights of Harlem Octor 5th 1776

Dr Sir

    Your Obliging favor of the 20th Ulto came duly to hand, and demands my best acknowledgments. I congratulate You Sir most cordially upon your appointment to the Government & with no less sincerity on your late recovery—Your Correspondence will confer honor and satisfaction, and whenever it is in my power I shall write to you with pleasure—Our retreat from Long Island under the peculiar Circumstances we then labored became an Act of Prudence and necessity, and the Evacuation of New York was a consequence resulting from the other—Indeed after we discovered the Enemy, instead of making an Attack upon the City, were endeavouring (by means of their Ships and a superior Land Force) either to intercept our retreat by getting in our Rear, or else by landing their forces between our Divisions at Kingsbridge & those in the Town to seperate the one from the other, it became a matter of the last importance to alter the disposition of the Army.

Liz jumped up onto Patrick Henry's desk as he read Washington's letter, interrupting him. His Ovid book was sitting there opened on the desk. He had just signed his name in the front next to Lord Dunmore's signature and was letting the ink dry. *Perfect,* mon *Henry!* she meowed.

Surprised, Patrick put down the letter and reached out a hand to scratch Liz behind the ears. "Hello, little Liz. What is so important that you must interrupt my reading a letter from the Commander-in-Chief?" he asked with a chuckle.

We shall not fight our battles alone, Liz meowed softly, quoting from Patrick's Liberty or Death Speech. *You've known since the beginning of tensions between America and Great Britain that the French would come to America's aid. I must leave you now to go make sure that your words come true. Who better than a French* chatte *to secure an alliance with France, no?*

Patrick wrinkled his brow at her lengthy meow and gave a curious smile. "It truly does seem like you are trying to tell me something important. I wish I knew what it was."

Liz nudged the Ovid and smiled. *Someday you will understand,* mon

Henry. But you have things well in hand here to lead Virginia. You are no longer an outlaw, but the Voice of the Revolution, and I know you will support the Sword of the Revolution as he leads his army to escape from New York. Do not be sad when you no longer see me. I shall return, mon *Henry.* She affectionately head-butted Patrick on the forehead. *Adieu.*

With that, the petite French cat jumped off the desk and left the room to use the family Bible in the parlor to reach the War Room, stopping first of course to dip her paw in a dish of milk.

Escaping Defeat

THE WAR ROOM

A l's head remained covered with a red cloth while Clarie set him down in a soft leather chair. He slowly lifted his paws to the long table and tapped the hardwood in multiple places to confirm that he was sitting in a solid place. "Sure, and that's a relief," he exclaimed, pulling the cloth down onto the sleek table with a goofy grin.

Gillamon sat smiling at the head of the table in the form of a very dirty, disheveled Mr. Atticus. His shirt was scorched and torn, his three-cornered hat had a hole in the rim, and his face was bloodied from a cut on his face. "Glad you could join us, Al."

"I'm always happy to join ye, when I know I'm joinin' ye in one piece," Al answered. His eyes widened in alarm to see Gillamon in such disarray. "But it looks like *ye* barely made it through the portal, lad! This is exactly *why* I be so scared to come here!"

Max shook his head at his scaredy cat friend. "Still doesn't get it even after all these years . . . daft kitty."

Gillamon chuckled softly. "I've just come from the battlefront in upstate New York where I must look the part to blend in."

"As must I," Clarie added, removing her hat, and mussing her dirty hair. Her clothes were stained with dirt and grime, and her face was blackened from gunpowder and musket fire. "I can't wait to take a bath."

Max sniffed the air and wrinkled his nose. "Aye, I can't wait for ye ta take a bath either. Ye an' Gillamon *both.*" He leaned over to Nigel and Al and whispered, "Humans can r-r-really stink."

"I think it makes them blend in, like Gillamon said," Al suggested.

"Right, well, um, I do say, it's utterly *thrilling* to have the old team reunited once again, what? Except for Liz, Kate, and little Jock, that is," Nigel chimed in, walking down the middle of the table with his paws clenched in dramatic form. "Here we are, serving on opposite sides of this tumultuous conflict and now bringing our sharp minds together via this War Council to unravel betwixt us the human strategic machinations of the war juggernaut barreling through New York!"

Al's mouth slowly moved, and he stared blankly as he attempted to decipher what Nigel had just said.

"Wha' the lad means, Big Al, is that Gillamon wanted ta br-r-ring us all together ta talk aboot wha's happened with the humans over the past month in the war, since he weren't with us," Max explained. "Jest tell wha' ye know an' saw aboot the Br-r-ritsh side of things."

Al pointed a fluffy paw to his head with a wink. "Sure, and ye're all in luck! I've brought me sharp mind to the table. What do ye want to know?"

Nigel and Max shared a tight-lipped look, stifling their mirth.

Clarie cleared her throat. "Ahem, perhaps Gillamon could first give us *his* news from the Battle of Valcour Island, and then we can fill him in on what has happened here in New York since the Battle of Harlem Heights?"

Gillamon nodded with a warm smile. "I think that's a grand idea, Clarie. Nigel, you may wish to step aside for a moment."

"Certainly, old chap!" Nigel quickly answered, scurrying over to where Max and Al sat.

Gillamon rolled out a map of upper New York with the border of Canada. He then spread out his fingers over the map, making it zoom into the scene of the battle at Valcour Island.

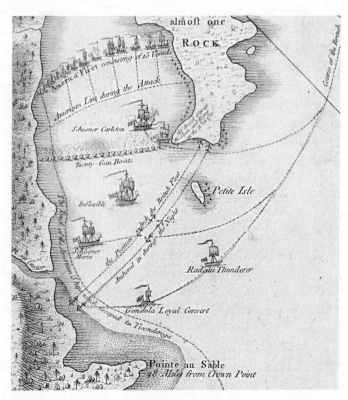

Gillamon then hovered his hand over the map, causing the corners to ripple, and a three-dimensional diorama came to life with moving water, bobbing ships, and mountains. Whitecaps crested on the water, and the names of the ships floated above them in the air.

"Now then, while you've been assisting the humans in southern New York, I've been assisting them in the uppermost reaches of New York, just south of the border with Canada," Gillamon explained.

"*Inflexible?*" Al asked, reading the name of one of the British ships. He reached out to dip his paw in Lake Champlain, but Max slapped it back with his burly paw, growling, "Not this time, kitty."

"In December 1775 the Northern Department of the Continental Army suffered a disastrous defeat in the Battle of Quebec, with General Richard Montgomery killed, General Benedict Arnold wounded, and Daniel Morgan taken prisoner along with four hundred other men," Gillamon began. As he hovered his hand over the map, each place he mentioned lit up with blue light. "Then in the spring of 1776, more than ten thousand British and Hessian troops arrived in Quebec. Canada's Governor, General Guy Carleton, and those British forces drove the Continental Army out of Quebec all the way back to Fort Ticonderoga and Crown Point."

"Fort Ti, where Jock got the guns with Henry Knox that dr-r-rove the Br-r-rits out of Boston," Max reminded them.

"Indeed. Over the summer, General Arnold proceeded to build an American Navy at Crown Point," Gillamon continued. "His men assembled a fleet of roughly sixteen vessels with seventy guns. Meanwhile, Carleton decided to launch a new offensive to reach the Hudson River near the southern tip of Lake Champlain by Crown Point with nine-thousand men and a fleet of two hundred vessels with ninety guns."

"Oh, dear, that does not sound like a fair fight at *all*," Nigel worried, his arms crossed as he saw the string of British ships sailing south. "But of course, the Continental Army is the David to the British Goliath!"

Gillamon nodded. "Right you are, Nigel. So, on October 11th, Benedict Arnold lured the British fleet into a strategic naval battle at Valcour Island."

"What happened? Did the Benedict win? Was the *Inflexible* flexible?" Al wanted to know, enthralled with the map of bobbing ships. He couldn't resist tapping the *Inflexible* with his paw, getting wet. He smiled at seeing the bobbing ship lean over, and quickly pulled back his paw, flicking saltwater in Max's eye. "Ha, it be *flexible!*"

"Gr-r-r," Max growled, tightly closing his stinging eye.

"Unfortunately, no, many of the American ships were damaged or destroyed," Gillamon reported. "The night following the battle, Arnold managed to sail the American fleet quietly by the British ships to start a retreat toward Crown Point and Ticonderoga. But bad weather hampered the retreat, and even more of the American vessels were either captured, grounded, or intentionally burned to keep them out of British hands."

"If only Jock had been there!" Max lamented.

"What did General Arnold do after that?" Clarie wanted to know, once again preventing Al from stretching out his paw.

"He decided they could no longer hold Crown Point as a defensive position against the British armada, so he destroyed and abandoned the fort, and moved those forces eleven miles south to Fort Ticonderoga with the rest of his men," Gillamon explained.

Nigel clasped his paws behind his back and rolled up and down on his back feet. "Right, so I presume that Carleton then occupied Crown Point? Does he intend to venture southward and capture Fort Ticonderoga?"

Gillamon nodded. "Carleton's forces indeed occupied Crown Point for two weeks, but he returned some of our prisoners to Fort Ticonderoga under a flag of truce rather than hauling them back to Canada. With the first snowfall on October 20th, it was clear to both sides that battle season was over and Carleton's forces needed to withdraw north back to winter quarters."

"So, it looks like Arnold failed, an' the patr-r-riots had ta r-r-retr-r-eat in northern New York jest like they had ta do with us in southern New York," Max realized with a disappointed sigh.

"Maybe he drank too much of the champagne in that lake," Al lamented.

"Lake *Champlain,* not champagne, old boy," Nigel corrected him.

Gillamon lifted a finger in the air and smiled. "On the contrary, Max. General Arnold *succeeded* in his attempt to delay the British forces from barreling down from Lake Champlain to the Hudson to join Howe's forces and crush the Americans."

Clarie clapped. "Huzzah! Now I see! If Benedict Arnold's forces hadn't delayed the British up there, this war would not just be hanging by a thread, it would be *over.*"

"Precisely, Clarie," Gillamon affirmed with a twinkle in his eye. "The northern army escaped defeat and lived to fight another day. Now, tell me about how things have unfolded in southern New York since the Battle of Harlem Heights."

"May I?" Nigel asked, lifting a paw as he looked to Max, Al, and Clarie, who nodded. "Right. Well, one could argue that the event of October 9th foreshadowed the doom of things to come. Three British ships once more sailed up the Hudson and past the American forts, again *proving* that Forts Washington and Lee are useless for their intended purpose. Washington observed the humiliating spectacle but made no changes to the American strategy. Then Nathanael Greene *doubled* his resolve that the army and forts were so strongly positioned that there was 'little more to fear this campaign.'"

"Fort Lee?" Gillamon asked.

"Forgive me, yes, Fort *Constitution* was renamed Fort *Lee* in honor of the hero from the Battle of Sullivan's Island, General Charles Lee," Nigel explained. "Lee arrived at New York on October 14th and resumed his position as Second in Command. I'm happy to report that Generals Sullivan and Stirling also returned through a prisoner exchange, so Washington was quite relieved to have his top commanders back by his side."

"I see. Al, can you tell me about the British side of things and what they did next?" Gillamon asked, withdrawing the map of Valcour Island so the curious cat would focus.

Al sat up and beamed to be asked his opinion, forgetting the map. "Glad to, Gillamon! I'll tell ye all aboot the British plan. Sure, Howe decided to follow Washington up, up, up Manhattan Island to try to defeat the rebel army once and for all. I were with them on October 12th when Howe sailed one hundred fifty ships through that scary Hell Gate in thick fog to make it to a funny place named Frog's Neck."

"Throgg's Neck, old boy," Nigel corrected him. "But in all fairness, that area is also referred to as Frog's Neck, I suspect due to the butchering of the name with phonetic reasoning."

Max rolled his eyes. "Gillamon, all ye need ta know is that it weren't a good landin' spot, an' a br-r-rave group of twenty-five American r-r-riflemen kept them Br-r-rits stopped in their tr-r-racks at the shoreline."

"I'll add that General Howe decided for the soldiers to reembark and wait for more supplies and reinforcements, which took another four days," Clarie interjected.

"General Clinton were really irritated about Frog's Neck and called it 'Tweedeldum business,' whatever that is. But he were happy when seven thousand brand new Hessians arrived with their new General Wilhelm von Knyphausen," Al reported. He then wrinkled his brow, deep in thought. "I didn't know frogs had necks. Their heads look as if they're attached at their bellies. So how can ye call a place something that don't exist?"

"Thr-r-rog's Neck or Fr-r-rog's Neck, don't matter wha' ye call it, daft kitty," Max huffed. "The point be that when they landed at the Froggy place, Washington knew they were sittin' in a tr-r-rap at Harlem Heights. Them R-r-redcoats only needed ta land up above them at King's Br-r-ridge," Max explained. "That's when he decided they best move eighteen miles north ta White Plains in Westchester County."

"Quite right. Might I add to the chronology of events that on Oct. 16th, Washington's War Council decided that despite the failure of obstructions to keep British ships out of the Hudson, that Fort Washington be retained as long as possible," Nigel added. "The point being to keep communications across the river to New Jersey open while the army retreated."

Al raised his paw in the air.

"Yes, Al?" Gillamon said with a grin.

"So THEN, on October 18th Howe landed at Pell's Point with four thousand British and Hessian soldiers," Al added. "That place must be named for pelicans because they have pointy beaks. And long necks, unlike frogs."

"I can report that at first British forces landed unopposed, but then Colonel John Glover saw what was happening and brought seven hundred fifty of his Marblehead men down to hide behind stone walls and fire on them," Nigel added with his arms raised as if shooting a gun.

"Aye, them Marbleheads gave the enemy a r-r-rout! The Br-r-ritish lost more at Pell's Point than in the Battle of Br-r-rooklyn, while the Americans lost a small number of lads," Max noted.

"General Clinton thought there must have been nearly fourteen thousand Americans firin' away at them. But unlike frogs, those Marblehead lads must have necks o' steel to support such heavy heads," Al interjected with a furrowed brow, again thinking deeply about things. He patted his fluffy head proudly. "I'm glad me head be as light as a feather, with a neck that's just right to sit on."

They all looked at one another and rolled their eyes. "Ye can say that again, Big Al. Ye be a bit light-headed then."

"Well, anyhoo, I can tell ye that the pell-mell at Pell's Point made Howe act like a turtle again and slow down," Al told the group. "He were worried there could be rebels hidin' behind every stone wall with rifles, so he moved his lads to the high ground at New Rochelle and stayed put until October 21st."

"Which allowed Washington time he desperately needed to get ahead of Howe and up to the safety of White Plains by October 23rd. White Plains is a quaint village of only seventy houses spread over 4,400 acres," Nigel added. "Washington made headquarters at the Jacob Purdy House in the center of the American lines and met with our brilliant Chief Engineer from Dorchester Heights, Colonel Rufus Putnam, on the best defensive position for the army to dig in. Putnam rode bravely to survey twenty-eight miles of land in fifty hours, even escaping capture as a spy to bring Washington a report!"

"Howe weren't in a hurry but wanted to try and get Washington to come out and fight on the open field there so he could whip the ragtag rebels in one big victory," Al explained.

"Washington an' the Americans dug in on the high gr-r-round along a line for a mile str-r-retched over Chatterton Hill, Purdy Hill, an' Merritt Hill," Max reported. "They had a natural defensive position with rivers an' wetlands between them an' the r-r-redcoats. Fr-r-rom the bottom of Purdy Hill almost ta the Br-r-ronx R-r-river there be thick swamps."

"While the Americans dug in, Howe thankfully waited ten long days before he moved. Then came the bright, crisp fall day of October 28th," Nigel recalled with a frown. "Veritas and I were astonished to see thirteen thousand Redcoats and Hessians marching up the main road to White Plains.

"Washington had aboot twenty-five thousand lads in his army, but only half were fit for duty," Max reported. "They looked out from their tr-r-renches an' saw Howe's army marchin' in two columns str-r-raight for Washington in the center. Howe, his officers, the Hessians, an' the 17th Light Dr-r-ragoons rode ahead in the left column."

"Perhaps another map would help," Clarie suggested, rolling another map out on the table.

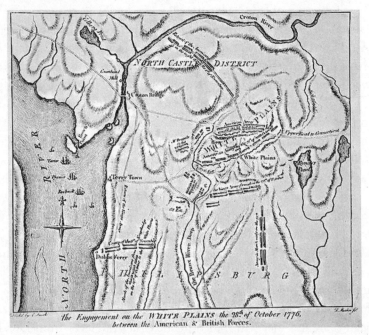

The Engagement on the WHITE PLAINS the 28th of October 1776, between the American & British Forces.

"Meanwhile, General Clinton commanded the right column led by Lieutenant Colonel William Harcourt's 16th Regiment of Light Dragoons, newly arrived from London," Clarie added. "As soon as Banastre Tarleton learned the 16th had reached New York, he immediately volunteered for duty. He was glad to serve in Harcourt's advance guard to instill terror in the Americans as the British approached."

"Sure, and that dragon lad always be the first to volunteer for action. He's all too happy aboot spreadin' fear, too," Al noted with a frown, waving an imaginary sword in the air. "He flashed his shiny saber as they galloped in front of the army."

"But then suddenly, one column turned sharp left to a higher point across the Bronx River at Chatterton's Hill," Nigel added. "It rises one hundred eighty feet to thickly wooded slopes but opens to clear fields at the top where the Americans were. I must say that it was quite a mesmerizing scene flying up above the sea of colorful uniforms, flags flying in the crisp sunshine, and the precision march of a well-trained, well-equipped, orderly, disciplined army. Military music wafted through the air whilst the guttural war chants of the fierce Hessians could be heard."

Max wrinkled his brow. "Mousie, ye make it sound like it were a scene pretty enough ta paint or something."

"I can't help myself, old boy," Nigel said with a jolly chuckle. "There's something rather elegant about such a resplendent army on the march. But back to our story for Gillamon. By noon the cannons opened fire on both sides and filled the air with smoke, the booms echoing to a deafening pitch! This time I can proudly report that our novice artillerymen and newly promoted Captain Alexander Hamilton performed admirably in manning two cannons against the dreaded foe."

"Aye, but sadly soldiers were maimed everywhere ye looked," Max interjected with a frown. "It were a horrible, bloody sight with musket fire, cannons, howitzers, an' mortars flyin'. Washington ordered more men ta Chatterton's Hill jest as thousands of Br-r-ritish an' them new Hessians, led by Colonel Rahl, charged str-r-raight up toward them through a smoke screen from the dry leaves set afire above them."

"Aye, it took three charges up the chatty hill, but it were all over in fifteen minutes." Al paused and puzzled a moment. "How do a hill chat, anyway?"

"Inevitably the militia and even veteran Continentals broke and ran, as did the new reinforcements, from the sheer volume of enemy soldiers coming against them," Nigel added, ignoring Al's latest ridiculous pondering. "With no bayonets, the Americans simply could not withstand mounted dragoons galloping toward them whilst slashing away with sabers. They simply had to give up the hill to the British. And once again, Howe did *not* pursue the Americans whilst they escaped over the bridge and along the eastern bank of the Bronx River to the safety of Purdy Hill."

"Howe gained Chatterton's Hill at a terrible cost of two hundred fifty men, twice what the Americans lost, just like when he took Bunker Hill," Clarie added. She held up the red cloth that Al had wrapped around his head to transport to the War Room. "But the Patriots proudly flew this flag that day." 'Liberty or Death' was stitched in blue letters across the top. A staff with a liberty cap on the end formed an 'x' as it crossed an unsheathed sword below.

"Patrick Henry's words continue to echo through this unfolding revolution," Gillamon told them. "He rallied a nation to independence with seven little words, and those words continue to rally her soldiers with each battle."

"I thought I'd bring the flag to Liz since it were taken from the battlefield as a prize by that dragon Tarleton," Al explained with a goofy grin.

"I'm sure Liz will appreciate your sentimental gesture, Al," Gillamon told him. "So, after the Battle of White Plains, what happened next?"

"Aye! So, after the battle, Howe were a turtle again and slowed down to wait for more reinforcements," Al reported. "Then it rained and rained and rained and rained."

"Thanks ta me gr-r-rand-lad, Jock!" Max announced with a nod of affirmation. "Washington then pulled back ta a higher spot."

"Then the two armies just waited and watched, wondering what the other would do," Nigel continued. "Finally on November 5th, much to the surprise of the Americans, the British war machine rumbled off, not to pursue Washington and the army, but southwest toward the Hudson River at King's Bridge."

"Some of our officers thought they were headin' ta Fort Washington, while others thought they were goin' ta board ships an' attack upriver," Max said. "But still most thought they were changin' their whole plan ta head on ta New Jersey an' gr-r-rab Philadelphia."

"Thankfully, General Howe did *not* accomplish his goal of capturing General Washington and destroying the Continental Army at the Battle of White Plains," Gillamon summarized. "But there was more for him left to capture. The forts, I presume?"

"Indeed, Gillamon," Nigel agreed, straightening his spectacles. "Washington wrote to Nathanael Greene that he felt it served *no* purpose to hold Forts Washington and Lee, but he ultimately left the decision up to Greene," the little mouse lamented, throwing his paws into the air. "Oh, how I wish Washington had chosen to be decisive about his instinct to abandon the forts!"

"Aye, everyone wishes that, Mousie," Max agreed. "When Greene decided to hold the forts, Washington decided ta split his army FOUR ways this time. He left the bulk of his army with seven thousand men under General Lee ta make sure the Br-r-ritish didn't attack New England. Then he left General Heath with three thousand men ta stay thirty miles north an' guard the Hudson Highlands at Peekskill, New York. Washington left with two thousand men ta cross over inta New Jersey, leaving Gr-r-reene in charge of Forts Washington an' Lee with the last two-thousand men."

"I find it quite interesting that Washington and Greene actually appear to have swapped their opinions about New York," Nigel noted. "Back in September, Greene thought the city should have been burned whilst Washington wished to hang on and defend it. Now Greene wanted to stay and defend the last post while Washington wanted to 'get out of town,' as it were."

"But why did Greene think he should hold the fort?" Al wanted to know.

"Well, he felt that the fort would allow the Americans to keep communications open across the Hudson whilst keeping the enemy occupied and thus prevented from marching on Philadelphia, and hopefully inflict another 'Bunker Hill' on them," Nigel reasoned. "He also felt that yet another retreat would crush the demoralized troops to a pulp. Greene also was confident in his commander in place at Fort Washington, Colonel Magaw."

Clarie frowned. "Well, all Fort Washington had going for it was that it was perched high up on a hill."

"Aye, it do have steep, rocky slopes, but it had no bar-r-racks ta shelter the tr-r-roops, an' no water supply," Max agreed. "Any water they got they had ta pull up the hill in buckets."

"And with winter approaching, that is *not* a good situation should the enemy lay a siege," Nigel noted. "But a siege isn't what the British had in mind, thanks to a revolting rat in our ranks!"

Al lifted a paw with an awkward frown. "I saw the rat meself, while Howe were still in White Plains. An American officer named William Demont came over to the British side and brought plans o' Fort Washington showin' where all the cannons were, and sayin' that the American army's spirits were low."

"So, the enemy knew *exactly* how ta attack the fort, an' decided ta send them tough Hessians for the job," Max told them.

"Actually, Max, Howe's plan had four parts," Nigel offered. "First, on November 15th, Howe sent under a white flag the same Colonel James Paterson he sent to deliver those wrongly addressed letters to Washington back in July. Paterson delivered a message to Colonel Magaw to surrender immediately or face imminent attack and death. Magaw had two hours to make a decision and return his reply."

"But that Magaw lad responded with br-r-ravery," Max gladly reported.

"He wrote Howe, '. . . give me leave to assure his excellency that actuated by the most glorious cause that mankind ever fought in, I am determined to defend this post to the very last extremity,'" Nigel quoted. "It was indeed a brave response, albeit an unwise one."

"Greene were at Fort Lee, an' as soon as he learned of Howe's ultimatum an' Magaw's answer, he sent a r-r-rider ta Washington, who were six miles away in Hackensack, New Jersey," Max told them. "Washington r-r-raced back, arrivin' at night. When he heard that Greene an' Old Put had r-r-rowed over the Hudson ta meet with Magaw at Fort Washington, he decided ta follow them in a boat. He met them mid-river on their way back. There, they discussed the situation in the middle of the r-r-river! Greene an' Putnam gave Washington an encouragin' report that the men at the fort were in high spirits an' were ready ta make a good defense. The three officers decided ta return ta Fort Lee for the night. Then they'd go be with their men the next day."

"Quite right. *But,* the next morning, November 16th, just as Washington, Greene, Old Put, and Mercer shoved off the bank of the river to head over to Fort Washington, the sound of cannons rippled across the water," Nigel reported. "They could see that the attack had already begun! They landed on the opposite shore and hurried up the slope to get a view of the attack from the Morris house. The officers urged Washington to return to the safety of Fort Lee while they proceeded on ahead to Fort Washington, but Washington thought it best that they *all* return to Fort Lee."

"Howe attacked with eight thousand troops from three directions after pounding the fort with cannon fire. The Hessians dragged themselves up the steep slope, pulling on beech-tree bushes to reach the top while under heavy fire from the Americans," Clarie interjected. "Meanwhile, British forces attacked the Morris house just fifteen minutes after Washington and the other generals departed!"

"The Americans were soon driven from the slopes back inside the walls of the fort, and by 2:00 p.m., Hessian General Knyphausen demanded their full surrender," Nigel added dolefully. "This time Magaw wasn't given even *half an hour* to decide. It was quite the hopeless sight from up above on the wings of Veritas!"

"Aye, Mousie. Washington watched in despair as 2,837 Americans marched out of the fort in between two r-r-rows of them fierce Hessian soldiers an' lay down their weapons," Max agreed sadly. "I'm the only one who saw it, but there were tears in the General's eyes, an' he quickly wiped away a tear that spilled down his cheek before the other humans noticed."

"Of all the humiliating defeats and retreats in the *entire* New York campaign, this was by far the *worst,*" Nigel said, shaking his head. "These poor American prisoners were marched off to join the other thousand men captured in Brooklyn, leaving four-thousand American soldiers in filthy, disease-ridden prisons, especially the horrid prison ships. Sadly, fifty-nine Americans lost their lives, and more than one hundred were wounded.

The British and Hessians lost nearly ninety killed and three hundred fifty wounded."

"An' it never should have happened, had they jest left the forts ta head over ta New Jersey," Max added.

"In addition to the loss of men, the army lost one hundred forty-six brass and iron cannons, weapons, supplies, and blankets, which they most certainly need as winter approaches," Clarie reported.

"Nathanael Greene was sick to his core about the horrific debacle of Fort Washington, and wrote a sorrowful letter to his dear friend Knox, needing his consoling voice," Nigel told them.

"How did Washington handle Greene after such a colossal failure?" Gillamon asked with a frown.

"Washington did not place the blame *by name* on Greene, nor did he relieve Greene of command or ship him off to some useless post," Clarie answered. "Washington, instead, decided to extend grace and faith to the young man he considers one of his most loyal generals. Washington *needs* Greene, and he realized that the decisions leading to the loss of Fort Washington ultimately were his as Commander-in-Chief."

"But General Lee was quick to place blame and has even started writing letters about how he predicted that this would happen," Nigel followed. "He was so mad he even pulled out some of his own hair! He wrote to Dr. Benjamin Rush, that, 'Had I the powers, I could do you much good, but I am sure you will never give any man the necessary power.'"

Gillamon leaned his grimy elbows on the table. "Hmmm, it would appear that General Lee is feeling out the Congressional waters to replace Washington."

"Over me dead body!" Max protested.

"Ye can't die, Max," Al reminded him.

"It be the sentiment, lad!" Max grumbled.

"I am happy to share that there was one hero from the day at the capture of Fort Washington, and HER name was Molly Corbin," Clarie told them. "She was the wife of a Pennsylvania soldier and fought by his side until he fell in battle. When he was killed, she took his place to load and fire a cannon until she also was wounded. The British allowed her to return home. Lassie power!"

Gillamon nodded with a smile. "I predict her act of heroism will be remembered in the history books. So, what happened to Fort Lee?"

"I got this one!" Al quickly volunteered. "Three nights later, Howe sent Cornwallis with four thousand British and Hessian troops in the pouring rain and in the dark to capture Fort Lee. Only a dozen American soldiers who had gotten drunk were captured. Maybe they drank some of the Lake Champagne."

"Lake Cham*plain*," Nigel reminded him. "Washington and his army are now retreating southward across New Jersey."

Gillamon leaned back in his chair, thinking a moment. "Once more, the Americans have escaped defeat, which is exactly what I told you we needed to help them to do. Well done, all."

Max, Al, Nigel, and Clarie shared uncomfortable glances.

"It don't feel much like a good job," Max confessed. "It feels like a defeat."

"Escaping defeat *is* a victory for the Americans," Gillamon replied. "Remember that Washington is adept at retreat, and this is perhaps one of the things that qualifies him the most for this post. All he needs to do is keep his army alive and live to fight another day."

"What's next for me Bow, Wow, Wow Generals?" Al wanted to know.

"You are of course referring to British Generals Howe, Burgoyne and Clinton, who sailed here before Bunker Hill on the *Cerberus* named for the Greek mythological three-headed dog," Nigel said flatly. "There must be some way to outwit *our* three-headed dog other than continually fleeing from the beast on the battlefield."

Gillamon reached over and picked up Al's red 'Liberty or Death' White Plains battle flag. "Well, how did Heracles handle that three-headed dog, Cerberus, in the mythical story?"

Nigel crossed his arms over his chest and tapped a finger on his chin, recalling the ancient Greek tale. "Hades told Heracles he could take Cerberus only if he *mastered him without the use of the weapons that he carried.*" Nigel suddenly brightened. "Heracles used his *lion-skin* as a shield and squeezed Cerberus around the head until he submitted!"

"Wouldn't that be *heads*, as in thr-r-ree?" Max asked.

Al's eyes widened in fear. "I may *look* like a lion, but they can't use me skin as a shield!"

"Not you literally, Al," Clarie assured him. "You simply inspired an idea."

Al's face relaxed, and he sat back, draping an arm over the chair. "Ye're welcome then."

Gillamon pointed to the stack of books on espionage that Nigel and Liz had studied. "If Washington can't beat the three-headed dog with the weapons he carries . . .

". . . He's going to have to master him without the use of the weapons he carries, meaning without guns, cannons, and men," Nigel enthused, running over to the spy gadgets sitting there. "'Around the head' in this case being *espionage* to outwit the three-headed dog? But certainly not with such ill-pre-pared spies as the tragic Nathan Hale."

"Precisely, old boy," Gillamon answered. "Not only does Washington need to keep his army alive by escaping defeat, but he must also develop a sophisticated spy ring as a new weapon to defeat the three-headed dog. He's going to need spies in New Jersey for what is to come, for this isn't over for the winter just yet."

Max gave a low grumble. "There's more tr-r-rouble ta come soon in New Jersey?"

"Aye, I could have told ye that, Max," Al offered. "General Howe ordered Cornwallis to clear out the rebels from New Jersey without a big fight and fast, before winter shows up." Suddenly he noticed a note addressed to him in Liz's handwriting. "A Liz letter!" He shot down the table and slid into the stack of books, knocking them off the table and picking up the note.

"Shall Liz be helping us with espionage in New Jersey, Gillamon?" Nigel wanted to know.

"No, she's gone to France!" Al wailed, plopping onto the table, sitting there with slumped shoulders and his pudgy arms resting on his pudgy belly. "I'll never see her again."

"She's with me Kate," Max reminded him.

"Of course, you will, Al," Clarie consoled him. "But I'll see her before you do."

Al's lip trembled. "Give her me love, will ye, lass?"

"Of course I will," Clarie told him, picking him up to hold the hefty cat in her arms. She picked up the flag and set it by the note. "I'll tell her you left her a surprise, and that it inspired a great idea to help Washington."

"Nigel, we won't have Liz, but Elsa will assist us (me as Mr. Atticus), as will someone you might not expect for this espionage assignment," Gillamon told him.

"Then I shall be wily as a fox," Nigel quipped. "Who else, Gillamon?"

"Archer," Gillamon replied.

Max laughed. "Ye mean that daft, one-ear-up doggie?"

Nigel lifted a finger in the air. "General Lee's 'shpechial' canine? How in the world shall he assist us?"

"We need to know what General Lee is planning," Gillamon told them. "And depending on what that plan is, to react accordingly. Clarie will get Archer back with General Lee. When heading north from South Carolina, Lee left his dogs in Virginia for safekeeping."

"I cannot believe we'll need that shpechial dog ta gather intelligence,"

Max replied, shaking his head with a laugh. He looked over at Al, who sat in Clarie's lap with a goofy grin on his face, kissing Liz's letter over and over. "But I've seen intelligence come fr-r-rom even less likely sources."

Gillamon chuckled softly. "Nigel, you'll also need to help Thomas Paine on another writing assignment. He served as General Greene's aide-de-camp at Fort Lee, but now he is simply retreating with the rest of the army. Since the Maker gifted him with the ability to inspire others, we feel he can best help the cause as a 'war correspondent,' if you will. Some dark days are ahead for the army."

"Indeed, these are the times that try men's souls," Nigel opined, preening his whiskers. "Quite the American crisis, I would say."

"Precisely," Gillamon agreed with a knowing grin. "Why don't you jot those words down to pass along to Mr. Paine? I think whispering in his ear at night such as you did with Handel to inspire *Messiah* will be sufficient to get his pen moving. Paine's pamphlet *Common Sense* gave Americans the inspiration they needed to pursue independence. Now soldiers and Patriots desperately need inspiration to keep fighting for it."

"Quite right," Nigel agreed. He lifted a quill to scribble the words on parchment. "I needn't play my violin in Paine's ear, but I shall happily fill his mind with a few words to get his pen flowing again." He paused to dip the quill in the ink. "They are no longer summer but *winter* soldiers now, and storm clouds have filled the sunny skies above every Patriot."

"Jot those thoughts down as well, Nigel," Gillamon told the brilliant mouse with a telling wink. He turned to Max. "Max, the storm clouds for Washington's confidence are building as well. Keep him encouraged as you protect him. Also, please fill Jock in on what is happening and let him know that he, too, will be busy in the weeks ahead. In addition to espionage, weather will be another weapon at Washington's disposal."

"Aye, I'll tell him, Gillamon," Max offered. "Will he need ta whip up some snow then?"

Gillamon's blue eyes twinkled, and he leaned forward. "Lots of snow. And ice. Washington's army is going to need it to escape defeat . . . crossing the Delaware."

PART FOUR

WILY AS A FOX

October 1776 – January 1777

44

THE CAT IS
OUT OF THE BAG

BRITISH EMBASSY, PARIS, FRANCE,
OCTOBER 15, 1776

"I s this really necessary, *mon amie?*" Liz asked, looking at Kate's small pouch lying on the ground.

"It is if ye want ta sneak inside the British Embassy an' other places without bein' seen," Kate answered. She then giggled. "Or I *could* carry ye by the scruff of yer neck like yer mum did when ye were a wee kitten. Gillamon said whatever (or whoever) I carry in me bag or in me mouth when I'm invisible will also be invisible."

Liz rubbed the side of her neck with her paw and looked up at the imposing building behind the black wrought iron gate, the flag of Great Britain flapping in the crisp fall breeze. She and Kate sat beneath a finely manicured green hedge nearby. "Well, I do not know if I can fit, but I believe I would prefer the pouch to your jaws clenched on my neck. Not to mention the dog saliva on my fur." She placed her dainty paw on Kate's shoulder. "No offense, *mon amie.*"

"None taken, lass," Kate answered, reaching into her sack to get a madeleine.

Liz watched in amazement as Kate slowly disappeared from view. *"Incroyable!* This new ability you have is fantastic, no? I am so happy that Gillamon gifted you with such a clever way to move about."

"Aye! I wish I'd been able ta do this over the centuries," Kate agreed. "It sure makes me job easier."

"Not to mention delicious, no?" Liz replied with a laugh. "We must not let Albert know about this."

"That's wha' Gillamon said!" Kate agreed. She opened the pouch. "Okay, little lass. Climb inside then."

Liz shrugged her petite shoulders. "Very well, here I come."

The double-chinned British Ambassador, Lord Stormont, frowned at reading the latest report from his spies stationed at seaports all over France, coupled with the verbal report of one of his new Parisian spies, who now sat in his office. He reached for a porcelain cup and took a sip, slurping loudly against the steaming hot tea while he continued to read, causing the spy to grimace. Stormont noisily replaced the cup in its saucer and mindlessly picked up a cookie from the silver tray and took a bite, crumbs falling onto his large belly, which stuck out like a shelf.

"A *Monsieur* Durand arranged for shipments to a warehouse in Le Havre, hmmm . . . Durand. Where have I heard that name, Durand?" Stormont asked, brushing the crumbs onto the floor.

"*Oui*, Durand is working with Roderigue Hortalez *et Cie*," *Monsieur* Simon replied. "They have just opened a new office on the Rue Vielle du Temple. And I've heard that *Señor* Hortalez hired that playwright Beaumarchais to run his office affairs." The spy snickered. "Evidently *Le Barbier de Séville* isn't as popular as Marie Antoinette has tried to make it sound if Beaumarchais must add to his playwrighting income as a trading house employee, no? That silly man is always her favorite party guest at Versailles."

Stormont raised his eyebrows above his charcoal-black eyes. "What else?" he asked with a scoff, fiddling with papers on his desk and reaching for another report.

"Well, *Monsieur*, that silly playwright has also been seen coming and going from the hotel of the American merchant Silas Deane," Simon added with a sneer.

Stormont's eyes flashed in anger. "Beaumarchais is no *mere* silly playwright, and Deane is no *mere* merchant." Tracing his finger down the page of a report, he began to read, emphasizing words as his exasperation grew:

> "But being known as a man of more *genius* than property, Mr. Deane for this and other reasons objected against the recommendation from *Count de Vergennes*; but the Count and his Secretary assured Mr. Deane that *Beaumarchais* would be properly supported and enabled to fulfill his engagements on the most advantageous terms to the *Congress*, and Mr. Deane therefore proposed to obtain from him a quantity of *ammunition* and other articles wanted by the *Colonies*."

He tossed the report back on his desk.

Simon's eyes widened. "You mean . . . Beaumarchais is working to supply Deane with arms to help the Americans?"

"How bright of you to connect the dots, *Monsieur*. And Vergennes and the French government are behind it all!" Stormont shouted, slamming a clenched fist on the desk, rattling his teacup and knocking a cookie on the floor.

"If you know this, why can't you complain to Vergennes about what you know to be true?" Simon asked.

"Because I cannot reveal the fact that *I know* this to be true," Stormont retorted. "Doing so would also reveal that we have a source in their inner circle and blow our informant's cover. So, I can only complain to Vergennes about what I see as *visible* evidence, such as what is happening at the ports. The timing of this disclosure must be handled delicately, as arming the Americans is an act of war."

"Oui, je comprends," Simon replied, nodding his head slowly as he considered the position in which Stormont found himself. "France wishes to help the Americans, while England wishes to prevent such aid. Yet neither country is prepared to go to war with one another over this issue, no?"

"Precisely. So, until that time comes, we will continue to gather intelligence on their movements so I can confront Comte de Vergennes with external proof of their actions," Stormont added. "Hopefully, the Howe Brothers will crush this American revolt once and for all in New York and prevent a wider conflict here in Europe." The Ambassador leaned forward. "Now, go pay a visit to Roderigue Hortalez and Company and see if you can find anything that would allow us to *prove* French aid to the Americans."

Simon got to his feet and bowed. *"Oui, Monsieur.* I will report back to you soon. *Au revoir."*

"Very well, *Monsieur* Simon," Stormont replied, reaching for another cookie. Finding the tray empty, he looked on the floor where he thought he had dropped one but didn't see it there. He got up from his desk and walked out of his office.

"Quick, Liz, we need ta see that report he read before he gets back!" Kate whispered to Liz from beneath the desk. "Yer paws will be better at turnin' the pages."

"Agreed, Kate!" Liz answered. "Get me up on the desk."

Kate jumped from the floor to the chair to the desk and Liz poked her head and paws out from the bag to rifle around on Stormont's desk. *"C'est ça!* Here it is, from Under-Secretary of State William Eden, head of intelligence in London!"

"Wha' else does it say?" Kate wanted to know, peering over Liz's head, nibbling on the cookie that Stormont had dropped.

Liz's eyes grew wide. "It is a full report by a Mr. Edwards, giving details of Silas Deane's arrival to France, his meetings with Vergennes and Gérard

. . ." She looked up at Kate. "The British in London know *everything* that is happening here in Paris and Versailles!"

Kate furrowed her brow. "Aye, Stormont has his own spies everywhere. One in every four servants in Paris be a spy! I knew aboot Simon but I don't know who Mr. Edwards might be. But if the report had ta be sent from London ta Stormont here in Paris, that means . . ."

"That this 'Mr. Edwards' isn't a spy who reports to Stormont. He is a high-level spy who reports directly to the head of intelligence in London!" Liz realized. "We will need to find out who this 'Mr. Edwards' is before he does more harm."

"Aye, but for now, get back in me pouch! Stormont's comin'!" Kate urged, pushing Liz's head back in the bag. She jumped off the desk and scurried out the door just as Stormont walked in.

Stormont looked down, feeling as if something brushed by his stockinged feet. Not seeing anything, he shrugged his shoulders. He walked over to his desk and took his seat, placing a fresh tray of cookies next to his cup and wearing a puzzled expression. There on his desk was a half-eaten cookie.

HÔTEL DES AMBASSADEURS DE HOLLANDE, PARIS, FRANCE, OCTOBER 16, 1776

"Poisson frais!" came the cry of a street vendor with a basket of fresh fish as a team of four horses went clip-clopping down the cobblestone street pulling a wicker chaise full of fashionably dressed women in their silk finery. Washerwomen clubbed their laundry with wooden batons on the quay of the Seine River almost in time with the bells that rang out from Notre Dame Cathedral. The aroma of fresh baked bread wafted into the air as a baker filled a tall basket with crispy boules next to an enormous wheel of cheese. Street vendors selling everything from newspapers to water to flowers called out their wares as butchers roasted meat, roaming minstrels offered to compose and sing a lively tune on a violin, and street barbers busily powdered and pomaded wigged clients in a hurry to make their next appointment. Contrasting with the beauty, buying, and busyness were raggedly dressed, smelly beggars sitting on the filthy streets reaching out their hands for a coin from passersby.

Liz closed her eyes in ecstasy as she took in the sights, smells, and sounds. "Ah, Paris! Is there any place like it in the world?"

"Not that I've seen. I prefer the highlands of Scotland, but ye would love it here, bein' a French lass," Kate answered, trotting down the busy Parisian street. "Now pay attention, Liz. I've shown ye how Stormont be snoopin' around with his spies. Now I want ta show ye Beaumarchais in action with his fake tradin' company."

"Pardon, Kate, *oui*, I am listening. Please continue," Liz said, her mouth watering as they passed the fresh fish seller. "You were saying that since Comte de Vergennes supplied Beaumarchais with the first million *livres* in June, he has been busy traveling?"

"Aye, Beaumarchais has travelled ta French seaports all along the Atlantic coast, includin' Le Havre, Brest, Rochefort, Nantes, an' Bordeaux. He's been lookin' for deep harbors an' large warehouses that can handle the huge amount of cargo he plans ta send to the Americans. He's been chattin' with harbormasters an' merchants who'll manage these shipments," Kate explained. "He got the second million *livres* from Spain an' raised a third million by sellin' shares in his Rodrigue Hortalez and Company ta some French businessmen, ship owners, merchants, an' bankers. The lad's been busy buyin' guns, muskets, cannonballs, gunpowder, clothin', camp supplies, ship supplies, an' jest aboot anythin' else ye can think of! He's got quite the busy business! But he never goes by the name of Beaumarchais, but *Monsieur* Durand."

"*C'est magnifique!*" Liz exclaimed. "So HE is the man that Stormont wondered about at the seaports! And he conducts all of this business now in the center of Paris?"

"Aye, he decided that rather than try ta hide from the British spies he knew are snoopin' aboot, he'd jest run his business right out in the open," Kate explained. "Vergennes told him that in order ta *appear* so, it must *be* so. Beaumarchais is a master of disguise so when he goes ta visit those seaside ports, he becomes someone else ta throw the spies off his trail. I'm tellin' ye, Liz, Beaumarchais will keep those English guessin', even if Stormont thinks he knows everything. Trust me, lass!"

"I cannot wait to see *Monsieur* Beaumarchais in person!" Liz exclaimed. "I like not only what he is doing to help the Americans, but I like *him*, no? He sounds like a simply charming human. I especially appreciate what he recently wrote to Vergennes:

Every time that I think how we hold in our hands the destiny of the world, and that we have the power to change the system of things—and when I see so many advantages, so much glory ready to escape, I regret

*infinitely not to have more influence over the resolutions of the councils,
and not to be able to multiply myself, so as to prevent the evil on one
hand, and aid the good on the other."*

"Hmmm, multiplyin' Beaumarchais would be a grand idea!" Kate
answered with her perky grin. "Welcome ta his Parisian abode."

They came to a corner across the street from a greystone baroque mansion with a large brass plaque by the front door: RODRIGUE HORTALEZ
ET CIE. A grand semicircular archway was perched above the double doors
with a bas-relief of two women and two winged deities on one side and
Romulus and Remus nursed by their she-wolf on the other. The massive
wooden front doors were adorned with carvings of Greek snake-haired
Medusas.

"This were the old mansion of the Dutch Embassy, but no one's lived
here for years," Kate explained. "Beaumarchais jest rented this mansion, an'
moved his family as well as his fake business here."

"It has impressive architecture," Liz noted, looking at the carvings.
"What is behind the front gate?"

"There be two courtyards leadin' ta the main building," Kate answered.
"The first courtyard be filled with sundials placed beneath the windows, an'
it leads ta the second, larger courtyard connected by a vaulted passageway.
It's filled with eight statues representin' dawn, twilight, an' the virtues of
strength, truth, prudence, justice, vigilance, an' wisdom."

"Let us hope those virtues watch over our friend Beaumarchais in this
important work," Liz noted. "I am eager to get inside!"

"Okay, Liz," Kate replied. "Let me eat a biscuit. Then ye know wha' ta
do. We'll wait for someone ta open the front gate."

Liz sighed. *"Oui,* Kate." She climbed into Kate's bag and they both soon
disappeared.

It wasn't long before Stormont's spy, *Monsieur* Simon, came to the front
door and knocked. Then Kate and Liz slipped invisibly inside behind him.

Liz gasped in awe of the beauty of the mansion once they got inside.
The walls were covered from floor to ceiling with murals depicting Greek
mythology and scenes of love and tragedy in rose and gold tones. The large
salon was lined with plush upholstered benches that sat on polished wooden
floors laid out in a diamond pattern. A marble staircase, trimmed with an
iron and mahogany banister, led to the next level.

Amid the beauty was a swarm of activity, with clerks, accountants, and
secretaries busy at their desks and interacting with the guests waiting their
turn for attention to their business at hand. At the far end of the reception

salon was a massive wooden door with a name plate posted outside: SR.
RODRIGUE HORTALEZ.

Kate slipped behind a large stone planter holding a miniature palm tree.
She whispered to Liz. "Beaumarchais should be here anytime now. Looks like
there be four or five real customers an' Stormont's spy here."

"Bonjour! Bonjour! Bonjour!" came the effervescent, lyrical voice of
Beaumarchais as he made a grand entrance into the salon. He was dressed
in a burgundy coat and breeches, trimmed in black satin, a white frilly shirt,
white stockings, silver satin shoes with ornate silver buckles, and a perfectly
powdered and curled white wig. He greeted the customers as he walked by
before making small talk with the employees.

"He is taller than I thought," Liz whispered with a grin. "He has such a
pleasant smile and playful, mischievous eyes."

Beaumarchais darted into his office for a few moments before emerging
and walking back by the waiting customers, slightly bowing with an upraised
finger. *"Un moment, s'il vous plaît."*

He proceeded to walk across the foyer to the imposing carved door of
Señor Hortalez. He knocked lightly with the back of his knuckles, announced
himself, opened the door, and slipped inside.

"Pardon, but have you ever met *Señor* Hortalez?" the spy Simon asked the
other customers in a hushed tone.

One man shook his head. *"Non,* I have never had such a great honor."

"Oui, he is in such great demand that few ever get to see him," another
man echoed. "But his voice is unmistakable."

"El comprador necesita ese envoi!" Hortalez demanded from behind the
door. They heard the sound of his fist slamming the table.

"It sounds like one of his bad days," one man added.

"Wha' did he say?" Kate whispered to Liz. "The lad sounds angry."

Liz frowned, then whispered, *"Señor* Hortalez said that the buyer needs
the shipment."

"Pas tout de suite, Monsieur!" came Beaumarchais's reply.

"Beaumarchais said it will not happen right away," Liz translated.

"Tienes que emplearte a fondo!" came Hortalez's thick Spanish accent.

"You must put everything you have into it," Liz translated.

"Oui, Señor, je comprends," Beaumarchais replied.

"Yes, sir, I understand," Liz translated again.

"¿Dónde están esos números que pedí?" Hortalez asked.

"Wha' did he ask now?" Kate wanted to know.

Liz listened intently and continued to translate, "Where are those numbers I asked for?"

"Je reviens dans un instant, Monsieur!" came Beaumarchais's reply.

"I'll be back in a moment," Liz translated.

Suddenly Beaumarchais opened the massive door to *Señor* Hortalez's office, quickly closing it behind him. He pulled a handkerchief from his pocket and dabbed the sweat from his brow, wearing a concerned look on his face. Walking by the customers sitting there waiting to see *Señor* Hortalez, Beaumarchais stopped and lifted a hand in the air and looked to the ceiling, suddenly remembering them.

"Ah, pardon *Messieurs!* I am *very* sorry, but *Señor* Hortalez is extremely busy today," Beaumarchais lamented. "I am afraid that he will not be able to meet with you. But I am happy to assist you on his behalf. If you will have a seat in my office, one at a time, I will be right with you, *s'il vous plaît.*"

The first French merchant waiting in line nodded reluctantly. *"Oui,* very well." He stood and followed Beaumarchais to the office with M. BEAUMARCHAIS emblazoned on a brass plaque outside his door. "I understand *Señor* Hortalez is an important, busy man. I appreciate your assistance, *Monsieur.* Please give him my regards."

Beaumarchais bowed and smiled broadly. *"Bien sûr!"* He picked up a stack of papers from his desk and held them in the air. "Allow me to get these numbers to *Señor* Hortalez and I shall return. *Un moment, s'il vous plaît.*"

Beaumarchais left the merchant sitting in his office while he once more walked across the shiny wood foyer to reach the office of *Señor* Hortalez. He tapped softly on the door before entering and slipped inside. Low murmuring could be heard for several moments. Then a deep laugh came from the mysterious Spaniard. Beaumarchais's high-pitched chuckle followed, and the conversation turned more light-hearted.

"It sounds like things are looking up for *Monsieur* Beaumarchais," one of the men whispered. "He must be relieved."

"Oui," another man agreed.

Simon looked down the line of customers who all whispered, in awe of the larger-than-life Hortalez with the booming Spanish voice behind closed doors. They would wait for as long as it took to accomplish their business here. They were legitimate merchants, traders, and financiers conducting legitimate business with Rodriguez Hortalez and Company. The spy questioned them on their specific matters of business and determined that there was nothing to indicate that neither they nor Hortalez was helping the Americans.

"Gracias y mantenme informado sobre ese envío," Hortalez finally told Beaumarchais.

"Thank you, and keep me informed on that shipment," Liz translated for Kate.

Beaumarchais opened the door and standing in the doorway, turned back to *Señor* Hortalez. *"Très bien. Merci, Señor."* He then hurriedly walked back across the floor toward his own office, calling over to the next customer waiting to see *Señor* Hortalez. "I will see you next, *Monsieur!"*

Kate and Liz sat there invisibly and watched as Simon looked from the office of Beaumarchais to the office of Hortalez and back to Beaumarchais. It would be a long wait. He wrinkled his brow, slapped a hand on his knee, shrugged his shoulders, and stood to leave. He quickly exited the salon and escaped into the courtyard.

"It would appear that *Señor* Hortalez has lost a customer, no?" Liz posed to Kate with a whisper.

Kate gave a knowing grin. "A fake customer, lass."

Liz's tail slowly tapped up and down on the floor. "I wish to see this mysterious man who is running *Monsieur* Beaumarchais's company."

"Okay, Liz, the next time Beaumarchais goes ta talk with him, I'll slip us inside," Kate suggested.

"Bon," Liz whispered.

After a while, Beaumarchais escorted the first merchant to the clerk and then brought the next customer to his office. Finally, he returned to the door of *Señor* Hortalez, and Kate slipped inside before he closed the door behind him.

Liz couldn't believe what she saw, or rather *didn't* see. There was no *Señor* Hortalez. There was only Beaumarchais! He proceeded to sit in a big leather chair and carry on a conversation with himself, laughing and discussing business with his feet propped up on the desk. She peeked her head out of the bag and looked at Kate, who was doing all she could not to laugh.

"Ahora, tengo algunas cartas que escribir," Beaumarchais said in a deep Spanish accent.

Liz rolled her eyes and shook her head with a giggle. "Now, I have some letters to write," she translated in a whisper to Kate.

With that, Beaumarchais jumped up from the desk and walked over to the door before bidding himself farewell with, *"Très bien, Señor* Hortalez." He left the office, leaving Liz and Kate alone.

"You knew, didn't you?" Liz asked with an amused tone, climbing out of the bag to stretch her legs. "He has indeed multiplied himself, no?"

Kate chuckled and nodded her head. "Aye, it's one of his grandest performances ever! He's not only Figaro, but Durand, Hortalez, and Beaumarchais all in one!"

"Who else knows that there really is no *Señor* Hortalez?" Liz asked.

"Only Beaumarchais's secretary Gudin, Gudin's brother the cashier, and his lady friend," Kate answered, wagging her tail. "Don't worry, Liz. Figaro will keep Stormont an' his spies guessin' for as long as it takes. His scheme ta help the Americans be in very good hands—all of them!"

"Bravo, *Monsieur* Beaumarchais!" Liz cheered, softly clapping her paws together and laughing at how she, too, was fooled by the brilliant playwright-spy-businessman. "The cat is out of the bag . . . in more ways than one, no?"

45

CUR NON?

PARIS, FRANCE, NOVEMBER 7, 1776, 1:00 A.M.

I must find a way, Lafayette drowsily thought as he fluffed his feather pillow and rolled over in bed. His restless sleep stemmed from racing thoughts about all that was going on in Paris. The American "merchant" Silas Deane wasn't just buying goods to ship to America. He was enlisting French officers to sail to America and fight alongside the rebels against the British army. Lafayette's former commander at Metz, the Comte de Broglie, had volunteered to help Deane meet these prospective soldiers. De Broglie hosted parties where young French officers came to make their interest known to him before he introduced them to the American. Everyone talked of little else than exacting revenge on their hated English enemies back on American soil. Lafayette, his brother-in-law Vicomte Louis de Noailles, and their best friend Louis-Phillipe Comte de Ségur were invited to attend one of de Broglie's parties the next night. It would not only be a lively event, but a setting where Lafayette could hopefully learn how he could also join the fight.

Lafayette, Noailles, and Ségur had been together with the Comte de Broglie at another lively event while training in Metz in August of 1775 with none other than King George III's brother, the Duke of Gloucester. Lafayette relived that dinner in his mind as he anticipated the conversation to come at tomorrow night's party. He slowly drifted off to sleep, replaying that life-changing night in his dreams.

Flames danced from the dripping candles in the gleaming silver candelabras lining the center of the long table as servants speedily reached around the guests to remove dinner plates from their gold chargers. Red and white wines and champagne were poured freely in multiple crystal flutes and goblets lined up with each sumptuous course, and the servants now brought out desserts of pear tarts, chocolate truffles, and creme brulée.

The Comte de Broglie sat at one end of the table, and the Duke of Gloucester at the other. A string of distinguished French officers sat between them, resplendent in their crisp, colorful uniforms, powdered wigs, shiny medals, *gorgets,* and decorative small swords. Lafayette, the Comte de Ségur, and the Vicomte Louis de Noailles sat near the Duke. Adrienne's uncle, the Prince de Poix, sat next to de Broglie. Multiple toasts were offered to the guest of honor, who graciously smiled and enjoyed the company of these proud Frenchmen who sought to impress the British royal by proving that their humiliating defeat at the Seven Years' War neither diminished their grandeur or their largesse at table. But while the guests' stomachs expanded and raucous laughter filled the room, the Marquis de Lafayette cared only about one thing at this sumptuous feast: the shocking words coming from Prince William Henry, Duke of Gloucester and Edinburgh.

"Je suis d'accord avec la cause des insurgés!" the Duke declared, slapping his hand on the table and causing the crystal glasses to tremble and clink. *"La politique de mon frère et de son cabinet est un désastre!"*

The Duke supported the American rebels and thought the policies of his brother and cabinet were a disaster. He had recounted all the events that had taken place in America following the end of the French and Indian War, including the Stamp Act, the Boston Massacre, the Boston Tea Party, the Coercive Acts leading to the closing of Boston Harbor, and the response of the colonists leading to the First Continental Congress. He decried Britain's unfair taxation of the colonies and applauded the resistance of the Americans against his brother the king. The French officers were enthralled with the accounts of Lexington and Concord, the capture of French guns at Fort Ticonderoga, and the siege of Boston.

"Do tell us, *s'il vous plaît,* what are the latest developments from America?" de Broglie asked.

"Just this morning I received shocking news from Boston," the Duke replied. *"Les Insurgents* built earthworks overnight on the heights of Boston at a place called Bunker Hill. Our forces responded in kind, and after a bloody day of fighting we gained 'victory,' but at a devastating loss of officers and men. The British officers considered their opponents as rabble, but it was *they* who were reduced to *rubble* by the end of the bloody day."

A current of almost palpable glee hovered over the table at the thought of arrogant British blood being spilled in such a crushing defeat.

"I have told my brother he should stop this fight with the Americans," the Duke continued, raising a hand in the air. "Give them representation in Parliament if they wish, give them independence if they wish, but end the argument and keep strong trade going to benefit both sides of the Atlantic."

"Great Britain is in dangerous waters of losing much of her commerce, one-fourth of her subjects, and half of British-held territory," the Prince de Poix stated, eyeing the young men.

The Duke nodded. "Indeed, but this matter of suppressing the freedoms of our own brethren must be settled once and for all." He looked around the table and caught the fixed gaze of Lafayette, who sat erect and nodded in agreement. "*Liberté, égalite, fraternité.* This is a struggle not only for the Americans, but for all of mankind."

"So, then what is the response from the king after this Battle of Bunker Hill?" Lafayette wanted to know. "Will he keep fighting, or will he take your advice?"

De Broglie leaned back in his chair and crossed his arms over his chest. He held a thumb under his chin, and rested his index finger on his mouth, studying Lafayette as he zealously waited for the Duke's answer.

The Duke swirled the wine in his crystal goblet and glanced around the table at the faces of the French officers, who leaned forward with eager anticipation to hear his response. What did it matter if the French received the answer directly from his lips as opposed to the string of spies gathering the identical information in the office of French intelligence in London? He took a sip of wine, set down his glass, and rested his elbows on the table.

"My brother believes he is completely in the right to crush the rebellion with an overwhelming show of force," the Duke relayed. "He and Parliament will fight to the death until the rebels are defeated, or until the strength of the British Crown is completely thrown off by the colonies, which of course is unlikely. As we speak, England is enlisting the aid of German mercenaries to wage war against the Americans."

The men murmured for a moment, discussing the fierce Hessian warriors.

"These Americans are not just content with words. We sit around and discuss the idea of *liberté,* but they are willing to *fight* for it," Lafayette whispered urgently to Noailles and Ségur.

"That war in America is the only war on the horizon," Ségur suggested.

Noailles nodded. "We have spent months training to fight, but we have no enemy to fight."

"What if we did? What if we were to help the Americans attain victory?" Lafayette proposed. "Would it not also be a victory for human *liberté? And* we could avenge the honor of France by defeating the British, who took it from us in the Seven Years' War!"

"I know you wish to avenge the death of your father who died at the hands of the British at Minden," Noailles added. "But this war in America is not our war."

"*Cur non?*" Lafayette replied with a flash in his eyes, echoing the Latin motto of his ancestors, 'Why not?' "America," he repeated softly, as if he were speaking the name of his love, Adrienne. "Such a glorious cause has never before rallied the attention of mankind."

Lafayette turned to face the Duke of Gloucester. "And who shall lead the Americans in their struggle for freedom?"

De Broglie, the Prince de Poix, and the Duke shared surprised looks to see this young, seventeen-year-old captain taking such a passionate interest in a conflict with a foreign country three thousand miles away.

"Their Second Continental Congress elected a Virginia planter by the name of George Washington as their Commander-in-Chief," the Duke replied, "but this General Washington has an army of farmers and militiamen from disparate colonies—not trained and equipped soldiers. They were fortunate at Bunker Hill, but they will come up against tens of thousands of professional soldiers who know how to fight a war. The Americans have heart but not the arms to defeat those professionals."

Lafayette's heart raced. He clenched his jaw as his hand instinctively drifted down to the handle of his small sword. He rose from his seat, slowly pulled his sword from its scabbard and held it proudly in the air. "Then I will give them *mine! Mon cœur et mon épée.*" He looked around the table. "From this day I give my heart to the Americans and will raise my banner and add my colors to hers!"

All eyes looked at Lafayette, stunned by his bold and impulsive declaration.

"Sit down, *Monsieur le Marquis,*" ordered de Broglie with a frown, motioning for the eager young man to sit. "Let us not bring declarations of war to this table, especially in the presence of our honored *English* guest."

Lafayette bowed respectfully, sheathed his sword, and took his seat. But the fire in his eyes would not be extinguished by the words of his commander or any other who would attempt to stop him from his noble quest. At that moment, all his childhood dreams of becoming a knight like his forefathers and finding glory on the field of battle illuminated his mind with vivid imagery.

Lafayette rolled over and muttered in his sleep: *"Cur non?"*

But Lafayette wasn't the only one dreaming of glory on the field of battle in America. Across the darkened streets of Paris lay another sleepless French officer who dreamed of leading the entire Continental Army.

"Who is this George Washington, but an untrained, failed Virginia colonel of backwoods militiamen, pfft?" the French officer murmured aloud to himself, staring up at the ceiling. "It was Washington's ineptitude that ignited the French and Indian War that eventually led to France's defeat in the wider Seven Years' War! *Non,* these Americans need *experienced* soldiers and officers to defeat the British. They need a *generalissimo* to lead them to victory, and after that . . . someone to lead the thirteen states—a new king to lead them. *C'est facile.*"

The French officer smiled in the darkness. *"Pourquoi pas moi-même?"*

Why not I?

NON, MONSIEUR LE MARQUIS

PARIS, FRANCE, NOVEMBER 8, 1776,
5:00 P.M.

L iz and Kate emerged into the sunlight from the darkened tunnel and allowed their eyes to adjust for a moment.

"We shall keep looking, *mon amie,*" Liz assured Kate, frowning at the dirt on her fur. She immediately started to give herself a bath as they sat on the wall overlooking the Seine River.

"Aye, I knew it were not goin' ta be easy ta find, with two hundred miles of tunnels down there," Kate agreed, looking up to the sky. She closed her eyes and soaked in the welcomed warmth of the sun. "If Charlatan does have his evil headquarters somewhere in those dark, dirty tunnels, wha' should we do once we find it?"

Liz stopped mid-lick and looked at Kate. "We inform Gillamon and follow his instructions, no?"

Kate nodded and looked at the angle of the sun making its descent. "Well, for now we'll follow his instructions for helpin' Deane an' Lafayette. Yesterday were a big day!"

"*Oui,* I am so happy that Deane *finally* received his official copy of the Declaration of Independence sent by Congress! He can finally meet with Vergennes not as a merchant but as the representative of an *independent* America," Liz agreed. She frowned, shaking her head. "But it remains a mystery as to what happened to the ship that sailed from Philadelphia in July with the *first* copy of the Declaration of Independence sent to Deane."

"Aye, that ship were lost at sea, never ta be seen again," Kate agreed with a worried look. "An' although Deane were happy ta get the official Declaration, he still didn't get the answers from Congress that he needed aboot enlistin' French soldiers ta send over for Washington."

"I find it remarkable that it was Arthur Lee who first suggested to Beaumarchais that the Continental Army needs European soldiers of excellent reputation," Liz added. "And then Beaumarchais in turn suggested it to Deane, who is now recruiting them, even though he does not have the approval of Congress to do so."

Kate nodded. "I guess he'll jest keep signin' commissions until he hears differently. So far, Beaumarchais has sent aboot thirty lads ta Deane, includin' a dozen artillery officers, a dozen engineers, and some infantry officers."

"*Oui*, I am especially interested in that young French engineer that Beaumarchais sent to Deane—Pierre Charles L'Enfant. I understand he is also skilled in architecture," Liz added. "But not all the officers sent by Beaumarchais are French, like that Irish-born Thomas Conway and Polish-born Casimir Pulaski. And not all the French officers coming to Deane will be beneficial to Washington. Many of them are bored, untested thrill-seekers who are greedy for high salaries and do not care about the American cause. I fear they may prove to be more of a burden and a problem for Washington, no?"

"At least that Bavarian-born Baron De Kalb were a good catch," Kate suggested. "Deane were especially glad when the Comte de Broglie brought him over for a meetin'."

"De Kalb speaks English, so that endeared him to Deane, I am sure," Liz offered with a grin. She curled her tail slowly up and down, thinking. "In fact, I believe that the Baron would be the perfect one to introduce Lafayette to Deane."

Kate wagged her tail. "I like that idea, Liz. Lafayette doesn't speak English, so De Kalb could also take our young Marquis under his wing on the trip ta America. The Baron an' the boy. But first, they have ta meet."

"So Comte de Broglie's party tonight will be the perfect place to begin," Liz added, wiping back her whiskers. "I know we shall be invisible *ce soir*, but I wish to look my best for this important *soiree.*"

"After all, ye penned their invitation for the lads," Kate pointed out with a wink.

HOME OF COMTE DE BROGLIE, PARIS, FRANCE, NOVEMBER 8, 1776, 9:00 P.M.

Lafayette, Noailles, and Ségur huddled together in a corner of the candle-lit room, scanning the French aristocrats and soldiers as they milled about. The room buzzed with energy, and no one talked of anything other than the war in America and who had been added to Deane's list.

"Baron De Kalb was only a lieutenant-colonel in the French army, but yesterday Deane gave him a commission to be a *major-general* in the American army!" Lafayette enthused.

"Plus, he will receive twelve thousand *livres* for his commission," Ségur added.

"*And* he will have an aide-de-camp to accompany him," Noailles added, pointing over to de Broglie. "The brother of de Broglie's secretary, Lieutenant Duboismartin will now be a major."

"De Broglie is the one who introduced the Baron to Deane," Lafayette shared with the group. "They have a long history of serving together."

"I heard that *Monsieur* Deane offers generous pay and seldom promises less than a captaincy," Ségur reported, lifting his glass to de Broglie, who noticed the three young men with a gracious nod of recognition. "How is the French government reacting to these appointments?"

"The king and his ministers are simply looking the other way," Noailles answered with a grin. "The French Ministry must keep up appearances of desiring peace with the British while winking at their officers who desire to go fight them across the Atlantic."

"And I am *one* of them!" Lafayette declared, looking his friends in the eye. "As I told you when we were in Metz, the Americans are not content with just words. We sit around and discuss the idea of *liberté*, but they are willing to *fight* for it." He gazed around at the soldiers dressed in their fine uniforms, wondering how many were in those uniforms simply because of who they were, not because of what they had personally accomplished. "Joining the Americans is finally an opportunity for me to achieve something on my *own*. I no longer wish to be dependent on Adrienne's family for a post or for advancement in the army because my father-in-law owns a regiment. Like the Americans, I wish to *fight* on my own for *my liberté*. I am going to America to find glory on the battlefield. Who is with me?"

Noailles and Ségur looked at one another, nodded, and then looked at Lafayette. "*Bon!* We're in. We shall go with you to America!"

"*Très bien!*" Lafayette exclaimed, happy to have his friends join him in his quest. "Then I will ask our former commander to introduce us to *Monsieur* Deane. Stay here." With that, the tall, red-headed marquis made his way over to the Comte de Broglie.

Liz whispered to Kate, "There he goes!"

Kate whispered back from where they sat beneath the bountiful table of food, "This should be easy for him! De Broglie is fond of the lad."

"*Bonsoir, mon général*," Lafayette greeted de Broglie with a courteous bow.

"Ah, *mon cher marquis!*" de Broglie replied, warmly patting Lafayette on the back. "I am happy that you three could come tonight."

"There is a great deal of excitement about the American, *Monsieur* Deane, and the commissions he is writing for French officers to join the fight in

America," Lafayette answered. "I understand that *félicitations* are in order, especially to the newly appointed *Général* De Kalb."

"*Oui,* Baron De Kalb is an exceptional recruit for *Monsieur* Deane. He fought under me in two wars," de Broglie replied. "King Louis XV awarded him the Knight's Cross Order of Military Merit. He has served the French Army for three decades, speaks English, and has also been to America."

"*C'est magnifique!*" Lafayette's eyes widened at hearing Baron De Kalb's resume. "So, he has been to America?"

De Broglie smiled and looked around them and whispered, "*Oui,* but it was for espionage for King Louis XV."

Lafayette raised his eyebrows and smiled. "Ah, then he must know a great deal about the colonies. And the Baron's rank makes him highly respected, no?"

"*Oui,* the rank of major-general. And in return, De Kalb has promised to recruit a group of volunteers to sail to America under his leadership," de Broglie further relayed.

Lafayette's boyish face lit up with a broad smile. "Then I wish to volunteer! *S'il vous plaît,* would you introduce me and my friends to *Général* De Kalb? We all wish to go fight in America."

"You declared this desire at a dinner in Metz, as I recall," de Broglie answered with a serious look.

"*Oui, Monsieur!*" Lafayette quickly answered. "I have thought of little else since that dinner! I remain committed to the glorious cause of the Americans."

De Broglie tightened his lips, took in a deep breath, and quickly exhaled through his nose. A frown appeared on his face. "My boy, I saw your uncle die in the war in Italy," he recalled, a firm hand gripping Lafayette's shoulder. "And I witnessed your father's death at the Battle of Minden." He clenched his jaw and looked into the eager eyes of the nineteen-year-old Marquis. "I will *not* be accessory to the ruin of the only remaining branch of your family."

Lafayette was crestfallen. "*Pardon, mon général,* but you will not help me . . . to meet Baron De Kalb . . . or *Monsieur* Deane?"

"*Non, Monsieur le Marquis,*" de Broglie answered. "You are a fine junior officer, and you trained with excellence in Metz, but you have never fired a shot in battle. Plus, you have a baby daughter and a young wife at home. I will not allow them to experience what your own mother endured when the British killed your father." He cleared his throat and patted the disappointed Lafayette on the back, leaving him to go talk to another guest.

Noailles and Ségur came up to Lafayette, standing there stunned by the disappointing answer of his powerful former commander. "Well?" Noailles asked.

Lafayette shook his head. "He told me, 'No.' Having seen my father and uncle die in war, he said he will not be responsible for killing off the last of the Lafayettes in battle." He clenched his jaw. "But what good is the name of Lafayette without glory attached to it, as my ancestors before me?! I will not give up my quest to go fight for America."

Noailles put a hand to Lafayette's back and looked between Lafayette and Ségur. "We are agreed that we *all* will go fight in America, together."

"*Oui,* but we are all minors and must receive permission from our parents as well as the military authorities," Ségur noted. "Plus, we must have the funds to pay for our passage and supplies."

"After I angered our father-in-law the Duc by ruining my position at court, I do not know if he would support my request," Lafayette lamented.

Noailles put his hand on his chest. "Leave this with me. I will discuss the matter with the Duc d'Ayen, and I will write to Minister of State Comte de Maurepas. He has great sway over Vergennes as well as our father-in-law."

"But we must proceed with secrecy and caution," urged Ségur. "The French volunteers Deane has enlisted so far have no standing in society. But *we* are noblemen."

Lafayette nodded in agreement. "*Oui,* when word gets out that three Frenchmen attached to the royal court have volunteered, it will rouse much attention, and possibly appear as a violation of France's neutrality with Great Britain. I do not wish to give the French Ministry cause to tell me 'No' as well."

"The Comte de Broglie's concern for the young Lafayette is kind, but is a rather surprising obstacle, no?" Liz whispered to Kate.

"Aye, a 'no' that the lad won't take sittin' down," Kate agreed.

HÔTEL DE NOAILLES, FRANCE, NOVEMBER 16, 1776, 5:00 P.M.

Kate sat on the settee next to Lafayette, licking his hand. He gently stroked her fur with his other hand and smiled affectionately. "If only people were as kind as you, Bibi. You always say '*oui*' to me, unlike everyone else."

Liz smiled from across the room, hidden under a raised bookcase. For once it was nice to be around the humans without having to be invisible inside Kate's bag. Kate was free to be with the humans, of course, but Liz still had to stay out of sight while in the Noailles home.

Suddenly Lafayette heard the voices of Noailles and their father-in-law, the Duc d'Ayen coming down the hall. Lafayette gently put Kate on the floor with a wink and a finger to his mouth. "We best not let the Duc see you on the furniture, no?"

Oui! Kate barked happily. She grinned and sat by Lafayette's side on the floor.

Lafayette stood and took a deep breath, anticipating the conversation to come. Noailles had already had several conversations with the Duc about his going to America, but the reticent father-in-law hesitated to give his approval. The two brothers-in-law decided to try again, but this time with Lafayette in the room to add his voice to the request.

"*Bonjour,* Gilbert," the Duc greeted Lafayette with a smile, taking his seat, as did Noailles. "*Comment va ma petite-fille ce matin?* I understand she has been rather sickly."

"*Bonjour,* Papa," Lafayette replied, sitting back down. "Your granddaughter Henriette is much better, *merci.* Adrienne is taking good care of our angel."

"*Bon, bon.* I am glad to hear it," Duc answered with a smile. "The weather is turning chilly, and I want her to be healthy and strong."

"*Moi aussi,* Papa," Lafayette agreed with a smile, locking eyes with Noailles, who gave a singular nod.

"Papa, I just learned that *Monsieur* Deane has now enlisted approximately a dozen officers to sail with Baron De Kalb to America," Noailles offered.

"He is *Général* Baron De Kalb now," Lafayette added with a finger in the air. "He has quite the impressive military record. Comte de Broglie shared with me his many achievements in the service of France."

Duc nodded slowly and tapped his hand on the arm of the upholstered chair. "*Oui,* Johann De Kalb is a fine officer, and a good family man."

"Thus, he will make an *excellent* leader, especially for the junior officers joining him," Noailles quickly added and then paused, locking eyes with a hopeful Lafayette, who willed him to press their father-in-law. "Papa, I know that if I served under De Kalb, I would be able to serve with distinction in America. I would ask you again, *s'il vous plaît,* if you would use your influence with Maurepas to allow me to enlist to fight for the Americans."

"*Moi aussi,* Papa!" Lafayette blurted out, unable to contain himself. He sat forward on the edge of his seat and became animated as he gushed out his deep desire that he could no longer keep bottled inside. "Ever since I learned about the American cause in Metz, I have wished to offer my sword to fight. *S'il vous plaît,* Papa, I would like to join my brother-in-law to volunteer and serve with *Général* De Kalb in this noble cause for *liberté.*"

In a flash, the Duc's face flushed with anger, and he pointed a finger at Lafayette. "I'll make *no* such request for you!" he shouted, standing to his feet. "You have already caused me great embarrassment with the royal court with your willful action to insult the king's brother to get out of the post that

I strategically endeavored to secure for you. I refuse therefore to ask them to allow you to pursue a military post that could ignite a war!"

With that, the Duc d'Ayen stomped off, leaving the two brothers-in-law sitting there, silent. Lafayette slouched down to rest his head on the back of the settee, as if he'd been kicked in the gut.

Kate gave a singular bark at the departing Duc, unable to contain her anger. She then jumped up on the settee next to Lafayette.

The poor marquis! He not only was rejected by his father-in-law but humiliated in front of his brother-in-law whom he admires so very much! Liz thought sadly.

"I am sorry, Gilbert," Noailles offered, letting go a breath. "I have tried, but without success."

"It would appear that everyone is determined to tell me, '*Non, Monsieur le Marquis!*'" Lafayette scoffed, raising his hands in the air and letting them fall to the couch in despair. He wrinkled his brow and stood up abruptly, buttoning his coat with angry determination.

"Where are you going?" Noailles asked.

"To ask the Comte de Broglie once more for help," Lafayette answered determinedly, putting on his three-cornered hat.

Noailles remained seated. "And if you receive another 'No'?"

"Then I shall give my new standard reply to everyone who tells me 'No,'" Lafayette answered, storming out of the room. "CUR NON?!"

THE DE BROGLIE INTRIGUE

HOME OF COMTE DE BROGLIE, PARIS, FRANCE, NOVEMBER 16, 1776, 8:00 P.M.

Charles-François de Broglie sat by the fireplace, reading a paper when a servant gently knocked on his study door. *"Oui?"*

"Monsieur, there is someone here to see you," the servant replied. "He said it is most urgent that he speak with you."

De Broglie looked up from his report. *"Qui est-ce?"*

"The Marquis de Lafayette."

The Comte raised his eyebrows and set his report aside, standing to his feet. "Bring him in."

Within moments Lafayette entered the room, removing his hat and bowing in respect to de Broglie. *"Bonsoir, mon général.* Forgive the late hour, but I must speak with you."

"Bonsoir, have a seat," de Broglie replied, his hand out to an empty chair as he also sat down. "What is this about?"

Lafayette sat down but remained on the edge of his seat. "As you know, it is my desire to volunteer my services to go fight for the American cause. And I know that you have tried to discourage me from going, *mon général,* but I am determined in my course, and my decision is made!"

De Broglie sat with his elbows on the arms of his chair, propping up his chin with the tips of his fingers as he listened to Lafayette plead his case, listing all the reasons he should be allowed to go.

"My brother-in-law and I have attempted to gain the approval of our father-in-law, the Duc d'Ayen, but he refuses to use his influence at court to help us. The Vicomte de Noailles has also written to Maurepas, but to no avail." He paused and shook his head, looking at the floor for a moment. "You alone, *monsieur,* are the only elder officer to whom I can turn. *S'il vous plaît,* I beg of you to help me! I must answer this call upon my heart to go fight in this noble cause!"

The fire popped, and the Comte put his hands on his knees and exhaled, saying nothing. He stood and walked over to the fireplace, lifting an iron poker to stir the embers. "I admire your zeal, *mon cher Marquis*. I see in you the same fire that burned within the hearts of your father and uncle. They were true warriors." He stirred the embers that were slowly dying out. "If they were the ones here speaking with you tonight, I believe they would cheer you on. They would tell you to go to America."

"Oui! I, too, believe this! A true Lafayette would answer the call and go to America, no matter the opposition he faced," Lafayette agreed eagerly. "Everyone keeps telling me, 'No,' but I refuse to accept that!"

De Broglie reached for a thick stick from the brass wood holder and held it up, turning to look at Lafayette. "Good! Get even! The fire of the Lafayettes must continue to burn," he said, setting the stick onto the embers. As he stoked the fire, sparks popped and crackled up into the air. The fresh glow of flame illuminated his smiling face and he turned to look at the desperate marquis. "Be the first to go to America! I shall take care of it!"

Lafayette was taken aback, surprised at the sudden turn of his former commander. He jumped to his feet, a lump of joy in his throat. *"Mon général!* You will help me? *Je vous remercie!* I shall not let you down!"

De Broglie replaced the iron poker and came to put a hand on Lafayette's shoulder. "I will send you to meet with Baron De Kalb." He walked over to his desk and lifted a quill to dip in the ink well, writing a note of instruction while Lafayette stood at attention, his heart about to burst with hopeful anticipation. The Comte rose to his feet and handed the paper to Lafayette. "Take this to De Kalb. After he has thoroughly talked through this matter with you, he will then decide when to introduce you to *Monsieur* Deane."

Lafayette eagerly took the paper in hand. *"Merci, mon général!* I will go to see him tomorrow!"

De Broglie stood and escorted Lafayette to the door. "I have no doubt you will convince him, just as you have convinced me. *Bonne chance, Monsieur le Marquis.*"

Lafayette bowed and happily walked to the door. "This is what I intend, no? *Merci et bonsoir, mon cher général!*"

"Je vous en prie. Bonne soirée, Lafayette," de Broglie answered, shutting the door behind the eager teenager. He went over and picked up the paper he had been reading and tapped it on the palm of his hand, smiling. He walked over to his desk and gazed at the now roaring fire. "Now to make sure nothing douses those flames." He picked up his quill to write another note to enclose with the paper—to Silas Deane.

MILON-LA-CHAPELLE, COURBEVOIE, FRANCE, NOVEMBER 17, 1776

Liz sat on the stone wall of Baron De Kalb's lavish estate five miles from the heart of Paris, the tip of her tail slowly curling up and down. Her gaze remained fixed on the beautiful house where De Kalb lived with his wife and three children. After retiring from the French army as a colonel in 1764, this son of a Bavarian merchant married late but well. His wife Anna Elizabeth was heiress to a fortune made from the manufacture of cloth. Thinking he would live out his days in retirement in this tranquil setting with his family, De Kalb unexpectedly became employed in 1767 by the Duc de Choiseul, Foreign Minister under King Louis XV.

De Kalb was sent on a covert mission to America following the end of the Seven Years' War, referred to by Americans as the French and Indian War. Given his ability to speak French and English, he was a perfect choice to assess whether the colonists might rebel against the King of England with the trouble brewing over unwanted taxation without representation. Choiseul was convinced that an American Revolution would come and pushed for the rebuilding of France's navy in the hope of using the colonies to strike the British lion. But De Kalb reported that although the Americans possessed an extraordinary spirit of independence, he did not foresee a rebellion any time soon. Choiseul abandoned his idea, and De Kalb returned home to the French countryside. But when Vergennes later came to fill the post at Versailles, he, too, had the same vision of employing an American rebellion to exact revenge on Great Britain.

Now, De Kalb was poised to once more take up arms and return to America, this time serving on the rolls of the Continental Army.

A squirrel suddenly bolted across the pebbled circular drive, but Liz took no notice. Kate came bounding up to her. "Ye must be thinkin' hard aboot somethin', lass. Wha's on yer mind?"

Liz blinked and looked down at Kate, who stood there with her head cocked. "*Oui,* Kate. I just do not understand why de Broglie had such an abrupt change of heart about helping Lafayette. At first, he was adamantly committed to protecting the young marquis from harm. Now he is all but pushing him out the door of France to get to America. Why?"

"Maybe Lafayette jest charmed his former commander with such a zeal for liberty that de Broglie was convinced he should help the lad," Kate suggested. "Or maybe he knew Lafayette wouldn't let him rest an' would pester him ta death until he got his way. Kind of how Al does when there's fish ta be had—he takes Jesus' words seriously: Ask an' it will be given ye; seek an' ye'll find; knock an' the door will be opened ta ye."

Liz grinned, thinking of her relentless Albert. "Perhaps, but I wish to better understand his decision."

Just then a carriage pulled by a pair of horses made its way up the drive to the front of the house.

"Well, for now, let's see wha' happens when Lafayette an' Noailles meet with the Baron. Ye should be happy for the lads! I've never seen Lafayette as happy as when he got home with his note from de Broglie!"

"Oui, I *am* happy, it's just . . . I cannot put my paw on it," Liz answered, jumping from the wall to the ground next to Kate.

"Maybe ye're jest feelin' off since their friend Ségur had ta back out of the plan ta go ta America with Lafayette an' Noailles," Kate suggested. "His parents weren't havin' any of it, objectin' ta the idea from the start."

Liz nodded. *"Oui,* Ségur himself was concerned that the French Ministry would not approve of the three musketeers' plan. He quickly stopped asking, seeking, and knocking. But this is not why I feel ill at ease, *mon amie."*

Kate took a madeleine from her pouch. "Well, keep thinkin' while ye hide. Let's go see wha' happens when Lafayette asks, seeks, an' knocks on *this* door."

"Very well, Kate," Liz answered. She stepped into the pouch, and together, the invisible duo followed Lafayette and Noailles as they exited the carriage and entered the home of Baron Johann De Kalb.

"Bonjour, messieurs," the burly De Kalb warmly greeted Lafayette and Noailles with a firm handshake, speaking French tinged with a Bavarian accent. Tall and built with a large boxy frame, the fifty-five-year-old Bavarian towered over the two young, slender Frenchmen. His bushy brown eyebrows arched over his large brown eyes like musical fermatas and rose when Lafayette presented the note from de Broglie. He scratched his dimpled chin that already looked as if he had a five o'clock shadow, even though he had shaved a couple of hours earlier. "Come, let's discuss vat you seek to do, *ja? Bon."*

"Je vous remercie," Lafayette enthused, stepping quickly behind the Baron, who led them into a large sitting room with a roaring fire. Given his wife's family cloth business, the furniture was covered in immaculate French upholstery. "My brother-in-law and I are grateful for your time."

"Oui, this is an honor, *Monsieur,"* Noailles added, taking his seat next to Lafayette on the settee.

"So, you vish to go to America and join the rebel cause," De Kalb stated, getting right to the point. "Vhy?"

"The cause of *liberté* is the universal right of mankind, no? The Americans seek to throw off the tyranny that has stomped upon that right," Lafayette offered. "Their cause is just, and we must fight against tyranny to restore that freedom."

"The American revolt is our opportunity to exact revenge for the humiliation that France suffered at the hands of the British," Noailles added. "We are trained soldiers who are ready and willing to join the fight."

"You are an idealist," De Kalb quickly observed, pointing at Lafayette. Turning his gaze and finger at Noailles, "And you are a realist."

Lafayette and Noailles looked at one another, chuckling and nodding in agreement.

"Unlike the other French soldiers who have come to me to enlist, you two are of the nobility," De Kalb observed. "The Duc d'Ayen is vell regarded in the eyes of the French court. Vhatever you do as his sons-in-law, it vill be known by the French court and by default, likely the British Ambassador, Lord Stormont. How does the Duc feel about your desire to go fight for the insurgents in America?"

Noailles quickly spoke up. "The Duc would *favor* our enlistment on the condition that we be given the rank of general officers."

"Oui, and nothing would please him or us more than for us to serve under you!" Lafayette followed. *"Félicitations* on your rank as major-general. We ask that you please introduce us to *Monsieur* Deane so we may join you in America."

De Kalb looked at the two eager Frenchmen for a moment, rubbing his chin. "Hmmmm. I know that you trained under Comte de Broglie at Metz, but I vill require seeing your full military records—your *livret militaire*— before I take you to Deane, *ja?"*

Lafayette eagerly nodded. *"Oui, oui, bien sûr!* We shall get those and return to see you. Is tomorrow convenient, *mon général?"*

"He sure didn't waste any time askin'," Kate whispered to Liz as the men talked among themselves. "An' he's already callin' De Kalb by his rank then."

"Lafayette is quick to ask," Liz whispered back. "This is one of the things I like about him, no? But Noailles leading De Kalb to believe that he and Lafayette already have the blessing of the Duc is a stretch."

"Aye, seekin' the truth may take a wee bit of diggin'," Kate agreed.

"Well, at least it appears that the door to *Monsieur* Deane is now open," Liz noted as the men stood and shook hands. "I wish to see if I can learn more about de Broglie's intentions by paying a visit to *Monsieur* Deane myself."

Deane's List

After their initial meeting, Lafayette promptly returned to see De Kalb and continued discussions with him nearly every day. De Kalb even came to see Lafayette at the *Hôtel de Noailles* where he met Adrienne but not the Duc d'Ayen. De Kalb assumed that Adrienne knew what they discussed and even approved of her enthusiastic husband's quest for an American military position.

Lafayette was eager to learn as much as he could about America and how the French would wage war with the Americans against the British. But within a few days, Noailles joined Ségur and dropped out of the scheme to get to America. He was unwilling to cross their father-in-law, as he was not only beholden to the Duc's good graces, but also to his money. Lafayette, on the other hand was independently wealthy, and was in no danger of being "cut off." While he, too, wished the blessing of his dear Papa, his determination was set in stone to forge ahead with his plans. Lafayette therefore avoided the topic of his father-in-law's approval as he was sure that the Duc would surely consent once the persistent marquis secured a high-ranking position with the American army.

Liz's insatiable curiosity kept her seeking further insights about de Broglie, but nothing had come to light. She knew she needed to access the correspondence of Silas Deane, but the sheer volume of papers and letters in his office was overwhelming, and the continual stream of humans in and out of his quarters complicated matters. Since De Kalb had arranged to finally bring Lafayette to meet Deane on December 7th, Liz insisted that Kate bring her to Deane's office ahead of that meeting.

"I will not give my approval until I feel good about Lafayette's situation, no?" Liz insisted before dawn to a very sleepy Kate. "Let us be going, *mon amie.*"

"Ayyyyyyye," Kate yawned and stretched in reply. Together they got to Deane's headquarters before sunrise.

Kate kept watch by the door while Liz hopped up on Deane's desk and located his pile of outgoing correspondence to the Secret Committee of Correspondence. He would write and accumulate packets of numerous letters to send to Congress, being diligent to make duplicate copies to send via different ships in case a ship was lost at sea or seized by the British.

"Wha' do ye see, Liz?" Kate whispered.

"A letter dated November 28th, let me see . . ." Liz said, scanning the letter.

> "*The apprehensions of the United States negotiating has done us much damage, and the interview at New York, said to have been between a Commission of Congress and the Two Brothers, however politik the step in America, was made use of to our prejudice in Europe, at this Court in particular, as it has been for some time asserted, by Lord Stormont and others, that a negotiation would take place, and as far as this is believed so far our cause has suffered and our friends have staggered in their resolutions. My opinion is that the House of Bourbon in every branch will be our friends; it is their interest to humble Great Britain.*

"Hmmm, it would seem that when John Adams and Benjamin Franklin met with Admiral Howe (representing the two Howe Brothers), it did harm to give even a hint that the Americans would consider negotiating with the British," Liz explained. "Evidently Lord Stormont is using that meeting as a tool to scare off the French court, but Deane still believes that France will stick with us."

"That's a relief," Kate said. "Jest because they met with Admiral Howe doesn't mean the Americans were goin' ta compromise. Wha' else does Deane write?"

Liz scanned further down the page. "He writes:

> "*I am well nigh harassed to death with applications of officers to go out for America. Those I have engaged are, I trust, in general of the best character . . .*
>
> "*Baron De Kalb I consider as an important acquisition, as are many other of the officers whose characters I may not stay to particularize, but refer you to Baron De Kalb, who speaks English, and to Mr. Rogers, who are generally acquainted with them.*"

"Nice ta see how highly Deane thinks aboot De Kalb," Kate noted.

"*Oui*, then on November 29th, Deane sings the praises of Colonel Conway, a native of Ireland. He believes him to be a fine officer who shall be of very great service," Liz relayed. She then flipped through a few more pages. "Here is a letter to John Jay dated December 3rd:

"A war in Europe is inevitable. The eyes of all men are on you, and the fear of your giving up or accommodating is the greatest obstacle I have to contend with. Monsieur Beaumarchais has been my Minister, in effect, as this Court is extremely cautious ..."

Scanning further down the letter, Liz read:

"Had I ten ships here I could fill them all with passengers for America. I hope the officers sent will be agreeable: they were recommended by the Ministry here, and are at this instant really in their army, but this must be a secret."

Liz wrinkled her brow. "But this does not make sense, as the French Ministry has not recommended these officers, no? In fact, they have *avoided* officially recommending them, just as Maurepas refused to recommend Noailles. If the French Ministry officially recommended officers and word leaked to Stormont, it would mean instant war. Hmmm, perhaps he means that an *agent of the French Ministry* recommended them."

"Well, since de Broglie has been sendin' them ta Deane, don't ye think he'd be the one that Deane means?" Kate asked.

"That is possible, of course, but at least Deane does indicate that it must remain a secret that these French officers are actually in the French army, but taking leave to come to America," Liz surmised. She skimmed further. "Ah, here is a note commending Dr. Bancroft:

"Doctor Bancroft has been of very great service to me; no man has better intelligence in England, in my opinion, but it costs something ..."

"I'm glad that Dr. Bancroft has been able ta be such a grand help ta his old tutor," Kate said happily.

"Oui, there are some letters from him in the stack of incoming mail to Deane," Liz noted. "He sends articles and information to Deane on a regular basis and hopes to return soon to assist him."

Suddenly they heard footsteps as Silas Deane made his way to the office to start work for the day.

"Hurry, Liz, get off the desk!" Kate warned. "Deane must be gettin' an early start before he eats breakfast!"

Liz slid the letter back in place and jumped off Deane's desk just as he opened the door. He proceeded to sit down at his desk, take out a fresh piece of paper, and begin a new letter to the Committee of Secret Correspondence. After a while he got up and went to a credenza on which sat piles of papers including the contracts he had signed with the French officers. He pulled from a stack several pieces of paper with a note attached. He took it back to his desk and sat for a few moments reading before setting it aside.

"Wha's he doin'?" Kate whispered.

"I believe he is thinking about what he just read," Liz whispered back.

Deane nodded once and picked up his quill to write again. After completing a paragraph, he blew on the ink and then stood, stretched out his back, and left it sitting there. He picked up the paper he had been reading and carried it with him, folding it as if he would discard it, but the attached note fell to the floor. When Deane left the room to go eat his *petit déjeuner*, Liz climbed out of the bag and jumped back up onto his desk. Kate, meanwhile, went to see the note on the floor.

"Now let us see what *Monsieur* Deane has freshly inked this morning," Liz announced, scanning the December 6th letter. "He has prepared a List of Officers of Infantry and Light Troops destined to serve the United States of America, giving their name, rank, and date of enlistment. Baron De Kalb is at the top of this list of sixteen officers, followed by a De Mauroy, who is also a major-general. The rest of the officers are lieutenant colonels, majors, captains, and lieutenants."

Kate's eyes widened as she read the fallen note. "Liz, I think ye better read this!"

Liz jumped to the floor and read the note:

Lafayette is an idealistic youth with vast wealth and important connections to court. He also has very little knowledge of the world. He might prove quite useful to my plan.

"Who wrote this?" Kate wanted to know.

"It definitely looks French. Let me see if I can make out this handwriting," Liz replied with a frown. She jumped up onto the credenza with the piles of contracts, along with letters of introduction. She compared the handwriting and suddenly her eyes landed on a note that matched.

"That note was written by none other than Comte de Broglie," Liz answered, swishing her tail furiously back and forth.

Kate wrinkled her brow. "But wha' plan is he talkin' aboot?"

Liz's mind raced and she jumped back over to Deane's desk to read more of the letter he had just penned to the Committee of Secret Correspondence. She read it aloud to Kate:

"I submit one thought to you: Whether if you could engage a great general of the highest character in Europe, such, for instance, as Prince Ferdinand, Marshal Broglie, or others of equal rank to take the lead of your armies, whether such a step would not be politic, as it would give a character and credit to your military and strike perhaps a greater panic in our enemies. I only suggest the thought and leave you to confer with the Baron De Kalb on the subject at large."

"Wait, wha' is Deane suggestin'? That Congress should replace General Washington with a general from Europe?" Kate asked. "Do he mean de Broglie?"

Liz wrinkled her brow. "I am afraid that is *exactly* what Deane is suggesting, on both counts." Her mind raced as she put the pieces together. She looked up at the ceiling quickly and then shook her head. "How did I not see this? De Broglie has enlisted De Kalb to recruit and take to America a contingent of faithful French officers to set the stage for him to then join them with a commission of his own—that of Commander-in-Chief. He wishes to take Washington's place!"

"If Max were here, he'd corner that schemer an' gr-r-rab his back side!" Kate exclaimed. "I suppose it's never dawned on de Br-r-roglie that maybe—jest maybe—America could produce a leader of her own who could lead her ta victory?" Kate ranted.

"Steady, *chère* Kate," Liz told her.

"An' I suppose de Br-r-roglie thinks a nation of farmers with pitchforks can't possibly take on the mighty Br-r-ritish Lion!" Kate growled. "Do he think he's some sort of messiah ta save the poor wee rebels?!"

Liz put her paw on Kate's back. "I understand your anger over de Broglie's plan, but to de Broglie and other experienced soldiers of war, it is only logical to assume that the Americans need help, no?" she tried to explain. "I am more shocked that *Deane* would even suggest such a thing. After all, he was one of General Washington's strongest supporters when he was elected to the post of Commander-in-Chief!"

"Aye, I can't believe it! Maybe Deane has been in France too long! How could he forget his Commander-in-Chief and friend George Washington so soon?" Kate wailed. "Deane's been dazzled by all the experienced French officers dressed in their fine uniforms an' shiny medals comin' ta see him every day. This news makes me mad *and* sad." Kate dreaded asking the next question. "Do ye think De Kalb's in on this plot, too?"

Liz frowned. "Well, he may not have been involved in devising the plan, but he must know about it. De Kalb served under de Broglie for thirty years and is extremely loyal to him. He is the one that de Broglie has used to create Deane's list of French officers. And Deane even writes that Congress should confer with *De Kalb* about a potential replacement for Washington when he arrives in America."

"But I truly like Baron De Kalb." Kate's eyes watered. "Wha' aboot Lafayette?"

"*Moi aussi.* I like *Monsieur* De Kalb very much, *mon amie,*" Liz replied softly. "Sadly, I am afraid that the only one who does not know about this plot is Lafayette himself. From de Broglie's note, it appears that he sees Lafayette as a useful pawn in his plan. This is why he so quickly changed his mind about supporting Lafayette in his desire to go to America. De Broglie apparently cares more now about how useful Lafayette can be to him in his coup."

Kate growled. "How dar-r-re he?! Mousie would say this be intoler-r-rable!"

"Kate, you are so angry you are rolling your r's just like Max," Liz noted with surprise. "But I understand, for I feel the same."

Just then Liz looked down to suddenly see a piece of parchment sitting on the desk with the Order of the Seven wax seal. She put her paw on it. "It's from Gillamon!"

"From Gillamon?! On Deane's desk?" Kate asked in surprise. "Better break the seal before Deane gets back!"

Liz grabbed the paper and jumped to the floor to be next to Kate. She pulled her claw across the wax seal, and together she and Kate vanished from the room.

THE PLOT THICKENS

THE IAMISPHERE

Liz and Kate entered the towering time portal where the sound of rushing wind and moving panels of time encircled them.

"And how are my two favorite lady agents in Paris?" Gillamon asked with a warm grin. He was in his true form of a mountain goat, his goatee blowing in the gentle breeze.

"*Bonjour,* Gillamon, but we are your *only* two lady agents in Paris, no?" Liz answered logically. "I assume Clarie is busy in America."

Kate rushed over to the wise team leader and buried her head in his chest. "I'm so happy ta see ye, Gillamon! We've jest learned some troublin' news."

"I know, Kate." Gillamon nudged the Westie with his nose. "There, there, little one. All will be well. I knew you could use some insights and some good news about the Lafayette mission."

Kate looked up hopefully. "Aye, good news would be grand."

"So, you know about this plot by Comte de Broglie to use De Kalb as his front man to take French officers over to America with the goal of replacing Washington?" Liz asked. "*C'est ridicule!*"

Gillamon nodded with a reassuring smile. "In times of war there have always been schemers who take advantage of the situation to elevate themselves to positions of power or to fill their pockets with money. De Broglie is no different. He has always been a schemer, and even served as head of King Louis XV's personal spy unit, the *Secret du Roi.* He reported directly to the king, and his unit's activities were not reported to the king's cabinet. He likes to hide in the shadows."

"Most schemers do!" Kate agreed.

"Because some of his actions with the previous king turned sour, King Louis XVI and his cabinet do not view de Broglie favorably," Gillamon further explained. "They see him as a dangerous man. Because he has lost opportunity for power in France, he sees an opportunity with the American Revolution, where his ambitions can thrive among people who will revere his valid military experience but not know the extent of his political failures."

"De Broglie *is* a dangerous man!" Liz warned. "He even appears to be toying with young Lafayette to use him for his ambitious plan."

"But in this case, what de Broglie intends for evil will be used for Lafayette's good," Gillamon replied with a knowing twinkle in his eyes.

Kate and Liz looked at one another with surprised looks of relief. "How so, Gillamon?" Kate asked.

"We'll get to that," Gillamon told them.

"And what about Baron De Kalb?" Liz asked. "We believe him to be a fine human, but his involvement with de Broglie's plot makes us wonder."

"De Kalb is indeed a fine human, although temporarily misguided," Gillamon assured them. "He will come around once he gets to America, meets Washington, and sees the situation with fresh eyes."

"Ah, wha' a relief, Gillamon!" Kate exclaimed happily.

"So, what are we supposed to do about this plot?" Liz asked. "Will you get word to Washington about these Frenchmen?"

"No need to alarm Washington about this particular plot. There will always be attempts to remove him from power as Commander-in-Chief, but no weapon forged against him will prosper," Gillamon explained. "As you know, Max and Jock prevented the assassination attempt on Washington's life in New York. Scheming men from within and without will seek to take his place, and we will deal with each one of them in turn. For now," Gillamon went on, walking over to the moving panels of time, "we're going to keep Beaumarchais' fleet from sailing with de Broglie's officers on board." He pulled a panel into view. It was Beaumarchais riding in a carriage toward the port city of Le Havre.

"But Gillamon! Washington and the Continental Army desperately *need* those weapons and supplies that Beaumarchais has worked so hard to acquire!" Liz protested.

"Aye! Why would ye keep them ships from sailin', even if de Broglie's men are on board then?" Kate added. "Those soldier lads desperately need guns, powder, an' clothes!"

"Never fear, the supplies will arrive as intended, albeit later than planned," Gillamon assured them. "But even the delay will serve to protect that precious cargo destined for the Patriots. The AOG reports that a fierce nor'easter is churning in the Atlantic."

"AOG?" Kate asked.

"Acts of God. It's the heavenly command center for weather and earthly events such as earthquakes and volcanoes," Gillamon explained with a knowing grin. "A team of angels is always at the ready to intervene and rescue humans from natural disasters. Humans will never fully realize the events they are saved from due to the Maker's delays."

"Why have we never heard of this AOG command center?" Liz wanted to know.

Gillamon leaned his head low to wink at Liz. "You've never asked."

Liz giggled. "Well, I would love to go there sometime and see the behind-the-scenes of weather events in action. *C'est magnifique!*"

"I'm afraid access is restricted to those in the spiritual realm," Gillamon explained.

"Do me grand-lad Jock's weather abilities come from the AOG?" Kate asked.

Gillamon grinned. "Something like that, Kate. Now, back to Beaumarchais. Our clever playwright will find a way to get his ships to set sail despite what we do, but they will *not* sail with de Broglie's men on board. It is not yet time for Lafayette to leave France, and we need to make sure that he doesn't 'miss the boat,' if you will. De Kalb must not sail to America without Lafayette. All of this will make sense in time."

"It always does, eventually," Liz answered with a confused look, trying to understand. "So, we will keep De Kalb and his officers from leaving France—for now—until Lafayette can sail with them?"

"Or until *they* can sail with Lafayette," Gillamon replied with a wink.

Kate cocked her head to the side. "An' jest how are we supposed ta do such a thing?"

Gillamon pointed to Beaumarchais nearing the city of Le Havre. "Tell me, why has British Ambassador Stormont been unable to protest what Beaumarchais has been doing with the fictitious company of Hortalez and Company?"

Liz thought a moment. "For one thing, Beaumarchais has brilliantly hidden his business dealings in plain sight in Paris from British spies so they cannot quite connect the dots to Deane and the Americans. Plus, he is a master of disguise, no?"

"Aye, he takes on different disguises when he travels ta various port cities as he prepares the ships ta sail ta America with the supplies," Kate added.

"So, he has kept his cover well hidden from Stormont's spies, even though he is *suspected* of collecting weapons and supplies to send to America," Gillamon replied. "Stormont knows that Deane has met with Vergennes and Beaumarchais, but he has not been able to connect the dots and *prove* that France is assisting the Americans. Because of his secret dealings and disguises, Stormont has not been able to present Vergennes with specific proof. So, if Beaumarchais was caught as the man in charge of these specific ships sailing to America with not only supplies but French officers on board who will fight alongside the Americans . . ."

Liz and Kate thought a moment, looking at each other. Liz's eyes suddenly grew wide.

"Stormont would be able to freely present to Vergennes *proof* that French aid and men are heading to America, which would be seen as an act of war!" Liz answered.

"If British spies catch Beaumarchais in the act, that's all the proof Stormont needs ta pressure Vergennes ta stop the ships from sailin'!" Kate added, then frowning. "So how do we get Beaumarchais ta blow his cover?"

Gillamon didn't respond but allowed them to think as he brought another panel into view. An elderly man with spectacles and thin, gray hair peeping out of a fur cap hobbled wearily down a stone jetty after getting out of a small fishing vessel. He walked with a cane, accompanied by two boys aged seventeen and seven who each carried baggage. "Benjamin Franklin landed in Auray, Brittany, two days ago with his grandsons, Temple and Benny. When his ship the *Reprisal* faced contrary winds that prevented them from sailing closer to Paris, he asked to be put ashore and travel by land, for he couldn't bear another day aboard. Our aged statesman needs time to recover from his long voyage. Over the next three weeks he'll wend his way to Paris via Nantes. Word will reach Versailles tomorrow, and nothing else will be talked about other than *why* Dr. Franklin has come to France."

"It will not take Lord Stormont long to connect the dots of France helping America once *Monsieur* Franklin gets in the public eye," Liz predicted, her tail curling up and down in thought.

"Indeed," Gillamon agreed. "Do you recall the purpose of Nigel's mission with Dr. Franklin thirty years ago?"

"*Oui!* It was to make Dr. Franklin a celebrity in France with his lightning experiment," Liz eagerly answered. "He is the most famous American in France! This is of course why King Louis sent the French spy Bonvouloir to secretly meet with Franklin in Philadelphia for the very first discussion between France and America last December."

"Aye, Dr. Franklin be the *key* ta unlock the door ta France's help for America!" Kate added.

Gillamon nodded with a grin. "That key was inserted into a lock that turned the knob; now Dr. Franklin has come to fully open the door to French aid beyond weapons and supplies—he will secure an official alliance with France. But it all was possible because of his *fame*. Tell me, what does Beaumarchais share with Benjamin in that regard?"

"Beaumarchais is a famous playwright who adores the spotlight with his popular play, *Le Barbier de Séville,*" Liz answered. "He loves to play the part of the crafty Figaro, not only onstage but offstage as well in his sneaky espionage and secret dealings."

"The lad has an irresistible passion for his plays an' characters," Kate added.

Gillamon brought another panel into view, of a small theater in Le Havre. Hammers were banging away on a set, actors were practicing their lines, and a young boy gathered up a stack of broadsides to go plaster them around the town, announcing the performance of *Le Barbier de Séville*. "We've arranged for Beaumarchais's play to be performed to coincide with his time in Le Havre." He looked at Liz and Kate with a coy grin. "And might I add that this particular troupe of actors are *less* than talented."

Liz's eyes brightened with understanding. *"Bon!* So, all we need to do is make sure that Beaumarchais knows about his play being performed, and resistance will be futile, no? He will not be able to help himself in giving direction to his pet work to improve the performance."

"An' once he does, it won't take long for the actors, audience, an' guests ta know that Beaumarchais, Durand, an' Hortalez be one an' the same human!" Kate followed. "Pride will get the best of Beaumarchais, as it do with most humans at one time or another."

"Precisely, ladies," Gillamon confirmed. "You may enter Le Havre directly through this panel. You'll have to act quickly, since you need to be back in Paris tomorrow for Lafayette's big day."

"Oui! Lafayette and De Kalb will meet with Silas Deane to receive his commission!" Liz enthused. *"Merci,* Gillamon. I will no longer be concerned that Lafayette will be led astray by that designing de Broglie."

"Je vous en prie, Liz," Gillamon answered with his warm smile. He handed Kate a piece of parchment. "Take this with you. It has the Seven Seal attached. You'll be able to break it, return here to the IAMISPHERE and simply select Deane's headquarters as your destination to travel quickly back to Paris."

"Thank ye, Gillamon," Kate said happily, putting the parchment in her pouch. "We'll be back from Normandy ta Paris in a flash."

Liz closed her eyes in delight. "Ah, my beloved Normandy! It will be heaven to be back in my home region of France, if only for a day." She turned to Kate excitedly. "Let us be going, *mon amie."*

"Bonne chance, little ones," Gillamon told them as they entered the panel of the theater at Le Havre. "Enjoy the drama to come . . . with the best act being the unmasking of Figaro."

50

UNMASKING FIGARO

L iz watched the feathery, white cirrus clouds swipe across the azure blue sky above the pebbled beach of Le Havre. The brisk wind blew back her whiskers, and her black fur soaked up the radiant warmth from the bright sunshine. She closed her eyes and inhaled the salty fragrance of the sea crashing into shore and fizzling down into the grayish-brown sand. Tiny crabs scurried among the pebbles and a swath of buttery-colored sea-foam lazily carried pieces of green seaweed to rest on a cluster of large rocks. The French cat sighed contentedly. *"Je t'aime, la Normandie."*

"Ye look happy, lass," Kate whispered with her peppy grin.

"Oui, je suis très heureuse, mon amie," Liz answered, her eyes still closed. "This port city was first called Havre-de-Grâce—'Haven of Grace,' and it is certainly living up to its name. In the middle of dealing with scheming humans and war, it is lovely to take what I like to call 'minute vacations.'" She opened her eyes. "They are like havens of grace, no?"

"Aye, it does a lass good ta catch her breath," Kate agreed. "Plus, it's always grand ta return home for a visit. Yer home were a bit down the coast as I remember, but it's been a long time since Craddock the whale brought us ta the beaches of Normandy on our way ta the Ark!"

"Oui, the humans now call my home Colleville-sur-Mer, which is west of here," Liz replied, looking down the beach. She giggled, "And as I recall, you, Max, and Albert *stormed* the beaches of Normandy when Craddock propelled you from his blowhole to reach the shore! No wonder *mon* Albert ran from fright until he reached my garden."

"Where the lad promptly destroyed everythin' in sight after eatin' the catnip!" Kate recalled. "I'll never forget Henriette scolding Al an' the fear on the poor kitty's face when she told him he'd have to explain his behavior ta the 'mad moiselle.' He thought ye'd be a terrifyin' beastie! But ye weren't mad at all, lass. Ye showed great kindness an' forgiveness that day."

Liz giggled. "Henriette was a bossy hen, but she meant well. Ah, but it was *l'amour* at first sight seeing pitiful Albert trying to apologize for ruining my garden. I was upset, *oui,* but forgiveness was necessary. Besides, the loss of my garden helped me to leave my beloved home to follow the fire cloud with all of you, no?"

"Things have a way of workin' out for the good of those who love the Maker an' are called accordin' ta His purposes, don't they, Liz?" Kate asked happily, paraphrasing her favorite verse. The white dog looked around the beach and harbor. "So how far are we from Paris then?"

Liz smiled and wiped the sea spray from her face. "We are approximately one hundred thirty miles west-northwest of Paris, at the mouth of the Seine River." She pointed out to sea. "England is only about ninety-three miles across *La Manche.*"

"Jest think how close King George an' the British really be ta King Louis an' the French!" Kate marveled. "Only a few miles separate these countries that fight like cats an' dogs." She put her paw on Liz's shoulder. "Good thing that phrase don't apply ta us lassies."

"Agreed, *chère* Kate," Liz told her fondly. *"Oui,* the close proximity of England and France has of course led to their many wars over the centuries. This is one of the reasons why François I established this port city of Le Havre, as protection from the enemy sailing down the Seine River to Paris." Liz walked over to jump up onto the rock jetty leading to the harbor. "But this port is easy for trading ships to access with the quay that reaches seventy yards into the deep harbor. Let us go inspect the ships that *Monsieur* Beaumarchais is loading to send to America."

"Except those ships won't be sailin' when the humans think they will after we do our work here today," Kate pointed out with a wink.

The two friends made their way to the massive stone wharf where three large ships bobbed in the water while tied with sturdy ropes to enormous iron cleats. Sailors and workers bustled to and fro from the warehouses along the waterfront, loading the ships like busy ants swarming an anthill. Barrels of gunpowder and sulfur sat in a line. A massive pyramid of cannonballs was replenished as quickly as it was dismantled by the busy sailors bringing twenty thousand of the four-pound balls from the warehouses to load onto the ship called *L'Amphitrite.* Two hundred older brass cannons and their brick-red gun carriages lined the quay and were slowly hoisted via pulleys rigged to the soaring masts above.

Kate's mouth gaped open as she saw the incredible amount of artillery being loaded onto a single ship. "Jest think! These guns will be fired in America by George Washington's Continental Army!" The Westie stopped at one of the cannons with ornate dolphin handles affixed to the barrel. "Maybe Jock will even be with Henry Knox when he fires this one."

"Quite possibly, Kate," Liz answered, tapping the cannon carriage with her paw. "These guns shall travel three thousand miles across the ocean to reach the Patriots," Liz added. *"C'est magnifique! Monsieur* Beaumarchais must be applauded for the incredible work he has done to help the Americans, no?"

"Aye, but we're here ta make sure he seeks applause from the *local audience* for his play," Kate answered.

"Oui, so it appears that the three ships we are here to stop from sailing—for the time being—are *L'Amphitrite, La Seine, and La Romaine,"* Liz noted, reading the names painted with gold flourish on the stern of each ship. "Now, to find Beaumarchais and deliver to him an invitation to his play."

Liz and Kate trotted along the quay, drawing smiles and chuckles from the sailors as they passed. They made their way up the hillside and into the town, which overlooked the harbor. After searching through several streets, they came to a mural emblazoned on the side of the building. A grinning Figaro was dressed in a harlequin costume and mask, holding a razor above a fat, older man sitting in a barber's chair, looking up at the mischievous barber with alarm. *"Le Barbier de Séville!* This must be the place."

Together they sneaked in the door that was propped open to allow fresh air because of the numerous candles and oil lamps that lit up the stage inside. They hid behind some chairs in the back of the darkened theatre and observed a disorganized disaster in progress. Actors were forgetting their lines, tripping over sets, and arguing over who was in charge.

"Gillamon were right, they don't seem ta be the best troupe of actors," Kate told Liz with a grin. "This will be easy. Now ta get one of those broadsides aboot the play." She looked around and noticed a stack of the flyers sitting on a table. She reached up and snagged one. "Got it!" she announced through gritted teeth.

"Bon! Now to find Beaumarchais," Liz cheered. Together they slipped out of the theatre and made their way back to the wharf.

"Where are these ships bound, *Monsieur?"* the local police lieutenant asked a tall, well-dressed man holding a leather folio and a pencil.

"Je m'appelle Monsieur Durand. These ships will soon sail to the West Indies, of course," Beaumarchais answered coolly, looking down his inventory list with the name HORTALEZ ET CIE written at the top. "We must equip our French forces in Martinique *et* Guadeloupe. Now, if you'll excuse me, *monsieur,* I have quite a number of items to inspect."

The police officer tipped a finger to his hat and walked on. Liz and Kate watched him depart and hurried to catch up with the busy Beaumarchais. He was a whirlwind of instructions, checking his list against the cargo manifest for each of the three ships.

"No, no, no! There are only supposed to be *fifty-two* brass cannons loaded on *L'Amphitrite,* along with fifty-two carriages," Beaumarchais barked. "The weight has been calculated to be evenly distributed among the three ships." He scanned down his specific list for this ship and mumbled as he read. "Powder and 20,000 cannon balls, 9,000 grenades, 6,500 muskets, 900 tents, spades, pickaxes, 320 blankets, 8,545 stockings, 4,097 shirts, and 1,272 dozen pocket handkerchiefs."

Liz raised her eyebrows. *"Très* impressive, no? He is an excellent manager with precise attention to detail."

"That he is, lass. I kin only imagine how he'll whip those actors inta shape for his play!" Kate answered.

"Kate, let me have the paper, *s'il vous plaît,"* Liz requested, seeing Beaumarchais walk over to a barrel to write some notes on his list. "I shall get up close and personal with our playwright."

"Okay, lass," Kate answered, handing the paper to Liz.

Liz's tail with its curlycue tip stretched high into the air as she sauntered over to the barrel. She jumped up and startled Beaumarchais, setting the paper on the top of the barrel. *Pour vous, monsieur,* she meowed.

Beaumarchais started, then laughed, delighted to see this beautiful, sleek cat. He reached over to pet her soft fur. *"Bonjour, ma douce petite chatte. Très jolie. Ça va?"* He then looked down to see in big, bold letters:

BEAUMARCHAIS
LE BARBIER DE SÉVILLE
12, 13, 14 DÉCEMBRE AU THÉÂTRE LE HAVRE

He quickly shot his gaze back to Liz with inexplicable surprise and delight. "How is it possible that you brought this to me?" He looked around and whispered in her ear. "For I am none other than Beaumarchais!"

Oui, monsieur, Liz meowed drolly. *I, of course, know this. And you shall do my bidding and go immediately to the theatre where you will discover that this play desperately needs your direction. You will then blow your cover identity and word will quickly spread to Versailles, Lord Stormont, and King George III himself that you are aiding the Americans. Tu comprends?*

Beaumarchais laughed and scratched Liz under the chin while he proudly read the broadside about his play. "What a funny little thing you are, and quite talkative, no?" He leaned over and got face to face with Liz. "I would love to continue our conversation, but I must go to the theatre and make sure that the coming performances are as ship-shape as these ships."

You are such an obedient human, Liz meowed with a coy grin. *Do not worry when your ships do not sail. Everything will work out,* monsieur. She jumped off the barrel and walked off to rejoin Kate.

"*Voilà,* it is done!" Liz reported. "Beaumarchais is on his way. Shall we follow him to observe the unmaking of Figaro?"

"With pleasure, lass!" Kate replied. Together she and Liz followed Beaumarchais as he wended his way through the bustling streets of Le Havre.

As they reached the theatre, laughter poured out from a café across the street, where French military officers waiting to board Beaumarchais's ships gathered. They bragged about the pummeling they were going to give the British in America. A British spy emerged from the café and spotted Beaumarchais as he proudly entered the theatre. The spy grinned, looked both ways, crossed the street, and slipped into the darkened theatre behind the suspected playwright.

Meanwhile, from the adjacent alley, the local police lieutenant took note of everything he saw.

51

Major General Developments

Lafayette's heart pounded as De Kalb knocked on Silas Deane's door with the tip of his walking stick. The young officer straightened his cravat and clasped his sweaty palms behind his back. Soon they heard footsteps coming to the door, and Lafayette let go a quick breath of nervous anticipation.

"*Bonjour,* General De Kalb," Deane greeted the burly man. Seeing Lafayette standing behind him, he gave a tired sigh. "Come in. I see you've brought yet another young officer with you."

"*Ja,* good day, Mr. Deane. Allow me to introduce the Marquis de Lafayette. Ve have come to discuss his vish to go to America," De Kalb explained, stepping in the door and holding his hand out to Lafayette. Turning to Lafayette, he spoke in French to introduce Deane. "*Je vous présente Monsieur Silas Deane.*"

Lafayette graciously bowed and smiled broadly. "*C'est un plaisir de faire votre connaissance, monsieur.*"

"He is honored to meet you, *Monsieur* Deane," De Kalb translated.

Deane smiled warmly and nodded his head, studying the young man. "*Enchanté, Monsieur le Marquis.* I have heard about you but am surprised to find you to be so young."

As the men made small talk, De Kalb kept a running translation going between Deane and Lafayette.

"*Oui,* with my youth I bring you the energy and vitality needed to wage war and fight for the justice of your cause, no?" Lafayette enthused with a confident smile.

Kate and Liz looked on, cloaked and out of sight while the men sat down in the parlor. They proceeded to have a lengthy discussion about the events leading up to the conflict with Great Britain and her colonies, the Seven Year's War and the loss of Lafayette's father, the current enlistments of French officers under the command of Baron De Kalb, and Silas Deane's role in granting commissions.

"The lad's eager ta sell Deane on why he should be allowed ta go ta America," Kate whispered.

Liz nodded. "I cannot help but think that young Gilbert must feel very much like young Patrick Henry did the day he found his voice in the Parson's Cause case. After failing at everything he tried, that court case was his last opportunity to prove to himself and to his father that he had what it took to be a lawyer and to realize his life's purpose. Thus far Gilbert has been unable to achieve anything on his own merit and has been faced with closed doors to *his* passion and life's purpose."

Kate nodded. "Aye, he must feel like this be his last chance ta escape any life but soldierin'. He's always strived ta be the best at whatever he did, whether it be school, ridin' a horse, or trainin' ta be a soldier. But every young lad must answer his true callin' by steppin' out on his own. An' Gilbert is aboot as eager ta realize his passion of soldierin' as any lad I've ever seen. He's dreamt of bein' like Lancelot with the Knights of the Round Table since he were a wee marquis!"

"I have thoroughly reviewed his military record. Lafayette trained with Comte de Broglie at Metz," De Kalb relayed with a knowing look. "He is a captain in the Noailles Dragoon Regiment."

"Very well," Deane answered as he made some notes to himself. "I understand you are now on reserve status. Let me confirm your leadership experience. As a captain, how many total men have you had under your command—sixty, one hundred?"

"Fifty," Lafayette answered nervously.

"*Fifty?*" Deane asked while Lafayette nodded quietly. He jotted that down and cleared his throat. "I see. Now, what is your age?"

Lafayette squirmed. "Nineteen, *monsieur.*"

Deane made a notation and did the math in his head of Lafayette's age and France's peacetime years. "So, I assume you haven't yet been to war?"

Lafayette frowned and shook his head, chagrined. "*Non.*"

Deane put down his pen, sat back in his chair, cleared his throat, and crossed his arms. "So why do you seek to go to America?"

"*Monsieur,* I come from a long line of warriors stretching back a thousand years! The Lafayettes have always answered the call to fight, whether it be fighting for the Crusades in the Holy Land, with Joan d'Arc in the Hundred Years' War, defending France from any enemy, or standing guard for the King himself." Lafayette sat on the edge of his seat and grew more animated with each sentence. "This passion and skill to fight as a soldier lies not only in my family's bloodline, but in my mind and heart! When I first heard of your glorious cause, I knew that I, too, wanted to be part of it. I not only give America my heart and mind, but I hereby give her my sword as well, to fight for her independence. I wish to fight and achieve glory on the battlefield, for America and for France!"

Deane raised his eyebrows and shared a look with De Kalb. "And no doubt glory for *yourself, Monsieur le Marquis.* Not to mention the fact that you would be glad to exact revenge for the death of your father at the hands of the British. You certainly are passionate."

"Deane does not seem convinced," Liz observed. "He is weary of the long train of French thrill-seekers who have walked through his door, no?"

Kate frowned. "Aye."

"He is vell connected at court with both the Lafayette and the Noailles families," De Kalb interjected.

"You are young, passionate, and well-connected, but you are *inexperienced,*" Deane stated matter-of-factly. "I have already extended many commissions to experienced officers, and I fear have *overextended* the coffers of Congress's ability to pay."

"He has lots of *money,*" De Kalb quickly offered. "He is vone of the vealthiest noblemen in France. Vast land holdings."

"Oui, so I will serve at my own expense!" Lafayette eagerly added.

Deane's eyes widened, and he sat up, once more very interested. "I see."

"Now he's interested in the lad," Kate said with a sneer. "Always follow the money with humans."

"What kind of commission do you seek then?" Deane asked. "I'm sure a captaincy . . ."

Lafayette looked at De Kalb and then at Deane. "I would consider nothing less than the rank of Major General."

Deane's eyes widened at this unexpected, huge request, holding his hand out to De Kalb. "My dear boy, you do realize that such a high rank is what I have extended to General De Kalb! He is thirty years your senior, and as an experienced soldier fighting for France, he *has* fought under fire innumerable times, earning medals of distinction! You are an inexperienced nineteen-year-old boy who has not commanded more than fifty men and has never fired a shot in battle! Yet you seek to command four to five thousand soldiers under fire from one of the most powerful armies in the world?"

Lafayette didn't bat an eye but confidently asserted, "My family will not consent to my departure without the rank of Major General, *monsieur.*"

"Huzzah! That's me lad! Shoot for the stars!" Kate cheered.

"C'est extraordinaire!" Liz echoed. "Our Marquis is bold to ask such a thing, no?"

De Kalb's arms were propped on the chair, and he brought a hand to his face, trying to stifle a smile even as he translated for the two men.

Deane seemed momentarily at a loss for words. He clasped his hands together and held them in front of his chest as he spoke. *"Monsieur le Marquis,* not only is this an extraordinary request of high rank, but you are a *nobleman,* as opposed to the other officers General De Kalb has presented to me. Your celebrity could present a problem with the rumblings of the British ambassador at court. Comte de Vergennes must give Lord Stormont no cause for alarm that the French government is sending its officers to aid the Americans."

Lafayette thought a moment but quickly spoke up. *"Oui,* but my connections at court could serve to convince the French government to fully support the American cause of independence! I am intimate friends with the inner court, including Queen Marie Antoinette and the brother of King Louis. Instead of being a negative, my celebrity could prove to be a *positive, Monsieur* Deane, in rallying the court and all of France. Especially when I am able to achieve victory and glory on the battlefield. I wish to prove to France that America's independence is worth fighting for."

Deane sat back in his chair and tilted his head, letting go a deep breath. *"Monsieur le Marquis,* you are truly different from the other officers I have interviewed. No one has expressed such zeal for our cause. You do not seek fortune, for you already have it. In fact, you willingly would sacrifice your personal wealth and comfort for a cause in which you only seek rank and glory. And you are confident that you will achieve what you set out to do."

"C'est vrai," Lafayette said with a look of serious consideration. He then leaned in with a grin. "So, you see, my departure for America would create quite a stir, no? I can *promise* you attention for the American cause with the Marquis de Lafayette fighting by her side."

Deane shared a look with De Kalb. "What think you, General?"

De Kalb rubbed his stubbly chin and rested his beefy hand on his knees. "It vould seem that the only vone vith something to lose vould be Lafayette. He offers you his sword at his own expense and backs up his commitment vith his connections and his vealth. *Ja,* the rank is certainly unusual for his age and experience but I vould allow the boy an opportunity to prove himself." He smiled at the eager young marquis. "I vant to see vhat he does."

"Give the boy a chance!" Kate whispered, willing Deane to say "Yes."

"Very well." Deane stood up, walked to his desk, and laid out two pieces of paper. He lifted two quills and handed one to Baron De Kalb, who took a seat in a chair on the other side of the desk. "General, if you would be so kind as to write down our contract in French for *Monsieur le Marquis* to review as I dictate and also write in English."

Lafayette stood at attention with a lump of excitement in his throat. He was about to realize his lifelong dream. De Kalb dipped the quill in the ink as Deane dictated the terms aloud:

"The desire manifested by the Marquis de Lafayette of serving in the Forces of the United States of North America and the interest which he takes in the justice of their cause have led him to desire opportunities of distinguishing himself in the war and of rendering such services as they may be within his power. Since, however, he cannot expect to obtain the consent of his family to serve in a foreign country and to cross the sea, unless in the quality of a General Officer," Deane paused and locked eyes with Lafayette.

"He *must* give him the desired rank!" Liz urged.

"I have concluded that I cannot better assist my country and those to whom I am responsible than by granting him, in the name of The Honorable Congress," Deane began again, smiling, "the grade of Major General, which commission I beg the States to confirm, ratify, and bestow upon him to hold and to rank from this day forward with the General Officers of the same grade."

Lafayette placed a hand over his heart and bowed his head in appreciation and humility. He fought back tears of joy, not wishing to show his emotion.

"Huzzah! The lad did it!" Kate cheered again, now hugging Liz.

"His noble lineage, his connections, the high dignities exercised by his family at this Court, his ample possessions in this Kingdom, his personal worth, his celebrity, his disinterestedness, and above all his zeal for the liberty of our Colonies have alone influenced me in promising to him in the name of the United States, the aforesaid rank of Major General.

"In witness whereof, I have signed these presents. Done at Paris, this seventh of December, One thousand, Seven hundred and seventy-six. SILAS DEANE."

De Kalb looked up and gave an affirming nod to the two men.

"Now, *s'il vous plaît,* dictate your agreement, *Monsieur le Marquis,*" Deane instructed Lafayette, holding his hand out to De Kalb. "Then we shall both sign our names."

Lafayette nodded and leaned over the desk slightly. "Upon the above conditions I stand ready and promise to depart, at such time and in such manner as *Monsieur* Deane shall judge advisable, to serve the aforesaid States without any allowance or special pay, reserving only the freedom of returning to Europe, when my family or my King shall recall me. Done at Paris, this seventh of December, 1776. THE MARQUIS DE LAFAYETTE."

Once De Kalb finished writing, he stood and held out the quill to

Lafayette with a broad smile. Lafayette's heart jumped as he took the quill and dipped it in the inkwell to sign his name:

Lafayette

"*Félicitations,* General Lafayette," Deane congratulated him with a grin, emphasizing his new rank as Lafayette placed the quill down.

Lafayette exhaled with a chuckle of surreal delight. "*Merci, Monsieur* Deane, for the confidence you have placed in me. I am honored and will do my best to live up to every promise." He turned to De Kalb. "*Et merci, mon général.* It will be my highest honor to learn from you and serve by your side in America."

De Kalb gave Lafayette a firm handshake. "*Félicitations, Général* Lafayette. I know you vill be a shining star in the cause of liberty."

"*Merci beaucoup,*" Lafayette exulted with great emotion in his voice. "When do you plan to depart for America?"

"Tomorrow my officers and I leave for Le Havre," De Kalb replied.

Lafayette stood there, stunned. "*Demain?*" His stomach dropped.

"Indeed, Beaumarchais has three ships ready to depart for America filled with men, weapons, and supplies," Deane added, looking over the contract they had just signed. He looked up, "Is there a problem, General?"

Lafayette smiled weakly and grabbed his hat. "No, no, pardon, but I must get going to prepare." His mind was racing. "There is much to do, no?"

"He does not yet have permission from the Duc d'Ayen to go to America," Liz asserted. "Even De Kalb does not realize that Lafayette is not free to depart tomorrow."

"I wish we could tell Lafayette that we have already solved his problem, an' that those ships won't be leavin' without him," Kate lamented. "At least *we* don't have ta panic, even while the poor lad does."

"*Oui,* now to see what happens as word reaches Versailles of Beaumarchais blowing his cover," Liz said. "Marie Antoinette won't need to spend money on the fireworks that are coming when Lord Stormont storms into Vergennes's office."

SLIPPERY SLEDS AND BLOCKED SHIPS

Comte de Vergennes sat at his desk, rubbing his temple as he read the morning news and correspondence. He could feel a headache creeping in with the amount of bad news spread out before him. The overcast, wintry skies outside his window only served to dampen his spirits. He sipped a cup of strong coffee as he read the chilling news from America published in a Parisian newspaper.

LES BRITANNIQUES REVENDIQUENT LA VICTOIRE À LONG ISLAND ET WHITE PLAINS, NEW YORK, FORCANT LES AMÉRICAINS À RETRAIR!

(British Claim Victory in Long Island and White Plains, New York, Forcing Americans to Retreat!)

The French Minister shook his head and thought, *Les Américains are no match for the British. All they can do now is retreat and lick their wounds while they wait for spring. I wonder if their army will even survive the winter.*

Vergennes tossed the newspaper and it slid onto the floor. He then picked up a letter from the local police lieutenant in Le Havre:

Monsieur Durand abruptly appeared at the theater, appointed himself interim-director, and showed even more proprietary interest in the play than in his munitions stockpile.

"Beaumarchais, what were you *thinking?!*" he murmured through gritted teeth. He picked up another letter that an officer wrote to Silas Deane about the now fully exposed playwright:

"He made himself known to the whole town by . . . making the actors rehearse, in order that they might play better," he read aloud. "All this has rendered his precaution he had taken to hide himself under the name of Durand useless." He tossed the letter onto his desk. *'Figaro' has foiled the entire cover of secret French aid to Les Américains. Perhaps we should never have bothered to assist them, especially now with their inability to hold New York.*

Vergennes got up from his desk and walked over to the window, continuing to rub his temple. He saw a team of men transporting to the stables one of Marie Antoinette's latest *menus plaisirs*, or small pleasures. It was an ornate, petite red-and-black carriage mounted on intricately decorated skis. After hearing that the previous French kings and their courts enjoyed sled races when Versailles was covered in snow and the Grand Canal frozen over, the queen was eager to bring sled parties back in fashion this winter. She ordered for herself a new sled and boasted of how she would race Madame de Lamballe around Versailles with the first snowfall. The Comte shook his head at the childish flippancy of the queen's priorities while he sought to keep France from sliding into war.

Vergennes's secretary softly knocked on the door and poked his head inside. *"Pardon, Monsieur,* but Ambassador Stormont insists on seeing you."

Vergennes took in a weary, deep breath. *"Oui,* of course he does. Send him in." He shook his head and went to stand by the ornate chairs where he would sit, and no doubt endure yet more bad news. Soon Lord Stormont was ushered in, and the two men sat down and exchanged the obligatory cordial greetings.

"I understand congratulations are in order for your government with yet another victory in New York," Vergennes said with a forced smile, trying not to choke on his words.

Stormont wasn't in the mood for games and got right to the glaring point. "It has been reported to me that suspicious ships are being loaded at the docks in Normandy. French roads are busy with the transport of munitions and weapons to the ports supposedly by a company by the name of Hortalez *et Cie.* These ships are reported to be sailing to Martinique and Guadeloupe, but . . ."

Vergennes casually crossed his legs and cut Stormont off. "How else would you propose that our French colonies in the West Indies receive supplies—by sled across a frozen ocean, *monsieur?"* He chuckled, hoping to deflect the coming accusation. "Of *course* private merchants such as Hortalez load their ships in Normandy and any other deep-water French port. We have no say over how they conduct business."

Stormont was having none of it. "An employee of Hortalez disguises himself as a merchant for Hortalez but assumes a different name in every port. Why would he need to do such a thing, *monsieur?* If he *truly* is an employee of Hortalez *et Cie*, why not be who he claims to be?" The British Ambassador sat forward on his chair, glaring at Vergennes. "He supposedly was a '*Monsieur* Durand' at the docks, yet he was quickly discovered to be someone else at the theatre in Le Havre. Can you guess *who?* Why, none other than the famed playwright of *Le Barbier de Séville!*" He threw up his hands in feigned surprise with a smile, then quickly grew a serious face as he hurled his accusation. "Your friend and courtier Pierre-Augustin Caron de Beaumarchais is running guns at the docks by day and directing his play by night."

Vergennes waved a hand off in the air and laughed. "All the world is a stage to Beaumarchais! He enjoys acting wherever he is, whether as a merchant by another name at the dock or Figaro on stage. He is a multi-talented, colorful fellow, no? Both onstage as an actor and offstage as a businessman."

"Spare me," Stormont scoffed with an upraised hand. "Beaumarchais is running guns as well as French officers! We know that he has met countless times with the American Silas Deane who has received scores of French officers who have been to see him! Soldiers are lining the docks and filling the cafés in Paris as well as Le Havre, bragging about how they will fight the British in North America! This, *monsieur,* is not just a silly playwright dabbling in business, but a front for the government of France to send aid to the rebel forces in the colonies! This, *monsieur,* is an act of war!"

Vergennes frowned and sat forward in his chair with a finger in the air. "The government of France in *no way* endorses sending French officers to aid the Americans. If soldiers are volunteering to go fight as mercenaries, it is not our doing, nor is it with France's permission."

"Well, I'm glad to hear it," Stormont said, quickly rising to his feet. "Then you will no doubt wish to prove it, *monsieur,* by preventing those ships, and all ships bearing munitions and French officers from sailing from those docks. Else I warn you of severe repercussions from London."

Vergennes got to his feet and straightened his waistcoat. He lifted his chin. "I will make known your concerns to the king, *monsieur.* We will of course do all we can to assure you of France's goodwill and friendship with your government."

"We shall wait. And we shall see." Stormont's eyes narrowed and he gave a singular nod. *Merci, Monsieur le Comte. À bientôt.*"

With that, Stormont left the room, leaving Vergennes standing there clenching his fists in anger. Ce n'est pas bien, he thought. *We are all on slippery sleds—Marie Antoinette, Les Américains, Beaumarchais, Silas Deane, and this court.*

Kate and Liz looked at each other, silently shaking their heads. They had witnessed the entire scene. They waited until Vergennes left the room but before they exited, Kate took the Parisian paper from the floor. *Somethin' tells me I need ta hang onta this.*

HÔTEL DE NOAILLES, FRANCE, DECEMBER 15, 1776

Lafayette bounced his baby daughter Henriette on his knee, pretending like she was riding a horse. He drew squeals of delight from the toddler whose tiny hands held tightly to his pointer fingers as she bounced along. The young father whinnied and lowered his leg to let her slide "off the saddle" to the floor.

"*Aimes-tu monter à cheval, ma petite fille?*" Lafayette whispered in her ear, giving her butterfly kisses. "I want my one-year-old to be happy on her first birthday!" He picked up a tiny cloth doll and handed it to the little girl. "*Joyeux anniversaire,* Henriette!"

Henriette giggled and patted her papa's cheeks with her chubby fingers. She held the doll to her chin and coughed. Lafayette immediately frowned, scooping the little girl into his arms. He held her close to his chest while she rested her small head on his shoulder, walking her around the room. "Shhhhhh, *tu vas bien, tu vas bien.* You *must* be okay." He tenderly kissed the girl and bounced her softly in the air as he carried her out of the room to go wake Adrienne. His young wife was resting after having been nauseous this morning. Little did Lafayette or Adrienne know, but she was pregnant with their second child.

"I haven't seen Lafayette this happy in days," Kate said to Liz when he was gone. "How he loves that wee birthday lass of his. I know the thought of leavin' her weighs heavy on his heart."

Liz stepped out from under the settee. "*Oui,* I cannot imagine how hard it will be for him to leave his young family to go venture off on such a hazardous mission to America, especially since Henriette continues to be sickly with that cough. *Quel dommage.*"

Kate frowned. "Aye. He loves the wee bairn. She's been a good distraction for him this week as he's been anxiously awaitin' word from de Broglie aboot wha' ta do with De Kalb an' his officers leavin' for America without him. Lafayette hasn't received a reply from the letter he sent ta de Broglie at his home in Ruffec."

"Well, the anxious Lafayette will not need to remain anxious for much longer," Liz answered. "De Kalb and his officers shall be back in Paris any day now since Vergennes sent the order from the king that no ships were to depart for America."

"Vergennes didn't have a choice, did he now? He had ta keep up appearances after Stormont stormed inta his office," Kate replied. "Those were some serious orders he gave the police, ta arrest any French soldiers who claim the

French government ordered them ta America."

Liz gazed out the window at the overcast sky. "At least Beaumarchais got the *Amphitrite* to sail before the orders to stop her arrived. I am sure that any delays the ship experiences will be arranged by the AOG to protect her from storms, no?"

"Aye, an' at least the bulk of weapons an' supplies, an' the officers under Major Coudray be on the way ta America," Kate agreed.

"The undaunted Beaumarchais ordered the other two ships unloaded. He'll change the names of the ships and reload them by cover of night," Liz said, grinning. "Gillamon said he will find a way to convince Vergennes to allow them to secretly set sail."

Kate joined Liz at the window. "I know all of these delays make Lafayette think aboot the risks he'll be takin' when he does leave his family for America, whether he has permission from the Duc d'Ayen or not. It weighs heavy on me heart for the lad, too. He'll have ta be separated from Adrienne an' sweet Henriette for who knows how long?"

"Lafayette could lose everything he has in wealth and possessions," Liz agreed with a furrowed brow. "This of course is nothing compared to the personal risks he faces with the voyage, no? He will risk storms, shipwrecks, pirates, illness, and disease. And if a British ship captures him, he could be taken to England, imprisoned, or even put to death!"

"An' if the French police catch him escapin' he could be thrown in prison for disobeyin' the king!" Kate added. "Then he'd face dishonorin' the Lafayette an' the Noailles family names, especially if he sets off a war between England and France!"

"Not to mention the risks of actually *fighting* in the war once he reaches America," Liz lamented, shaking her head. "He could be wounded or even killed on American soil, yet Lafayette is willing to spill his blood for her. He is willing to do all of this . . . for that priceless jewel of *liberté,* as *mon* Henry calls it. "

"I think the young lad somehow feels the same as young America, both tryin' ta stretch their wings an' fly like Cato the eagle had ta do," Kate noted. "He's seen how America's cries for freedom were rejected by tyranny, for he's felt that, too. America knows she's not strong yet, an' she doubts her powers while dreadin' the enemy comin' for her. All of this grabbed the knight inside of Lafayette, who wants ta go fight as her champion, an' at the same time, earn his own wings an' strength."

Liz put her dainty paw on Kate's shoulder. "He sees this as a fight not just for himself, or for America, but for all of mankind. It is a just, exalted cause that is good and that the young minds of this enlightened age love."

"An' all at the age of nineteen," Kate said with a fond smile. "He's an unusual lad, an' I'm happy I've had the joy ta be with him all his life."

"Well, *mon amie,* the marquis is just getting started on his bold adventure of life!" Liz told her with a wink. "Lafayette will accomplish what he sets out to do, or you would not have been assigned to such an important human in HIStory."

"Aye! So, once De Kalb an' his officers return here ta Paris, they an' Lafayette will have ta find another way ta sneak out of France," Kate said. "Stormont's spies will be watchin' Silas Deane, Beaumarchais, an' Vergennes even more closely than before."

"Not to mention watching Benjamin Franklin when he arrives in Paris, which could also be any day," Liz reminded her. "The French court is already buzzing about why Dr. Franklin is coming, and Lord Stormont will be ready to accuse Vergennes of an alliance with America with someone as important as the famous Benjamin Franklin visiting him at court."

Kate thought a moment. "Liz, Lafayette has lots of money. Why can't he jest buy his own ship an' take them all ta America himself?"

Liz's eyes brightened. "Brilliant, *chère* Kate! Why did I not think of this? Of course, this is what he must do! But this will require a great deal of planning to purchase the right vessel, equip the ship with provisions, select the right port from which to set sail, and find the perfect window of time to depart."

"An' once the date is set," Kate shared with a confident grin, "it will require a secret escape."

TRYING MEN'S SOULS

General Charles Lee grumbled to himself as he sat at his desk working on correspondence. He scratched out a line he had written to General Washington and then threw down his quill, grabbing the paper and crumpling it into a ball. "Ahhh!" he shouted in frustration. The fire popped, and an ember jumped from the fireplace onto the wooden floor. Lee got up and strode over to the fireplace on his skinny legs, stomping the ember to vent his anger. He then tossed the unfinished letter into the fire and gazed at the flames devouring the paper as he gripped the mantel with both hands. "What am I to do with that indecisive man?" he said to himself. *I have command of Washington's largest contingency of seven thousand men. He foolishly divided his army because he didn't know what Howe's next move would be and instructed me to follow him should Howe invade New Jersey.* "But he never gave me an outright order." He shook his head. "The Patriot cause is all but lost . . . unless I can rescue the army from annihilation under Washington's pathetic leadership."

A knock sounded on the door.

"Come!" an irritated Lee shouted, still watching the fire.

The door opened, and Lee heard the unmistakable sound of his high-stepping dog with the skinny legs running toward him, his nails clicking on the wooden floor. "Archer?!" Lee exclaimed in surprise as the dog whined and repeatedly jumped up on the general's legs.

I'm shpechial! Archer cried happily, his mouth wide open in an exuberant grin of joy. *Did you miss me?!*

"Is this your dog, Sir? I found him on the road near your headquarters," Clarie told him. She was in the form of a continental express rider. "I've heard you have several dogs with you at all times."

General Lee squatted with a knee to the floor, allowing Archer to lick his face as he threw his head back, laughing. "Dogs are much more preferable to humans!" He looked up at Clarie with unexpected joy. "Yes, Archer is my dog, but I don't understand how he got here to New York. I left him in

Virginia." He instantly thought back to the moment when he rode next to Washington in Cambridge over a year ago; Mr. Atticus had delivered General Washington's dog Max, also claiming to have found him on the road. *My dogs would follow me to the ends of the earth,* he told Washington, affirming the notion that dogs had been known to travel long distances to be reunited with their masters. He gave Archer a tight hug. "I'm glad to have a dog back with me. Finally, someone worth talking to."

"Archer obviously missed you, Sir," Clarie observed with a grin. She reached into her knapsack and retrieved two letters, acting surprised to see the second one. "I bring you a letter from General Washington, and, . . ." she said, pausing to look at the unexpected letter in her pouch, "it appears his aide-de-camp Colonel Joseph Reed also slipped a letter in the post for you, Sir."

Lee got to his feet and took the letters in hand. "Thank you. Dismissed." He turned and walked over to the settee. Clarie winked at Archer, who returned a nod, and left the room, closing the door behind her. Lee patted the settee. "Come sit with me, boy. Let's read these letters."

Archer jumped up next to Lee and sat there happily, one ear up and one ear down, watching as the general opened the first letter from Washington. Lee mumbled as he scanned the letter. "The Commander-in-Chief and his staff concur that I should cross the Hudson with my troops to join his army." He scratched Archer behind the ear. "But Washington still did not *order* me to come."

Lee tossed Washington's missive on the settee and picked up Reed's letter. He cracked the seal and began to read aloud to Archer. *"I do not mean to flatter nor praise you at the expense of any other, but I confess I do think that it is entirely owing to you that this army and the liberties of America . . . are not totally cut off."* Lee raised his eyebrows and lifted his chin, sniffing proudly through his massive nose. *"You have decision, a quality often wanting in minds otherwise valuable."* He read silently and turned to smile at Archer. "Colonel Reed credits *me* for the army's escape from Manhattan over to King's Bridge and believes the garrison from Fort Washington would still be ours had *I* been in charge. Of course, it would."

Okay! Archer agreed happily, his tongue hanging out. *Whatever that means!*

Lee's eyes suddenly widened as he read the next line aloud. *"Oh! General— an indecisive mind is one of the greatest misfortunes that can befall an army . . . as soon as the season will admit, I think yourself and some others should go to Congress and form the plan of the new army . . . Nor am I singular in my Opinion—every Gentleman of the Family the Officers & soldiers generally have a Confidence in you—the Enemy constantly inquire where you are, & seem to me to be less confident when you are present."* He let the letter fall to his lap, his mind racing. "Some other officers close to Washington agree with Reed. And they are *right!* Washington is no longer worthy to remain Commander-in-Chief given his repeated failures in New York and the disintegration of the army. And he does not *deserve* my unquestioning obedience. I must keep my distance and maintain an independent command for as long as possible. If Howe's forces crush Washington's tiny army, the decision for Congress will be all too clear of *whom* to put in charge." He mussed Archer's head. "ME!"

Archer, with a furrowed brow, cocked his head. *That sounds kinda like betrayal to me. With lots of pride thrown in.*

"But I'll have to be careful, or I could shoot myself in the foot with Congress," Lee thought out loud. "I cannot blatantly *disobey* Washington's orders. So, let's hope he remains too intimidated by my experience and too indecisive to give me a direct order to join him in New Jersey." Lee grinned and rubbed his hands excitedly. He jumped up from the settee and went to his desk. "Now to write a reply to Reed."

Archer rested his head on his front paws. *Whatever you say. But I'll have to tell Clarie what you're up to.*

NEWARK, NEW JERSEY, NOVEMBER 22, 1776, 8:00 P.M.

Thomas Paine leaned against a tree, his head wrapped in a woolen scarf beneath a three-cornered hat, looking at the scene around him. Exhausted cold wet soldiers were curled up next to a fire, trying to get dry and warm. Others were trying to sleep. They hadn't stopped running from the British since they left New York, and their retreat was just getting started. Today they engaged a Hessian *Jäger* company and two British grenadier battalions in a skirmish before crossing the Passaic River over a dilapidated bridge. Washington ordered the destruction of the bridge behind them while the 16th Light Dragoons followed uncomfortably close. The army suffered a long march through the cold rain while Washington rode at the end of the column, encouraging the men to press on.

What Washington and Paine didn't know was that Cornwallis remained in Hackensack, New Jersey, with the main body of the army and had thankfully called off the pursuit of Washington's army for now while they foraged for food and supplies.

Paine heard one soldier sounding a wet, choking cough. Paine's heart filled with compassion as the young man shivered and pulled his thread-bare, muddy coat over his shoulders. Two other soldiers shivered and pressed their backs together to try to get warm. Next to them slept a drummer with his drum sitting off to the side, his sticks in his pocket. The light from the fire illuminated the side of the drum painted with a rattlesnake and DON'T TREAD ON ME.

The almost forty-year-old Briton reached into his pocket for a handkerchief to wipe his red nose and felt the wooden pen in his pocket. For two nights he'd had the same dream, as if someone were whispering in his ear. He pulled out the pen and held it close to his face. With it he had written his pamphlet, *Common Sense*. Published earlier this year in January, it had sold over 150,000 copies; its words spread across the globe with hope for the oppressed and with irritation for the oppressors. His words were just what the American people needed to finally decide to declare independence. Now in the fierce, devastating struggle to back up those words with action, the American spirit was gasping for breath. *It's time to write something new,* he thought. *I hate war with a passion. But some evils in this black time of 1776 are worse than war, including tyranny. The American people must wake up again and realize what they are truly warring against!*

Paine reached into his knapsack and lifted a small leather journal. He then considered the drum that he could use for a writing desk. He stood and walked over to bring the drum back to the tree, taking his seat once more. He unwound the slim leather strap and opened the journal to a fresh page. The firelight seemed to dance on the page, eager for what he would write. As did Nigel who clung to the side of the tree, peering over Paine's shoulder. *Finally!* Nigel thought. *Now to see if you've been listening to my nighttime words of inspiration.*

These are the times that try men's souls: The summer soldier and the sunshine Patriot will, in this crisis, shrink from the service of his country; but he that stands it NOW, deserves the love and thanks of man and woman. Tyranny, like hell, is not easily conquered; yet we have this consolation with us, that the harder the conflict, the more glorious the triumph. What we obtain too cheap, we esteem too lightly:—'Tis dearness only that gives every thing its value. Heaven knows how to set a proper price upon its goods; and it would be strange indeed, if so celestial an article as FREEDOM should not be highly rated. Britain, with an army to enforce her tyranny, has declared, that she has a right (not only to TAX) but "to BIND us in ALL CASES WHATSOEVER," and if being bound in that manner is not slavery, then is there not such a thing as slavery upon the earth. Even the expression is impious, for so unlimited a power can only belong to GOD.

It was all Nigel could do not to shout, 'HUZZAH!' with every word he read from Paine's fluid pen. *He's off to a splendid beginning! I daresay this work may even surpass* Common Sense *on the best-seller list.*

After Paine wrote for a while, the weariness of the day's march finally caught up with him, and his eyelids grew heavy. He closed his journal, slipped it back into his knapsack, and returned the drum. He wrapped his cloak tightly around his shoulders and headed for his makeshift lean-to.

"Good evening, 'Common Sense'! I see you've been busy penning another tome. I'm getting caught up on my letters," said a young lieutenant, using the moniker given to Thomas Paine by the army. He was also writing by the light of the fire.

"I find it beneficial for both writer and recipient to keep the ink flowing," Paine answered, holding up his ink-stained hand. He yawned and winced against a cold gust of wind.

"Indeed," the young man replied. He held up a mittened hand. "I've wanted to thank you for using your profits from *Common Sense* to buy mittens for the army. It was extremely generous of you."

Paine's brilliant blue eyes lit up with a warm smile. "You're welcome. I only wish I could do more."

"Just keep writing, Sir," the officer suggested. "It's making a difference."

Paine nodded and patted his manuscript. "I shall. Good night."

"Good night, Sir," the young officer answered.

Curious, Nigel scurried to peer over the shoulder of the eighteen-year-old Virginian far from home on this bitter cold night. *Hmm, he's writing about General Washington. Let's have a look at how this young officer views the Commander-in-Chief amid this retreat.* The little mouse adjusted his spectacles and read:

> *I saw him...at the head of a small band, or rather in its rear, for he was always near the enemy and his countenance and manner made an impression on me which I can never efface. His deportment so firm, so dignified, so exalted, but yet so modest and composed, I have never seen in any other person...*

Nigel smiled and thought, *I say, Washington is setting an example of calm leadership for the next generation. I shall wait to see his signature to learn this young man's name.* A few moments passed, and the officer signed his letter:

> *James Monroe*

"Bravo, Monroe!" Nigel squeaked as young James Monroe put away his writing materials. "I pray other young officers are equally inspired by Washington's example, for they are America's future leaders, huzzah! Betwixt Washington and Paine, perhaps they shall give the lifeline that this army needs to survive this crisis." With that, he scurried off into the night to give Max and Jock an update.

WASHINGTON'S HEADQUARTERS, COCHRANE'S TAVERN, NEW BRUNSWICK, NEW JERSEY, NOVEMBER 30, 1776

"NOTHIN'!" Max grumbled. "Washington spent several days in Newark hopin' that some New Jersey militia would decide ta get off their bums an' come *help* him fight this war, but wha' did they do after Washington's call ta arms? NOTHIN'! All they did were murmur an' desert the cause!"

"Sadly, I've just read what Washington wrote to Hancock about the dire situation," Nigel agreed. "He holds no hope for support from New Jersey militia coming, plus he wrote that the New Jersey assembly has fled and will soon dissolve, leaving the state without a government. Plus, the College of New Jersey in Princeton has shut down, the president fleeing on horseback and the students scattering everywhere. I daresay it appears we are on the eve of despair and ruin, with the Hound Cornwallis relentlessly chasing the Fox Washington across New Jersey!"

"On top of all *that* happy news, Washington still hasn't heard back from General Lee, whose seven thousand soldiers could change everythin'!" Max piled on. "Washington don't even know where Lee be. I jest don't understand why Lee be ignorin' his commander."

"Gillamon did mention his suspicion of Lee's intentions," Nigel reminded him.

Jock frowned. "Isn't that why he said he'd get Archer involved? I wonder if he's gathered any intelligence."

"Ha!" Max laughed. "I doubt it. When we pushed south here ta avoid the Br-r-ritish outflankin' us, Washington expected ta be joined by Lee's army ta form a defensive line. He were shocked ta get a letter from Lee yesterday that he hadn't even broken camp! Desperate for soldier lads, Washington sent his aide Colonel Reed an' other officers off ta go find r-r-recruits wherever they can."

Suddenly they heard the heavy footprints of George Washington coming down the hall. Just as he reached the door, an express courier strode up behind him. "Sir, letters for you just arrived."

"Thank you," Washington replied, taking the letters in hand, dismissing the courier. It was Clarie. She winked to Max, Jock, and Nigel and left the room.

Washington thumbed through the stack until his eyes rested on a letter from General Lee, but it was addressed to Colonel Joseph Reed, his aide-de-camp. Raising an eyebrow, Washington took the letter in hand. "Perhaps there is updated news about Lee's whereabouts," the general muttered to himself, sitting down in a chair by the fireplace.

Max and Jock looked at one another and shared a glance with Nigel, who had hidden behind the copper matchbox.

Washington broke the wax seal on Lee's letter to Reed and unfolded the paper. As he began reading, the animals could see waves of emotion crashing over the Commander-in-Chief:

> I received your most obliging. flattering letter. and lament with you that fatal indecision of mind which in war is a much greater disqualification than stupidity or even want of personal courage. Accident may put a decisive blunderer in the right. but eternal defeat and miscarriage must attend the man of the best parts if cursed with indecision.

The general clenched his jaw and leaned forward to rest his elbows on his knees, his heart racing with what was clearly the response to a scathing letter from Colonel Reed to General Lee about Washington. He didn't have to see what Reed had written to Lee. Lee's response was enough to understand the gut-punching betrayal taking place behind his back. He let the letter fall to the floor and cupped his hands over his nose and mouth, sitting in stunned silence. His most trusted officer had lost confidence in him. And his most highly regarded general distrusted and had decidedly abandoned him.

Max quietly walked over to Washington and nudged his leg, looking up soulfully at the hurt man. Washington dropped a hand to Max's head and gave a sad smile. "There *is* one thing Lee and I do agree on. Dogs are faithfully man's best friend." He tightened his lips. "Men will disappoint at every turn. I'm glad you're here, Max. You're about the only one I can personally trust and confide in anymore. A shortsighted Congress hasn't delivered the number of soldiers we need, nor the supplies to keep them fed, clothed, and armed. They are reduced to nothing, and the people of New Jersey won't help feed us, deserting the cause to serve the British. The states themselves are not answering the call to help us with recruits. My reputation is destroyed from failure and retreat. I tremble for Philadelphia." He shook his head. "No man ever had a greater choice of difficulties and less means of getting out of them than I have. I fear the game is pretty much up, boy."

Max looked over and mouthed to Nigel, *Wha' do the letter say?!*

Nigel shrugged his shoulders but held up a finger for Max to wait. Washington stood up from the chair, straightened his waistcoat, and reached down to angrily scoop up the biting letter from the floor. He walked over to the desk and took a seat, setting the letter aside while he lifted a quill to dip into the inkwell. Nigel scurried over and hopped up on a window ledge behind Washington, reading Lee's letter while the general penned a new note:

The inclosed was put into my hands by an Express from the White Plains. Having no Idea of its being a Private Letter, much less Suspecting the tendency of the Correspondence, I opened it, as I had done all other Letters to you, from the Same place and Peekskill, upon the business of your office, as I Conceived and found them to be.

This as it is the truth, must be my excuse for Seeing the Contents of a Letter, which neither inclination or intention would have prompted me to.

I thank you for the trouble and fatigue you have undergone in your Journey to Burlington, and Sincerely wish that your labours may be Crowned with the desired success. My best Respects to Mrs Reed, I am, Dear Sir, your mo. obt servt.

Washington then took the note and folded it together with Lee's letter, addressing it to Colonel Reed. He picked up a stick of wax and held it over the candle until it began to melt. He then put a glob of the wax onto the letter and impressed into it his official brass seal. Tossing the seal aside and blowing out the candle, Washington got up and left the room, taking the letter with him for a courier to deliver immediately to Reed.

Nigel jumped down from the desk and scurried back over to Max and Jock.

"Well? Wha' were that all about?" Max wanted to know. "I know it weren't good."

"Colonel Reed evidently wrote a letter to General Lee behind Washington's back, praising Lee as the superior commander and denigrating Washington as an indecisive buffoon," Nigel explained, lifting his spectacles to rub the emotion from his eyes. "So, Washington explained to Reed that he mistakenly read Lee's letter, thinking it was of a military nature. He then thanked that 'Judas' Reed for his service and signed it as the gentleman of integrity he is. Rarely does one see such largeness of character in a human. I thought

I admired Washington before this day. Now he has my undying respect and loyalty for how he has handled this treacherous betrayal. Utterly astonishing, our George Washington."

Jock frowned. "That's terrible! Washington is such a good man! He's doing all he can to hold this army together! And this is the thanks he gets?"

Max growled. "That no good R-r-reed! How dare he backstab the general at a time like this! Did ye hear how bad everythin' be? Washington said I were the only one he could talk with aboot personal stuff. While I'm glad ta do it, he needs a human by his side ta talk with now that he's lost R-r-reed's confidence."

"What about Lafayette?" Jock asked. "Aren't Liz and Kate trying to get him get over here to help Washington? Maybe he'll become the general's new best friend he can trust and talk to."

"Aye, Gillamon said that gettin' Lafayette over ta America were crucial for the war," Max agreed. "But I think he meant more for fightin' an' his connections with France."

"I daresay it would be quite extraordinary for the Marquis de Lafayette to befriend our stoic Virginia gentleman on such a deeply personal level," Nigel posited.

"Well, Washington never had a son of his own, and Lafayette lost his father, right? I know what it's like to be an orphan," Jock said. "Maybe they could give each other what they're both missing. Sounds like it would be a closer friendship than most. Maybe the Marquis is meant to do both things to help Washington—connect us with France to fight while becoming the son Washington always wanted." The young Scottie nudged his grandsire. "It happened to me, after all."

"Aye, that it did, lad," Max agreed with a smile.

"I look forward to seeing if your Lafayette hypothesis comes to fruition, but meanwhile we must provide the Commander-in-Chief with as much support as we can," Nigel suggested. "But a more devastating blow shall hit Washington in mere hours. Almost half of his remaining army will simply walk away as their enlistments expire."

"Aye, an' then most of those left will expire in a month," Max grumbled. "Plus, them Br-r-ritish dr-r-ragoons an' light infantry be headin' this way. Cornwallis's army ain't stoppin' the chase. We'll be headin' ta Pr-r-rinceton with the Hound on our tail."

"Washington and the cause of Independence must both experience revival from defeat, as it shan't come from victory," Nigel suggested. "I *know* for a fact that Washington has a core of men who still believe in him, like Greene, Knox, and that young Lieutenant James Monroe. The wretched remains of the broken army need a jolt of Patriotism, and I have high hopes for Mr. Paine's essays to assist in that endeavor. He shall soon have it printed in Philadelphia once we are safely on the other side of the Delaware River."

"What's he calling it?" Jock wanted to know.

"*The American Crisis,*" Nigel answered.

"The lad sure does know how ta name things," Max remarked. "Calls it like he sees it, aye?"

WITH THIS SWORD

THE IAMISPHERE

The sounds of splintering wood echoed off the walls of the circular time portal as Gillamon and Clarie viewed the panel of time unfolding along the banks of the Delaware River. It was dawn on December 8, 1776, and a few dozen men in the rear of Washington's retreating army urgently labored to destroy bridges and fell trees to impede the pursuing British army. Washington had ordered every boat seized or sunk by the Continental Army for forty miles up and down the east side of the river. Only one, sixty-foot Durham boat remained on the bank below where George Washington and Delaware Captain Enoch Anderson stood, waiting to take the final group of men across the cold river.

"They look like canoes, tapered at each end, but those heavy, flat-bottomed Durham boats are working beasts, aren't they?" Gillamon noted. "What a clever vessel the humans designed for transporting fifteen tons of heavy iron and cargo downstream to Philadelphia. They range from forty- to sixty-feet long and eight-feet wide, but they only need twenty inches of water even when fully loaded. I'm sure Noah himself would be fascinated by such a design."

Clarie giggled. "He would. And just five men with oars can navigate those shallow-draft boats, sped along by the current. Washington knew about the Durham boats when he gave the order to round them up a week ago. And just as he did in escaping Brooklyn across the East River, the General waits with the last boat to carry his men across the Delaware River to the safety of Pennsylvania."

A pioneering soldier let go an icy breath and wiped the sweat from his brow after repeated attempts at felling a sugar maple tree as Washington approached him. "Care to have a go, General?"

Washington grinned slightly and took the ax in hand, giving the tree several more whacks before it severed from its trunk and crashed to the ground. A chorus of cheers rose from the ranks of these battered, exhausted soldiers who had faithfully followed their Commander-in-Chief across New Jersey. The soldiers hefted the fallen tree and threw it on the pile of brush that blocked the road behind them. Washington then ordered them to load the boat, stepping last into it himself.

"Chopping wood was good for Washington to vent his frustration over the obstinate Lee, who has refused to join him," Gillamon noted with a grin. "Blades are useful things, and the Sword of the Revolution has been sharpened with every difficult turn in 1776. He may not yet realize it, but General Charles Lee has been one of Washington's best sharpening tools."

Clarie's brow was furrowed. "Well, despite Lee's irritating behavior, I know that Washington has gained the esteem of his men through his selfless bravery of standing between them and the enemy on this retreat."

"And he has refused to panic throughout repeated losses and the hounding from Cornwallis's army," Gillamon added.

"Speaking of which!" Clarie exclaimed, pointing to the scene of Hessian *Jägers* and light infantry approaching the outskirts of Trenton shortly after Washington and his men pushed off for the opposite shore. "Washington's timing amazes me, Gillamon! That was a close call!"

"Yes, but the long retreat from New York is finally over, and now Washington has bought his ragtag army precious time," Gillamon said, pointing to a scene of campfires dotting the river for twenty-five miles. The exhausted soldiers collapsed in makeshift camps throughout the woods and out of sight of the Delaware. "Washington directed the sick and wounded to Morristown, New Jersey while on retreat, and other invalid soldiers have now been sent to a Moravian monastery hospital in Bethlehem, Pennsylvania. But the rest of his men here are sick, hungry, cold, and miserable. They can at least catch their breath with the river between them and the enemy. But Washington knows that the river will only hold back Howe's forces for just so long."

Gillamon pointed to another scene of General Howe and Cornwallis now standing at Trenton, discussing their next course of action. "Howe is quite pleased with Cornwallis's command of the pursuing army after choosing him to replace General Clinton. Howe again rejected Clinton's proposed strategy, this time to encircle Washington's small army before the winter snow, or even attack Philadelphia and capture the Congress. Howe instead sent Clinton to Rhode Island with six thousand troops to capture Newport and squash the efforts of rebel privateers attacking British supply ships. Clinton took the city without a battle, so that now makes a third colony that has fallen to the British. I think that Howe is almost as happy to have his difficult subordinate out of his wig for the winter as to have Rhode Island, New Jersey, and New York in British hands."

"General Cornwallis appears to have done everything right so far," Clarie agreed. "He pursued Washington as far as New Brunswick with ten thousand men but halted to wait for further instructions, as Howe had ordered. Washington also escaped *that* town hours before Cornwallis arrived!"

"So now Cornwallis has scoured the Delaware for thirteen miles looking for boats, but thanks to Washington, he has found none," Gillamon relayed. "The British and Hessians could wait until the ice thickens and march across the river. Philadelphia is only one day's march away, but Howe has already decided to put his army into winter quarters. Still, he has ordered several outposts in New Jersey to protect the Loyalists and to keep an eye on Washington's army this winter. He'll keep four thousand men in New Brunswick, three thousand in Princeton, and the forward positions of Trenton and Bordentown will be manned by three thousand Hessian forces. The oh-so-confident Howe and most of his subordinates think that they have crushed the rebellion and that this war is practically over."

Clarie wore a defiant expression. "But *we* know better. The British and Hessians think that by crushing the people of New Jersey along their march they've subdued their spirits—but they have stirred up a hornet's nest by cruelly plundering their homes and farms, and horrifically abusing and murdering her citizens."

"Indeed, what man intended for evil, the Maker intended for good," Gillamon agreed. "Even though Admiral Howe issued yet another proclamation to the citizens of New Jersey to return their loyalty to the protection of the king, their own army's behavior destroyed such goodwill. Public support for the fight for independence had steadily waned with each defeat in New York, followed by this humiliating retreat. But cries of 'Don't Tread on Me' revived because of the enemy's harsh treatment of the citizens of New Jersey."

"What Washington and the Congress have been unable to do in recruiting soldiers, the *enemy* has accomplished for the Patriot cause in rallying men to take up arms to fight against them!" Clarie added happily. "The British simply don't understand the American spirit. If you threaten their land, their possessions, or their rights, they *will* respond to defend them!"

Gillamon nodded. "With those new recruits plus the scattered parts of the Continental Army slowly joining Washington in Pennsylvania, the Commander-in-Chief will soon miraculously have a decent fighting force again at his side."

"Except for General Charles Lee, that is," Clarie countered. "Despite Washington's pleas to join him immediately in Pennsylvania, Lee has taken his time, contemplating his own moves, like launching a surprise attack against the British at Brunswick or Princeton. Lee doesn't think the British will cross a frozen Delaware River to attack Philadelphia."

"And Lee is *right,*" Gillamon interjected. "Howe and his officers will return to the warmth and comfort of New York for the winter, trusting in the Hessian outposts to keep watch on the rebels. Then, whatever remains of Washington's army, they believe they'll easily eliminate in the spring. But just as the brutal tactics of the enemy have re-ignited public support for the Patriot cause, so too has Lee's defiance of Washington *helped* the American army."

Clarie's eyes widened. "How in the world has Lee's behavior *helped,* Gillamon?"

"Cornwallis is very much aware of the size of General Lee's army, and it is only *Lee* who concerns him, not Washington," Gillamon explained. "Cornwallis is plagued with the idea of Lee lurking behind him with ten thousand men, ready to pounce from behind. He doesn't yet know that Lee's forces have also been reduced to three or four thousand men due to expiring enlistments. So, Lee's dallying in New York slowed the pursuing British and Hessian army, since Cornwallis had to keep an eye on his flank. Slowing down Cornwallis gave Washington's army just enough time to escape across the Delaware."

"Huzzah! I love it when the Maker brings good from bad." Clarie clasped her hands together expectantly. "I've positioned Archer with Lee as you instructed. What comes next?"

Gillamon smiled and touched another panel of time, showing General Cornwallis assembling his Council of War now on December 11, 1776. "Lee finally ordered his army to march to Morristown, New Jersey, as he could no longer ignore Washington's repeated instructions. Cornwallis wants to know exactly where Lee is, and this Council of War will soon make Archer's role very clear. Watch."

Clarie and Gillamon looked on as Cornwallis discussed the British position in Pennington, New Jersey, eight miles north of Trenton.

"We simply *must* know what General Lee is doing," Cornwallis stressed, looking around the room at his assembled officers. Spread out before him on a table were numerous pieces of intelligence. He held them up, one by one, as he posed Lee's possible moves. "Our supply lines have been harassed and attacked, but has that been the work of Lee or the local rebel militia? Has General Howe spread our outposts too far apart in New Jersey, possibly exposing us to an attack by Lee at any one of them? Could General Lee possibly be posturing a return to New York to protect New England?" He paused a moment and picked up the latest bit of intelligence. "Or is the traitorous Lee heading to join his forces with those of Washington across the Delaware?"

An uncomfortable moment of silence lingered in the air above the perplexed British and Hessian officers. Cornwallis sat in his red coat trimmed in gold, drumming his fingers on the table as he searched their faces.

Suddenly a young officer cleared his throat and stepped forward from where he stood in the back of the men assembled. "General Cornwallis, might I offer a suggestion?"

Cornwallis lifted his chin approvingly and motioned for thirty-three-year-old Lieutenant Colonel William Harcourt to step forward. "Please, Lieutenant Colonel."

Dressed in a handsome scarlet uniform with dark blue facings, the impressive Harcourt commanded the 16th Regiment of Light Dragoons, known as the Queen's Rangers. They had arrived in New York from England in early October after a rough thirteen-week voyage, during which they lost thirty-nine horses and four of their four hundred ninety men. Harcourt's regiment consisted of mounted as well as unmounted troopers, as he had only brought enough horses for half of his men. Banastre Tarleton wasted no time in contacting the well-connected Harcourt to volunteer for service in his regiment, and after their week of rest, Tarleton rode with the Queen's Rangers in the Battle of White Plains. It didn't take long for the 16th to earn a savage reputation through the final New York campaign and then into New Jersey under Cornwallis. They were ruthless with the sword.

"My Lord, I wish to offer my services to find out the enemy's situation by means of a patrol," Harcourt offered. "My regiment has performed numerous patrols, but I feel we must penetrate deeper into enemy territory to determine Lee's intentions."

Cornwallis's eyes widened, and he held out a hand with a broad smile to Harcourt as he glanced around the room. "Lieutenant Colonel Harcourt not only commands the Queen's Rangers, but he is a personal *friend* of Queen Charlotte, having escorted her from Mecklenburg-Strelitz to England. And he has just *proven* what a friend he truly is by volunteering for such a dangerous mission." The general turned to Harcourt, his brow wrinkled. "You do realize that such a far-reaching patrol shall require an overnight stay in hostile territory, possibly all the way to Morristown? You shall be under constant threat of rebel militia ambushing your patrol from hidden positions."

Harcourt tightened his lips and gave a quick nod, gripping his black leather helmet under his arm. "Understood, my Lord."

"Very well. Take a small portion of your regiment," Cornwallis instructed, pointing to a map of New Jersey. "No more than thirty-two troopers. Have them ready to ride tomorrow morning. And Lieutenant Colonel, choose some of your more . . . brutal troopers for this mission."

Clarie turned to Gillamon. "Don't tell me. I think I know who will be the first to volunteer to ride with Harcourt's patrol."

Gillamon nodded as they watched Harcourt receive his final orders from Cornwallis and leave the room. Once outside, he was immediately approached by none other than Banastre Tarleton.

"I was just coming to find you, Cornet Tarleton," Harcourt told him. "We ride in the morning."

"Sir? Ride where?" Tarleton asked.

"To find General Lee," Harcourt answered with a slight grin. He pointed to Tarleton's saber. "What was that claim you made back at the Cocoa Tree?"

Tarleton gave a mischievous smile and pulled his saber from its sheath. "With this sword, I will cut off the head of General Charles Lee!"

"Come with me," Harcourt ordered, walking away briskly with Tarleton toward their regimental quarters.

"Get to Archer immediately and prepare him for what is heading his way," Gillamon instructed Clarie. "Make sure he knows exactly what is at stake with General Lee."

ROO THE DAY

"Roo-roo-roo-roo-roo!" Archer cried happily, trotting along next to the four-mile-long column of men who plodded south in the muddy road. A morning snowfall had now turned to slush from rising temperatures and the marching footprints of four thousand soldiers. Archer loved splashing mud everywhere while running in every direction. He also knew it provided great entertainment to the weary soldiers.

"The general's dog doesn't bark, does he?" a soldier whispered as Archer ran past.

His friend laughed. "No, he 'roo's.' What a funny dog!"

"I'm shpechial!" Archer agreed, now bolting off to run as fast as he could back to where Lee rode in the rear of the column. The soldiers laughed at the dog, enjoying some comic relief in the midst of their misery. Some of them didn't have shoes and had tied strips of leather around their feet. Some coughed as they walked, and others still shivered with hands folded under their armpits.

"Hush, Archer!" Lee hoarsely scolded the dog as he came bounding up, covered in mud. "We're operating on a strict mode of silence. HUSH!"

Archer clamped his mouth tight and mumbled, *Whatever you shay!*

Twenty-seven hundred Continental soldiers and thirteen hundred militia made up Lee's army marching in the direction of General Washington. Over the past three weeks, the Commander-in-Chief had sent eight letters to General Lee to join him in Pennsylvania—they progressed from suggesting to entreating and finally to ordering Lee to come with the last dispatch from an exasperated Washington. Lee had no choice but to finally order his army to march.

Lee's second in command, General Sullivan, looked up at the sun getting lower in the sky as they came to a fork in the road. "What are your orders, General Lee?"

"Tomorrow we'll swing west to cross the Delaware at Tinicum," Lee answered. "We'll skirt the sizable British forces in the south. You men pitch tents here for the night. I've located a small inn nearby in Basking Ridge, a

Widow White's Tavern. I'll take my aide Major William Bradford, fifteen guards, and those two new French volunteer officers."

"Understood, Sir," Sullivan answered with a bit of a curious tone. "You will be about three miles from the army then? Do you wish to gather your personal baggage from the supply wagon?"

Lee shook his head. "No need to take it. I'll join you in the morning. Good night, Sullivan."

With that, Lee and his small band of men peeled off the main road. Darkness soon enveloped Lee's party with the sun setting on the way to Basking Ridge. After about a mile, Archer picked up a foul scent in the air. He lifted his nose and looked around but saw nothing.

"Oh, boy! A ta-vern, a ta-vern, we get to stay in Widow White's Ta-vern!" Archer cheered loudly. "Roo-roo-roo-roo-roo!"

"ARCHER!" Lee again scolded. The goofy dog once more clamped tight his mouth and rooed under his breath.

From the shadows, a set of huge paws followed along behind. "General Lee is going to rue the day he ever let that pathetic mutt come to live with him," Espion predicted smugly. "Or rather, 'roo' the day. That dog's stupid mouth led me straight to General Lee." The invisible wolf followed until Lee and his entourage set foot inside White's Tavern, and after watching the general send sentries to stand guard for their position. "Now to tell Rafe exactly where Lee is."

WIDOW WHITE'S TAVERN, BASKING RIDGE, NEW JERSEY, DECEMBER 13, 1776, 4:00 A.M.

Nineteen-year-old Major James Wilkinson galloped up to the front of the tavern and dismounted his chestnut horse, tying it to the post. He wiped his runny nose from the chilly night ride and hurried to the front door. He hesitated, but then rapped the door with his knuckles. After no one answered, he knocked more persistently.

In moments, Mary White cracked open the door, asking, "Who's there?" A flicker of candlelight danced over her wearied face.

"Major Wilkinson, aide-de-camp to General Gates, with an urgent message for General Lee," the young man quickly offered.

The widow pulled her shawl tightly around her shoulders and opened the door. "I'll take you to him," she said quietly as she led the young man up the creaking staircase to the second floor.

When they reached the upstairs, there lay Lee's officers asleep on blankets spread out before a roaring fire in the common area. They tiptoed by the men over to the door of Lee's bedchamber.

"General Lee," Mary White hoarsely whispered, rapping on his door with one hand, holding a candle in the other. "General Lee! You have an urgent message."

Wilkinson and Mary looked at one another as they heard Lee murmur and shout a grumbly, "HUH? COME!"

Mary opened the door and held out her hand for Wilkinson to enter, following behind him to light the candle on General Lee's nightstand. Archer sat at the foot of the bed, his tail slapping the blanket happily, as he always did when anyone approached. Lee sat up, his hair askew in all directions. He gave a low grumble and rubbed his eyes with one hand before letting it fall to the bed. "What is it?"

"Sir, it's Major James Wilkinson. I apologize for waking you, but I feel General Gates's dispatch is most urgent," the young man quickly offered, handing the letter to Lee.

Lee snarled and snatched the letter from his hand and looked at the inscription. "This is addressed to General *Washington!*" he snapped, attempting to hand it back to Wilkinson.

"Yes, Sir, it is. But the reason for my bringing it to you is that Gates sent ahead of him three Continental regiments from upstate New York in Albany, which he then followed with four more regiments," Wilkinson began. "We encountered a blinding snowstorm on December 11th in the New Jersey hills, and General Gates sent me to find General Washington to determine the best route to take to join with his army. On my way here I discovered that Washington had already crossed the Delaware and removed all the boats from the ferries. I then proceeded toward Morristown, where I located one of your aides, Joseph Nourse, who directed me here to find you for instructions."

Lee scratched his stubbly chin and swung his skinny legs to the floor, grunting as he slipped his bare feet into the worn-out slippers sitting by the bed. "Very well," he replied as he broke the wax seal of Gates's letter and held it to the candlelight. "Hmmm," he finally said after a moment, tapping the letter on his knee in thought. "Go rest for a while by the fire with the other officers, Major. You can brief me more on the situation later this morning."

"Thank you, Sir," Wilkinson answered, stepping out of the bedroom to join Lee's officers by the crackling fire. He took a blanket from a cupboard and spread it out on the floor, letting go a deep exhale of relief. He closed his eyes and quickly fell asleep from exhaustion.

Archer stood on the bed as Lee got up and stretched out in his nightshirt. The old general leaned over to scratch the dog behind the ears. "Keep sleeping, boy. No cause for alarm. I just need to think."

Well, thinking's always a good thing to do, Archer thought with a wide yawn, circling around to find a cozy position, and laying his head back down on the blanket.

"If I join my army with Washington's army, plus Gates's army, any blow struck against the enemy will give all the credit to General Washington," Lee surmised with a frown. He then grinned and held a bony finger in the air. "But if I can strike against the British on my own, I alone would get all the glory. I must make my decision before we leave after breakfast."

Archer frowned. *I've always found that thinking on an empty stomach makes you think dumb thoughts.* He yawned with a yelp. *So does thinking without sleep. You best wait until after breakfast then. You wouldn't want to do anything dumb now, would you?*

SOMERSET COURTHOUSE, NEW JERSEY, DECEMBER 13, 1776, 4:45 A.M.

Banastre Tarleton turned over and breathed in the scent of straw, followed by the pungent smell of burning wood. His eyes fluttered open, and he sat up straight with a start, trying to remember where he was. He looked around in the darkness and felt the straw-covered earth around him. Suddenly the previous day came rushing back into his mind. He and thirty-one troopers from the Queen's Dragoons had ridden with Colonel Harcourt on the expedition to find General Charles Lee, on special orders of General Charles Cornwallis. They left Pennington and headed northeast toward Morristown, New Jersey, along with a guide who knew the area well. They rode roughly eighteen miles without incident and stopped to rest for the night just south of Hillsborough, where two companies of the 71st Regiment were quartered. Sleeping soundly in a comfortable house, they were rudely awakened at 1:00 a.m. by screams of "FIRE!" Filing out of the house, the rangers took shelter in a barn as the house burned to the ground. Quite mysteriously, no one knew what had caused the fire.

Tarleton shook his head, rubbed his eyes, and pulled on his black leather boots, kicking Cornet Francis Geary, who slept near him. "Wake up!" Tarleton got to his feet, picked off pieces of straw clinging to his red jacket trimmed in blue, and dusted off his white breeches. He secured his black leather helmet with its horsehair plume, strapped on his saber, and made his way outside the barn. The embers of a small fire remained in a circular stone pit in the courtyard. The young cornet threw a few pieces of wood on the pile and stoked the fire, bringing it back to life. He gazed into the hungry flames and smiled. *Today is the day.*

"Good morning, Tarleton," came Colonel Harcourt's voice. "You always seem to be the first on any scene, even after a sleepless night. Impressive."

Tarleton tugged the hem of his jacket and stood at attention. "Thank you, Sir! I wish to serve my king well. I'm eager for the day ahead."

An aide sounded the call for all troopers in the Queen's Rangers to saddle their horses. Harcourt warmed his hands by the fire and grinned. "I'm sure you are, Cornet Tarleton. Let's go find Lee."

Soon the entire patrol mounted their horses and galloped off as the sky slowly turned from grey to pink with streaks of fiery red marking the horizon. They rode two miles north to Hillsborough, crossing the Millstone River, and then reached the Raritan River, hugging its southern bank as they rode east. As the sun rose above the horizon, the impressive sight of these red-clad horsemen filled the drab winter landscape with shocking color and explosive sound as the hooves of their athletic horses tore through the dirt of the New Jersey countryside.

Harcourt called a halt to the patrol and motioned for Tarleton. "Cornet Tarleton, you shall take six dragoons and ride as our advance guard."

Tarleton's heart raced with excitement and pride. "Yes, SIR!" he exclaimed. He pulled his saber from its sheath and held it in the air as his men gathered behind him. Thrusting it forward, the ambitious dragoon dug his spurs into his horse and galloped ahead.

It wasn't long before Tarleton's men came across a rebel sentry. The thirst for blood quickly overtook reason, and a dragoon cut down the man with a sword without even an inquiry. "Pity," Tarleton exclaimed, spurring them further toward their target, "but we're getting close."

Two miles behind Tarleton, Harcourt came across a man in the road who flagged him down. Harcourt lifted his hand in the air to halt the advance of his dragoons.

"You looking for that General Lee?" the man inquired of Harcourt.

"Indeed, we are," Harcourt answered, gazing at the man with curiosity. *How did he know?*

The man pointed in the distance. "He's naught but four or five miles ahead at an inn." He stepped forward to stand before Harcourt's horse. Harcourt smelled a foul stench coming from the man in the road. "Better watch the way you came from. Them rebels done cut off your retreat."

Harcourt cast an anxious glance behind and called out to Captain Nash, who sauntered up to him. "Take four dragoons and see if rebel militia are blocking our escape route."

"Yes, Sir!" Nash answered, galloping off.

Harcourt turned to address the man in the road, but he was gone. The

Colonel wrinkled his brow but saluted his thanks, anyway, galloping ahead to give Tarleton the news. "We're not just going to *find* General Charles Lee. We're going to *capture* him."

Tarleton felt as if he were on fire. "YES, *SIR!*"

Riding another three miles ahead, Tarleton and his dragoons came upon two rebel sentries in the road. The men tried to run but Tarleton galloped ahead of them and quickly dismounted, pulling out his saber and pressing it against the neck of one of the men. Drops of blood oozed against his blade. "Now, rebel, you WILL tell me where I will find GENERAL CHARLES LEE, or you will die . . . instantly."

The Patriot sentry's forehead beaded with sweat, and he almost collapsed from terror. Only Tarleton's saber at his throat kept him standing upright. "He's . . . about a mile off," the man sputtered out with a quivering mouth, swallowing gingerly against the steel pressed against his neck.

Tarleton leaned in and whispered in the man's ear. "And how *large* is General Lee's guard?"

The Patriot sentry trembled and sank for a moment before Tarleton's blade made him stand on his toes, his voice rising in pitch. "Ahhhh, he only has ahhhh a small guard around him . . . maybe a dozen?"

"You have been *most* helpful to volunteer such useful intelligence," Tarleton told the man with dripping sarcasm. He stepped away and shoved the rebel sentry to the ground, quickly mounting his horse once more as he ordered one of his men to detain the two rebels. He then doubled back to report to Harcourt what he had discovered.

Harcourt furrowed his brow, concerned about being encircled by Lee's men. "We best ascertain our situation before proceeding ahead. Take two men to the top of that ridge and observe what you can."

"Yes, Sir!" Tarleton exclaimed, taking two men with him. The bold cornet could smell it. Lee was close, and soon the traitorous general would be his.

WIDOW WHITE'S TAVERN, BASKING RIDGE, NEW JERSEY, DECEMBER 13, 1776, 8:00 A.M.

"Washington has made one poor decision after another!" Lee ranted to Wilkinson, now sitting at a long table in the common area. They had been discussing the situation of the northern army, and now of Washington's ineptitude. "If I hadn't arrived from the Carolinas in time to save the main army from capture on Manhattan, this war would already be over!"

The young major sat there listening to Lee's diatribe of Washington when footsteps sounded on the stairs. Several members of the Connecticut Light Horse regiment appeared, led by Colonel Elisha Sheldon.

"What is this about?" Lee demanded to know, slamming his bony fist on the table at the interruption.

Archer sat by the fireplace and listened as the men offered up one complaint after another. They needed forage and shoes for their horses, and one dared to bring up the fact that he was owed back pay. *Oooooooooh, they better watch it around old 'Boiling Water'!*

Sure enough, Lee jumped to his feet, arguing with the dragoons before sending them out of the house with a shout. "Your wants are numerous, but you have not mentioned the last—you want to go HOME! And you shall be indulged, for you do no good here! Be gone with all of you!"

As the men stomped back down the stairs and out of the tavern, Archer shook his head and thought, *Lee's always been called a "pot of boiling water," but something tells me he's the one who's going to get burned with that temper today.*

After only a few moments, another officer arrived. This time, it was Colonel Alexander Scammell, the same officer who had been deceived by Charlatan or Rafe the night of Washington's escape from Brooklyn. Now he served as General Sullivan's aide-de-camp. Archer sat on one of the chairs next to Lee as would any of his officers. Before him was a bowl of scraps, and Archer licked his chops happily, wagging his tail as the young officer approached.

"Sir, I come to receive marching orders for General Sullivan," Scammell told Lee, giving a curious grin to the dog casually dining next to Lee.

Lee pointed to Scammell's leather knapsack draped over his shoulder. "Do you have a map of the country there?"

"Yes, Sir," Scammell answered, pulling out the map and laying it on the table.

Lee traced his finger along the map, first in a route of Sullivan's position in Vealtown to Pluckemin and down to Princeton, then from Pluckemin to Brunswick. Archer leaned forward, watching Lee's finger on the map.

"Colonel Scammell, tell General Sullivan to move down toward Pluckemin, that I will soon be with him," Lee instructed the young man.

Archer's eyes widened as he realized exactly what Wilkinson also understood by Lee's instructions taking the army on a different course. *Uh-oh! Lee isn't planning to march to meet Washington anymore! He's going to make a raid on Princeton, against Washington's orders! He's gonna be in bi-i-ig trouble!*

After Scammell left, Lee scribbled out another note for General Sullivan and called for an express rider named Samuel McIlrath waiting downstairs. Archer looked out the upstairs window and watched as McIlrath galloped away from the tavern to deliver the message. Mary White then brought in a tray of breakfast for Lee, Wilkinson, Bradford, and the two French officers.

Lee ate quickly and wiped his grimy hands on the tablecloth, swirling his tongue around his mouth to clean his teeth. "Saddle my horse. I've got to finish a letter to Gates, which *you,* Major Wilkinson, are to take to him immediately."

"Yes, Sir!" Wilkinson answered as Lee walked over to the writing desk, Archer at his heels.

Lee glanced over the letter to General Horatio Gates that he had begun the night before, rubbing Archer's head as the dog jumped up on a box next to him. He read along as Lee added a few lines:

December 12/13 1776

My Dear Gates:
The ingenious maneuver of Fort Washington has unhinged the goodly fabric we had been building. Entre nous, a certain great man is most deficient. He has thrown me into a situation where I have my choices of difficulties. If I stay in this province, I risk myself and army, and if I do not stay the province is lost forever. I have neither guard, cavalry, medicines, money, shoes, or stockings. I must act with the greatest circumspection. Tories are in my front, rear and on my flanks. The mass of the people is strangely contaminated. In short unless something which I do not expect turns up we are lost. Our counsels have been weak to the last degree. As to what relates to yourself if you think you can be in time to aid the General I would have you by all means go. You will at least save your army. It is said the Whigs are determined to set fire to Philadelphia. If they strike this decisive stroke the day will be our own, but unless it is done, all chance of liberty in any part of the globe is forever vanished.

Archer shook his head sadly. *It's too bad you don't have any faith in Washington. I happen to know he's been chosen by the Maker for this job. But you DID say one good thing there, Boiling Water: 'In short unless something which I do not expect turns up we are lost.'* He jumped off the box and sauntered out of the room to go outside. *I'm counting on it.*

**NEAR WIDOW WHITE'S TAVERN, BASKING RIDGE,
NEW JERSEY, DECEMBER 13, 1776, 10:00 A.M.**

Tarleton held up a spyglass to scan the rolling countryside when suddenly he spotted a lone rider galloping toward them. "Yankee light horseman!" he exclaimed before taking off after the rider.

Within moments, Tarleton had Samuel McIlrath in the identical position of Lee's sentry. His saber was at the express rider's throat. "You will come with me, NOW."

Soon McIlrath stood before Colonel Harcourt, spilling everything he knew about General Lee and his lodgings at Widow White's Tavern.

"I . . . I am taking an express message to General Sullivan," McIlrath gushed out.

Tarleton pressed his blade against the rider's neck. "And just how many guards does General Lee have with him?"

McIlrath attempted to swallow, his heart racing inside his chest. "M-m-maybe twenty . . . no th-th-thirty men. I, I can show you where he's staying."

"Excellent," Tarleton whispered in McIlrath's ear. The brutal cornet cast a glance at Colonel Harcourt, awaiting his instructions.

Harcourt called for Captain Eustace, Cornwallis's aide-de-camp. "What do you think we should do? Are we strong enough in numbers to take the risk? If we maintain the element of surprise, perhaps we can overcome Lee's men with sabers before their men have time to fire."

Eustace thought a moment and nodded. "I believe your men are *fully* capable, Colonel. I would advise you to proceed."

Harcourt nodded and turned to lock eyes with Tarleton. "Proceed, Cornet. Go capture General Lee."

Tarleton gave a wicked grin, saluted, and took off at full speed.

WIDOW WHITE'S TAVERN, BASKING RIDGE, NEW JERSEY, DECEMBER 13, 1776, 10:30 A.M.

"Why is Lee so angry all the time?" asked Rusty, Major Wilkinson's horse. He was still tied to the post outside where Archer now sat. Two sentries stood by a wagon parked near the entrance to the inn.

"He had an unhappy childhood," Archer explained. "He was hurt so much as a boy that he grew up fighting everyone and not trusting anyone but us dogs."

"That's sad!" lamented Rusty.

"Some humans just seem to be happier choosing to be miserable," Archer answered, shrugging his shoulders. Suddenly he lowered his one upstanding ear to the ground. "You hear that?"

Rusty pawed the ground as he, too, felt the vibrations and heard the distant noise. "Yep!"

"It's felt like half of forever, but . . ." Archer said, turning his gaze to the window above them. " . . . company's coming!"

Upstairs General Lee looked over his letter to General Gates one last time before signing it:

Adieu. my dear friend. God bless you.

Charles Lee

Lee folded the letter and affixed a wax seal to the front. "Take this to General Gates immediately," he instructed, handing the letter to Major Wilkinson. "It's time we all depart."

As Major Wilkinson took the letter in hand, he suddenly heard horses' hooves and glanced out the window of the second story room. His eyes widened at the sight of a party of British dragoons turning a corner to charge at top speed toward the inn, swords raised high in the air. They quickly covered the hundred-yard lane situated between thick woods and an orchard. "Here, sir, are the British cavalry!"

"Where?" Lee shot back in alarm.

"Around the house!" Wilkinson exclaimed, watching as the dragoons swarmed the premises.

"Where are the guard? Why don't they fire?!" Lee asked, rushing to the window. "Do, Sir, see what has become of the guard."

"Right away, Sir," Wilkinson answered, picking up his pistols from the table and thrusting Lee's letter into his pocket.

Mary White and her sister ran into the room. "General! Please hide in the bed!"

Lee scoffed at the women and waved them off in disgust while Wilkinson raced to the opposite end of the house where the guard had stayed. The major saw their arms in the room, but the guards were not there. He quickly made his way to the back door leading outside and saw the guards scattering in every direction. They had evidently gone outside to enjoy the sunshine of this balmy morning. Only one or two of them had muskets and attempted to fire off a shot while the others fled in a panic.

Above the whinnying of horses and shouting, Banastre Tarleton cupped a hand to his mouth and ordered, "FIRE ON THE HOUSE THROUGH EVERY WINDOW AND DOOR! CUT UP AS MANY OF THE GUARD AS YOU CAN!"

"Do *not* shoot," Lieutenant Leigh warned a guardsman struggling to load his musket. He drew a pistol and aimed it at the guard's head. "If you fire, we will blow your brains out."

Two other guards were savagely cut down by dragoons wielding their deadly sabers as ordered by Tarleton.

Suddenly the house was riddled with carbine shot as the dragoons fired from atop their horses. Bullets shattered glass and pinged off a mirror, tore through furniture, and sent feathers flying from an upholstered settee in the front parlor. Rusty tried to rise on his hind legs but was tethered to the post. Archer bolted to a nearby tree to hide. Inside, Major Bradford and the two French officers Lieutenant Colonel Boisbertrand and Captain de Virnejoux fired out the windows. Lee paced about the room calmly while Wilkinson hid in a back-room fireplace.

Mary White ran from behind the house to where Banastre Tarleton sat atop his horse. She fell to her knees, peering up at the fierce dragoon. "Please spare our lives! General Lee is in the house!"

A corner of Tarleton's mouth upturned with pleasure to hear that Lee was inside, assuring him that he had the traitor cornered. Harcourt's men joined Tarleton's advance guard and fired seventy shots into the house.

After about eight minutes Tarleton rode confidently up to the portico and fired into the front door. "I know General Lee is in the house! If he surrenders himself, he and his attendants will be safe. But if he refuses my orders and does not surrender immediately, we will burn down this house and put every person to the sword—without exception!"

While Tarleton paused to listen intently to voices coming from inside, out of the corner of his eye he saw an officer attempting to escape out the back. He took off after Boisbertrand and quickly captured him with his sword, inflicting wounds on the Frenchman's head and arm.

Lee tightened his mouth and gripped the back of a chair. "No help is coming, Major Bradford. Go down and tell them that I will submit."

Bradford swallowed and nodded gravely. "Sir." He made his way downstairs, but as he started to open the door, another round of fire whizzed past his head and grazed his hand. "WE ARE COMING OUT! GENERAL LEE WILL SURRENDER!" he shouted, gripping his bloodied hand in a fist. He hurriedly wrapped a kerchief around his wound and cautiously opened the door.

This is gonna be awkward! Archer thought when he saw to whom Lee would be surrendering.

General Charles Lee and Major William Bradford stepped out into the sunshine of this crisp December morning. Lee looked around at the mounted dragoons surrounding him and slowly walked toward Colonel Harcourt. He knew the officer well. Harcourt had served under him when Lee himself had commanded this same Burgoyne's 16th regiment of light dragoons as a British officer serving in Portugal.

"I surrender myself as a prisoner of war," Lee told Harcourt. "I trust I shall be treated as a gentleman."

Harcourt nodded. "You have my assurance, Sir." He pointed to Rusty and ordered a dragoon to mount Lee on the horse.

Lee felt his bald head with a bare hand. "Sir, may I request that my aide retrieve my hat and cloak from inside?"

Harcourt nodded, and Lee motioned for Bradford to go retrieve the items. Bradford slipped inside but instantly decided on a ruse to keep himself from being taken prisoner as well. He quickly changed into the clothes of a servant and then set Lee's hat and cloak outside on the front stoop before escaping back inside.

A dragoon grabbed the items and shoved them into Lee's hands as he forced the general to mount the chestnut horse. Rusty glanced worriedly over at Archer, who shouted, "I'll catch up, don't worry!"

With that, shouts rose into the air, and a bugle sounded for the patrol to leave. Tarleton came riding up behind Harcourt and General Lee, his French prisoner in tow. Boisbertrand was one of the first French officers to be captured by the British, angering the redcoats with evidence of French aid for their rebelling colonies. Together the patrol of thirty dragoons thundered back down the lane shouting cries of victory as they carried off their prize.

Tarleton eyed Lee with icy satisfaction, his bloodied saber in its sheath, for now.

TARLETON'S PRIZE

"THIS IS INTOLERABLE!" Nigel fumed, tugging on his whiskers as he stomped up and down the table. "That dense-headed canine and his loud-mouthed verbosity allowed the enemy to learn *exactly* where they could find General Lee! Now the Continental Army has lost its finest military mind! We've been ruined by that 'sphechial' dog! Ruined, I say!"

"R-r-roo-ined be more like it, aye?" Max huffed.

Nigel, Max, and Jock had come to the War Room on the invitation of Gillamon. They sat around the table watching the single panel of time on the wall showing General Charles Lee now held as a prisoner at Cornwallis's headquarters in Pennington, New Jersey. Banastre Tarleton and his fellow dragoons were boisterously celebrating their prize. They lifted bottles of rum, shouting toasts to every officer in the British army they could think of. When they ran out of names, Banastre Tarleton had an idea.

Tarleton pulled his saber from its sheath and held it high in the air. "Back in London at the Cocoa Tree, I vowed to cut off the head of Charles Lee with this sword!"

The group of soldiers gave a collective "Ooooooh!"

Rafe cupped a hand to his mouth and shouted, "DO IT!" Uncomfortable laughter and murmuring rippled through the room.

Tarleton shook his head, laughed, and picked up an unopened bottle of rum with the other hand. "Being a soldier of dishcipline, I always obey my commanding occifer. While I would *love* to remove the head of that traitorous Lee with this sword, he is considered too valuable by my Lord Howe, despite the worthiness of my vow." He proceeded to use his saber to clip off the cork of the rum bottle, almost losing his balance as he tried. "The ancient Romans would parade their captives through the shtreets of Rome for all to see the spoils of war. And because of Lee's horshe, we were able to parade that spoiled, defeated general into camp today!" He lifted the bottle of rum high in the air for another toast. "To Lee's horshe," he slurred, "for carrying Lee into our camp jusht like the Romans!" The tipsy dragoon took a swig and wiped his mouth. "I think Lee's *horse* deserves a drink!"

The animals watched in dismay as the soldiers broke out in laughter, guffawing as Tarleton poured rum into the horse's water trough. Archer hid behind the horse's legs, his ears down. Soon the horse was lapping up the water.

"That mean Rafe is there celebrating with them!" Jock exclaimed. "It looks like the bad lads have beat us this time."

"I thought ye wanted us ta see somethin' *happy* an' encouragin', Gillamon," Max huffed. "Not only did the enemy capture General Lee, but now they be gettin' his horse dr-r-runk!"

"Uh-oh, Archer's drinking the spiked water, too," Jock noticed. Sure enough, Archer stepped up to the trough and thirstily drank.

Gillamon and Clarie sat there grinning but said nothing.

Rusty swayed his head back and forth like a rag doll. "I don't know what he put in my trough, but I feel kinda funny!" he whinnied, almost stepping on Archer. "Ssssorry there, little doggie," he slurred, followed by a hiccup.

Archer smacked his lips. "That Ban-ban-man poured shomethin in your water, Rusty. I feel kinda funny, too!"

"It's too bad you had to get pulled into all of this messh with me," said Rusty.

"Oh, I wasn't *pulled* into it! I was a shecret agent to *help* it alllllllllll happen!" Archer confessed. "I told the bad guy invisible shpy exactly where the British could find Lee—Boiling Water was trying to take Washingtonsh job, sho we had to get him out of the way." He gave a long, drawn-out belch. "Jusht in time for Christmas! I love Christmas, don't you? I helped give Washington a bigggggggggg preshent!"

"No kidding? I would've never picked *you* for a spy!" Rusty remarked with a snicker.

"I told you I was shpechial!" Archer exclaimed, slurring his words with a goofy grin. "Merrrry Christhmash!!!"

"What . . . did . . . he . . . just say?" Nigel slowly asked, gob smacked, holding out a paw in disbelief.

Suddenly Rafe's face fell, and his eyes filled with fury at overhearing Archer's drunken confession. He slammed his fist into the wall and stormed out into the night, away from the revelry.

"Rafe has just learned what you all are now learning," Gillamon finally said, standing next to the panel of time. "It was all a set-up. Archer loudly spilled the news of Lee's whereabouts so Espion could then inform Rafe, who then informed Harcourt, and ultimately Tarleton."

"BUT WHY!?" Max grumbled. "I know Lee were tryin' ta weasel inta Washington's job but allowin' the Br-r-rits ta capture our best general seems like it will *hurt* the Patriot cause more than help it!"

"Agreed! This seems like too drastic a measure to remove a threat to Washington," Nigel agreed.

"On the contrary," Gillamon countered, pointing to his head. "The biggest threat to George Washington lies between his ears. The Sword of the Revolution needs to be sharpened into the leader the Maker has called him to be. Ever since Washington was appointed Commander-in-Chief, he's lived in the shadow of the much more experienced Lee. He's known that Lee was a wiser military leader, and he's been too intimidated by Lee's prowess to make a move unless he first ran it by Lee."

"And as you've seen, Washington couldn't even bring himself to order Lee to join him in New Jersey, then Pennsylvania," Clarie interjected. "He begged Lee to come multiple times before he built up the nerve to *order* him to bring his army to Pennsylvania."

"Exactly right, Clarie," Gillamon agreed. "Plus, Lee was already positioning himself with Congress, using men surrounding Washington, such as his trusted aide, Colonel Reed. You see, if Tarleton hadn't captured General Lee at White's Tavern, Lee may have convinced the Continental Congress to select *him* as the Continental Army's new Commander-in-Chief. General Washington would have been demoted to serve as Lee's subordinate."

"Now Washington is liberated from all of that," Nigel noted. "I finally understand the supreme wisdom of this turn of events! The British believe they've just dealt a death blow to the Continental Army, but they have in fact provided the *perfect* opportunity for Washington to rise to the occasion and stand on his own two feet."

"Aye, not on them skinny Lee legs," Max agreed.

"America's independence must be won by an American at the helm," Clarie added. "General George Washington is now fully in charge with no one to make him second-guess his decisions at every turn."

"Before they fled Philadelphia, Congress declared a day of fasting and prayer before officially giving Washington full power to prosecute the war," Gillamon told them. "They've also listened to Washington's pleas to finally enlist a standing army, so he won't have to keep losing men with short-term enlistments as he fights this war. But before that happens, Washington is faced with an army whose enlistment is up, and who can and *will* likely walk away."

"So, what now, Gillamon?" Jock asked. "Archer said he helped give Washington a Christmas present. What about us? What can we give him?"

"Now we must give Washington an unexpected event to save the army, the cause of independence, and Washington's honor," Gillamon answered. "He'll open this gift in front of the Continental Army, Congress, the British, the Hessians, France—the entire world."

"That sounds like a big Christmas for 1776!" Jock cheered.

"Oh, it shall be a *very* big Christmas, little one," Gillamon assured him with a wink. "We'll all have parts to play to deliver our best Christmas gifts to Washington and the Continental Army."

Gillamon unfurled a map of Trenton with the Delaware River on the long table. He hovered his hand over the map, and it slowly turned into a moving water map. "Now, little Jock, what did Henry Knox desperately need *last* Christmas to deliver the guns from Fort Ticonderoga the day he found you?"

"Snow!" Jock answered. "And I gave Knox a white Christmas! Can I give one to Washington?"

"Yes, when the time comes, you can give him snow, with lots of ice," Gillamon answered. "For now, blow on the river, Jock."

Jock wagged his tail excitedly and blew across his paw, which became frosty white. His icy breath hovered in the air for a moment before settling on the banks of the Delaware River. Ice chunks formed as snow fell over the river and its banks. "How's that, Gillamon? It sure is a lot less work on the map than in real life!"

Everyone gazed at the ice floes filling the Delaware River, and the large snow drifts building on the shoreline all the way to Trenton.

"All that snow an' ice will keep the Br-r-ritish an' Hessians fr-r-rom expectin' an attack," Max offered.

"Precisely, so that is exactly why Washington will cross the Delaware to do just that," Gillamon said, smiling broadly and pointing to Trenton, turning it blue on the map. "Now it's our turn to sharpen the Sword of the Revolution."

57

FROM FOX TO HOUND

TRENTON, NEW JERSEY, DECEMBER 14, 1776

The smell of skillet-fried bacon and boiled egg yolks over thick toast wafted through the air as servants hurriedly brought in fine bone-china plates to set before the British, Hessian, and Scottish officers. General Howe wore an immaculate scarlet coat trimmed in gold, and sat at the head of the long breakfast table draped with fine linen. He was now 'Sir' William Howe following his knighthood for his victory in the battle of New York. He lifted a crystal glass of small beer and gave a broad smile. "Good morning, gentlemen. It is a glorious day to be in the service of His Majesty, King George III, is it not? We routed that Fox Washington and his rebels in New York and chased them all the way across New Jersey until they scampered across the Delaware in fear for their lives!"

"Huzzah!" the British officers exclaimed, slapping the table heartily enough to make the flatware jump and the crystal goblets clink.

"There is nothing more despicable than Continental Troops!" General Grant shouted, his double chin quivering while he laughed until his face was as red as his woolen coat.

The two Hessian commanders looked around the table, not understanding them. Colonel Johann Rall wore his blue-black regimental uniform and sat opposite Hessian Colonel Carl von Donop dressed in his *Jäger* green. They simply picked up their crystal goblets of small beer and drank, understanding the general merriment of victory that filled the room. They knew their combined forces had achieved victory thus far.

"But *yesterday* came an unexpected and tremendous bonus victory," Howe exclaimed, lifting a hand to Cornwallis. "Why don't you share your good news, General?"

"Thank you, *Sir* Howe," Cornwallis replied with a nod of respect. He lifted his chin high in the air and wore a broad smile. "We have eliminated the only real threat facing us. I sent out a scouting party, led by Lieutenant Colonel Harcourt, to locate the traitor General Charles Lee." Cornwallis held out his hand to the commander of the Sixteenth Light Dragoons. "Why don't *you* share the good news, Colonel?"

"Thank you, my Lord," Harcourt answered. He sat up straight and looked around the room of expectant faces that leaned in to hear his report. "We didn't just *locate* General Lee. We *captured* him thanks to the swift action of Cornet Banastre Tarleton. Lee is now our prisoner locked up in Pennington!"

The room erupted with "HUZZAHS!" as more hands pounded the table in celebration. Al sat under the table; his ears flattened to avoid hearing the bad news. "Sure, I knew that bad dragon lad would be nothin' but trouble."

"Tarleton and his men even got Lee's horse drunk!" Harcourt shouted above the din of laughter.

Howe lifted a hand to quiet the officers. "So, you see, gentlemen, there is nothing more that needs to be done for this 1776 campaign. We've defeated the rebels and decimated their army, captured the only true military leader they had, and have taken New York, New Jersey, and Rhode Island. Winter is upon us, and I doubt there will be anything left of Washington and his pathetic little band by springtime. It is time for us to enter winter quarters, but we will keep an eye on the rebels. I have personally scouted up and down the Delaware to assess rebel positions and have decided to hold the river with three brigades." He motioned for his engineering officer Captain John Montresor to pass around the map he had designed.

Rall and Donop couldn't speak English, but they could read a map, and began to study the markings.

"Each brigade will be spread six miles apart to offer mutual support yet provide sufficient coverage of defenses," Howe told them. "Colonel von Donop will oversee all forward outposts with three Hessian battalions at his central post at Bordentown; Colonel Stirling will garrison at Burlington with the Forty-Second Highland Regiment and a Hessian battalion, and Colonel Rall at Trenton with three Hessian regiments. Twelve miles behind them at Princeton will be a full brigade of light infantry and light dragoons under General Alexander Leslie, and behind them will be fourteen garrisons across New Jersey. I'm placing General Grant in overall command at headquarters in Brunswick while General Cornwallis returns to England on leave. I shall, of course, return to New York."

"Where much feasting, dancing, and merrymaking shall begin!" Grant exclaimed, lifting his glass.

Al reached up his paw to the bountiful table only to have it slapped away by General Cornwallis. "How does this cat follow me everywhere I go? He must have slipped into my carriage. Take this feline out of here," Cornwallis ordered a servant. He looked over at the heavy-set Grant and grinned. "Although I have grown quite fond of the ever-hungry cat, I know the perfect place for him to stay while I'm in London—with General Grant."

Al's face erupted in a smile as he glanced at the corpulent Grant, knowing where he'd now be stationed. The servant lifted the crazy cat and set him outside where Nigel, Veritas, and Elsa were waiting for him behind a hedge.

"Halloo, Al!" Elsa exclaimed, licking her chops to see the delicacy that Al held in his paw. "I am *so* very happy to see you, *ja?*"

"Good day, Al. We've been eagerly awaiting the latest British update," Nigel added.

"Top o' the mornin', all. There be lots o' news, Mousie," Al told him. "Howe be headin' to New York, Cornwallis be headin' to England, and them Hessians be stayin' put here in Trenton and Bordentown this winter," the cat reported, chewing on the piece of bacon that he snagged on his way out of the room. "They're puttin' troops in Princeton and other spots, with Grant in charge o' things in New Jersey. But it be a Bow-Wow-Babel in there."

"Whatever do you mean, old boy?" Nigel wanted to know, straightening his spectacles.

"Well, the British officers speak English, but them Hessians don't," Al began, pointing his bacon at Nigel, then Elsa and Veritas as he spoke. "The Brits think that as long as they *shout* in English really loud, them Hessians will know what they say. General Howe sends out his orders in English and French. Donop writes in French to English officers, and in German to his fellow Hessians, but he can't really *speak* English. Rall don't speak English or French, only rough German. Plus, those two Hessian commanders can't stand each other, so they don't even *want* to talk. Then there's that Scottish Colonel Stirling—he writes in English but speaks Gaelic with his Highlanders. I'm tellin' ye, Mousie, they be one miscommunicatin' mess o' soldiers like that Tower o' Babel."

Elsa wiped the drool from her mouth, staring at Al's fried bacon.

Nigel put a paw to his mouth, trying to follow Al's report. "Remarkable that they've achieved any coherent battleplan thus far! This bodes well for setting up confusion in their lines of communication should a sudden attack ensue."

"Aye, plus they won't be able to talk well to each other if something happens real quick like," Al said, drawing a shaking facepalm from Nigel. "But that General Grant don't hear anybody, no matter what language they speak."

Nigel furrowed his brow. "Do you mean the same General James Grant who boasted to Parliament that with five regiments he could march though the colonies and defeat the rebels? Has the old chap fallen deaf?"

Al scratched his head. "Aye. I don't know aboot fallen, but he chooses not to listen to whoever he doesn't want to hear from, especially them Hessians. He's a big, gouty lad from Scotland, and while Howe and his upper officers like him, everybody beneath him hates the fat laddie. Except for me, that is. I love to be beneath him, under the table!" He waved his bacon proudly. "If ye think *I* love food, ye should see how crazy *Grant* be for food. He has his own chef named Baptiste and makes him sleep in the same room with him to be ready at any moment to get the fat lad's menu order for the next meal!" Suddenly Al stopped and thought for a moment, blinking back joyous tears. "I never knew I could love a human so much. I know the fat lad's a pompous buffoon, but I'm willin' to look past all that, for the cause."

Elsa walked right up to Al and nabbed the bacon from his paw. *"Danke* for sharing!"

Al rubbed his belly. "Ye're welcome, little fox lass. I'll have plenty more where that came from now that I'll be livin' with fat laddie Grant. Cornwallis wants him to look after me while he's gone across the pond."

"Vell I for vone am happy about this plan, *ja?"* Elsa said, gulping down the bacon.

"Right, now that we have the British plans confirmed, we must move to the next part of *our* mission," Nigel told them. "Gillamon has requested that Elsa and I give a hunting demonstration in the snow for General Washington whilst he converses with him as Mr. Atticus."

"What kind of a hunting demonstration?" Veritas asked. "I'm a better hunter than this little fox."

"Not *under* the snow," Elsa countered. "You may be able to *see* above ground, but I can *hear* below it."

"Precisely! Which is why I shall *pretend* to be your prey under the frozen tundra, and you shall *pretend* to catch me on the hunt," Nigel explained.

Elsa cocked her head in question. "You mean I vill pounce on you *und* grab you vith my pointy teeth?"

"Yes, but again, this shall merely be a feint, a ruse, a demonstration for the Commander-in-Chief," Nigel offered with a nervous chuckle. "You shall not indeed *eat* me. But I shall willingly put myself in your dainty mouth whilst Mr. Atticus makes his point."

"Mousie's been in me mouth before, lassie!" Al admitted with a goofy grin. "In fact, me mouth met Mousie before the rest of me did."

"Al tends to think with his stomach first and ask questions later," Nigel scoffed with a frown. He raised a paw dramatically in the air. "There I was in the dark, murky cavern that smelled of fish and bananas, with only my tail exposed to the outside world. But I escaped the jaws of death and lived to tell the tale."

Elsa's eyes widened, marveling at the tiny mouse. "How did you escape the deadly kitty jaws of death, Nigel? Did you pry open his mouth with a tiny svord?"

Nigel gave Al a look of scorn through his spectacles. "Do you wish to tell her, or shall I?"

Al gave a weak grin. "Me lass Liz told me to drop him. She said he weren't no ordinary mouse since he were readin' a scroll of funny Egyptian writin'. But Mousie were makin' the papymoose wiggle, and we kitties can't stand anythin' to wiggle without a pounce."

Elsa wrinkled her brow and cocked her head. "Funny Egyptian writing? Vhere vould you be reading such things but in Egypt?"

"I've found it's best not to ask them about stuff like that," Veritas interjected.

"*Papyrus,* not papymoose," Nigel corrected Al. He cleared his throat and waved off the question to change the subject, not wanting to get into the matter of ancient Egypt and their mysterious immortality. "'Twas only a scroll of hieroglyphs, my dear. Just a hobby of mine. But let us discuss this another day. Shall we get back to the matter at hand?"

"I'd rather get back to the bacon at hand, but I'm all out," Al lamented.

"Right. General Washington is vacating his headquarters at the Barclay house just across the river there at Trenton Falls and shall head ten miles north to be closer to the main body of his small army," Nigel explained. "Whilst he is en route, we shall meet him for the fox hunting lesson."

"Only *I* vill be the fox who is hunting," Elsa added with a smile.

BUCKS COUNTY, PENNSYLVANIA,
DECEMBER 14, 1776

Blueskin snorted icy puffs of breath as he galloped through the wintry countryside. Washington needed some time alone to think and decided to gallop on ahead of his supply wagons, which were moving his headquarters to the William Keith House. He was glad for the move, as his other officers were quartered nearby on the west bank of the Delaware. Greene was stationed at Merrick's only a quarter of a mile from Keith's, and Knox was at Chapman's. All headquarters were in the vicinity of Jericho Mountain, which was now stripped of its leaves and from its heights provided sightlines for signaling up and down the river. Washington needed his military family close by, especially with the continual defiance of General Lee to join him. He also terribly missed Martha's company and wisdom. The Commander-in-Chief felt very much alone.

"Let's give you a rest, boy," Washington told Blueskin, pulling on the reins and coming to a halt. He patted his faithful white horse and dismounted, leading Blueskin to a small creek for a drink of water.

Washington looked up at the tall trees towering above him, stretching to the pink sky as the sun began its descent. He had enjoyed the warmth of the sun and the clear day after the recent snow showers. But he suddenly felt an overwhelming sense of his smallness and lack of control, coupled with the weight of all that was upon him. Instinctively he dropped to one knee and knelt in the snow. "Dear God in heaven . . . please, show me what to do."

"It appears that Max and Jock are traveling on the supply wagons today," Gillamon, as Mr. Atticus, observed. He peered out from behind some trees with Elsa and Nigel by his side. "Are you two ready?"

"*Ja,* I am ready for the hunt *und* the lesson for Vashington," Elsa answered happily, peering over at Blueskin. "I vonder if the horse that is blue becomes bluer vith this cold."

Nigel tapped the fox on her forearm. "Remember this is just a *ruse* requiring delicate handling, my dear."

Elsa lowered her head and got eye to eye with the concerned mouse. "Trust me, *meine kleine maus.*"

"Your little mouse, quite right," Nigel answered with a nervous chuckle. "Very well, Mr. Atticus, do proceed so we can get this over with. I shall go make myself scarce."

Gillamon chuckled as Nigel scurried off and disappeared in the snow. "Elsa, your prey is getting into position, and I shall get into mine."

With that, Mr. Atticus quietly approached Washington, his footsteps crunching the snow. Washington lifted his head and smiled to see his old friend. He got to his feet and lifted a hand in greeting. "Mr. Atticus. We seem to meet at the most unusual times and places."

"I don't mean to interrupt you, General," Mr. Atticus replied. "I never want to interfere with a man's communion with the Almighty."

Washington brushed the snow from his breeches and looked around them, taking in the magical winter wonderland. "It certainly is easy to commune with the Almighty out here."

"I agree. I enjoy coming out here to forage for food as I am today," Atticus explained. He reached in his knapsack and pulled out some nuts, offering them to the general who gestured 'no, thanks.' "It's busy in camp, with soldiers doing the best they can to endure the conditions. You don't hear them complaining though. Here we are in the middle of war yet walking a little way up the mountain, it's as if nothing is amiss. Nature continues her course regardless of what men do."

"I'm glad to hear the men are in good spirits," Washington answered.

"Indeed, the rhythm of the natural world continues. It is predictable. Our enemy, however, is not."

"Pardon, Sir, but it seems to me that General Howe *is* predictable," Atticus offered. "He doesn't have a problem defeating us. He just has a problem *finishing* us."

"Indeed, after all the routs Howe has given us, starting at Bunker Hill, he is content with victory in the moment while our army escapes to fight another day," Washington noted. "That certainly is a significant flaw. He followed us to the banks of the Delaware and stopped his pursuit. While we snatched up every boat up and down the Delaware, if Howe had truly pressed on, there is lumber enough in Trenton to have built boats for his army to keep up the chase. And yet, he stopped his pursuit with the arrival of winter."

Atticus nodded. "The British hounds have allowed their Fox to escape, haven't they, General?"

Washington gave a singular laugh and shook his head. "I must admit that I have a greater sympathy for the foxes I have hunted over the years."

"Once the hunter stops the chase, it is the *fox* who then goes on the hunt," Atticus said with a grin. "Have you ever seen how a fox hunts in the snow, General?"

Washington pursed his lips and pulled out his pocket watch to check the time. "I can't say I have, no."

"Foxes live, eat, sleep, and work alone. As you know, they can bark like a dog, purr like a cat, but they are neither," Atticus informed the General. "They can run fast and swim, but the main thing they use to hunt is their hearing." He pointed to Washington's ticking pocket watch. "A fox could hear that some forty yards away. They hear everything. They listen, and they wait for the opportune moment to strike." Suddenly they saw a flash of red and in the distance observed a fox bounding through the snow. "Well, would you look at that?"

"What are the odds?" Washington asked in surprised delight. "A fox!"

"You don't fox hunt in these conditions, do you, General?" Atticus asked. "Look how the hunted now becomes the hunter. She is using the very thing that called off her pursuers to now hunt her prey: snow and ice."

Together Washington and Atticus watched as Elsa sat with her tail wrapped around her feet, sitting quietly in the snow to keep herself warm. She cocked her head to the side and listened intently.

"What is she listening for?" Washington whispered.

"She's listening to her prey that has made tunnels to burrow under the snow," Atticus explained. "Likely a little field mouse."

After a moment they watched Elsa jump high into the air and dive headfirst several feet away into the snow. Only her tail and hind legs were visible as she stayed there motionless for a moment. Then she righted herself and scuffled out of the snow with Nigel in her mouth, his tail flicking back and forth. Blueskin snickered behind them at the scene. Elsa then trotted off with her prize, disappearing into the forest.

"So, the fox could hear her unseen prey scurry under the snow and pinpoint exactly where to strike," Washington observed.

"Not only *where* to strike, but *when,*" Atticus answered. "Timing is everything to the fox. Her attacks must use stealth, surprise, speed, and shock. The same applies to you as Howe's 'Fox.' Without the pursuit of the Hound, you are free to go on the hunt."

"I want nothing more than to find an opportunity for a counterstroke," Washington admitted. "I'm tired of doing nothing but retreating and escaping."

"Plus, you have a reputation that I'm sure you feel needs saving," Atticus suggested, peering into Washington's eyes. "The question is, are you content to work alone like our fox? Meaning, to be the solitary hunter who decides how, where, and when to strike?"

Washington clenched his jaw and wrinkled his brow. "I must hear from my officers in the field, especially General Lee . . ."

Atticus interrupted him. "Excuse me, Your Excellency, but do you believe in yourself?"

The General shot Atticus a swift look of indignation, but then immediately softened. Strangely, this old soldier was the only individual whom Washington allowed such pointed familiarity. But Washington knew he needed frank counsel and plainspokenness. "I do."

Atticus nodded. "And do you believe in the justice of our cause? That the smiles of Providence are upon us?"

"Indeed, Sir, I do," Washington replied.

"Well then, either you are the Commander-in-Chief, or you are not," Atticus boldly posed. "You can't be the Commander-in-*Least* and expect to lead this ragtag army. Of course, you need to hear from your officers, but you need to direct *them*. It's time you silence all those critics who see you as little more than a helpless fox that is mercilessly hounded and cornered to the sound of the horn. *You* are the one in charge of what happens next. Not Lee, not Greene, not Gates, and certainly not General Howe."

"I thank you for your vote of confidence, Mr. Atticus," Washington answered. "And I appreciate your wisdom and honesty."

Atticus smiled. "I know you're itching for a fight, General. So are the men. And they'll follow where *you* lead."

"But not for much longer. If we're going to go on the offensive, it must be before their enlistments expire in the next two weeks," Washington stated plainly. "My greatest concern is that General Howe will attack Philadelphia."

"Ah, then there's the first key, to your *timing*. I understand Old Put is holding the fort in Philadelphia," Atticus noted. "What's the word there, General?"

"Yes, I sent General Putnam with a force of men to provide security and succor to the citizens there, but he informs me that the arrival of British and Hessian forces to Trenton has caused widespread panic," Washington answered. "Half of the city has fled, along with the Congress." He paused a moment, gazing out to where Elsa had sat and listened in the snow. "We can't hear as well or as far off as a fox, but we need a keen ear to hear all that is going on in the enemy camp. I must order all officers to gather intel every way they can and spare no expense to send spies carefully behind enemy lines."

"Very wise, General. There's much to be gained by espionage, especially from a spy who doesn't just go behind enemy lines briefly, but one who lives among the enemy," Atticus offered.

"Like Dr. Benjamin Church did with us back in Cambridge. Our most trusted physician!" Washington lamented with a frown, feeling again the sting of that betrayal. "We didn't have any idea he was passing intel to the enemy."

"Hiding in plain sight is the most effective way to gather intelligence. The ideal would be a local living among the Hessians to give us information," Atticus suggested.

Washington nodded. "Do you have anyone in mind?"

"I do, actually," Atticus admitted, looking off at Elsa in the distance. "I'd be glad to see what I can find out, General."

"I've always found you to be trustworthy, Mr. Atticus," Washington told him. "I would very much like to hear what you discover, but I implore you to take the greatest care in doing so. And I would ask you to please keep any such information between us alone. I feel it best to have a few select informants who report directly to me."

"I'd be honored, General Washington." Atticus removed his hat and bowed. "You have my word. I'll only come straight to you."

"Excellent, Mr. Atticus. I'm grateful for this chance encounter, with you *and* the fox," Washington told him. "We shall keep our ears open and wait for the opportune moment to act."

Atticus pointed to his right ear. "If I have anything to tell you, I'll give you this signal. And I'll sign any correspondence as Mr. Fox."

"Understood. Very well, I must get going to headquarters at the Keith House," Washington told him. "Godspeed."

"And *that* is the second key, to the kind of speed we need," Atticus quipped, sending Washington walking back to Blueskin with a smile.

Gillamon smiled at Washington. "Now, to give Elsa her orders. Who better to gather intelligence from the Hessians than a German fox?"

58

VICTORY OR DEATH

KEITH HOUSE, BUCKS COUNTY, PENNSYLVANIA,
DECEMBER 15, 1776

Washington sat in the main front room of the two-story stone house, poring over his correspondence. Yesterday, Max and Jock sat next to the fireplace and watched as Washington wrote letter after letter to his officers in the field. Nigel obtained the aerial view of Washington's correspondence from the windowsill. He smiled as he read the general's letters to Heath and Gates, asking them to hasten their arrival to join their armies with his:

> *If we can draw our forces together, I trust under the smiles of Providence, we may yet effect an important stroke, or at least prevent General Howe from executing his plan.*

"The General has written a flurry of letters to his commanders at the various fords along the Delaware, instructing them to spare no expense to gather intelligence," Nigel told them. "Mr. Atticus's pep talk seems to have invigorated him to begin thinking about that counterstroke. Sadly, he did also write a ninth pleading letter to General Lee, which of course shall never reach the wretched man."

"Aye, but Washington should hear the good news aboot Lee's capture any time," Max noted.

This morning, Max, Jock, and Nigel remained by the fireplace, waiting to see his response.

"Looks like that time is now!" Jock suggested as an express rider hastily delivered a December 13th letter from General Sullivan. They watched as Washington opened the letter:

> *My Dear General: It gives me the most pungent pain to inform your Excellency of the sad stroke America must feel in the loss of General Lee, who was this morning taken by the enemy near Vealtown ..."*

Washington shot to his feet and paced about the room as he tried to absorb the news. When he finished reading, his hand dropped to his side. "Unhappy man! Taken by his own imprudence!"

Suddenly, the words of Mr. Atticus filled Washington's mind: *Either you are the Commander-in-Chief, or you are not. You can't be the Commander-in-Least and expect to lead this ragtag army. Of course, you need to hear from your officers, but you need to direct them. It's time you silence all those critics who see you as little more than a helpless fox that is mercilessly hounded and cornered to the sound of the horn. You are the one in charge of what happens next. Not Lee, not Greene, not Gates, and certainly not General Howe.*

Washington tapped the letter in his palm and shook his head. But while he was filled with alarm, he suddenly felt an unusual feeling of release. *I can rely on my own instincts and judgments from now on. Any failures going forward will rest on my shoulders, but at least they will be definitively mine.*

CONTINENTAL CAMP, BUCKS COUNTY, PENNSYLVANIA, DECEMBER 20, 1776

"These are the times that try men's souls: The summer soldier and the sunshine Patriot will, in this crisis, shrink from the service of his country; but he that stands it NOW, deserves the love and thanks of man and woman. Tyranny, like hell, is not easily conquered…"

Washington and Knox sat atop their horses in the distance, listening as one of the Continental captains read aloud Paine's *American Crisis* to a group of battle-weary soldiers gathered near a fire. It was printed in a Philadelphia paper the day before and sent by an express rider for wide distribution among the army. Max, Jock, and Nigel sat with Gillamon as Mr. Atticus by a tree, listening in as well.

"I call not upon a few, but upon all; not on THIS State or THAT State; but on EVERY State; up and help us; lay your shoulders to the wheel; better have too much force than too little, when so great an object is at stake. Let it be told to the future world, that in the depth of winter, when nothing but hope and virtue could survive, that the city and the country, alarmed at one common danger, came forth to meet and repulse it. Say not, that thousands are gone, turn out your tens of thousands; throw not the burthen of the day upon Providence, but "shew your faith by your works," that GOD may bless you. It matters not where you live, or what rank of life you hold, the evil or the blessing will reach you all. The far and the near, the home counties and the back, the rich and the poor, shall suffer or rejoice alike. The heart that feels not now, is dead: The blood of his children shall curse his cowardice, who shrinks back at a time when a little might have saved the whole, and made *them* happy. I love the man that can smile in trouble, that can gather strength from distress, and grow brave by reflection. 'Tis the business of little minds to shrink; but he whose heart is firm, and whose conscience approves his conduct, will pursue his principles unto death ..."

"Ye done good, Mousie," Max told Nigel. "I like the lad's words."

"Yeah, if this doesn't boost the soldiers' spirits, I don't know what will!" Jock added.

Nigel twirled his whisker and grinned. "I must say, I'm terribly pleased at the final outcome of Paine's new tome."

"It's just the shot in the arm that these men needed," Gillamon told them. "And not just the soldiers, but the people throughout America. This will rally Patriot hearts everywhere, both now and in the future. Well done, Nigel."

"I relish the compliment, Gillamon," Nigel answered with a graceful bow. "I say, any word from Elsa on the state of Hessian affairs?"

"Yes, they are being harassed to death by the New Jersey and Pennsylvania militias," Gillamon reported. "In fact, I best go give General Washington my report. Things are coming together, and he'll be ready to act soon."

"Aye, now that Sullivan ar-r-rived with Lee's forces an' Heath made it here as well, plus Ewing's Pennsylvania Flyin' Camp an' Cadwallader's Philly Associators, Washington's forces be up ta aboot six thousand lads," Max reported. "Though not all of them be fit for duty with sickness r-r-runnin' thr-r-rough their r-r-ranks."

"Excellent. Stay alert, lads," Gillamon told them. He then wended his way over to Washington and Knox.

"Ah, good day, Mr. Atticus," Knox greeted him with a wide grin. "What do you think of Paine's latest writing?"

Mr. Atticus touched a finger to his three-cornered hat. "Good day, Sirs. It's a grand piece of writing that will inspire the men, no doubt. I hear our New Jersey and Pennsylvania militias have finally sprung into action of their own accord, going about the other side of the river harassing the Hessians. They certainly are no sunshine Patriots."

"Indeed, Mr. Atticus, plus Knox has our artillery doing the same," Washington told him.

"Our artillery is lined up all along the western riverbank and has forced the British to extend the line of their outposts for thirty miles on the east side of the Delaware," Knox told them. "Rest assured, Your Excellency, our artillerymen are quick to give fire to any British or Hessian skirmishers who venture near the water."

"Sounds like you'll be wearing them down in no time," Atticus posed, touching a hand to his ear, and slipping a note to Washington where Knox couldn't see. "Good day, Sirs. Keep smiling in trouble."

"Good day, Mr. Atticus," Washington answered, slipping the note into his pocket with a knowing grin.

COUNCIL OF WAR, KEITH HOUSE, BUCKS COUNTY, PENNSYLVANIA, DECEMBER 22, 1776

"The New Jersey and Pennsylvania militias have risen up to take back their country, thanks to the brutality of the Hessians during the retreat," Washington announced gladly to the group of officers assembled. "The Hunterdon men have attacked Hessian foraging parties and picked off so many of Rall's men that Rall was forced to send dispatches to Princeton with an escort of one hundred troops."

"They've done this of their own accord?" General Greene asked.

"Yes, and while the Hunterdon men have attacked upriver from Trenton, Ewing's six hundred Pennsylvanians have launched raids across the river in small boats and attacked a *Jäger* outpost at the Trenton ferry landing," Washington reported. "They hurry back across the river before Rall knows what hit him. Ewing's men continue these daily raids, and it is taking its toll. Last night they made a river crossing with blackened faces and set fire to several houses before they vanished and returned to their post across the river."

"Do we know the reaction of the Hessians, General Washington?" Heath wanted to know.

"The Hessians are badly shaken. Rall has ordered his exhausted men to turn out before sunrise and haul a cannon to the ferry landing each day, but they must pull it back before dawn," Washington explained.

"If I may, General, the Hessian guards appear to have been ordered not to gather at the ferry in daylight, as our artillery will fire at them," Knox added.

"The end result is that Rall is beginning to lose control of the town, and his men are sleep-deprived, exhausted, sick, and anxious with the relentless harassment from our men," Washington summarized. "Their morale is very low. Now that our forces have doubled in size with the arrival of our scattered troops, it is time for us to make a counterstroke against the British and the Hessians."

The officers looked around at one another in approval as Washington continued his briefing.

"In Trenton there are fifteen hundred Hessians filling the hundred or so houses, taverns, jails, school, churches, post office, Friends Meeting House, and stone barracks," Washington told them. "There are another fifteen hundred Hessians garrisoned in Bordentown, six miles south."

"Do we know if Colonel Rall has sent for reinforcements?" Greene asked.

"My sources inform me that he has sent multiple messages asking for assistance from Donop, Leslie, and Grant, but only Leslie in Princeton has replied by sending light infantry to support Rall in Trenton," Washington told them. "But they were strangely ordered to march back to Princeton. Grant has not taken Rall's concerns seriously and assures Rall that he is quite safe from us Americans since we 'have no shoes or stockings and are naked without blankets.'"

"So General Grant's contempt for both the Hessians and the Americans is hanging Colonel Rall out to dry, as it were?" Knox surmised with a wide grin.

"Yes, and today I received a letter from Colonel Reed encouraging us to make an offensive attack as he feels the opportune moment has come," Washington added. "So, gentlemen, I agree the time has come to cross the Delaware and attack one of the enemy's posts. But where shall we strike? Trenton? Bordentown? Whatever our plan, it must utilize stealth, surprise, speed, and shock. I welcome your thoughts."

As Washington's officers debated the possible routes and methods of attack, Max, Jock, and Nigel listened in with glee.

"Washington sure sounds like a Commander-in-Chief, huzzah!" Nigel exulted.

"Aye, he's got lots of intelligence now," Max agreed. "Gillamon gave him all sorts of information aboot the Hessians an' Grant."

Jock beamed. "All thanks not to a little bird, but a little fox."

Over the course of the next two days, Washington and his officers consulted with Colonel John Glover about the river and the boats available for a surprise crossing. Glover assured Washington that his Marblehead boys who had rescued the Continental Army from Brooklyn in one night on the East River back in August would be able to manage the icy Delaware River as well. When news came that a third militia group of Jerseymen skirmished with Donop's men, pulling them away from Bordentown to Mount Holly, the plans for the surprise attack came together. Washington called together his Council of War at the Merrick House to map out their plans for a four-pronged attack. Among those in attendance were Greene, Sullivan, Stirling, Fernoy, Mercer, Stephen, St. Claire, Sargent, Stark, Glover, Knox . . . and unbeknownst to them, a British spy.

Late on Christmas Eve, Washington again called his council together, when they mapped out their final plan of attack in detail. This time, it was a smaller group of officers to keep the plans as secretive as possible. The attack was scheduled to take place in Trenton the morning of December 26th, following a Christmas night crossing of the Delaware. It was time for the Epic Order of the Seven to go into action as well.

MCCONKEY'S FERRY INN, BUCKS COUNTY, PENNSYLVANIA, DECEMBER 24, 1776

"Blankets, stockings, muskets, powder, and lead!" exclaimed a soldier who climbed up on the wagon to pull back the tarp. "This wagon is full!"

"This one, too!" exclaimed another soldier on a second wagon.

"Merry Christmas," Clarie muttered under her breath with a grin to Nigel. She was dressed as a militia man, and together they watched the exuberant soldiers surround the supply wagons that had just arrived from Philadelphia. Wealthy merchant Robert Morris tirelessly supported Washington and the Continental Army by gathering coin to pay the troops and amassing supplies to send to the scantily clad men. He found wagons and arranged teamsters to deliver these much-needed supplies that had arrived on the Continental sloop *USS Independence* from Martinique. But it was Clarie who enabled the ship to escape a British frigate and then a British blockade for safe passage to Philadelphia.

"Bravo, my dear. It's as if the Magi themselves have come to town, what?" Nigel cheered with a jolly chuckle. He and Clarie stood outside the stone house belonging to Mr. McConkey. Washington currently used it for his headquarters as his troops readied to cross the Delaware for the attack on Trenton. "And I understand our Governor Patrick Henry has rallied the entire state of Virginia to also send needed supplies. He's written to the head of every single county militia, using his eloquence to appeal to the better angels of their nature. I was quite taken with his words." The little mouse cleared his throat and lifted a paw to quote Henry's plea for blankets and rugs. *"When it is considered that those who are defending their country are in the extremest want of blankets, and that our Army cannot take the field without a supply of that article, I have hopes that our worthy countrymen will spare from their beds a part of that covering which the exposed situation of the soldier teaches him to expect from the humanity of those for whom he is to fight.'* Poetry, I say! Sheer poetry!"

Clarie giggled at Nigel's passion over words. "You're right, Nigel. Washington is grateful that his dear friend governs the largest state in America to help equip the Continental Army. If anyone can move people to action with words, it's Patrick Henry."

Just then they saw Dr. Benjamin Rush ride up to the house and dismount from his horse.

"Ah, our fine physician from Philadelphia has arrived," Nigel noted. "Washington has requested surgeons to be on hand, anticipating the worst for the upcoming battle. I shall wend my way inside to listen in on their conversation."

"You do that, Nigel. Max and Jock are inside," Clarie encouraged him, slipping behind a tree to reemerge as a lady dressed in a lovely green silk gown and a red woolen cape and hand muff. "We have a few busy nights ahead, and I need to get back to my post in Mount Holly. I've been gone long enough, but I had to make sure these supplies arrived for the men in time for Christmas."

"Mount Holly?" Nigel asked. "You look as lovely as a sprig of holly yourself, my dear. Whatever are you doing there?"

"Keeping the Hessians under the command of Colonel Carl von Donop occupied and far away from Colonel Rall," Clarie explained, batting her eyes. "Yesterday, Donop led his men out of Bordentown to skirmish with the Jersey militia on the outskirts of Mount Holly. Of course, the Americans quickly retreated, but Donop decided to stay the night in a town vacated by its citizens. I just so happen to be the only beautiful young widow left in Mount Holly who graciously offered her warm, comfortable home for Donop to stay."

Nigel chuckled. "Don't tell me! May I assume that our Hessian colonel has a weakness for beautiful young widows, and wishes to extend his stay to enjoy Christmastide at her bountiful hearth?"

"Yes, you may!" Clarie answered with a wink. "I shall keep him entertained through Christmas Day with sumptuous feasting, dancing, and merrymaking. He will be unreachable when Rall seeks help from Washington's attack. Instead of being only six miles from Rall at Bordentown, he and his troops are now a full day's march of eighteen miles away from Trenton."

"That takes the Hessian biscuit, my dear!" Nigel cheered, bowing to the lovely widow. "Utterly brilliant! Who would have guessed that a pretty face could eliminate an entire Hessian regiment from battle? I daresay, this one interference could decide the outcome of the entire war! Huzzah for perfume and petticoats!"

"Lassie power!" Clarie exclaimed, giving a low curtsy, and extending her hand. "I shall see you in Trenton."

"Right! Cheerio, my dear!" Nigel answered, kissing her hand. "Until Trenton!" With that he scurried inside the stone house as Clarie vanished.

"I thank you for coming to make medical preparations for our army, although I pray your services shall not be needed," Washington told Dr. Benjamin Rush. "Thank you also for your assistance to Mr. Paine to get his

American Crisis printed in Philadelphia," Washington told him, not looking up from the table where he sat scribbling on pieces of paper. "It was circulated among the men throughout all the camps along the Delaware, and shall no doubt have the effect of galvanizing their spirits. I pray their despair and gloom will be replaced by hope and bright optimism, inspiring the men to want to fight on."

Nigel beamed with pride and preened his whiskers. "Another publishing triumph, if I do say so myself."

"Aye, Mousie," Max whispered with a grin.

"It is my honor, General. I, too, pray my services shall not be required. And I was more than happy to help Mr. Paine, especially after seeing how *Common Sense* rallied Americans to the cause of liberty," Dr. Rush answered, nodding slowly, studying Washington.

"Colonel Knox shared with me something that one of our young captains of artillery said about liberty," Washington remarked, dipping his quill into the inkwell. "Captain Alexander Hamilton is called 'The Little Lion' by his men. He told Knox, 'There is a certain enthusiasm in liberty, that makes human nature rise above itself in acts of bravery and heroism.'"

"It would appear that Captain Hamilton might also have a future wielding a persuasive pen as does Mr. Paine," Rush supposed with a surprised expression.

"The thought occurred to me as well," Washington answered. "But for now, he wields a six-pound cannon against the enemy as he has done with excellence on the long retreat from New York. He was studying law at Kings College, but now shivers in the cold with black powder caked under his nails as a common soldier. I wonder what the impact will be of this war on the next generation as they take up arms to fight for liberty."

"It will make 'Little Lions' grow into fierce, *roaring* ones," Rush answered, sitting forward in his seat. "Our republics cannot exist long in prosperity. We require adversity and appear to possess most of the republican spirit when most depressed." The physician paused in thought for a moment. The fire crackled, and the dancing flames cast their shadows on the wall. "Just as young Hamilton put away his law books to fire cannons, and as I put down my scalpel to pick up a quill to sign the Declaration of Independence, and as you, General, walked away from your quiet farming life at Mount Vernon to serve at your own expense and lead this volunteer army to accomplish the impossible task of defeating the British lion, each man and woman who decides to fight for liberty must do so with all their might, or experience the death of everything else."

One of Washington's papers fell to the floor and Rush leaned over to pick it up. He raised his eyebrows as he read what Washington had written for the call sign the army would use with the coming conflict:

Victory or Death

Rush handed the paper back to Washington. "Exactly," Washington answered.

"But *everything* will depend on the element of surprise," Nigel noted.

"Aye, so it's time ta whip up that white Chr-r-ristmas, lad," Max told Jock.

"I'm ready!" Jock barked, standing up and wagging his tail, gazing out at the night sky. "Snow, with lots of ice, coming right up!"

59

Two Icy Rivers, Two Scots, and Two Choices

MCCONKEY'S FERRY, BUCKS COUNTY, PENNSYLVANIA, DECEMBER 25, 1776, 3:30 P.M.

Christmas morning dawned cold with bright sunshine, but slowly the clouds of a winter storm began to swirl above the banks of the Delaware River. The grey haze of winter overtook the blue sky, and by late afternoon, weather conditions deteriorated quickly.

"So, what's the plan?" Jock wanted to know, jumping on the frozen snow to test it out. "I've made Washington's Christmas snow and ice heavy, like Gillamon told me to do."

"Aye, good job, me gr-r-randlad," Max told him with an approving wink. "Washington ordered the lads in all the camps ta cook up thr-r-ree days of r-r-rations ta take on the march," Max explained. "Also, the lads each have ta have their guns, flints, gunpowder, an' sixty r-r-rounds of musket balls in good order. They're supposed ta start loadin' up the boats here after sunset, but they don't know where they're headed. The officers will put white pieces of paper in their hats so their men can find their leaders—they'll be leadin' fr-r-rom the fr-r-ront. All of Washington's forces will cr-r-ross the Delaware tonight an' attack Tr-r-renton a wee bit before dawn. Mousie, why don't ye tell Jock wha' the humans have planned?"

"Right. This shall be a four-pronged attack on Trenton with four vital elements: stealth, surprise, speed, and shock," Nigel began. "First, Washington shall cross the Delaware with twenty-four hundred men here at McConkey's Ferry, then march approximately nine miles to attack Trenton from the north and west. Second, Colonel Ewing shall take eight hundred Pennsylvania militia and cross to the south side of Trenton at the falls and hold the enemy's only southern escape route over the bridge at Assunpink Creek. Third, General Cadwalader shall cross twelve miles below Trenton near Burlington with twelve hundred Philadelphia Associators and six hundred Continental

488

soldiers as a diversion to occupy von Donop's Hessian brigade, although I already know this shan't be necessary," the mouse chuckled. "Finally, if General Putnam is able, he is to wend his way from Philadelphia and cross with a force to join the South Jersey militia south of Mount Holly. All the while, the troops must operate in *profound* silence once they land over in New Jersey, and no man is to quit his ranks."

"Wow! That's a lot of stuff happening all at the same time!" Jock exclaimed. "Why won't Cadwalader's part be necessary?"

"Clarie informed me that she already has a different sort of diversion well in hand," Nigel explained with a wink. "Whilst all this is happening, I shall perform aerial reconnaissance with Veritas to observe the moving parts of the attack on Trenton. But everything depends on *timing*. Each part must move precisely like clockwork or else the plan will *fail.*"

"Aye! Jock-lad, ye an' me will stay close ta Washington an' Knox ta keep them safe fr-r-rom harm," Max added. "Ye best be sure them bad beasties will be out in full force tonight."

Jock scooped up some snow with his nose and tossed it in the air. "Huzzah! I can't wait! When do we go?"

"All forces must soon be at their crossing points before sunset at 4:41 p.m. for darkness to hide their movement from the dreaded foe, hence the *stealth* part of the plan. Washington plans to have all forces across the river by midnight to march to Trenton and attack by 5:00 a.m., which of course is the *surprise* part of the plan," Nigel answered, suddenly drawing a concerned look. He pointed to Washington and Knox observing the river and Washington checking his pocket watch. "*Speed* comes next in the plan, but I wonder if there is an issue." Together, he, Max, and Jock got within earshot of the men.

George Washington and Henry Knox gazed at the turbulent waters of the Delaware River and frowned to see floating chunks of ice beginning to appear. It had been snowing heavily but up until now, the river had remained clear. Now it was wild and overflowing its banks, with debris filling the river, along with the dangerous, jagged ice.

Colonel John Glover came up to the two officers. "Sirs, the westerly winds have shifted to the northeast. We can feel the weather changing." He pointed to the thin clouds and the wildly swaying trees. "The weather is going to get worse, and fast."

"Understood. Thank you for the report, Colonel Glover," Washington told him, glancing at his pocket watch. "Have the boats ready on schedule."

Glover and Knox quickly glanced at one another before Glover saluted. "Sir, yes, Sir." He trailed off toward the riverbank where his men readied the Durham boats for the men, and ferry boats for the horses and artillery.

"Sir, if I may," Knox began with a big frown. "This much ice will only worsen as the sun sets and temperatures drop." A huge gust of wind blew, and snow hit them in the face. "I'm concerned about delays or if we can even cross tonight. These are far different conditions than when we crossed a few weeks ago. It took us *five days* to cross a normal river—yet we are attempting to cross an ice-choked river in a single night."

"Oh dear, this isn't good at all," Nigel said, shaking his head. "Perhaps the weather will be too much for the crossing tonight."

"I've done as Gillamon told me, but none of the humans seem happy about it," Jock lamented. His ears flattened, and he looked at his frosty paws, now almost white from the storm he had created. Tears filled his eyes to hear his human Henry Knox so upset as he talked with Washington. "I must have overdone it! I've ruined everything!" The little Scottie went running off into the snow, crying. He didn't understand that his tears would only increase the severity of the storm.

"I didn't mean to upset you, dear boy!" Nigel called after him. "I'm terribly sorry, Max."

"It's not yer fault, Mousie," Max told the mouse. "It'll be alr-r-right, ye'll see. I better go fetch the lad."

Washington watched Max and Jock running through the snow toward the large tree that hung low over the riverbank. He pointed a finger at the two Scotties. "I've crossed an icy river before, back when I was on mission for Governor Dinwiddie to deliver a letter to the French."

Knox raised his eyebrows. "Ah, shortly before the French and Indian War?"

Washington winced and nodded. His memory still smarted as scenes flashed across his mind of how his actions had unintentionally ignited that war. "Yes, I was just a twenty-one-year-old Major, venturing through the rugged wilderness. My guide Gist and I built a raft to cross the Allegheny River, which was choked with such ice that we became stuck halfway across . . . at night."

Knox's eyes widened. "Stuck? Whatever did you do, General?"

The now forty-four-year-old Washington eyed the Delaware River as he remembered that bitter cold, icy night. "We used our setting poles to try to push ourselves away from the floating chunks of ice that had built up all around us. I slipped and fell into the icy water, and the cold immediately gripped my lungs to where I could scarcely breathe. It felt like thousands of needles sticking into my skin, and my muscles contracted. Gist was able to pull me back onto the raft, but there was no getting across the river that night."

Knox gulped as he considered the horrible scene. "How were you able to survive?"

"Our raft somehow momentarily broke free of the ice and we were able to wedge it against an island in the middle of the river," Washington explained. "We were wet, freezing, and exhausted, but at least we were on dry land. The strangest thing happened next. A pair of terriers evidently had walked across the ice from some nearby farm and came up to us. We held onto them all night and they kept us warm. In the morning, Gist had some frostbite, but I was completely fine. I didn't even suffer a sniffle from the cold."

"Your Excellency, that is a remarkable story!" Knox exclaimed. "Two Scots? Just like Max and little Jock." Little did Knox or Washington realize that it was Max himself plus Kate that night who kept Washington and Gist warm. He and Kate had also worked with a team of beavers to free the raft from the ice.

Washington smiled as he recalled that following morning, watching Max and Jock running through the snow. "I told Gist that if I ever have to cross an icy river at night again, I'll want a pair of Scots to go with me."

"Like those two?" Knox noted, pointing, and smiling at Max and Jock. His smile then faded as he saw a massive chunk of ice float by. "General Washington, should we reconsider crossing tonight?"

"Colonel Knox, you hauled those cannons from Fort Ticonderoga to Boston across frozen rivers, and you've since hauled them across multiple rivers on our retreat here from New York," Washington replied, not answering his question. "You've become quite an expert on crossing rivers with heavy guns, which is why I'm putting you in charge of this crossing tonight. I have complete faith in you. That booming voice of yours will carry to direct the men over any nor'easter that blows against us."

Knox bowed his head in humble gratitude. "I'm honored, Your Excellency. And I thank you."

Suddenly the drums began to beat for the men to assemble at the ferry. Washington pointed at the river. "When I crossed the icy Allegheny River at night, it was eight hundred *yards* across when we got stuck halfway." He leaned in to lock eyes with the hefty Knox. "The Delaware is only eight hundred *feet* across. What say you, Colonel Knox? Can we get our men and guns across, given that liberty is at stake?"

Knox clenched his jaw and lifted his chin. "Absolutely, General Washington! Victory or Death."

Washington gave the big man with the booming voice an approving nod. "Victory or Death."

MCCONKEY'S FERRY INN, BUCKS COUNTY, PENNSYLVANIA, DECEMBER 25, 1776, 5:00 P.M.

Major James Wilkinson was cold and wet after a perilous ride from Philadelphia. He had passed camp after camp of soldiers marching to the assembly points. He couldn't get out of his mind the image of what he saw. *Blood already in the snow, but not from gunfire.* He had seen footprints of blood dotting the snow from the feet of men with broken or makeshift shoes, or no shoes at all.

Up ahead he spotted Washington getting ready to mount Blueskin to take him to the ferry. Wilkinson hurried up to the Commander-in-Chief. "Sir, I have a letter for you!"

"What a time is this to hand me letters!" Washington answered.

"My apologies, Your Excellency, but I am following the orders of General Gates," Wilkinson explained, handing him the letter.

"General Gates!" Washington exclaimed, growing agitated by the delay, and slowly reaching out his hand to take the letter. "Where is he?"

"I left him this morning in Philadelphia," Wilkinson answered.

Washington's brow was furrowed. "What was he doing there?"

"I understood him that he was on his way to Congress," Wilkinson answered, bowing, and turning to leave. He hurried to the river to volunteer for the crossing.

"On his way . . . to Congress," Washington repeated with disgust, looking skyward in disbelief. He broke open the seal and began to read by the light of a lantern hung from the post.

Days before, Washington had asked Gates to take command of part of their attack on Trenton. Gates pleaded ill and requested to go to Philadelphia. Washington reluctantly agreed but urged him to stop in Bristol to handle issues with the Continentals and militia. Again, Gates refused, claiming he was too ill to stop.

"Why that insubordinate, lyin', schemin' coward!" Max growled, hearing the conversation. "Gates be too sick ta help fight the enemy, but not too sick ta r-r-rat on Washington ta Congr-r-ress! He's no better than Lee, goin' over Washington's head ta tr-r-ry an' take Washington's job! An' now? George had ta find this out *now*, as he's gettin' r-r-ready ta cr-r-ross the Delaware?!"

"Steady, Max," came Gillamon's calm voice. He was in the form of Mr. Atticus. "Washington needed to be free of Lee *and* Gates for what is to happen in Trenton. Don't worry about this now."

"What about Washington?" Nigel worried. "It appears *he,* instead of his foes, is experiencing shock at the moment."

Together they watched Washington calmly fold the letter and slip it into his pocket, clenching his jaw, yet gathering his emotions. "The General's remarkable self-control and discipline will help him return to the task at hand," Gillamon told them. Sure enough, Washington mounted Blueskin and galloped off to the ferry. "Now, it's time for us to get on that ferry as well."

Jock came walking up with big, sorrowful eyes. "They won't want me on that ferry. I'm the one who's making this hard on everyone. Everything is going to fall apart because of me!"

Gillamon squatted down and scooped up Jock in his arms. "Nonsense! Don't you know that Washington said the next time he crossed an icy river, he'd want two Scots with him?"

"I tr-r-ried ta tell him, Gillamon," Max insisted.

"You'll see, young one," Gillamon assured Jock, walking toward the ferry. "Things aren't going to fall apart because of you; they're going to fall *together.*"

A group of artillerymen waiting to board the ferry looked up at the now darkened sky when they heard an unusual sound. "That's thundersnow," a young private named Malcom told them. "Ever heard it before? That means this storm is going to strengthen." Suddenly they could see a flash of lightning through the thick clouds. "You had best be ready. We're in for a wild night."

The snow was now mixed with sleet and hail, as the temperature had risen slightly. The river was packed with ice floes, and the wind howled and cut like a knife through the men, strafing their faces with needle-like pellets. The men shivered from the wet, raw conditions. Those who were fortunate enough to have claimed the newly delivered blankets pulled them tightly around their shoulders. Others trembled not only from the wind, but from the cold snow that caked their feet and crept into their makeshift shoes. As Wilkinson had witnessed, some men only had rags wrapped around their bloody feet. They were not only miserable, but on edge with where they were going. Anxiety began to seep into the ranks as quickly as snow into their shoes.

The banks of the Delaware teemed with activity. Soldiers began boarding the high-walled Durham boats while Glover's Marblehead men brilliantly handled the ice-choked currents. One by one, the Durham boats shoved off and slowly crept out into the darkness to reach the far shore, ice scraping the sides of the flat-bottomed boats as the mariners poled them across. Meanwhile, the flat ferry boats began loading the horses and artillery.

Together Malcom and his comrades shuffled to the landing and stepped into the ferry boat that rocked from the turbulent water. But it also rocked from the weight of the hefty Henry Knox, who next stepped foot aboard. He made his way to one of the eighteen cannons making the journey and tapped it with confidence. He held up a small lantern and saw the unmistakable form of Washington's cape blowing in the wind as he dismounted Blueskin.

"Your Excellency, we're ready for you," Knox called out to Washington.

"My boys, shall we cross?" Washington asked as he stepped onto the ferry, leading Blueskin gingerly across the ice-slick, soaked boards.

Malcom's eyes widened at seeing the Commander-in-Chief joining their group of soldiers. "Yes, Sir, Your Excellency!"

As he maneuvered his way through the tightly huddled men, Washington looked at their faces, barely illuminated by the lantern glow. These men were clearly anxious about the conditions and the crossing. Undoubtedly, few of them knew how to swim, and falling into the icy clutches of this churning water could be deadly. As Washington came to stand next to the heavy Henry Knox, a wry grin appeared on his face. "Colonel Knox, move over a bit, but slowly, or you'll swamp the boat."

With that the men broke out in snickers and big smiles, laughing under their breath. Washington locked eyes with Knox, and they shared a slight grin and a nod. The Commander-in-Chief had just given the men a much-needed moment of levity as they cast off into the dark, icy, turbulent waters of the Delaware, not knowing what lay ahead.

"Aren't ye comin' with us?" Max whispered to Gillamon as they got to the ferry. Nigel hopped on board and hid in the shadows.

"I have much to do tonight, Max," Gillamon told him. "I'll see you both soon."

"Two more passengers, General?" Mr. Atticus called out, putting Jock onto the ferry as Max hopped on board just as the ferry began to pull away. "Your two Scots, as requested. They'll help to herd the nervous horses along the march."

Washington stared quizzically at Mr. Atticus, dumbfounded. *How in the world did he know about that?* "I . . . thank you, Mr. Atticus," he stammered, reaching down to give Max a scratch. "Blueskin can be a bit skittish around artillery."

Don't ye worry aboot a thing, lad, Max thought. *I'll keep him movin'.*

Knox reached down, picked up Jock, and gave a hearty laugh. "My Commander tells me you're just what we need for an icy crossing. You've never let me down before in these conditions, Jock Frost Knox."

Jock hid his face in Knox's thickset arms, hiding from the wicked wind barreling down upon them with heavy, wet snow. *I hope I don't let you down now.*

POTT'S HOUSE, RALL HEADQUARTERS, TRENTON,
NEW JERSEY, DECEMBER 25, 1776, 4:00 P.M.

Colonel Rall sat before his checkerboard with his American host, Stacy Potts, and studied his next move. The fire whistled and popped, and a gentle snow fell outside the window. He picked up his steaming hot cup of wassail and slurped loudly, not taking his eyes off the board for a moment. The peaceful scene was interrupted when an express rider arrived and banged on the door. Rall's aide answered the door and quickly took the note translated in German from the rider. It was an urgent dispatch to Colonel Rall from General Grant. The spy who attended Washington's war council on Christmas Eve reported to Grant everything that was said:

Washington has been informed that our troops have marched into winter quarters and has been told that we are weak at Trenton and Princeton, and Lord Stirling expressed a wish to make an attack on those two places. I don't believe he will attempt it, but be assured that my information is undoubtedly true, so I need to advise you to be on your guard against an unexpected attack at Trenton. I think I have got into a good line of intelligence which will be of use to us all.

Rall crumpled the letter with a huff and tossed it on the floor. He picked up his checker and forcefully jumped over two of Potts's checkers, shouting, "*Lass sie kommen! Wir werden sie mit dem Bajonett angehen!*"

Elsa crouched outside below the window and heard Rall's shouted answer to the threat of a surprise attack. *Let them come! We'll take them on with the bayonet!* Her eyes widened to hear his brash defiance. Rall knew the rebels were coming, but he didn't seem worried. *I must tell Gillamon!* thought Elsa.

NORTH TRENTON, NEW JERSEY,
DECEMBER 25, 1776, 11:00 P.M.

The snowstorm was so heavy and blinding that Elsa could hardly see where she was going. She stopped and listened. She soon heard the unmistakable sound of Mr. Atticus's footsteps and went bounding toward him as the two took shelter beneath a rocky outcropping near the cooper house where Hessian guards were posted outside.

"I think Jock might have overdone it a bit vith his Christmas gift to General Vashington!" Elsa exclaimed, shaking the snow from her face, and wrapping her tail tightly around her body. "This is the vorst storm I have ever seen! How can Vashington's men get through this veather?"

Atticus chuckled and pulled his collar up high around his face. "It may seem like it's too much, but you'll see that it is exactly the kind of weather Washington needs. This weather is keeping Loyalists inside their homes, so they won't be keeping an eye out like usual to see what the Continental Army does tonight. Tell me what you've heard from Rall and the Hessians this afternoon."

"Rall has received several varnings about the coming attack, from American deserters, a doctor, another man, *und* even in a letter from General Grant, all vith the same varning," Elsa told Gillamon. "But his response vas, 'Let them come! Ve'll take them on vith the bayonet!'"

Gillamon wrinkled his brow. "Does Rall show *any* sign of concern about a surprise rebel attack?"

"*Ja,* that is vhat is funny about Rall," Elsa answered. "Vhen von Donop ordered him to erect redoubts *und* fortifications around Trenton, Rall ignored him. He is very confident that he *und* his men can handle Vashington *und* his army in a fight, just as they did in New York, but he still keeps his men on high alert. Each day *und* night, Rall keeps vone of his regiments ready to muster *und* take up arms at a moment's notice. But he makes all his regiments sleep in their full uniforms *und* equipment. They don't even remove their belts vith those little cartridges!"

"That certainly would make for sleepless nights for the Hessians," Gillamon noted.

"*Ja, und* vhen you add to that the harassment by the rebels day *und* night, these Hessians have reached their limit," Elsa concluded. "Rall wrote to Donop that his brigade is vorn out from the veather *und* being on constant alert, *und* that he only has two officers in his own regiment that are fit for duty. Rall told him that he must have reinforcements soon."

"But still Rall blusters to 'let them come,'" Gillamon reiterated, shaking his head. "Did he allow his men to celebrate Christmas?"

Elsa shook her head. "No! Unless they vere very sick, every man vas put on patrol duty today! Rall ordered patrols to constantly march, *und* seven outposts vith sentries like this vone have been on guard duty. Even when a group of Americans attacked an outpost a little vhile ago, Rall rode his horse up here to see his six vounded men, but the Americans vanished back into the voods. Rall ordered the outposts strengthened, *und* even hauled a cannon as they looked for the rebels, but the Hessians could not find them.

So, Rall vent back to the Hunt house *und* is there playing cards now."

Suddenly they heard the approach of a rider who stopped at the picket house. He shouted to be heard above the storm. *"Frohe Weihnachten!"* He got off his horse and said a few more things to the sentries in German.

Elsa listened closely and her eyes widened. She turned to Atticus with a wide grin. "You vere right, Gillamon! Lieutenant Viederholdt is alloving his men to take shelter in the picket house tonight because of the storm! *Und* he said that Major Dechow has cancelled tomorrow's predawn patrol! They don't think the enemy could attack in such veather. *Mein Hundebaby* made the perfect vinter storm to make the Hessians relax for the first time in over a veek!"

"That's exactly what I've been waiting to hear, little one! Well done, Elsa," Gillamon told her. He picked up the little fox and held her close. He kissed the top of her head. *"Frohe Weihnachten,* sweet fox."

Und this is vhat I've alvays vanted . . . to be held vith such love, Elsa thought. She closed her eyes with a smile, happy in the warmth of Gillamon's embrace. "Merry Christmas, Gillamon."

ASSEMBLY AREA, JOHNSON FERRY, NEW JERSEY, DECEMBER 26, 1776, 2:00 A.M.

Washington sat on a wooden crate that had been used as a beehive and stared dolefully into a small makeshift fire, his mind in anguish over what to do. For hours, men had pulled down nearby fences and scavenged any wood they could find to make fires. They miserably turned on their heels repeatedly like roasting chickens on a spit to try to stay warm as they huddled together before the fires. Above the roar of the wind, everyone could hear the booming voice of Henry Knox directing the infantrymen spilling out from the Durham boats, and ordering artillerymen to hitch the draft horses to the carriages and move the cannons away from the riverbank. The movement of men and materiel was painfully slow, and they were already way behind schedule.

We will soon be four hours behind, Washington thought as he looked at his pocket watch. He clenched his jaw and shook his head. *We have already lost the element of surprise, since we will not arrive in Trenton until after sunrise. What should I do? Turn back?* He looked at the last infantrymen struggling to get ashore and although they were chilled to the bone, they were in surprisingly good spirits. He glanced at the ice-caked river and couldn't bear the thought of sending those men back without having accomplished anything. *There is certainly no making a retreat without being discovered and harassed on repassing the river.*

True to their word, the tough mariners did as they promised, and not one man was lost to the icy Delaware. One man fell in but was quickly snatched from the river and saved. Glover's men had finally gotten all the infantry safely over to the New Jersey shore. It would be another hour to get the artillery fully across, and likely another hour still to have the entire column organized and ready to pull out at 4:00 a.m.

And what of the other columns attempting to cross the river tonight? Washington wondered. He had earlier received word that General Putnam would not be able to join his forces with Washington. *Have Ewing and Cadwalader been able to make it through the treacherous water? And if so, might they engage the Hessians in Trenton before we can arrive to help them?*

Suddenly the general felt Max and Jock pressing against him to keep him warm. Max looked up at Washington with soulful eyes and willed the torn commander to press on. *The last time we cr-r-rossed an icy r-r-river at night, ye got up the next morn an' walked out across the ice—the very thing that str-r-randed ye became yer br-r-ridge ta victory. Tr-r-rust that the Maker will do the same with this ice. Ye've only got two choices, lad. Either ye turn back or ye press on.*

Washington looked at the terriers and thought back to that night long ago. He gave Max a scratch behind the ears and rose to his feet. "There is only one way out of this storm, and that is *ahead.*"

Little did he know that weather conditions ten miles south were so bad for Ewing, Cadwalader, and Putnam that their crossings were called off. Washington would face the Hessians alone.

A Glorious Day
For Our Country

JACOB'S CREEK, DECEMBER 26, 1776, 4:45 A.M.

The moon was full but hidden behind the thick clouds that produced a steady torrent of snow, sleet, and hail. Washington's army slowly trudged through the darkness in a mile-long column along the frozen, rutted road. The men had to keep their gaze down to avoid getting struck in the eye by sleet as the wind slapped their faces. The only light for their path shone from artillery torches mounted on the gun carriages. The men could hear the flames sizzle and flare as the fire struggled to stay lit against the wintry mix. And they could see the crimson trail left in the snow by the bleeding feet walking ahead of them.

At the head of the column were local guides mounted on horseback. They led the army up a steep, winding, narrow road through the dark woods. After a mile and a half, they came to a crossroads at the Bear Tavern and turned right, instantly getting relief from the wind, no longer blowing directly in their faces. The road also leveled out, which made the march easier, although it was still slippery. They were now able to pick up the pace, until they came to Jacob's Creek.

"Halt! Unharness the horses and prepare the artillery!" ordered Henry Knox.

"What's happening?" Jock whispered to Max and Nigel.

Nigel was perched on Max's shoulders. "We have come to a big stream called Jacob's Creek, and it appears to have a deep ravine. It is impossible to use the horses to pull the guns up and down the steep sides of the ravine, so they must unharness the animals to lead separately whilst men use ropes against trees to lower the guns down one side and up the other."

"Oh, I remember we had to do this coming back from Fort Ti," Jock answered. "That's when a cannon got loose and almost hit Knox, who slipped and fell. The bad invisible wolf beastie Espion caused it."

Washington rode atop Blueskin, encouraging the men all along the column in a deep and solemn voice. "Soldiers, keep by your officers. For God's sake, keep by your officers."

Max eyed Blueskin and then looked down to see huge pawprints in the snow along the shoulder of the road. A low growl entered the dog's throat as he caught a whiff of a foul stench in the air. "I think that wolf beastie has come back ta r-r-repeat history. Nigel, stay here with Jock!"

Nigel hopped onto Jock's back as Max took off running toward General Washington. As Max reached Blueskin he saw fresh pawprints emerging in the direction of the horse. "BLUESKIN!" Max barked. "Br-r-race yerself, lad!"

Suddenly Blueskin felt something grab his hind legs. "MAX! Help!" he neighed as he started to slip from the top of a steep bank. Max immediately darted behind the horse to brace his hind hooves against the slippery bank as best he could. It was only for a moment, but that moment was just enough. Max then also began to slip and clambered down the embankment. He took off running to chase away the unseen beast in case it was still close by.

In that same instant, Blueskin then began to fall, but Washington locked his fingers tightly in Blueskin's mane. "Steady, boy," the general calmly muttered to the terrified horse. He pulled Blueskin's head up while balancing his own weight to counteract the gravity pulling against horse and rider. Blueskin was able to find his footing well enough to make it to solid ground. Washington's skill and strength caused the men to gape in awe at their Commander-in-Chief, who maintained full control in a perilous moment.

Washington patted the rattled horse on the neck. "There you are, boy. There you are. Steady."

"What an utterly brilliant feat of horsemanship!" Nigel called out against the howling wind as he and Jock trotted up. "Whatever happened?"

Blueskin's heart was racing. "Why, something pulled my hind legs out from under me."

Jock lifted his nose in the air. "I bet I know what it was!"

"Aye, it were that invisible wolf beastie!" Max exclaimed, breathing heavily as he rejoined them. "I chased it off. Are ye alr-r-right, horsie lad? That tumble could've killed both of ye!"

Blueskin snorted and nodded his big head, his mane flying against the stiff wind. "I am alright now, thanks to you and Washington. You gave me just enough of a brace before Washington pulled me up."

"Is Espion gone, grandsire?" Jock asked fearfully, getting next to Max.

"Aye, he's gone for now, but I'll stay on me guard," Max assured him.

"Good show, old boy!" Nigel cheered. "And look how unfazed Washington is after that harrowing event," Nigel marveled, watching as Washington calmly continued to encourage the men up and down the column. "Extraordinary."

The army pressed on and soon came to another ravine requiring the drag ropes and the Herculean strength of exhausted soldiers to lower the artillery and haul it up the far slopes again. But they pressed on and gradually moved ahead down the road toward Trenton. They came to a small village called Birmingham at the bottom of the hill. The first rays of light began to emerge from behind the clouds. Washington quickly grew concerned with the coming sunrise. He pulled out his pocket watch. *Nearly six o'clock. And we're only halfway to Trenton.*

Nigel observed Max sniffing the air. "Oh, dear, is the dreaded foe back to harass the column?"

Max smiled. "No, Mousie, this time it's jest breakfast."

"Huzzah!" Jock cheered. They were in front of the Benjamin Moore home. "That nice family is bringing Washington something to eat and drink, but he doesn't have time to get down from Blueskin."

"I'm quite pleased that he has accepted much needed sustenance to keep up his strength," Nigel noted. "It appears he is having an impromptu War Council with his breakfast in the saddle."

"Aye, they be confimin' their plans," Max agreed. "The army is goin' ta split up here. General Greene will take the Upper Ferry Road headin' up an' away from the r-r-river ta the Scotch an' Pennington Roads. His lads will enter Tr-r-renton from the north. Washington will be with them."

"Right, meanwhile Sullivan's column shall continue on the River Road and enter the town from the west," Nigel added. "Greene's route is more difficult and shall take a bit longer, so Sullivan has been ordered to halt and wait for a while when he reaches Trenton."

"And ahead of *both* columns are the advance parties whom Washington sent on ahead last night to put up roadblocks and cut off communication around Trenton," came Gillamon's voice as Mr. Atticus. "Good morning, little ones."

"Gillamon! Where've ye been all night?" Max wanted to know.

"Here and there," Gillamon replied with a wink. "I had to arrange for a local physician's dogs to rouse the good doctor from his bed to meet the advance party with Lieutenant James Monroe. Dr. John Riker brought them food and volunteered to help Monroe's infantry, saying he might 'be of help to some poor fellow.'"

Nigel's ears perked up. "Lieutenant Monroe? I was quite impressed with his pen when I was assisting Mr. Paine with the *American Crisis* by the campfire. He's a fine young Virginian serving with General Washington's distant cousin, Captain William Washington."

"Indeed, and he shall do a great deal more than write, so I needed to make sure all was in place for his watch care today," Gillamon explained. "Nigel, see if you can mount up on Veritas to keep watch from above. I know conditions will be difficult with this storm, but it's crucial that you keep an eye on Monroe as the battle unfolds. I'll be blocking the Hessian retreat at Assunpink Creek if you need me."

Nigel gave a salute. "Understood, Gillamon! We shall do our best to stay airborne above the fray. Where is our fine feathered friend Veritas?"

"He'll meet us on the outskirts of Trenton," Gillamon answered, pointing to Washington. "I'll stay with you until then. I've already slipped Washington a note from 'Mr. Fox' so he has perfect intelligence about the Hessian outposts. Let's listen in."

"I expect the Pennsylvania and New Jersey units to arrive from the south and east. If they were unable to cross the Delaware, Sullivan, you are to move quickly into town and seize the eastern roads. We must enter Trenton and push directly into town with great speed and force before the enemy has time to form and respond," Washington told his officers. Max, Jock, and Nigel watched as Washington then ordered his senior officers to remove their pocket watches. "Please set your watches by my time, and we shall attack at precisely the same moment."

"I do say, I believe we are witnessing the first synchronized military movement in history," Nigel told them. "That takes the biscuit!"

A young officer came riding up to Sullivan, and the senior officers gathered on horseback. Sullivan chatted a moment with the young man and frowned with a nod. He turned to the Commander-in-Chief. "General Washington, word has come from Glover's Marblehead regiment that their best secured arms are wet and not in firing condition. Snow and sleet have melted into the carriage boxes. What is to be done?"

The officers looked from one to another, and Arthur St. Clair lifted a hand. "Sir, if I may. You have nothing for it but to push on and charge."

Washington tightened his mouth and nodded. "Advance and charge."

"Why can't the men fire their muskets?" Jock asked, once again becoming upset about his winter storm. "What if they can't protect themselves?"

"You see, dear boy, attempting to keep their gunpowder dry in these wet conditions is terribly difficult for soldiers," Nigel explained. "But cannons are *foul-weather* weapons. Big guns can more easily be loaded and fired whilst the snow, sleet, and rain swirl about, as opposed to the infantry with muskets. So, Alexander Hamilton and Knox's other artillerymen have taken great pains to keep the cannon touch holes as dry as possible."

"Aye, so ye see, it's a good thing yer Knox br-r-rought the *big* guns that ye helped him get from Fort Ticonderoga," Max noted.

"The few men who have bayonets shall use them and wield their muskets as swords rather than fire them," Nigel further explained. Jock's ears drooped at the thought.

Max nudged the young Scottie. "Hopefully Knox's big guns will do most of the fightin'. Chin up, ye'll see it will all work out, Jock-lad."

"He's right, Jock. And I'll let you in on a secret," Gillamon said as he knelt in the snow and got eye to eye with Jock. "I was with Elsa when we heard the Hessians say that they think the weather is too much for the Americans to attack. They cancelled the dawn patrol and let their guard down—because of *your* storm."

A big grin appeared on Jock's face. "You mean, I haven't ruined things after all?"

"Quite the opposite, little one," Gillamon answered with a chuckle. "Several unexpected things overnight including your weather are helping everything fall into place."

"Huzzah!" Jock cheered, jumping up and down in the snow. "Should I make some more snow?"

"NO!" Max, Nigel, and Gillamon exclaimed in unison. A massive gust of whirling snow enveloped them.

"We've got jest the r-r-right amount as it is, lad," Max quickly added. "But I'm pr-r-roud of ye."

"When we get to Trenton, Jock, we'll need you to shift the direction of the wind to be at our *backs* and in the face of the Hessians," Gillamon added. "For now, let's join the humans. The army is again on the march."

SCOTCH ROAD OUTSIDE TRENTON, NEW JERSEY, DECEMBER 26, 7:30 A.M.

"Press on! Press on, boys!" Washington shouted as he trotted along the line. The Commander-in-Chief urged the men to move along quickly. Timing was critical.

Just then they heard a shout from the front of the column. Washington and Greene looked at one another in alarm and rode to the front. It was a party of fifty Virginia militiamen coming from the direction of Trenton.

"What is this about?" Washington demanded to know.

Captain George Wallis led the men. "Sir, one of Adam Stephen's men was killed by a Hessian *Jäger* on Christmas Eve, so he sent us to take revenge. We attacked a Hessian outpost and they came after us but we escaped back into the woods."

Washington clenched his jaw. "Bring Stephen to me immediately."

Max whispered, "That Stephen lad be a long-time thorn in Washington's side. He were Washington's undisciplined second-in-command in the Fr-r-rench an' Indian War. Sounds like he went off ta fight his own war with the Hessians last night. This don't sound good, Gillamon."

"It's actually quite good, Max," Gillamon answered. "I'll explain in a minute."

"YOU, SIR, may have ruined all my plans by having put them on their guard!" Washington raged against Stephen. The General was furious at yet another instance of insubordination and lack of discipline by his men and continued to rant while the animals looked on.

"I'm on the edge of my Scottie, Gillamon!" Nigel exclaimed, wide-eyed and sitting atop Jock's head. "Do tell me how this can *possibly* be good? Washington has clearly lost the element of surprise and secrecy with the Hessians due to his own men, no less!"

"Aye! How in the name of Pete will *this* help?" Max agreed.

Gillamon held out a hand to calm them. "Our resident spy fox *also* learned that Hessian commander Rall was warned by multiple sources, including General Grant that an American attack was imminent. When Rall rode out to see what had happened when these very men attacked his outpost, what do you suppose he thought?"

"I know!" Jock answered. "Rall thought that the militia attack was *the* attack he was supposed to expect?"

"Precisely," Gillamon answered, giving Jock a pat. "So, not only has Jock's storm made the Hessians let down their guard, so too has this unexpected surprise attack by these undisciplined militiamen."

"Brilliant!" Nigel cheered with a fist in the air. "Huzzah for weather hazards and hapless Hessians!"

"And look. Our Washington is already back in control of his emotions and addressing these bewildered Virginians," Gillamon noted.

Washington turned aside from Stephen and went to address Captain Wallis and his men. He did not berate them as he had their commander, but instead kindly invited them to join his column to return to Trenton and fight the Hessians.

"Well, I'll be a Scottie's uncle . . . or gr-r-randsire, as it were," Max marveled with a wide grin. "There's not another human like George Washington. He's the best leader the Patriots could ever have."

"The Maker knew what He was doing when He chose and prepared

Washington for this calling," Gillamon answered. "Now, let's go help him win this battle so the rest of the world will know it, too."

COOPER'S SHOP, TRENTON, NEW JERSEY, DECEMBER 26, 1776, 8:00 A.M.

Freezing rain pinged against the windows of the cramped cooper's shop filled with Hessian guards under the command of Lieutenant Wiederholdt. The stale air and smoky fire from the brick fireplace made eyes water, as did the smell of seventeen soldiers who were long overdue for a bath, not to mention their clothes. A few soldiers had just returned from patrol to report that they saw nothing unusual. Wiederholdt listened but wasn't entirely convinced that his patrol was as thorough as he wished. Who could blame them in such foul weather as this?

Wiederholdt decided to look for himself. He opened the door and was hit by a gust of cold, wet wind. He blinked against the snow flurries that quickly landed on his eyelashes as he gazed out at the bordering fields along Pennington Road. He squinted, then saw something move. Was it swirling snow? He listened and kept scanning the fields. Suddenly his eyes widened when he saw that the movement came not from swirling snow, but rebel soldiers sprinting toward him. *"Der Feind! Der Feind! Heraus!"* he shouted, running back into the cooper's shop.

"What did he say?" Veritas asked Elsa. who sat there with Nigel at the rocky outcropping to shelter from the storm.

"'The enemy! Turn out!'" Elsa translated. "This is it! It is time for the Battle of Trenton to begin, *ja?*"

"Right! Gillamon charged me with keeping watch over a young soldier named Lieutenant Monroe and to alert him of any issues whilst he battles at Assunpink Creek. Although I don't know if we shall be able to take flight for an aerial view of the battle," Nigel answered, looking at the sky and then at Veritas. "What say you, bald chap?"

Veritas frowned, stretched his wings, and shook his tail feathers. "Sorry, Nigel. This morning's flight is grounded. Jock's storm is too strong for me, I'm afraid."

Elsa cocked her head and wore a coy grin. "But it is not for *me!* I vill carry you, Nigel. Vhat must ve do?"

Nigel tapped Veritas on the wing. "There, there, old boy. I'm dreadfully sorry to leave you, but I simply *must* get to the theater of battle. Perhaps when the storm lifts we can have a flight above, what?" The little mouse then hopped onto Elsa's back. "To the streets of Trenton!"

Elsa took off running, and Veritas watched as she easily jumped over obstacles and disappeared into the storm. He grinned. "I've been outfoxed." Suddenly musket fire erupted behind him, and the bald eagle lifted off to reach the safety of nearby trees in an apple orchard.

The stunned Hessians spilled out of the cooper's shop and feverishly attempted to load their muskets. General Greene's men were quickly advancing in three columns, now firing a third volley of musket balls that whizzed by their heads. Wiederholdt then heard cannon fire from River Road and soon realized the rebels were approaching from both flanks. He quickly ordered a retreat. The Hessians got off a shot here and there as they made their way down the road, firing from behind houses.

Washington couldn't believe what he was hearing. Sullivan's guns were firing just as Greene's column attacked. *The timing worked!* he thought, a rush of adrenaline coursing through him. *Both wings of our army attacked the Hessian positions of Trenton at precisely the same time, just as we planned.* An exuberant Commander-in-Chief took off galloping on Blueskin in pursuit of the enemy. He was fearless as the bullets whizzed toward him, leading the charge of the center column. The air filled with swirling snow and smoke, the smell of gunpowder, and the guttural sound of Hessian soldiers shouting the alarm as German drums beat to arms. A nervous Blueskin, on the other hand, knew that Max followed close behind to keep him moving through the barrage of fire.

At the top of King and Queen Streets on the northern end of town, Knox's gun crews including Alexander Hamilton went rapidly into action to set up six-pounders and howitzers. They kept up a relentless volley of shells into the Hessian positions. Knox couldn't believe the hurry, fright, and confusion of the enemy. "This is not unlike that which will be when the last trump shall sound!" he bellowed over the roar of the guns.

Jock looked on and jumped with each boom of cannon fire. "This must be the shock part of the mission!" he barked.

A group of Sullivan's men led by John Stark, who had valiantly commanded at Bunker Hill, collided with a Hessian outpost behind a grand estate house known as the Hermitage. Supporting fire power from across the Delaware sent the *Jägers* fleeing and dropping their knapsacks after firing a single shot as the sounds of splintering wood, breaking glass, and groaning men filled their ears.

Colonel Rall was suddenly awakened by his aide shouting, *'Der Feind! Der Feind!'*, having slept through the booming cannons and musket fire now coming closer as rebels spilled into the alleys, lanes, gardens, and houses. *"Was ist loss?"* the gruff commander shouted as he leapt from his bed in his nightshirt and gazed out the window. His eyes widened to see the carnage unfolding in the streets of Trenton with house-to-house combat. He hurriedly pulled on his uniform and darted outside to order eighteen Hessian artillerymen and their teams of horses to position field guns to answer the rebel cannon fire. They let loose a few shots before Knox's guns found their mark, killing several of their horses. Rebels now took up positions inside houses to hurriedly dry off their flints and muskets and break out the windows to unleash sniper fire against the Hessians in the streets. Within moments, nearly half of the Hessian artillerymen lay dead or wounded, their blood turning the white snow deep red. The rest of them dropped their artillery sponges and fled.

Rall immediately mounted his horse and regrouped two of his regiments behind St. Michael's Church. He then ordered them to advance across Queen Street where an apple orchard stood.

Washington pulled out his spyglass from the top of the town and watched what Rall was doing. "He's attempting to counterattack from the east! Send a force of riflemen to block their approach on our left flank!" Within moments of their withering fire, Rall turned his men back to the center of town, uncertain of what to do next.

Suddenly Rall's men ran after two cannons that rebels had claimed after their artillerymen fled. Knox quickly ordered New England gunners and the Virginia infantrymen under Captain William Washington to attack with drawn swords and bayonets. Captain Washington's hands were quickly wounded in the attack, and he was forced to retreat from the field. Elsa and Nigel peered out from an overturned barrel when they spotted young Lieutenant James Monroe taking the lead in the fight.

"Is that the Monroe?" Elsa asked.

"It is!" Nigel clenched his fists as if fighting along with an invisible sword, willing the young Virginian to strike a blow. Just then a musket ball hit Monroe in the upper chest and shoulder, sending him flying backward into the snow, his blood spilling out. "He's been hit! Oh, dear, he's been hit! He needs immediate attention!"

"Let's go!" Elsa exclaimed, grabbing Nigel, and hurling him onto her back. She darted out from the barrel and ran into the fray of bullets screaming past them, dinging off the cobblestones and sending chunks of brick walls flying. They hurried to the bridge at Assunpink Creek where Gillamon fought with Sullivan's men to keep the third Hessian Knyphausen Regiment from retreating. "I see him!"

"Mr. Atticus!" Nigel screamed as they neared the fray, knowing his tiny voice couldn't be heard.

Miraculously, Gillamon turned and saw Elsa's red coat against the white snow and Nigel waving atop the fox. He hurried over to them.

"Monroe has been hit badly over by the Hessian guns on King Street!" Nigel exclaimed.

"On my way!" Gillamon answered, disappearing in a flash.

"Hang on, Nigel!" Elsa shouted as she took off running toward the apple orchard. "I vill get us up in a tree!"

"You can climb trees?" Nigel asked with surprise.

"Of course, it is vhat foxes do!" Elsa answered, darting down an alley.

Rall wheeled his horse around, surrounded by cannon blasts and gunfire coming at him from every direction. Suddenly he was hit by two bullets and was knocked from his saddle onto the hard street. Immediately two Hessians pulled their bleeding commander into the church, where he gasped for breath.

Two of the battling Hessian regiments slowly retreated to the apple orchard under the incessant fire of the rebels, who pressed in on them with field pieces and musket fire. Washington ordered the gunners to switch from round to canister shot, but suddenly Captain Forrest spotted Hessian hats held up with sword points, and soldiers laying down their colors and grounding their arms.

"Sir, they have struck!" Captain Forrest told Washington.

"Struck!" Washington repeated.

"Yes, their colors are down," Forrest confirmed.

Washington looked over at the scene of the Hessians surrendering with their proud, colorful flags no longer flapping in the fierce winter breeze but lying surrendered in the snow. "So they are," he exclaimed, riding off to the apple orchard.

Soon Major Wilkinson rode up from the bridge at the creek with the news that the third Hessian regiment had also surrendered. Washington extended his hand to the young officer. "Major Wilkinson, this is a glorious day for our country."

As Elsa jumped and climbed up the barren apple tree, there sat Veritas. His mouth fell open. "Are you telling me you can climb trees? But you're a *fox.*"

"*Ja,* of course! I have claws *und* can do many things like a cat," Elsa answered, nudging the bald eagle.

Veritas shook his head at the surprising little red fox sitting next to him. "Just when I think I've seen everything."

"But look at vhat the humans have done! Vashington *und* his army have made the Hessians to surrender!" Elsa exclaimed, waving at Blueskin. "The General is sitting on his horse that is blue!"

"Huzzah! Victory at last!" cheered Nigel. "I find it utterly fascinating that our gentleman farmer Commander-in-Chief Washington essentially employed the same tactics that Hannibal used with his Carthaginians to defeat the Romans in the Battle of Canae in 216 B.C.," the well-read mouse offered. "It was a double envelopment strategy, bravo!"

Elsa and Veritas shared a knowing grin.

Elsa blinked her eyes in disbelief. "I vill not even ask how you know this."

"Good idea, little fox," Veritas told her with a wink. "Elsa."

"And, although he did *unintentionally* start the French and Indian War, a young George Washington learned from that carnage the brilliant use of guerrilla warfare tactics used by the Indians to take the methodical European warriors by surprise," Nigel added with a fist of victory raised in the air with a jolly chuckle. "Now *that* is the epitome of learning from one's mistakes, what?"

"Whatever you say, Nigel," Veritas remarked, spotting Max and Jock trotting over to where they were. "Here come the others . . ." He stopped when he saw a blood-covered Mr. Atticus walking up as well. "Gillamon looks like he was hit!"

"Oh, no!" Elsa cried, jumping down from the tree. "Are you okay, Gillamon?"

"I'm fine, little one. This is not my blood, but that of Lieutenant James Monroe," Gillamon explained.

"Did our young warrior survive?" Nigel asked hopefully, scurrying down the tree.

"Thankfully, yes. The bullet severed Monroe's artery, and he was in great danger," Gillamon explained. "Our volunteer physician Dr. Riker was able to save his life just in time."

"So, that doctor lad r-r-really did end up bein' 'of some help ta some poor fellow,'" Max noted with a smile. "Now I see why ye had ta make sure he were with Monroe's party."

"Why is James Monroe so important, anyway?" Jock asked.

"Mein Hundebaby!" Elsa exclaimed, smothering Jock with kisses. "You have made quite the storm! I vas vorried that it vas too strong, but it vas exactly vhat Vashington needed, *ja?*"

"Hi, Elsa!" Jock gave a shy smile. "I was worried, too, but Gillamon was right. And Washington's army won, huzzah!"

"But where in the world is Clarie?" Nigel wanted to know. "She said she would see me in Trenton."

Gillamon rubbed his bloody hands with the snow and dried them with a kerchief. "And so you shall, Nigel."

"Wha' do ye mean, Gillamon?" Max asked with a frown.

"The only British unit here in Trenton were twenty troopers of the 16th Light Dragoons. They managed to escape across the Assunpink Creek bridge while it was still in Hessian control," Gillamon told them. "No doubt they are galloping at top speed to Princeton. Once General Grant and the British high command in New York know what happened here today, we can expect a prompt response. Clarie left for New York after her Hessian 'guests' departed Bordentown."

"You mean there will be more fighting here in Trenton?" Nigel worriedly asked.

Gillamon wrinkled his brow and looked on as Washington made his way to Rall's headquarters. "The Fox is still in danger. This isn't over yet."

61

Ten Crucial Days

THE WAR ROOM

"Shouldn't we be out there with our humans?" Max asked in a panicked voice, looking around the Epic Order of the Seven's secret room at Gillamon, Clarie, Nigel, and Al. "Them r-r-redcoats could attack any minute! Washington's havin' his War Council r-r-right now ta decide wha' ta do! Plus, we didn't br-r-ring Jock!"

Gillamon smiled and nodded, in the form of Mr. Atticus. "Cornwallis and his officers are also having a War Council to decide what to do. Since Washington and Cornwallis are both doing so, I thought we should have our own War Council as well. Remember, Max, that just as the IAMISPHERE is a time portal outside of time, so too is this War Room, even though we only have one panel of time here to view. We will reenter human time at the same moment, so don't worry. We haven't left anything behind by coming here."

Al looked behind himself and snapped his tail back and forth, making sure it was still attached. "That's a relief. I always think I'll leave somethin' behind, but me behind be all there." His ears flattened. "Although I *did* leave behind a piece of mutton."

"Al!" Clarie protested. She was dressed as a colonial lady camp follower in a blue petticoat with a flowery red, white, and blue boddice and red wool cape. "How *could* you?"

Al gave a weak smile. "Sorry, lass. I hope it weren't anyone ye knew. I were jest eatin' Grant's leftovers!"

"I'm afraid I echo Max's concerns," Nigel said, ignoring Al's poor taste. "Please tell us what necessitated such urgency as to draw us away from Trenton at such a pivotal moment," he asked Gillamon.

"You may not realize it, but we are on the eve of the last of what will become known as Ten Crucial Days. These ten days aren't just crucial for America in 1776, but the world—for all time," Gillamon began. He walked over to the single panel of time and touched it. The Delaware River came into view, and the men were loading the boats to cross on Christmas night. "Before we enter the tenth day, I want us to review the first nine days. You must understand the importance of these days and how what happens tonight and tomorrow will change history."

"So, Day One of the Ten Crucial Days was Washington and the army crossing the Delaware on December 25th," Clarie noted, watching as Mr. Atticus put Jock onto the ferry with Max. "I'm happy to see this since I was busy keeping von Donop and his Hessian regiment occupied in Mount Holly."

"Bravo on your exquisite performance, my dear!" Nigel told her. "Had von Donop been able to get to Trenton, the outcome of Day Two would likely have been quite different."

"What happened on Day Two at Trenton, anyway, besides getting Bow-Wow-Howe so upset?" Al asked.

"The Americans suffered minimal losses, only two men, who stopped on the march and froze to death, plus two officers and two privates wounded in the battle," Gillamon reported, swiping the panel to show the Battle of Trenton. "But many of Washington's men were sick and later died of exhaustion and exposure. About four to five hundred Hessians were able to escape, but the Hessians lost twenty-two killed, eighty-three wounded, and eight hundred ninety-six taken prisoner by the Americans. Colonel Rall was killed, but Washington met with him before he died, and promised him that his men would be treated humanely."

"And so they have. The Hessian prisoners were marched to Philadelphia and have been amazed by the kind treatment they've received," Clarie told them. "Washington's army captured all their muskets, bayonets, swords, and powder, which was enough to equip several brigades. Plus, Knox added six excellent German cannons to his inventory."

Gillamon nodded. "Indeed. Washington then called a Council of War in Trenton to see if they should attack another post, hold their ground, or retreat. His officers agreed that the best course was to take the prisoners and plunder and regroup." He swiped to the scene of the nine-mile-long march back to Johnson's Ferry and re-crossing of the Delaware that night.

"I daresay that re-crossing the Delaware that night was even worse than the first time," Nigel added, shivering. "Look at what those weary soldiers did for the cause of liberty! Extraordinary!"

"Aye, Washington's poor lads had marched sixty hours thr-r-rough Jock's snow, r-r-rain, sleet, and hail," Max recalled. "Why didn't Jock come here with us, Gillamon?"

"I've got him working on another weather assignment tonight," Gillamon explained. "But as you know, Jock thawed things out on Day Three with warmer temperatures, but things also got hot inside the British high command that day after Clarie couriered the news from Trenton." He swiped the panel to show a scene of General Howe and General Cornwallis in New York:

British officers were laughing and toasting one another at an elaborate dinner celebrating Howe's Knighthood, and Cornwallis's successful pursuit of Washington's army.

"To my brother, *Sir* William Howe! Congratulations on your appointment by King George III for your victory over the rebels in the Battle of New York!" Admiral Howe exclaimed, lifting his glass. The men cheered and drank to his health.

"And here's to General Cornwallis, who hounded the old Fox Washington all the way to Pennsylvania!" Sir Howe replied with another glass lifted. "Godspeed on your voyage home to see your beautiful wife Jemima in London."

Cornwallis bowed his head gratefully and wore a proud, relieved smile. "I thank you, my Lord. My bags have been loaded on the *HMS Bristol* and I am due to depart this very evening."

Suddenly Admiral Howe's secretary Ambrose Serle rushed up to the Howe brothers at the dinner table and whispered the news of Trenton. The men who were gathered around the table watched as looks of shock quickly turned to fury. Howe rose to his feet and pressed his knuckles on the table, hanging his head for a moment. He slowly lifted his gaze to the officers seated there. "The rebels attacked Trenton yesterday morning and destroyed the Hessian garrison there. They killed Colonel Rall and took nine hundred men prisoner." Audible gasps of disbelief rose from the proud British officers. Howe turned his gaze to Cornwallis. "Your leave is cancelled. I'm sending you immediately back to Trenton. You are to find the rebel army, strike quickly, and DESTROY IT!" He slammed his fist on the table, rattling the goblets.

Cornwallis's face fell, and he clenched his jaw in disbelief and indignation.

Al covered his eyes at the scene. "I don't want to watch this part. I don't like it when humans get mad."

Max wore a big grin. "I *love* this part, Big Al! Serves them pompous Br-r-rits r-r-right. Now they'll think twice aboot Washington an' his army."

"Not only the British, but everyone is thinking differently, Max," Clarie told him. "As news has spread about Trenton, many Americans feel it is a sign from God that the Continental Army is His instrument for their just Cause. This Patriot victory has had a huge impact on the people. A week ago, they had almost given up the Cause for lost. Now they are all 'liberty mad' again, and men are volunteering to fight in droves. People who had signed Howe's loyalty oath to the king are changing their minds and returning to support American independence."

"Meanwhile, the British are blaming the Hessians, and the Hessians are blaming the British," Gillamon told them. "Every British leader has denied responsibility, and I must say that von Donop was especially shaken by the news. But while the British lion was roaring in New York on Day Three, Washington and his generals had a Council of War at the Harris House back in Pennsylvania." He swiped to a panel showing Washington, Knox, Greene, Sullivan, and others celebrating around the table.

"Jock were happy that his Henry Knox were made a Br-r-rigadier General that night!" Max exclaimed.

"That promotion was *well*-deserved, huzzah!" Nigel cheered. "This Day Three Council also decided that the victory in Trenton was not sufficient, and the army needed another victory to prove that it wasn't a one-time event."

"Yes, they realized that they have awakened the British lion, who will seek revenge, and so they decided to plan another attack. They based their decision on intelligence gathered by Colonel Cadwalader after he and his Philadelphia Associators finally succeeded in *their* crossing, not realizing that Washington's army had returned on December 26th," Gillamon added. "They found that the enemy was fleeing in a panic, abandoning Burlington and Trenton. Cadwalader saw this as an opportunity to attack and drive the British from West Jersey. So, Washington issued orders for the troops to prepare to recross the Delaware yet *again.*"

"Is Day Three over yet?" Al opened his eyes. "What happened on Day Four?"

"Daft kitty," Max grumbled. "On Day Four Washington were busy wr-r-ritin' all sorts of letters ta r-r-rally militia companies all over New Jersey, Pennsylvania, Connecticut, Massachusetts, an' New York."

"Right, and Washington wrote to the New Jersey Militia in Morristown, instructing them to begin harassing the enemy's flanks and rear, just as the militia did here in Trenton to wear the Hessians down to a frazzle," Nigel reported, pulling on his whiskers excitedly. "I hope they give those husky Hessians the what-for until they pull out their wooly whiskers!"

Gillamon chuckled and swiped the panel to another scene of Washington's army crossing back over the Delaware. "Days Five and Six involved eight different ferry crossings, but with great difficulty due to more snow and freezing conditions. This was not Jock's doing, but just the regular New Jersey winter. Washington also received troubling news from the commissary officers that the army was running out of food. New Jersey has been swept clean of food reserves by both armies."

"No food? TURN BACK! Tell the lads to turn back now while they have a chance!" Al exclaimed, his paws up to his mouth in horror. "I bet that havin' no food alone will drive Grant from New Jersey!"

Clarie giggled and petted Al. "This is another surprisingly *good* thing that has brought Americans together in a Continental effort for the Cause. Commissary General Joseph Trumbull is working hard with Virginia to supply bread and New England to supply salt meat to keep the army fed and alive. Our dear Robert Morris in Philadelphia is truly an unsung hero to also gather money and supplies tirelessly."

"Gillamon, I hereby volunteer to work directly with that Trumpet lad to gather food for the Cause," Al offered, raising his paw in a solemn vow.

Max and Nigel rolled their eyes at one another. "I might add that Washington held another Council of War at his headquarters in Trenton on Day Six. There they decided that whilst the first Battle of Trenton was a bold *offensive,* a second battle would be of a *defensive* nature. Washington's intelligence of the enemy told him there were about six thousand British and Hessians in New Jersey, with another four thousand soldiers marching in for support."

"I could have told him that," Al remarked nonchalantly.

"Well maybe ye *should* have then, kitty!" Max huffed. "So, the Council agr-r-reed not ta build up fortifications in Tr-r-renton, but ta make their defensive stand at Assunpink Creek."

Nigel frowned. "That location was chosen to make it a costly attack for the enemy, just as it was when they attacked Bunker Hill and other Patriot positions on the heights. Such is the ugly business of war, to cause the most casualties to one's adversary."

"Meanwhile, Washington finally added some cavalry," Clarie reported. "The First Troop of Philadelphia Light Horse is a volunteer group of smartly dressed, wealthy young gentlemen serving at their own expense who succeeded on their first mission for Washington. He wanted to find out what was happening in Princeton, so he sent Colonel Reed with them to find out, since Reed grew up in the area and knows it well."

"I'll take it from here, lass," Al told her, clearing his throat. "Swipe to the scene please, Gillamon." Max and Nigel looked at one another with surprised smiles as Gillamon brought the scene of a farmhouse into view. "I *love* mincemeat pies, so when Grant's chef made some for the Christmas celebrations, I accidentally ate the whole batch. Sure, and he were a wee bit mad when he saw them missin'. He didn't have time to make more pies with everything Grant ordered for his menu, so he ordered a parcel of them to be sent from a baker in Princeton. Well, it jest so happens that a dozen of those 16th dragon lads at Princeton smelled them mincemeat pies bakin' and couldn't help themselves. They raided the house and were in there eatin' the whole bunch when Washington's horse lads surrounded the house and caught them." Al patted his belly. "I never knew I'd have anything in common with dragon lads, but now I do. Mincemeat pies, aye."

Gillamon chuckled at the scene of Washington's dragoons taking the British dragoons back to Trenton for interrogation. "It was from these captured dragoons that Washington learned the British plans of concentrating eight thousand soldiers at Princeton to then attack Trenton."

"Brilliant, Al! Who knew food could be such a useful weapon!" Nigel exclaimed with a jolly chuckle.

Max shook his head good humoredly at their fluffy feline friend. "Ye done good, big Al. Yer appetite be one of our best secr-r-ret weapons."

"In addition to *that* intelligence, Cadwalader's men came across a *mysterious* 'intelligent young man' in Princeton who told them that Princeton was protected on all sides but one," Clarie added, eyeing Gillamon with a knowing grin. "He told them that the town could be approached by back roads from Trenton, and Cadwalader drew out a map for Washington. Based on this *mysterious young man's* information, Washington sent a thousand men with six guns halfway to Princeton on the Post Road to delay any British movement toward Trenton, isn't that so, Gillamon?"

Al looked from Clarie to Gillamon a couple of times before a goofy grin broke out on his face. He shook a paw at Gillamon. "Why ye sneaky little mysterious young man, ye!"

Gillamon shrugged his shoulders and nodded. "Of course, I had to change my appearance to reduce my age by thirty years or so, but it did the trick."

"I say, what a brilliant maneuver, old boy!" Nigel cheered. "Did they ever get your name?"

Gillamon shook his head 'no.' "And no one will ever know my identity in history."

"I love it when that happens," Max said with a wide grin. "It keeps them humans guessin'."

"Thus, Day Six was an *extremely* busy day, what?" Nigel noted. He then hit Max with the backside of his paw as Gillamon brought Day Seven into view. "Ah, but Day SEVEN, December 31, 1776, is a day I shan't forget for its Patriotic magnitude. Max and I were enraptured over Washington's speech!"

"Aye, Washington were aboot ta loose his whole army on New Year's Day," Max added.

"Sir, the men are assembled as ordered," General Greene told Washington.

The Continental regiments under Greene and Sullivan stood at attention on the banks of the Delaware. Clouds hovered above them but had paused their deluge of rain and snow. Washington slowly rode Blueskin to stand in front of the veteran warriors who had already given their all for the Cause. He drew in a deep breath and scanned their faces, making eye contact with each one he could.

"Soldiers of the Continental Army, you have fought the good fight in our righteous cause of liberty," Washington began. "You have served valiantly and without complaint through many hardships—the Battle of New York, the long retreat across New Jersey, the midnight crossing of the icy Delaware, the long march to Trenton, the Battle of Trenton, the long march and crossing back to Pennsylvania, and once more recrossing the hazardous Delaware to stand here at Trenton." He pointed his riding crop up and down the line. "You have dealt the enemy a devastating blow! But we cannot stop at one victory in Trenton. We must press on, for although any action we take involves danger, *inaction* now could be far worse; while action involves the risk of defeat, *inaction* will surely invite disaster upon us and the Cause."

The men kept their gaze on their Commander-in-Chief as he rode forward a few steps on Blueskin. "I know that you wish to return home to your warm hearth and home, to your families and to the bounty of your tables. I know you are worn down from fatigue and want of sufficient food and clothing. Your enlistments are up, and you of right can leave our noble army, but I am begging you to stay. Your services are greatly needed, and you could do more for our country now than you ever could at any future date. I *implore* you—please. Stay with us a while longer. I promise you ten dollars if you agree to stay for six more weeks." Washington then looked at Greene and Sullivan and gave a singular nod.

Greene lifted his chin and shouted, "All who would stay, please step forward."

The drums beat for volunteers, but the line of weary soldiers didn't move. The uncomfortable silence of the men rippled throughout their ranks. Greene and Sullivan looked at one another and then at Washington with silent dismay as not one man stepped forward.

Suddenly Washington wheeled about on Blueskin and rode along in front of the regiment, willing the men to answer him. "My brave fellows, you have done all I asked you to do, and more than could be reasonably expected; but your country is at stake—your wives, your houses, and all that you hold dear. You have worn yourselves out with the fatigues and hardships, but we know not how to spare you. If you will consent to stay one month longer, you will render that service to the cause of liberty and to your country, which you probably can never do under any other circumstances."

Washington then silently rode Blueskin back down the row of soldiers as some of them began to whisper among themselves. The drums rolled again.

"I'll stay if you will," one soldier told another.

A grimy soldier with threadbare breeches clenched his jaw and shook his head, gazing out across the town of Trenton. The Hessians were gone, but everyone knew it was only a matter of time before the British responded to what the Patriots had done here. "We cannot go home in these circumstances." He slapped his hat to his thigh and stepped forward.

Then another stepped forward. And another. All down the line, men made a choice to continue the fight for liberty.

"God Almighty inclined their hearts to listen," Greene told Sullivan with a hopeful smile as one by one, men stepped forward to agree to stay.

"HAPPY HUZZAH NEW YEAR!" Nigel cheered with both fists pumping in the air. "To watch General Washington move those men to action with his inspirational words was a glorious moment for the history books!"

"The money didn't hurt, though," Max admitted. "That Robert Morris actually went ta the house of a r-r-rich Quaker who had a chest of coins buried in his yard, an' got him ta dig it up so Washington could pay the lads as pr-r-romised."

"Hooray!" Al clapped his fluffy paws together. "How many lads did Washington get to stay?"

"He convinced 3,300 soldiers to stay, plus the militia is now pouring in from all over," Clarie answered. "Meanwhile, the thousand men Washington sent halfway to Princeton to stall the British arrived under cover of darkness on Day Seven and were ready to skirmish with the enemy as Day Eight dawned." She pointed to the scene as Gillamon brought the time panel into view.

"Now that's the way to start a new year, with a BOOM!" Al exclaimed, wide-eyed to see the carnage on New Year's Day.

"The Americans inflicted a heavy toll on the British and Hessians, and the enemy had to call for reinforcements," Gillamon told them. "But this skirmish warned the enemy that the rebels were out in full force and were fighting well to inflict casualties on them while keeping their own losses low."

"I'm sure *that* frazzled the dreaded foe!" Nigel cheered. "I daresay, our infant army has suddenly grown into a feisty adolescent!"

"Aye! So, while those boys were fr-r-razzlin' the enemy, Washington had a New Year's War Council ta figure out wha' ta do next," Max shared. "They knew the Br-r-ritish were comin' an' now they had ta decide wha' they'd do aboot fightin' or r-r-retr-r-reatin' somewhere else ta fight."

"Right, so our rotund General Knox suggested they hear from Dr. Benjamin Rush, who had just arrived," Nigel added. "The good doctor told the

Council that the Philadelphia militia would be happy to serve under the command of Washington and would instantly obey a summons to join the troops in Trenton. So, after deliberating a bit longer with his officers, Washington handed Dr. Rush a letter to take immediately to Colonel Cadwalader seven miles away. Mind you, it was 10:00 p.m., and the night was dark and the roads muddy. It took Dr. Rush three hours to reach Cadwalader, but the Colonel mustered his men to march immediately to Trenton. It was a difficult march due to the warmer temperatures making the roads turn to muddy sludge."

"Were that Jock's doin', Gillamon?" Max wanted to know.

Gillamon grinned, swiping the time panel to reveal Day Nine. "Yes, I had your grandlad turn up the temperature to turn the hard, icy roads into mud. But that mud was not meant for Cadwalader's men." A scene of British redcoats and Hessians trudging through knee- and thigh-deep mud emerged. Guns and horses were repeatedly getting stuck in the muck.

"I know this one, too!" Al piped up. "The muddy roads were meant for *Cornwallis* and all his redcoats and Hessians. I should know, as I weren't even recognizable by the time we arrived from mud splashin' me on the back of the wagon. It took me hours to clean meself off."

"Day Nine, today, started off badly for General Cornwallis's men in the mud," Clarie noted. "Not only was his army slowed down by mud, but they had to skirmish with the American pickets along the way, preventing them from reaching Trenton until thirty minutes before sunset. The Hessians are furious over what happened in Trenton last week, and von Donop ordered his men to not give any quarter to rebels on pain of scourging."

"In other words, the Hessians were ordered to kill every rebel, or else be punished themselves," Nigel added somberly.

Gillamon swiped the time panel to show the next scene of ninety-five hundred British and Hessian soldiers entering the north end of Trenton as the Americans under Edward Hand and Forrest's artillery unit retreated in perfect order toward the Assunpink Creek bridge. Washington sent some Rhode Island men to cover their retreat through town. "Alas, in the confusion, some Americans were left behind, including an elderly Scottish Presbyterian chaplain named John Rosbrugh, whose horse had been stolen." Suddenly the image of Rafe wielding a bayonet came into view as he grabbed the chaplain and called over to a group of Hessians. They began to make a game of killing the man as he fell to his knees and prayed. "I'll spare you the scene, but they took everything from him, including his money, watch, and clothes, and left him dead with thirteen bayonet wounds and saber cuts to his head. Rafe immediately celebrated the clergyman's death, holding up his wolf gun in celebration."

Max growled. "Ye can be sure that wherever that evil R-r-rafe be, there be death!"

Gillamon swiped to a touching scene of Washington sitting on Blueskin on the Assunpink Creek bridge as the Americans retreated. "But in the midst of the ugliness in battle, there was also seen honor, valor, and confident leadership on display by the Commander-in-Chief."

"It was an utter marvel to watch as Washington sat quietly atop his noble steed, calmly welcoming each man who passed by with the assurance that they were now safe under his watch," Nigel remarked. "He spoke to many of them. Blueskin was so close to the bridge railing that some of the men brushed the general's boot as they passed. They were in awe of the man and instantly were inspired by his example of resolute bravery in the face of an oncoming enemy."

"And come the enemy did," Gillamon stated as together they watched the Second Battle of Trenton unfold before them. "General Knox has double the amount of artillery pieces he had in the first Battle of Trenton, with ample powder and shot. And it was on full display this evening."

"Once the men were across the bridge, Washington placed his sixty-eight hundred men in their defensive positions along the Assunpink Creek. He assigned his brave Virginia regiment under Colonel Scott to hold the most important post at the bridge, 'to the last extremity,'" Clarie relayed. "At twilight Cornwallis first attempted some probing attacks at some of the fords of the creek."

"But Jock's weather had made the water high an' fast so it were hard ta cr-r-ross," Max added proudly. "Then Knox's big guns an' the firin' Patriot lads made the enemy fall back."

"Then the British attempted two more attacks on the bridge," Nigel pointed out, "and that's when things got terribly bloody. Knox's eighteen guns let loose a barrage that has never been seen on these American shores. The enemy fell back, regrouped, and advanced, but soon it was over. The bridge became red with blood and redcoats covering every inch."

Al covered his eyes with his paws. "I couldn't watch then, and I can't watch now. How many laddies were killed out there this evenin', Gillamon?"

"Washington lost fifty Americans, but Cornwallis lost five hundred killed and captured," Gillamon answered. "So, the Second Battle of Trenton ended, and at 7:00 p.m. the guns fell silent. Both sides dropped to the ground in exhaustion at their camps, and our twenty wounded men have been taken to a house where Dr. Rush is doing the best he can for those poor fellows."

"Which brings us to where we were when we began this Epic Order of the Seven War Council," Nigel gathered. Gillamon swiped the panel to show Washington's War Council.

"Which is why I wanted to show you the contrasting councils of Washington and Cornwallis," Gillamon began. "Both commanders have their patrols out this evening. The poor British infantry have been sent out in twenty-degree weather along the Assunpink Creek to keep watch but are not permitted to even light a fire so as not to give away their positions."

"Even I feel sorry for them," Max admitted, watching the men shiver in the cold. "So, it looks like ye made Jock dr-r-rop the temperature fast, Gillamon. Why?"

"Look," Gillamon said, pointing to Washington's council gathered in the quarters of General Arthur St. Clair in the Douglas House on Queen Street.

The officers were gathered around a wooden table with wax dripping down the candlesticks that illuminated a map of Trenton and Princeton. Washington, Greene, Sullivan, Cadwalader, Mifflin, Ewing, St. Clair, Hitchcock, Mercer, Stephen, Knox, and Reed sat with mud-caked boots and weary faces from the difficult day of battle. Local citizens had been invited to attend and offer their input. Washington reviewed the situation in which they found themselves.

"Battle tomorrow is certain," Washington began. "Defeat is a high probability, given the enemy's numbers and their determination. A retreat down the river would be difficult and precarious. But the loss of the corps I command might be fatal to the country. I now ask your advice given these circumstances."

The officers began to murmur and offer up varying opinions. Some preferred a retreat. Others wished to risk it all for a direct battle. Suddenly General Knox spoke up. "I believe a general engagement would be hazardous in the extreme, Your Excellency. If that were to happen, I predict that our right wing might give way and the defeat of the left wing would be inevitable, then throwing the whole army into confusion or pushing it into the Delaware, which is unpassable by boats. Our army is cooped up like a flock of chickens."

More murmuring over the two options: retreat or fight.

Washington wrinkled his brow, considering his dilemma. He wanted a fight, but he knew what was at stake. His newly amassed army gifted to him from the hope of their one victory in Trenton a week ago was on the line. But so was the fate of America. It could all be over tomorrow.

Just then, General St. Clair spoke up. "General Washington, might I propose a third option?"

"Please," Washington eagerly answered.

"My brigade was on the extreme right of our army today, and we patrolled the country lanes beyond our flank. Some of these paths lead north by a roundabout route to a crossing at a place called Quaker Bridge. It's near a Friends meetinghouse in the woods," St. Clair began. "If the army could reach that point unobserved and unopposed, it then could proceed almost due north to Princeton, about six miles distant from the bridge. From Princeton, the main roads could then be used turning left of the enemy, gaining a march upon him, and proceeding with all possible expedition to Brunswick."

"He's right!" Reed quickly affirmed. "I know the area well, and when I led the Philadelphia Light Horse on patrol, we saw no enemy on the back roads to Princeton."

Washington raised his eyebrows. "It would avoid the appearance of a retreat, which is of consequence as I wish to give reputation to our arms."

As the officers began a vigorous discussion of the plan, consulting the locals for their opinions, Gillamon turned to face the group. "St. Clair has offered the one solution that no one considered, and that is slipping away from Cornwallis and attacking his rear at Princeton."

"It's utterly brilliant!" Nigel exclaimed. "This is a way to allow Washington and the army to escape whilst giving them a potential victory as a result."

"Observe how Washington has learned to listen and bring the best minds and ideas to the table," Gillamon told them. "This Commander-in-Chief has earned their loyalty and respect for the way he has elevated every one of them to a new standard of conduct in an army. He treats his men as gentlemen, not for their social status, but for their conduct of honor. And he gives value to their opinions, yet every man in that room understands that Washington is in charge. These men know that their general has made many mistakes since he took command, including his failures in New York. But they also see his emerging genius in strategy, but even more so, his example of leading from the front."

He tapped the panel, which shifted to the War Council of Cornwallis and his officers. The British commander was surrounded by red-clad men in polished uniforms who were gentlemen of the aristocracy holding the exclusive status of connections to King George III himself. They were "chums" who had schooled together and been well bred together, sharing benches in Parliament and long histories together on the battlefield.

"What do you first notice?" Gillamon asked.

Al held up his iron claw and punctuated the air as he counted. "There be fewer of them at Cornwallis's table than at Washington's. Of course, Grant could count for two officers."

"Right, Al," Gillamon answered with a grin. "Cornwallis's council is small and tight. They address him as 'Lord' for he is not just their leader but the one who rules the moment. Unlike Washington, he is not interested in hearing what his army *should* do. Cornwallis already knows what he *will* do and is simply telling them what *shall* be."

"Those skulking peasants are skilled only in the art of running away!" General Grant blurted out, his double chin shaking with laughter at his diatribe aimed at the Americans.

"They seem quite cheeky in their expectant victory," Nigel noted as the men laughed over several bottles around the table. They discussed the risks they faced, but maintained confidence in their arms and experience.

Only General Sir William Erskine spoke up with caution. "My Lord, should we not consider disposing of the American army quickly with a sudden attack? If you trust those people tonight, you will see nothing of them in the morning."

Cornwallis waved him off to dismiss his suggestion. "No, Wooly, there are many reasons *not* to attack tonight. In general, I do not like night attacks, for they are too unpredictable. And tonight is exceeding dark, with very little starlight. The ground is too soft, and this terrain is unknown to me. Our men are exhausted from the day's march from Princeton, and they have been under arms the whole day. They are languid and require rest." The general shifted in his seat and picked up a goblet to swirl his wine. "I was surprised by the strength of the American artillery today. I therefore wish to reinforce our artillery before a further engagement and have already sent orders for men and guns to be brought from Princeton on the morrow. No, dear Wooly, the troops should make fires, refresh themselves, and take repose. I have the enemy safe enough and can dispose of them in the morning."

General Erskine, whom Cornwallis referred to as 'Wooly,' frowned but submitted to the British commander without another word. The matter was settled.

Cornwallis leaned back in his chair, and an impish smile grew on his face. "We've got the Old Fox safe now. We'll go over and bag him in the morning."

Gillamon closed the panel of time and rested his hands on the table. "Everything that has happened over the past nine days will either save the Continental Army and American Independence, or it will bring it all crashing down around them. "Tomorrow is Day Ten."

"An' old foxes aren't easily caught," Max interjected with a grin.

62

A Fine Fox Chase

TRENTON, NEW JERSEY, JANUARY 3, 1777, MIDNIGHT

"Where do you think we're going?" one private asked his friends as they sat around their small campfire. He gingerly wrapped his frozen, swollen feet in fresh cloth that Clarie had given to him when making her rounds through the camp, giving soldiers aid and comfort. He then slipped his feet into the boots he had taken off a dead Hessian in the streets of Trenton. They were a little large, but his bloody feet at least now had some sort of covering, and he was grateful. He was fortunate. Countless soldiers still had no shoes, and their bloody, cracked feet would once more have to carry them on the march. "I heard the supply wagons are on their way to Burlington. They wrapped the wheels with rags so they wouldn't be heard."

"Maybe we're going to attack the enemy in the rear, north of Trenton," his friend answered. He had a bloody bandage wrapped around his left hand and winced as he tried to examine it in front of their small fire. It ached as much from the cold as it did the wound. "I hope I'll be able to hold a musket, much less fire one."

"I bet we're heading to Princeton," a third private remarked, sounding a wet, raspy cough. He looked up at the dark sky and stood to kick the fire. "Only the General knows. It's so pitch black out here we won't be able to see where we're going anyway."

"Shhhhh, keep your voices down," Major Wilkinson whispered to the young men. "Fall in with your unit. We're moving out. Leave your campfire burning."

The three young soldiers nodded but shot a puzzling glance at the major. They hurriedly slipped their knapsacks over their chests and picked up their muskets to fall in line with the long column of Washington's army. The first soldier hobbled along on his sore feet, aided by his friends.

"It's fr-r-reezin' out here," Max whispered once the men were gone, his icy puff of breath rising in the air. "Jock did good, but why did ye want such fr-r-rigid temperatures, Gillamon?"

Gillamon as Mr. Atticus stomped the hard ground that yesterday had been soft and muddy. Within hours of the rapidly dropping temperatures, it became solid, packed ground. "Which kind of road would be easier for the army to make its midnight escape with horses and wagons—mud or hard pavement?"

Max shook his big square head. "Aye, of course. I get it now. The lads won't sink ta their knees in the muck as they march."

"Yes, but they undoubtedly shall find it terribly difficult to see where they are going," Nigel pointed out. "Once they leave the brightness of these fires, their eyes will have to adjust to the pitch black of the night."

"At least the enemy won't be able to see us since we're pitch black to begin with," Jock said with a grin. "But why are they leaving these fires burning? And why did the major tell those soldiers to be quiet when other lads are over there making such a racket?"

"Washington is keeping a rearguard of troops behind with fires burning to trick the enemy into thinking the army is still in place," Gillamon explained. "They are noisily using pickaxes and shovels to make the British *think* that the army is digging in when in fact, it is moving out. These rearguard soldiers will follow along when daylight nears."

"Ohhhh, I get it. Just like he did in Brooklyn," Jock replied, his eyelids getting droopy. "That's clever."

"Washington's bein' sneaky as a fox," Max told him with a grin. "But the lads have a long night of marchin' ahead. We best get on the r-r-road with 'em."

Jock yawned and shook his head. "How long will we be marching tonight? I'm sleepy."

"It's sixteen miles to Princeton, and it will be a long, hard march for the humans, especially for the men in Mifflin's and Cadwalader's brigades. This will be their second night march in a row, and they are already exhausted. They'll snag a minute of sleep here and there as the column stops to move the artillery over obstacles in the road, but several of them will almost no doubt be sleepwalking," Gillamon explained. He smiled and picked up Jock. "But I'll carry you, little one. You've expended a lot of energy on this weather."

Jock yawned again and laid his head over Gillamon's shoulder. "Aye, I was hoping you'd say that."

Nigel hopped up onto Max's back and patted the Scottie's shoulder. "Right, and I am terribly grateful for your transport as well, old boy. Do you mind if I take a snooze whilst you trudge on? There's a good chap."

"No r-r-rest for the Scot," Max sighed, looking up at Jock, who was already drifting off to sleep. "At least, not for this one."

QUAKER BRIDGE OUTSIDE PRINCETON, NEW JERSEY, JANUARY 3, 1777, 7:22 A.M.

Jock heard men chopping wood and drowsily opened his eyes. He lifted his head to see the first streaks of dawn giving light to a magical winter wonderland spread out before him. Hoarfrost covered everything in sight. As the emerging sunshine hit the frozen snow-covered ground and frosty trees and shrubs, its feathery appearance glittered like diamonds. Jock blinked and smiled. "I even make frost in my sleep. Where are we?"

"Good morning, little one. Six miles south of Princeton," Gillamon answered. "We're at the Quaker Bridge, but the humans had to quickly construct a second bridge to support the artillery."

"Good mornin', lad. We were gettin' r-r-ready ta wake ye," Max said. "The army be splittin' up here in two wings. General Greene will take a small division on the left wing, an' General Sullivan will take the main body of the army on the r-r-right wing."

"The plan is for Greene's division to head west and attack Princeton from the north of the town while Sullivan's division attacks from the south," Gillamon explained. "Both divisions will have Continental troops in the front and rear with militia in the middle."

"Part of Greene's men are ta keep the Br-r-ritish fr-r-rom either leavin' Pr-r-rinceton or arrivin' from Tr-r-renton with r-r-reinforcements," Max added.

"Like how Washington did in Trenton?" Jock asked. "He sent his army in two columns, with one drawing attention while the other attacked from another direction."

"Splendid observation, Jock *Frost* Knox! He shall attempt yet another double envelopment," Nigel exclaimed, looking around at the beautiful morning landscape of this cold, crisp day. "We appear to be in your namesake territory." He breathed in deeply and spotted Veritas coming in for a landing. "I shall soon take flight to keep my aerial vigil of the day. Good morning, old boy."

"It won't be good for long," Veritas told them. "You better come along with me. There's a column of British redcoats and artillery heading from Princeton toward Trenton on the Post Road."

"Those must be the reinforcements that Cornwallis ordered last night," Gillamon surmised, setting Jock down on the frosty ground. "Things are happening earlier than I expected. Everyone be ready. It won't be long before both armies spot one another. Stay with your humans!" Suddenly he ran off, leaving them as he headed out with Greene's column.

"Oh, dear! Let's be off then!" Nigel exclaimed, climbing onto the bald eagle's back. Veritas flapped his massive five-foot wings and lifted off from the ground.

"Let's find Washington an' Knox," Max told Jock. "Keep yer nose r-r-ready!"

POST ROAD AT STONY BROOK, NEW JERSEY, JANUARY 3, 1777, 8:00 A.M.

"Hector! Apollos!" Colonel Mawhood shouted, calling his dogs to stay near his position.

Commander of the Fourth Brigade at Princeton, Lieutenant Colonel Charles Mawhood sat atop a brown pony and grinned at his two black-and-white springer spaniels playing in front of him. "They haven't a care in the world. How pleasant it would be to have no knowledge of this dreadful war," he remarked to Captain Hale, who rode alongside him. "I lament this American contest and lay it squarely at the feet of Lord North himself. *That villain* caused this war."

Grenadier Captain William Hale of the Forty-fifth Foot wore a non-committal expression, not being a Whig like Mawhood, and certainly not as freely spoken regarding politics. "I understand that you had said if you were General Washington, you would attack several outposts at once since we are weak. It's as if the rebel commander heard you, Colonel."

Mawhood lifted a hand in agreement and nodded. "You see?" He gestured to the long column of seven hundred men marching ahead of them. "Trenton was so weak that the rebels took it handily. Even with more than nine thousand men there now, Cornwallis has *still* called for our reinforcements after fighting them yesterday." Although Generals Howe and Cornwallis held Mawhood in high esteem, his confidence in them was slipping.

A tapestry of colors and textures draped the column, from red to dark blue jackets with white, buff, or green facings paired with black high grenadier caps or small helmets to kilts with feather bonnets. The proud colors of the various Royal Artillery, Light Dragoons, Light Infantry, and Highlander units fluttered in the crisp January air. They had been on the march since before sunrise and had just crossed the bridge at Stony Brook. As they came to the top of a hill by Cochran's house, they suddenly spotted Washington's two columns behind them.

"Sir! Rebel troops about a mile distant on our left!" called Ensign Inman.

Mawhood spurred his horse around, pulled out his spyglass and gazed at Washington's army entering a wooded area that they had just passed. "They are clearly heading toward Princeton and Brunswick." He lowered his spyglass and thought for a moment. "Get this column turned around."

OUTSIDE PRINCETON, NEW JERSEY,
JANUARY 3, 1777, 8:00 A.M.

Major Wilkinson rode at the front of Sullivan's column, admiring the beauty of the winter landscape when out of the corner of his eye he saw a flash of light. He turned and gazed out to the distant Post Road and spotted a long column of redcoats, the sun catching their long bayonets affixed to their shouldered muskets. He immediately turned and raced to notify Washington's military secretary, Colonel Harrison. Soon the officers were studying the movement of the British column.

"Look, the British are marching in quick time toward Princeton!" Nigel told Veritas. "Oddly enough, it appears their commander has a pair of dogs with him!"

"And it looks like the Americans in Sullivan's wing have spotted them," Veritas answered. He could clearly see the faces of the American officers huddled together, pointing in the direction of the oncoming redcoats.

"But what about Greene's column?" Nigel wondered.

Veritas circled overhead to observe the British force advancing east toward Sullivan's main body. "Greene's division is travelling a sunken road in a ravine of Stony Brook and doesn't seem to see the British."

"Nor do the British appear to see Greene's column!" Nigel surmised. "They only see Sullivan's column. Neither Greene nor the British realize they are heading directly toward one another!"

Veritas scanned the long column and spotted Max and Jock trotting toward Washington. The eagle then spotted Washington looking through his spyglass. "Well, Washington sees exactly what is happening." He observed a moment longer and saw Washington send a messenger galloping toward Greene. "Looks like he's sending word to Greene."

Within minutes, Washington's messenger reached Greene. Greene in turn immediately ordered General Hugh Mercer to lead his brigade out of the ravine to confront the approaching British troops, with Cadwalader's unit following behind. Mawhood sent some light-horsemen to reconnoiter, and they soon discovered Greene's column. Now each side knew about the other.

"It appears that Mawhood is sending about four hundred fifty men toward the Americans," Nigel observed. "And Mercer's unit of one hundred twenty riflemen and Continentals is advancing to that barren apple orchard at the Clarke Farm! Oh, dear, Mercer shall be quite outnumbered!"

"They're lining up for battle," Veritas observed.

Soon musket fire erupted, and men began dropping into the snow while the ice-laden tree branches splintered, and twigs went flying all around them. Mercer led the charge of his unit, which seemed at first to drive back the British, but both sides continued to add more troops and return volley after volley of fire. A cloud of smoke began to cover the battlefield that was quickly becoming riddled with fallen men gasping in agony. Because the ground was so frozen, the blood pooled on the surface, turning the field into a red sea.

"What's happening? I can hardly make out the scene with all that smoke," Nigel said, squinting to see.

Veritas peered through the gun smoke and saw the unmistakable flash of bayonets charging from the British column. "This isn't good. The Americans don't have bayonets and those long blades are coming for them."

Suddenly Mercer's horse was hit by a musket ball, sending Mercer falling to the ground. "Retreat!" Mercer cried as his men recoiled in fear and confusion from the bayonet charge. He drew his sword next to his horse, which was writhing in pain.

Just then Veritas spotted a gun he had seen many times before—at Lexington and Concord, Bunker Hill, and Brooklyn. "It's Rafe, and he's heading right for Mercer."

"Oh, no, not that evil minion!" Nigel cried.

They looked on in horror as Rafe went right up to Mercer and shouted, "Surrender, you traitor!"

"I shall never surrender!" Mercer defiantly retorted, lunging at Rafe with his sword.

Rafe's face contorted with rage, and he hit Mercer in the head with his wolf gun, splattering the handsomely dressed general with blood as he fell back onto the now-slick ground by his horse. The fierce grenadier stepped back and pointed to Mercer, shouting to the British troops, "Look! We've taken Washington!" With that bald-faced lie, several British infantrymen came in for the kill with fury.

"Call for Quarters, you rebel!" one British soldier raged.

"I am no rebel," Mercer answered, wincing and holding his head in agony.

With that, the group of British soldiers bayoneted Mercer seven times, shouting, and cursing at him before leaving him mortally wounded.

"What a tragic loss!" Nigel cried. "General Mercer was both Washington's dear friend and neighbor, and one of America's bravest officers!"

Mercer's other officers attempted to step in and rally the brigade, but they were killed: Colonel Haslet from Delaware (the only man who fell into the Delaware River the night of the Crossing), Captain Fleming from Virginia, Captain Neil from New Jersey. The Americans broke and ran as their leaders fell, and the British came after them with the bayonet, chasing them through the orchard. Cadwalader's men rushed onto the field, but even their line fell apart as Mercer's retreating men ran into them. The American line continued to falter until some guns were brought to fire against the enemy. Mawhood answered with his own field guns, and an artillery duel ensued for the next few minutes.

"Look! More American soldiers are taking the field," Nigel cheered. A group of Cadwalader's Pennsylvania Associators formed a line to face the British column. "Those brave lads are simple merchants, artisans, and mechanics, not trained soldiers. Yet look at them! They choose to stand and fight against skilled soldiers! Oh, what valor they possess!"

"I don't know if they'll be able to last long, despite their bravery," Veritas worried. "But I spy five more brave ones. Gillamon and Clarie are carrying Mercer off the field to shelter under an oak tree, and Max and Jock are running alongside Washington right toward the carnage."

"Bravo! The British commander has two dogs at his side, and so does the American Commander-in-Chief!" Nigel exclaimed.

"Washington must have seen exactly what was happening," Veritas surmised. "The British 17th Regiment of Foot completely broke Mercer's small band of men and overran a company of New Jersey artillery. Now they're after Cadwalader's band of militia."

"If the British destroy Cadwalader's men, they'll split the American force asunder," Nigel feared. "But look! Captain Moulder's artillery is firing shot and canister against the oncoming redcoats!"

"Looks like it's halting their advance," Veritas added. "The British can't tell how many Americans are hiding behind the Clarke house and farm buildings firing at them."

Suddenly George Washington came galloping on Blueskin right between the lines on the hottest part of the battlefield just as Cadwalader's and Mercer's demoralized men were starting to retreat. Following behind Washington were Continental reinforcements from Sullivan's division.

Washington took off his three-cornered hat and waved it in the air, exclaiming, "Parade with me, my brave fellows! There is but a handful of the enemy, and we will have them directly."

The American forces were in awe of the fearless Washington, who dared to ride directly in the line of fire to rally them to fight on. Musket balls whizzed by his head, and cannon fire exploded around him coming from both sides, fully encasing him in smoke.

Washington's aide, Colonel Fitzgerald, immediately put his hat over his face, unable to watch his beloved commander cut down in the field.

"I can't watch!" Nigel cried, also covering his eyes.

What was only seconds felt like hours. Veritas dove down for a clearer view, and suddenly had a lump in his throat. "Open your eyes, Nigel!" he shouted excitedly.

The little mouse dared to look down when suddenly Blueskin pranced out from the cloud of smoke with Washington waving his hat, completely unscathed. Immediately, the men turned on their heels and followed their Commander-in-Chief, leveling a withering volley of musket fire as they advanced against the enemy. Washington led the way, continuing to rally the men with shouts of encouragement.

"HUZZAH!" Nigel exclaimed, almost falling off the eagle as he raised both of his tiny fists into the air, tears of joy filling his eyes. He quickly grabbed Veritas's feathers. "He's done it! Washington has turned the army around!"

"Not only that, but with the men Washington brought, the Americans now outnumber the British three to one!" Veritas exclaimed. "The redcoats are stubbornly fighting back, but Washington's troops are cutting them down right and left."

"Some of the Americans with bayonets are even charging at the dreaded foe with those steel blades!" Nigel exulted. "Washington's fearlessness has filled every man on that field, huzzah!"

An elated Washington ran alongside the soldiers charging with their bayonets and proudly exclaimed, "It is a fine fox chase, my boys!"

"Well, what do you know? The hunted has become the hunter," Veritas observed. He suddenly caught sight of Elsa sitting off to the side of the field, watching Washington gallop after the enemy before his men had to rein him in. She wore a wide smile with her red tail wrapped around her feet.

"The Fox has indeed become the Hound!" Nigel cheered, watching British Regulars now fleeing from the Continentals in open combat. Cheers erupted from the American lines as Mawhood's men scattered in every direction.

Veritas heard musket fire at the College of New Jersey and scanned the other emerging battle scene. "General St. Clair's men are driving the enemy from Frog Hollow to the college."

"Do take us over the college, old chap," Nigel directed him. "We need to see the end of this business."

WOODS NEAR CLARKE FARM, NEW JERSEY, JANUARY 3, 1777, 9:00 A.M.

The scene of carnage left behind on the Clarke Farm was unimaginable. Dead and wounded soldiers and horses from both sides lay across the frozen ground in pools of blood. After he was struck down, Gillamon and Clarie managed to carry General Mercer to the oak tree in front of the Clarke farmhouse so he could be tended to, and per his request, so he could watch his men fight on. After the battle, Mercer was taken inside the farmhouse where Dr. Rush attended to his mortal wounds the best he could.

Gillamon, Clarie, Max, Jock, Nigel, Veritas, and Elsa had regrouped in the woods by the farm after the horrible yet hopeful hour of battle.

"Is there any hope for General Mercer, Gillamon?" Jock asked hopefully.

"As a physician and surgeon himself, Mercer knows he won't survive," Gillamon lamented. "His wounds are too extensive, but he is in surprisingly good spirits. He is proud of his men. He has always been a brave warrior, as far back as 1745 at the Battle of Culloden in Scotland before coming to America. He fought with Washington in the French and Indian War and jumped into the fray with the Patriots at the outset of the American Revolution." Gillamon paused, as he knew that Mercer would linger for nine days before he finally succumbed to the savage wounds he received. "But at least Mercer's daughter is safe."

"His daughter? Vhy in the vorld vould his daughter be involved vith this battle?" Elsa wanted to know.

Gillamon wore a sad smile. "Forget I said it, little one. Mercer's daughter and family are safe back in Virginia."

"Sometimes Gillamon knows tidbits from the future that he can't share with us," Clarie interjected. "But even I am curious. Might Mercer's daughter give birth to someone important?"

Gillamon gave her a knowing look. "Several important someones, but there will be *one* especially important Mercer legacy that you all will meet on another battlefield, in another war, on another continent. But that's for another time."

Veritas whispered in Elsa's ear. "Remember, the less you know the better. Just stay in the moment, little fox."

"The cunning of the fox is as murderous as the violence of the wolf," Nigel quoted. "Thomas Paine penned those words in his *American Crisis*, but I never imagined such a poignant illustration on this battlefield today. Rafe slayed Mercer with his violent wolf gun, but the Fox Washington slayed the British lion with his cunning."

"Vhere I come from ve have a proverb: Vhat the lion cannot manage to do the fox can," Elsa shared with a wink.

"I'm pr-r-roud of our Old Fox! Forty-five minutes," Max realized. "That's all it took for Washington's army ta win victory over them r-r-redcoats! I stayed by his side, but I don't think anythin' would have touched the general today. The Maker hisself was watchin' out for our br-r-rave Fox."

"What happened over at the college, Nigel and Veritas?" Clarie asked. "We were needed here but knew things were well in hand there."

"Right, well in a nutshell, Sullivan managed the double envelopment, and the British knew their position was unsustainable," Nigel began. "Once Mawhood's 55th Regiment of Foot saw the bloodied 17th fall back, they also retreated."

"While those redcoats retreated, General St. Clair's men, who were marching toward Princeton, came to Frog Hollow Creek where they ran into the 40th Regiment of Foot," Veritas further explained. "The Americans fired, and those men fled into the College at Nassau Hall, busting out windows to try to defend it."

"But young Captain Alexander Hamilton fired his mighty cannon at the Hall and blasted through a wall," Nigel exulted with a fist of victory in the air. "It didn't take long before the British surrendered, and it was all over."

"Huzzah!" Jock cheered. "Knox's team ended the battle!"

"I guess Day Ten ended with a boom!" Max added happily. "So, Gillamon, looks like Washington and his army made it thr-r-rough these ten cr-r-rucial days with flyin' colors."

Gillamon nodded proudly. "Indeed, today we witnessed not only the saving of Washington's army but of American independence. The British suffered forty-five percent casualties today with one hundred killed and four hundred wounded or captured. The Americans lost forty killed and forty wounded."

"But this war is far from over," Clarie reminded them. "In fact, we need to get moving. Washington and the army can't linger in Princeton. Cornwallis will no doubt be here soon, so the Fox must escape north to Morristown."

"Will the Americans finally get to rest for the winter?" Jock wanted to know.

"Well, 'rest' is a debatable term, because both armies will need to fight a forage war this winter, but in terms of general action fighting, yes, they can 'rest' for the winter," Gillamon answered.

"But Vashington vill need to remain as vily as a fox," Elsa quipped.

Gillamon chuckled. "That's right, little one. Wily as a fox."

PART FIVE

THE GREAT ESCAPE

France,
December 1776 – April 1777

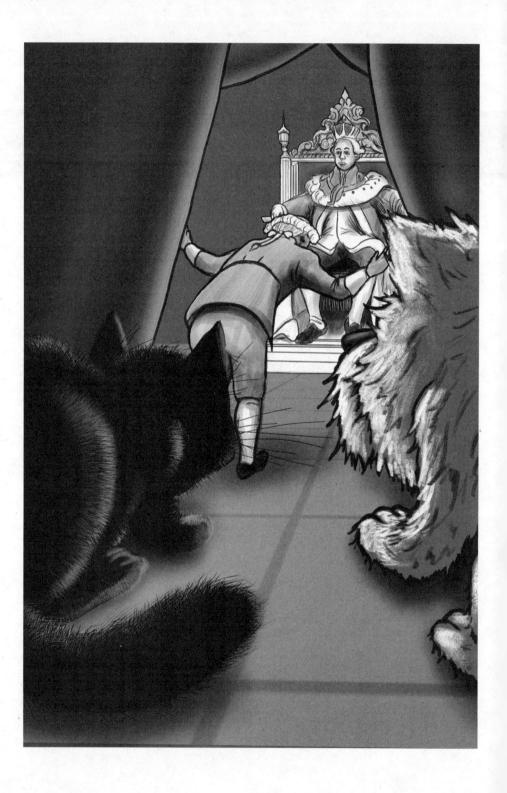

63

EVIL BELOW
AND SPIES ABOVE

CIMETIÈRE DES INNOCENTS, PARIS, FRANCE,
DECEMBER 21, 1776

L iz grimaced and held her paw up to her nose. "I am glad we did not begin our search here, *mon amie*. The stench is terrible! I cannot believe the humans operate *Les Halles* market right next to this cemetery! No wonder this street is called *Rue D'Enfer!*"

"Aye, remember how I told our team aboot the recent collapse that happened here at 'Hell Street' right at the cemetery?" Kate answered before sneezing from the smell, and shaking her head. "It's been comin' for a long time. When the Romans were here in the first century, they discovered limestone in the soil of the left bank of the Seine River. It were perfect for buildin' walls, so they dug lots of quarries outside the city. But come the twelfth century, the humans started diggin' underground quarries so they could still use the surface above ta grow the city. Over the centuries, the quarries were abandoned while the humans continued buildin' houses, streets, an' all sorts of buildings on top, includin' this old, over-used cemetery."

"Ah, *oui*, so the collapse into those quarries below ground was inevitable," Liz surmised, understanding. She looked at the crumbling wall surrounding the cemetery. "Just how many humans have been buried here?"

"Aboot two million," Kate answered with a frown. "It started out bein' a private place for humans ta lay their loved ones ta rest, but with the famines an' plagues that hit Paris, they started diggin' mass graves ta bury thousands of poor souls. Plus, they buried the homeless paupers with no place ta go, but they ran out of space. They've put some of the centuries-old bones in the walls ta make more room, but the humans never use enough dirt. I've heard it said that the smell has poisoned the air so badly that it turns milk sour!"

"This is a *grave* situation in more ways than one, no?" Liz answered with wide eyes, shaking her head. *"C'est tragique!* I can think of no better place for Charlatan and his evil minions to feel at home than below a place of so much death. Poisoned air makes me especially think of Kakia. She must love it here." The petite cat shuddered, bristling her fur. "So, what are the humans doing about this terrible situation—both the collapses of the ground, and this overused cemetery?"

"King Louis has first ordered the mapping of all the tunnels an' caves beneath Paris before they decide wha' ta do," Kate answered. "If the humans are smart, they'll do like the Romans did in Rome an' turn those tunnels inta catacombs ta bury the poor humans."

"*Oui,* hopefully the humans will come to this logical conclusion, and get rid of this terrible place," Liz agreed, walking to look for a tunnel entrance. "Well, I am eager to get away from here, so let us be going. Since we do not yet have the humans' tunnel map, we shall have to continue our search for Charlatan's secret headquarters on our own."

"Aye, I had hoped we could find it elsewhere, but this smelly place should have been where we started," Kate lamented, following Liz. "I were dreadin' wha' we might find."

"*Je comprends,*" Liz agreed. "It took me a long time on the Ark to approach Charlatan's dark, smelly stall. I also did not want to face what could be there where he was."

Soon they came upon a small opening and made their way down into the darkened, damp tunnel. The pair allowed their eyes to adjust and then walked along some rubble scattered about. Their voices echoed off the walls.

"We should talk quietly, in case we encounter the enemy, no?" Liz suggested in a whisper.

"Aye," Kate whispered back.

They proceeded down one tunnel, then turned when they came to a fork, which led to another fork, and another turn. It was a never-ending maze of nothing but dark, smelly tunnels. After what seemed like hours, Kate's paw walked across something crinkly, and she stopped. "Liz! I found somethin'! Ye can see better than me in the dark. Wha' do you think it is?"

Liz picked up what appeared to be a strip of printed paper.

solved; and that as FREE AND INDEPENDENT STATES, they have full Power to levy War, conclude Peace, contract Alliances, establish Commerce, and to do all other Acts and Things which INDEPENDENT STATES may of Right do. And for the Support of this Declaration, with a firm Reliance on the Protection of divine Providence, we mutually pledge to each other our Lives, our Fortunes, and our sacred Honor.

Signed by ORDER and in BEHALF of the CONGRESS,

JOHN HANCOCK, PRESIDENT.

ATTEST.
CHARLES THOMSON, SECRETARY.

PHILADELPHIA: PRINTED BY JOHN DUNLAP.

She squinted and read, "Reliance on the Protection of divine Providence." Liz quickly looked at Kate in alarm. "Kate! This is the Declaration of Independence! It was torn from one of the Dunlap broadsides that Congress first had printed to distribute throughout the colonies."

"Isn't that wha' Congress sent over ta Deane here in France?" Kate asked.

"*Oui,* but the ship carrying it never arrived," Liz answered pensively.

Kate sat down. "Why would this be down here?"

Liz's tail curled up and down as her mind raced. She looked up at Kate. "What if the ship disappeared at sea because it was *sabotaged* to prevent Silas Deane from receiving the good news and instructions from Congress?"

"An' who else would have wanted that other than Charlatan hisself?" Kate added, looking around. "He would've kept the Declaration as a trophy."

"But he tore it into pieces like Dr. Franklin's dismembered snake!" Liz suggested. "If this is true, then your hunch about Charlatan's evil headquarters being below Paris was correct! He has always sought to be near places where the Maker helps humans in crucial points of history."

"Aye, an' with France helpin' America, he'd want ta stop everything from happenin' here in Paris," Kate agreed. Her nose twitched as a fresh wave of stench washed over them. "Do ye smell that?"

A trickle of dirt started falling on their heads from above. They looked up and suddenly felt a rumble as cascading rocks and debris crashed down around them.

"Watch out!" Kate shouted before grabbing Liz by the scruff of her neck only seconds before a large boulder barreled into where they had just been standing. More debris fell as a section of the tunnel collapsed, sending a shower of pebbles and dirt over them. They clung to each other until everything stopped. The air filled with dirt and dust, causing them to cough and gasp for breath.

"*Merci, mon amie,*" Liz coughed and shared, "we could have been pinned under that rubble!"

Kate nodded her head and coughed. "It looks like the tunnel be completely blocked now. Look."

Liz looked to see that the passageway they had walked on was now blocked by boulders and debris in both directions. Suddenly they heard muffled sounds from a loud crowd echoing above ground. "Listen!" She looked up and could barely make out a tiny stream of light. "I believe we can make our way out up there."

Kate nodded. "Aye, always follow the light! Follow me, lass!" The Westie climbed up the pile of rubble, and as they reached the top, she used her paws to shove rocks out of the way. She pushed with her nose until she could sniff the fresh air above. "Almost there!" The little dog continued pushing and digging until finally her head popped out into a gravelly courtyard. "Grab me tail, Liz!"

"I have it!" Liz shouted back, hanging on tightly as Kate pulled them both out of the tunnel. Together they fell onto the ground, panting. A cloud of dust swirled around them from the dirt that was caked to their fur. They coughed and shook from tip to tail. Liz looked at Kate, who was anything but white now. "Bravo, Kate! You saved us! But you look more like a grey Westie."

Kate grinned as she panted, her tongue hanging out. "An' ye look more like a grey tabby cat!"

"Well, at least we are safe now," Liz replied, wiping the dirt off her face. "We must have reached another overbuilt area of Paris that caused another collapse."

"Clarie said she'd help us look for Charlatan's headquarters," Kate offered. "It may be best ta have her with us next time we search, in case we can't get out."

"Agreed, *mon amie,*" Liz replied, nodding. "We must report what we found to Gillamon in the War Room." She looked up at the sky and listened to cheering coming from a distant street. "I wonder where we are. And what is all this noise?"

They saw a crowd lining the street beyond the courtyard and made their way to stand at the feet of the humans. People lined both sides of the street and held little paper kites on sticks, waving them in the air.

"*Peux-tu le voir?*" a man asked another man next to him.

"*C'est ça, oui!*" the other man replied, pointing to an approaching carriage, jumping up and down excitedly.

"Wha' are they sayin'?" Kate asked Liz over the roar of the crowd. "An' why are they wavin' kites?"

"One man asked the other if he could see a man, and the other pointed to a carriage and said, "Yes, here he comes," Liz translated. She snaked her way through the forest of legs and peeped her head out to see exactly who they were watching for. She smiled and looked back at Kate. "It is none other than Benjamin Franklin! He has finally arrived in Paris! I see Silas Deane with him, as well as Franklin's grandsons."

"*Docteur* Franklin! *Docteur* Franklin!" shouted the crowds as the carriage drew close. Liz jumped up onto a stone horse mounting block to get a better look. She could see behind the glass window of the carriage the unmistakable grinning, round face of Benjamin Franklin, spectacles on his nose, and fur cap perched on top of his head. He held a hand in the air and waved at the crowds as he passed by. "*Bienvenue, Monsieur* Franklin!" Liz cheered along with the crowd.

Kate hopped up next to Liz, wagged her tail, and barked her welcome to the famous American inventor and statesman. "Look how the Frenchies love him! He's a celebrity, all from Mousie's kite idea!"

But from behind them in the courtyard, a dark figure made its way through the crowd. ⚜

HÔTEL D'ENTRAQUES, PARIS, FRANCE, DECEMBER 22, 1776

"My dear Dr. Bancroft!" Benjamin Franklin exclaimed, vigorously shaking the hand of his long-time friend and protégé. "I am delighted to see you! I bring the gratitude of the Congress for your assistance thus far to our American delegation."

"Welcome to France, Dr. Franklin!" Bancroft answered with a hearty grin, removing his hat. "It has been my honor, sir, and I look forward to further assisting you and Mr. Deane."

"And *me*, Bancroft," came the sulky voice of Arthur Lee. "I am also part of the three-man delegation appointed by Congress to negotiate an alliance with France. I just arrived from London this morning."

"Lee is Thomas Jefferson's *replacement*," Benjamin Franklin interjected with a look of regret. "Mr. Jefferson declined the appointment due to his wife's ill health."

Bancroft turned to see Lee and shook his hand. "Good day, Mr. Lee. I arrived yesterday myself, but with the tumult in Paris with Dr. Franklin's arrival, I waited to make my way here today. I am at your service," he said, bowing before the men, "all three of you."

"The three commissioners are technically equal in rank, and two must agree before any official action is taken," Liz explained. "But due to Dr. Franklin's age, experience, and working knowledge of the French language, he will naturally be the head of this American delegation, and *Monsieur* Deane will slide into second place," Liz noted. "Franklin and Deane get along brilliantly, but I am afraid that cranky Lee will always be the odd man out. There is some distrust of him, as Lee has friends on both sides of this conflict at the same time, depending on what the politics of London are at the time."

"Not ta mention that Lee has already angered Vergennes with his rude letters, *tellin'*—not askin'—the French how ta handle the American cause," Kate added. "Aye, this won't be a strong cord of three Americans, I can tell ye that."

Silas Deane stepped forward. "It has been a hectic couple of days. When I heard Dr. Franklin had arrived at Versailles, I went to meet him to escort him to Paris." He turned to Benjamin. "I hope this second-floor apartment will be suitable for you and the boys. I am on the first floor of this hotel." Turning to Bancroft, "You can lodge with me, Bancroft. Your assistance will become even more valuable now with the entire delegation here." He noticed a canvas bag by Bancroft's feet. "What do you have there?"

"Thank you, Mr. Deane," Bancroft answered. He hefted the canvas bag with a grin and gave it to Benjamin. "Dr. Franklin's admiring public not only lines the streets of Paris with paper kites but also sends their written regards. This bag was at the front desk when I arrived, and I am certain more will follow."

Benjamin shook his head with a grin. "My plethora of printed words have come back to me in abundance."

"Not only do Parisians love and quote your words from *Poor Richard's Almanack,* but the ladies have also taken to styling their hair 'coiffure à la Franklin' after your marten-pelt fur cap," Arthur Lee noted, holding his hand above his head.

"But the Franklin madness goes beyond that," Deane followed with a chuckle, his hands in the air. "I must warn you that you shall meet your face coming and going, wherever you step foot, Dr. Franklin. I've heard that the French have put your likeness on everything from ladies' gloves to engravings for display on mantels, snuff boxes, countless prints, and—dare I say it—chamber pots!"

"As long as their aim is true, I will be honored," the seventy-year-old Pennsylvanian drolly replied, laughing. "They think I am a Quaker by my homespun dress, which of course I am not. But Quakers are fashionable in France and are admired for their gentle, honest, humble disposition. So, I shall humor them and play the part of a New World philosopher in my rugged, simple, linen clothes." He winked at the men. "What better way to stand out among the powdered heads of Paris?"

Kate and Liz sat invisibly in the parlor as the four men wasted no time getting one another up to speed on everything that had happened or was coming on both sides of the Atlantic.

"Dr. Franklin is as brilliant in painting himself as the naïve image of the New World as he is in his cunning diplomacy," Liz noted with a grin. "It shall be fun to watch him charm every Parisian in the salons all the way to the court of Versailles."

Kate wagged her tail. "How grand ta have the entire team finally together here in Paris! I'm glad Dr. Bancroft is back ta help them get ready ta meet with Comte Vergennes. From the looks of it, he'll be busy jest helpin' with Dr. Franklin's fan mail!"

"*Oui,* but I imagine it will take several days before they have their ducks in a row to present to Vergennes the proposal for a Treaty of Unity and Commerce from Congress," Liz agreed.

"Now I must warn you, Dr. Franklin, that mixed in with your admirers shall no doubt be spies watching your every move," Deane warned him. "Dr.

Bancroft here wrote to me about some Americans in Paris who are actually British spies. If you would, sir, please relay to these gentlemen what you shared with me."

Bancroft sat forward, collecting his thoughts. "Indeed. One spy is an American gentleman by the name of Hugh Williamson, who arrived in Paris in September. He's been sending letters back to London reporting about Deane's activities in France and even warning Whitehall about me as a close associate of Mr. Deane! Another is Colonel George Mercer, who is a former lieutenant governor of North Carolina. He fled to London yet declared that he was a staunch supporter of the American cause. But the British ministers sent Mercer to Paris to meet with Lord Stormont and collect information on Deane. I implore you all to *please* be on your guard, as you will be assailed by every shape and form of deception."

Arthur Lee piped up. "I have no doubt these hotel walls will grow ears, and every keyhole will grow eyes."

Franklin leaned back on the silk-upholstered couch, sinking into its comforting form, unconcerned by what he heard. "I have long observed one rule which prevents any inconveniences from such practices. It is simply this: to be concerned in no affairs I should blush to have made public, and to do nothing but what spies may see and welcome." He looked around at the men, locking eyes with each of them. "When a man's actions are just and honorable, the more they are known, the more his reputation is increased and established." He then chuckled. "If I was sure, therefore, that my valet was a spy, as he probably is, I think I should probably not discharge him for that, if in other respects I liked him."

Liz and Kate shared shocked looks, as did Deane, Lee, and Bancroft.

"I'm surprised that Dr. Franklin would have such naïve thoughts aboot spies!" Kate whispered. "Charlatan may be below Paris, but Stormont's spies be everywhere above."

"Unless our good doctor is thinking countless moves ahead of everyone in a strategic game of chess." Liz studied the astute Franklin, who wasn't naïve about anything. "But I believe more remote headquarters for this American delegation would be better than a Paris hotel. A house perhaps, between Paris and Versailles where Stormont's spies would be less plentiful."

"Good idea, Liz," Kate agreed. "Passy might be a good choice. It's a charmin' little village, an' Deane wants ta introduce Dr. Franklin ta *Monsieur* Chaumont, who's been supplyin' most of the war supplies for America. He has a grand estate in Passy with lots of room."

"*Bon.* But meanwhile we must also keep our eyes out for spies, including that 'Mr. Edwards,' whose letter we discovered while in Stormont's office," Liz suggested. "He's the one spy who has me worried more than all the others, for he is with the British high command."

"We lassies sure do have lots of seekin' ta do for this mission—spies, evil headquarters, secret plots," Kate noted. "An' now we need ta find Lafayette a ship."

"We should go to the War Room and leave an update for Gillamon," Liz answered. "There we can research the ideal port for Lafayette's ship, no? We need to find a Bible."

Kate picked up her invisible pouch. "Let's be goin' then."

"Where to?" Liz asked.

"Ta Notre Dame," Kate answered. "Let's go seek wee Jesus in their nativity scene. It will remind us aboot the spies an' plots we dealt with against him in Bethlehem, an' how he escaped every one of them. Then we'll use one of their Bibles ta transport ta the War Room."

"*C'est très bien, chère amie!*" Liz enthused. "*Oui,* and like the wise men, wise *lassies* still seek him."

64

LA VICTOIRE

NOTRE DAME CATHÉDRAL, PARIS, FRANCE,
DECEMBER 22, 1776

L iz and Kate gazed up in awe at the soaring ceilings of the magnificent French cathedral designed in the shape of a Latin cross. A rainbow of color washed over them from the large, stained-glass rose window as they walked stealthily between rows of empty pews. Exquisite draperies and tapestries depicting the Christmas story hung from the nave and the choir loft. A group of robed singers stood with opened music folders while they followed the upraised hand of the choir director. Their harmonious voices filled the cathedral with beautiful music.

"'Our Lady of Paris' is so very lovely, no?" Liz said to Kate, not bothering to whisper. "It never ceases to amaze me how the humans built this beautiful cathedral more than six hundred years ago."

"Aye, she's a bonnie church, especially at Christmastide," Kate said, admiring the stunning architecture. "I think I see wee baby Jesus on the altar then."

Liz looked over to see a small figure of baby Jesus lying in an ornately carved bed draped in purple fabric, his tiny arms raised in the air, and an angelic look on his face. He was surrounded by countless candles. Not far from him sitting on a pedestal was a Bible opened to the Gospel of Luke. "While I appreciate how humans pay honor to Jesus with such beautiful depictions of art, they simply do not portray the scene as it really was in that cave on the hillside above Bethlehem. Ah, but Jesus was so beautiful and the light that surrounded him was divine!"

"Aye, I'll never forget that night. Jesus' wee hand touched sweet Clarie's face, healin' her blemish, an' makin' her feel worthy," Kate remembered, her eyes brimming with happy tears. "But these humans weren't there ta see him like we were, lass." Suddenly the music reached a crescendo. "The organist an' the choir will be all warmed up for tonight's Christmas festival. The music durin' this week be the prettiest all year."

"If only Nigel were here to enjoy this with us. He would love it," Liz imagined with a smile. "Before we transport to the War Room, I would very much like to see the organ up close as well as watch *Monsieur* Couperin play. Nigel indicated that he is an exceptional organist as well as composer."

"Mousie's our music expert, but if he were here, we'd never get ta the War Room as he wouldn't want ta leave!" Kate pointed out with a chuckle. "Come on then, ta the organ loft."

Soon Kate and Liz stood behind the organist. His hands sailed across the keys while his feet danced along the foot pedals, filling the mammoth pipes with rich, deep tones. He seemed lost in the ecstasy of the music that rose and filled the cathedral. Liz studied the organist for a moment and then noticed some sheet music lying behind him on the floor, spilled out from a folder that had slipped off the bench where he sat. Curious, she crept out of the bag to see a booklet of music.

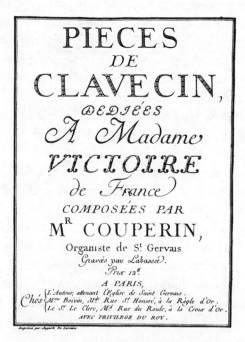

"*Monsieur* Couperin composed and dedicated several harpsichord pieces to King Louis's aunt, *Madame* Victoire," Liz noted. "Didn't you tell me that Beaumarchais taught her to play the harpsichord?"

"Aye, that he did." Kate peered at the booklet of music with her. "I've always thought she had an interestin' name, Victoire."

"*Oui,* it obviously means 'victory' but what an odd name for a human," Liz replied. "Of course, it was a perfect name for the statue we saw on our mission with Paul in Samothrace. I adored that statue, even though it was of the pagan goddess Nike."

"Didn't Gillamon tell ye that ye'd see that statue someday here in France?" Kate asked.

"*Oui,* and that remains a mystery," Liz answered. "I just do not understand why and how a statue overlooking the Aegean Sea in Greece would come to France."

"Well, the Libertas statue sailed from Israel ta Rome ta France," Kate reminded her. "An' now she's sittin' in Lafayette's garden in Versailles."

"*Oui,* and Gillamon said she would take on new meaning, from something pagan to something good, which I am now beginning to see," Liz agreed.

"Aye, Lafayette loves that Libertas statue as a symbol of freedom, not as a goddess," Kate reminded her. "As far as the Winged Victory statue in Greece comin' ta France, time will tell. It always do."

"You are right, *mon amie,*" Liz agreed with a smile, opening the booklet. She raised her eyebrows. "Speaking of which, Couperin's first piece is entitled 'La Victoire.'" She gazed at the name of the composer and placed her paw on the music. "And look, Kate! His full name is Armand-Louis Couperin. I do not think I have met an Armand since our Roman centurion Armandus."

"How grand! No wonder he be such a talented human, with a name like Armand," Kate enthused happily. "Ye've always been the expert with names, Liz. Since we're going to help Lafayette find a ship, how important do ye think the name of the ship will be?"

"The name will be *très important, mon amie!* Names mean things, and humans have named ships since ancient times. It serves not only as the identity of the vessel, but can relay the ship's purpose as well," Liz explained.

"I've heard sailors can be very superstitious an' think havin' a female on board brings bad luck," Kate suggested with a frown.

"But strangely enough, they believe that giving a ship a *female* name brings them *good* luck, fortune, and protection for the vessel, crew, and passengers," Liz explained. "Humans even give ships 'godmothers' to christen and watch over the vessel. They have ceremonies to reveal the ship's name followed by the godmother breaking a bottle of champagne on the bow of the ship before its maiden voyage."

"So how do the humans pick names then?" Kate wanted to know.

"Well, many ships in ancient times were named after goddesses and other mythical figures, but mariners today sometimes name their vessels after women they hold dear," Liz answered. "But not all ships are named for women; some are named for the overall purpose of the vessel and its mission. Some ships are renamed as they change owners."

"Well, when we find a ship for Lafayette, she'll need a good name." Kate looked at the sheet music. "*La Victoire* has a nice ring to it, don't ye think?"

Liz's eyes brightened at the suggestion. *"Oui!* Kate, what a marvelous idea! Not only is *Victoire* the name of a *woman,* but it is also perfect for what Lafayette seeks, no?"

Liz and Kate looked at one another and exclaimed, "Victory!"

Suddenly the organist hit the final notes of the musical piece and lifted his hands from the keyboard. He raised his hands high over his head to stretch and then wiggled his fingers before placing another piece of music on the stand to begin playing again.

"We best get goin' now, Liz. Get back in the pouch an' I'll take us ta the Bible down below," Kate suggested. "Get yer quill ready."

"As you say, *madame,*" Liz answered as she climbed into the pouch. "I shall dip my quill into the travel vial of milk."

Kate stealthily made her way back to the front of the church and the altar where baby Jesus lay in his beautiful manger and jumped up onto the pedestal. Liz then carefully turned the pages from Luke 2 back to Genesis 3, hoping the humans wouldn't notice the pages flipping on their own. *"Joyeux Noël,"* Liz whispered as she blew a kiss to baby Jesus before writing a 'w' on the page. In a flash, they left Notre Dame.

THE WAR ROOM

"Looks like ye got Christmas flowers from Al," Kate observed with a smile as she and Liz opened their eyes. Sitting there on the table was a branch of mistletoe and a scribbled note:

Dear Liz,

I thought o' ye when I were hidin' in a tree next to this mistletoe when Banastre Tarleton brought General Charles Lee to headquarters. But don't worry. Mousie said Lee's been schemin' to take Washington's place as Commander-in-Chief, so he won't be a problem for a while then. At least that dragon lad didn't do as he said in the chocolate house in London when he threatened to take off Lee's head with his sword. I guess he were happy enough to make the general a prisoner and get his horse drunk. Archer accidently got drunk, too, when he drank from the same trough. It weren't a pretty sight, I can tell ye that! Anyway, I sure wish I could kiss ye under this mistletoe. Don't eat the berries, though. Me tummy don't feel so good. Happy Christmas, me bonnie lass.

Love,

Al

Liz giggled. "My poor Albert! He did not know that *phoradendron leucarpum* causes stomach upset but is also poisonous."

"Then why do the humans hang it up an' kiss under it?" Kate asked.

"It is one of their strange traditions, but I find it rather lovely, no?" Liz answered, touching the mistletoe fondly. "But these are startling developments about General Lee's capture!"

"Aye, but like Gillamon told us before, no weapon forged against Washington will prosper," Kate reminded her. "Amazin' how the Maker allowed the enemy ta help Washington with that scheme against him! Jest like de Broglie's scheme will help Lafayette, although we don't understand it yet."

"*Oui,* what man intended for evil, the Maker intends for good," Liz marveled. "But ooh-la-la, that Archer gets more 'shpechial' with every news report."

Kate shook her head. "The poor dears! That Banastre Tarleton be a bad lad!"

"Well, let us be about our business," Liz suggested, taking out a fresh piece of paper. "I shall leave Gillamon a report of our findings in the tunnels below Paris, of Dr. Franklin's arrival, and of our next steps to assist Lafayette. Why don't you look over the map for the best possible port for Lafayette's ship?"

Kate walked over to the map of France and studied all the port cities. "Well, we know that Le Havre be crawlin' with Stormont's spies, an' it's close ta Paris, so I'd cross that one off the list right away." She scanned the map with her paw. "Marseilles, no. Too far ta reach the Atlantic. Nantes, maybe. Hmmm, Bordeaux. There be lots of ship builders an' sellers there. An' when Gillamon sent me ta Bordeaux ta meet Silas Deane, he showed me a bonnie lass he said would someday help Lafayette. She's an innkeeper's daughter named Madeleine."

"So she lives in Bordeaux?" Liz asked, finishing up her report.

"No, she were jest there for the day," Kate answered. "She's from St. Jean du Luz, near the border of France an' Spain."

Liz came over to study the map with Kate, tracing her paw down the southern border of France. "Well, it is only logical that if she is to help Lafayette, she would do so from this region, no? And Bordeaux is a long way from Paris, so this would be a safer place for Lafayette to leave France, far from the eyes of Stormont's spies, Versailles, and the reach of the king."

"An' Lafayette's *father-in-law,*" Kate added.

"*Bon,* then I say we search in Bordeaux for *La Victoire,*" Liz suggested. "This is rather exciting. I have never been ship-shopping before!"

Kate wagged her tail. "I want ta make sure she's the perfect bonnie lass of a vessel ta take me marquis across the ocean."

"And to take *you* as well, *mon amie,*" Liz told her. "You will of course accompany Lafayette to America, no? You will make the perfect godmother for *La Victoire.*"

"Ye mean *dog*-mother," Kate answered with a chuckle. "I'll be happy ta sail an' watch over Lafayette an' the ship. Jest think, when Lafayette joins Washington, I'll be reunited with Max an' Jock!"

"That will be a happy day!" Liz answered. "Before we search for the ship in Bordeaux, let us first see what is happening with Lafayette, De Kalb, and de Broglie."

Kate nodded. "De Broglie hasn't replied ta Lafayette's letter for advice an' instructions, but De Kalb an' his men are headin' ta Ruffec ta figure out wha' ta do now that their voyage was cancelled."

"*Bon,* then let us go to Ruffec," Liz suggested, walking over to the globe. She winked at Kate. "And then we shall show them what to do, no?"

CHÂTEAU DE RUFFEC, FRANCE, DECEMBER 23, 1776

"The plan to sail to America *must* proceed," de Broglie insisted, pacing in front of the large fireplace. "We have worked too hard to lose these hand-picked men. What a fool Beaumarchais was to ruin everything with his play in Le Havre, *pfft! C'est ridicule!*"

De Kalb leaned back in his chair and let go a breath of frustration. "*Ja.* I hope that Deane can secure a ship before all the officers who vere supposed to sail vith me scatter all over France."

Duboismartin, de Broglie's secretary nodded. "Well, I do know that Lafayette will not abandon this venture to go to America while we wait. I have never seen such a determined young man. He still awaits an answer from you, *Monsieur le Comte.*"

"*Oui,* Lafayette's mind is made up, but I do not plan to answer him until we know what we will do," de Broglie answered. "Johann, I understand *Docteur* Franklin has arrived in France. I want you to ask Deane to share our plan with him."

Liz and Kate looked at one another. "Dr. Franklin will never agree to de Broglie's scheme!" Liz whispered to Kate.

"Deane would be a fool ta share it with him!" Kate agreed. "I wonder why it doesn't dawn on these three men that Lafayette can buy a ship?"

"Your younger brother also vill not abandon this venture, *ja?*" De Kalb said to Duboismartin. "He vas supposed to have gone vith me as a major and aide-de-camp. Vonce ve got to America, I planned to send him back here with news if I was able to secure from Congress de Broglie's appointment to replace Vashington."

Liz thought a moment. "None of these men are sailors, but *petit* Duboismartin *is*. He spent eleven years as a sailor before entering the army. He knows about ships and would be the perfect human to make the purchase for Lafayette." She turned to Kate. "I will write an anonymous note to Lieutenant Duboismartin."

"Wha' will ye write?" Kate asked.

"Oh, something to the effect of how Deane will be unable to buy a ship, but how eager and wealthy Lafayette is," Liz answered with a coy grin. "I have a feeling he will not need much of a nudge to cooperate."

"Aye! For now let's go celebrate Christmas with Lafayette," Kate suggested with a wink. "Then we'll make sure Dr. Franklin's first meetin' goes well with Vergennes, an' *then* we'll go ship-shoppin."

Liz let go a sigh. "Starting with the first Christmas, this has always been the most hectic time of the year, no?"

A Newsworthy Diversion

BORDEAUX, FRANCE, JANUARY 5, 1777

A stiff breeze lifted Kate's fur as she looked out at the ships moored in the harbor. "Well, it's a new year, but so far we haven't found a new ship for Lafayette," she lamented. "We've looked at every ship in dry dock as well as in the harbor. They're either too big, too small, or too old. Maybe *La Victoire's* not here in Bordeaux after all."

Liz jumped up on the seawall next to her friend. "Do not lose heart, *mon amie!* It may be that she is just not here *now.* "

"Wha' do ye mean, Liz?" Kate asked. "Have ye found somethin'?"

"Oui, while you walked around the last ship here, I researched listings of ships for sale that are currently at sea but expected back in Bordeaux soon. The description of one merchant ship caught my eye," Liz began, growing more excited with every word. "She was built in 1771, has three masts, weighs two hundred-twenty tons, is seventy-three feet long, twenty-five feet wide, and has two cannons. She is on her way back from her *fifth* ocean voyage. So, she is the *perfect* size, the *perfect* age, and she is *perfectly* seasoned with an experienced captain and crew!"

"Mousie would say 'She takes the biscuit!'" Kate's eyes brightened with expectancy. "She sounds perfect, lass!"

"Plus, one of the finest shipping firms in Bordeaux has their eye on her, and they are sympathetic to the American cause!" Liz added. *"Monsieur* Pierre Reculès heads up Reculès de Basmarein et Raimbaux and is already outfitting two other ships with armaments to send to America—*La Duchesse de Mortemart* and *Le Meulan. C'est magnifique!"*

"Wha' could be more perfect than the *right* ship operated by the *right* firm that has the *right* heart toward the Americans?" Kate cheered, wagging her tail. "So wha's the name of this ship?"

"She was first christened *La Comtesse de Richemond* by a *Monsieur* Pierre Rivière, but when *Monsieur* Labat de Serène bought her, he renamed her *La*

Bonne Mère," said an enthused Liz, placing her paw on Kate's arm. "Her name means 'the good mother!' What could be more perfect for you as her 'furry dog-mother'?"

"Oh, Liz, I think ye've found our perfect, bonnie lass! When will she return ta Bordeaux?" Kate asked happily.

"She is sailing back from Santo Domingo and should arrive early next month," Liz answered. "This will give us plenty of time to get the humans organized. *Petit* Duboismartin should be sufficiently impatient with the delays of de Broglie's plan and ready to set things in motion."

"We'll have ta find the perfect way ta inspire Lafayette for her new name," Kate pondered, jumping off the seawall. "Let's get back ta Lafayette then. I know he won't understand a word I say, but I jest have ta tell him all aboot *La Victoire!*"

CHÂTEAU DE RUFFEC, FRANCE, JANUARY 20, 1777

Snow began to fall as the elder Duboismartin walked beside the frozen pond with his younger brother, Lieutenant Duboismartin, also known as *petit* Duboismartin, who had come to visit him here in the French countryside, away from the noise of Paris.

"Monsieur Deane has done *nothing* for a month, other than continually receive more French officers who wish to go to America," the young lieutenant scoffed, irritated.

"Oui, but he hasn't been able to secure a ship to send those officers to America, so they are not going anywhere," Duboismartin offered. "Nor has he yet found a ship to send you with de Broglie's men. I know you are impatient to rejoin your regiment in Santo Domingo now that it seems as if things might not go through with our plan, but I implore you to wait. This venture to America with Comte de Broglie's men could be the opportunity of a lifetime for you."

Petit Duboismartin blew out an exasperated, icy breath, watching it rise into the air. *"Mon frère,* having sailed for over a decade, I can tell you that there is *always* a way to find a ship for transport. If I had the money, I would buy one myself!" He stopped and picked up a rock to throw into the pond, trying to break the ice. "If *Monsieur* Deane cannot secure a ship, why not ask the Marquis de Lafayette to purchase one for us? I understand he is the most eager of us to go, even though he knows nothing of de Broglie's plot. Isn't he the wealthiest young man in France?"

Duboismartin stopped in his tracks and looked at his little brother, the snowfall now covering their woolen capes. His eyes grew wide with under-standing, and a grin appeared on his face. "*C'est ça!* That is exactly what we should do, *petit frère!*" He thought for a moment. "Tell me, when you recently arrived in Bordeaux from the West Indies, hadn't your commander specif-ically instructed you to purchase supplies for your regiment back in Santo Domingo?"

"*Oui,* I already have made connections with some of the shipping firms and suppliers in Bordeaux," *Petit* Duboismartin replied.

"*Therefore,* you would not fall under the suspicion of British spies if you were to purchase an additional transport ship and supplies as part of your standing orders," the elder brother suggested, growing more excited. "*Bon,* I want you to write out a plan of how you will buy this ship, and I will take it immediately to Lafayette. Then I will bring him to meet with us at your hotel in Paris."

The younger brother grew a wide smile. "*Finalement,* we have a solution. *C'est simple, no?*"

"*Oui, c'est simple,*" Liz echoed, leaving footprints in the snow next to Kate. "Lafayette will of course agree to this plan, and Lieutenant Duboismartin will soon head to Bordeaux. He is even more perfect for this task than I realized, after hearing this conversation! He may already have met Reculès, so now I shall provide him with specific information about *La Bonne Mère* ahead of his arrival there."

"We must make sure that no one finds out aboot this plan for Lafayette ta buy a ship, especially the Duc d'Ayen," Kate cautioned.

Liz nodded. "*Oui,* he forbids Lafayette to sail to America on any ship, much less on one the young marquis would purchase himself, no?"

"Aye, so we may need ta split up, lass," Kate suggested. "I best stay with Lafayette while you go ta Bordeaux ta make sure young Duboismartin picks our *La Victoire.*"

Liz stopped and thought. "Knowing Lafayette, he will be so excited about this plan that he will wish to meet continually with Deane and De Kalb. It will not take long for his family to grow suspicious, not to mention the Paris police who will no doubt notice his movements."

"We need a diversion for the lad," Kate said. "A short trip while he waits."

"Somewhere that would be the least obvious place for a French officer to go who is planning to escape France, sail to America, and fight against King George III," Liz agreed. A mischievous grin grew on her face. "London, perhaps?"

Kate grinned. "An' I think I know how ta get him there."

CHÂTEAU DE NOAILLES, FRANCE, JANUARY 23, 1776

Lafayette hummed to himself as he hurriedly got dressed, smiling as he tied the cravat under his chin while gazing into the mirror. He slipped on his boots, put on his heavy woolen cloak, and positioned his wig before donning his three-cornered hat.

"I don't think he slept a wink last night," Kate whispered to Liz.

Liz yawned. "I do not blame him, after last night's meeting. I cannot wait for him to tell Deane the good news."

Soon they followed Lafayette to the waiting carriage and hopped onto the back as the coachman snapped the reins, steering the horses toward Paris. Before long they were in front of the American headquarters at *Hôtel d'Hambourg* on *Rue Jacob*. As Lafayette exited the carriage to go inside, one of Stormont's informers took a small book from his pocket and made a notation.

"Bonjour, Messieurs!" Lafayette heartily greeted Silas Deane and his aide, William Carmichael.

Thirty-seven-year-old Carmichael was from Maryland and had been living in London when Arthur Lee sent him to America with papers for the Congress. But instead of heading west, he traveled to Paris and befriended Silas Deane. Deane and Franklin sent him on frequent errands to port cities to check on shipments, or to carry dispatches to ship captains. He also spoke French, which was invaluable for Deane as he continued to struggle with the language.

"Bonjour, Monsieur le Marquis," Carmichael responded, taking the role of interpreter for Deane.

Lafayette looked around, removing his hat and cloak. "Is *Docteur* Bancroft present?"

"No, he has returned to London, as his family is still there," Deane explained. "We hope for him to move his family and join us in Paris soon, which will be a tremendous help with our workload now that Dr. Franklin is here. We will all relocate soon to new headquarters in Passy, which will be a much better location for us all to meet."

"Très bien," Lafayette answered. "Well, I shall get right down to why I have come. Last evening, I met with *Les Messieurs* Duboismartin, and we have come up with a plan." The young Frenchman's eyes danced with excitement as he looked from Carmichael to Deane. "Up to now, sir, you have witnessed only my zeal. But now I am going to turn it to some account. I am buying a boat to transport your officers. Let us not give up our hope yet; it

is precisely in time of danger that I want to share whatever fortune may have in store for you."

Deane lifted his eyebrows as Carmichael translated. "I must say, *monsieur,* that I am very impressed! This is good news indeed. When do you expect to have this vessel?"

"*Petit* Duboismartin departed for Bordeaux last evening and informed me that he will send word once he has found the right ship," Lafayette explained.

Liz winked at Kate and whispered. "She has already been found, no?"

"Excellent!" Deane answered, clapping his hands once in an enthused cheer.

"I do not believe it will take him long to make the necessary arrangements," Lafayette continued. "Therefore, we can begin to discuss plans with General De Kalb and the other officers who shall depart with us."

"I will make arrangements to meet with De Kalb as soon as possible," Carmichael assured him.

"In the meantime, might I suggest that you and Carmichael communicate with one another away from this hotel so as not to arouse the attention of the French authorities?" Deane offered. "Carmichael will keep me in the loop on developments."

"*Oui, je comprends,*" Lafayette answered. "*Monsieur* Carmichael, I can pick you up in my carriage to simply ride while we discuss our plans."

"*Très bien,*" Carmichael agreed. "It will be very important to keep this plan quiet."

Lafayette rose to his feet. "*Bon,* I will not stay. I have another appointment with an artisan in Paris. I have decided to make some changes to the Lafayette family crest before I sail to America. I shall add a motto that has served me of late against all who would stop me in my quest."

"Oh? And what might that be?" Deane asked as he and Carmichael stood.

An exuberant Lafayette smiled and answered, "Cur non?"

As the men bid one another farewell, Kate quietly slipped from her pouch a newspaper and placed it on Carmichael's desk.

PARIS, FRANCE, JANUARY 31, 1777, 3:31 P.M.

The clip-clop of horses' hooves echoed against the houses lining the narrow Parisian street. Inside the carriage, Lafayette and Carmichael swayed to the movement as they carried on a conversation—as they had done numerous times over the past week. The two men had become fast friends, and Lafayette leaned on the older American as a true confidant, not only for the logistics of their plans, but to freely express his growing ardor for the American people.

The chill of this January day was tempered by abundant sunshine casting brilliant rays onto the two men who secretly discussed new dangers to their plans.

"So, your family's suspicions led them to ask Minister Maurepas to intervene?" Carmichael asked in alarm. "What happened?"

Lafayette, his brow furrowed, nodded. *"Oui,* Maurepas sent the Prince de Montbarey to find out what I am up to. He is a high official in the war office, so you can imagine how intimidating this was for me, no? I told him what I intended to do with going to America, and in my panic, I promised to abandon my plans."

Carmichael raised his eyebrows. "And will you?"

Lafayette shook his head. "Of course not! I panicked, and the words gushed out, *mon ami.* I will *never* give up this mission! I do not think Montbarey believed my words anyway, which he will report back to the French ministry."

"They will likely wash their hands of it and tell your family that they did all they could do to discourage you," Carmichael assured him. "At least this has deferred their questioning for now, but we may need to take other precautions."

As the carriage rounded the corner, two members of the Paris police took note of who was inside, just as they had done all week.

CHÂTEAU DE NOAILLES, FRANCE,
FEBRUARY 4, 1777, 1:00 A.M.

"Bonsoir, I received your note to meet here," William Carmichael whispered. *"Pardon* for the late hour, but I felt it best that we meet while Paris sleeps."

"Bonsoir," Lafayette whispered as he let Carmichael in the door, noticing the paper in his hand. "I am always happy to see you no matter the hour, *mon ami! Merci* for coming to see me here rather than in Paris. I am not sleeping much lately with so much excitement!"

Carmichael slipped inside, and the two men sat down in the parlor, keeping their voices down so as not to arouse the household. Kate sat by Lafayette's feet, her nose peeking over the table and smiling to see the newspaper. *Good lad! He brought it!*

"Have you the latest news?" Lafayette asked eagerly as Carmichael unfolded the paper.

"It is actually *old* news but is newsworthy for our purposes," Carmichael whispered, opening the October 1776 *Gentleman's Magazine.* *"Marquis de Noailles,"* he read aloud, tapping the paper. "Isn't that your wife's uncle?"

Wednesday 23.
Count de Noailles, who succeeds the
Count de Guignes, as Embassador from
France, arrived at his house at Whitehall,
from Paris.

"Oui," Lafayette answered, leaning over to see the newspaper and spotting the name of Noailles. "I recognize the name, but unfortunately, I do not read or speak English. What does it say, *Monsieur?"*

"It is a notice about his arrival on October 23rd to London as the new Ambassador from France," Carmichael answered. He pointed further down the page. "He was presented to King George two days later."

Friday 25.
This day his Excellency the Marquis
de Noailles, Ambassador from France,
had his first private audience of his Majesty, to deliver his credentials.

"Ah, *oui,* the Duc d'Ayen is *very* proud of his brother's appointment as Ambassador," Lafayette said, nodding his head. "Adrienne's cousin, the Prince de Poix, has asked me to go with him to visit the Marquis de Noailles in London. But I have not wanted to leave Paris with all that is happening, so I have declined his invitation."

"Perfect! This makes our plan even more valid," Carmichael exclaimed with a big smile. "We know that the Paris police are aware of everything that is going on with your comings and goings to meet with us, even in our carriage rides. Your family remains suspicious as well. If you continue to decline the invitation to accompany your cousin-in-law to London, it will only increase their suspicions . . ."

Lafayette nodded, and then his eyes widened with understanding. "But if I go with him to London, it will throw everyone off the scent of my plans of going to America! I can do this while I wait for news on my ship, no?"

"Excellent! When can you make arrangements to leave?" Carmichael asked.

"Certainly not until after *Carnaval,* ending with Mardi Gras," Lafayette quickly answered. "The queen will hold many balls and dances and I regretfully must be in attendance."

Carmichael nodded with understanding. "Very well, let's set the plan in motion."

Thank ye, dear David. Yer Gentleman's Magazine *helped us again!* Kate thought. The editor was none other than Patrick Henry's cousin, David Henry. *Now for Lafayette ta see the other paper!* She ran to get the December Parisian paper she had stashed away from Vergennes's office and brought it over to the men, wagging her tail and nudging Lafayette's shin.

"What do you have there, Bibi?" Lafayette asked with a laugh, scratching Kate on the head and gently lifting her to the couch next to him. "She must think we wish to read more news." He took the paper from her mouth and his eyes landed on the headline:

LES BRITANNIQUES RECONNAISSENT LA VICTOIRE À LONG ISLAND ET WHITE PLAINES, NEW YORK, FORCANT LES AMÉRICAINS À RETRAIR!

(British Claim Victory in Long Island and White Plains, New York, Forcing Americans to Retreat!)

"She brings us old yet newsworthy news as well," Carmichael noted with a resolute expression. "Washington and his forces need our help now more than ever."

"Oui. This makes me wish I could leave today!" Lafayette answered in frustration. "While in London I suppose I will have to mingle with British officers who have returned from *leur victoire* in New York," he posed with a frown, clenching his jaw at the thought of Washington's army retreating at the hands of the British. "But I shall not shy away from expressing my opinions."

Carmichael held out a hand of caution. "Carefully weigh your words, Gilbert. *Especially* if you meet King George."

"Je comprends, mon ami," Lafayette answered, nodding and tossing the Parisian paper on the top of the stack. "I do not wish to be with those I will soon call my enemy and to hear them gloat over *leur victoire,* but I understand it will be the perfect cover for our plans. And I will be able to quickly receive word as soon as my ship is ready."

"Indeed," Carmichael agreed. "Have you a name for your ship? *Cur Non,* perhaps?"

Lafayette stared at the paper. He leaned over and re-read the headline. *"Victoire,"* he whispered to himself. Kate eagerly licked his hand. He looked up at Carmichael. "I shall name her for what I hope to bring to General Washington and the Americans with this noble quest . . . *La Victoire!"*

Kate barked once happily and then realized she might wake the house.

"Bravo, General Lafayette," Carmichael answered with a smile. "I like the name as well as your enthusiasm."

"Moi aussi!" Lafayette exclaimed, now growing even more excited about his ship.

I thought ye would, Kate said to herself, grinning as Lafayette rubbed the Westie's back.

Lafayette
in the Lion's Den

CHÂTEAU DE VERSAILLES, FRANCE,
FEBRUARY 11, 1777

"*La reine va s'écraser dans la fontaine!*" Ségur exclaimed, elbowing Vicomte de Noailles that the queen was going to crash into the fountain. Marie Antoinette was laughing wildly as she steered her ornate sled along the snow-covered gardens of Versailles.

Noailles's eyes grew wide. "*Oui,* but she is determined to beat Madame de Lamballe with her new sled!" He laughed and cheered along with the crowd of adoring courtiers at this outdoor pre-ball event. He nudged Lafayette, who wasn't even looking in the direction of the queen's wintry race. "Gilbert! Are you even watching?"

Lafayette turned and feigned a smile of interest. "Hmm? Ah, *oui, bravo.*"

"Lafayette's head is in the clouds, as usual," Ségur joked, clapping as the queen neared, the jingle bells of her horse sounding her fast approach.

"*Bravo!*" Noailles cheered, clapping and giving a sideways glance to his brother-in-law. "What is with you today?"

Lafayette gave an elusive grin. "Just enjoying the fresh air."

"Well, I suggest you get your head back to the queen before tonight's masquerade ball," Noailles told him. "Especially if she asks you to dance!"

Normally such a threat of dancing with the queen and making a fool of himself would cause Lafayette to bristle, but not today. He had just received word that Lieutenant Duboismartin had found a ship including her cargo for 112,000 *livres,* from *Reculès de Basmarein et Raimbeux* of Bordeaux. He could think of little else than *La Victoire* and had written to Duboismartin to purchase and rename her. Lafayette then hastily wrote to Carmichael, letting him know that the ship had been found and would be ready to set sail mid-March. *I hope to be able to take to your country the zeal that animates me for their happiness, their glory, and their liberty.*

Marie Antoinette came racing by, spraying the three young Frenchmen with snow. *Encore cinq jours et je serai libre de Versailles,* Lafayette thought. *Five more days and I will be free of Versailles.*

CHÂTEAU DE NOAILLES, FRANCE,
FEBRUARY 16, 1777

Lafayette held Henriette close to his chest and kissed her hair softly. *"Au revoir ma petite fille."* He handed the toddler over to Adrienne and smiled sadly. He then enveloped his pregnant young wife in a tender embrace, closing his tired eyes. He only had an hour of sleep since returning in the wee morning hours from Marie Antoinette's final Mardi Gras ball. But this morning his adrenaline ran high. He opened his eyes and looked around the room, taking in the beauty and comfort of this safe place one last time. After a moment he kissed Adrienne on the forehead and picked up his hat, turning to leave. *"Au revoir, mon amour."* He hesitated, as if searching for the right words. But he had none. His innocent wife knew that he was going to London for a short trip, but nothing more.

"Au revoir, mon cher," Adrienne answered sleepily, blowing him a kiss. "I will see you soon."

Lafayette tightened his lips, nodded, and quietly slipped out the door.

Kate waited for him in the foyer. Before Lafayette stepped outside to join the Prince de Poix in the waiting carriage, he knelt to scratch the little dog behind the ears. He whispered, "Bibi, take care of my little family while I am away. I don't know when I will see them again."

Sorry but I can't do that, lad, Kate thought. *I'm goin' with ye.*

As Lafayette walked outside, Kate scarfed down a madeleine and hopped invisibly onto the back of the carriage with the luggage which would soon be transferred to a small ship.

Lafayette did not know that while he possessed the zeal to sail to America, he did not possess the sea legs to get there. Waves of nausea washed over him as the small vessel plowed through the rising salt-water swells crossing from France to England. Kate felt sorry for the young marquis. *If he's this sick for a short sail across the channel, how in the world will the lad survive the three-thousand-mile trip across the Atlantic Ocean?* The Westie gazed at this same water she had crossed on Craddock the whale so long ago with Max when Al was just as seasick. *It's* déjà-vu *all over again, as Al would say.*

FRENCH EMBASSY, LONDON, ENGLAND,
FEBRUARY 27, 1777

"I don't think he's goin' home before he sails ta America," Kate told Liz in hushed tones, getting her up to speed. "I think he's goin' ta wait on word that *La Victoire* is ready, an' then go straight ta Bordeaux. Ye should have seen him strugglin' ta tell Adrienne good-bye. He knew he'd be gone longer than a few weeks."

"I can imagine our young marquis has many conflicting emotions about this adventure, no?" Liz asked. "But I am sure that Lafayette will stop in Paris to pick up Baron De Kalb on the way to the south of France. When I left Bordeaux, Duboismartin was working with De Kalb to finalize details of their voyage."

"I'm glad ye got *La Victoire* squared away so ye could join me here, lass," Kate said happily.

"*Moi aussi,*" Liz answered with a smile. "I could not miss seeing Lafayette meet the king of England! I am happy I got here in time."

Just then they heard a knock. A servant opened the door, and in walked Dr. Bancroft.

"*Bonjour,* Dr. Bancroft!" Lafayette greeted him. "What a delightful surprise!"

"*Bonjour, Monsieur le Marquis,*" Bancroft replied with a firm handshake. "When I heard you were in London, I wanted to wish you well, especially on this important day." He leaned in with a knowing smile. "It is not often that one gets to meet the King of England."

Lafayette nodded and smiled. "*Oui,* it is an honor. *Monsieur* Deane sends his regards and looks forward to your return to Paris."

Bancroft clasped his hands behind his back and nodded. "As do I, I assure you."

"I wonder how Bancroft knew Lafayette was here," Liz whispered as the men continued conversing in French.

"All of London knows by now, with all the parties an' dinners we've attended," Kate explained. "The lad has danced at the home of Lord George Germain an' dined with Horace Walpole. Today he meets King George an' next week he'll attend the opera. He's a busy French bee!"

"And all the while he knows that he is getting ready to sail to America and fight against this British lion," Liz answered, shaking her head good-humoredly. "Our marquis is dancing in the lion's den."

"Aye, but *this* time he knows how ta dance with grace. I have ta brag on me marquis," Kate reported. "He was invited ta tour the Portsmouth shipyards where the navy ships are bein' prepared for the war in America, but Lafayette wouldn't go. I think he didn't want ta do anythin' that might be seen as spyin', especially for his uncle's sake."

Liz raised her eyebrows. *"Très bien!* This is a testament to his good character. Once Lafayette sails to go fight in America and word reaches Paris and London, such a visit will not reflect well on Ambassador Noailles. Our young marquis chose wisely."

"I also wanted to bring you some good news, if you hadn't heard," Bancroft told Lafayette. "On Christmas night, General Washington led a surprise attack on the Hessian mercenaries in Trenton, New Jersey, capturing the city. It was a much-needed victory for the Americans."

Lafayette's eyes widened, and he grabbed Bancroft by the shoulders to enthusiastically kiss him on each cheek, startling the American. *"Merci* for this glorious news! *C'est magnifique!* Bravo, General Washington!" Lafayette looked around them and then whispered into his ear. "I look forward to congratulating him in person, no?"

Bancroft gave a knowing grin. "I will of course forward this good news to Mr. Deane in Paris."

"Did you hear that? Oh, I cannot wait to hear the details of Trenton!" Liz exclaimed.

"Aye! Max, Jock, an' Nigel had as busy a Christmas as we did, then," Kate agreed.

ST. JAMES'S PALACE, LONDON, ENGLAND,
FEBRUARY 27, 1777

As they waited to be admitted into the drawing room of King George III, Ambassador Noailles tugged on his silk waistcoat, straightened his wig, and then looked over his nephews to make sure they looked perfect in their full court dress. *"Très bien,* after I present you to the king, we will exchange a few brief words and then be dismissed. Remember that as my nephews you reflect on me, and thus you reflect on France. Follow my lead on gestures. *Comprenez-vous?"*

"Je comprends," Lafayette quickly answered, nodding humbly.

"Bien sûr," de Poix agreed.

"Bon, allons-y," Noailles said as the gilded doors opened, and two royal attendants stood at attention as the Frenchmen entered.

One side of the drawing room was lined with floor-to-ceiling windows framed by red and gold fringed draperies. Ornate tapestries lined the opposite wall between portraits of members of the royal family dating back centuries. At the far end of the drawing room was a red, boxed canopy suspended from the ceiling over the gilded throne. Thirty-eight-year-old King George III sat beneath the canopy while a line of eager courtiers were presented to him by name. Men and women filled the room in their elegant attire and freshly powdered wigs. The women's hoop dresses took up considerable space while their feather-adorned wigs stretched high in the air.

As they walked into the room oozing with British nobility, Lafayette gazed up at the portraits of past kings and nobles and couldn't help but wonder which of his own French ancestors faced them in battle. He smiled at the thought that now it was his turn to carry on the Lafayette tradition of fighting this ancient foe.

"The Ambassador of France the Marquis de Noailles, the Prince de Poix, and the Marquis de Lafayette," announced the official court presenter to the king.

King George sat dressed in his striking red Windsor uniform with the sash and star of the Order of the Garter emblazoned on his coat, studying the three Frenchmen as they approached the throne.

"Your Majesty," Ambassador Noailles said, arms wide and bowing before the king. Lafayette and de Poix mirrored him and did the same. "It is an honor to present to you my nephews."

King George's elbows rested on the arms of his ornate chair. He nodded and lifted one hand in the air to greet the French entourage. *"Bonjour, Prince de Poix et Marquis de Lafayette."*

Lafayette was surprised to hear the king speak in his language, as he had not met many British men who did so. But the king had been taught French and Latin as a boy. *"C'est un honneur, sire."* Lafayette's eye landed on the Order of the Garter pinned on the king's coat, and he pointed to his own chest, cocking his head to read the inscription. *"C'est une médaille impressionnante."*

"He said it is an honor to meet him, and that his medal is impressive," Liz translated for Kate.

King George touched the star-shaped medal and lifted his chin proudly. "The Order of the Garter, so named by King Edward III in the medieval era. He was so inspired by tales of King Arthur and the chivalry of the Knights of the Round Table that he established his own group of honorable knights."

Lafayette nodded as Ambassador Noailles gave a running translation as the king spoke in English. Finally, he smiled and answered the king while Noailles translated. "I, too, love the tale of King Arthur and the Knights of the Round Table."

"No doubt your favorite is Lancelot, the *French* knight," King George surmised with a grin.

"*Oui*, sire, for I come from a long line of French knights," Lafayette answered eagerly. "*Je suis un chevalier aussi.*"

"He told the king that he also is a knight," Liz translated. "Although technically he is a Marquis."

King George tilted his head at Lafayette and grinned. "No doubt King Louis prizes your sword—your *sheathed* sword."

Ambassador Noailles put his hand on Lafayette's elbow to usher him along with a parting bow to the king.

"I was honored to dine with the Duke of Gloucester while training for my king in Metz," Lafayette quickly interjected. "He differs in his opinion about how to handle the American colonies."

King George's grin faded. "Indeed, my black sheep brother would foolishly grant them independency were he king which he is *not*, and never shall be." He made a fist. "Because I love my rebellious people, I shall keep them harassed, anxious, and poor, until the day when, by a natural and inevitable process, their discontent and disappointment will be converted into penitence and remorse."

Lafayette raised his eyebrows, tapped his chest, and read the motto of Latin words surrounding the king's medal. "*Honi soit qui mal y pense.*"

"'Shame on him who thinks this evil,'" King George said with a smile. "*Exactement, Monsieur le Marquis.*"

"Thank you, your Majesty, for your time," Ambassador Noailles quickly said, bowing and nudging Lafayette to do the same.

King George gave a departing wave to the three Frenchmen and looked to the next courtier in line waiting to be presented.

"I cannot believe yer Al lived here with this tyrant!" Kate scoffed.

"*Oui*, the king's buffet was the only thing that kept Albert sane," Liz agreed.

As they walked away from the throne, Lafayette wore such a broad smile that de Poix leaned over to ask, "Did you enjoy meeting King George as much as it appears, cousin?"

"*Bien sûr,*" Lafayette replied, then thinking to himself with a grin, *Shame on me for thinking this evil. I may take too much pleasure in mocking the tyrant I am about to fight.*

THEATRE ROYAL, COVENT GARDEN, LONDON, ENGLAND, MARCH 5, 1777

"Oh, Kate, I have chills to be in this theatre again," Liz whispered, gazing up at the ornate chandeliers illuminating the grand hall. "It is hard to believe that it has been thirty-four years since we came here for the debut of Handel's *Messiah*."

"Aye, an' thirty-two years ago for the play, *Cato*," Kate agreed, looking around as they invisibly trailed along behind Lafayette, de Poix, and Ambassador Noailles. Just then she spotted General Henry Clinton. "I think we'll have some grand entertainment tonight with Lafayette. Look who's back from America."

Liz drew in a quick breath. "*Oui*, this should be an interesting encounter!"

Ambassador Noailles spotted Clinton at the same moment and whispered to Lafayette. "I see General Henry Clinton, recently arrived from his *victoire* in New York. He sailed to Boston with Generals Howe and Burgoyne in 1775 and has not returned to England since."

"Wasn't he the British general who said something to the effect of the Battle of Bunker Hill being such a dear bought 'victory' that another such one would ruin them?" de Poix asked.

Lafayette's head snapped to attention. "Where is he? I would very much like to meet him, this victor of New York and Bunker Hill."

Ambassador Noailles nodded in Clinton's direction. The forty-seven-year-old general wore his sharp red military dress uniform, his dress sword on his hip, shined and polished to perfection. "He is the only child of a British admiral, and spent his early years in New York, where his father served as the royal governor."

"So, he knew the topography of New York well. No doubt his superior officers sought his input for the battle," Lafayette assumed.

"Actually, my sources tell me that Clinton has poor interpersonal skills and is politically weak. He is supposedly the most experienced soldier and strategic thinker of the three generals, but his irritating manner causes his suggestions to go unheeded. Plus, his suspicious nature keeps him guarded and his colleagues guessing, as he is always thinking about the next move," Noailles explained. "His superiors have repeatedly ignored his advice in America, such as fortifying the heights of Boston, taking action early at the Battle of Bunker Hill, pursuing the retreating rebels after the battle, and abandoning Boston before winter. Howe sent him south to take Charleston, but Clinton was not allowed to organize things as he would have liked, and the mission ended in defeat in the Battle of Sullivan's Island."

A slight grin appeared at the corner of Lafayette's mouth. *"Quel dommage."*

"Howe did finally heed Clinton's advice, and Clinton was indeed the mastermind of the Battle of Long Island," Noailles added. "But when he wanted to finish off the Continental Army after British forces had them cornered in Brooklyn, General Howe denied his request, allowing Washington's forces to escape across the river."

"Imagine Clinton's disappointment," de Poix offered. "After he defeated *les insurgents*, his *victoire* was squandered in a single night due to fog!"

"Jock's fog!" Kate whispered to Liz.

"Quel dommage," Lafayette muttered again sarcastically, inwardly rejoicing at Washington's escape. "He must especially feel the sting now with Washington's surprise *victoire* in Trenton."

"Oui, I've heard rumors that General Clinton tried to resign from his assignment in America since returning to England, but King George denied his request," Ambassador Noailles noted. "You should know, Gilbert, that among Clinton's few close friends is Major-General William Phillips." He looked at Lafayette, frowning. "Phillips was the artillery commander at the Battle of Minden."

Kate instinctively growled. "It were Phillips's firing orders that killed Lafayette's father."

Liz's paw went to her mouth. "Oh!"

Lafayette's eyes narrowed, and he clenched his jaw, walking in Clinton's direction. "Will you introduce me to General Clinton, *s'il vous plaît?"*

Ambassador Noailles and de Poix quickly followed Lafayette. The Ambassador rushed between them to make their introductions, translating for them all.

"General Clinton, please allow me to introduce members of my family from Paris," Noailles began. "My nephew, Philippe Louis de Noailles, Prince de Poix."

"C'est un plaisir de faire votre connaissance, monsieur," de Poix said with a gracious bow.

Clinton nodded courteously. *"Monsieur."*

"And my nephew-in-law, the Marquis de Lafayette," Ambassador Noailles added with his hand out to Lafayette.

"Monsieur," Clinton acknowledged the young Frenchman with another courteous nod.

"Enchanté, Général," Lafayette replied with a forced smile.

"What brings two Frenchmen to London?" Clinton asked the men.

"It is an honor to visit our uncle in his role as ambassador to represent France," de Poix answered with a smile.

"I have never traveled outside of France," Lafayette followed, staring at Clinton's red coat. He lifted his gaze to the British general. "But I look forward to even more opportunities to do so."

Liz grinned. "Our young marquis is enjoying speaking between the lines with his adversary."

"Well, I hope you have a pleasant stay," Clinton replied disinterestedly, looking around the room.

"I truly admire the quality of your fine uniform, *Général*," Lafayette told Clinton, studying his scarlet coat with deep blue facings, trimmed in gold stitching, gold epaulettes, and engraved gold buttons. "It appears to be a deeper *rouge* than the uniforms of some of your more junior officers I have met."

"Yes, British wool is of course the *finest* one can buy anywhere in the world," Clinton answered smugly, lifting his chin, and holding his arm out for Lafayette to touch his coat. "Our senior officers' coats are made with expensive dyes that give their coats a more vibrant, scarlet hue than the lesser ranks."

"*Magnifique.* Where might I find your tailor here in London to purchase such exquisite British wool?" Lafayette asked as he ran his hand along the rich fabric.

Clinton smiled. "My tailor is located on Cork Street in Mayfair along with the best tailors in the world."

"*Merci,*" Lafayette answered, halting a moment, then pointing to the deep blue cuffs of Clinton's jacket. "I understand that the Americans' uniforms are this shade of *bleu.*" He looked up with a forced smile at the smug general. "No doubt you saw a sea of *bleu* retreating in fear before you during your *victoire* in New York. *Bleu* and . . . I do not know the color of *Général* Washington's officers' uniforms."

Clinton slowly pulled back his arm and studied the young Frenchman, his dark, bushy eyebrows covering his furrowed brow. "Indeed, a sea of blue . . . and buff."

"Ah, *bleu et chamois.* I read that you captured some of *Général* Washington's officers in New York," Lafayette noted. "No doubt you saw their *inferior* uniforms up close."

Clinton's eyes narrowed. "It is not just their *uniforms* that are inferior, but their skill in battle."

"Except for surprise escapes, no? I understand that the Americans escaped from Brooklyn and later caught the Hessians off guard in Trenton," Lafayette retorted, drawing a frown from Clinton.

"Another cheeky shot across the bow," Kate whispered with a grin.

Ambassador Noailles quickly stepped in to change the subject. "*Général* Clinton is soon to be knighted by the king for his victory over the Americans in the Battle of Long Island."

"*Félicitations* for such an honor on the field of battle," de Poix offered, playing the etiquette game.

"Thank you, *monsieur,*" Clinton responded with a cordial nod of his head.

"*Oui, felicitations,*" Lafayette echoed hollowly. "When I spoke with the king last week, we discussed his brother's differing views on the Americans' quest for independence."

"So will you be returning to fight in America?" Noailles quickly interjected, not wanting this conversation to continue.

Clinton gave a subtle frown. "Yes, I shall return to America next month."

Then I shall see you there, Lafayette thought with a grin. He gave a slight bow, locking eyes with Clinton. "*Je vous souhaite bonne chance dans la poursuite de la Victoire.*"

"*Monsieur le Marquis* says that he wishes you good luck in your pursuit of victory," Ambassador Noailles translated.

"A subtle invitation to chase his ship?" Liz said with surprise. "Lafayette seems eager to play a game of cat and mouse."

"But in this case, he's toyin' with a lion," Kate agreed.

Clinton bowed slightly in return. "*Merci.* Enjoy the opera." He then turned and walked away while Lafayette's eyes bored into his back.

"I can only imagine what is going through Lafayette's mind," Liz whispered to Kate. "But I have a feeling he will visit Clinton's tailor to purchase uniform cloth tomorrow."

"Aye, blue and buff," Kate answered. "An' he'll be wearin' it when he next meets Clinton—in America."

LONDON, ENGLAND, MARCH 9, 1777

Lafayette lit a candle and sat down at his desk to again read the exciting message he had received from Baron De Kalb. *La Victoire* was outfitted and ready for an ocean voyage to America. It was time for him to return to Paris. In the morning, Lafayette would have to tell his Uncle Noailles that he could not attend the ball in his honor tomorrow evening, but that he had business to attend to in Paris. It would be up to the ambassador to make the excuse of why the Marquis de Lafayette was absent from the king's reception.

The teenage Frenchman had written a flurry of letters to Adrienne during his stay in London but sitting on his desk was a letter he had not yet mailed to his father-in-law, the Duc d'Ayen. He now would deliver it when he returned to Paris. Lafayette lifted the letter to read it once more by candlelight.

"You will be astonished dear papa at what I have to tell you," he whisper-read aloud, letting go an anxious breath, anticipating how his father-in-law would respond as he read these words. "My word has been given, and you would not respect me if I broke it. I have found a unique opportunity to distinguish myself and to learn my profession. I am a general officer in the army of the United States of America." Lafayette smiled, once more in awe of what he was getting ready to do.

"My zeal for their cause and my sincerity have won their confidence. For my part, I have done all that I can for them, and their interests will always be dearer to me than my own," he continued, scanning the page as he recounted that he would embark upon a vessel he bought, accompanied by Baron De Kalb, "a major-general in the United States service like myself," he repeated with a giddy lump in his throat. "I am filled with joy, at having found so beautiful a chance to accomplish something and to learn. I know very well that I am making enormous sacrifices and that it will hurt me more than anyone else to leave my family, my friends, you, my dear papa, because I love you more tenderly than anyone has ever loved before. But this voyage is not very long. People make longer ones every day for pleasure alone, and besides I hope to return more worthy of all those who will be so good as to miss me."

Lafayette nodded, pleased with his naïve eloquence. *"Bon."* He signed his name and yawned. The hour was late. He rubbed his eyes, got up from the desk, and promptly fell into bed. Morning would come quickly, and he would cross the channel back to France.

Once Lafayette was asleep, Liz and Kate jumped up on the desk to read what he had written to his father-in-law. "Little does Lafayette know, but before he fights the British lion in America, he will need to escape the French one who will roar when he reads this letter."

THE FIRST ESCAPE

CHAILLOT, FRANCE, MARCH 15, 1777, 9:00 P.M.

The old man turned when he heard two horses galloping up the road behind him. He picked up his little dog, holding him close so he wouldn't be trampled underfoot, and sat down on the low stone wall in front of his house. From his darkened position across the street, he watched as the two cloaked riders rode up to the home of the local gardener in this quiet village on the outskirts of Paris. They quietly dismounted their horses, looking around them while they secured the reins to a post. A moment later the door opened, and they slipped inside.

"Did you see anything, Papa?" came the eager voice of his nosy wife behind him, holding a lantern and gazing across the street.

The old man set the little dog on the ground and rested his hands on his knees. *"Non.* Just two riders. *Pourquoi?* What do you care, *madame?"*

"Un homme mystérieux arrived there two days ago while Marie and I were talking," she answered, squinting to try to make out movement from the darkened house.

"Gossiping, you mean," the old man quickly added with a huff, waving a hand in the air.

She ignored his jab and continued her story. "The mysterious man quickly entered the house without speaking, even though he saw us," the old lady answered, gesturing to the darkened windows. "Since then, he hasn't left the house. BUT he's had visitors! Marie and I asked the gardener, but he won't tell us anything. He says he's just 'the gentleman on the first floor' and wishes to remain anonymous."

"Pfft, then let him *remain* anonymous!" the old man scoffed, standing, and grabbing his wife's elbow to usher her inside. "It is none of your business *who* he is."

She looked over her shoulder as he moved her along, clucking his tongue and calling for their dog. "Come, *chien.* Before she sends *you* over to investigate, eh?"

From inside the house, William Carmichael let the curtain fall from his hand where he had observed the old couple fussing across the street. "They're gone."

Baron De Kalb lit a candle, and the dark shadows vanished, illuminating the faces of himself, Carmichael, and Lafayette.

"My gardener has some very interested neighbors," De Kalb noted. "I thought you vould better be able to stay anonymous here rather than at my house."

The young marquis let go a breath of relief. "It has been hard to remain anonymous with so many guests coming to see me. But it is necessary, no? Basmarein came yesterday to settle the purchase details for *La Victoire.*"

"This is why I cannot bring Dr. Franklin to meet you as I had hoped, *mon ami,*" Carmichael said, pulling up a chair to join them at the wobbly farmhouse table. "He would draw too much attention."

"Dommage!" Lafayette answered, a hand on his heart. "How I wanted to meet him before I left."

"Dr. Franklin will forward a letter of endorsement on your behalf to General Washington," Carmichael assured him, pulling out a stack of letters. "Meanwhile, here are letters of introduction from Mr. Deane for you both as well as some for the officers sailing on *La Victoire.* Gilbert, this one is for you to deliver to Robert Morris for your banking needs once you reach Philadelphia. Like Dr. Franklin, Mr. Deane will send letters directly to General Washington and to the President of the Continental Congress, John Hancock, commending you both."

"Bon, and do you have the final list for the voyage?" De Kalb asked, rifling through the letters.

"Oui, besides you and Lieutenant Duboismartin, there are three officers from the original Le Havre expedition plus the new names we agreed upon," Carmichael explained, handing him the list. "With Lafayette, that makes a total of fifteen. They will all meet you soon in Bordeaux."

"Merci, cher ami," Lafayette told him. "I am grateful to you and *Monsieur* Deane for all of your diligent work to get us ready to depart."

"Ja, merci, Monsieur Carmichael," De Kalb agreed. He turned to Lafayette. "Are you ready to depart in the morning?"

Lafayette eagerly nodded. *"Oui,* after I see to a couple of things. I will come to your home to board the coach and we shall be on our way!"

"Bon, then ve vill go now," De Kalb answered, standing to his feet. "I vish to spend as much time as I can vith my vife on this last night together in France. *Bonne nuit.* Get some rest."

"I will try, but I am far too excited to sleep!" Lafayette answered with a laugh.

Carmichael held out his hand to Lafayette. *"Bon voyage, mon ami. Et bonne chance."*

Lafayette grabbed Carmichael by the upper arms and eagerly kissed him on both cheeks. *"Merci, mon ami!* I shall write to you from Bordeaux."

"A demain, Lafayette," De Kalb whispered, blowing out the candle before opening the door. Together he and Carmichael slipped outside.

Liz and Kate sat in the shadows and watched the men mount their horses and ride off into the night.

"Lafayette has stayed hidden for three days, an' aside from the nosy neighbors, no one has found out that he's back from London," Kate whispered. "Tomorrow we'll be on our way ta Bordeaux!"

"C'est bon. But I think we need to split up again, *mon amie,"* Liz suggested. "I feel I must stay in Paris should anything go wrong once Lafayette's secret escape is no longer a secret. I will join you in Bordeaux once things are clear here."

"Ye're right, lass," Kate agreed. "Lafayette will be droppin' off his letter for the Duc d'Ayen on his way out of Paris. I'm dyin' ta know wha' happens with Lafayette's family an' the French court when they find out he's gone."

"Not to mention the other players who would wish to foil Lafayette's escape—that spy 'Mr. Edwards' is still at large. As is Charlatan."

PARIS, FRANCE, MARCH 16, 1777, 7:00 A.M.

Ségur was in a deep sleep, dreaming of riding a horse in an open valley. Suddenly the door to his room opened, rousing him, but he didn't open his eyes. He could hear soft footsteps creaking along the floorboards. He slowly licked his lips and swallowed, reluctantly waking. He rolled over, and his eyes fluttered open. There sitting by his bed was the Marquis de Lafayette, grinning at him.

"Bonjour, mon ami," Lafayette whispered.

Ségur raised up on one elbow and whispered, "What are you doing here?!"

"I've come to give you some news and to bid you *adieu,"* Lafayette answered. He leaned forward, giddy to reveal his secret. "I'm going to America!"

Ségur rubbed his eyes and shook his head, sitting up in disbelief. *"What?!* How?"

"I secured a commission from *Monsieur* Deane as a major-general in the Continental Army! Since the Court has forbidden Beaumarchais's ships from sailing, I have purchased a ship and named her *La Victoire.* I am transporting Baron De Kalb and a dozen other officers who have volunteered to fight for *Les Insurgents."*

"*C'est incroyable!* I am in shock, *mon ami,*" Ségur replied, shaking his head in disbelief, unable to find the words. "*Félicitations!* But how did you get the Duc d'Ayen's permission?"

Lafayette grimaced. "My father-in-law does not know. Nor does Adrienne. *No one* knows, *mon ami,* and I need for you and Noailles to *keep it that way* until I am gone. I know I can trust you two—my best friends—to keep my secret."

Ségur nodded solemnly. "*Oui, je comprends.* We will do as you wish. When do you leave, and from where?"

"*Ce matin,*" Lafayette answered, rising from his chair. "De Kalb and I leave for Bordeaux when I reach his home. But first, I must tell Noailles."

"I admit that I am jealous. I wish I were going with you, *mon ami!*" Ségur confessed, getting to his feet. He gripped Lafayette by the arm. "*Adieu,* Gilbert. Go make us proud, and return covered in glory."

Lafayette, with a lump in his throat, embraced his best friend. "*Merci, cher ami.* I will! *Adieu.*"

"*Bon courage,* Lafayette," Ségur told his friend, who turned to slip out the door. "*Courage.*"

CHAILLOT, FRANCE, MARCH 16, 1777, NOON

Lafayette sat in the carriage and watched De Kalb as he told his wife goodbye. Emotion caught in his throat as he considered how Adrienne would feel once she learned that he not only was not coming back from London but was sailing to America. He looked down at the letter he had prepared for the Duc d'Ayen. He tapped it in his hands and then decided the least he could do would be to write a quick note to Adrienne. He reached into his leather valise on the floor and lifted a blank piece of paper and a pencil.

De Kalb gave his wife a parting kiss and walked over to the carriage where a servant opened the door for him. He took his seat with a grunt and saw that Lafayette was hastily writing. "Do ve need to vait for this message?"

Lafayette looked up. "No, *merci,* but I do need to stop by *Hôtel de Noailles* to drop off this note to Adrienne and a letter for my father-in-law."

"Are you sure you don't vish to stop and tell her farevell?" De Kalb asked. "I'm sure your family vould like to see you off, *ja?*"

"No!" Lafayette answered with a start. "Uh, no, no, *merci.* No, if I were to see Adrienne it would be a scene of tenderness and heartache that I would not wish to endure." He raised a hand to the baron. "Just watching the sadness in your wife's eyes to bid you *adieu* makes me wish to avoid such a scene."

Kate's eyes widened from her invisible perch on a shelf inside the carriage. *He hasn't told De Kalb that he never got the Duc's permission ta leave, or that Adrienne doesn't know he is leavin'!*

De Kalb pursed his lips and nodded. *"Ja, je comprends."* He reached his hand out the window of the carriage for the servant. *"Hôtel de Noailles."*

The carriage pulled away from the front of his home and Lafayette's heart raced. He had one more stop to make before he escaped Paris without his family or the French court stopping him. His palms were sweating as he finished the note to Adrienne. When they reached the gate of the *Hôtel de Noailles,* he dared not exit the carriage for fear of being seen. He asked De Kalb's servant to deliver the letters the following morning. Once that was done, the two new major-generals of the Continental Army settled in their seats for the bumpy, three-day journey to Bordeaux.

CHÂTEAU DE NOAILLES, FRANCE, MARCH 17, 1777

Vicomte de Noailles wore a pained expression as he met Ségur in the foyer. *"Merci* for coming. I wanted you to witness the Duc's reaction. This will not be pleasant."

"It is *I* who should thank *you, mon ami,"* Ségur answered with a broad grin as the two young Frenchmen made their way to the parlor where the Duc d'Ayen sat reading the morning newspaper. "I wouldn't miss this for the world."

Noailles frowned. "You don't have to be so excited about what Lafayette has done."

"Cur non?!" Ségur retorted with Lafayette's motto, slapping Noailles in the chest with a playful back of his hand. "Gilbert has done what neither of us dared to do, no? He alone had the courage to defy everyone and pursue the glorious cause. He has every right to rub our faces in it. Lafayette will be *le Générale de division! C'est incroyable!* You should be proud of him!"

Noailles nodded reluctantly. *"Oui,* I *am* proud of him, but I must admit that I am also *jealous* of him. I wish I were going, too. But I can't show my approval in front of my father-in-law or the family."

"Well, perhaps you'll be able to join the fight when Lafayette returns from America covered in glory!" Ségur whispered with a laugh, patting Noailles on the back as they entered the parlor.

"Ah, *bonjour,"* the Duc greeted the young men with a smile from his leather high-backed chair. He was in a chipper mood, enjoying his favorite morning delicacy of warm cocoa. He lifted a hand toward the tray with a steaming pot and several porcelain cups. *"Chocolat?"*

"Bonjour, Papa," Noailles answered with a weak smile, taking a seat on the

settee, spotting the stack of mail a servant had just delivered. Lafayette's letter sat on top. *"Non, merci."*

"Bonjour, monsieur le duc! Merci, oui, I would love some *chocolat,"* Ségur eagerly answered, pouring himself a steaming cup. He sat down in a chair, ready for the fireworks to begin. He took a sip of the chocolat. "I read that the Grand Duke of Tuscany, Cosimo III of Medici, created a recipe that was to die for—sometimes literally!"

"What do you mean?" Noailles asked.

"His 'Medici's Elixir' was sometimes found to be served with added poison for unsuspecting enemies in Florence," Ségur explained, taking another sip with a grin.

The Duc raised his eyebrows. "Indeed? I shall have to make sure that our servants do not get that recipe while we are in Florence." He chuckled and poured himself another cup.

"How are the plans coming for your trip to Italy, Papa?" Noailles asked. "Is it still to be with your sister and her husband?"

The Duc swallowed his sip of *chocolat* and nodded. *"Oui,* there is much to do. We will be gone for ten months. We shall depart in a few weeks when the weather turns warm."

"Florence! *Magnifique.* Meanwhile, I imagine the Prince de Poix and Lafayette are having a marvelous time in *London,"* Ségur interjected. "Have you had any news from them?"

Noailles shot a perturbed glance at Ségur, rolling his eyes.

"Oui, we've had three weeks of nothing but positive news from London. My brother presented de Poix and Lafayette to King George III, and all of London has celebrated their presence." The Duc smiled contentedly, set his cup down on the saucer, and leaned over to pick up the letter sitting on top. "Let us see if there is more good news in today's mail." As he broke open the seal and unfolded the letter, Ségur winked at Noailles with eager anticipation.

The Duc reached for his cup as he began to read Lafayette's letter. "You will be astonished dear Papa at what I have to tell you," he read aloud. He suddenly stopped, holding his cup in mid-air as his mouth moved silently. Noailles's heart raced with dread. The Duc's face began to turn red, and he dropped the cup on the table, spilling the *chocolat.* He grabbed the letter with both hands as he shot to his feet. *"C'est un scandale! Comment ose-t-il faire ça?!"* he roared.

Noailles cleared his throat, feigning ignorance. "How dare who do what, Papa?"

The Duc slapped the letter on his thigh. "Lafayette! He is no longer in London but is on his way to America to fight for *Les Insurgents!"* He handed the letter to Noailles and gripped the sides of his head, pacing the room. "The boy . . . *bought* . . . a . . . SHIP!"

"A ship?" Noailles asked innocently. Ségur got up and quickly went over to read Lafayette's letter over Noailles's shoulder.

"This situation is worse than before when the three of you were asking the French ministry to give you permission to go to America, which *was* and *still is* out of the question!" the Duc snapped, pointing at Noailles and Ségur. "For Lafayette to show such blatant support for *Les Insurgents* just days after having been a guest at the Court of St. James in London is an insult to both King George III and Louis XVI! And how will this reflect on my brother as the French Ambassador?"

Noailles didn't quite know what to say, so Ségur jumped in. "I am sure the English can be made to see that Lafayette acted without the knowledge of the Ambassador."

"Mon cher, what has happened?" came the Duchess d'Ayen, walking into the room and seeing the Duc's flushed face.

Noailles jumped to his feet and went to take her hands in his, kissing them. *"Maman,* do not worry. Gilbert sends news that he has left for America to fight in their army as a Major General."

The Duchess's eyes widened, and she shook her head slowly in disbelief. "But . . . Adrienne . . ." was all she could say.

"No son-in-law of mine is going to abandon his wife and child and run off to a war that is none of France's business!" the Duc shouted. "This is the second time that boy has put me in the humiliating position of having to fix things with the Court—first, insulting the Comte de Provence to get out of his courtier position, and now *this.* I shall go to Vergennes and demand that the king forbid his departure . . . and arrest him if need be!" He stormed out of the room, shouting orders for servants to ready his carriage.

Noailles leaned over and picked up the letter for Adrienne and handed it to the Duchess. "Perhaps you should give Adrienne this letter and tell her the news."

"Oui," she replied quietly, still stunned at the news of all that was happening. As she left the room, Liz waited a moment until the coast was clear to follow her.

"Well, given the Duc's temper I think Lafayette should avoid any *chocolat* offered him by his father-in-law after my Medici comment," Ségur said sarcastically.

Noailles frowned and shook his head, not laughing. "What if Gilbert is arrested? The king might throw him into the Bastille!"

"Knowing our Gilbert, he will find a way to escape the king," Ségur offered with a hand on Noailles's back. "It's your *father-in-law* that he has to worry about."

"*C'est vrai,*" Liz agreed from under the bookcase. "But we will make sure he escapes them both."

Liz left the two friends and stealthily made her way down the hall to Adrienne's apartment. The Duchess d'Ayen had just calmly shared the news of what was happening with Lafayette. Having been raised in a convent, she led a very pure life and raised her five children to also be pure and devoted to God. Her demeanor was one of calm hope. She handed her daughter the note that Lafayette had hastily scribbled.

Adrienne unfolded the note and read aloud for her mother to hear. "*Do not be angry with me. Believe that I am sorely distressed. I had never realized how much I loved you—but I shall return soon, as soon as my obligations are fulfilled. Goodbye, goodbye, write to me often, every day . . . It is terribly hard for me to tear myself away from here, and I do not have the courage to speak to you.*" She dropped her hands in her lap and welled up with tears. "Oh, *Maman!* What will happen to my Gilbert? Father is so angry! And what if the king does call for his arrest?"

"Shhhh, I will handle your father. I have a feeling that he is far more upset than the king or the French ministry will be," the Duchess assured Adrienne with a squeeze of her hand. "I think what your husband has done speaks to his noble character. While he is going about it in a very, how should I say, *unorthodox* manner, I believe he is doing what he believes in his heart to be right. I know nothing of conquests or glory, but in my heart, I am sure Gilbert will achieve both."

Adrienne smiled through her tears, dabbing the corners of her eyes with a handkerchief. "*Merci, Maman.* I am happy that you believe in Gilbert as I do. *Il est mon brave chevalier.*"

"We will pray for his safety. Gilbert is in God's hands, no?" the Duchess d'Ayen said, gently kissing the young woman's forehead.

"*Oui*, he is in God's hands," Adrienne answered softly. "And there is no safer place for him to be."

"*Très bien!* Lafayette has these two godly women praying for him—Lassie power!" Liz whispered quietly to herself from the shadows. "Adrienne and the Duchess are praying for him, Kate is with him, and I shall do what I do best—write for him. It will only be a matter of time before Lafayette's secret escape becomes public, but the timing and delivery must be perfect. I will give the Parisian papers something to rally the people to Lafayette's side, for humans love cheering for a noble, brave outlaw on the run."

A Public Secret

The stiff wind kicked up whitecaps in the harbor, sending sea spray into the air as waves hit the long stone quay in the bustling port city of Bordeaux. De Kalb and Lafayette walked along the wet quay, having arrived the previous day, but not yet able to go aboard *La Victoire*.

"I thought ve vould find the rest of our officers here. I'm surprised that ve vere the first to arrive," De Kalb muttered. The older man pointed out to *La Victoire*. "And your ship is not fully ready as ve hoped. You must be anxious to get to your boat, but ve cannot board until ve sign in vith the port officials and get a certificate."

Lafayette didn't say anything but walked along with his hands clasped behind his back, and his head down, deep in thought.

De Kalb stopped and put his walking stick out to stop the young Frenchman. He leaned over and slightly tipped up Lafayette's hat, frowning. "Or perhaps you are *not* anxious to get aboard your ship."

Jest tell him yer secret, lad, Kate thought as she followed invisibly along behind them. *Ye'll feel better once ye tell him!*

Lafayette clenched his jaw and let go a heavy sigh. He looked down at his boots, only now noticing the sea spray that covered them. He then looked up at De Kalb and gave a weak grin. *"Oui,* I *am* anxious to go aboard *La Victoire,* but . . ." he finally said, looking out at the beautiful ship bobbing in the harbor. He looked around them, making sure no one was nearby. "I need to tell you something, *Général.*"

De Kalb folded his arms and tilted his head to the side. *"Ja,* vhat is it?"

The truth always comes out eventually, lad, Kate thought.

Lafayette cleared his throat. "I had hoped we would be able to quickly set sail when we arrived, but now we will be delayed until the other officers arrive," he began. His heart raced, and he cleared his throat again, knowing he could no longer hide his secret. *"Je suis désolé,* but with this delay I fear that the Paris authorities might now have time to act and stop us."

De Kalb furrowed his brow. "And vhy vould they stop us?"

The teenager exhaled, quickly looked around them again and spilled his secret. "I did not get the consent of my father-in-law to go to America. I told him about my commission in the letter I left for him before we left Paris. Adrienne didn't even know, and I told her as well in my note."

De Kalb's eyes widened, and his eyebrows rose, a look of shock covering his face. It quickly turned to frustration. "You should not have kept this from me, *Monsieur le Marquis!*" He gripped his walking stick and tapped the ground with it. "You led *Monsieur* Deane to believe that you vould only get the approval of your family if you received the rank of major-general, *ja?* That vas three months ago, and you have just now told them?!"

"Je sais, je sais, je suis vraiment désolé!" Lafayette lamented. "I should have told you when we were in Paris. This is the main reason I did not wish to return home—it wasn't just to keep the French government or British spies from discovering our plans. I am afraid that my father-in-law will ask the French ministers to stop our voyage."

De Kalb blew a raspberry and shook his head. "Vell, ve need to *know* what is happening, not just fear vhat *could* be happening."

Lafayette nodded. *"Oui,* I agree. I could send a courier to Paris to find out from a family friend exactly what the reaction of the Duc d'Ayen has been." He thought a moment. It needed to be someone other than Noailles or Ségur so as not to get them in trouble if they weren't already. "I will send word to Vicomte de Coigny and ask him what is happening with my family and the French ministers."

"Ja. Bon," De Kalb agreed. He looked out at *La Victoire.* "Let us hope your ship vill be able to do more than just sit in this harbor."

Another idea dawned on Lafayette. "Adrienne's great-uncle, the Marshal de Mouchy, lives here in Bordeaux as the lieutenant-governor of Basse-Guyene. After we send the courier, I will go pay him a visit and wait there to see if my family happens to send word about me there."

The two men turned and hurriedly walked toward the dispatch office to send a courier. Kate slipped in the door with them as they made their request and noticed there was only one rider sitting there while the manager conducted business with Lafayette. He had striking blue eyes and kept looking in her direction, smiling. She looked down at her fur to make sure she was still invisible.

The manager whistled, and the courier got to his feet. "I will send *Monsieur* Clary *tout de suite."*

"You must ride at top speed to Paris," Lafayette instructed him, pulling out his money pouch to hand some coins to the young man and writing out the note for de Coigny. "Wait for his response and return here to Bordeaux immediately."

"Oui, monsieur, I'll ride there in record time," the courier answered, looking in Kate's direction. "I shall leave right away."

"Bon, merci," Lafayette answered, sharing a nod of relief with De Kalb.

Kate's eyes narrowed, and she slipped out the door, following the courier. She stayed quiet as he saddled up his horse. He looked around and then down to where she stood. *"Bonjour,* Kate. Gillamon sent me to see if I could be of assistance."

"Clarie!" Kate gushed. "I thought that were ye! I'm so happy ye're here ta hand deliver Lafayette's message. I feel better aboot this now jest knowin' ye're the courier. But how kin ye see me?"

Clarie laughed. "I'm a spiritual being, remember? I can see hidden things." She leaned down and gave Kate a quick pet. "I'll go ahead and tell you that Versailles is in an uproar, and Liz has a front-row seat. But don't worry—all will work out."

"I knew it wouldn't be pretty!" Kate answered. "Gillamon told us that de Broglie's plot ta replace Washington would actually help Lafayette escape France. How is that goin' ta happen?"

"You'll see, sweet Kate," Clarie assured her with a wink. "Keep an eye on things here, and I'll be back before you know it."

"Okay, lass. Gillamon's always right," Kate answered with a grin. "But Lafayette an' De Kalb will be antsy 'til ye get back."

Clarie stood and mounted her horse. "The other officers are arriving today, so at least they'll feel like they have safety in numbers. Oh, and we arranged for Carmichael to send a young American born in Europe named Edmund Brice to teach Lafayette English on the voyage."

"How grand!" Kate cheered. "I've learned some French, but I look forward ta Lafayette learnin' English."

"Lafayette's ability to speak English will be one of the most important things for Washington in terms of his usefulness," Clarie told her. "Well, I'll be on my way. Once the officers arrive, they'll start getting their boarding passes for *La Victoire* so they can be ready to sail any day."

"I can't wait ta get underway," Kate replied. "Ride safe, lass!"

Clarie nodded. "Will do. See you soon!"

Later that night, De Kalb sat down to write his wife as he tried to do faithfully as often as possible. He let go a sigh and dipped his quill in the ink.

Nothing is more uncertain than this voyage . . . The marquis is greatly disturbed by the delay, and I think he is right. It is possible that we shall not sail.

BORDEAUX, FRANCE, MARCH 22, 1777

"It is the law of France that every passenger obtains a certificate, signed by the proper port official. You must give your place of birth, age, and your general appearance. Santo Domingo is our destination, as we will first sail to the West Indies before America," Lieutenant Duboismartin explained to Lafayette and a group of French officers assembled outside the port commander's office. "*Général* De Kalb and several officers signed in here with the port authority yesterday, and today you shall do the same. Then you can go join them aboard the ship."

Kate watched as Lafayette nervously bit his lip. He stood in line with the others while Duboismartin conversed with the port official who readied a new page of the logbook of passengers to depart Bordeaux aboard *La Victoire*. Soon the port official motioned for Lafayette to step up to the desk.

The busy attendant dipped his quill in the ink and glanced up at Lafayette. "*Nom* and place of birth?"

Lafayette lifted his chin and declared, "Gilbert du Motier, Chevalier de Chavaillac."

That's a proper name for him, aye, but most humans wouldn't recognize it as Lafayette. Kate cocked her head as the man scribbled down the answer. *Chavaillac is an older spellin' of Chavaniac, but it should check out.*

"*Âge?*"

"*Vingt ans,*" Lafayette replied.

True, the lad's in his twentieth year, so it's jest a stretch sayin' he's twenty instead of nineteen, Kate thought, breaking out into a big grin. *He's coverin' his tracks on paper so the Frenchies can't find him!*

"*Apparence?*"

Lafayette hesitated a moment and then answered. "*Tailles hautes, cheveux blonds.*"

Kate grinned at Lafayette's attempt to disguise himself. *He's tall for a human, but blond hair? Let's hope the man doesn't see Lafayette's red hair stickin' out of his wig!*

"*Signez votre nom ici, s'il vous plaît,*" the man instructed Lafayette, turning the book around so he could sign his name on the official logbook.

Lafayette took the quill and dipped it in the ink, leaning over the desk. He signed his name as Gilbert du Motier, much smaller than he usually would sign Lafayette. When finished, he smiled and handed back the quill.

The man scribbled a certificate and handed it to the young Frenchman. *"Merci."*

The outlaw quickly turned and let go a breath of relief. He was in the book and had his pass. Now to wait on the courier to return, and hope the French police weren't riding with him.

AMERICAN DELEGATION HEADQUARTERS,
HÔTEL VALENINOIS, PASSY, FRANCE, MARCH 22, 1777

"What a mess!" Silas Deane wailed, removing his cloak and hat. He stomped down the hall to where Benjamin Franklin and William Carmichael sat in the airy sundrenched room overlooking the eighteen-acre garden leading down to the Seine. The doors were open to allow an unusually warm breeze of early spring air inside. Dr. Bancroft hurried along behind him, bringing the notes from their meeting with Vergennes's secretary Gérard at Versailles. "It's all unraveling!"

Franklin looked up, calm and seemingly unconcerned. "Like a cat with a ball of yarn, or a disappearing garment leaving our marquis exposed?"

Deane stopped and wrinkled his brow at Franklin's odd question. "I don't know what you mean, Dr. Franklin, but the Duc d'Ayen made it clear to the French ministry that Lafayette left *without* his permission. Lord Stormont has now heard about this and is on the warpath, crying foul against the standing public order of the king forbidding French officers to sail to America. All of Versailles is in an uproar!"

"A cat unraveling a ball of yarn is of no consequence. It makes a mess, but ultimately is harmless," Dr. Bancroft posited. "An unraveled garment, however, cannot cover or protect a person. I believe Dr. Franklin seeks to discern the ultimate nature of the uproar's effect?"

Franklin's smiling eyes looked through his spectacles perched on the end of his nose. "Indeed, Dr. Bancroft. When things unravel, they are either a nuisance or a threat. I submit that the only one who is *truly* upset is Lafayette's father-in-law, not the French ministry. Vergennes will need to keep playing his cat and mouse game with Stormont, but I cannot imagine he truly cares. He knows that his comments are reported to Stormont, so of course he said he discouraged Lafayette's departure."

"Vergennes announced that the king has issued a *lettre de cachet*—an arrest order for Lafayette," Deane explained. "That would appear to be a true threat to me! Maurepas and the Duc d'Ayen came up with the idea to order Lafayette to report to Marseilles. There the Duc, his sister, and her husband will meet the marquis and together go on a ten-month tour of Italy. They think that should cool his ardor for the American cause."

Franklin chuckled. "I'm sure the young marquis sees traipsing around Italy behind three old aristocrats as a threat not only to his *liberté* but to his sanity. Such a threat will have the opposite effect, I assure you, and only spur him on to escape from France."

"Has the arrest order been sent to Bordeaux?" Carmichael asked, more concerned than Franklin.

"A courier should depart any time now," Bancroft answered. "Mr. Deane has been asked to write to General Washington, asking him to disallow Lafayette's commission."

Carmichael's eyes widened, and he tapped the paper on the table in front of them. "What about for the rest of the officers on this list?"

"They were not mentioned thus far," Deane answered.

Liz watched from the door and decided to take the opportunity to boldly make her presence known. Now that they were in the Parisian outskirts, she could play the part of a stray and make herself at home without hiding. She lifted her curlycue tail and walked right into the midst of the American men. *Bonjour,* she meowed.

Franklin smiled broadly. "As if on cue! A French cat to illustrate my point?"

You have no idea, monsieur, Liz meowed.

He reached down to scratch Liz behind the ears. "Cats keep pests at bay, as I'm sure this little one does with the orangery outside. And I predict that this entire matter is nothing more than an unraveled ball of string. A nuisance but nothing more."

Oui, *and if I may borrow your writing materials* ce soir, *I will play with the ball of yarn called public opinion, no?"*

Deane looked at Carmichael and Bancroft, shaking his head at Franklin's assessment of the situation.

Liz waited until the humans were in bed and then made herself at home on Franklin's desk. She picked up a quill and tapped it on her chin, thinking about what to write to the Parisian paper. "I shall stick to the basic facts, for they are newsworthy enough to weave a colorful story in the public's mind. I'll throw in a bit of confusing intrigue about the Italy trip as well."

One of the richest of our young nobility, the Marquis de Lafayette, relation of the Duc d'Ayen, between nineteen and twenty years of age, has, at his own expense, hired a vessel and provided everything necessary for a voyage to America with two officers of his acquaintance. He set out last week, having told his lady and family that he was going to Italy. He is to serve as a Major General in the American Army.

"*L'affaire Lafayette* will be the talk of Paris," Liz smiled and said, putting the quill back in the inkwell. "Once I deliver this to the newspaper office in Paris, Lafayette's secret will be a public one—and they shall love him for it!"

BORDEAUX, FRANCE, MARCH 25, 1777

After a week of unfavorable wind, fair breezes finally returned, enabling ships to depart the port city. All the officers from their list had arrived, so Lafayette and De Kalb decided not to wait any longer for the courier to return from Paris. They would sail ahead. But just as they were at the dock and ready to step into the launch to take them back out to *La Victoire,* they heard a horse galloping up to them, shouting, "*Monsieur le Marquis!* I have your reply!"

Lafayette turned to see the courier, and his heart jumped a beat. "Ah, here he is!" He quickly stepped down the dock as Clarie raced up to him, carrying a sealed envelope.

"From *le Comte de Coigny,*" Clarie said, handing him the note, a finger to her hat.

"*Merci, monsieur,*" Lafayette replied, taking the letter in hand and giving her a few coins. He turned and walked back to the launch.

Clarie squatted down as if to fix her shoe and whispered to Kate, "I have new instructions for you from Gillamon. I'm taking you to St. Jean-du-Luz to wait for Lafayette there at Madeleine's home. You can go ahead and take a sip of water now. They're rowing out to the ship."

"I don't understand, lass," Kate answered, lapping up some water. She slowly started to reappear and shook from tip to tail. "They're gettin' ready ta sail! Don't I need ta be on the ship?"

Clarie smiled and shook her head. "Not now. When Lafayette opens that letter, it will change everything. You'll see him again soon, and once *La Victoire* finally sets sail for America, you have permission to come out of hiding for the voyage."

Kate beamed. "I'm happy aboot that! I guess that will make me his *third* white dog then."

"That's right," Clarie answered with a scratch behind Kate's ears. "Now, let's get going. We need to find the perfect horse for Lafayette."

"A horse? Why?" Kate asked.

"If Lafayette wants to be a knight like Lancelot, it's only fitting that he should make his final escape on a white horse," Clarie answered with a wink. She scooped up the Westie and they watched from a distance as Lafayette sat in the launch reading his letter.

"Vell? Vhat does he say?" De Kalb inquired eagerly.

Lafayette's mouth hung open, and he slowly shook his head. "My family, the French ministers, and the king have all expressed displeasure and are taking definite measures to stop me! He says there is even some talk of a *lettre de cachet!*"

De Kalb frowned. "A *lettre de cachet* is a very serious matter. The king can imprison anyvone for any length of time vithout specifying the reason," he shared, leaning in to make eye contact with the anxious teenager, "including keeping the sons of vell-known families from disgracing themselves."

Lafayette clenched his jaw and dropped the letter to his lap in a huff. "Pfft, well, it is too late to turn back now. Maybe Coigny's perception of things is different than what is *really* happening, no?" He folded the letter and stuck it in his pocket. "We are already on our way. We must at least get out of France. Let us sail to the Spanish port of San Sebastian. It is not far. We can go there and await further developments and decide what do to next."

De Kalb lifted a hand in the air and let it fall. "As you say, but . . ." he paused, not finishing his sentence.

"It is settled. *Bon.* Here we are, *Général,*" Lafayette reported as the launch reached the ship.

La Victoire creaked against the rope holding its anchor, as if she was as ready as Lafayette to get out of Bordeaux. The men got out of the launch and climbed up the rope ladder to get on deck. Within moments, the captain gave the orders to hoist the anchor. A beehive of activity ensued with the crew releasing the sails that filled with the fair winds to take her down the Garonne River.

Lafayette beamed as he gazed at the sun dancing on the water like diamonds. His stomach lurched from a mixture of anxious excitement and uncertain dread. Ever the optimist, the young marquis proudly gripped the railing of his ship, knowing that somehow everything would work out.

But as *La Victoire* crested over the horizon, a second courier galloped into Bordeaux. And in his bag, he carried a letter for the Marquis de Lafayette, sealed with the royal seal of King Louis XVI.

AN UNEXPECTED
TURN OF EVENTS

SAN SEBASTIAN, SPAIN, MARCH 31, 1777

**YOU ARE FORBIDDEN TO GO TO THE AMERICAN
CONTINENT, UNDER PENALTY OF DISOBEDIENCE,
AND ENJOINED TO GO TO MARSEILLES
TO AWAIT FURTHER ORDERS.**

L afayette swallowed hard, a wave of fear crashing over him as he read the official directive. He knew what disobedience to the French Crown meant: imprisonment. And he knew the power and wrath of the French Court that could be unleashed on those who disobeyed. His hand trembled, and he next picked up a letter from his father-in-law with equal fear. He took a deep breath and broke the seal, dreading its contents.

When the king's courier reached Bordeaux as *La Victoire* sailed over the horizon, he went to see the commandant of the port for further instructions.. *Monsieur de Fumel* sent the courier riding by land for another 125 miles to find Lafayette at the Spanish port of San Sebastian.

"I have orders to go at once to Marseilles to join my father-in-law and his sister the Comtesse de Tessé for a tour of Italy," Lafayette told the General, numbly handing the letters off to De Kalb in disbelief. "What should I do?"

"Ve are now in *Spain,* out of reach of the Duc d'Ayen." He lifted an exasperated hand out to the endless horizon. "There is nothing stopping us from setting sail for America this very day. If ve do not leave soon, ve vill not arrive to the field of battle before the spring campaign ends." He looked down at the water lapping against *La Victoire* and shook his head. "But my boy, I think you must go back to Bordeaux and settle this matter, *ja?*"

"I value your opinion and your wisdom, *monsieur,*" Lafayette replied, looking out to sea. "I of course am upset that my family, my government, and my king are displeased with me. I confess that I am fearful and torn as to what to do. Part of me wishes to sail away this moment!" He turned and looked at De Kalb with a look of anxious uncertainty. "But I cannot. It is not only my conflicted feelings that need to be settled, but also honor that compels me to clear up this misunderstanding. Although I go to join the Americans, I am first an officer of the King of France, so it is my duty to be obedient to my sovereign. I cannot leave without *some* form of approval."

"But if you do this, I do not believe you vill be able to rejoin me," De Kalb answered gravely. "I vould advise you to sell *La Victoire* back to the ship owners at a sacrificial price to at least get some small portion of your money back."

"I cannot sell her!" Lafayette quickly answered with a frown. He gripped De Kalb's arm. "I must be certain that at the end of this venture, forgiveness will be granted to me before I put an ocean between myself and my country. You may think me foolish to stop now after working these past six months to reach the point of setting sail for America." He clenched his jaw, resolute in his decision. "But I must wait until I can gain the assurance I seek."

De Kalb tightened his mouth and nodded in understanding. "If it be said that you have done a foolish thing, it may be answered that you acted from the most honorable motives, and that you can hold up your head before all high-minded men." The older officer tapped the ship's rail, as if to punctuate that Lafayette's decision was made. He leaned against the railing, his back to the sea. "So vat vill you do once you reach Bordeaux?"

"I will try to understand more of what the court wishes of me," Lafayette answered. "I will write more letters to the ministers and to my family. If necessary, I will return to Paris and meet with my father-in-law or proceed on to Marseilles to clear up this matter."

De Kalb gave a singular laugh and shook his head at the young Frenchman. It was already crystal clear what the government and Lafayette's family wished from the letters they had already sent. "In other vords, you vill stubbornly keep asking, 'Cur non?' until you can convince them to agree vith *your* plan."

"*Oui,*" Lafayette answered, a smile growing. "Cur non? But you must not sail to America without me until you receive definite word on what has been decided."

De Kalb lifted his hands and shrugged his shoulders. "*Ja,* of course. It is *your* boat, *Monsieur le Marquis.*"

"*C'est vrai!*" Lafayette heartily agreed. "*Bon.* Let us go eat dinner in town, and I shall then be on my way to Bordeaux."

OUTSKIRTS OF ST. JEAN-DE-LUZ, FRANCE, APRIL 1, 1777

Lafayette sat in the darkened coach, jostled back and forth as they rode along the bumpy road hugging the coast. It would be a three-day journey by land back to Bordeaux—three days to think about everything that had happened, everything that could happen, and everything he wished would happen. The young Frenchman tried to sleep, but sleep would not come. He gazed out the window at the lights dotting the passing hillside, mentally processing everything he faced.

This voyage to America was the only thing his heart had truly longed to do ever since he was a boy and went on the quest to kill the Beast of the *Gévaudan* and free the terrified people of Chavaniac. Ever since then, he was made to do the bidding of everyone else instead of charting his own course . . .

He was so disheartened that the high rank he had been granted as a major-general was not enough to impress his father-in-law or prove to him how serious he was in this quest to seek glory in America . . . If France finally went to war with England, he could return with respect and accolades of achievement on the battlefield to take up arms to defend France . . .

Now was his moment to stake his claim and become his own man! If he yielded to the wishes of others, there would be nothing left for him to do except follow along behind his elders, dragging his feet aimlessly around Italy. . . But if he disobeyed and got arrested, he could be locked away in prison. He would be humiliated and branded a fool by his friends, the court, and his family . . . And there was the loss of friendship with his new American friends who would now view him as a failure, since he was unable to keep his word to them . . .

How valiant the Americans are in their quest for freedom! General Washington is perhaps the wealthiest man in the colonies, and he is risking his life, his property, and his reputation by openly defying King George's forces, knowing he could be tried and hanged for treason. He is risking it all for liberté, *he thought. Shouldn't I do the same, as one of the wealthiest men in France? Isn't freedom worth such sacrifice?*

Suddenly the coach stopped, and Lafayette looked out to see that they were back in France, in the small town of St. Jean-de-Luz. He yawned and shook his head, rubbing his face and his tired eyes. He felt physically and emotionally drained.

The coachman jumped down and lowered the steps for Lafayette to get out. "We have stopped so I can get fresh horses, *monsieur.* and we will be on our way again. You can enjoy your *petit déjeuner* at this inn while you wait."

Lafayette stepped out and stretched. *"Oui, merci, monsieur."* He looked around the beautiful coastal town that was starting to come to life on this new day. He breathed in the fresh sea breeze and yawned again, trying to come awake. He made his way over to the inn door and stepped inside. He looked around the welcoming room and smiled. A cozy fire blazed in the white brick fireplace, the aroma of fresh-baked bread filled the room, and tiny vases of fresh flowers were set out on the handful of tables. Morning sunlight poured in through the windows framed by cheery blue, yellow, and white curtains.

"Bonjour, monsieur," a petite young lady greeted him with a radiant smile, wiping her hands on a linen towel. She had a tiny waist, beautiful brown locks, striking facial features of a square cut jaw, chiseled French nose, and blue eyes. It was Madeleine. *"Petit déjeuner?"*

Lafayette smiled and nodded gratefully. *"Oui, merci, mademoiselle."*

She smiled and led him to a wooden blue table by the window that overlooked the small, crescent-shaped harbor lined with white and terra cotta-roofed buildings. Small fishing boats bobbed just offshore as the local fishermen checked their lobster pots for their overnight catch. The little town filled with people starting their day.

After Lafayette took a seat, she set before him a large cup of steaming *chocolat,* a basket of warm bread, butter and jam, and a plate with two brown boiled eggs, an apple, and several slices of cheese. He raised his eyebrows in delight, thinking of how his *grand-mère* fed him this simple breakfast each morning in Chavaniac as a child. *"Merci!* This looks delicious, *mademoiselle.* It reminds me of home."

Kate sat invisibly in the corner, giddy with joy. *I knew ye'd like it here, lad.*

Madeleine smiled, placing a hand on her hip and tilting her head. *"Je vous en prie, monsieur.* I am happy to hear it. You look weary from your journey. Where is home?"

"My family comes from the Auvergne region in the south of France," Lafayette answered, closing his eyes in delight as he tasted the warm, fresh-baked crusty bread. He nodded and held up the bread. *"Délicieux!"* He took a big gulp of *chocolat* to wash it down. He was feeling better already.

"Ah, the Auvergne, *oui.* The rugged volcanic land where Vercingetorix made his last stand against the Romans," Madeleine remarked with a feisty hand in the air.

Lafayette's eyes widened. He liked her spunk. *"Oui!* I am surprised to hear a lovely young lady first refer to the history of that place instead of the famed *fromage* of the Auvergne."

Madeleine giggled and refilled Lafayette's cup. *"Mon père* taught me to love *l'histoire.* Especially France's heroes."

"Vercingetorix has always been *my* hero," Lafayette agreed happily. "I admire how he led the people to fight against the tyranny of Rome. It took great courage to go against Julius Caesar, and it ultimately cost him his life."

"And yet here we are, speaking of his bravery for doing such a noble thing, more than eighteen hundred years later," she noted with a smile. "Anyone who fights for *liberté* is a hero worthy of *la gloire,* no?"

"*La gloire, oui.*" Lafayette couldn't believe what he was hearing. How was it possible that he had been forced to take a coach back to Bordeaux, only to stop in this simple inn to be refreshed and encouraged by this lovely daughter of France? "*Oui,* nothing is more important than *liberté.*" He nodded and smiled to himself. He, too, wanted to achieve glory in the fight for freedom. "I think Vercingetorix would be a perfect name for a horse, *n'est-ce pas?*"

"*Oui, c'est perfect,*" Madeleine answered. She gestured out the window. "In addition to this inn, *mon père* is the postmaster across the street. He must keep *les chevaux* ready for post riders and coach riders in our barn. But he has a new stallion that no one seems to be able to control. I think he would give it away if he could!"

"Oh? Perhaps it was ill-treated before it came here," Lafayette surmised. "What kind of horse?"

"A wild white Camargue, recently brought here behind a transport from Saintes-Maries-de-la-Mer," Madeleine answered. "*Mon père* was told that its speed is unmatched, but he is yet to ride him."

Lafayette sat back in his chair. "The Camargue are an ancient, majestic breed. They've lived for thousands of years in the harsh wetlands of the Rhône delta. They love to run in the sea, which gives them great stamina and agility. They truly are quite beautiful animals."

"You obviously know a great deal about *les chevaux, monsieur,*" Madeleine answered with delight.

Lafayette did not want to reveal that he had been a black musketeer for the King of France and was in the Noailles cavalry regiment of dragoons. "*J'aime les chevaux.*"

"Perhaps *you* could tame him, *monsieur!*" Madeleine suddenly heard other guests enter the room and needed to attend to them. She pointed to Lafayette's plate. "*Pardon, monsieur. Bon appétit.*"

"*Merci, mademoiselle,*" Lafayette said with a nod. He savored his delicious breakfast, enjoying the beautiful view of this small town and the delightful encounter with the innkeeper's daughter. *Vercingetorix would have to be a magnificent horse—a perfect horse that at the sight of a whip would have the pluck to throw off its rider and escape to freedom.* He wondered about the wild horse in the postmaster's barn.

When Lafayette finished, he dabbed his mouth with his napkin and grabbed the apple to put in his pocket. *"Merci, au revoir!"* he called as he left, giving Madeleine a courteous bow of gratitude.

"Au revoir et merci, monsieur," Madeleine answered back with an upraised hand. *"Liberté!"*

"Liberté!" he answered with a big smile and a wave. Walking back outside, he found the coach ready to go, equipped with fresh horses and the coachman standing by the open door.

"I hope you enjoyed your time here, *monsieur,"* the coachman said, lowering the steps for Lafayette. He had striking blue eyes and Lafayette did a double take, for he somehow seemed familiar. "Are you ready to resume our journey?"

"Oui, merci, monsieur," Lafayette answered, coming to rub the necks of the new brown and black horses. "Did you see the white horse in the postmaster's barn?"

Clarie nodded. *"Oui,* he is a wild one, but a magnificent beast. Would you like to see him?" She held out her arm in the direction of the barn.

Lafayette nodded and started walking toward the barn. *"Absolument."*

The loud whinny of a horse greeted Lafayette as he entered the barn. A pair of swallows chased each other, chirping, and delivering straw to the nest they built high in the rafters. A single ray of light shone in from an open window, illuminating a swirl of dust suspended in its beam. The familiar smells of hay, manure, and old wood brought a smile to Lafayette's face. How he loved being around horses. Multiple stalls lined the walls, mostly empty except for the two horses that Clarie had exchanged, and the far stall at the end of the corridor that housed the white Camargue horse.

As Lafayette approached, he could hear the heavy breathing of the untamable stallion that paced its ample stall. He quietly stood in front of the gate with his hands behind his back, studying the handsome horse.

The white stallion was young, only fourteen hands high, and appeared to weigh about 700 pounds, as was typical for this smaller breed of horse. But despite his short stature, he was incredibly sturdy. He had a square head with a flat forehead, well-chiseled cheek bones, and bright, expressive, wide-set dark eyes. His small, short ears were set well apart, and his forelock was full. An abundant silvery-white mane fell from his short neck. His muscular, deep chest and rugged, compact body were supported by long, powerful legs and well-muscled hindquarters.

Clarie came up next to him and whispered, "I noticed he doesn't have horseshoes."

Lafayette kept his steady, calm gaze on the horse, who now appeared to be studying *him.* "Camargue horses have hooves that are hard and tough, with large, wide soles which are suited to their marshy habitat. Because they've had to adapt to a wet environment, their hooves easily withstand moisture and they do not develop hoof problems as do other breeds. This is why it is not necessary to put horseshoes on these horses," he explained softly. He smiled, locking eyes with the beautiful white horse. "Legend has it that the Camargue horse was a gift from Neptune to be man's faithful companion. They have been nicknamed *'cheval de mer,'* because of how much they love the water."

Sea horses, Kate thought with a grin, eyeing the horse.

"Ah, je comprends," Clarie answered. "They must love to live free, galloping along the seashore."

"C'est vrai," Lafayette answered. "They can travel long distances, go extended periods without food, and can withstand hazardous conditions. They are extremely brave and intelligent and usually have an even temperament. I wonder if something has traumatized this horse."

Lafayette slowly moved toward the stall, his hand sliding into his pocket. The horse snorted and pawed the dirt. His muscles bristled at Lafayette's approach, but he maintained eye contact.

"Shhhhh, I will not hurt you," Lafayette calmly whispered to the horse as he approached. He pulled out the apple and took a bite, the juice dripping down his chin. He then held out the apple to the horse. The horse didn't budge but kept staring at Lafayette. He calmly took another bite and draped his arms over the rail, making himself at home in the horse's space.

Just then, Madeleine came into the barn, a basket of fresh eggs draped over her arm. She came up behind Clarie and Lafayette. "I saw your carriage still outside."

Clarie nodded. *"Monsieur* wished to see your wild stallion before we left."

"He does not appear to be very wild at the moment, no?" Madeleine observed with a warm smile.

Lafayette maintained his gaze, taking another bite of the apple and holding it out to the reluctant horse. "It is all about respect, *n'est-ce pa?* In order to communicate with a horse, you must be calm and serene inside. Horses are deeply sensitive, spiritual creatures. They constantly scan humans and can tell if you have a bad spirit inside." He took another bite, and the horse took one step forward. "When a horse doesn't know a human, it first assesses their nature. If the human proves himself, he can go from being a threat to a protector for the horse."

Lafayette again stretched out his arm and held the apple for the horse. *"Tu veux une pomme?"*

The horse shook his mane and pawed once more, but then took a step forward, then another. He came right up to Lafayette and began nibbling the apple. The teenager smiled and gently rubbed the horse's neck. *"Bon, bon, cheval. Bon."* He turned and looked back at Madeleine and Clarie. "Once a horse realizes it can trust you, only then will it begin to look to you for leadership and do what you ask. And they have excellent memories. Once they meet someone or learn something, they never forget it."

"Bravo, monsieur," Madeleine exclaimed with a broad smile. "You have a gift of whispering to horses."

Lafayette looked the horse in the eye. "He is such a magnificent creature. How I wish I could ride him, but we must be on our way."

Madeleine stepped up to the stall and haltingly lifted her hand to pat the horse on the neck. "Such a horse seems worthy of the name Vercingetorix. Bold, brave, defiant, no? What do you think, *monsieur?"*

Lafayette nodded. "Indeed, *mademoiselle. C'est parfait."* He rubbed the horse on the nose. *"Au revoir,* Vercingetorix." He turned and placed his hand on his chest with a bow. *"Et au revoir, Mademoiselle.* It has been a pleasure."

"Pour moi aussi, monsieur," Madeleine answered. *"Bonne journée."*

Lafayette yawned as he walked back to the coach. But he now had a full stomach and a renewed focus of why he was doing what he was doing. He felt he could now get some shut-eye as they traveled.

Once Lafayette was inside the coach, Clarie motioned for Kate to come along as she folded the steps back into place. She lifted the invisible dog and placed her up on the coachman's seat next to her. She snapped the reins, and off they went, back to Bordeaux.

As they once more traveled along the bumpy coastal road, Lafayette soon fell asleep, dreaming of Vercingetorix.

70

THE NEXT ESCAPE

OFFICE OF PORT COMMANDANT,
BORDEAUX, FRANCE,
APRIL 3, 1777

"*M*onsieur, I alone am responsible for all of this misunderstanding. I wish to set things right and request to go to Paris for two weeks to see my wife and family," Lafayette declared with lifted chin, ready to face the music.

Port Commandant de Fumel frowned and shook his head. *"Non, Monsieur le Marquis,* you must go to Marseilles as ordered by the Court at Versailles and wait for your father-in-law before proceeding to Italy." He wagged his finger at the teenager. "And you *must* be there by the fifteenth. Now, if you will excuse me. I have other matters to attend to." He walked off, leaving the chagrined marquis awkwardly standing there.

Lafayette hung his head, reeling with despair. Once more he was told, *'Non, Monsieur le Marquis.'* There would be no further discussion, at least not with the commandant here in Bordeaux. De Fumel had his orders from Versailles and was charged with making sure that Lafayette did as he was told. The prodigal would either get in a coach bound for Marseilles, or he would be arrested. It was as simple and awful as that.

Lafayette stepped outside and angrily kicked up the dust in the street. *I will not give up so easily! I will write to Prime Minister Maurepas, begging him to reverse the order, but I will word it in such a way to let him know that I have returned to Bordeaux, and am compliant, but I have not given up.*

But once he planted himself behind the desk at the home of Adrienne's great-uncle, the Marshal de Mouchy, he didn't stop writing. He wrote letter after letter to everyone he knew who could intervene or at least support him in his predicament. He wrote to Deane, to Carmichael, to Adrienne, and to de Broglie. He sent off courier after courier, and eagerly awaited just one hopeful reply.

RUFFEC, FRANCE, APRIL 7, 1777

Comte de Broglie fumed, listening to the latest news from Versailles and reading the latest Parisian gossip lauding the rogue Marquis de Lafayette, who had returned to France after sailing to Spain. Everything he had worked for months to set in motion was falling apart.

"If that boy does not turn around and get back on that ship, he will not be the only one who becomes a laughingstock of France. I will be as well!" He paced in his office as his secretary Duboismartin stood by. "If *La Victoire* does not sail from Spain, this entire plan will fail just as it did with Beaumarchais at Le Havre. De Kalb and my officers will not get to America and be able to set the stage for me to become commander of the American Army."

"Agreed. So, what do you think would put Lafayette at ease to convince him to set sail?" Duboismartin asked.

De Broglie crossed his arms and stared out the window. "If he believed that the French ministers had only acted out of respect for the Duc d'Ayen and the Noailles family, and that neither the king nor any of the Court were *truly* angry with him for so noble an enterprise." He turned and put his hands on the back of a chair, thinking out loud. "This is in large part, true. Maurepas and Vergennes have needed to keep up a good front with Stormont and the English, claiming a desire for peace as they prepare for war. So, they have *officially* condemned French officers for volunteering to fight with *Les Insurgents* while *unofficially* winking at us to proceed. They've granted military leave to the officers we have enlisted to go to America, so it is clear they do not object to French soldiers joining the fight! But when the Duc d'Ayen stormed into Versailles and raised such a loud fuss over Lafayette, it put the ministers in the delicate position of making an even greater show of disapproval." He paused and slowly nodded as he realized what he needed to tell the French outlaw. "If Lafayette knew that no consequences would follow him if he set sail, I believe the boy would proceed on, for that is what he truly wants to do."

Duboismartin nodded. "Then tell Lafayette just that. And send someone to tell him in person. Someone he would trust, coming directly from you."

"Give him the specific assurance he seeks," De Broglie echoed, nodding. He thought a moment and then snapped his fingers. "Like Lafayette and De Kalb, Vicomte de Mauroy was also given a major-general's commission by Deane. He was supposed to sail with De Kalb back in December, but he was not included with the officers sailing on *La Victoire.*" He looked up at his secretary, and a broad smile grew over his face. He picked up the Parisian paper applauding Lafayette's exploit. "Send Mauroy immediately to Lafayette in Bordeaux with good news from Paris that all of France is behind him. Have him tell Lafayette that all is well with everyone except his protective father-in-law."

"*Très bien,*" Duboismartin responded with a grin. "I'll make sure Mauroy leaves tomorrow morning."

Liz's eyes widened when she heard this conversation from the shadows. *This is exactly what Gillamon had said would happen! The very man scheming to replace Washington is the very one who will help Lafayette to escape. Bravo!*

BORDEAUX, FRANCE, APRIL 13, 1777

"Lafayette's exploits are now known in every café and salon in Paris! He has the public's sympathy and approval," Liz reported, now back with Kate and Clarie. The three of them sat at the water's edge in front of the dispatch office, waiting for Lafayette. He was back in the port commandant's office, begrudgingly getting his passport papers stamped for Marseilles. "The French people already loved what the Americans are doing in their fight for *liberté,* but Lafayette's passion and willingness to risk everything to share in their cause has only increased their enthusiasm for *Les Insurgents.*"

"But you say that the people *disapprove* of the behavior of the Duc d'Ayen and of the French government?" Clarie asked. "I'm happy to see that Lafayette has clearly won the publicity battle."

"He's doin' exactly wha' he set out ta do with publicity!" Kate cheered. "First with the Frenchies, an' next he'll do it with the Americans."

"*Oui,* so Maurepas, Deane, d'Ayen, and even Stormont were relieved to hear that Lafayette returned to France. They all think that his adventure is over—that he has given up his dream of sailing to America!" Liz relayed to Kate and Clarie. "But Maurepas did not correctly read between the lines of Lafayette's letter. He most certainly did *not* give up!"

"So Gillamon were right," Kate cheered. "De Broglie will be the only one ta help Lafayette escape!"

"Of *course* Gillamon was right," Clarie added with a clap. "He's *always* right."

"*Oui,* but sometimes it is hard to understand how such things are possible. We are just simple creatures, no?" Liz answered with a wink.

"Won't Lafayette be surprised when Mauroy gets here?" Kate asked happily, wagging her tail. "He's been so sad, an' dreads ridin' on ta Marseilles, but he can't wait any longer for a hopeful word. When the last courier returned without a reply from Maurepas, Lafayette assumed that the prime minister must've thought his request ta change the king's orders didn't even deserve a reply. So, he's decided ta go on ta Marseilles an' try one last time ta convince his father-in-law ta give his consent."

"And you are his coachman, Clarie?" Liz asked.

Clarie tipped her hat. "At your service, little lady! I've played the part of his courier, his coachman from San Sebastian, and now his coachman to Marseilles."

"Ye can join me up on the seat." Kate enthused with her perky grin. "But it will be a short ride, for Lafayette anyway."

Liz wrinkled her brow, curious. "What is the plan? I assume Commandant de Fumel will wish to make sure that Lafayette shows up in Marseilles as ordered."

"Aye, Liz, he's plannin' ta have Lafayette's carriage followed just ta be safe," Kate offered with a wink. "But we've got alternate transportation all worked out for the lad."

"Just in time." Clarie stood up and pointed to the approaching horses. "Mauroy's carriage is here. After he gives Lafayette the good news, things will happen quickly."

A crestfallen Lafayette came walking toward the coach, tucking his passport into his coat pocket, and dragging his feet.

"*Monsieur le Marquis!*" came Mauroy's voice from his approaching carriage, startling Lafayette.

He looked up, surprised to see his friend now stepping out of the carriage. He rushed over to him, clasping him by the hand. "Vicomte de Mauroy? What are you doing in Bordeaux?"

Mauroy held up a newspaper with Liz's article. "I've come with good news for you, *mon ami!* Comte de Broglie sent me to tell you that all is well, and that you can return to *La Victoire* without concern. *You* are the talk of Paris! All of France applauds what you are doing!"

Lafayette's eyes widened, and his heart skipped a beat. "*Je ne comprends pas!* How can this be true?!"

"After your father-in-law stormed into Vergennes's office requesting that you be recalled, the French ministers of course had to make a big show of disapproval, especially when Lord Stormont and the British ministry learned of your departure," Mauroy explained. He leaned in with a grin and whispered, "Vergennes *did* send official notices to stop you at the ports and on ships to the West Indies, but it is all only for show. The truth is that the French Court has no real issue with you. It is only your father-in-law who remains upset. So, I am to sail on with you to America!"

Lafayette grabbed Mauroy by the shoulders and kissed him on either cheek, ecstatic and stopping himself from jumping up and down. *"Mon ami,* this is glorious news! *C'est magnifique!* We must leave right away!" He patted his pocket. "I have my passport for Marseilles, but *Monsieur* de Fumel made it *very* clear to me that he expects me to leave without delay and threatens my arrest if I disobey."

Mauroy looked around them and spoke quietly. "We can take the road to Marseilles and change course once we are a safe distance from Bordeaux."

"Oui, but I think we should take greater precautions in case we are followed," Lafayette answered. "Even if the French Court sent out arrest orders for show, the police don't know that. They would throw me into prison, and who knows how long I could be locked up." He paused a moment, thinking this through. "I have an idea, but before we depart, I must write to Prime Minister Maurepas, clarifying my actions for sailing to America," Lafayette told Mauroy. "I will tell him that I understand that the king's orders were only for show, and when I did not receive his reply in a timely matter, I took his silence to mean his *consent* to proceed, no?"

"That is what you call *selective hearing,"* Clarie muttered under her breath to Kate and Liz. "Teenagers are masters at this technique."

"Coachman, please transfer *Monsieur* Mauroy's baggage to my coach," Lafayette instructed Clarie. "He will now be accompanying me to Marseilles. We will be back momentarily."

"Très bien, monsieur," Clarie answered, quickly jumping into action. She winked at Liz and Kate, lifting them up to her seat while the men stepped inside the dispatch office for Lafayette to send his letter.

"What is this alternate transportation?" Liz asked, looking from Kate to Clarie.

"A perfect seahorse," Kate told her with a grin. "The plucky kind that Lafayette wrote aboot when he were a wee marquis."

Monsieur de Fumel stood outside the dispatch office, arms folded across his chest, watching as Lafayette and Mauroy got ready to climb into the coach bound for Marseilles. Two Bordeaux police officers stood next to him.

Lafayette looked up at the port commandant and waved his hat, his white wig catching the sunlight. *"Adieu, Monsieur de* Fumel! We'll be on our way to Marseilles now."

Fumel raised a non-committal hand in farewell. *"Monsieur* Lafayette is suddenly quite happy about this journey to Marseilles. *Pourquoi?"* The commandant's eyes narrowed as he watched Lafayette climb cheerfully into the coach. When Clarie lifted the steps and climbed up into the coachman's seat, Fumel turned to the officers. "Follow them, and make *sure* they get to Marseilles."

Clarie snapped the reins and the horses clip-clopped ahead, out the entrance gate of Bordeaux.

Lafayette and Mauroy looked at one another and simultaneously let go their anxious breaths. Clarie looked behind them and saw the two police officers on horseback following along behind but keeping their distance.

"This road goes southeast toward Marseilles for about twenty-five miles," Lafayette told Mauroy. "When we get to Langdon, the road splits off to head southwest toward Bayonne and San Sebastian."

"So that's where we'll turn?" Mauroy asked.

Lafayette nodded, leaning his head back on the seat. "That's where we'll do more than turn." He grinned, pointing his thumb toward the countryside. "We'll make sure anyone following us gets a complimentary meal."

For mile after mile, they passed one endless blossoming vineyard after another through this region of France famous for its luscious grapes. The Garonne River slowly narrowed as they traveled further away from the coast. After three hours they entered the town of Langdon, and Clarie pulled the coach up to a tavern providing lodging and stables. She hopped down from the seat and opened the door for the men. Lafayette and Mauroy stepped out and stretched.

"Monsieur, we will go inside this tavern to eat. After an hour, meet me in the stables out back," Lafayette instructed Clarie. He stared at this coachman's outfit, which was just like the clothes of the courier whom he had first sent to Paris. He wore burgundy breeches, a black cotton shirt, black boots, a long charcoal gray coat with high collar, and a wide-brimmed three-cornered hat. "We appear to be the same size."

"Very well, *monsieur,"* Clarie replied with a tip to her hat.

She watched for about forty minutes and noticed Fumel's officers ride into town. The sun was beginning to set. They dismounted their horses and went inside the tavern. She grinned up at Kate and Liz. "This should be fun. Stay here."

At the appointed time, Clarie met Lafayette in the stables. He came to the chestnut mare in one of the stalls. "We have a change of plans and will now travel to Bayonne. I will pay you handsomely for your trouble and cover your expenses back to Bordeaux once you have dropped off *Monsieur* Mauroy with our baggage." He patted the mare on the neck. "I have bought this horse, which I will ride ahead of the coach to meet you at Bayonne."

"*Je comprends, monsieur,*" Clarie answered innocently. "Are you aware that you may have been followed from Bordeaux?"

Lafayette grinned. "*Oui,* and I have taken care of that. I have paid for the meals of every patron in that tavern this evening. That should slow them down, no? After I leave, stay behind for a while, and then depart with *Monsieur* Mauroy." He took off his hat, wig, and coat. "Quickly now, change clothes with me, *monsieur.* I will pay you for these items. I also need your leather messenger bag."

"As you say, *monsieur,*" Clarie agreed, playing along with Lafayette's new disguise.

Once they changed outfits, he slipped the leather bag over his head and held out his arms. "How do I look?"

"Like a common courier, *monsieur,*" Clarie said with a smile.

"*Bon!*" Lafayette exulted, opening his pouch and filling Clarie's hand with gold and silver coins. "This should cover everything." He walked over to the horse and untied the reins, slipping them over its head. He climbed up into the saddle and patted the docile horse. "She is no Vercingetorix, but she should deliver me to the next town. *Merci, Monsieur.* I shall see you in Bayonne."

"*Bonne chance, monsieur!*" Clarie exclaimed, opening the stable door for the marquis. She grinned as he rode off into the night. "Vercingetorix will be waiting."

BAYONNE, FRANCE, APRIL 16, 1777

Over the next two days, Lafayette tried to stay off the main road as much as possible, sleeping in barns and staying out of sight as best he could. He played the part of a courier, switching horses along the way at post depots. It was dusk as he entered Bayonne. He stopped to water his horse and quickly get something to eat at a tavern. When he came out, he saw the coach pulling into town with Mauroy inside, the coachman wearing his own blue coat. He grinned and started making his way to the inn where he saw them stop. Mauroy stepped out of the carriage and lifted a hand in greeting, smiling broadly to see Lafayette.

"*C'est bon!* We've both made it!" Lafayette greeted him. "How was your journey?"

"Uneventful," Mauroy answered. "I'll have you know that *Monsieur* Fumel's officers enjoyed their fill at the tavern in Langdon."

Lafayette grinned. "Well then, I am sure you were able to get quite the head start and throw them off our trail."

"Oui, but they may have doubled back once they rode a while in the direction of Marseilles," Mauroy answered with a worried look.

"Monsieur Mauroy is right," Clarie interjected. "The officers would be sure to check each town for our presence and record of horse exchanges on the road to Marseilles. If they discovered that we did not travel along that route, it is possible that they figured out our new course and will follow us here."

Mauroy nodded. "I must attend to some business before we travel the last thirty-odd miles to reach San Sebastian."

"Je suis fatigué," Lafayette followed with a yawn, rubbing his tired eyes. "I must rest. I will take cover in a nearby stable for the night. Let us meet back here in the morning."

"Bon, a demain," Mauroy agreed.

"And by tomorrow afternoon, we will finally board *La Victoire!"* Lafayette determined, leading his horse away with an expectant fist of victory raised in the air.

Kate and Liz followed along invisibly behind him. They weren't about to let him out of their sight on this, his last night in France.

71

VERCINGETORIX AND THE OUTLAW

BAYONNE, FRANCE, APRIL 17, 1777

Pink ribbons streaked across the lightening purple sky, causing the half-moon to slowly fade from view. A single dust-swirled beam of sunlight crept into the hundred-year-old barn as a rooster strutted back and forth across the entrance. His head jutted forward with each step, and he emitted a quiet 'bawk, bawk, bawk,' to warm up his vocal cords.

Liz stifled a giggle at the iconic French rooster. The sleek black cat lifted her dainty paw and smiled. "Whenever you are ready, *monsieur.*"

"Bon, madame," the rooster answered, stopping in place, and blowing her a kiss with the tip of one of his wings. Then he threw back his head, took a deep breath, and closed his eyes. "COCK-A-DOODLE-DOOOOOOOO!"

Lafayette moaned, hearing the rooster greet the day. But he didn't budge.

"Do it again, if ye don't mind," Kate whispered to the rooster. The little white dog smiled. "I know how ye like ta own the morn."

"Avec plaisir, madame," the colorful rooster proudly answered with a gravelly French accent and a wink to the white Westie. "It is what I do best, no?" He cleared his throat, lifted his red beak high in the air, and stretched out his blue-green metallic wings for the windup in order to really belt it out. His red throat feathers flared out and violently shook as he let it all go, screaming, "COCK-A-DOODLE-DOOOOOOOO! COCK-A-DOODLE-DOOOOOOOOOOOOOOOOOOO!"

"Oui, I heard you the first time," an irritated Lafayette muttered, rolling over on the straw. "And the second, and the third . . ." His sleepy mumble trailed off. In a moment he let go a snore.

Kate frowned, shaking her head at the exhausted young Frenchman who refused to wake up. She looked from Liz to the rooster and shrugged her shoulders.

"Humph! I know when I have been insulted!" the rooster huffed, embarrassed by the teenager who ignored some of his best work. *"Adolescent typique, pfft!"* he blustered as he lifted his chin and strutted out of the barn toward the farmhouse. He would press on, crowing to rouse the rest of the local inhabitants in this ancient town perched on the southwest coastal border of France and Spain.

"*Le coq francaise typique, no?*" Liz said, sharing a giggle with Kate.

"Aye, jest like Jacques," Kate answered. "Yer typical French rooster."

"*Oui,* and a typical teenager, as our rooster friend said of our marquis," Liz agreed, gazing at Lafayette's black shirt and burgundy breeches as he nestled comfortably in the hay. Her tail curled up and down, and she looked around the old barn, thinking.

"He needs ta get up," Kate uttered with a frown. "We don't want ta get caught here after how far we've come. We're almost there!"

"Do you know what the local Bayonne peasants did in the mid-seventeenth century when conflicts arose with the Spanish, and they ran low on gunpowder and projectiles?" Liz asked, walking over to a bench with tools.

Kate cocked her head. "Nooooo, Liz. Ye know I enjoy yer history lectures, but I don't think this be the time . . ."

"They simply attached long hunting knives to the barrels of their muskets, and *voila* they had makeshift spears," Liz continued, ignoring Kate's comment. She picked up a small, iron spike and turned, wearing a big grin. "And do you know what the peasants of Bayonne called them?"

Kate sighed, "Um, *no,* lass."

"Come, *mon amie,* think!" Liz encouraged her excitedly. "*C'est simple!*" She walked over to Lafayette and held the spike close to his back side.

Kate's eyes widened as she saw Liz lift the spike in the air. "Bayonets!"

"*Oui,* which is the *point* of this lecture!" Liz answered gleefully, poking the spike into Lafayette's behind, causing him to bolt upright and shout as she darted behind a barrel.

Lafayette frowned and rubbed his back side, looking around him. He saw no one, only the sun now pouring into the barn and the hay scattered about. All he heard was the rooster crowing in the distance and his brown horse in the far stall, seemingly snickering at him. He shook his head, his red hair mussed and dangling around his shoulders. He felt around the hay and his hand landed on an iron spike. "Ah, I must have rolled over this." He chuckled, tossed it back into the hay, and stretched out his arms and back, trying to come to life.

Kate stepped outside the barn because she heard something that Lafayette hadn't yet heard—the sound of a swift pair of horses galloping up the road. Alarmed, she ran to the hedge and spotted what she had hoped she would not see. It was Fumel's men!

"It's them!" she barked, alerting Liz. "They've followed us here!"

Lafayette heard a dog barking and hurriedly slipped on his boots. He walked over to peek out of the barn and spotted the two horsemen as they passed by. He withdrew into the barn, his heart racing as he leaned his back against the old wooden door. *They've followed us here!*

The nineteen-year-old quickly put on his long, charcoal coat and three-cornered hat and ran to the stall to grab the horse by the reins. "Shhhh, we must be quiet, *cheval.*" He gently rubbed the horse's neck and led him to the entrance of the barn. He mounted the horse and looked both ways. No sign of the horsemen. He exhaled and directed the horse onward. Once he got to the road, he frowned. "We cannot meet Mauroy and the coach back at the inn as planned. Fumel's men will surely be there," he muttered to his horse. "He will have to figure it out and meet me at San Sebastian." He patted the horse on the neck. "I know you are tired from our long journey yesterday, *cheval,* but I need for you to ride a bit longer, as fast as you can." The horse whinnied, as if protesting the coming ride. Lafayette clicked his tongue, squeezed his legs tight, and hoarsely whispered, *"Allons-y!"*

Liz ran out to meet Kate, and they watched the Marquis de Lafayette gallop away from Bayonne. "We must get to Clarie and the coach to let her know he has gone on ahead!" Together the two friends ran down the dirt path to the town center to find their friend.

The sun was high overhead now, and Lafayette kept looking behind him as he rode his horse hard and fast toward San Sebastian. It was twenty-eight miles from Bayonne to reach the port city where his ship awaited him. It had been three weeks since he left *La Victoire* in the care of General De Kalb and the shipload of officers waiting for him to sail to America. After all he had overcome to reach this point, he could not afford to be apprehended by those police officers. They were only following orders, but the orders they followed were to arrest the outlaw, and they were issued by none other than King Louis XVI of France.

The gravity of his escape weighed heavily on his mind, spurring him on to escape arrest, to escape the king, to escape his father-in-law, and to escape a meaningless existence at the Court of Versailles. If he could finally make this one great escape, he would not only win liberty for the Americans, but also for himself. The Marquis de Lafayette would attain glory on the battlefield fighting for a righteous, glorious cause.

Lafayette slowly felt his horse begin to struggle with the pace he had held now for twelve miles. The horse's breathing grew labored, his pace slowed, and he began jerking his head against the reins. *"Je sais, je sais, mon cheval,* you have run so far, and so well," Lafayette consoled him, slowing to a walk. Lafayette frowned and patted the horse's neck, feeling how drenched it was with sweat. The horse's heavy breathing mixed with an occasional wheeze. He needed watering, and now.

Suddenly Lafayette heard behind him what he most dreaded, especially at this moment. A pair of horses were galloping toward him, kicking up the dust a mile distant. "No, no, no, no!" Terror filled his eyes and he looked down at the struggling horse. He quickly looked around to get his bearings when he saw a welcome sight. There in the distance was a small, crescent-shaped harbor and the little town of St. Jean-de-Luz. He leaned over into the horse's ear. "One mile more, *mon cheval!* Then you can rest. But for now, I need you to run!"

The young Frenchman snapped the reins, pressed his knees into the horse's side, and once more took off at a fast gallop. Lafayette leaned over the horse as low as he could, his coat flying behind him in the air. His heart pounded as hard as his horse's hooves against the road. He looked behind him and it appeared that the men were gaining on him. "Almost there, *cheval!*" he shouted.

Within a few moments, he galloped into town and hurried to the familiar barn behind the inn. He quickly dismounted and brought the horse inside to a watering trough. His chest heaved and he put his hands on his knees, trying to catch his breath. His legs felt weak from fear as much as the rigorous ride. He stood up and wiped his face with his upper arm. He then leaned over and stroked the horse's neck, burying his head gratefully into its black mane. *"C'est bon, c'est bon. Merci, mon cheval. Merci."*

"Monsieur?" came the soft voice of a lady at the entrance to the barn. She had a basket of fresh eggs draped over her arm.

Lafayette snapped his head up quickly, and his face flooded with relief. It was Madeleine. Her eyes suddenly widened with recognition, but then frowned, as she saw that he was now dressed like a common courier, not a gentleman. She tilted her head in question, but before she could say anything more, the two police officers came clip-clopping up the street in front of the barn. Lafayette quickly put a finger to his mouth and then raised a fist in the air, mouthing the word, *"LIBERTÉ!"*

"Mademoiselle! Have you seen the rider that came this way?" one of the officers asked.

"He rode a brown horse," the other officer added.

Madeleine didn't bat an eye but walked over to join the men in the street, diverting their attention away from the barn. *"Oui,* I've just seen him. He wore a long, dark coat and burgundy breeches, no?"

The officers looked at each other and nodded. *"Oui,* that's him!"

The young French girl smiled and pointed in the opposite direction. "That way."

"Merci, mademoiselle," the men answered in unison, tapping a finger to their hats. In seconds they galloped off in pursuit of the elusive outlaw.

Lafayette heard the horses ride off and closed his eyes in relief. He slumped down to the cool stone floor, drawing his knees up and resting his head on his arms.

Madeleine reappeared in the door. "I did not expect to see you again . . . especially dressed like that, plus not in your carriage . . . and being chased by riders." She wore a look of suspicion. "Who were those men, *monsieur?"*

Lafayette looked up and smiled, a sweaty mess with his damp red hair sticking out from his hat. "I cannot begin to thank you enough, *mademoiselle.* You are an angel sent from God!" He looked up and gave another exhale of relief and then got to his feet. He took her hand in his and kissed it. *"Merci, merci, merci!"* He smiled and clasped his hands together as if praying. *"S'il vous plaît,* believe me, I am not a criminal. There has been a terrible misunderstanding, and those men have not yet received word to explain things. I cannot go into the details, but I am in pursuit of doing something noble."

Madeleine tilted her head and smiled. "Noble like Vercingetorix? *Liberté?"*

"Exactement!" Lafayette exclaimed with a hand up. His eyes widened. "Veringetorix!" He ran to the stall belonging to the wild white stallion. "He is still here!"

"Oui, he is still here," Madeleine answered.

"You have already done more for me than I could ever ask, but I must ask you for one more favor," Lafayette implored. "Please, allow me to exchange my brown horse for Vercingetorix. I must continue on my way, especially if those men come back looking for me here. I cannot allow you to experience trouble on my behalf."

"But *monsieur,* we are yet to ride him! You remember that he has bucked off every man who has tried," Madeleine answered.

"Did they use whips?" Lafayette asked, now staring at the horse, who walked right up to him.

"Oui, I believe so," she answered. "How else could they control him?"

Lafayette looked the beautiful white horse in the eye and stroked his nose. "Do you also want *liberté,* Vercingetorix? Let me take you away from here, *cheval."* The horse didn't flinch but kept his gaze on the young Frenchman, who slowly opened the gate of the stall, stepping inside. Lafayette went over and gently rubbed the horse's side, allowing the horse to smell him and get reacquainted with him.

Madeleine looked on and marveled at how the young man and the horse interacted. "Are you certain you wish to take him?"

Lafayette slipped his arm under the horse's head, standing close while the horse nuzzled him. *"Oui,* I can ride this horse. Plus, I do not have a choice. I must escape from here." He whispered in the horse's ear. "Show me that you are the fastest *cheval* in France."

Madeleine shrugged her shoulders with a grin. *"Très bien. Mon père* will be relieved to have you take the horse off his hands."

"Merci beaucoup, mademoiselle!" Lafayette exclaimed, patting Vercingetorix. *"Bon!* Let me move the saddle and harness, and we will be on our way." While he took care of the horses, he told her, "You were quick on your feet to tell those men I rode in the opposite direction."

"I did not exactly do that, *monsieur,"* she answered with a sly grin. "I told them I had just seen you—which I had, in the barn—and then I simply pointed and said, 'That way.' I didn't say you had *gone* that way."

Lafayette threw back his head and laughed. "You are an angel indeed!"

Soon he was ready to mount up and handed her several gold coins. *"Pour vous, merci."*

"Merci beaucoup, monsieur!" she exclaimed, wide-eyed with the money he gave her. "You honor Vercingetorix—both of them!"

Lafayette bowed with a hand over his heart. *"Merci. Au revoir."*

Madeleine curtsied and grinned. *"Au revoir, et bonne chance, monsieur."*

With that, Lafayette guided the white horse out of the stall. He calmly put a foot into the stirrup, grabbed the mane and pulled himself up. The horse whinnied and moved his head side to side, a bit anxious. Lafayette calmly patted his neck and spoke to him. "Shhh, *bon cheval, bon cheval."* He gently applied pressure with his knees and Vercingetorix started walking forward. Lafayette and Madeleine exchanged glances of delight. Once he was at the door, he tipped his hat to the young lady and rode outside.

Within moments Lafayette and Vercingetorix raced down the street toward San Sebastian. "But first, *mon cheval,* I will take you to *la mer."*

The white horse gave a neigh of exhilaration as they took off toward the sea, his mane flying behind him. He snorted with anticipation, smelling the salt air he longed for. Lafayette had never ridden a faster horse! He guided him down the coast and to a remote beach below the craggy shoreline where the cliffs towered above the azure sea below. When they got to the beach, Vercingetorix ran right into the water, galloping happily along. Lafayette threw his head back, laughing with joy. He already was madly in love with this horse that shared his craving for freedom.

Lafayette allowed the horse to go where he wished, back and forth and up and down the beach, frolicking. After a while, Vercingetorix slowed and simply stood in the water, gazing out to sea, panting. He snorted and bobbed his head up and down.

Lafayette leaned over and rubbed the horse's shoulder. *"Mon cheval de mer."* He sat back up. *"Bon,* now we must get to *La Victoire."*

It was now nearing dusk, and the pink ribbons in the sky that began the day started to appear, this time bringing the half-moon back into view as the light started to fade.

Once Fumel's men had ridden a few miles, they decided to backtrack, having seen no sign of Lafayette anywhere on the main road. They decided that if the outlaw were going anywhere other than Marseilles, it would be to San Sebastian to catch his ship. Off they went, now in the direction of the port. If they didn't find the ship, they would head back to Bordeaux. Once they crossed over into Spain, they would be out of their jurisdiction to arrest Lafayette. At least they could report what they learned, but their aim was to catch the outlaw before he reached the border.

As Lafayette neared San Sebastian, he suddenly heard the two riders in the distance. He turned to see them a mile behind him. Had they spotted him? He quickly pulled on the reins and directed Vercingetorix off the road and into a cluster of trees in a thicket near the cliff. He prayed a quick prayer for an answer of what to do next.

If they caught him here, his dreams of sailing to America would be over.

Soon the men passed by, continuing to San Sebastian. Lafayette took a deep breath and jumped down from the saddle, taking Vercingetorix by the reins, and walking out from the trees to get a view of the distant port. The road that the men traveled now veered away from the shoreline and curved farther inland, so they would not have a view of the sea for a while. Lafayette looked down the coastline and suddenly saw something he didn't expect.

There, sitting in a secluded, tiny harbor of Los Passajes five miles northeast of San Sebastian was *La Victoire!* "De Kalb must have moved her there for safety!" Lafayette exclaimed, looking up to the heavens. *"Merci, mon Dieu!"* There could have been no greater answer to prayer than an unexpected escape to such a safe haven.

LOS PASSAJES, SPAIN, APRIL 17, 1777

De Kalb grinned broadly as he stood on the bow of *La Victoire* and saw Lafayette being rowed in a launch out to the ship. The young marquis waved his hat and wore a huge smile. The general slapped the railing with joy. "Lafayette *est arrivé!*"

The other officers and crew swarmed to the side of the ship and leaned over to see Lafayette's approach. They cheered and readied the rope ladder to welcome him aboard, including Mauroy, who had made it to the ship before Lafayette. When the coachman took them on an alternate route to San Sebastian, he "just so happened" to see *La Victoire* moored here.

As Lafayette triumphantly set foot on deck, De Kalb gripped him by the hand. "*Bonjour, Monsieur le Marquis!* I am happy to see that you have returned safely." He leaned in with a coy grin. "Am I to understand that you are finally ready to sail to America?"

"*Bonjour, Général! Oui!* I am an outlaw, but I prefer to fight for the *liberté* of America rather than lose my own *liberté* and languish in a French prison," he exclaimed with a low bow to the laughs and cheers of the officers gathered around him. "So my friend, we shall be comrades in arms after all."

Liz, Kate, Clarie, and Vercingetorix stood on the shore and listened to the distant voices of the men cheering Lafayette's arrival. When Lafayette found the coach here at the shoreline, he left the horse in the coachman's care for the moment. It would take a couple of days to unload the baggage, ready the ship, and purchase fresh provisions for the voyage.

"We have not been properly introduced," Liz said, sauntering up to the white horse. "I am Liz. Lizette Brillante, from Normandy." She lifted a paw to Kate, who wagged her tail and smiled. "This is Kate, and this human is named Clarie, but she is not really a human. She just looks like one at the moment. You saw them both at the barn. *Comprenez-vous?*"

Vercingetorix looked from Liz to Kate to Clarie and back to Liz. He said nothing for a moment. Then he leaned his head down to whisper in Liz's ear. "*Bonsoir,* Liz. You mean I can talk in front of this human?"

"*Oui, mon ami!* We have much to explain to you, but just understand that we are on mission from the Maker to help humans," Liz answered. "Clarie is actually a lamb, but she can take any shape or form. Welcome to the mission to help the Marquis de Lafayette!"

The horse lifted his head with surprise and looked at Clarie, dressed as the coachman. He snorted and then laughed. *"Bonsoir,* Clarie. Humans talk to me all the time, but I never talk back with words."

"Aye, but ye an' Lafayette have learned ta talk easily," Kate said, wagging her tail.

"He's the first kind human that's really known how to talk to me," the horse replied, nodding his head. He looked out to sea. "I like him, but it looks as though he's left me."

Clarie came up to the horse and petted him on the neck. "No, dear one, you will be traveling with Lafayette on an exciting voyage across the sea."

"Moi? Across the sea?" Vercingertorix asked. *"C'est bon!"*

"Aye, I've got ta stow away on board, but I'll soon come out ta see Lafayette an' be with ye!" Kate said happily. "Ye'll be me big seahorse!"

The horse leaned down and nudged Kate with his snout. *"Avec plaisir."*

ABOARD *LA VICTOIRE*, LOS PASSAJES, SPAIN, APRIL 19, 1777

As they prepared to get underway in the morning, Lafayette busied himself with several final letters to Adrienne, telling her not to worry and that he loved her very much. He begged her to forgive him for leaving. He told her to take good care of Henriette and their baby on the way. Finally, he penned one last letter, to William Carmichael:

Here, Monsieur, is the last letter which you will receive from me in French…The fear of doing some harm to my friends forced me to make a cruel sacrifice. Now the fear is over, I have not lost a single moment, and I leave full of joy, of hope and of zeal for our common cause. I am told that Lord Stormont has shown some bad humor at my leaving. On the whole, this affair has produced all the éclat which I desired and at this moment, when all the world has its eyes on us, I shall try to justify that celebrity. I can vouch for it that the English will not take me, and I hope that you will not be worried.

Do not worry about my family or even about the order which I received. Once gone, everyone will approve my action; once victorious, everyone will applaud my enterprise. It is from your recommendations that I expect the means of securing all these advantages. I hope that I shall prove as good a general as I am a good American and I shall forget nothing in order to justify your friendship and the public esteem. I hope too it may be a way to prove the tender and eternal attachment, with which I have the honor to be Monsieur, your very humble and very obedient servant,

Lafayette

⚜

LOS PASSAJES, SPAIN, APRIL 20, 1777

The sun was making its way onto the horizon, and it was time for them to be on their way.

Vercingetorix had already been taken to the ship and hoisted on board, only with the calm reassurance of Lafayette. Clarie drove off with the coach, heading back to Paris where she would further investigate the city's underground tunnels that Kate and Liz had told her about while searching for Charlatan's headquarters. While they waited for the last launch that would take the remaining supplies and crew back to *La Victoire,* Liz and Kate spent a few minutes saying farewell.

Liz smiled. "Lafayette has defied his king, declared his independence, and is taking up arms to defend liberty. He already sounds like an American."

"Aye, he's goin' ta fit right in!" Kate agreed happily. "All is well now, lass. Lafayette is safely in Spain, he's got the blessin' of the people, the French government secretly wants him ta set sail, an' his family won't interfere any longer." Kate put her paw over her heart and smiled. "Lancelot would be proud of Lafayette. He may be a naïve, sometimes confused young lad, but way down in his heart, he's truly a gallant knight."

"*Oui,* so I shall wish you *bon voyage, mon amie,*" Liz replied sadly. "I must return to *mon* Henry in Virginia."

The two friends put their heads together for a parting embrace.

Kate pulled back, her eyes brimming. "It's been a grand adventure, lass. Thanks for all yer help with Lafayette's escape from France. I'll miss ye."

"It has been my honor and joy, *chère* Kate. I shall see you in America," Liz answered, wiping away a tear. "*Au revoir et à bientôt.*"

As Kate watched Liz walking away, she nibbled a madeleine, turned invisible, and stepped into the little boat just before the remaining crew members arrived to row out to *La Victoire.*

But none of them noticed the shadow that slipped onto the launch and under some canvas bags, out of sight.

A Word from the Author

"GIVE ME FACTS OR GIVE ME DEATH AS A CREDIBLE HISTORICAL AUTHOR!"

I t is vitally important to me that I share with you background information on my research that fills the pages of my books, and the liberties I take to tell the stories. The genre I write is historical fiction fantasy, in that order. This means the first layer I begin writing is the *history*. This foundation layer must be rock solid historically, down to the most minute detail. I exhaust my sources of books, online research, site visits, and interviews with historical experts on people, places, and events. Once the bedrock history is laid, I then add the layer of *fiction*, which must be *plausible*. For instance, the fictional words I put into Lafayette's mouth, as well as his actions, must match his character and the cultural setting. Once the historical fiction is as pure as I can make it, I add the layer of *fantasy* where the animal characters come into play. I look for those "unknowns" in the story of things that did happen (but we don't know how or why) or that *could* have happened. I allow my animals to affect the events of the story without ever giving away their true identities, which makes it fun. Once all three layers are set, the book is an accurate, educational, enjoyable (I hope) read intended to make history come alive for the reader.

I've compiled a great deal of background information that I hope you will find fascinating, but with a few spoiler alerts for this book and the next. It will fill in some details I cannot possibly cover with an already lengthy manuscript. I wish I could write about everything that was going on concurrently in America, France, and England during these exciting years, for there is far more that occurred than what I've presented here. In some ways I feel I am just scratching the surface, believe it or not. I highly encourage you to read nonfiction books and biographies that cover this amazing historical period to increase your understanding of and appreciation for our founding fathers and the American Revolution. A fantastic resource for maps to visualize each battle I describe is located at author Rick Atkinson's website from his superb book, *The British Are Coming:* https://revolutiontrilogy.com/maps-timeline/. Please reference my bibliography for his book and others that I hope will get you hooked on learning about the players and events of America's birth. With every book you finish, I hope you'll quote my dear friend Richard Schumann (Colonial Williamsburg's Patrick Henry) who says, "This bears further discovery."

You can find this background information, resource links, plus fun research pictures, videos, and interviews on my website. Please visit the MARQUIS web page at www.epicorderoftheseven.com or use the QR code below:

BIBLIOGRAPHY

Allen, Thomas B., and Cheryl Harness. *George Washington, Spymaster: How America Outspied the British and Won the Revolutionary War*. National Geographic, 2004.

American Revolution and Its Era: Maps and Charts of North America and the West Indies, 1750–89 | Digital Collections | Library of Congress. Library of Congress, https://www.loc.gov/collections/american-revolutionary-war-maps.

André, John. *Major André's Journal: Operations of the British Army under Lieutenant Generals Sir William Howe and Sir Henry Clinton, June 1777 to November 1778*. 1968.

Andrlik, Todd. *Reporting The Revolutionary War: Before It Was History, It Was News*. Sourcebooks, 2012.

Anonymous. *A Complete History of the Marquis De Lafayette: Major-General in the American Army in the War of the Revolution Embracing an Account of His Tour Through the United States to the Time of His Departure, September 1825*. General Books, 2010.

Appleby, Jayce Oldham, et al. *The American Republic to 1877*. Glencoe/McGraw-Hill, 2005.

Atkinson, Rick. *The British Are Coming*. HarperCollins Publishers, 2019.

Auricchio, Laura. *The Marquis: Lafayette Reconsidered*. Vintage Books, 2015.

Bailyn, Bernard. *To Begin the World Anew: The Genius and Ambiguities of the American Founders–1st. Ed*. Knopf, 2003.

Bakeless, John. *Turncoats, Traitors, and Heroes*. Da Capo Press, 1998.

Bass, Robert D. *The Green Dragoon; the Lives of Banastre Tarleton and Mary Robinson*. Holt, 1957.

Bass, Streeter. "Beaumarchais and the American Revolution." *Central Intelligence Agency*, Central Intelligence Agency, 5 Aug. 2011, https://www.cia.gov/library/center-for-the-study-of-intelligence/kent-csi/vol14no1/html/v14i1a01p_0001.htm.

Bearce, Stephanie. *The American Revolution: Spies, Secret Missions, & Hidden Facts from the American Revolution*. Prufrock Press Inc., 2015.

Beck, Derek W. *Igniting the American Revolution: 1773–75*. Sourcebooks, 2016.

Beck, Derek W. *War before Independence: 1775–76*. Sourcebooks Inc, 2017.

Becker, John P. *The Sexagenary: or Reminiscences of the American Revolution*. J. Munsell, Albany, NY, 1866, https://archive.org/details/sexagenaryorremi00beckiala/page/n3.

Bemis, Samuel F. "British Secret Service and the French–American Alliance." *The American Historical Review*, vol. 29, no. 3, Apr. 1924, https://doi.org/https://doi.org/10.2307/1836521.

Bernier, Olivier. *Lafayette: Hero of Two Worlds*. E.P. Dutton, 1983.

Bobrick, Benson. *Angel in the Whirlwind: The Triumph of the American Revolution*. Simon & Schuster, 2011.

Bolton, Charles Knowles. "Letters of Hugh, Earl Percy, from Boston and New York, 1774–76 : Northumberland, Hugh Percy, Duke of, 1742-1817 : Free Download, Borrow, and Streaming." *Internet Archive*, The Library Shelf, 1 Jan. 1970, https://archive.org/details/hughearlpercybos00nortrich.

Bonk, David, and Graham Turner. *Trenton and Princeton, 1776–77: Washington Crosses the Delaware*. Osprey, 2009.

Borneman, Walter R. *American Spring: Lexington, Concord, and the Road to Revolution*. Back Bay Books, 2015.

Boston and the American Revolution: Boston National Historical Park, Massachusetts. Division of Publications, National Park Service, U.S. Department of the Interior, 1998.

Boudreau, George W. *Independence: A Guide to Historic Philadelphia*. Westholme, 2012.

Brandt, Keith, and Scott Snow. *Lafayette, Hero of Two Nations*. Troll Associates, 1990.

Bris, Gonzague Saint, and George Holoch. *Lafayette: Hero of the American Revolution*. Pegasus Books, 2011.

"THE BRITISH ARMY AT THE OUTBREAK OF THE REVOLUTION: A GENERAL SURVEY." *The British Army—Chapter One*, http://www.american revolution.org/britisharmy1.php.

Broadwater, Jeff. *George Mason, Forgotten Founder*. University of North Carolina Press, 2006.

Brooks, Noah. *Henry Knox, a Soldier of the Revolution: Major-General in the Continental Army, Washington's Chief of Artillery, First Secretary of War under the Constitution, Founder of the Society of the Cincinnati, 1750–1806*. G.P. Putnam's Sons, New York and London, 1900.

Brown, Richard H., and Paul E. Cohen. *Revolution: Mapping the Road to American Independence, 1755–83*. W.W. Norton & Company, 2015.

Butler, Judge Edward F. "A Biographical Sketch of REV. / LT. COL. WILLIAM MC CLANAHAN and the Culpeper Minutemen." *Sons of the American Revolution— PATRIOT REV./LT. COL. WILLIAM MCCLANAHAN*, 13 June 2009, http://judge-ed-butler.sarsat.org/Genealogy/REVLTCOLWILLIAMMCCLANAHAN.htm.

Byrd, James P. *Sacred Scripture, Sacred War: The Bible and the American Revolution*. Oxford University Press, 2017.

Cahn, Jonathan. *Book of Mysteries*. Frontline, 2016.

Carson, Jane, and Edward M. Riley. *Patrick Henry, Prophet of the Revolution*. Virginia Independence Bicentennial Commission, 1979.

Carter, H. *The Marquis De Lafayette: Bright Sword for Freedom*. Random House, 1958.

Castrovilla, Selene, and Drazen Kozjan. *Revolutionary Friends: General George Washington and the Marquis De Lafayette*. Calkins Creek, an Imprint of Highlights, 2013.

Catel, Patrick. *Soldiers of the Revolutionary War*. Heinemann Library, 2011.

Chaffin, Tom. *Revolutionary Brothers: Thomas Jefferson, the Marquis De Lafayette, and the Friendship That Helped Forge Two Nations*. St. Martin's Press, 2019.

Charles River Editors, *Marquis De Lafayette and Baron De Kalb: The Lives of the Legendary Foreign Soldiers Who Sailed to America Together to Fight in the Revolutionary War*, 2021.

Chartrand, René, and Richard Hook. *American War of Independence Commanders*. Osprey, 2003.

"Chateau De Versailles Mobile Application." *Chateau De Versailles*, 2018, http://en.chateauversailles.fr.

Chernow, Ron. *Washington—A Life*. Penguin Books Ltd., 2011.

Clary, David A. *Adopted Son: Washington, Lafayette, and the Friendship That Saved the Revolution*. Bantam Books, 2008.

Cocca, Lisa Colozza. *Marquis De Lafayette: Fighting for America's Freedom*. Crabtree Publishing Company, 2013.

Cocking, Lauren. "The Rambunctious, Elitist Chocolate Houses of 18th-Century London." *Atlas Obscura*, Atlas Obscura, 28 Nov. 2018, http://www.atlasobscura.com/articles/history-of-gentlemens-clubs.

Collins, Kathleen. *Marquis De Lafayette: French Hero of the American Revolution*. Rosen Central Primary Source, 2004.

Cook, Charles, and Nancy Cook. "Blueprint for a Revolution: The Spies at Carpenters' Hall." *Carpenters' Hall*, http://www.carpentershall.org/blueprint-for-a-revolution.

Cook, Jane Hampton. *Battlefields & Blessings: Stories of Faith and Courage from the Revolutionary War*. God and Country Press, 2008.

Cornwallis, Charles, and Charles Ross. *Correspondence of Charles, First Marquis Cornwallis: Edited with Notes, by Charles Ross, Esq., in Three Volumes*. Chadwyck-Healey Ltd., 1987.

Cote, Jenny L. *Epic Order of the Seven. The Declaration, the Sword & the Spy*. Living Ink Books, an imprint of AMG Publishers, 2020.

Cote, Jenny L. *Epic Order of the Seven. The Voice, the Revolution & the Key*. Living Ink Books, an imprint of AMG Publishers 2017.

Couvillon, Mark. *Patrick Henry's Virginia: A Guide to the Homes and Sites in the Life of an American Patriot*. Patrick Henry Memorial Foundation, 2001.

Couvillon, Mark. *The Demosthenes of His Age: Accounts of Patrick Henry's Oratory by His Contemporaries*. The Patrick Henry Memorial Foundation, 2013.

Covington, Richard. "Marie Antoinette." *Smithsonian.com*, Smithsonian Institution, 1 Nov. 2006, https://www.smithsonianmag.com/history/marie-antoinette-134629573/.

Daigler, Kenneth A. *Spies, Patriots, and Traitors: American Intelligence in the Revolutionary War*. Georgetown University Press, 2015.

Daughan, George C. *Revolution on the Hudson: New York City and the Hudson River Valley in the American War of Independence*. W.W. Norton & Company, 2017.

"Declaring Independence: Drafting the Documents Exhibition." *Exhibition— Declaring Independence: Drafting the Documents | Exhibitions—Library of Congress*, 4 July 1995, https://www.loc.gov/exhibits/declara/.

Dick, Jimmy. *Silas Deane: Forlorn and Forgotten Patriot*. Journal of the American Revolution, 28 Oct. 2013, https://allthingsliberty.com/author/jimmy-dick/.

Doren, Carl Van, et al. *Secret History of the American Revolution; An Account of the Conspiracies of Benedict Arnold and Numerous Others Drawn from the Secret Service Papers of the British Headquarters in North America, Now for the First Time Examined and Made Public*. The Viking Press, New York, 1941.

Drake, Francis S. *Life and Correspondence of Henry Knox: Major-General in the American Revolutionary Army*. 1873.

Dunaway, W. F. "The Virginia Conventions of the Revolution." Vol. 10, no. 7, 1904, pp. 567–86. *JSTOR*, https://doi.org/10.2307/1100650. Accessed 12 Nov. 2019.

Duncan, Mike. *Hero of Two Worlds: The Marquis De Lafayette in the Age of Revolution*. PublicAffairs, Hachette Book Group, 2021.

Durand, John. "New Materials for the History of the American Revolution: Beaumarchais, Pierre Augustin Caron De, 1732–99 : Free Download, Borrow, and Streaming." *World Cat*, London: F. Warne; New York: Scribner, Welford, and Armstrong, 1 Jan. 1889, https://archive.org/details/newmaterialsforh00beauuoft /page/n3.

Edward Bancroft (@ Edwd. Edwards), Estimable Spy. Central Intelligence Agency, 8 May 2007, https://www.cia.gov/static/750b6cacc27ec291177e7f33e693727b /Edward-Bancroft-Estimable-Spy.pdf.

Ellis, Joseph J. *His Excellency: George Washington*. Alfred A. Knopf, 2004.

Empreinte Digitale / Ligeo-Archives - https://www.empreintedigitale.fr, · Christophe Grosvallet, historian. "Bordeaux and American Independence." */ - Revenir à L'accueil*, https://archives.bordeaux-metropole.fr/expositions/ salle-recules-de-basmarein-raimbaux-et-compagnie-21/n:21.

The Eno Collection of New York City Views—NYPL Digital Collections, https://digital collections.nypl.org/collections/the-eno-collection-of-new-york-city-views ?keywords=&sort=sortString%2Basc#/?tab=about&scroll=6.

Ferling, John E. *Almost a Miracle: The American Victory in the War of Independence*. Oxford University Press, 2009.

Fewster, Helen, editor. *The American Revolution: A Visual History*. Smithsonian DK Publishing, 2016.

Fischer, David Hackett. *Washington's Crossing*. Oxford University Press, 2006.

Fisher, Robert I. C., and Thomas A. Chambers. *The Thirteen Colonies: Travel Historic America*. Fodor's Travel Publications, 2003.

Flexner, James Thomas. *Washington, the Indispensable Man*. Back Bay Books, 1994.

Fontaine, Edward, and Mark Couvillon. *Patrick Henry: Corrections of Biographical Mistakes, and Popular Errors in Regard to His Character. Anecdotes and New Facts Illustrating His Religious and Political Opinions; & the Style & Power of His Eloquence. A Brief Account of His Last Illness & Death*. Patrick Henry Memorial Foundation, 2011.

Ford, Paul Leicester. "Lord Howe's Commission to Pacify the Colonies." *The Atlantic*, Atlantic Media Company, 24 May 2022, https://www.theatlantic.com/magazine

/archive/1896/06/lord-howes-commission-to-pacify-the-colonies/635446/?utm
_source=copy-link&utm_medium=social&utm_campaign=share.

"Founders Online: The Committee of Secret Correspondence: Instructions to Silas..."
National Archives and Records Administration, National Archives and Records
Administration, https://founders.archives.gov/documents/Franklin/01-22-02-0222.

Franklin, Benjamin. "'The Morals of Chess', [before 28 June 1779]." *National
Archives and Records Administration*, Reprinted from The Columbian Magazine, i
(December, 1786), 159–61; Incomplete Copy:6 American Philosophical Society,
1786, https://founders.archives.gov/documents/Franklin/01-29-02-0608.

Freedman, Russell. *Lafayette and the American Revolution*. Holiday House, 2010.

Fritz, Jean, and Ronald Himler. *Why Not, Lafayette?* Puffin Books, 2001.

Fritz, Jean, et al. *Where Was Patrick Henry on the 29th of May?* Puffin Books, 2010.

Gaines, James R. *For Liberty and Glory: Washington, Lafayette, and Their Revolutions*.
W.W. Norton, 2009.

Gallagher, John J. *The Battle of Brooklyn 1776*. Heritage Books, 2004.

Gerson, Noel B. *Statue in Search of a Pedestal: a Biography of the Marquis De Lafayette*.
Dodd, Mead, 1976.

Gilbert, Oscar E., et al. *Patriot Militiaman in the American Revolution, 1775–82*.
Osprey Publishing, 2015.

Gillis, Jennifer Blizin. *Patrick Henry*. Heinemann Library, 2005.

Gottschalk, Louis. *Lafayette in America*. University of Chicago, 1975.

Green, Dr. Matthew. "How the Decadence and Depravity of 18th-Century London
Was Fueled by Hot Chocolate." *The Telegraph*, Telegraph Media Group, 25 Jan.
2018, https://www.telegraph.co.uk/travel/destinations/europe/united-kingdom
/england/london/articles/surprising-history-of-london-chocolate-houses/.

Green, Raleigh Travers, and Philip Slaughter. "Genealogical and Historical Notes
on Culpeper County, Virginia: Embracing a Revised and Enlarged..." *Full Text
of "Genealogical and Historical Notes on Culpeper County, Virginia: Embracing a
Revised and Enlarged..."*, University of Michigan, https://archive.org/stream
/genealogicaland00slaugoog/genealogicaland00slaugoog_djvu.txt.

Greenwood, John. *The Revolutionary Services of John Greenwood of Boston and New
York, 1775–83*. HardPress Publishing, 2010.

Groberg Films. "First Freedom: The Fight for Religious Liberty." *PBS*, Public
Broadcasting Service, 2012, http://www.pbs.org/video/first-freedom-first-freedom
-fight-religious-liberty/.

Grose, Francis. *A Classical Dictionary of the Vulgar Tongue*. Printed for S. Hooper, 1785.

Grote, JoAnn A., and Arthur M. Schlesinger. *Lafayette: French Freedom Fighter*.
Chelsea House Publishers, 2001.

Hamilton, Alexander. "Founders Online: The Farmer Refuted, &c., [23 February]
1775." *National Archives and Records Administration*, National Archives and Records
Administration, https://founders.archives.gov/documents/Hamilton/01-01-02-0057.

Hannings, Bud. *Chronology of the American Revolution: Military and Political Actions
Day by Day*. McFarland & Co., 2008.

Harmon, Daniel E. *Lord Cornwallis: British General.* Chelsea House Publishers, 2002.

Harris, Michael C. *What Is the Declaration of Independence?* Penguin Workshop, an Imprint of Penguin Random House, 2016.

Hart, Stephen. *Cant: a Gentleman's Guide to the Language of Rogues in Georgian London.* Improbable Fictions, 2014.

Hayes, Kevin J. *The Mind of a Patriot: Patrick Henry and the World of Ideas.* University of Virginia Press, 2008.

Henrickson, Beth. *The Marquis De Lafayette and Other International Champions of the American Revolution.* PowerKids Press, 2016.

Henry, Patrick, and James M. Elson. *Patrick Henry in His Speeches and Writings and in the Words of His Contemporaries.* Warwick House Publishers, 2007.

Henry, Patrick, et al. *Official Letters of the Governors of the State of Virginia. The Letters of Patrick Henry.* Vol. 1, Virginia State Library, 1926.

Henry, William Wirt, and Patrick Henry. *Patrick Henry: Life, Correspondence and Speeches.* Vol. 1, Kessinger Publishing, 2010.

"History.org: The Colonial Williamsburg Foundation's Official History and Citizenship Website." *Colonial Williamsburg Digital Library,* http://research.history.org/library/.

HM 10th Foot in America, http://www.redcoat.org/.

Hoffman, Renoda. *It Happened in Old White Plains.* S.n., 1989.

Hoffman, Renoda. *The Changing Face of White Plains.* R. Hoffman, 1994.

Hoffman, Renoda. *Yesterday in White Plains: A Picture History of a Vanished Era.* R. Hoffman, 2003.

Hogeland, William. *Declaration: The Nine Tumultuous Weeks When America Became Independent, May 1–July 4, 1776.* Simon Et Schuster Paperbacks, 2011.

Holoch, George. *Lafayette: Hero of the American Revolution.* Pegasus Books, 2010.

Howe, Archibald Murray. "Colonel John Brown, of Pittsfield, Massachusetts, the Brave Accuser of Benedict Arnold." *The Project Gutenberg,* Project Gutenberg, 2008, http://www.gutenberg.org/files/24581/24581-h/24581-h.htm.

Howe, Archibald Murray. An Address DELIVERED BEFORE THE FORT RENSSELAER CHAPTER OF THE D.A.R. AND OTHERS AT THE VILLAGE OF PALATINE BRIDGE, NEW YORK September 29, 1908.

Hyde, Mr, director. *The Rise and Fall of Versailles.* https://www.youtube.com/watch?v=8ti8bcaYuQ4.

Idzerda, Stanley J. *France and the American War for Independence.* Cornell University Press, 1975.

Idzerda, Stanley J., and Roger E. Smith. *Lafayette in the Age of the American Revolution.* Vol. 1, Cornell University Press, 1977.

Isaacson, Walter. *Benjamin Franklin: an American Life.* Simon & Schuster, 2003.

Jefferson, Thomas. "Translation of the Declaration of Independence by Thomas Jefferson." *La Declaration D'indpendance Des Tats-Unis Du 4 Juillet 1776,* 1776, http://www.axl.cefan.ulaval.ca/amnord/USA-hst-declaration_ind.htm.

Jones, Gareth, editor. *Military History: The Definitive Visual Guide to the Objects of Warfare.* DK Publishing, 2015.

"Journals of the Continental Congress." *A Century of Lawmaking for a New Nation: U.S. Congressional Documents and Debates, 1774–1875*, Library of Congress, https://memory.loc.gov/ammem/amlaw/lwjc.html.

Karsch, Carl G. "The Unlikely Spy." *Carpenters' Hall*, http://www.carpentershall.org /the-unlikely-spy.

Kelly, C. Brian., and Ingrid Smyer-Kelly. *Best Little Stories from the American Revolution: More than 100 True Stories*. Cumberland House, 2011.

Kelly, Jack. *Band of Giants: the Amateur Soldiers Who Won America's Independence*. Palgrave Macmillan, 2014.

Kennedy, John F. *A Nation of Immigrants*. Harper and Row, 1964.

Ketchum, Richard M. *The Winter Soldiers: The Battles for Trenton and Princeton*. Henry Holt, 1999.

Kidd, Thomas S. *Patrick Henry: First Among Patriots*. Basic Books, 2011.

Kilmeade, Brian, and Don Yaeger. *George Washington's Secret Six: The Spy Ring That Saved the American Revolution*. Sentinel, 2013.

King James Bible. Holman Bible Publishers, 1973.

Kite, Elizabeth S. 'LAFAYETTE AND HIS COMPANIONS ON THE 'VICTOIRE.' *Records of the American Catholic Historical Society of Philadelphia Vol. 45, No. 1 (MARCH, 1934), Pp. 1–32 (32 Pages)*, JSTOR, 2 Apr. 2021, https://www.jstor.org /stable/44209160.

Kite, Elizabeth S. *"Beaumarchais and the War of American Independence."* Google Books, R.G. Badger, 1918, https://books.google.com.

Knight, John. *War at Saber Point: Banastre Tarleton and the British Legion*. Westholme Publishing LLC, 2020.

Kramer, Lloyd S. *Lafayette in Two Worlds: Public Cultures and Personal Identities in an Age of Revolutions*. University of North Carolina Press, 2000.

Kukla, Jon. *Patrick Henry: Champion of Liberty*. Simon and Schuster, 2017.

Lossing, Benson John. "Patrick Henry's Commission." *The American Historical Record*, vol. 2, no. 13, Jan. 1873, pp. 32–33, https://babel.hathitrust.org/cgi/pt?id=hvd.3 2044094455078&view=1up&seq=43.

Lafayette, Marie Joseph Paul Yves Roch Gilbert Du Motier, and John Quincy Adams. *Oration on Life and Character of Gilbert Motier De Lafayette Delivered Dec. 31, 1834*. Printed by Gales and Seaton, 1835.

Lafayette, Marie Joseph Paul Yves Roch Gilbert Du Motier. *Memoirs of General Lafayette*. Robbins, 1825.

Lafayette, Marie Joseph Paul Yves Roch Gilbert Du Motier. *Memoirs, Correspondence and Manuscripts of General Lafayette*. Saunders and Otley, 1837.

Latzko, Andreas, and E. W. Dickes. *Lafayette: a Life*. Literary Guild, 1936.

Lefkowitz, Arthur S. "French Adventurers, Patriots, and Pretentious Imposters in the Fight for American Independence." *Journal of the American Revolution*, 5 June 2021, https://allthingsliberty.com/2021/06/french-adventurers-Patriots-and -pretentious-imposters-in-the-fight-for-american-independence/.

Levin, Jack E. *George Washington: Crossing, The*. Threshold Edition, 2013.

"List of Delegates to the Continental Congress." *Wikipedia*, Wikimedia Foundation, 18 Mar. 2018, https://en.wikipedia.org/wiki/List_of_delegates_to_the_Continental_Congress.

Lumpkin, Henry. *From Savannah to Yorktown: The American Revolution in the South.* To Excel, 2000.

Mackesy, Piers. *The War for America: 1775–83.* University of Nebraska Press, 1993.

MacNiven, Robbie, and Adam Hook. *Battle Tactics of the American Revolution.* Osprey Publishing, 2021.

Maier, Pauline. *American Scripture: Making the Declaration of Independence.* Vintage, 1999.

Maloy, Mark. *Victory or Death: The Battles of Trenton and Princeton, December 25, 1776–January 3, 1777.* Savas Beatie LLC, 2018.

"Maps Division." *The Library of Congress*, https://www.loc.gov/collections/american-revolutionary-war-maps/?dates=1700/1799.

Martin, Joseph Plumb. *Memoir of a Revolutionary Soldier: The Narrative of Joseph Plumb Martin.* Dover Publications, 2006.

May, Robin, and G. A. Embleton. *The British Army in North America, 1775–83.* Osprey Military, 1997.

Mayer, Henry. *A Son of Thunder: Patrick Henry and the American Republic.* Grove Press, 2001.

McBurney, Christian M. *Kidnapping the Enemy.* Westholme, 2014.

McCants, David A. *Patrick Henry, the Orator.* Greenwood Press, 1990.

McCullough, David G. *1776.* Simon & Schuster Paperbacks, 2006.

McCullough, David G. *John Adams.* Simon & Schuster, 2001.

McGaughy, J. Kent. *Richard Henry Lee of Virginia: a Portrait of an American Revolutionary.* Rowman & Littlefield, 2004.

McManus, John C. *U.S. Military History for Dummies.* Wiley, 2008.

McNab, Chris. *The Improbable Victory—the Campaigns, Battles and Soldiers of the American Revolution, 1775–83: in Association with the American Revolution Museum at Yorktown.* Osprey Publishing, 2017.

McPherson, Stephanie Sammartino, and Nicolas Debon. *Liberty or Death: a Story about Patrick Henry.* Carolrhoda Books, 2003.

Meade, Robert Douthat. *Patrick Henry: Practical Revolutionary.* Lippincott, 1969.

Medved, Michael. *The American Miracle: Divine Providence in the Rise of the Republic.* Crown Forum, 2017.

Meltzer, Brad, and Josh Mensch. *The First Conspiracy: The Secret Plot to Kill George Washington.* Flatiron Books, 2020.

Meltzer, Brad, et al. *The First Conspiracy: The Secret Plot to Kill George Washington.* Roaring Brook Press, 2020.

MEMOIR, CORRESPONDENCE, AND MISCELLANIES, FROM THE PAPERS OF THOMAS JEFFERSON. Project Gutenberg, 2005, http://www.gutenberg.org/files/16781/16781-h/16781-h.htm#linkcontents.

Miller, Nathan. *Spying for America: The Hidden History of U.S. Intelligence.* Marlowe & Co., 1997.

Miranda, Lin Manuel. "'You'll Be Back' from the Musical Hamilton." New York, Richard Rogers Theater, 2015, https://atlanticrecords.com/HamiltonMusic/" https://atlanticrecords.com/HamiltonMusic/.

Moore, Frank. *Diary of the American Revolution, from Newspapers and Original Documents* Vol. 1, Privately Printed, New York, 1865.

Morgan, George. *The True LaFayette*. Lippincott, 1919.

Morgan, George. *The True Patrick Henry: with Twenty-Four Illustrations*. Lippincott, 1907.

Morrill, Dan L. *Southern Campaigns of the American Revolution*. Nautical & Aviation Pub. Co., 1994.

Morris, B. F. *Christian Life and Character of the Civil Institutions of the United States*. Benediction Classics, 2010.

Morrow, George. *War! Patrick Henry's Finest Hour, Lord Dunmore's Worst*. Telford Publications, 2012.

Murray, Stuart. *DK Eyewitness Books: American Revolution: Discover How a Few Patriots Battled a Mighty Empire from the Boston Massacre To*. Dorling Kindersley Publishing, Inc., 2015.

Nagy, John A. *Invisible Ink*. Westholme, 2011.

"Naval Documents of the American Revolution." *Naval History and Heritage Command*, https://www.history.navy.mil/research/publications/publications-by-subject/naval-documents-of-the-american-revolution.html.

Niderost, Eric. "Benjamin Franklin: Revolutionary Spymaster." *HistoryNet*, 24 Jan. 2018, http://www.historynet.com/benjamin-franklin-revolutionary-spymaster.htm/2.

Norman B. Leventhal Map & Education Center at the Boston Public Library. *Digital Collections*, https://collections.leventhalmap.org/.

O'Donnell, Patrick K. *Washington's Immortals: The Untold Story of an Elite Regiment Who Changed the Course of the Revolution*. Atlantic Monthly Press, 2016.

"Official Website." *Palace of Versailles*, 10 Jan. 2019, http://en.chateauversailles.fr/.

O'Reilly, Bill, and Martin Dugard. *Killing England: The Brutal Struggle for American Independence*. Henry Holt and Company, 2017.

O'Toole, G. J. A. *Honorable Treachery: a History of U.S. Intelligence, Espionage, and Covert Action from the American Revolution to the CIA*. Grove, 2014.

Paine, Thomas. *Common Sense*. Dover Publications, 1997.

The Papers of George Washington Digital Edition. The University of Virginia Press, 2008, https://rotunda.upress.virginia.edu/founders/GEWN.html.

Paterson, Mike. "Gambling in London's Most Ruinous Gentlemen's Clubs." *London Historians' Blog*, 5 June 2014, https://londonhistorians.wordpress.com/2014/06/05/gambling-in-londons-most-ruinous-gentlemens-clubs/.

Patriot Tours NYC. "The Battle of Brooklyn 1776—Exhibit at the New York Historical Society." *YouTube*, Patriot Tours NYC, 2 Mar. 2021, https://youtu.be/lbkgUbqRvLQ.

Patterson, Benton Rain. *Washington and Cornwallis: The Battle for America, 1775–83*. Taylor Trade Publishing, 2004.

Payan, Gregory. *Marquis De Lafayette: French Hero of the American Revolution*. PowerPlus Books, 2002.

Perkins, James Breck. *France in the American Revolution*. B. Franklin, 1970.

Philbrick, Nathaniel. *Bunker Hill: a City, a Siege, a Revolution*. Penguin Books, 2014.

Philbrick, Nathaniel. *Valiant Ambition George Washington, Benedict Arnold, and the Fate of the American Revolution*. Penguin Books, 2017.

"A Plan of the City and Environs of New York in North America." *NYPL Digital Collections*, https://digitalcollections.nypl.org/items/5e66b3e8-f38d-d471 -e040-e00a180654d7.

Plumb, J.H. "The French Connection." *AMERICAN HERITAGE*, 1974, https://www .americanheritage.com/french-connection.

Polmar, Norman, and Thomas B. Allen. *Spy Book: The Encyclopedia of Espionage*. Random House Reference, 2004.

Puls, Mark. *Henry Knox: Visionary General of the American Revolution*. Palgrave Macmillan, 2010.

Putnam, Rufus, and Rowena Buell. "The Revolutionary War." *The Memoirs of Rufus Putnam and Certain Official Papers and Correspondence*, Nabu Public Domain Reprints, pp. 56–58, 2010.

Ragosta, John A. *Patrick Henry: Proclaiming a Revolution*. Routledge/Taylor & Francis Group, 2017.

Randall, Willard Sterne. *George Washington: a Life*. Henry Holt & Co., 1998.

Reit, Seymour. *Guns for General Washington: a Story of the American Revolution*. Gulliver Books, 2001.

Rose, Alexander. *Washington's Spies: The Story of America's First Spy Ring*. Bantam Books, 2007.

Ruppert, Bob. "America's First Black Ops." *Journal of the American Revolution*, 19 Aug. 2017, https://allthingsliberty.com/2017/09/americas-first-black-ops/#_edn15.

Savas, Theodore P., and J. David Dameron. *A Guide to the Battles of the American Revolution*. Savas Beatie, 2013.

Schaeper, Thomas J. *Edward Bancroft: Scientist, Author, Spy*. Yale University Press, 2012.

Schecter, Barnet. *The Battle for New York: The City at the Heart of the American Revolution*. Penguin Books, 2003.

Schellhammer, Michael. "The Daring Departure of Lafayette." *Journal of the American Revolution*, 28 Aug. 2016, https://allthingsliberty.com/2013/11/departure-lafayette/.

Scotti, Anthony J. *Brutal Virtue: the Myth and Reality of Banastre Tarleton*. Heritage Books, 2007.

"Second Continental Congress." *Wikipedia*, Wikimedia Foundation, 18 Mar. 2018, https://en.wikipedia.org/wiki/Second_Continental_Congress.

Smith, David. *New York 1776: The Continentals' First Battle*. Osprey Publishing, 2008.

Smithsonian, The. *The American Revolution: A Visual History*. DK Publishing, 2016.

Spivey, Larkin. *Miracles of the American Revolution: Divine Intervention and the Birth of the Republic*. AMG Publishers, 2010.

Spy Letters of the American Revolution. http://clements.umich.edu/exhibits/online/spies /index-timeline.html.

Staib, Walter, and Paul Bauer. *The City Tavern Cookbook: Recipes from the Birthplace of American Cuisine*. Running Press, 2009.

Stevens, Benjamin Franklin. London: Malby & Sons, 1889, *B.F. Steven's facsimiles of manuscripts in European archives relating to America, 1773–83: with descriptions, editorial notes, collations, references and translations*, https://catalog.hathitrust.org/Record/101739764.

Stewart, Chris, and Ted Stewart. *Seven Miracles That Saved America: Why They Matter and Why We Should Have Hope*. Shadow Mountain, 2009.

Strum, Richard M. *Henry Knox: Washington's Artilleryman*. OTTN Publishing, 2007.

Symonds, Craig L. *A Battlefield Atlas of the American Revolution*. Savas Beatie, 2019.

Holy Bible, New Living Translation. Tyndale House Publishers, 1996.

Tucker, Phillip Thomas. *George Washington's Surprise Attack: A New Look at the Battle That Decided the Fate of America*. Skyhorse Publishing, 2014.

Unger, Harlow G. *Improbable Patriot: The Secret History of Monsieur De Beaumarchais, the French Playwright Who Saved the American Revolution*. University Press of New England, 2011.

Unger, Harlow G. *Lafayette*. Wiley, 2003.

Unger, Harlow G. *Lion of Liberty: Patrick Henry and the Call to a New Nation*. Da Capo Press, 2011.

Van Horne, John C. "Federal Procession." *Carpenters' Hall*, http://www.carpentershall.org/federal-procession.

Van Vlack Milton C. *Silas Deane, Revolutionary War Diplomat and Politician*. McFarland & Company, Inc., 2013.

Washington, George. "Founders Online: From George Washington to Lt Col Joseph Reed, 28 & 30 Nov, 1775." *FoundersOnline*, National Archives and Records Administration, https://founders.archives.gov/documents/Washington.

We the People: Documents and Writings of the Founding Fathers. Sweetwater Press by Arrangement with Race Point Publishing, 2014.

Weitzman, David M. *Living a Life That Matters: a Memoir of the Marquis De Lafayette*. Liberty Flame, 2015.

Wells, James M., and Carris J. Kocher. *The Christian Philosophy of Patrick Henry*. Bill of Rights Bicentennial Committee, 2004.

Werther, Richard J. *A French "King of America"?* Journal of the American Revolution, 12 Sept. 2019, https://allthingsliberty.com/author/richard-j-werther/.

Wilbur, C. Keith. *The Revolutionary Soldier, 1775–81: An Illustrated Sourcebook of Authentic Details about Everyday Life for Revolutionary War Soldiers*. Globe Pequot Press, 1993.

Willison, George F. *Patrick Henry and His World*. Doubleday, 1969.

Wilson, Hazel Hutchins, and Edy Legrand. *The Story of Lafayette*. Grosset & Dunlap, 1952.

Wirt, William. *Sketches of the Life and Character of Patrick Henry*. Published by James Webster, No. 24, S. Eighth Street, Philadelphia. William Brown, Printer, Prune Street, Philadelphia, 1818.

Wood, W. J. *Battles of the Revolutionary War, 1775–81*. Da Capo, 2003.

The Wreck of the HMS Somerset (III) British Man-Of-War, 1746–78. https://www.nps.gov/caco/learn/historyculture/somerset.htm.

Wright, Robert K. *The Continental Army*. Center of Military History, U.S. Army, 1984.

Glossary of Words
and Phrases

Gillamon as the Dutchman:

Al is de leugen nog zo snel,
de waarheid achterhaalt haar wel.
However quick a lie may be, the truth will overtake it.

Beter ten halve gekeerd dan ten
hele gedwaald.
It's better to change direction halfway than to be wrong all the way.

Gladjakker
A smooth talker who tells you what you want to hear

Het leed is geleden.
The suffering is over.

Van de hand in de tand leven
Living on very little money, without a steady source of income, living 'hand to mouth'

Eighteenth Century Slang:

Cat's Paw
To be made a cat's paw of; to be made a tool or instrument to accomplish the purpose of another

Cat's Sleep
Counterfeit sleep: cats often counterfeit sleep, to decoy their prey near them, and then suddenly spring on them

Cheeking
Taunting or jeering at

Crikey
Expression of amazement, surprise

Flip
Shoot

Flush in the pocket
Has a lot of coin

Hot or Cold
Ways of attacking. By shooting (hot) or by bayonet (cold)

Hug
To hold a gun close; to hold onto something tightly as you're afraid to let it go

Huzzah
Hurrah

Keep your hair on
A command not to get excited, or "Keep your hat on"

Liberty-man
Sailor

Miry
Swampy, muddy

Nesh
Frail, tender, especially as regards susceptibility to the cold

Padding the hoof
Walking

Rookie
New recruit

629

Sly boots	Cunning fellow
Tibby	A cat
Wolf in the stomach	Hungry

Select French Terms:

À bientôt	See you soon
Absolument	Absolutely
A demain	Tomorrow
Âge?	Age
Aimes-tu monter à cheval, ma petite fille?	Do you like to ride the horse, my little girl?
Au contraire	On the contrary
Ami/amie/amies	Friend (masc./fem./plural)
Allons-y!	Let's go!
Au revoir	Goodbye
Avec plaisir	With pleasure
Beaux reves	Sweet dreams
Bien sûr!	Of course!
Bienvenue	Welcome
Bon	Good
Bon appétit	Enjoy your meal
Bonjour	Hello/Good day
Bonne chance	Good luck
Bonne journée	Good day/Have a nice day
Bonne nuit	Good night
Bonsoir	Good evening
Bon vol	Good flight
Bon voyage	Good voyage
Ce matin	This morning
Ce n'est pas bien	This is not good.
Ce n'est pas pour tout de suite	It won't happen right away.
Ce soir	This evening
C'est ça	That's it!
C'est extraordinaire	This is amazing.
C'est incroyable	It is incredible.
C'est magnifique	It is magnificient/incredible.
C'est mon brave chevalier	He is my brave knight.
C'est qui?	Who is it?
C'est ridicule	It is ridiculous.
C'est simple	It is simple.

C'est tragique	It is tragic.
C'est un honneur de vous rencontrer	It is an honor to meet you.
C'est un plaisir de faire votre connaissance	It is a pleasure to meet you.
C'est un scandale! Comment ose-t-il faire ça?	This is an outrage! How dare he do this?
C'est vrai	It's true.
Cher/chère	Dear
Chocolat	Chocolate (used for hot chocolate)
Comment va ma petite-fille ce matin?	How is my granddaughter this morning?
Comprenez vous?	Do you understand?
Déjà vu	This has happened before.
Demain	Tomorrow
Dieu	God
Et	And
Exactement	Exactly
Excusez-moi, Mesdames… Je vais prendre l'air	Excuse me, ladies . . . I'm getting some air.
Faux pas	A blunder, especially a social blunder
Fête	A grand party or celebration
Femme	Wife
Félicitations	Congratulations
FEU!	Fire!
Finalement	Finally
Frais	Fresh
Grand-mère	Grandmother
Je comprends	I understand.
Je ne comprends pas	I don't understand.
Je ne sais pas	I don't know.
Je regrette	I regret that.
Je reviens dans un instant	I'll be back in a moment.
Je sais	I know.
Je suis désolé!	I am sorry.
Je suis vraiment désolé	I am truly sorry.
Je suis très heureuse	I am very happy.
Je viens à vous, Amérique!	I'm coming to you, America!
Je vous en prie	You are welcome.
Joyeux Anniversaire, aux Etats-Unis d'Amérique	Happy Birthday to the United States of America
Joyeux Noël	Merry Christmas

Juste	Just
L'amour	Love
La galerie des Glaces	The Hall of Mirrors
Le petit prince	The little prince
Les cochons	Pigs
Leur victoire	Their victory
Liberté	Liberty
Livre	French currency, equivalent to a pound
Lorsque, dans le cours des événements humains	When in the course of human events
Ma/Mon	My
Madmoiselle	Miss
Madame	Mrs.
Menus plaisirs	Small pleasures
Merci/beaucoup	Thank you/very much
Mes amis	My friends
Messieurs	Misters
Moi aussi	Me, too
Mon ami/amie	My friend (masc./fem.)
Mon Dieu	My God
Mon frère	My brother
Mon Général	My General
Mon professeur	My teacher/professor
Mon roi	My king
Monsieur	Mister
N'est-ce pa?	Isn't that so?
Nous somme arrivés	We have arrived.
Oui	Yes
Oui, le voilà!	Yes, there he is!
Quel dommage	What a pity.
Qui est-ce?	Who is it ?
Pain	Bread
Petit déjeuner	Breakfast
Petit frère	Little brother
Peux-tu le voir?	Can you see him?
Poisson	Fish
Pour moi aussi	For me also
Pourquoi pas moi ?	Why not me ?
Premier commis	Chief secretary
Puis-je vous présenter	I am pleased to present

Réveillez-vous	Wake up
S'il vous plaît	Please
Soiree	Party
Soupe/potage	Soup
Touché	Used to acknowledge someone has made a clever or witty remark in an argument
Toi aussi	You, too
Très bien	Very well
Très jolie	Very pretty, very nice
Tu veux une pomme?	Do you want an apple?
Un(e) chat(te)	A cat
Un homme mystérieux	A mysterious man
Un moment	One moment
Une chienne	A dog
Une chose de plus	One more thing
Un moment	Just a minute
Vingt ans	Twenty years
Voici! L'ennemie	The enemy is here!
Voilà	To call attention, to express satisfaction or approval, or to suggest an appearance as if by magic

Award-winning author and speaker

JENNY L. COTE

developed an early passion for God, history, and young people, and beautifully blends these three passions in her two fantasy fiction series, *The Amazing Tales of Max and Liz*® and *Epic Order of the Seven*®. Likened to C. S. Lewis by readers and book reviewers alike, she speaks on creative writing to schools, universities, and conferences around the world. Jenny has a passion for making history fun for kids of all ages, instilling in them a desire to discover their part in HIStory. Her love for research has taken her to most Revolutionary sites in the U.S., to London (with unprecedented access to Handel House Museum to write in Handel's composing room), Oxford (to stay in the home of C. S. Lewis, 'the Kilns', and interview Lewis' secretary, Walter Hooper at the Inklings' famed The Eagle and Child Pub), Paris, Normandy, Rome, Israel, and Egypt. She partnered with the National Park Service to produce Epic Patriot Camp, a summer writing camp at Revolutionary parks to excite kids about history, research, and writing. Jenny's books are available online and in stores around the world, as well as in e-book and audio formats. Jenny has been featured by FOX NEWS on Fox & Friends and local Fox Affiliates, as well as numerous Op-Ed pieces on FoxNews.com. She has also been interviewed by nationally syndicated radio and print media, as well as international publications. Jenny holds two marketing degrees from the University of Georgia and Georgia State University. A Virginia native, Jenny now lives with her family in Roswell, Georgia. Official website: www.epicorderoftheseven.com.

Same Characters, Two Award-Winning Series

The adventure begins with the two-book prequel series: *The Amazing Tales of Max & Liz®*, where the Maker begins building His team of animals to be His envoys through pivotal points of history. Max, Liz, Kate, and Al launch the adventure in book one, *The Ark, the Reed, and the Fire Cloud*, and are joined by their British mouse friend, Nigel, in book two, *The Dreamer, the Schemer, and the Robe*. With book three, *The Prophet, the Shepherd, & the Star*, the team of seven animals is finally complete, and known forevermore as the Order of the Seven in the *Epic Order of the Seven®* series. Working behind the scenes in the lives of Noah, Joseph, Isaiah, Daniel, those in the Christmas story, Jesus, the Disciples, Paul and the early church, the team will pass through Biblical and world history up to modern times with Patrick Henry and the Revolutionary War, and C.S. Lewis and World War II.

Keep up with Jenny and her latest news by subscribing to Epic E-news at www.epicorderoftheseven.com

These Titles Now Available on Audio Book
(with more on the way!)

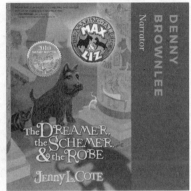

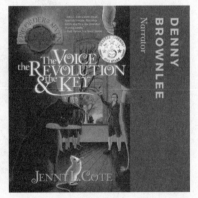

Find them on www.audible.com.

Listen to the *Epic Order of the Seven, The Podcast* with behind the scenes insights and chats with your hosts Max, Liz, Nigel, Jenny L. Cote and narrator Denny Brownlee as he plays chapters from the audiobooks.

Season One: *The Ark, the Reed, and the Fire Cloud*
Season Two: *The Voice, the Revolution, and the Key*

Tune in here:
epicorderoftheseven.com/podcast
or podcasts on Apple, Google and Spotify

The Epic Revolutionary Saga
Available in Print, eBook, Audio, Study Guide and Podcast

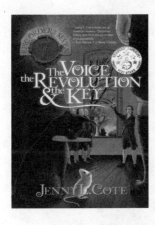 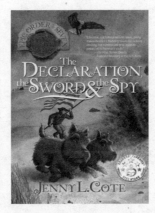 

The Voice, the Revolution, and the Key: 1743-75
The founders as kids, events leading up to the eve of Revolution

The Declaration, the Sword, and the Spy: 1775-76
Lexington and Concord, Bunker Hill, siege of Boston through
the Declaration of Independence

The Marquis, the Escape, and the Fox: 1776-77
The Battle of New York, Trenton, Princeton, escape of the
Marquis de Lafayette from France, and France's secret aid to
America

More titles to follow to complete the entire story of the
American Revolution and the founding of the
United States of America.

Learn more at *www.epicorderoftheseven.com*.

A Companion for *The Voice, the Revolution, and the Key*

- For general study, digging deeper, or for history and literature curriculum, spanning a semester or more.
- Offered in print (Amazon or the Epic Store, 444 pages, $24.95) or digital download (the Epic Store $14.00).
- Provides Chapter Guide questions for three levels (Eaglet, Fledgling and Eagle) that parents and readers can select based on age, grade, or reading level.
- Includes fun Bonus material projects with two beloved book characters, Nigel and Cato.
- Includes Answer Keys.
- Includes digital "Eagle Feathers" readers earn for completion of Chapters and Bonus projects.
- Includes four Book Part Tests and Final Examination with Answer Keys for use as a transcript credit.
- Visit www.epicorderoftheseven.com.

Schedule Jenny L. Cote to Speak to Your Group

Award-winning author Jenny L. Cote opens the world of creative writing and history for students of all ages and reading levels through fun, highly interactive workshops. Jenny has appeared to thousands of students at homeschool groups and conferences, lower, middle, high schools, writing conferences, book clubs, and universities in the US and abroad. Jenny's workshops correspond to her specific books, showing students exactly how she crafts her books, from research to character development to imagery. It gives students real hands-on tools used by an author, with a behind the scenes look at how a book comes together. Surprising grand entrances, fun props, and humorous questions keep students engaged from the first minute, with smiles and hands raised to be chosen to do the next fun thing!

Learn more at www.epicorderoftheseven.com/schools-groups.

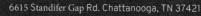